ON EMERALD DOWNS

ON EMERALD DOWNS

Patricia Shaw

headline

First published in 2002
by HEADLINE BOOK PUBLISHING

10 9 8 7 6 5 4 3 2 1

Cataloguing in Publication Data is available from the British Library

ISBN 0 7472 7048 1 (hardback)
ISBN 0 7472 7050 3 (trade paperback)

Typeset in Times New Roman by
Avon DataSet Ltd, Bidford-on-Avon, Warks

Printed and bound in Great Britain by
Clays Ltd, St Ives plc, Bungay, Suffolk

HEADLINE BOOK PUBLISHING
A division of Hodder Headline
338 Euston Road
London NW1 3BH

www.headline.co.uk
www.hodderheadline.com

To Debbie, Sterling, Lilly and Jaxson Daniher, with love.

Chapter One

The man, Ilkepala, watched the raid on Montone Station from the cover of trees further up the hill. He was a tall, powerfully built man of middle years with hard, expressionless features, thick hair that hung in strands plaited with snakeskin and a chunk of beard that jutted from an already prominent jaw. His body was laced with cicatrices, reminders of painful initiations, but unlike the other men with him, he wore no paint. Ilkepala had no need of decorations of any sort, for he was a magic man, a keeper of knowledge, confidant of the spirits. His people respected and feared him . . . his enemies knew him not. Few white men had ever heard of Ilkepala, let alone set eyes on him. Jack Drew, the man he was watching now, was one of the privileged few.

Jack Drew, white man, absconded convict, had sought shelter among the Aborigines some ten years ago and his presence among the families had been brought to the attention of Ilkepala by hostile clans. They wanted the rogue killed, disposed of without delay, but his friends and his lover, Ngalla, pleaded for his life, claiming he was a good man, worthy of their pity. Ilkepala didn't know about that. Drew did not have the face of a good man, it seemed to him; his eyes were too sharp, always hunting about, wary. Shark's eyes. But then it was true that he had escaped from his own kind and was afraid to go back. Some Kamilaroi men had come forward to say the troopers had tracked the fellow through the bush for days when he first escaped, and they certainly would have hanged him had they caught him. In which case, he would have no love for the white authorities . . . Perhaps it would be a good idea to let him stay awhile. Observe him. There was much he could teach the families about the white man's world if he made the effort to do so.

On that note, the matter rested. Jack Drew, though he did not know it, was under the protection of Ilkepala, who could have ordered his destruction at any time, but who instead became intrigued by this white fellow, the first one he'd been able to study at close range. He found Drew a mass of contradictions . . . bold and brash in his talk, mean and selfish at times, but a born leader. He was a fighter, in his own style, but no warrior, keeping clear of confrontations by resorting to jokes and humble apologies which, Ilkepala observed, were in fact meaningless. This white man did

1

not suffer from loss of face at any time; such a condition did not exist in his terms, he just got on with his days. And there was his strength. He tried to fit in, was kind to his woman, made an effort to learn the language, and all the time unconsciously he was teaching them the white men's ways.

Ilkepala issued instructions to the men who shared their campfires with Jack Drew, that they were to listen to him and learn. Question him as much as they liked because it was obvious he enjoyed answering. By his side they were able to learn about the white men and their ships, and the good men they called 'convicts' who were their slaves. They learned about horses who were good fellows and cows that you could eat, and sheep too, but their fur made the best coverings. All sorts of things were to be heard by his side, even that white women were the same as black women when their massive coverings were removed, and that was rather a disappointment.

Ilkepala even knew about Jack's plan to find the yellow stones, known as gold, much prized by white men. He was always asking about gold, especially of tribesmen passing through, and though many brought him samples of what they thought he might be seeking, it was only recently that they had actually found some for him. What he intended to do then was of great interest to Ilkepala. He hoped Jack would stay, his fount of knowledge important in these terrible times. And had not Drew suffered too? His wife, Ngalla, and many of her family members had been murdered by white men when they ignored his pleas and went back to their sacred places. He had warned them that even a peaceful walkabout in country inhabited by whites was dangerous, but they could see no harm. He had begged them not to go, explaining that he couldn't risk returning to that district with them, for fear he'd be captured, so he had waited in the hills for the loved ones who never returned. After that he linked up with another family, travelling north, keeping ahead of the terror, and eventually was permitted to attend a corroboree, where he had the privilege of glimpsing some of the powers of magic men.

'Who is that?' he'd asked fearfully, when Ilkepala himself had appeared, first on a nearby ridge and in a second rearing up among them, a giant breathing fire, his voice like that of a great spirit, echoing throughout the valley. The demonstration had been necessary to force the various clans at this meeting place to concentrate on the dangers, casting aside all of their differences. The time had come to make decisions. Those who could would go forth and join with the Tingum warriors. Since the Tingum and Kamilaroi peoples were not known to be the best of friends, this caused some mutterings, but Ilkepala roared his displeasure, frightening them into silence.

'This is a time of great danger. You will heed me! Who dares turn his face away? Warriors go to Tingum country, families travel further into the shelter of the bush, keeping away from the whitefeller tracks!'

Later he gave instructions that Jack Drew was also expected to move to

2

Tingum country and was astonished when he heard the white man had declined, arguing that he was not a warrior. Which was obvious, Ilkepala allowed with a snarl. Then he realised that the fool didn't know any tribal boundaries; most of the time he'd hardly known where he was.

'Just see that his travels take him towards Bussamarai's camp,' he ordered, and so it was done.

Many moons later, when he returned from conferring with worried northern tribes, he found Jack Drew living uneasily on the fringe of a large war camp, unable to obtain permission to depart.

'What's the point of having him here if you don't use him?' Ilkepala demanded of the chief.

'I've been busy. I can't be bothered with renegade white men.'

'You'd better be bothered with this one. How many men have you lost lately? More than forty, and plenty wounded from the guns. That Jack Drew knows how the white men do battle, see what he can teach you.'

'I won't ask a dirty white man for help!'

Ilkepala gave a grim smile. 'You won't have to ask. Just bring him into the circle when you plan raids. Let him listen. The man is incapable of shutting his mouth. It is my belief he'll be telling you your business in no time, such is his cheek. He may have things of interest to divulge.'

From that day on, Chief Bussamarai's fortunes took a turn for the better. He had always been able to keep the white men out of his lands near the Wide Bay, but he was failing in his attacks on the settlers who were gradually surrounding him. Now the tide was turning. With Drew mapping out plans of attack, refusing to allow the traditional ways to take precedence, Bussamarai's men were becoming the scourge of the district, driving white men out of their homes and rousting their sheep and cattle.

Ilkepala remembered the first time that Jack Drew had intervened in a discussion about a raid. He'd attended that meeting himself, unseen by the white man, because he had reason to be nervous. Jack Drew wasn't proving to be at all helpful; he'd just squatted there, for the third night in a row, with his mouth firmly shut. Bussamarai was not impressed, nor would he lower himself to ask for this fellow's opinion.

But just when Ilkepala had about given up and was considering asking Drew's friends to give him a nudge, the man had exploded, butting in in a most violent manner.

'You fools!' he'd shouted, jumping up to face them. 'There's nothing brave about running at bullets. Your shields are useless against bullets. You're all mad!'

The chief's face blazed with anger at this outrage. Insult upon insult in only a few words. Ilkepala feared for Jack's life. Quickly he conjured a thick curl of smoke from the central fire and a voice was heard to commend the chief for his wisdom.

'A wise man hears all opinions and digests them,' the voice added.

Never again did these warriors line up with their flimsy shields and

3

spears to do battle. From Jack Drew they learned to value cunning above valour. To seek out and kill their main enemies . . . troopers. To forgo their war cries and bullroarers and attack in silence. From cover. To stampede herds, burn houses . . . Oh, he had a bagful of tricks did Jack Drew, tricks he paraded with great glee. Ilkepala thought he enjoyed the planning more than the battles.

The raid on Montone Station meant a lot to Bussamarai. His attack on this place last summer had been a disaster. Not only had the first row of his warriors been cut down by gunfire, after the battle the white men went among the fallen and slashed at those still alive with swords. Then they threw the bodies in a pile and set fire to them. To add to the chief's anguish, as far as he could make out there were no casualties among the white people. Certainly there followed none of the usual funerals they normally observed.

Ilkepala felt a rush of exhilaration when he saw the Tingum men filtering through the scrub surrounding the homestead and the outbuildings on Montone Station, creeping up on white folk the way Jack Drew had advised. Though Jack Drew and the chief had become friends, if this second attack failed it would be a serious blow to the chief's reputation, and it was possible that Jack Drew would have to carry the blame. Ilkepala shuddered. His own reputation could also be damaged. He tapped on the totem stick he carried to remind the spirits of his need for good fortune here.

But then Bussamarai led the attack and Ilkepala leapt up to watch. He saw the chief break cover and race forward with his spear and tomahawk as the station dogs began to bark, his men darting out from all sides.

A white woman emerged from the bird house carrying a basket and was immediately killed. As she fell, eggs toppled from the basket and smashed all about her. Ilkepala sighed. The attackers had raced on, the caged birds shrieking and cackling in a panic, and those good eggs were wasted. He had become particularly fond of the eggs those strange birds laid, and always gave special blessings to any person who could bring one to him.

But what was this? Jack Drew was in among the first wave of warriors, and already guns were blazing from the windows. He dodged between buildings, soon making it to the main house, keeping up with Bussamarai.

'What's he doing there?' Ilkepala demanded of his own men.

'The chief's rule,' Moorabi said. 'All his men have to fight.'

'But not him. He'll just get in the way.'

'Bussamarai wanted him to fight, to show loyalty.'

Ilkepala shook his head. He didn't imagine Jack Drew would be happy about this, since he'd always managed to avoid fighting, and had never taken part in raids before. He didn't have the strength or agility of the black men. Quite possibly, the magic man mused, Bussamarai was testing him, forcing him to confront his own people. An interesting experiment, but a waste.

The whites were resisting strongly, keeping up a steady fire, causing many casualties, but Tingum men were dashing over to a veranda, racing along, battering at doors, finally breaking in. Guns were banging like thunder. Someone had set fire to the outbuildings and was running with a flaming torch to fire the main house but was shot down. Another man rushed forward and picked up the torch. Nothing could stop the assault now.

The defenders obviously knew that too. Ilkepala saw them making a run for it. There was a woman with them. They dodged from the house still firing their guns, and ran across to a long building, which wouldn't protect them for long, Ilkepala thought, as he lost sight of them. But all of a sudden a mob of horses could be seen bearing down on the house from a front paddock, racing wildly, he thought, in as much of a panic as the caged birds.

The homestead was burning now. For a few minutes he lost sight of the main action and could only see more of Bussamarai's men converging on the house. But suddenly, over past the long building, he glimpsed a group of white people making their escape on horseback, the big animals, fleet of foot, flying down the track with warriors racing after them, spears hurled hollowly into the dust.

'Get down there and find Jack Drew,' he told his two followers, and they sprinted away.

Bussamarai had won! The whites might have escaped but their station would not survive. All the buildings and that big haystack were afire, and celebrations had begun. There would be a great feast to mark this success. Later. Much later. Jack Drew had warned that if they won this battle they should get away fast, for this was the best of the sheep stations in the district and posses of gunmen and troopers would soon be on their tails, seeking revenge.

Smoke was curling into the sky and casting away into the breeze, that in itself enough to alert other whites in the area. Someone would come to investigate, and indeed there would be great anger over this day's work, but it had to be done. Ilkepala had no false hopes about who would win the final battle in this part of the country. The Tingum days were numbered, as were those of the Kamilaroi nation before them and all the other tribes and nations in the south, but he could allow himself to believe that the more warlike tribes in the north would survive either by force or through disinterest by the whites. After all, they surely didn't need all of blackfeller country.

He dropped down the slope in time to see the two men carrying Jack Drew towards the trees, and even from that distance he could see the man was in trouble, blood colouring his chest.

'Fool,' he muttered. 'Playing at heroes. He could have hung back, gone off looting and firing sheds, as many a timid man would do.'

They placed him gently on ground softened by thick ferns and shook their heads as Ilkepala approached, so he was prepared for the bad chest wound, but the burns shocked him.

'He was lying face-down in the house,' they apologised. 'What can we do for him?'

'Take him from here as fast as you can, before he wakes up and the pain attacks him and he starts screaming. Put him in the cave behind the falls.'

'Will he live?'

Ilkepala did not reply. He could not afford to be wrong. Maybe, he thought, maybe not.

He was half alive, but teetering between the worlds. They washed dust and debris from his sun-browned body, a peculiar sight with its white patches under arms, between thighs and toes and at the nape of his neck, protected by his shaggy hair, but his blood was normal, and plentiful. He had lost so much, his face, what could be seen of it, was paling to grey. Ilkepala sighed. The man was a shocking mess. The bullet had smashed into his shoulder and gone right through, fortunately not on the heart side, but that side of his face was badly burned, as were his left shoulder and arm, his hip and part of his leg. Roasted. As if on a spit. He wondered if it might be kinder to help the fellow die peacefully. But then he was a medicine man; here was a good chance to test various salves. First, though, the wound.

He packed it with poultices of ground tubers and herbs, front and back, hushing the man as he came awake, groaning and trying to free himself from the hands that held him still, as Ilkepala turned to the burns. He applied a protective skin of honey and weak sap, sending Moorabi, one of his helpers, into the bush to find more wild honey, a lot more. He would need a supply to keep tending all the burns on this big man. Then he reached into his dilly bag for a small pouch of ground fungi and fingered some into Jack's mouth. It was strong medicine; it would ease the pain for a while.

The blue eyes snapped open as Drew spat out the foul-tasting powder and jerked his head away.

'Who are you?' he groaned.

'I am Ilkepala.'

'Oh, Jesus! That's all I need. Get away from me!'

It surprised his physician that Jack Drew was speaking English, rare for him over the last few years, but he took the meaning as the fellow thrashed about and had to be held tighter. After all, the only other time this whitefeller had ever set eyes on him was back at that corroboree, where he learned to fear him. And he would have heard the name many times since.

Of course, with that effort, the pain really surfaced and Drew was writhing in pain and starting to yell, so Ilkepala forced the powder into his mouth this time, holding it closed until it would have dissolved.

'Be still. The more you move, the more you suffer.'

* * *

Jack screamed in rage. Who was doing this to him? Who had put his body into this inferno? Into hell! That was where he was. Hell! 'Oh, Jesus. Spare me. Don't do this to me.'

A hand clamped over his mouth and he bit it. Who was this, trying to choke him? If he could only get up he'd kill the bastard with his bare hands. His tongue was swelling. It was growing like a thick lump of dough, right there inside his mouth, swelling. Jack panicked; he grabbed an arm, to beg for help, mute now, helpless, dying, gagged by his own tongue.

'Be still,' a voice said, settling him down, soothing him, and the panic wave flowed past him, taking with it the great burden he was carrying. Jack was so relieved, tears of gratitude flowed as he tried to think who his rescuer might be. A friend, he supposed, but what friend? He didn't have any friends on this ship. Stuck down here with a hundred stinking felons, none of them worth spit, with no room to move. No wonder they said be still or you'll suffer more. He would have to remember that. In this hell it was every man for himself, and Jack kept to that rule. By God he did. They moved aside pretty smart for Black Jack if they knew what was good for them.

He could hear them talking now, in a strange language. Who were they, for Christ's sake? Maybe the ship had docked at Sydney Cove, the strange new land, and this was the local language. He guessed that would be right. They must have arrived to be placed in prisons from which there was no escape. Since when? He chortled. He'd be off first go.

'Is he getting better?' Moorabi asked. 'He seems better.'

'No.' It had been five days. The powders were working, so Ilkepala retreated to the cool springs above the falls. They could not stay here indefinitely; Moorabi and his brother had to guide a contingent of their clan to new and safer lands, and he himself had to make a difficult journey into the dividing mountains to meet elders from the mighty Kalkadoon nation. He had serious business to discuss with these difficult and dangerous men who never grew out of the warrior stage, no matter what their years. Most of them had never even seen a white man, and all of them were convinced that their own power and magic made any sort of threat from the invaders laughable. It was Ilkepala's job to be sure they heeded his warning, and – he took a deep breath now, for courage – to lodge a formal request for Kamilaroi and Tingum people to enter their land, where they would at least be safe for many years to come.

As he worried about the reaction of the Kalkadoons to such an outrageous proposal that didn't even carry the incentive of trade, since his people had nothing much left to trade, he made short message sticks for Moorabi to take with him. The sticks were hewn to the size of his middle finger, the marking etched in and daubed with white paint. They were unmistakably from the great magic man, so few would dare disobey the instructions to assist and protect the traveller.

That chore completed, he returned to the cave and found Moorabi, a good and kind man, patiently brushing persistent flies away from the patient with a fan of leaves.

'Is he awake?' he asked, and Moorabi nodded.

'We have to go soon. Two more days. That is all we can spare.'

'Yes.'

Eventually time was up. Moorabi awaited instructions.

'Get a canoe,' Ilkepala said slowly, forming a plan as he spoke. 'We can't carry him and we can't leave him. The river down there connects with the big river. I want you two to put him in a canoe and take him as far away from this place as you can. He must not be associated with this raid or they'll kill him. That is, supposing he lives long enough.'

'I'll bloody live,' the Englishman whispered, and Ilkepala thought he might just too, he was contrary enough. Wounded, burned, barely able to breathe properly let alone take care of himself, Jack Drew had the cheek to make that cranky remark a threat. As if it were Ilkepala's fault he was in this mess.

The magic man called Moorabi aside. 'He must be kept quiet on your journey so I'll give him some heavy sleeping juice when you're ready. I want you to go quietly down the river, as close as you can get to the big settlement, and leave him on the riverbank where he can be found. He will be in the hands of his own spirits then. They may help him, if they haven't forgotten him.'

He cleaned the wounds again and smoothed on a lotion gleaned from the stalks of moonflowers, to produce a numbness and reduce pain while he worked. He had hoped to leave the maggots in place for a while yet, to continue their work of cleansing, but there was no more time. He would just have to sew up the wounds as they were and hope for the best. He searched his dilly bag for the twine and some fine slivers of bamboo, and started stitching, first the chest wound; then, as Moorabi gently turned the patient over, he closed the hole in his back. That done, he covered the wounds with clay and bark to stay the bleeding and hopefully protect them from further injury. The clay set hard within minutes. Next he turned his attention to the burns. They were coming along fairly well, the honey mixture hardening over them, giving the skin a chance to dry out and regrow.

The patient had gone back into his head again, muttering, arguing, cursing, and as Moorabi dripped water into his mouth, Jack Drew shifted restlessly, clutching at his chest. Ilkepala removed the hands firmly. 'It might be a good idea to bind those hands to stop them pawing at wounds that have to be given peace,' he told Moorabi.

As the early-morning mists drifted over the mangroves, he watched his two followers carry Jack Drew down to the log canoe and place him on a kangaroo skin crushed into the narrow base. They gave him a mantle of bark for shade and squatted front and back of him, their oars propped in the mud. Quickly Ilkepala pushed them off and the canoe shot out into the stream.

They all had to make up time now, not least Jack Drew. He had lost ten years of his whitefeller life; it would be hard for him to find his way back. If he lived. But he would have to do that, because he'd never find his blackfeller families again. They'd disappeared into strange new worlds.

He was back on the transport ship, in that hold again, water sloshing against the timbers, listening to O'Meara belabouring his friends over the need to watch for every chance to escape, since they'd heard the *Emma Jane* was right now sailing in Sydney Cove and due to drop anchor this very morn. It was hot in here, stinking even more than usual, but Brosnan was laughing at something. He was one of O'Meara's mob. Politicals, they were called. Sent away from Ireland for raising hell. Jack liked that. The politicals were the only ones he found worth his time as the weeks passed, a cut above the rest of the scum. He liked the way they talked, the things they talked about, your rights and all that stuff that Jack had never known existed. He had his own rights. Me first they were, not as complicated as the Irish rules. But that Brosnan, he was always laughing, even in this hell, and to Jack's astonishment, he could make him laugh too. Who would have believed it?

He felt a terrible pain in his chest and his hands flew but he couldn't move them, they were bound. No, it was the bloody chains, they were all chained, and suddenly it was pitch black and silent and Brosnan was no longer there. He could hear O'Meara asking for Brosnan, and he told him. He was weeping, God help us, Jack Drew never wept over anyone, but there . . . Brosnan was dead. Shot. That's right, they were at the Mudie farm, working for the bastard Mudie, and there was an escape on. But poor bloody Brosnan didn't make it.

Someone was giving him water to drink, and slopping it on his face. Maybe the ship wasn't moving at all, maybe he'd imagined that, and he was only on the prison hulk in the Thames and he'd been here for years and years and years.

'Let me out,' he screamed. 'Let me out!' But it wasn't to be; they held him down, the chains were heavy. He could still hear the water slopping, slopping out there. It sounded so cool, so inviting, he wished he could drown in it, drown all this pain. Die. Who cared? He was sick of life.

The two black men kept on, skilfully avoiding bracken and debris in the wide reaches, and days later they swung out on to the big river that wound its way out to sea, and dug the heavy oars deep to push their unwieldy craft into the current.

For Moorabi it was a sad journey. He loved Meerwah, this wide river, but his people were moving away. At every stroke he took in the landmarks he knew so well . . . the leisurely bends in the river with their quiet leafy reaches, deceptive in their way, for great torrents had been known to surge down this river and engulf the land; the abundance of food and the endless beauty of bush often reflected in the waters. He remembered their favourite fishing spots, looking out for them, and the places where they'd often crossed to the south side, leading down to Bundjalung country.

Each day they swung to shore, quietly lifting the white man out of the canoe and into the water, as Ilkepala had instructed, to clean him up and keep him cool, for so far he was free of fever, thanks to the great man's medicines. Then they deposited him in thick grass to dry off.

He would wake, muttering again, trying to move about in a drunken and ungainly way, but that was good for him, to avoid stiffness of the limbs and encourage his blood to flow evenly. This was the reason for the short stop. They too needed to exercise their limbs and muscles while they searched about for some food, but soon they were on their way again.

As they passed, Moorabi kept his eyes on the bush along the shores. The countryside seemed deserted; everything was so quiet, so normal, but he knew it was not. There were still tribal folk living here, refusing to leave, wary of strangers and hostile to white men, and troopers patrolled the area, watching for escapees from their prison, and any blackfellers they could find and shoot. It was dangerous country. Though Ilkepala had given them no fixed instructions, they had decided to keep going through the night because the moon was high and the river was running fast after the recent heavy rains. They estimated it would take only a couple more days to reach the outskirts of the white settlement, and the sooner they were in and out of there, the better. They could turn back then, dump the canoe and head north across country at a much faster pace.

It was a mystery to him why the white men built their houses, like the place that had just been burned to the ground, so far inland, in such isolated areas, when food was so plentiful down here. He was not to know that the inlanders were moneyed men who claimed huge areas of land for themselves and their cattle, for he had no concept of private ownership. But these were matters for thought as the hours passed, for hadn't Ilkepala advised that there was much to learn if the people were to survive? So they skimmed along in the darkness, hardly making a sound, the waters seeming to be smoother, more restful with just the stars overhead and the world at rest, and the white man mumbled in his sleep again.

One afternoon they rounded a bend and saw a house high on a hill. His brother lifted his oar and looked back to Moorabi.

'Where are we? I thought you said we had another day to go before we came close to them.'

'So I did.' Moorabi was confused. How could he have made such a mistake? He peered about him. He knew exactly where he was . . . There were the two bunya trees at this bend, exactly where they should be, and on the other side a sandy beach below the rocky outcrop. Behind it, he knew, was an ancient cave, a Dreaming place, very sacred. A sanctuary, Ilkepala had told him, for goodness against evil. But what was this? A whitefeller house up there on the rise, and part of the hill now bald!

'They're here,' he said dismally. 'I never expected to see them this far up the river.'

'So we put him down here?'

'Yes. This would be the place.'

Once again they lifted the whitefeller out of their canoe, and took him up the high bank. Moorabi tapped his forehead, hoping his words would penetrate.

'We have to leave you now, Jack Drew. You did good with us. Our people will remember.'

Chapter Two

'Come and look here,' Bart, the post digger, yelled to the five men in their work party. 'There's a dead nigger down here on the riverbank. And not a stitch on him. Come and see.'

They rushed down to stare, but Albert, the gang boss, ventured closer, bending down to turn the body over and pulling back in shock. 'Christ almighty, get a load of that. He's been bashed and burned, the poor bugger. One of them high-and-mighty bosses might have got him. They don't like blacks hanging about.'

The others moved down, but suddenly Bart screeched: 'Look out! He ain't dead. I saw him blink.'

'Ah, get out,' someone said. 'You couldn't see a horse blink.'

'I did so, by God. Go on, Albert, you do a listen, see if you can hear him breathing. I reckon he's still with us.'

Reluctantly Albert went down on one knee to investigate, feeling for a pulse, for a heartbeat, in the bare battered chest, but then the man moaned.

'Cripes, Bart's right,' Albert said. 'The poor bugger is still alive. We'd better take him up to the barn. Bring up the dray, you blokes.'

'Then what?' Bart said. 'He looks more than poorly to me and we ain't got no doctor.'

'Doctors don't come to blackfellers anyway,' Albert retorted. 'Help me get him over to the dray, we can't leave him here.'

'Wait till I get them cords off his wrists. Looks like he's been bound and broke free. He could be a prisoner, Albert, we don't want any trouble. They'll be looking for him.'

'What else can we do? Leave him here to rot? Come on, grab hold of him. Careful now, poor feller.' Albert leaned down to lift the man's shoulders, wincing as he groaned in pain. 'Have we got anything to cover him?'

'Hang on. Down here.' Bart held up a kangaroo skin. 'Here's his clobber, but I can't make out how it stays on him.'

'Never mind. Bring it along. Now grab hold.'

They carried him up to the track and placed him on his side in the dray to avoid aggravating the burns on his other side, then covered him with the kangaroo skin.

'We might as well quit for the day,' Albert told them. 'It'll be dark before we get back. Put all the tools on the dray and don't leave anything behind. I don't want a repeat of yesterday. You know everything has to be handed in, axes, crowbars, the lot. Don't even leave a spade out, never mind you'll be using them tomorrow. They all have to be accounted for, every bloody night.'

Albert was worried as they tramped up to their barracks. They were all convicts from Brisbane prison, employed on this farm by Major Kit Ferrington, who had very strict rules. They were paid a few shillings a month, given food, meagre though it was, and lodgings, but they were not chained or locked in at night. Unless Ferrington was prepared to pay full-time guards, there was no point in that, since the convicts could escape at any time during the day if they wished. If they wished to be murdered by blacks or hunted down by troopers, Albert reflected. The farm was on the outskirts of the town, deep in the bush. There wouldn't be much point in trying to escape from here. Nowhere to go but downriver, back to Brisbane.

Ferrington had what he called an honour system, to ensure his workers stayed on the job, and it was terrifyingly simple. He only employed men with good prison records who were nearing the end of their terms, and that made them vulnerable. Any transgressions and they were sent back to face a magistrate and probable flogging or extension of their sentence.

More blackmail than honour, Albert thought as they left the one-mile track through the bush and headed across open country that they had already cleared. There was no doubt this place, Emerald Downs as it was known, had the makings of a splendid farm in time . . . once it was fully established. It had good soil, plentiful water and acres of space. Some said there were farms in this country a hundred times bigger, but Albert thought this ten thousand acreage was monster. It would do him and then some. Right now, though, there was the problem of this poor bloke. Ferrington had more rules than you could poke a stick at, but there were none for this situation. He hoped he was doing the right thing, bringing in the blackfeller . . . What else could he do? But somehow he knew it wouldn't go down too well with the boss, who, fortunately, was away. He often left the farm without advising anyone and returned without notice, ready to pounce on anyone who displeased him, so there was a fairly regular turnover of workers and a general malaise of anxiety among those who managed to hang on, with their imminent freedom at risk.

There were twelve men working the farm at present, five clearing and fencing, two carpenters working on the house, and the rest clearing blocks for ploughing and taking care of the dairy herd. Everyone worked hard, by God they did, desperate for their freedom. Albert was aware that had he been a free man, he would have had the title of overseer, and been paid a fair wage, but that wouldn't do for a convict. He was simply the gang boss who lived in a dingy iron shed with the rest of the farm workers, and lined up morning and night for meals served to them from the kitchen window by a cranky Chinese cook known as Tom Lok. In all, though, Albert sighed, it wasn't so bad here. Anything was preferable to more jail time. He kept his mind firmly fixed on the future; only a year to go and he'd be free. He'd decided to find a job as a clerk for a start; not too many 'government men' could read and write as well as he could . . .

'Put him in the barn,' Bart was saying. 'Isn't that what you said, Albert?'

He nodded, knowing that canny old Bart was covering himself. 'Yes. I'll go up to Polly and see if she'll look at him. She'll know what to do, he's terrible sick.'

The homestead was far from finished. It was being built section by section.

'Wings' the Major called them. This part, this wing, Albert corrected himself, had all you'd need in a house and more, but Ferrington was just the one to want all the trimmings. The plans showed big reception rooms and a wing for guests, even a gaming room. Albert was impressed. His family back home in Liverpool had never lived in a real house, only dark rooms, jammed in the back of tenements. They never even owned any furniture; that is, until young Albert, aged twelve, had bought himself a bed. An iron bed with a springy wire base to hold a mattress, when he had one. Most times he'd used an old piece of carpet. But that bed, he reflected, had been his pride and joy; he'd dragged it with him every time the family moved, which was often. He'd had that bed right up to the time he was arrested, and he wondered who had it now.

Already Ferrington's house was a flash place. It was all timber, with a shingle roof. From the front veranda there was a fine view across hill and dale, and he had a passage running straight through the house to catch the breeze, with rooms off either side, rooms that could shelter whole families. Though he'd never admit it in a million years, Albert loved this house. He'd watched it going up, stick by stick, enjoyed seeing the carpenters and plasterers at work, there being no end of talented tradesmen available in the overcrowded prison, and fairly drooled at the splendid furniture the carriers brought to the door. Wouldn't he just love to have a house like this.

Fat chance, he told himself as he made for the kitchen at the rear of the house. But then you never knew what was ahead; stranger things had happened in this wild country. One pleasurable strange thing . . . Some years back, Captain Logan, Commandant of the Moreton Bay prison, had been murdered by blacks while on a shooting expedition out in the bush. Or so it was told. Wiser heads whispered that it was his convict bearers who'd done the deed, an act of revenge for Logan's sadistic cruelty, but nothing could be proved. Whoever it was deserved a medal, the prisoners, and many free settlers, agreed. That recollection put a smile on Albert's face, and he looked up at the sky.

'All blue,' he murmured ruefully, 'not a single cloud in the sky. Not one!' Except for that poor nigger, he reminded himself anxiously.

* * *

14

Mrs Pohlman, known as Polly, was the Major's housekeeper and cook, and she occupied a room set between the kitchen and the laundry.

Apparently the Major had tested quite a few convict women for this job, placing a priority on cleanliness, and then he set out to find a woman who was also a really good cook.

Polly, a thin and wiry Irishwoman in her early thirties with prematurely grey hair and fierce green eyes, wasn't the type to stir his blood, but she bragged openly that she was the best cook he'd ever find. And obviously the Major agreed.

'I've got a job for life here,' she told Albert.

That surprised Albert. 'But your term will be up soon. Like the rest of us. You'll be able to go free.'

'Where to? I can't afford to pay my own way home, and I'm not sure I'll be wanting to. What's there to go home to except heartbreak to see all the poor hungry folk around me? And haven't I got me own room and all? I'd be a fool to leave. It's beautiful here, a darling place and so quiet. Hardly any people here to go spoiling everything.'

Years in a crowded female factory and then Moreton Bay prison after a horrific voyage in the hold of a transport ship had Polly dreaming of space, of room to move about without having to touch the flesh of another. She'd become obsessive about cleanliness in an environment where the means did not exist, and now that they did . . . she kept herself scrubbed clean, couldn't even tolerate a grimy fingernail after she'd worked in the vegetable garden. The kitchen shone and every corner of the Major's house gleamed. Polly vowed she'd stay on here, even if he couldn't be persuaded to pay her better than the convict wage.

She was in the vegetable garden, out beyond the laundry, plucking a bunch of leaves from some strange plants, when Albert appeared.

'What would you be wanting at this hour?' she asked him.

'Just a word.'

'That's cheap. Smell these.' She brushed the leaves under his nose. 'Lovely, aren't they? He brings me new herbs nearly every time he comes home.'

'Smells good. Sort of clean and happy.'

'So it should. It's called basil, to make the lamb tasty. What was it you're wanting?'

'We've got a sick man in the barn. I thought you might have a look at him.'

'What's wrong with him? And what's he doing in the barn? Has he got somethin' catchin'?'

'No. He's been hurt. Got burned and all. Real bad.'

'God help us and save us! I don't think I can do much for burns. Wait here, I'll get my bag and some bandages.'

As they hurried down the path, Albert told her a little more. 'We found him down by the river. At the boat ramp. We thought he was dead . . .'

15

'Ah, dear God!' She strode out, faster now.

'And there's one more thing . . . the poor bloke. He is real bad, you know. No one to help him. He's a blackfeller.'

'He's what!' She stopped in her tracks and shoved her medicine bag at Albert. 'I wouldn't know what to do with a blackfeller. I never touched one.'

'They're no different from us, Polly.'

'Who says so? They frighten the daylights out of me. I'm not going near no blackfeller.'

'Oh come on. Just come down. I'll go in and see how he is, and call you. Poor bloke'll probably be dead by this, and you fretting about touching him.'

He had her walking again, reluctantly, and all the way she kept insisting she wouldn't touch him. 'I'll tell you what to do, if I can. But I'm not going near him, not on your nelly.'

But then Bart came running towards them, stumbling on the steep path in his excitement. 'He's not a nigger! He's white, true he is. Unless he's piebald,' he added with a grin.

Albert pushed past him. 'Piebald? What are you talking about? Of course he's a nigger.'

Now curiosity brought Polly along behind them as Albert charged into the barn.

He couldn't see much as the shadows lengthened, so he lit an oil lamp.

The fellow was black! His skin was like old leather. He didn't look much like a blackfeller now because he had sharp features and a hook nose, but who was to say? None of them knew much about blackfellers.

Bart pranced eagerly about the man on the floor, and pulled off the kangaroo skin covering him. 'Take a look at his armpits. They're white. And here between the legs, round the bollocks . . .'

Forgetting he was dealing with a seriously injured man, Bart grabbed the fellow's thighs to part them, taking hold of a badly burned leg.

Jack was barely conscious, only now beginning to emerge from the heavy drugs that Moorabi had been administering, but that strong hand gripping him brought out a roar of pain and he lashed wildly with his fists.

'Get away, you bastard!' he shrieked. And fainted.

Hearing the English voice, Polly came rushing in, only to veer away at the sight of the naked body that looked like a nigger to her, after all.

'I don't know about this,' she said. 'What will the boss say? He don't like strangers, you know.'

It took a while to convince her, since she rejected Bart's offer to show her more of the patient than she wanted to see, but in the end, when they prised open an eyelid and showed her the pale green iris stationed there, she relented, more from curiosity than pity.

'He's got more than burns,' she said accusingly. 'Looks like he's been shot. What's going on here?'

16

No one answered. Most of the men shrugged, turning away, the excitement over.

'Go on down to the cookhouse after you check in the tools,' Albert told them, 'and don't mention this bloke in front of the Chink. We better keep quiet about him being here.'

'The other blokes will find out. They have to come in here; you can't keep them out.'

That was true. The barn was huge, a repository for animal feed, farming stores and implements.

'Tell them to keep their mouths shut too. And try not to disturb him until . . .'

'Until what?'

'Until he is well enough to go on his way,' Albert said uncertainly, hearing a grunt of irritation from Polly.

'Don't know when that'll be,' she said grimly. 'The burns are bad, right down this side, even on his face. His hair's burned off this side. I'll bring down me scissors and cut it neat. Someone's put a real hard ointment on the burns, like a crust, see. It's falling off round the edge. For all I know it might be doing some good so I'll leave it. Smells like honey.'

'Who'd smear honey on a dying man?' Albert asked anxiously.

'Who says he's dying? He seems to have trouble staying awake. Might be the pain, tiring him.'

For all the apparent clumsiness of her large, ungainly hands, Polly had a delicate touch. She examined the wounds on the man's chest and back with care, washing off the mud that had set over them and standing back with a gasp of surprise to find they'd been stitched.

'Bring the lamp closer! For God's sake look at this. I'd say a bush doctor has helped him. Stitched the wound. Let's see the back. The bullet's gone right through, that's obvious, but look here again. More stitches.'

Albert glanced quickly at the wounds and then moved away. He could smell the antiseptic she was using and hear the bloke moaning. Coming to again, he supposed. But what then? A bullet wound could mean only one thing. He was on the run, whoever he was, and that made the situation worse. They could go up for harbouring. He was mentally wringing his hands as he took another bucket of clean water over to Polly when she asked for it, and then a small beaker so she could give him some water to drink. Then he had to help her bandage his chest, apologising to her for the nakedness.

'Yes, you'd better go and get him some clothes, Albert. Come what may, he has to have some trousers and a shirt at least. He can't be runnin' about in that bearskin.'

'Will I go now?'

'Yes. And get a move on. I don't want to get caught in here.'

As soon as Albert had left, she leaned over the stranger and whispered

17

to him: 'Listen to me, mister. Are you escaped then? If you are, you can't stay here. The boss'll turn you in. He's a high-up military man.'

Jack opened his eyes and stared at the woman. Who the hell was this? He groaned again. Christ, it hurt to bloody breathe. What had happened to him? Last thing he remembered he was on the prison ship. No, wait, he was at Mudie's prison farm.

'They shot Brosnan,' he told her, his tongue thick and unwieldy.

'Where? Where was this?'

'Mudie's.'

'Mudie's? Major Mudie's?' Every convict in New South Wales knew about Mudie's prison farm. A truly brutal labour camp, mainly for chain gangs.

'Who are you?' he asked.

'Never mind now. You just try to stay still, and rest up. I'll get Albert to find you a bunk.'

'What's the matter with me?'

'You got shot. And you've got some bad burns. I'll give you some laudanum to help you sleep.'

Jack struggled to remember. 'They didn't shoot *me*,' he tried to tell her. It was Brosnan they shot, but she wouldn't listen. He tried to convince her but his voice was fading. It was as if he'd fallen, dropped into a deep pool. He struggled up but sank again, then resurfaced, in and out of consciousness so often that he was unable to separate dreams and memories from reality. His body had turned into a torture chamber, his mind mud, quicksands, from the sustained pain someone was inflicting on him. All thoughts treacherous. But Jack Drew was a wily fellow, and there was a small section in his brain, way up there in the gods, that knew when to listen, or even just when . . .

Maybe it was a warning signal, preset, that came to his aid when all else failed. It had happened recently with the voice that had warned him to be still, and now here it was again; that small listening device had picked up another warning. He knew he was in danger, and he kept hold of that information as he sank down again.

They were moving him somewhere. Lifting. The woman fed him something warm and sloppy and comforting to his stomach, and then his mind shut down again under a strangely familiar odour.

'He's a bolter,' she told Albert. 'He says he comes from Mudie's prison farm.'

He laughed. 'That's a tall one. They haven't got convicts there any more. It got shut down years ago. Went back to England, did old Mudie.'

'That's what he said. Must have been a lie. Though a mysterious one if you ask me.'

'What's mysterious? He's on the run. Got shot. But what do we do with him?'

'He'll just have to take his chances. We can't tip him out, poor sick feller like that. I'm betting troopers will be riding in here any day, looking for him.'

'Yeah. He was probably in a bush work party. And they shot him while he was trying to escape across the river.' Albert frowned as he contemplated that scenario, knowing that somehow it didn't fit.

'That'd be right,' she said sarcastically. 'And on the way across he dressed his own wound and stitched it up and packed clay—'

'All right then. Be smart. I was only trying to work him out. He must have been helped by the blacks. He got shot. They looked after him for a while . . . those burns aren't new . . . and brought him here.'

She nodded. 'But if the troopers come here, I'm not going back for harbouring him. If they ask me, I'll be pointing up this away, I'm sorry to say. Best I can do is to keep out of their way, but you're in the firing line, Albert. You won't get away with keeping him hid.'

'I know that,' he retorted angrily. 'I know that.'

At first light Polly ran down to the shed, half hoping that by some miracle the stranger would have managed to up and leave, but he was still there, sitting on the side of the low wooden bunk, head drooping as if holding it up would take too much effort.

'I brought you some porridge,' she said, and he squinted at her as if he didn't understand.

'Porridge?' he echoed. 'Porridge?' But he made short work of it as she spooned it into him.

'You're looking better today,' she said. 'How do you feel?'

'Giddy. My head's spinning and my chest hurts like hell. What happened to me?'

'I already told you. You got shot. And you've suffered burns as well.'

'Jesus!' He could only shake his head as if that astonished him.

'What's your name?'

'Jack Drew,' he said absently. 'You got any more food?'

'I can get you some bread and sausage. I didn't know if you'd want to eat, you being so sick. Or even if you could eat much yet.'

'I'm hungry,' he said simply. 'I could eat some more of that porridge stuff too.'

'Right you are,' she said, 'I'll go get it for you.'

Jack watched her go and then dragged himself to his feet. They'd put trousers on him, the first he'd worn in years, and they chafed in the crotch and dragged painfully across the burn sores on his legs, but he gritted his teeth and began to walk, hanging on to the wall. He knew he couldn't stay in this place, so he would have to make his body get itself fixed; it was

19

only a matter of beating the pain. Obviously the gunshot wound wasn't going to kill him, nor were the burns, which felt as if hot coals were embedded in his skin, so there was no excuse. He'd seen the blacks beat shocking injuries this way, by grit and concentration, and now it was his turn. And he could do it, he bet he could. Bloody oath.

He wished he hadn't given the Irish woman his name. But he'd been carried away by the wondrous sweetness of whitefeller food, after all this time, and let it slip. It probably wasn't a good idea to reveal his name, since he was an escaped convict, but then who would remember him now? No one. Surely. They'd more likely have given him up for dead.

Albert hurried over to see him that night. 'How are you feeling, mate?'

'Sore and bloody sorry. Where am I?'

His voice sounded strange. As English as the rest of them, born near the Bow bells true enough, but slow he was, as if he was having trouble getting the words out, chewing them up a bit. The sickness, he supposed; the poor feller would have been right sick the day he collected these injuries.

'Emerald Downs farm, outside of Brisbane. Polly says your name is Jack Drew?'

'Yes. Brisbane? Where's that?'

Albert stared. 'Brisbane? Why, it's the port. Grew up around the Moreton Bay prison settlement. It's thirty miles from here.'

He saw Drew's eyes narrow and a frown crease the leather-smooth forehead. 'You own this farm?' he asked.

'Cripes no! We just work here. Compliments of the prison bosses. Seeing out our time. I hope you don't mind me asking, but are you on the run, mate?'

'No.'

'That's a relief. Troopers would soon grab you here, if you were. We'll do our best for you, the boss being away, but he doesn't take to strangers . . .'

Drew struggled up. 'I'll be out of here as soon as I can. I don't want to cause any trouble.'

'You have to stay put a while, mate . . . you're not fit to travel yet. Where did you come from?'

But Drew sank back on the thin mattress, his eyes closing wearily. 'A long way,' he sighed. 'A bloody long way.'

For four days he found solace and safety in sleep, dragging himself out in the dead of night to test his strength, and explore this farm, accompanied by two suspicious dogs. They weren't sure what to make of him, these wiry, half-starved animals, but crusts from his plate tipped the scales enough for them to allow him to limp quietly about their domain.

The woman, Polly, fed him, clucking over his injuries, marvelling that they were healing so fast, and answering his questions.

'I don't know who's got the most questions, you or me, Mr Drew, since I can't make out where you come from and you can't figure out where you are.'

She clipped his thick, matted hair, and delicately shaved off the scorched and frayed beard . . . 'Because you can't be having a half-beard and a half-head of hair,' she argued, when he tried to object, and he supposed she was right, but it was so long since he'd been clean-shaven, he'd forgotten the look of his own face.

'There now,' she said. 'You're not a bad-looking bloke after all. Myself, I took you to be the wild man of Borneo. But tell me now, Mr Drew. How did you get shot? Who would do that?'

Jack had been consolidating his story. He was a free man. He had come out to the colony to do some exploring and ended up living with the blacks for years.

He tried it on Polly and she was amazed.

'You don't say! Couldn't you get away from them?'

'No need. I liked living with them.'

'Lord above! What were you exploring before you went native?'

Ah. Think quickly. Easy! 'I was prospector . . . prospecting.'

'What for?'

'Gold.'

The minute he said that, his world seemed to explode.

'Gold!' he cried out, grabbing her arm. 'Where's my gold?'

'What gold? You didn't have no gold. You had nothing, Mr Drew. Not even a stitch of clothes. Albert had to get you into a shirt and trousers, you only had that kangaroo skin. Nothing . . .'

But Jack wasn't listening. Suddenly he knew. It came to him in a burst of rage.

He remembered the raid on Montone Station. The fighting . . . he'd had to take part, shoved into the thick of it by Bussamarai . . . caught up in the excitement then, fighting his way into the house like a bloody lunatic, on into a bedroom where a woman . . . the face was familiar . . . was cringing against the wall in terror. She'd thought he was a savage.

'Stay there,' he'd hissed, and slammed the door quickly, turning to lead his black comrades away from that room, but he'd run into the station boss, who had a gun . . . and from there . . . Blank. No. The fire. The house was on fire and he was lying there, bloody fool . . .

Perspiration dripped from his face as he struggled to remember and the woman, Polly, fretted over him, wiping his face with a damp rag, moaning about him being feverish now.

'Don't be upsetting yourself,' she said. 'You're all of a dither.'

'The fire,' he said. 'I got burnt.'

'Yes. That's right now. The burns are healing remarkable, but you'll have scars. Even on your poor face. Shouldn't be too bad though. On your cheek and forehead mostly. But what about the gold? And where was the fire?'

Ilkepala was here somewhere. He'd always been terrified of that ugly bugger with his magic spells. Jack had seen the old rogue perform some terrifying acts. He could make himself a giant, he could be seen in two places at once . . . but none of that mattered any more. Where was his gold? It had been hidden in the thick leather belt he'd made with his own hands. Thick and strong that belt, and with the gold sewn into it it weighed a heap, but he never took it off.

'A bush fire,' he told her. A lie.

The blacks must have seen him get shot and dragged him out of the house before the fire finished him off. He guessed they would have fired the house, as planned. Frantically, he felt around his middle again. Uselessly. The belt had come off, fallen off somehow, the ties broken or burned. He never was able to find a buckle. It wouldn't have occurred to the blacks to pick up his belt. It would still be there in that house! Bloody hell. That was the last he'd see of it. The owners would go back and rake over the ruins, looking to see what they could retrieve from the wreck . . . and they'd find it. Molten or rock solid, they'd find it. His gold.

'Reckon it's gone,' he said miserably.

'Your gold? Gone where?'

'To the bastards who robbed me,' he lied again. 'A man can be unlucky. I spent ten years prospecting for gold. Finally had my hands on it . . .' this was turning into a suitable tale, 'and I was making my way back to civilisation when two blokes ambushered . . . ambushed me. Robbed me and I thought I'd die in the bush fire. If my blackfeller mates hadn't found me I'd be dead meat by now.' That bit was true enough. Someone had patched him up, one of their women probably.

'That's the sorriest thing I ever heard,' she moaned. 'Would you know those fellers again?'

'Might do,' he said wearily, 'but it wouldn't do much good, would it?' The conversation was tiring him. Everything was tiring him. Where could he go from here? And where was he anyway?

'I'm still in the dark, missus,' he added, leaning on his good side. 'Can you tell me about this Brisbane place? Where exactly is it?'

'About thirty miles from here as the crow flies.'

'Yeah. But how far from Sydney Town?'

She looked at him aghast. 'Sydney Town! By God, you have done some roaming, Mr Drew. It's a long ways off. Could be five or six hundred miles to the south, they say. Us government people were all brought up to Moreton Bay by ship.'

Jack hid a grin, surprised that he could find anything amusing in his situation, but 'government people' tickled him. Even the convicts could put on airs now. Maybe they were treated kindly these days . . . that'd be a miracle, but this lot didn't seem too badly off. No boss in sight and no chains. Hard to believe.

'I couldn't walk back to Sydney Town then?'

'Don't think so. Not in your state anyways.'

That was what she said, but Jack knew she was wondering about his story. How had he got this far north if he didn't even know of Brisbane? A port, obviously.

'I came up thisaway inland,' he told her. 'Just kept moving on over the years, always on the lookout for gold. Reckon I lost count of where I was.'

'Yairs,' she said. Left it at that. Left unsaid more questions. Jack was good at picking up the unsaid. A lot of that stuff he'd learned from the blacks when he was struggling to learn their language. No alternative. Learn to fit in with them or go back to gaol and very nasty punishments for bolting. White men couldn't survive in the bush. He'd been lucky that the first blacks he'd met had seen with their own eyes that he was being tracked by troopers, a lone man struggling blindly through the bush, trying to get away from them. So . . . they'd come to his aid, those savages! He'd been scared of them too, especially when they let him know they'd speared the three troopers! Killed them! Life with the blacks had started with a jolt.

He thought about walking to Sydney Town. That was all he could think to do at the minute. Nowhere else to go. And he could cover a lot of territory in a day now. Just like the blacks. He reckoned he could walk that thirty miles into Brisbane in half a day if he set his mind to it. Easy. He'd had plenty of practice. Feet like leather.

Sydney Town! He'd only really got a glimpse of it, but over the years in all his back-country wanderings he'd dreamed of going back. A man had to carry something with him to hold on to, for his identity, like, and he was bloody sure it wasn't London and the grimy life he'd lived there.

He liked to reminisce about the day they'd disembarked from the transport ship, the *Emma Jane*, in Sydney Cove.

For a change the prisoners were assembling in an orderly manner, like waifs who might be denied an outing. The short-term men were frisky, boasting they'd only have to stick it out in this port for a few years and then they could take off back to the Old Country. But the Irish politicals, Brosnan and Court and O'Meara, were giving them the sneer for being fools, asking if they were planning to walk back over the oceans, because no ship would take them.

'You're all banished like us,' Brosnan laughed. 'So give 'em hell, lads.'

But Jack had his own plans. He had heard that a man could get over the hills beyond Sydney Town and make his way to China, so he was anxious for the slow-moving line to take him up to the deck so that he could see those hills for himself.

Chains clanking, he climbed to the deck in his turn, and there under the impossible blue skies of New South Wales he had his first glimpse of this prison. He looked about him in amazement.

There were people on the docks, waving and cheering as if royalty, not a bunch of felons, was disembarking. They sang and shouted

23

encouragement as the prisoners wobbled on to the docks, while their shore escort of soldiers in red jackets stood in an untidy line awaiting instructions.

An array of tall masts lined the wharf like an avenue of willows in winter. The waters of the harbour glittered so blue in the warm sunshine that Jack imagined if he dipped a hand in them it would come up blue.

And then a strange thing happened. Jack Drew, robber, highwayman, one of the meanest characters the captain of the *Emma Jane* had ever had to deal with, found himself smiling.

He looked out over the stretch of the harbour with its vivid green shores, back to the white buildings of the town and off to the distant ring of blue hills, and he experienced, for the first time in his life, a sense of space. Of being able to reach out endlessly in an uncluttered world.

Overhead, gaudy birds wheeled lazily and then swept towards the hills. All about him now, from ship to shore, there was a burst of activity as officers shouted instructions, men were shoved and pushed into line and the onlookers fell back from the raucous voices of authority, but Jack was no longer part of it. To him, these people were intruders in the grand landscape.

'Ah,' he sighed now. The picture always pleased him. He'd carried it with him all these years, even though he'd come across magnificent scenery in his travels through the blackfeller-country. This one was his own picture.

He never bothered to revisit what had followed . . . the public floggings, the reminders that they were the scum of the earth and would be treated accordingly . . . except to recall that O'Meara and a little fellow called Scarpy had also escaped from Mudie's prison farm and gone their own ways. Jack often wondered if they had managed to stay at large too, and what had become of them. Maybe they were back in Sydney Town. The only white people he could lay names to in the whole bloody country.

Rum, that. Come to think of it, he was like a newborn. Pity he'd given the name Jack Drew, which had been an alias in the first place. If they'd known they had Jack Wodrow, highwayman extraordinaire, in their court, he'd have got the rope, not transportation. But his alias was still a convict's name. He just hadn't been thinking fast enough. He should have told them something classy like Wellington or Marmaduke, and John instead of rough old Jack.

Ah, well. Suddenly he realised he was feeling a lot better. Must be the grub she's feeding me, he thought.

More days dragged past and he could feel the tension as Polly and Albert worried about the return of their boss, though Jack could see no reason why this bloke should take offence at a wounded man being cared for. But as soon as he told Albert he ought to be on his way, they brought him a bedroll, which they called a swag, with goods tied up inside it.

'Looks like you've got a lot to learn, mate, if you don't even know what a swag is,' Albert said, and Jack managed a response.

'I didn't waste any time. I got to Sydney, heard there was gold in the hills and went straight out fossicking. I knew the streets wouldn't be paved with gold like they said back home.'

'That's a terrible thing about your gold. Where did you find it?'

'That's the trouble. I didn't. Some blackfellers knew I was looking for yellow rocks and eventually found some for me. Don't know where they found it. But then I was off home. Made my fortune, I thought. Lost it a month or so later.'

'Shocking,' Albert groaned, feeling the pain of a loss like that. 'And you can't think where it might have come from?'

'Only a general idea.'

'By Jove, if you ever need a partner to go searching for it again, don't forget me.'

'I won't. But I've had enough of the bush for a while.'

Albert handed him some pages torn from a ledger. 'I've drawn some maps for you. This one is the road into Brisbane. This next one is a mud map of Brisbane itself, on the bend of the river, showing where the docks are, and this last one I drew of the coastline.'

Jack peered at him. 'You draw well, real neat. Which reminds me, what did you get sent out for?'

'Stealing books. I was a clerk. I didn't want the books, I only borrowed them so I could learn to copy my employer's signature and lift a little of his profits.'

Jack nodded. 'A good man with the pen, eh? You paid a high price for the borrowing.'

'No use crying over it now. I'll be free soon and I reckon I'll do all right. Got a few ideas, I have. But look here . . . see this coast map. That's the best I can do. It shows where Brisbane is from Sydney and there's a couple of ports in between. I guessed at the miles, but I'd say they're close.'

Jack studied it carefully. 'Hell! I didn't know I'd come this far! But tell me, are all the workers here from the prison?'

'Every one. Even Polly.'

'If it's a prison farm, how are you able to walk about free the way you do?'

'No chains and no guard here, Jack. We break one of the bastard's rules and we're back before the magistrate for an extended sentence. He only picks workers with a short time left. And we only get fed the same as if we're sitting in the cells. It's hard here, but worth it.'

'Polly seems to be able to get her hands on food. Why doesn't she . . . ?'

'Because our Chinese cook would tell the boss. The Chink doesn't know you're here, and we can only hope he doesn't find out. He's a snoop. As for Polly, she has to account for all her rations, she can't help us.'

Albert came back after their evening meal to wish him well and Polly brought him tea, and a billy to boil water, and bread and cheese to pack in his swag.

'I'm sorry I can't do better, Mr Drew, but you know how things are.'

25

'I won't starve in the bush,' he said. 'Plenty of food out there.'

Albert was interested. 'Is that right? I never knew that. They've always told us it's worse than a desert for food.'

'You have to know what to look for, so don't try it. You'll prove them right. But thank you kindly for looking after me, Polly. I ought to come back and marry you.'

She hooted with laughter. 'Get out with you. He's surely a lot better now, Albert, I never thought to see him on his feet so fast. Which way are you going, Mr Drew?'

'It's Jack. Thought I'd take a look at this Brisbane place. I'll be out of here before the sun comes up, so you can breathe easy.'

They slipped away and he was left to his own thoughts. While they were talking he'd remembered the name of that prison. Moreton Bay. Newly arrived convicts were constantly reminded of the horrors of the place, and threatened that re-offending, including absconding, would see them sent straight there. It was a prison for hardened criminals and re-offenders.

Jack eased himself down on the bunk for a few hours' sleep before he took to the track. What price Albert's story? It would take more than stealing a couple of books to have him sent on from the Sydney prison to that hellhole. But that was his business.

He thought about the day ahead, nervously now. He was still bloody weak, cracking hardy for their benefit, but he was improving. What to do when he did reach Brisbane? This was a very real problem. At least he wasn't wearing convict garb, but these rough farmhand clothes weren't much better. And he had no boots. The thought of marching into a town full of people and vehicles and things already had him so intimidated, he was almost inclined to head back to the bush. But he couldn't do that. It was over, the bush life, and not before time. The poor buggers out there were at war now, a running, uneven war, forced on them unless they kept retreating. No place for Jack Drew any more. But where *was* his place?

Chapter Three

'Who the hell are you?'

A lantern was shining in his eyes. A boot lashed out and kicked the bunk from under him. Jack tumbled on to the floor with a gasp of pain, but he was on his feet swiftly, feeling for the knife he kept in his belt ... except there was no belt, no knife. In a second he had disappeared into the dark recesses of the barn, waiting for an opportunity to strike back as his hands found a pitchfork.

But then there was a shot, the noise so sudden in the quiet of the night it was deafening to Jack's ears.

'Come out,' the voice said. 'Give yourself up or I'll just keep firing. I might get a couple of possums as well, but I'm as sure as hell I'll get you at this range.'

Jack obeyed, walking into the lamplight and on towards the door, his hands over his head, keeping his eyes on the dark glint of the gun barrel that moved with him. No doubt this was the boss, and in his hand was a revolver, so he hadn't been joking about firing at random.

As he edged out of the barn he heard a man growl:

'You said he was a nigger!'

'That what they say, master,' a thin voice whined. 'I hear them whispering orrighty.'

Jack sighed. The Chinaman! 'You can put the gun down,' he said firmly. 'I wasn't doing any harm.'

'Shut your mouth and start walking.'

The Chinaman ran ahead of them with the lantern, Jack following, and the man with the gun behind him.

'The lockup,' he ordered, and the Chinaman bobbed. 'Yes, master.'

He hurried to open the door in another building at the rear of the barn, and turned to give Jack a push, but he pulled back.

'I'm not going in there! I'm a free man. A citizen. You can't lock me up!'

'You're a trespasser and a thief,' the boss said, nudging Jack in with his boot. 'Get in there.'

They slammed the heavy wooden door and shot the bolt.

'I'll have the law on you,' Jack shouted as he heard them move away, but his voice bounced off the walls in this confined space. He felt around him, fighting the mild panic that this was causing him. Ten years of living without walls had left their mark, he noted. The barn hadn't been a problem, but this, not much bigger than a broom cupboard, was really upsetting him. Sweat was pouring off him, moisture he couldn't afford to lose since they'd not left him water, so he groped around the floor to take his mind off this unexpected reaction. Jesus, he thought. They won't want to put me back in gaol. I'd go off my head now if this is how being shut in affects me. I'll have to be bloody careful.

There were lumps of metal in the corner among some rags and pieces of hessian, some sharp, and feeling them in the pitch dark he managed to identify them. A rake without its handle. Butt end of a shovel. Manacles, for Christ's sake! Chains. Hobbles. All covered in dust. Obviously they didn't use this lockup too often. He felt calmer now, but he had to get out of here. Albert was right. He'd guessed this bastard wouldn't even give him the chance to explain.

'Bloody hell!' he said, spitting dust, and picked up the spade that had lost its handle. This could be a weapon, but as he'd been spouting for so long to the blacks, useless against a gun.

The boss was home!

Though it was only just after midnight, the clang of the fire bell and the dizzying shrieks of Tom Lok, the cook, roused them from sleep and had them stumbling out on to the cobbled square, to line up awaiting trouble, for naught else would cause this assembly.

Having performed that duty, Tom rushed around, grinning gleefully as he lit the wall lamps on the corners of the buildings. First the barracks, then the cookhouse, then the stables, and lastly the long shed that housed the master's office and storerooms. He had waited a long time to get his own back on these ingrates, these criminals who had the nerve to complain about his cooking. And they never stopped teasing him, angering him . . . they even cut off his pigtail . . . and for that he'd never forgive them. A joke, was it? Look at them now, shambling into line, blinking like weak rabbits. Bullies all of them. Englishmen bullies. And the master was a bigger bully. By right, of course. He had the right. Not this scum.

That was what the boss called them when he came down from the house. 'Scum! Thieves! The lot of you. Harbouring one of your scurvy mates in my barn again. Feeding him my food. Giving him clothes from my store. Well, it's late, so I'll cut this short. You're on half-rations for three weeks.'

He ignored their groans. 'As for you, Albert, I left you in charge and you let me down.'

'No, sir,' Albert called. 'The man was badly injured. We did but take him in, as you would have done yourself.'

'Do not presume to think for me. You are getting above your station.

Obviously you are not to be trusted. I gave you a chance and it didn't work, therefore you will have to go back to prison for further sentencing.'

Albert fell to his knees. 'Please, sir, don't do that. I did no wrong.'

'Liar!' Major Ferrington slammed his riding whip down on a hitching post. 'I got back just in time, didn't I? Were you intending to ask that felon to repay me for food and shelter? I think not. You were helping him to steal away scot-free. And why? Because you knew that troopers were after him. So I'll see they find this felon, but there's you.'

He took out a silver case, selected a cheroot and lit it, sucking in the aroma with obvious enjoyment as they watched nervously.

'Albert! You don't want to go back to prison? I guess not. Pity you didn't think of that earlier. But I'll give you a choice. You can take sixty lashes at the triangle out there, or go back. That's straightforward. What's it to be?'

Albert closed his eyes and took a deep breath. What a choice! Sixty lashes with the cat could tear a man's back up. Half of the men here had the scars to prove it, but he'd managed to get through the years with his back unscathed. Malicious warders had knocked teeth out, one had broken his leg, leaving him with a limp, and inflicted various other injuries upon him, but he'd never been flogged. He'd witnessed them, though, plenty of them, sickening bloody affairs they were. Albert had seen and heard enough of them to put fear in him at the very mention of the word. He groaned silently. His freedom was at stake. Maybe a kindly magistrate might only imprison him again without adding to his sentence. Might not, too.

It was a warm night. A pleasant breeze drifted up from the river. An owl hooted. Men shuffled. A dog barked. Clouds banked in high white mounds against the dark sky seemed to shift a little, as eyes tried to focus on them rather than on his comrades. The taste-charged aroma of that cheroot wafted across to them. A man sighed.

'I haven't got all night,' the Major snapped.

Albert stepped forward. 'I'll take the whip, sir.'

Then it was Polly's turn.

She was frantic. He'd come home late, not unusual for him, and banged on her door, which meant she had to dress quickly and dash into the kitchen, light the stove and get him supper as quickly as she could.

No sooner had she placed the kettle on the stove than she heard him talking to someone outside. The someone, she realised, straining her ears, being Tom Lok.

'Here? In my barn?' the Major shouted. 'By Christ, we'll see about that.'

Polly flew to the door in time to see him load that Collier revolver he was so proud of, and march furiously out of the house.

She heard the fire bell clanging not long after that, and guessed the boss had them all out again, one of his favourite tricks when he was in a bad mood, but this time the situation was serious. Obviously he'd found Jack, and dragged the poor man out. She wished Albert had left her alone, then she wouldn't have gone anywhere near the barn. Why hadn't she minded her own business?

'Oh God, spare us,' she prayed, and hurried about his supper.

He was in the sitting room, the French windows open to a light breeze, reading a newspaper and drinking wine, when she brought his tray in. He had been away for ten days so there was little in the larder in the way of fresh food for him, but she had baked that morning, thank God. She presented him with fresh buttered bread, cold corned beef, a cheese platter with country biscuits, slices of her pork brawn with pickles and a pot of tea, and bobbed gratefully when he lifted the teacloth to check his supper, and nodded.

'I'll make some beef pies for you tomorrow, sorr, your favourites. And roast a goose,' she rushed to tell him. To please. 'And now you're back, I'll back up some marble cake, the one with pink icing, you know?'

He ignored her so she crept back to her kitchen to await further instructions.

Eventually he rang the little silver bell and she hurried back.

'I'll have more tea, and more pickles.'

'Yes, sorr.' She reached for the teapot.

'Just a minute. I believe you've been feeding a felon from my kitchen.'

'Oh no, sorr,' she cried, the china pot a lead weight in her hands. 'Only a few morsels. Some porridge. He was sick and all, you know . . .'

'Your excuses don't interest me. And the only thing that saves you from being sent back to prison is your cooking and the fact that you're able to clean house, unlike the rest of your sort, so you'd better not let me down as Albert has done.'

She gulped. 'Oh no, sorr, I will not, believe me now.'

'I'm not finished. There's your punishment . . . the room you occupy. I want you to move out.'

'Yes, sorr. Where should I be moving to?'

'Please yourself,' he said loftily. 'The men will move up for you, I'm sure.'

'Oh sorr, please, I couldn't . . .'

'No, I suppose not. Their quarters are already crowded. Tell you what. You move into the barn, there's a bunk by the door. That was good enough for your friend . . . What's his name, by the way?'

'Drew, sorr. Mr Drew.'

'Ah yes. On the run, I believe?'

'Not that he says. A free man he is, been gold-prospecting. And found gold he did, and all, but then wasn't he bushwhacked and left to die in a bush fire?'

'Rubbish! Go and get fresh tea. And don't forget the pickles.'

* * *

The boss, Major Kit Ferrington, dropped the newspaper on the floor, yawned, and sat looking out over his starlit domain. All was well in his world, his ten thousand acres of beautiful pastures, bought for a song and the signature of no less a personage than Sir George Gipps, former Governor of New South Wales, in return for his years as aide-de-camp to the gentleman.

It was during his stint at Government House that Kit had come across valuable information.

Despite opposition from the military, the Governor had decided to close down the notorious Moreton Bay penal settlement.

'It's a frightful place,' he had said, 'totally at odds with its surrounds, which are quite beautiful, sub-tropical you know, set by a grand river. If I allow that penal settlement to expand, it will forever ruin the reputation of Brisbane, a struggling little river port which I think has a good future if we look after it.'

'Convicts are still being transported, sir. The prison authorities claim they need Moreton Bay.'

'Then let them build a normal prison. I will not have an area of that size out of bounds to civilians as it is now. The perimeter of the convict settlement is huge, a waste. Then when I've cleared that out, we'll open the area for settlers. Yes. That is the agenda, Major. And I'll have no quibbles over it. No debates either. I ought to get surveyors up there now, to have a look about. Come to think of it, you should take a couple of our surveyors up there right away. Get some preliminary work done so they'll be ready as soon as the edict is published.'

'Yes, sir, I'll get on to it right away. And I wonder if you'd mind, sir, if I bought a couple of blocks of land up there myself, when they're ready for sale?'

Sir George peered at him over his spectacles. 'No law against it.'

In the heady gubernatorial atmosphere, meeting Sydney's elite, who held sway over huge estates, Kit had seen that a man could aspire to a lifestyle far beyond the means of a military man, unless he were a Wellington, showered with estates and riches, and that wasn't likely. These colonials, inferior in his mind to the true-born Englishmen, were known as squatters. They had expansive country estates set in private parklands, as well as ornate mansions in Sydney, and they entertained magnificently! Kit enjoyed their company and desperately aspired to that lifestyle in his own right, not as an aide to the Governor.

First, though, he had to find cheap land, but where could one look in New South Wales now? The squatters had collared the best a generation ago. It seemed the only land available at a price he could afford was hundreds of miles away, way out in the far west, and that was out of the question. He had no intention of burying himself far from civilisation at the mercy of the elements and wild blacks.

In the mean time, he had discovered that sleazy customs officers were stealing confiscated liquor held in warehouses on the wharves, and further investigations revealed that those warehouses contained hundreds of casks and bottles of wine and spirits. All were left there until duty was paid, or the owners volunteered, as smugglers, to claim their property. An unlikely turn of events. Most of the liquor was forgotten, gathering dust, providing an occasional tipple for customs men.

Major Ferrington did not report the gentlemen for pilfering; instead, he made a deal with them to take large quantities off their hands, to make room for the next shipments. It didn't stop the pilfering, that was understood, and they were happy to accept a few shillings from him to overlook large gaps on the warehouse shelves from time to time. Kit had noticed that the official documents were chaotic, so he had no qualms about removing the liquor, but it was not for his own use. He made tidy profits selling it to a woman who owned a sly grog shop in the heart of the harbourside slums, known as The Rocks.

He was cheered, thinking of Bonnie Hunter. What a one she was! Sly grogger. Money lender. Pawnshop owner. Brazen, gleeful, saucy, bold . . . ah, she was bold, and still a beauty closer to thirty, his own age, than the twenty she claimed. He'd come across her a few times during slumming jaunts with fellow officers, and then sought her out for advice on the disposal of quantities of liquor he had stored in a disused cellar.

From then on they'd become 'bosom' friends, as she liked to tease him. He wished he could bring her up here; she was exciting company, so lewd and sexy she drove him wild. What a romp they could have here, instead of having to meet in her miserable rooms behind the pawnshop. But it wouldn't do. Bonnie knew her place. She was his mistress, proud of it too, but that was all. Even though she insisted she was saving to buy her way out of those stinking streets, their worlds could never conjoin, she understood that. She knew about his fiancée, Jessie Pinnock, the only daughter of wealthy Parramatta pastoralists, and about this property; in fact, she'd loaned him money to help him pay for it, and that was all right. Bonnie was a good stick. But this side of his life was closed to her.

A bird squealed, and there was a scuffle high in nearby trees. Some cockatoos, crisp white against the dark sky, sailed into the air over the trees, screeching crossly at the disturbance before returning fussily to their roosts. Kit took off his shirt, dropped it to the floor and made for the crystal decanter on the sideboard. He poured himself a goblet of claret and went back to his chair, enjoying his reminiscences since there was no one to talk to.

He'd gone north with the surveyors, taken little interest in the place, rejecting an offer to buy cheap town allotments at the first sale. They weren't what he'd been looking for.

'It's land I want. Good farmland,' he told them.

'Too soon for here, Major. Over the other side of the ranges, squatters coming north on the inland trails are grabbing massive blocks,

32

but they're beyond the bounds of civilisation and prone to attack by the blacks.'

'Why can't we do the same here?'

'Give us time. Until we get rid of the penal settlement, no one can come within fifteen miles of this place, unless they have special permission, as we do.'

But Kit wouldn't give up. 'All right. I want land past the perimeter. Twenty miles out. What's out there?'

'According to old maps, the Brisbane River winds and winds, like a snake's path, so fifteen miles is still a good way upriver, and for all we know it could be mangrove country. Useless unless you could afford to drain it.'

Disappointed, Kit left it at that. 'Let me know when the real work starts and I'll come back.'

He'd accomplished much since then, not least finding the confidence to woo and win Jessie Pinnock, with the blessing of her grandfather, Marcus Pinnock, an influential squatter, and his friend Sir George Gipps. The latter was delighted that Kit had decided to stay in the colony.

'English gentlemen are greatly needed here, Kit, as the population expands. I am sure you'll do well. Are you still interested in taking up farming one day?'

'Oh yes. One of these days, when I can find the right property.'

'If I were you I'd take another look north. Buy your land on the outskirts of Brisbane while you still can.'

'I was hoping the surveyors might let me know what was available . . .'

'And I suggest you don't delay. I believe a new colony is to be founded in the north. Settlement there is too far from Sydney to be workable as part of New South Wales, and of course the land up there goes on for ever.'

Kit had no wish to invest in land that went on for ever out in the wilds, but his interest in the Brisbane River valley remained.

'Yes,' Governor Gipps was saying, 'I believe the new colony is to be called Queen's Land when they get round to it, and if I were you, Kit, I'd try to buy land before the rush. A new colony will mean Brisbane becomes the capital city.'

That rat's nest a capital city! Kit thought, amazed. But he didn't remark. Instead he took the Governor's advice, went to Brisbane and collared one of the surveyors for his personal explorations. Not long after that, a superb tract of land along the river was pegged out as belonging to Major Ferrington.

And just in time, he reminded himself.

Gipps was a quiet, retiring man. He relied on the Major to smooth his way through the whirl of social engagements that were part and parcel of his office, but when it came to the business of governing, he was decisive and single-minded to the point of pigheadedness, or so said his detractors.

The penal settlement was long closed, but then came the argument

33

about education. Gipps believed, demanded, that all children in New South Wales, rich and poor, must have free access to the education system, while leading citizens decried such an idea. They claimed the colony could never afford such fantastic largesse, but their petitions and complaints were ignored. The Governor ordered that schools be built.

When Kit arrived, triumphant, from Brisbane, deeds to ten thousand acres now secure in the bank, he found an even worse row had erupted. This time the Governor's demands sent shock waves through the community. He ordered a second trial of the men who had been accused of the cold-blooded murder of some forty or fifty blacks, including women and children. The crime was known as the Myall Creek massacre. The second trial upended the first jury's verdict and they were found guilty, most of them hanged. Right up to the last minute, reprieve for those white men was expected. But none came. The Governor was adamant on the punishment for the crime of murder.

Gipps was so unpopular by this that he was forced to return to England. 'And that's how old Gippsy and I came to the parting of the ways,' Kit murmured. 'It was time for me to strike out on my own.'

The Governor had arranged one last favour, an introduction to the chief warden of the Brisbane prison, who, he said, 'could be helpful in finding labourers for your farm. It is still legal to employ volunteer convicts only, so this fellow would be your man, in choosing workers.'

As it turned out, Rollo Kirk was very handy finding healthy workers for him, but he was also a villainous creature, and worse, a leech, claiming the Major as a great friend, presuming far too much. He was apt to call in uninvited whenever he was passing, and was damned hard to get rid of. Then again, it was Rollo who'd given him the true background to the Heselwood disaster long before the facts became known.

Kit finished off his wine, picked up the lamp and went through to his bedroom, congratulating himself that he'd had the good sense to stick to his guns and take up land close to the coast, even if the great expanse the other side of the hills was going at half the price. Lord Heselwood was a prime example. Sir George had warned the big squatters like Jasin Heselwood that to go too far out, too soon, was dangerous. But they wouldn't listen, too eager to grab huge swags of land beyond the boundaries of civilisation.

Jasin Heselwood had found out the hard way. The blacks had pounced, a woman and six stockmen were killed, his Montone homestead burned to the ground . . .

Kit shuddered. Madness to go too far west too soon. At least folk were safe here. The few blacks who still lived in the district were relatively harmless, he recalled grimly. His problems were with his own workers. He seemed to have been at war with them ever since his first convicts arrived. Instead of appreciating the absence of chains and locks, they were insolent and destructive to a degree that shocked the Major. He complained to

Rollo Kirk that they smashed farm implements, fouled their quarters and stole supplies, often selling them to tramps and absconders he would find skulking about his property.

Rollo took eight men back to prison and had their sentences extended; erected a triangle and carried out the first of the floggings, shaved the heads of the two bawdies who'd claimed to be cooks, and sent out replacements. Then it was up to Kit to maintain control, and he did so by following Rollo's example. They soon learned that the boss never deviated from his rule: offenders had a choice of swift punishment or a return to prison.

It had been a long haul, he sighed wearily, but at least the workforce had settled down to a reasonable routine, and oddly, they'd begun to treat him with something akin to respect.

He was relieved that he'd managed to punish Albert and Polly without having to get rid of them. They were indispensable to the smooth operation of this farm-in-the-making. When they were due for release he intended to offer them better pay to stay on. He might have blown his chances with Albert after tonight, but you never could tell; those types knew their place. Albert had broken the rules after all . . .

Escape was the first order of the day, Jack determined. To get out of here before anyone woke, but how? The walls were heavy timber, rough-hewn; they smelled old and musty. He was very aware of smells now that he'd returned to the white world. Where at first he'd been repelled by the odour of the rancid fat the Aborigines smeared on their bodies, now he found the whites had a stink of their own, stale and sweaty, not helped by the pissy smell of their clothes. Had Jack been in better health, Ferrington would never have caught him. He remembered the pong that had preceded the boss when he entered the barn, but he'd been too weary to interpret the warning in time. It won't happen again, he told himself, and then shook his head at his own foolishness.

'It won't happen again?' he muttered. 'You'll be smelling like the rest yourself soon enough.'

He leaned against the wall and tried to plan the attitude he would take when troopers arrived to collect him. No losing your temper, he warned. You've got to be polite, insist on your rights as a citizen, but be respectful, don't even criticise this Major fellow. Kid them you think the gentleman believed he was doing the right thing. Above all, keep calm. He thought about the new house up there, that had a smell all of its own. A good smell of fresh timbers and plaster; he hadn't come across that for a long time, by God. Then it hit him.

Fresh-sawn timbers! This shed was old. Rough-hewn. He bet this door didn't have metal hinges; they'd have used leather. He felt the door jamb, and sure enough, the hinges were home-made, smooth and old, sweet to the touch. Soon he was rubbing and scraping through them with his piece

35

of metal as fast as his hand would work, for fear someone would come by and catch him. They hadn't left a sentry, so he didn't have much to worry about, except . . . except, he thought, what the hell am I going to do when I get out? If I take off, this bastard boss could raise the alarm and I really would be on the run again . . . in a bloody country where the buggers shoot first when they're on the track of a native or convict. Maybe I should just go up to his house and dispose of him while he's asleep. That'll give me time to work out what to do next. Suddenly he felt the door lurch. The hinges had given way.

He set the door aside, climbed out, replaced it, then moved silently up towards the house. He circled the building in the darkness, taking note of the surrounds as well. Most of the rooms opened on to a wide wraparound veranda, and he easily located Ferrington's bedroom; the boss had gone to sleep and left the lamp on. And there on a tall chest of drawers was that gun. Kind of him.

Swiftly Jack entered the bedroom, turned out the lamp, took the gun, pleased to find it was loaded, and calmly sat on the side of the bed, whistling quietly. When that didn't wake the gentleman, he pressed the barrel of the revolver under his chin, forcing his jaw up, until Ferrington woke with a snap, and a yelp of fear.

Naked, he cringed against the bedhead, legs drawn up. 'Who are you?' he whispered, terrified.

'I'm your guest, Major. But you weren't treating me too kindly. I was just sitting here thinking of shooting you.'

'No! God no! Please don't shoot me. What do you want? Money? I've got some money here. You can have it . . .'

Jack stood and backed away from him, still undecided what to do for the best. For the long term, he worried. I could shoot the bugger, rob this place, grab a horse, and be gone before anybody wakes up. And I could end up in prison again.

'Don't worry,' he said, a kindly smile in his voice. 'I won't shoot you unless I have to. Get up. We have to talk.'

'What about?' Ferrington asked nervously, edging off the bed.

'About me, of course. I am a good citizen, not a felon or a thief as you say, and it was wrong of you to lock me up without even giving me a hearing. So we will have the hearing now. Stand up.'

Ferrington stood. 'Can I light the lamp?'

'No, I'm more comfortable in the dark. What are you doing?'

'I'm just reaching for my trousers.'

'Leave them. I'm not much used to trousers either.'

'Who the hell are you?'

'Come outside and sit on the step.'

That done, still holding the gun, Jack stood facing the Major and began his own interrogation. 'First things first. Who are you? I suppose you're an ex-warder from that prison?'

'I am not! I am Major Ferrington, recently retired from the service, and former aide to the Governor himself.'

'And who might he be?'

'It was Sir George Gipps. The present Governor is Sir Charles FitzRoy, not that it would mean anything to you.'

Jack nodded. 'That's true. Don't get too cheeky, though. I still have the gun.'

'And if you use it you'll hang.'

'True again. But if I can't talk some sense into you, I won't have any choice. Now you want to know who I am. The name is Jack Drew. I've been prospecting out in the bush for years and years, and I'm back now.'

'Why now?'

'Ha! I reckon you've heard about my gold. You don't have to tell me, I know what you're thinking. Is his story true or is it not? But forget about the gold for now; there's a war raging out in the bush between the blacks and the whites, so I reckoned it was getting too hot for a peaceful man. Time to head into civilisation.'

'And I'm supposed to believe that?'

'You have to believe it. You'll look a right fool if you try to make me out as an escaped convict. How many of your gaolbirds have been living in the buff for years and got sun-browned skin to prove it?'

'You could still be an absconder.'

This was the question Jack would have to confront with care. He leaned forward and put a foot on the second step. 'Listen here. I'm the one holding the gun. You're the one looks stupid, not me. If I was an absconder, I'd be shot of this country years ago. I could have taken a ship out of any port between here and Sydney.' He was grateful for the little extra bit of knowledge he'd only lately gleaned.

'But did you find gold?'

Jack grinned. He had him. He could feel the Major bursting to hear more about the gold, which could be his trump card if he played it right.

'Sure I did, and lost it just as fast. If I ever find them buggers, I'll carve 'em up and cook 'em.'

He saw the Major flinch at that, as he had intended, needing to remind him that the newcomer really could be dangerous. A cannibal even.

'But now, Major, what to do with you?'

'I insist you allow me to dress, it's nigh on dawn.'

'So it is, but for your life, what can you offer me?'

'You can go. Leave here. But if you decide to talk about where gold might be found, I won't send troopers after you.'

Jack sighed, 'And here I was thinking I could trust you as a gentleman. See that stump over there? It's riddled with bull ants. I could tie you and your bare arse to it and watch you dance until we make a deal, but you won't stick to the rules. You make me an offer,' he said, suddenly angry. 'An offer that you'll keep, or I won't be the only one limping round here.'

'Who let you out?' Ferrington demanded.

'Your stupidity. The hinges are leather, as you'll see if you live to check. I'm getting bloody sick of this chit-chat.'

'All right. I accept that you are a free man. You can stay here for a while on condition that you explain to me where that gold came from. And how you came to be washed up here anyway.'

Jack nodded. It was the best he could do for now. He didn't trust this bloke, but then Ferrington would be mad to trust him. A standoff.

'Can I go in and dress now?'

'Go ahead!'

'I'll have my gun back,' the Major said as he hurried inside, Jack following this time.

'Ah no, it's a bit soon for that. I don't doubt you've more guns here and there, so this will keep us even. But I tell you what, I'm bloody starving; the least you can do is offer your visitor breakfast.'

Ferrington scowled as he pulled on breeches and a shirt, both of fine cloth, Jack noticed with a pinch of envy. Still, that can be remedied, he mused, if I can get sorted out proper.

'I'm having a whisky,' Ferrington snapped, walking through to a dining room.

'That too,' Jack said evenly, trying not to look impressed as he took in the comforts of this grand room.

'Where do you come from?' Ferrington demanded, thumping a small glass of whisky on the table in front of this ruffian, and pouring a larger one for himself.

'London, of course. My folks were savers of souls. Me, I rathered look out for myself.'

Though still furious at being ambushed in his own home, Kit was less inclined to be concerned about Drew now, even if he did have the gun. Any felon worth his salt would have been on his way by this, robbery and maybe even murder in his wake, so it was fairly obvious Drew was telling the truth about being a prospector, if not necessarily about finding gold. In which case it seemed he did have a down-and-out tramp on his hands, and one who could possibly prove useful.

At this point Polly stuck her head round the door. 'I thought I heard . . .' She stopped short with a gasp at seeing Jack Drew sitting at the dining room table, drinking whisky with the boss.

'I'm ready for breakfast,' Kit snapped, dismissing her.

'So am I,' Drew called after her, but she knew better than to turn back.

Kit glanced at Drew, interested to see that the gun had disappeared from the table in a swift and tactful removal before Polly spotted it, a move that met with his approval. In the early light he saw the fellow clearly for the first time, noting the shrewd eyes and strong features, and was momentarily taken aback by the burns on the side of his face, weeping between the scabs.

'Those burns,' he said, ignoring the reappearance of the gun. 'Were they from the bush fire?'

'Yes. Got me down the side, arm and leg. Hurt like buggery.'

'There haven't been any bush fires around here lately.'

'The fires were back in the hills. I was bad hurt and some blackfellers looked after me. They couldn't do much so I asked them to take me downriver to the white folks. I reckon they must have tooken me at my word, kept coming till they saw white men in the fields, close 'nuff to find me. So they dumped me quicken before they got fired on. They weren't to know farm workers don't carry guns.'

Kit nodded. Probably true. No other explanation. He found Drew's sudden mispronunciations strange, considering that on the whole he spoke quite well for a tramp, and wondered if that had anything to do with the fellow's tale that he'd been living in the bush for ten years.

'You expected to see a doctor?' he asked.

'Of course I did. Why didn't your men send for one?'

'Because they're prisoners. They have no authority to do so.'

'You want to hope you don't get crook, mate.'

Kit ignored that remark and pointed to the gun. 'You might as well give me that. You can't follow me around all day, and I do have other firearms. But tell me this. If you lived with the blacks as you claim, can you speak their language?'

Drew nodded. 'Marl boolar gooliba boolarboolar boolargoolibar gulibaguliba.'

'What's that?'

'One two three four five.'

'How do I know it isn't what it sounds? Gobbledegook.'

Drew shrugged. 'You don't. And I'll keep the gun so we can stay even. I'm not getting locked up again.'

'I said you can stay.'

'Where?'

Kit couldn't allow the tramp to move into his house, nor did he want the fellow mixing with his workers. He was too much of a smartmouth.

'There's a room off the kitchen,' he said, with a smug smile. 'Polly will show you. I'll talk to you later. You won't be staying here scot-free; I've got a job for you.'

Polly looked tired. 'He had Albert flogged,' she whispered when Jack came into the kitchen. 'And the men are on half-rations . . .'

'I'm sorry.' He held his sore arm bent across his chest, as if nursing it, but he was actually nursing the gun against his chest under his loose shirt. He could have given it back; the Major was right, it was pointless to keep it now, but he liked the feel of it. He was looking forward to examining it in private.

'The boss said I could have a room off the kitchen. Is that it out there?'

39

He peered out of the window to the building across the other side of a small garden.

She stared. 'He's putting you in there? How come he let you out and you so pally with him now?'

'I think he knows I could be useful. Someone must have told him about my gold.'

She flushed. 'So we all get punished? Albert's down there in agony and you get the welcome, eh? That's the thanks we get. Your room's over there, *Mister* Drew. Are you taking breakfast with him, Your Honour?'

'No. In the room,' Jack said angrily. The punishments had been meted out. It was too late to do anything about them. He'd said he was sorry. What more did the woman want? Should he go back to that useless lockup to make them happy? Bloody hell!

The small room was neat and smelled of her cleaning. The iron bed had a mattress and pillow and sheet and blanket. He touched them gingerly. A plain table and chair sat on the cold stone floor and a curtain across a corner was meant as a closet, he supposed. Years back he would have thought this a little palace, but now it was too restricting. He opened the window as wide as it would go, took the chair and propped it against the door to keep it open, and retreated to seat himself on the edge of the bed, telling himself he would have to get used to this. Be a normalty . . . normal person again. He heard himself stumble over the English, but it didn't bother him. He was his own man, he could talk how he liked.

Just then Polly came tramping over with a tray which she dumped on the chair at the door.

'Your breakfast, *Mister* Drew!' she called angrily, and stormed back to her kitchen.

Jack was upset that she was still angry with him, making him feel guilty, but he didn't know how to redeem himself. He lifted the tray cloth and stared at delicious burned chops, bread and butter and a pot of tea. And the white man's eating tools! He picked them up carefully, mouthing, 'Knife, spoon, cup and, er . . . fork? Yes.'

He knew about them all right, but did he have to bother now? He was right hungry.

Quietly he closed the door, put the tray on the floor and fell upon this banquet with his fingers.

The meal finished, Jack gave a belch of pleasure and turned his attention to the revolver. It was a beauty, with a silver-embossed butt, smooth bore and muzzle loading. The cylinder held five chambers. He had seen revolvers like this in his holdup days, but had never owned one as neat and expensive as this one. Funny he should be reminded of his career as a highwayman when he hadn't thought about those times, not even about England, for years. He'd run away from home at thirteen, run away from his parents, a sanctimonious pair, full of cant and sham, who'd presided over a dockside seafarers' mission, hell-bent on saving souls.

'With whip and cosh,' he growled as he lowered himself on to the bed.

Ordinary seamen, discovering that charity came at a price, avoided the Wodrow Mission, but weaker characters, cajoled into confessing their sins, allowed themselves to be severely beaten by the Reverend while his wife sang hymns over them. And of course the violence didn't stop there. Their two little sons, Jack being the elder, were subjected to daily whippings and clouts. So much so that Jack, in whispers, referred to their mother Clara as 'Clout', since she could hardly pass them without lashing out at them. She regarded them as sinners who had to be brought to the Lord by harsh measures, and was even more callous in her treatment of the children than their father was. Sometimes when they were cold and shivering, refused access to the warm kitchen, Father would try to explain to them that their mother was a good woman, and was only doing her best for them.

Jack scowled, remembering. 'Poor fool, young Hector,' he muttered. 'He believed that tripe.'

More realistic than his young brother, Jack thought the woman was simply vicious, and their father, Mervin Wodrow, a plain idiot. He'd seen how it pleased the Reverend Wodrow to hurt and humiliate gullible seamen, and he'd also seen the other side of the man, sucking up to the nobs, usually wealthy do-gooders, who came down to the docks to view his good works, and, Jack soon realised, get a thrill out of peering into London's wicked underbelly.

Nearly all of them donated to the mission, not realising that most of the money went into Clout's moneybox, the one she kept locked in the heavy oak cupboard upstairs in her bedroom. The do-gooders were under the impression that the Wodrows lived in the tiny stone dwelling behind the waterfront mission, because they'd see the two boys there, poring over their lessons, but they were wrong. Once the mission closed of an evening, the family would flee the area, hurrying on past the canal to their home, a neat stone cottage behind a high wall, fully a mile and a half away.

As for the do-gooders, having ventured into a known crime-ridden area, there was anger but not surprise when many of them lost their purses or other valuables to pickpockets, but there would have been surprise on the part of all of them, including his parents, had they known the pickpocket was the Reverend's elder son, well taught by local exponents of the trade.

Having saved several pounds for his getaway money, Jack had intended to take Clout's moneybox with him as well, but he'd left it too late. She'd finally taken the plunge and banked their considerable funds for fear they could be robbed while they were away during the day. By then, though, their son had had enough of them, so he could delay no longer. He tried to persuade his ten-year-old brother to come with him, but Hector was too frightened to attempt such a radical move. He was afraid Jehovah would strike him dead.

Jack came up from these recollections, his head a little fuzzy, to find

41

himself sitting on the bed, still nursing the revolver. It was a shame to have to do this, he admitted ruefully, but he'd better give it back. Obviously the Major treasured it, and there was no point in irritating or even threatening the man by hanging on to it. After all, he grinned, I could easily search out his other weapons if I put my mind to it.

He padded through an open door and went on to the dining room to plant the gun on the table in front of his host, who simply nodded and went on eating a huge piece of steak.

'What's the job?' Jack asked.

'I do not like to be interrupted during a meal. And you may not enter my house in future without knocking. And you will address me as sir. Have you got that?'

'Yes. I'll wait outside on the veranda. I've got plenty of time.'

He walked out of the French doors, wishing he could cast off these clothes because they were rubbing against wounds that were already feeling like mounds of wasp stings, and stood looking down the valley. In the distance men were burning piles of cleared scrub, the smoke curling lazily in the humid air, and an eagle circled overhead watching for prey disturbed by the heat.

Polly came out. '*Mister* Drew, sorr, the Major wishes me to show you to the bathroom. He says you are his guest and you need a bath.'

Jack didn't bother to respond; he simply followed her curiously down the centre passage to a room tucked on the end, beside a large water tank. He had never seen a bathroom in a private house; he'd only frequented bath houses in London, in his heyday, when he'd worn snappy clothes and the swish hats befitting his profession.

This place had a high-backed tin bath set in the middle of the room, with a large tap hanging over the end.

'Here's a towel,' she said. 'You put the plug in and turn the tap on. You don't need hot water today, it's too hot.'

The latter sounded like a punishment, and Jack grinned. 'Cold will do. You gonna wash me?'

'Oh surely,' she snapped sarcastically. 'I suppose you had black women to do that, your lordship.'

'Yes,' he said, as he turned the tap, while Polly, snorting her disgust, rushed away.

'I was only joking,' he called after her, but there was no response.

The tap took a while to provide enough water for a bath, and eventually Jack climbed in, nursing a large bar of soap, which did help to remove the mud that had accumulated since his arrival on the riverbank like Moses. He wished he could tell the story to his parents, of their son being delivered up to King Ferrington and taken in like a little prince. They could make a good sermon for the believers out of that one.

He looked up when Ferrington came in.

'Thought you'd turn up.'

'You needed a bath. You smell.'

'So do you.'

'I brought you some clothes. I can't have you up here dressed like a convict. Boots you can get from the store.'

'I don't need boots.'

'Please yourself.'

While they were talking, the Major was checking up on him as Jack had guessed he would. He now took note.

'The wound on your shoulder. That's not a burn.' He stepped quickly round the bath to look at his guest's back. 'I thought so. That's a bullet wound.'

'That's right. I got ambushered . . . ambushed.'

'Shot?'

'You'd have a bit of trouble chucking me into a fire if you didn't shoot me first. I got shot. So?'

'So who were your attackers?'

'I don't know. You want to have a look at my behind. I've got a scar from a spear there.'

'Running from *them* too?'

'No. It was a game. I lost.'

The Major was peering out of the window. He stuck his head in the air with a sniff. 'Very well. You ought to bandage that arm, it seems to have taken the worst of the burns.'

With that, he left, and Jack looked down at his toes.

'What do you know? I think he believes you.' He still didn't know what the job was about, but it occurred to him that the high-and-mighty bossman could get a bit lonely here, mightn't mind having someone to talk to.

'Crikey,' he said, as he jumped out of the Major's bath, 'I wonder if he plays cards? It's a long bloody time since I saw a pack, but I surely wouldn't mind learning again.'

A sudden downpour swept in from the surrounding hills, and Jack stood moodily at the window, trying to remember something about this valley that was stirring in his mind. He was certain he'd never been here before, but he might have passed the outskirts when travelling out there on the other side of those hills. His last memory before this place was of Montone Station, and he hoped to God it wasn't nearby. The reminder of that station, and the raid, was painful, not only physically, but for the too-sudden separation from his friends and, of course, the loss of his gold.

He began to dress, pulling on the trousers, not new, but good cloth, he noted, and studying the white cotton shirt. To pull it on over the weeping burns on his arm would ruin the shirt; bandages were needed. So reluctantly, he had to ask Polly.

'You're wanting bandages for your arm, is it?'

He nodded, watching as she ferreted in a bag of rags and came up with some torn sheeting.

'That should do you.'

'How is Albert?'

'How would you think? Lyin' flat on his stomach for the fun of it?'

'Is there anything I can do for him?'

Polly glanced at him resentfully. 'Ask him yourself!'

He retreated to the room, managed to bandage his arm, and sat staring at the rain that had now set in, with rolls of thunder warning of heavier falls to come. He felt very tired and feverish, thanks to a lack of sleep, and though the bed with its white sheets was more intimidating than inviting, he was too exhausted to put up an argument. Soon he was asleep, with the blanket over his head to shut out the light.

Even then he could find no rest, his sleep interrupted by confused dreams and the discomfort of his injuries. He thought he could hear a woman screaming. It was dark, he couldn't see her, but he knew it was the woman in that bedroom, caught up in the tumult of the raid. The scream was agony, mingling with his own soundless screams, and then there was the fire, and he was trying to get back to her, knowing that they'd kill her, show no mercy on these raids, not even to women, and why should they? Their women and children were being slaughtered by the hundreds in this war. Hadn't they even killed his own wife, Ngalla, shot her down, an innocent with her family, guilty only of being black. But where was the woman? What had happened to her?

Jack threshed about trying to get to her. The door was open now but she was no longer there, and the fire was advancing; he thought he could hear her calling him and he lurched up, almost falling off the low bed. He was drenched in sweat, and he knew he was suffering from a high temperature. Groggily he looked about him. The rain was thudding down, the room was still and quiet, and very dry. He wiped his hand across his forehead and swept off the sweat as if flinging away that dream, but the woman's face was still there. He'd had the same dream, or something like it, recently, and guilt shivered within him again, that he'd been part of her final torment.

Sometime in the wavering between darkness and light, that time of confusion before they set him adrift down here, he'd heard Moorabi say that Montone Station had been razed to the ground. Burned down, ruined. They'd won. Bussamarai's reputation was intact. He'd heard that and been relieved. Until the woman confronted him in a dream. Upsetting him. What else could he have done to save her?

He thought of Albert, now suffering after a vicious flogging. And asked himself the same question: what could I have done? Nothing. And it was too late for anyone to help. But guilt remained, fanned by Polly's attitude. Though he was feeling a little wobbly, he decided to go down and see Albert; a walk in the rain might cool the furnace at work behind his forehead.

*　*　*

44

He was only halfway down the hill when he met the Major, who exploded.

'Where the hell do you think you're going?'

'Down there.' Jack pointed.

'The workmen's quarters are out of bounds to you. Go on back.'

'I heard you flogged Albert for taking me in.'

'I didn't flog him; two of the men attend to those things. But he deserved it. He broke the rules.'

'Bloody tough rules, when all he did—'

Ferrington interrupted angrily. 'Standard procedure! He had a choice. Back to prison or take the whip. And he's smart enough to know that if I sent him back he'd probably get flogged there anyway.'

'But you didn't have to give the order to flog him.'

'And you mind your own bloody business. I have to keep that pack of cutthroats in order, and I do it without chains or locks. You say you're not a convict, you came out here a free man, in which case you know nothing of these matters, so keep your nose out.'

It suddenly occurred to Jack that there'd be another reason for Ferrington to invite himself into the bathroom and inspect him, especially his back. To see if he carried the scars of a flogging! Dead giveaway for convicts. He thanked his stars he'd managed to steer clear of the whip before he escaped . . .

'The job,' Ferrington said, gesturing for Jack to go on ahead of him to a side veranda, out of the rain. 'I want to discuss this with you.'

Jack wished he had the courage to demand to see Albert, though such a measure wouldn't alleviate the poor bloke's pain. He wished he had the resources to tell Ferrington to go to hell, and walk away from this place.

'Right,' the boss said, when they were safe under cover. 'As soon as the rain stops I want to do some exploring around here. I haven't had time before this. Further out there are the really big stations taken up by inlanders. Did you see any of them?'

'Saw some houses, not many,' Jack said. 'I was a long way north, I think. Travelled from Sydney out west over the ranges, then worked north wherever the black families were going, so I had sustenance.'

'What's it like the other side of these ranges?'

'Much the same as this side.'

'I heard it was desert.'

'Desert? No, desert's a long way west.'

'Well, my plan is to follow the river valley. Have a good look around. See what and who is there. I always wanted to do that . . .'

Jack listened to him rattle on about the valley and its surrounds, and the advantages of knowing all there was to be known about it, if one were to be a successful pastoralist. He had already guessed his own role. Obviously this character had no one to accompany him besides convicts, and that would be demeaning and maybe asking for trouble. And then trouble was easy enough for a lone traveller to stumble on in the bush, especially if he ran into cranky blackfellers. Not all of the blacks would be shoved out of here by the whites; they'd probably pulled back into the heavily wooded hills. Ferrington would know that and would appreciate a guide who knew the language.

'What's the name of this river?' he asked.

'The Brisbane River.'

'Is that all? The name in blackfeller words might have given me a hint on where I am.'

'I can't see what difference that will make. I can show you exactly where we are. Come inside and look at my maps.'

Yes, Jack thought, you know on paper, but the blacks call places different names. I know by landmarks. With luck I'll recognise something, since it looks as if I'm to be the guide. He smothered a laugh, thinking of language ... Can I speak blackfeller language? Sure I can. I can speak one, only one, of the Kamilaroi, and that a dialect. Don't you know there are hundreds of languages and hundreds of dialects, you bloody fool? How do I know which one we've got here?

He shrugged and followed the Major inside, passing a dresser that featured an ornamental mirror. He saw someone in the mirror, realised it was himself, ducked back with a grin to have a better look and stood, rooted to the spot in shock ... The face before him was that of an old man. His hair was peppered with grey and his heavy eyebrows had a white shading as if snow had lodged on them. He brushed at them, but the white stayed. His face was leaner, his eyes serious, intent; they seemed to have lost the squint of humour they once owned. His skin was leather, and the burns on his cheek were horrible. Ugly as sin! But worst of all, he looked so bloody old.

He totted back. Forty, I'd reckon. Only bloody forty and I look sixty. More!

Ferrington was waiting for him. 'Admiring yourself, Drew?'

Jack turned from the mirror very slowly, still dazed. 'No. I was just thinking how bloody hard I did those ten years living native.'

'Why did you stay so long?'

'I was certain I'd find gold.' And that was the truest part of his fragmented tale, he admitted to himself with a sigh. Turned yourself into an old man in the doing.

He didn't ask Drew to come with him, and offer the opportunity for refusal. He deliberately took it for granted that the fellow would accompany him, thus avoiding any decision-making. Drew was a stubborn character, that was obvious, stubborn almost to the point of madness, if he'd hung on so long in his quest for gold. He had not accepted the necessity for Albert's flogging either, which meant he remained critical of his boss, but that was common among the working class, so one had simply to take note and be aware. But his presence on a tour of the district would be reassuring; a man needed backup and this fellow was ideal.

The Major walked through to the parlour and watched the plasterers at work, as proud of the delicate roses at the cornices as if he'd formed them with his own hands. From there he marched out the back and across muddy fields to begin his daily inspections. He'd been caught up in Brisbane much longer than he'd expected, waiting for drovers to bring a large mob of cattle to the saleyards, but they hadn't eventuated. He was furious when he learned that the drovers had sold them en route without even bothering to let waiting buyers know.

'Bound to happen,' Rollo Kirk told him, 'with all these new settlers coming through town. You'd better use a stock agent.'

He walked by a hedge of grevilleas, their red flowers like flames flickering in the greenery, and thought how much Jessie would appreciate them. Looking about him now, despite the misty rain, he thought his property was pretty as a picture, everything so green, the white house nestling on the hill as if it belonged there from the beginning. The tall gum trees that bordered the long drive out to the road were like sturdy sentinels; they looked quite wonderful. Kit himself had marked each one for preservation. Instead of pushing the drive through the forest, straight from road to house, he'd insisted it wind around the huge old trees, and the result pleased him. The drive was a half-mile long, the house hidden by a hill until one rounded a bend and came upon it. His treasure.

The dairy was clean, well swabbed out. Tom Lok was busy in there separating the milk. Kit gave him a nod and went on through to the stables, where he saddled his horse and headed down the track to see how the land clearing was progressing. He really enjoyed living here now, everything was going so well. It seemed to him a great nuisance that he'd undertaken to travel to Sydney to bring Jessie and her mother up to view the property and discuss plans for the wedding. And then, when the date was set, to have to return. There for quite some time, to meet social requirements prior to the wedding day.

As he rode along the track by the river he decided it would be a good idea to build a jetty by the boat ramp. To put a more substantial structure there. But getting back to the wedding, he reminded himself . . . why go to all that trouble? Why not go down just the once? Get married. Come back. Bring his wife back with him. This house with its lovely surrounds was ideal for a honeymoon. He knew Jessie and her interfering mother had been discussing a honeymoon in the Blue Mountains, which would keep him away from the farm even longer, and run him into even more expense. Well, it wouldn't do. He would explain to Jessie, if he had to, that they simply did not have the money to waste on trivialities. Stocking the property was their priority.

He almost turned the horse there and then, but decided to keep the men on their toes by riding over, shouting a few orders about tree roots not properly hauled out and the necessity to leave some trees as a windbreak. Soon enough he was back in his office looking over the yard, composing a

47

letter to Jessie about revised plans. She'd be thrilled. And he was too, for that matter. He'd been too long on his own here. A wife would make all the difference. He grinned. You could say that again. Sex on call. Jessie looked a lusty young lady, properly rounded. She'd make a good wife for a lonely man. By God she would. And her dowry would make a difference. Not to mention her future inheritance.

He drew out a sheet of stationery and embossed it across the corner with his initials . . .

My dear Jessie, he wrote in his full, flowing hand.

Chapter Four

Adrian Pinnock was angry with his grandfather for keeping them late. He'd been looking forward to the luncheon at Government House, even though he'd been commandeered into escorting his young sister.

'What are you making such a fuss about?' she asked him.

'Sir Charles hates people to be late.'

'We won't be seated for another hour yet, we've plenty of time.'

'I don't want to rush, be just in time to hit the trough. I like to socialise, to talk to people.'

'Anyone in particular?'

'Cecilia Dignam, if you must know. I hear she wants a word with me.'

'Cissie Dignam! That stuck-up ninny? What does she want to talk to you about?'

'I believe she'd like me to escort her to the military ball,' he said proudly.

'Really! Wait until I tell Mercia she has to *ask* boys to escort her!'

'You can be so juvenile, Jessie! It's nothing to do with Mercia, so mind your own business.'

He paced the drawing room angrily, pausing every so often to adjust his black silk cravat in the long mirror and jerk his frockcoat into place. Jessie was amused by this fussing. Her brother hadn't had the slightest interest in smart clothes until they moved from Parramatta to Sydney, where he'd met up with the military crowd. She supposed it would be difficult for a young man to have to compete with the army officers stationed here; they were always resplendent in their uniforms and many of them were very handsome. One in particular, she sighed. Her very own Major Ferrington, to be exact. Tall, fair-haired and fair of face too, she recalled with a warm smile.

She missed him so much, her dear fiancé, it was almost too hard to bear, especially since he wasn't much of a correspondent. His courting had been wonderfully romantic when he'd been an aide at Government House. There'd been so many enjoyable social functions to attend that Jessie had found herself in a complete whirl, capped by his sudden proposal of marriage. She still couldn't believe that it had happened. That she, only a country girl, was to marry Kit Ferrington, the most dashing and popular officer in Sydney.

He'd often talked about acquiring a farm and Jessie had found that sensible; after all, the Pinnocks were graziers themselves, so she'd be happy on the land. It hadn't occurred to her, though, that it would take so long for him to find the right land and get it established for habitation. And it was rather disconcerting to learn that his final choice was so far away, best accessed by ship. It seemed to Jessie that they were moving to another country, and though she accepted her future husband's decisions, she was a little sad to be leaving her mother, a widow, and Grandfather Marcus, who was getting old now. But, she sighed, it had to be. She wished Kit would write more often, though. He'd only been back to Sydney once in six months.

'Rome wasn't built in a day,' Grandfather had said. 'Give the man time. My pater took years to clear our properties; he couldn't even afford convict labour. Thanks to his hard work and foresight we're sitting pretty for generations, and that's what Kit is trying to do for you.

'At least we should be,' he added grumpily, 'as long as that brother of yours does the right thing.'

Jessie's mother and her grandfather were always at odds over Adrian. He claimed that his grandson was lazy and irresponsible, while Blanche Pinnock defended her son.

'If you'd give him some responsibility he'd settle down. But no, you like to run everything yourself, without ever referring to Adrian. No wonder he's spending more time in town than at the station.'

'His father never complained at how I run things. He pitched in and worked; he knew what to do without being asked.'

'Adam had a different temperament, Marcus. You know that.'

'What are you saying? That Adrian is not fitted for hard work? Then he'd better find out quick smart what he *is* fit for, apart from playing the dandy.'

'I didn't say he isn't a hard worker. You'd see that he is if you'd stop being so critical!'

The argument went round and round, Jessie reflected, never-ending. Just then her mother came in to tell them that a message had come from Marcus to say he'd been held up at the meeting of the hospital board and for them to go on ahead.

'Marcus has the carriage, so we'll have to take a horse cab now,' she said, fixing her wide hat in place. 'Run up and get one, Adrian.'

'No need. I'll get my new brougham, Mother. You'll have to ride in it now. You'll love it. Hang on, I'll be back in a tick.'

Blanche shook her head. 'Your grandfather is furious with him for buying that vehicle. It was so expensive and we don't need it.'

'Yes we do,' Jessie laughed. 'For occasions like this. Adrian is so proud of it, Mother, and I think it's fun to ride in. It's very light and Adrian says it's easy on the horse because the forewheels can turn so sharply.'

'Why would one want to do that if not using excessive speed, I'd like to

50

know. If we need another vehicle as you say, another small carriage would have done us quite well. I wouldn't say this in front of your grandfather, but Adrian should be reminded that the Pinnocks do not need to show off. I find that vehicle quite vulgar.'

The brougham was comfortable, Blanche had to admit, with well-padded upholstery and everything of good quality, even the lacquered rug boxes and side lamps, but as they spun down South Head Road, she called to Adrian: 'Slow down! This is not a race.'

He eased the horse back a little. Only a little, she noticed, but it would have to do, so she sat back, well out of sight, not needing to be seen in this flashy lightweight conveyance, even if they were all the fashion.

'Gloves on, please,' she said to Jessie.

'I will, but we're not there yet. It's too hot.'

'Then keep your hands out of sight.'

Jessie looked lovely today, Blanche mused, her dark hair complemented by the summery blue georgette gown that the dressmaker had finished only yesterday. It was perfect for today's elegant gathering, as was the lovely chapeau she was wearing. And to think Blanche had had to insist she buy it, because she claimed it was too fussy! Absently, Blanche smoothed the lapels of her own grey silk dress with its white satin trim. Her favourite. It was so cool and so understated.

Unlike her daughter, Blanche loved clothes. And jewellery. She had two rooms set aside for her wardrobe in the Rose Bay house, and another two in the Parramatta homestead. Barney, her dear late husband, had found her preoccupation with clothes amusing.

'Some ladies,' he used to say, 'enjoy gardening or needlework or uplifting reads, while others tinkle a piano or trill a tune, but Blanche's hobby is fashion.'

'That is not strictly correct,' she'd told him. There was fashion and fashion! Oversized skirts and hats and gaudy colours, for instance, were oft cited as fashionable, where Blanche found them hideous.

'Everything has to conform to one's sense of good taste, first and foremost,' she would say, but no one listened. It was disappointing that Jessie, who could look an absolute picture in the right clothes, for she was a good-looking girl, preferred comfort before couture.

They were travelling down busy Macquarie Street now, past the hospital, and on towards the botanic gardens, the pride and joy of all Sydney. She really did love living here, but she wondered now if it had been a mistake to move from the country after Barney died. A mistake when it came to her son and daughter. Adrian had got in with a fast crowd, mainly military gentlemen, if many of them could be called that, and to her horror, Jessie too had become part of their set.

She glanced at her daughter. Jessie was headstrong, and a little too outspoken for her own good, but a sensible girl. If the truth were known,

51

far more down-to-earth than her brother. Blanche had remonstrated with her about the company she was keeping, but Jessie had laughed.

'Don't worry, Mother. I know they're all a bit ratty.'

'Shallow, I would say.'

'Maybe. But they can be very nice and most amusing. They're all from Britain or India, so it's most interesting to talk to them.'

She could hardly refuse to allow Jessie to mix with her brother's new crowd, but the girl did have other friends whom she saw regularly, so Blanche expected this stage to pass. Until Major Kit Ferrington loomed up on the scene, handsome, a social lion due to his vice-regal connections, and ambitious. And, Blanche thought, calculating.

But no one agreed with her, of course. Even Marcus liked him. Said he was a gentleman and a man of foresight. 'Investing in that land up north is a brilliant move, pioneering again, just like my pater did. I can't believe you would object to him marrying Jessie.'

'Mother,' Adrian called now. 'Please!'

She looked up, startled to find that they had arrived at the impressive entrance to Government House, and a flunky was waiting, holding open the door of the brougham.

Sir Charles and Lady FitzRoy were still in the hall welcoming their guests when the Pinnocks arrived, but no sooner had Lady FitzRoy greeted them than she was called away.

'Then may I have the honour of escorting you, Mrs Pinnock?' her host asked. 'There don't seem to be any more comers.'

'Thank you,' Blanche said as they moved down the crowded hall. 'I did so want to speak with you, Sir Charles. Have you had word of Georgina and Jasin Heselwood?'

'Oh my dear! I have. I've been telegraphing Brisbane, where they are resting quietly. Certainly Georgina would need that after such a shocking experience. Jasin says she was very brave. Rode hard with the men to escape, with those savages on their heels.'

'Oh my goodness! Is she all right?'

'Yes. They did intend to come back to Sydney on the first available craft, and of course my wife issued them an invitation to stay here, but apparently there's been a change of plan. I don't know quite what at the moment. Poor things, their fine new homestead burned to the ground.'

A voice behind them interrupted: 'They've still got that land, Sir Charles; you can't burn down land. I hear it's a splendid property.'

Sir Charles turned. 'Marcus! Glad to see you. I was becoming concerned that I should have to find a stand-in for your speech. But you're right. I believe Montone *is* quite splendid. I suppose they'll go back one day. If Georgina is up to it. His lordship isn't one to surrender.'

* * *

52

The drawing room was crowded and Jessie looked about her with a touch of sadness. Government House and its lovely setting overlooking the harbour was so familiar to her. These gracious rooms, so beautifully furnished, were always a joy, but more so in Kit's company. And as an aide, he'd known it all so well, even showing her which china and cutlery were used for various functions, depending on their social standing. She guessed the third best would do for today, this luncheon being held to raise money for the hospital, with no very important personages present apart from His Excellency. Cissie Dignam and her brother Sam came over to join them just as the crowd began a slow surge into the ballroom, where tables were set for lunch.

'We ought to swap partners,' Adrian teased. 'You take Jessie, Sam, and I'll look after Cissie.'

'You will not,' Blanche said crossly. 'You will seat yourselves exactly where you were placed.'

'He was only joking, Mother,' Jessie said, but Sam Dignam grinned. 'I thought it was a good idea.'

So did Blanche, but she couldn't allow young people to upset table arrangements, especially not here, where Lady FitzRoy went to so much trouble. She wondered what made the fates so contrary. Sam had always been fond of Jessie. He was a kind and thoughtful young man, and wealthy in his own right, thanks to family bequests. Exactly the opposite of Kit Ferrington, she mused sourly. Then there was his sister, Cecilia, who was chasing after Adrian, a silly girl who had grown embarrassingly snobbish over the last few years. Where that had come from, Blanche couldn't imagine. Their parents were also pastoralists, decent people, never given to such rudeness as their daughter often displayed.

Blanche wished she had a magic wand with which to transfer Cecilia's affections towards the Major and Jessie's to Sam, but since she had no control over such matters, she sighed and meekly took her place beside Marcus, who didn't appear to be well. His face was flushed.

'Are you all right?' she whispered.

'Yes. Just a bit hot. I walked up Macquarie Street.'

'Oh dear. You shouldn't have! Not on a day like this.'

'Shush . . . His Excellency is about to speak.'

Sir Charles was in fine form, congratulating the committee members on their hard work, and Lady FitzRoy, for her guidance. He announced that the target of one hundred pounds had been raised, but if any ladies or gentlemen present might care to double the sum in aid of a children's ward at the Sydney Hospital, hands up anyone who would object.

Amid laughter, no objections were heard, and two gentlemen doubled the sum, taking the amount to two hundred pounds and then to four, for which the second gentleman received a hearty ovation.

Then Marcus Pinnock, chairman of the hospital board, delighted by the additions to the hospital finances, walked up to the small stage beside the Governor to give his address. He thanked their hosts and the good people who cared enough to ensure that Sydney Hospital offered the best possible treatment, and then took a little time to wipe perspiration from his face, apologising for the delay. He began his speech again, but cut it short, going straight to the last few lines.

Blanche was distressed; she knew he'd laboured over that speech for days because he wanted support for stricter registration for doctors in New South Wales, to counter the many quacks who were hanging out shingles. He hadn't mentioned any of that.

She watched as the old man began to make his way back to the table, but suddenly he veered away and lurched for the door leading to the kitchen.

Blanche was beside her father-in-law almost before he fell, but he was a big man, and though she did try to halt his fall, he crashed to the floor just as a waiter carrying a tray of dishes approached. He went sprawling too, creating a terrible din.

Sir Charles himself rushed over, ignoring the smashed china all round them, to lift Marcus up.

'So sorry, sir, so . . .' Marcus tried, then he collapsed again.

The Governor made way for Dr Bob Austin, a luncheon guest, who quietly told His Excellency that it appeared the old gentleman had suffered a heart attack.

Two footmen carried Marcus into a private sitting room and placed him on a divan. Jessie and Adrian came hurrying to the door.

'How is he?' Jessie whispered to her mother.

'Not good. Bob will arrange for him to be taken to hospital shortly. Poor Marcus, he is barely conscious. It was a terrible shock to see him collapse like that, and he was so concerned. I hope they're going on with the luncheon,' Blanche said.

'Yes, they are,' Adrian said. 'But the spark's gone out of it, I'd say.'

They returned home late that evening, a weary trio, desperately worried about Marcus, and frustrated that there was nothing they could do but wait until the morning, when a verdict might be forthcoming.

'He's sleeping now,' Bob had told them eventually. 'You might as well go on home.'

As she walked through the vestibule, Blanche picked up a letter from a tray on the hall stand, and saw it was for Jessie. She hoped Ferrington had made a better effort with this one, after the few unimaginative lines he had allowed the girl last time.

'A letter,' she called to Jessie, who was following her inside. 'I think it's from your fiancé.'

Jessie was thrilled. She grasped the letter and ran upstairs to her room.

54

It was quite long for Kit, two pages. He hoped she was well, and told her the house was progressing and was very smart for this area . . . 'if I do say so myself', he added.

He wrote that he was taking Marcus's advice and turning to cattle, since it appeared this district was too wet for sheep. And he said he'd been in Brisbane on business, and whilst there had hoped to catch up with Lord and Lady Heselwood, but apparently they were recovering from their ordeal and not receiving for the time being. 'The attacks by blacks are all the talk here, but rest assured we're in a safe area.'

Jessie glanced over to the bottom of the second page, hoping for a little more than his usual 'yours affectionately', but there it was again. Recently she'd been permitted to read a letter Mercia Flynn's sister had received from *her* fiancé, and had been cross with envy. He'd called her 'my darling' and 'my darling lover' and smothered her with kisses, signing off with 'everlasting love'.

Why couldn't Kit do that? Perhaps she should mention this in her next letter. Maybe not. Not since, following his example, she'd been shy about expressing her love for him. She never wrote smothering him with kisses either. She dared not. Which was sad.

With a sigh she turned back to the letter, learning that the weather was still hot but bearable.

Then he explained that he was kept busy here, and . . . 'since I almost have everything in readiness for my bride, I see no reason why we should not be married as soon as possible. I shall be in Sydney next month. Don't you agree we could be married then? Do let me know if this plan is suitable and kindly suggest a date if so. I still have the Irish cook and I think you will agree to keep her on . . .'

'Mother! Where are you? Where are you? I have the most marvellous news!'

Blanche rushed out of the dining room as her daughter hurtled down the stairs. 'What's happening? What are you yelling about, Jessie?'

'Kit and I are to be married next month. Next month! Isn't it just wonderful?'

'For goodness' sake, Jessie, settle down. What's all this about?'

'I told you!' Jessie said, hugging her mother in her excitement. 'We're to be married next month. Kit says the house is ready . . .'

'How can it be ready when we haven't had any measurements for drapes and curtains and floor rugs? Measurements he promised to send.'

'Oh, don't worry about that. The thing is, Kit says he'll be down next month and we ought to be married then. I mean, it's so sensible, Mother. Poor man, he can't be sailing up and down the coast all the time.'

Blanche frowned. 'That wasn't the arrangement, Jessie. We were to visit, you and I, when the house was ready, so that you could see your

55

future home and decide, once and for all, that that was where you wanted to spend the rest of your life.'

'No,' Jessie said angrily. 'That was your arrangement. I didn't need to decide once and for all, as you say. I had already made up my mind to marry Kit; there was no necessity for any of that.'

Blanche took her into the parlour and closed the door so that the servants wouldn't hear them arguing. 'Quieten down, miss. That was the original agreement I had with Kit. Now he's asking you to break it, without referring to me.'

'I know. But please, Mother, I'm sure he doesn't mean to be disrespectful. He's only being practical, and you really can't argue with that.'

'He's making it difficult. He must know perfectly well that it takes time to organise a formal wedding, there's so much to do, and anyway it's certainly not feasible now, with your grandfather so ill. Surely you haven't forgotten him?'

Jessie blushed. 'Oh Lord, I hadn't really . . .'

'Of course not. So you'd better write or telegraph Kit straight away. Thank him, but let him know about Marcus, and say that any such arrangements are out of the question now. But we look forward to his visit next month . . .'

Jessie walked over to the window, disappointed. Then she turned back to her mother. 'I can't believe you're doing this. Next month isn't tomorrow. Kit can't be sailing up and down from Brisbane all the time to please you. We have managers on our properties. And overseers. He doesn't have help like that. He has to look after everything himself.'

'I know. But he agreed to the original arrangement.'

'You never did like Kit. You're just doing this to delay the wedding.'

'I see. I also arranged for your grandfather to have a heart attack so as to delay the wedding. There just isn't time right now, Jessie. We can't even consider celebrations with Marcus so low.'

'You can't, but I can,' Jessie said stubbornly. 'I shall write to Kit that I agree. Grandfather will understand. If you're not up to helping me arrange my wedding, leave it to me. I'll organise everything myself.'

Sam Dignam called by the hospital early the next morning to enquire after Marcus Pinnock, distressed to hear that the old fellow had suffered some paralysis and loss of speech. He waited around, hoping to see Jessie, and was not disappointed initially, but soon after she arrived with her mother, she gushed that her marriage was to take place the following month. He left the hospital thoroughly depressed, bought himself a newspaper and sat in nearby gardens pretending to read while he digested this latest bit of bad news.

He disliked Kit Ferrington, not caring that jealousy could be half of his attitude, because he had heard some strange stories about the fellow, mainly that he'd been involved with a disreputable woman and with sly grogging

56

operations in The Rocks district. They were only rumours, though, and in all conscience Sam couldn't repeat them, not even to Adrian, though he'd been tempted often enough.

He did know that it had been Kit Ferrington who'd introduced Adrian to the dance hall girls from the Bijou Theatre, with the result that Adrian, all of nineteen, was now madly in love with Flo Fowler, the magician's assistant. Flo was a pretty little thing, all curls and curves, and Adrian was no match for her wide-eyed prettiness.

Sam turned his attention to the paper and read that a new paper known as the *Moreton Bay Courier* had begun publication in Brisbane. That interested him. He was a journalist, presently working for the paper he was reading.

Wouldn't it be fun to get a job there? he mused. No one could say I'm chasing after Jessie. I'd have a legitimate reason to keep in touch, even if she's married.

Realising his own foolishness at being so in love with a girl about to be married, Sam did spare a minute's pity for Adrian and his obsession with the Bijou girl whom he kept out of sight, but shrugged it off. At twenty-two, he felt older and wiser than Adrian. He'll get over Flo Fowler, he said to himself, but I won't get over Jessie. Ever.

By mid-afternoon he had written an application for a position with the *Moreton Bay Courier*, and posted it. He strolled down George Street telling himself that this new appointment would get him out of the doldrums, wake him up to a career more interesting than the Sydney rounds. Brisbane was only a small port as yet, but it was the gateway to the huge lands beyond, and a promise of adventure. Passing a store, he peered at a pile of books in the window, and spotted Leichardt's latest, *Journey of an Overland Expedition in Australia*, and immediately purchased it.

'Might as well learn something about the north country,' he said to the woman who served him, and she agreed, vacantly.

He called in at the bar of the Australian Hotel, his favourite haunt, and heard that Leichardt had left the Darling Downs, near Brisbane, to attempt to cross Australia from east to west. Sam had been offered the chance to join the expedition because he'd grown up in the bush and explored large areas of western New South Wales with his father, a man of insatiable curiosity when it came to new lands, but he'd had to pass on that opportunity. His father believed such an expedition was too dangerous, too huge a proposition, with thousands of miles to cross and no backup. He claimed such trips should be done in stages, bringing on fresh horses and supplies every two or three months. He was probably right, Sam thought, but now that the famous expedition was actually on its way, he wished he'd gone. What an adventure! To be the first to see the distant mountains and deserts and who knew whatever else was out there!

Adrian Pinnock joined him at the bar, depressed about his grandfather's sudden illness, and other matters.

'I wanted a word with you anyway, Sam. I've been all over the place looking for you,' he said eventually. 'Do you suppose you could lend me a couple of hundred pounds?'

'No,' said Sam without hesitation, and Adrian was taken aback.

'No? Just like that? Hear me out at least.'

'I don't need to. You'll only put it back on the tables or at the races, so I'm saying no. No more.'

'But why? I always pay you back.'

'Yes. Most times. But you're already into me for a hundred and you're getting famous around town for your gambling debts. It's time to pull up, mate. Give it away.'

'Thank you for nothing. Some friend you are! Couldn't you even lend me a hundred?'

'No. Can I buy you another drink?'

'Don't bother!'

Adrian stormed away and Sam returned to his drink, unconcerned. He'd done his duty. Only this morning, after all the important news about her forthcoming marriage, Jessie had taken him out into the corridor so that her mother couldn't hear them, and accused him of encouraging Adrian to gamble.

'I do not!' he said. 'And what's more, he doesn't need any encouragement, believe me.'

'But you lend him money. I know you do.'

'Some. Only a bit here and there.'

'Well it has to stop. Don't lend him any more! Mother would have a fit if she knew he's spending so much. He's cleaned out his allowance already and I know Mr Messenger at the bank is looking for him. You talk to him, Sam. Tell him he shouldn't be gambling.'

'I don't think he'll listen to me.'

She sighed, exasperated. 'Surely you could try.'

'To please you, my love, I shall try,' he'd grinned, bowing.

'There's no need to make fun of me, Sam Dignam. Just do it. I've got enough worries right now without you teasing.'

Who was teasing? he asked himself now, as he declined another drink and the bartender swept his empty glass away. And what worries besides Marcus? Trouble with Ferrington, he hoped.

He saw a group of men walk past the open doors of the bar and watched them curiously. They were squatters, he'd bet. The wide hats and country clothes, including well-polished boots, were uniform among these men. For some of them, he mused, stubborn insistence on looking like well-dressed bushmen was simply preference, and a resistance to town fashions, but for others, younger men, their outfits were a status symbol, denoting membership of the elite and powerful pastoralist society.

Sam hurried outside, wondering why they were all looking so earnest, and where they were going, and with a reporter's nose for news, he strode out after them.

He noticed Edwin Flynn was with them and fell into step beside him.

'And where would you lot be off to this fine day?' he asked, and Edwin turned to him, surprised.

'We're going down to have ourselves a meeting with his lordship.'

'Sir Charles?'

'The very one. Arranged and all.' His eyes twinkled. 'Not like the old days, when we'd come calling on governors with hammers.'

'What's up then? What's on today's agenda, wool prices?'

'No. Ahead there is Ossie Jackson, and ahead again two of his mates. Jackson's cattle station up north was attacked the same time as Heselwood's, and his homestead burned to the ground too. They want protection. The police chief up there in Brisbane says he can't spare men, he's undermanned already.'

'What does the Police Commissioner say?'

'There's no such thing up there. Our fellow down here, Donnelly, he's in charge. He keeps saying he'll send more men but never does. Fobbing them off. So we're a delegation, you could say, to back up Jackson. Our families have been through those experiences. We had to fight to get troopers out to the back country to help us get established; we're just trying to lend him a hand. If the Commissioner won't listen, the Governor might.'

'Interesting. Can I tag along?'

'Sure you can. You might get a piece in the paper about it too, if you think it will help.'

'Yes, I might be able to.' Sam was sure that he could. The Heselwood story had been big. Headlines! Aristocrats, and a lady to boot, forced to ride for their lives. Their female cook murdered, as well as several stockmen. This delegation was an extension of the same story. All part of what Sam liked to call the Black Wars, though he was howled down by friend and foe alike for giving insignificant country 'scuffles' with blackfellows such importance.

Sir Charles welcomed the delegation in his usual charming manner, though Sam thought he was wary, and even more so as the gentlemen began to file in and he recognised Sam.

'I wasn't expecting the *Sydney Morning Herald*,' he said with a smile.

'No, sir, I suppose not. I was invited by members of the delegation.'

'His family are squatters too,' said Flynn.

'Then you are not here in your capacity as a reporter, Mr Dignam?'

'A bit of both?' Sam asked.

'I'm afraid not. This is a private meeting. We don't want the public reading more into what's going on in the north than is needed. Not that you would exaggerate, Mr Dignam, I'm sure. But we are endeavouring to attract good settlers to the area, which, I am sure you'll know, will be a separate colony in the near future. I would prefer this discussion to remain just what it is. A discussion. Not worthy of your journalistic skills.'

Sam knew that as a reporter he was being asked to leave, so he fell back on Flynn's explanation.

'Completely off the record, sir, if that suits you? I should like to remain, though, because pastoralists like my father and brothers are rightly concerned over these matters.'

Sir Charles had no choice but to admit him, and so they were ten. Ten men seated on chairs in the Governor's pleasant office, looking over the east terrace and the lovely gardens beyond. It struck Sam as being incongruous to hear them discussing savage and bloody fighting in such sanguine surrounds. As if the stories they were spilling to the Governor in lurid detail were of darkest Africa. Not this civilised new outpost of the empire.

Sam had heard it all before, the ambushes, the attacks by the blacks, and noticed that no mention was proffered of similar attacks on the blacks by white men. Of the known massacres of black families at Myall Creek that had caused so much dissension in the community. And part of the downfall of the previous governor.

Sir Charles was more flexible than Gipps had been, but he was still sharp, and he didn't miss much. He would have been well aware of the other side of this story, but obviously deemed it would serve no purpose to discuss what they obviously knew to be fact. Sam had the impression that he was letting these men have their say, giving them his full attention in the hope that they would get their gripes off their chests and go away. Just as the Police Commissioner had done.

This was a guerrilla war, Sam had always insisted, a hit-and-run affair on both sides. Settlers needing to advance. Aborigines needing to protect their lands. He spoke for the first time.

'Sir. There's a war going on out there, though no one will admit it. Can't we somehow arrange a truce, so the killings, on both sides, can cease? Then we could draw up a treaty . . .'

'A treaty?' Sir Charles said. 'Who with? I understand we're dealing with black nations. I have it on good authority that these nations are made up of tribal, clan and even kin divisions. Do you know any of the chieftains of these nations? Who they might be? Where we could find them?'

Sam was taken aback, realising that Sir Charles was, astonishingly, better informed than he'd thought.

'I have people out there making enquiries for me, Mr Dignam; I don't want to see further bloodshed any more than you . . .'

'Excuse me, sir. I think you're missing what we're here about,' Ossie Jackson insisted. 'We know there's tit-for-tat going on, but things have changed. That raid on my station wasn't the usual mad yellin' and screamin' run at the place chucking spears. Oh no, sir. This was a well-planned assault. They crept up on the place like as if they've finally woken up that guns kill. They remained well hidden until someone gave the order and

60

then they overran the house, killing my son . . . my nineteen-year-old son . . .' His voice faltered, but he pushed on.

'We were only starting up in a small way. Me and the missus. Two stockmen, who were coming back over the hill saw the attack from up there. They said at least thirty blacks sprang from cover all round the house, at the same time. Nothing they could do against a mob like that with spears and clubs. They smashed in the doors and windows and finding no one else around, looted the house before they burned it.'

'How fortunate that you and Mrs Jackson weren't home,' Sir Charles murmured.

'But we were,' Jackson said. 'We were in the stables. They came so suddenly, screams and shouts like you never heard, but by then they were on top of the place. Our Johnny got a few shots off before we heard no more of him, and by then me and Mrs Jackson, we'd loaded up and picked off a few of the devils, but our horses took fright and barged out before we could grab them and make a run for it. Then we saw why: the blacks had set fire to the stables behind us. Looked like they were keen to cook us, but we had a cellar in the stables with some supplies, safety for my missus and any ladies who might be about, and I tell you, sir, I was glad to jump down there with her.

'We stayed down there for fear they might be lurking, until our stockmen came back to tell us they'd cleared off. But we all knew our Johnny would have to be over there in the ruins,' he sighed. 'And he was. Dead: up in the chimney where he must have jumped in the hopes they wouldn't find him.'

Sir Charles interrupted. 'Mr Jackson. Would you care for a cold drink, or a cup of tea?'

'Thank you, sir, but no,' Jackson said stoutly. 'We came to convince you that the blacks are getting organised. Someone is leading them into planned actions like a war, and now you tell us that you know they have chieftains and you're looking for them. Well, so are we.'

His companions added noisy 'hear hears'.

'That's right,' Flynn said. 'Jackson here says there has to be a boss man planning these raids. This one happened at the same time as the attack on Montone, as you know, and on other stations in the district.'

'People are fleeing the area,' Jackson added. 'When we headed back to town, we met a column of refugees pulling back into Brisbane, determined to stay there until the police declare the area safe. So what we want to know is, what are you going to do about it? No one seems to care that some blackfeller has claimed back a huge area from the Gimpi Gimpi hills right down to the Brisbane River valley.'

'I reckon troops ought to be sent to find this chief and pull him in.'

'And hang him,' someone added.

'You can't let this go on, Sir Charles,' Edwin Flynn said. 'The more time is wasted, the more blacks will congregate.'

61

Jackson turned excitedly. 'That's what Jasin Heselwood said. He claims they weren't all local blacks, and for all we know this chief fellow could be recruiting. There are plenty more tribes north of us, tribes that'd think nothing of sending a few hundred warriors down to give him a hand.'

'I hardly think that could happen,' FitzRoy said, but the growl around the room caused him to pick up a file and open it as if he could find a solution within. When it was obvious that nothing came to mind from that source, he reached for the old well-worn response:

'I shall have to put this matter to Whitehall. In the strongest terms, of course, and see what can be done. At earliest.'

He rose from his chair, the move a signal for them to depart, but a voice from the back of the room shouted: 'What? Is that it?'

'No bloody fear it's not,' Jackson snarled. 'Not by a long shot.'

The delegates remained seated, waiting.

'I will also,' Sir Charles added hastily, 'be discussing the matter with the Police Commissioner . . .'

'We've already done that. What will you tell him to do?' Flynn asked.

Sir Charles was not one to bluster, but Sam guessed he was close to it this fine morning. 'I think perhaps more police are needed there, but I do know the force is undermanned. The Commissioner is doing his best to recruit and train more, but it takes time. The trouble is, as you gentlemen would surely understand, that settled areas are expanding so quickly, it is difficult to have government services, such as police, keep pace.'

Jackson shook his head. 'We don't want police galloping about two by two, and getting themselves lost in the bush. We need soldiers. Troops, to go out and engage this chief's pack of wolves before he turns it into a full-blown army.'

'Don't think it can't happen, sir,' an elderly squatter said, turning the rim of his hat round in his hands as if it were a small wheel. 'I've been a fair way north up there, found a way to make chit-chat with the occasional blackfeller, and I can tell you with certainty that there aren't hundreds of blacks north and west of Brisbane, there are thousands. Ossie's right. They need troops urgently.'

'Troops? If you really believe there is imminent danger of our few soldiers running into an army of thousands of blackfellows, sir, then the Aborigines might just as well get on with it. We don't have enough troops in the whole of New South Wales to engage in such an action.'

'You must have enough to run down and destroy the blacks already rampaging up there. It has become a no-go district for whites, be they settlers, prospectors or loggers. Everyone has to detour around it now, hundreds of miles into unknown territory, making the trails even more dangerous.'

'I don't know if we can promise that. We only have sectors of regiments in service in New South Wales, and a changeover is in progress at present.'

Some of the men drew together to discuss this response, while Sir Charles waited patiently, seemingly unperturbed, and Sam watched, intrigued.

Eventually Flynn, as spokesman, stood. 'With respect, Your Excellency, that is unacceptable. We need the troops and we need them now.'

'How many would you suggest?'

'At least a hundred. Maybe two.'

'Out of the question.'

The elderly gentleman, who Sam now remembered was Harry Spicer, remarked, as if in an aside: 'Then you should go after the Queen Bee.'

'I beg your pardon, Mr Spicer?' the Governor asked kindly.

'The Queen Bee. This chief they were talking about. Find out who he is and grab him, like you were saying in the first place. That would only take an officer with a bit of knowledge of the area, and a small party of mounted troops to get in there and find out what's going on, without being belligerent or upsetting people. And it would surely head off any civilian posses, which are more trouble than they're worth.'

'That is a possibility, Mr Spicer. Indeed it is. A reconnaissance job, eh? I will put that to Colonel Gresham. I have spoken to him before about the unfortunate situation up north, when they were having trouble with black marauders on the Darling Downs. He was able to send them some troops, but the other problem that arises now is that we don't have the officers we need. Not only can the officers already serving not be spared, but I don't know of any with knowledge of the area. Most of these chaps are from the new lot, landed only recently.'

'What about one of your aides? They're officers!' Flynn said bluntly to the Governor, as if to say they were wasted here. His Excellency ignored the impertinence.

'I shall have to talk to the Colonel. I don't know anyone I could recommend off the top of my head.'

'What about Major Ferrington?' Sam asked. 'He's an officer on the spot. Lives in the Brisbane valley. He won't want the black hordes descending on him.'

'Ferrington?' Sir Charles mused. 'Major Ferrington? But of course! I'll look into it, gentlemen. Yes. I think the Colonel might be able to help you after all. Our Major Ferrington would be ideal!'

Sam couldn't use the story just yet, so he went up to the Hyde Park Barracks and made an appointment to see Colonel Gresham in the morning.

The sergeant in the lobby told him that the Colonel was free now, if he wished to see him, but Sam wanted to give him time to accept a summons from the Governor. In the meantime he could write the story, add Gresham's interview and be free to print it.

Back at the *Herald* offices he met a fellow wandering the halls. A tall, well-dressed chap, in his late thirties, Sam guessed.

'Are you looking for someone?' he asked.

'Yes. I'm looking for the room where one can place advertisements.'

'Ah, no trouble. Turn back, go left, down to the end of the corridor, find a glass-panelled door that reads ENTER. That's it.'

'Thank you. You're very kind.'

The gentleman raised his hat and departed, and Sam gave him no further thought beyond a fleeting curiosity about what he might be selling. He had something else on his mind. The baffling question of why in the world he'd spouted Ferrington's name like that. He couldn't even try to kid himself that his sudden brainwave had been an innocent endeavour to help solve the impasse. He hadn't forgotten, not for a fleeting minute, that the Major was set to marry Jessie. His Jessie.

'I was only half serious,' he muttered, as he threw his hat on to an old peg and slumped into the worn chair at his desk. It was a joke, he told himself. Everyone knew Kit Ferrington had never moved beyond a desk job, except to ponce about as Gipp's lady-in-waiting.

Sam Dignam began to laugh. He laughed until tears ran. Ferrington leading soldiers into the bush! The toy soldier wouldn't like that appointment one little bit, but he could hardly refuse. And yet he didn't know a damned thing about the bush, and he'd be leading a party of soldiers no wiser than himself. The blind leading the blind!

His editor, Tom Grabble came by. 'What's so funny?'

'Just something I thought of.' Sam knew this was one joke he couldn't possibly share with anyone. 'But listen, I've got an appointment with Colonel Gresham tomorrow; there's a good story brewing if ever I heard one.'

'About what?'

'Tell you tomorrow.'

Hector Wodrow wasn't selling anything. He was searching.

He was given a form marked off in boxes, to contain his words, and relegated to a corner bench and high stool to consider his message.

'You can have another form if you muck that one up,' the clerk called magnanimously, but Hector didn't need one. His message, rehashed for months now, was clear in his mind. He took up the indelible pencil, gave it a lick, and set to work.

ANYONE KNOWING THE WHEREABOUTS OF JACK WODROW
AGED 40 YEARS FORMERLY OF LONDON PLEASE ADVISE
HECTOR WODROW AT THE TRAVELLERS INN PITT STREET.

* * *

Mervin Wodrow was dying. And not soon enough for him, with all the pain he'd had to endure the last few months, except that he would have liked to see young Jack again.

'He's a one, that Jack,' he murmured to his wife, Jane. His second wife. Clara had died years ago.

'He used to call Clara . . . Clout . . . thought I didn't know. Ran off, he did.'

'Yes, dear, I know.'

Jane had been at the mission the day Clara had taken a turn and gone into a fit, sicking up, a proper mess, and had rushed away to find a doctor, but there wasn't much he could do for Clara. She died two days later, something wrong with her insides. But Jane was there. She'd been kind, helping him and young Hector over the bad time, though he couldn't recall that Hector ever shed a tear. He was fourteen and working at the chandler's down the street.

Me either, he mused slyly. For a long time he'd had a lady friend, Bridget, who used to come in nights when he stayed to clean up, sending Clara on ahead to get the supper ready. Bridget didn't like him being a missionary, used to complain something awful that it wasn't no job for a man. And to upset him, she'd say that he wasn't no oil painting anyway in the first place and lucky to get her drawers off. She could be cruel, Bridget. Always threatening to dump him if he didn't shake off the wife – she hated Clara – and get a man's job. He only held on to her by buying her presents and giving her a little change here and there, but she was worth it, Lord she was. In the end she ran off with her landlord, leaving his wife and kids penniless, and then Clara upped and died.

'See, she should have waited,' he said to Jane.

'Yes, dear.'

But then Jane was there to help. And she was a widow. A well-off one too, which was why she used to come down to the mission with her lady friends, doing their charitable duty. She was kind, and Mervin became quite fond of her.

Soon they were keeping company officially and Mervin closed down the mission, thinking he would find a new job, a man's job. Jane must have misunderstood him, because she began helping him look about for a better parish. A parish where they could do pastoral works together rather than missionary, somewhere near her home, perhaps.

Well! Once he got a look at her house, her mansion up there in Victoria Street, he'd have worked anywhere at any job if she'd asked. And in the end she did the asking. Mervin made sure of that, to keep a firm hand, stringing her along the way Bridget had strung him. She bought him presents every time he 'forgot' to call or write. But when he sold his house and told her he and Hector were off to China to work as missionaries, she jumped right in to stop him.

Soon they were married and living the good life. Mervin never did bother to look for a new parish; instead he sent Hector off to learn to be a proper minister of Jane's high church. Then they had the big house all to themselves. He dismissed the servants, telling her it was sinful to use other souls in that manner . . . though he didn't rightly care one way or the other, but it was a good way to save a heap of money. And relieve him of

65

the necessity to work at all. Anyway, she fell for it, and they'd had a good enough time together . . .

'We had a good enough time together, didn't we?' he asked her.

'Yes, dear.'

'Now you'll look after my boy, won't you?'

'Yes, dear. Hector's doing well. He's got his own parish now.'

Bugger Hector. It was Jack he was talking about. When Clara died he'd gone looking for Jack, to tell him. Found him all right. Found out he was a robber. An out-and-out robber! Working the highways and byways. And word had it round the inns that he haunted in his search, that Jack was doing all right for himself.

Then he saw him. All dressed up. Fit to kill. Laughing his fool head off. Women hanging after him.

He wanted to speak with him. Not necessarily now to tell him about Clara, just to have a bit of a talk. But he dared not. He remembered why Jack had called her Clout. He remembered Jack's defiance when beltings were being handed out, how he snarled and spat and copped even more, and fear overtook him. The man he saw was a seasoned criminal, hard-faced despite the jollity. How would he react to a man who had beaten him daily, for a good reason, mind you, but caused the kid to run away?

This time it was Mervin who ran, a voice echoing in his ears . . .

'Hey, mister! Wasn't you looking for Jack?'

Mervin ran all the way down the muddy road, afraid Jack might have recognised him and come after him with a whip. Or a gun even.

Back home he changed his story to himself. I couldn't have spoke to him. Couldn't have. Would have had to ask him home. What would Jane say if she found out Jack was a robber? That'd be the last of Hector and me. She'd shake us off like a pair of fleas.

A long time later he met up with Bridget again. Down on her luck she was, charging for her favours now, and he'd become an occasional customer, but immune to her pleas for extra shillings. It was Bridget who told him she'd met Jack Wodrow in her travels.

'Your son, I reckon.'

'Never heard of him.'

'Go on, he's your son all right. Looks like you too, with them cold green eyes. Bet that don't sit too good with Plain Jane wot you married.'

No more was said. No more was ever said about Jack Wodrow round the town, until curiosity pushed Mervin to ask Bridget what had become of him.

'Jack?' she said, as if she knew him well, which somehow Mervin doubted. 'Oh, he did well for himself. Made a heap of money at his trade.' She winked. 'Then I heard he'd shot through. Gone to live in Australia, wherever that is. Got clean away. Retired now, they say.'

'Knew no one would beat Jack,' he said to his wife.

'Yes, dear.'

'When I die,' Mervin whispered to Hector, 'I want you to find Jack and tell him I was asking after him.'

'Jack? I wouldn't know where to find him.'

'Australia.' Mervin grinned gummily, proudly. 'Australia.'

'How do you know?' Hector was astonished.

'I know. You go and find him. Jane,' he wheezed, 'make him promise. On the cloth.'

'Yes, dear.'

'He's done well, he has,' the old man gloated. 'He's rich. I've done well too.'

'Yes, dear.' Jane accepted the compliment tearfully. 'Yes. Thank you, dear.'

Hector didn't have to promise. He was delighted to have a chance to find his dear brother at long last. And to be able to take a long sea voyage as part of the promise, if he could afford to do so. He'd had no idea the pater had this secret, and was touched that the old sinner could now repent of the treatment he'd meted out to Jack. Hector himself, now ordained, had already forgiven him. Or liked to think he had.

Mervin had saved the day by marrying this kind and foolish woman, who spent most of her life down on her knees, scrubbing and polishing the three-storeyed house, and cooking for him, the well-established master of the household. All for the love of God, she'd told her stepson, who could only shake his head in wonder.

The day of Mervin's funeral, his son resigned his ministry, bade farewell to his childless wife – another silly, pious wretch – and booked passage to Australia. He'd been astonished to discover that Mervin had left him a small fortune. Money, he found, that had begun with his parents' joint account, been added to by the sale of their house and improved upon by the simple means of bleeding Jane's account into his own over the years.

Now, he guessed, Jane Wodrow would soon discover that she was broke, the foolish woman. But she still had her house. Her sparkling clean house. And good luck to her.

Hector threw off his clerical collar and marched into a gentlemen's outfitters, to purchase a wardrobe suitable for a person travelling first class to the other side of the world. Just as his brother must have done.

Chapter Five

The sun came up fast, streaking the wide horizon with pinks and reds, ready to take on damp earth only just emerging from overnight rain. Mist rose from the deep green pastures as Jack tramped down to the stables, sniffing the spongy air.

'Good day for a walkabout,' he said, then he laughed, correcting himself, '. . . rideabout.'

Today, he and the boss were off on their exploring expedition, and though he'd never admit it, Jack was excited. Not so much because of the chance to figure out where he was in relation to his former travels, though that was important, but because of the horses. He hadn't been on a horse since he left England. Since before he was thrown into Newgate prison, to be exact. Out here, or anywhere for that matter, convicted felons didn't get mounts . . . they hoofed it. In chains, in his day.

He watched the 'government men' filing out of the cookhouse, and saw them glance at him, neither ignoring nor acknowledging, their movements so regular, so eerily practised, as if their chains were still in place. He wondered how long it would take for them to shake off that certain motion and step out like ordinary citizens. In his case it had been fast, born of necessity, the necessity to run and keep running for dear life. Blindly, he recalled, through that murky bush with troopers on his tail.

'Where's Albert?' he asked, and a thumb jerked towards the men's quarters.

He strode across the square, sparing a second glance at familiar cobbles – he hadn't seen such things in a long time – and found Albert slumped on the wooden steps, his shirt across his knees as if he were readying himself to dress. His back was a mass of lacerations, still weeping, and small furrows were already yellowing with infection.

'How are you?' Jack asked, and Albert jumped.

'I didn't hear you coming,' he snapped. 'Sneaking about barefoot like a bloody blackfeller.'

He looked pale, and weak, but just the same, Jack knew, he should have been up and out to work. Flogging allowed one day off, one day and no more, yet here he was sitting in the sun, probably hoping the heat would dry out the wounds.

'You need more salt wash on that back. Can I swab it for you?'

'You can mind your own bloody business.'

'I'm getting that from all directions, Albert. I'm real sorry I got you into strife.'

Albert stood up and shoved him aside. 'Get out of here, you bastard! Didn't take long for you to switch sides! Toadying up there!'

Abruptly Jack turned away. He knew better than to prolong this sort of argument, reflecting that he'd had to cope with unreasonable men like this among the blacks too. Only the black men were more dangerous. Or were they? He conjured up Albert's eyes and studied them. They were not the eyes of the kind man he'd encountered previously; they were hard. Callous. He stared into them and shook his head sadly, because he'd seen madness. Convict madness. Savagery and solitary had done the damage here.

Nodding to himself as he walked into the stables, he wondered if the boss knew that his man Albert wasn't all there. But then, he mused, as they said around here, 'Mind your own business.'

A stablehand led out two tall, powerful horses and Jack jumped back. He'd forgotten the size of these animals up close.

The stablehand sneered. 'Never been around good horses, eh?'

'No.' Jack let him have his fun. He marvelled as the horses were saddled up, provisions were packed into saddlebags and bedrolls were slung over the horses' rumps. There were other additions, billycan and pan for cooking, and of course, water bottles. Jack wondered how long they would be away, but then it didn't matter, he had no other plans.

Then the Major came along, all gussied up in an expensive tweedy jacket and white moleskins, and Jack pondered his strange circumstances. He'd never known an upper-class bloke personally before, and where once he would have treated Ferrington with the same mistrust that the Major handed him, now he didn't care one way or another. He didn't consider himself Ferrington's equal, far from it, but nor was he intimidated by him. Maybe it was just part of trying to ease himself back into the white world, he mused, having to figure out where he fitted in, that had him a step removed from it all. Like a *bukuta*, he grinned, an old owl, just sitting there watching.

Ferrington was wearing his fancy revolver in a holster slung around his hips, but he also brought out a rifle which went into its holster by his saddle, and Jack couldn't resist . . .

'Are we going to war?'

The Major ignored that, yelled for Tom Lok, and gave him some letters to post.

'Where's the post office round here?' Jack asked the stablehand.

'We ain't got none. The Chink gets to ride about ten mile back up the track to the Saxby store, and the mailman collects it from there. Can you get yourself in the saddle,' he sneered, 'or do you have to have a leg-up?'

Jack led the horse away from him, leapt into the saddle with ease and dug his feet into the stirrups. Soon he was riding down the long tree-lined drive towards the road with Ferrington, and he felt on top of the world. He was looking forward to this outing, especially since he had a clear path and a horse to do the work. No more trudging along blackfeller tracks for days on end. This is the life, he smiled, sheer bloody luxury!

They rode for miles, and Jack had plenty of questions he wanted to ask but didn't dare. Questions like how far to Brisbane by river? And what sort of money do they use here? He'd never yet been privileged to receive pay for his labours in this country, though they'd worked Jack Drew the convict harder than he'd ever imagined a man could be forced to toil. Amazing that he'd stood up to it, he mused, since prior to that experience he'd never put in an hour's work in his life.

Rum that he should be thinking of a job now, he supposed, but he'd learned how if nothing else, and he needed to keep well away from the authorities. Keep his head down, so there'd be no more lawbreaking. He grinned: I'm turning into a bloody saint! Old Clout would love that! 'Crime doesn't pay,' she'd be saying, and for once in her ugly life she'd be right.

He looked at Ferrington, who was riding well ahead of him, and wondered when *his* questioning would start. The Major wouldn't have forgotten about the gold. Even though he seemed to have lost interest, he'd be biding his time, trying to figure out the best way to go for it.

They took a road that veered away from the river and headed inland, but once they reached the foothills the Major called out to him to look out for loggers' tracks.

'Following the tracks will help us to get higher uphill,' he explained to Jack, who hadn't been told that they were on their way into the hills, or why, but he nodded, not bothering to mention that they'd already passed several loggers' tracks, as well as blackfeller ones. The latter fresh. For some reason, knowing that blacks were still in the area reassured him, as if he had some friends left. At least he hoped they'd be friendly. Time would tell. He still missed his woman, Kana, but she'd gone north with her family when the real fighting had started over a year ago. He had sent her away himself because he wouldn't allow her to face the same dangers that had killed Ngalla, his first wife. She'd known then that they'd never meet again, but she was strong and probably knew that it was time she took herself a husband from her own people.

'Who sewed up that wound in your shoulder?' Ferrington asked suddenly as they rode across a cleared hillside.

'What? Where I got shot? Oh, one of the black women, I suppose. I was out to it.'

'You sure it wasn't a white woman?'

'What gives you that idea?'

'I can't see how black gins would know how to sew up wounds.'

'Well they do.'

'Without needles?'

'They use bamboo and fine thread, and other stuff. They got plenties of their own medicines, they can fix people good, I tell you.'

The Major left that subject, but when they were forced to dismount and lead the horses up steeper slopes, he wanted to know if Jack could find his way back if he found himself out in the bush again.

'Depends,' Jack said. 'If I got brought in dead to the world, sick and sorry for myself, no.'

'I wasn't talking about your latest circumstance,' Ferrington said testily. 'I asked a simple question. Many people find distances in the bush confusing because of the sameness. Difficult to establish landmarks.'

'Do they? Well, I dunno about that. I never see a sameness, there's so much going on, trees, plants, stars, creeks, you wouldn't know where to start if you had to list them.'

As they progressed, he tried to tell Ferrington some of the things he'd learned, like how the sides of an anthill indicated directions, birds could take you to water, and trees were never the same; simple things, but he could see his boss had lost interest, he'd only needed the affirmative, that Jack could do it. Another step closer to that gold?

Eventually cliffs and crevasses barred their way, so they had to hobble the horses and leave them until they could explore the area and find an easier track, but Jack was nervous about leaving them. The higher they climbed, the more evidence he'd gleaned of the presence of blacks; a few families, he thought. There were patches of destruction on the hillsides where logging had taken place, ugly bare spots where nature, as if ashamed, was trying to cover the nakedness with high grasses and tiny wildflowers. But the loggers had taken their timbers and moved on. The hills were still heavily wooded in these high rocky areas where it had proved too difficult for the loggers to work, so those families would be left in peace up there. He prayed they had enough sense to stay hidden. And peaceful.

'Why don't we call it a day?' he said. 'It's getting late. We could figure out how to get to the top in the morning.'

'Call yourself a bushman,' Ferrington laughed. 'I made up my mind to get to the top today, and by God I will.'

The blacks would know they were here, Jack worried. They had to know. And those horses would be vulnerable for mischief, payback for this intrusion, if only by undoing the hobbles and letting them go. They never seemed to understand that whitefellers had no sense of humour at all about joke tricks they pulled.

He thought of warning Ferrington of this possibility, but knew the guns would come out, so in the end he shrugged. Maybe the resident blacks would simply ignore them. With luck.

'You carry the rifle,' Ferrington said. 'I can't leave it here.'

'Why not? You're leaving the horses.'

'No one will steal the horses.'

'Well I'm not carrying a bloody rifle. I'm not a foot soldier. I'd break my neck climbing round here with that thing slung on me.'

Ferrington handed it to him. 'Put it on.'

They began the climb to the peak then, Jack leading and Ferrington coping remarkably well.

'This is topping,' he called out as they edged along an embankment. 'I used to do quite a bit of mountain-climbing back home. In Scotland, actually.'

'Ah!' Jack gave a gasp of sheer pleasure when he looked out from that point, the afternoon glow lending extravagant hues to an astonishing landscape, but one that he recognised instantly.

The Major puffed up behind him, equally impressed by the three peaks that rose so suddenly from the treetops.

'I say,' he marvelled. 'What strange shapes they are! I knew we'd have a magnificent view if we could get past these hills, but I never expected oddities like this. At a guess I'd say they're the cores of worn-down mountains, or volcanoes. Something like that. But I thought I'd be seeing sweeping plains now, I never expected thick forest again.'

'It's not as heavily forested as this side, though it seems like it from up here.'

'You know this district?'

'Yes,' Jack said simply, thinking, why not? Nothing to hide. 'That is Beerwah, the blacks say. She's the mother of Tibrogargan, the first peak, and Coonowrin, the crooked peak.'

'Is that so? Well, they're certainly very sedate and dignified.'

'Landmarks they are. You can see them from all directions. We'd better get back down now, before it gets dark. Them rocks are slippery.'

He was also worried about the horses, but the Major wasn't. He was still excited about the panorama before him, with those peaks towering over the land.

'You know, I think we're looking at the Glasshouse Mountains. I recall reading about them. They can be seen from out to sea – Captain Cook named them.'

Jack didn't know who Captain Cook was, but he was surprised that the brother peaks could be seen from the ocean. 'From right out there? By gee, I didn't know that. I suppose the blacks would, they know everything.'

For a minute there the two men seemed to share a camaraderie, a mutual appreciation of this phenomenon, but then the Major had to add his query.

'They must know where gold can be found. I reckon you know full well where it's hidden, and I don't accept this tale of yours that you're not going to try again. I think you're just using my place as a convalescence camp until you can disappear back there.'

Jack scowled. 'Let's get this straight. Blackfellers have seen gold; I reckon they've seen plenty of diamonds and rubies too, you can bet your life, but they don't mean nothing to them. I nagged them for years to keep an eye out until someone actually did bring me the real thing instead of the useless stones they'd pick up, hoping to please me. And if you think I'm just using your place as a camp, well that's true. I'll be off any time you say, unless you've got a job for me, like you said.'

The Major didn't move from their lookout; he didn't seem able to tear himself away from this safe vantage point until he'd had his questions answered.

'Would there be wild blacks out there?'

'Yes. A few. A lot. I don't know.'

'Could you pass through their ranks without harm?'

'Probably, but I'd rather steer clear of their wars.' As he watched the horizon becoming awash with colour, Jack suddenly regained that wonderful experience he'd felt when he'd gazed ashore from the crowded transport ship in Sydney. That sense of peace, and space. And freedom. Where he'd known that freedom was possible even if he'd been silly enough to believe that China was just over these hills. The hills he'd learned were called the Blue Mountains. For those few seconds he yearned to go back to the bush, to that running-free feeling, but he knew now that no matter where he went or what civilisation he chose, there were rules, savage rules. Liberty wasn't perfect anywhere.

He set off downhill ahead of Ferrington, admitting that the bush had given him years of contemplation. This wasn't the same Jack Drew who had absconded, who never gave anything a second thought but finding a quid and having a good time. He was a little ashamed of that fellow. He'd never told any of his Aborigine family or friends that he'd been a thief, a robber. They would have been shocked.

He realised what he'd been trying to tell himself since he was brought in, by water again, and deposited on strange soil for the second time. This time he had to get it right.

An hour later, as he approached the clearing, he knew that blacks had been around, but he could smell the horses from afar and gave a sigh of relief that they were still there. When he finally came to them, he found another problem. The saddlebags were gone. They had no food.

'Bloody hell!' he said, peering about him. 'Bloody hell!

'What?' Ferrington yelled. 'What do you mean, gone? Who'd take them? By God, I'll thrash the living daylights out of the bastards! It must have been blackfellows. There aren't any white people living up here. Unless there are tramps sniffing about. Ah, dammit! You light a fire while I water the horses.'

'Why do you want a fire?' Jack asked. 'You want to drink hot water?'

He could hear the boss cursing all the way over to a small stream, and decided to follow him and fill his stomach with water. He wasn't bothered by this short-term lack of food; he'd been eating well at the farm for a good while now. His stomach couldn't complain.

'Not even any tea!' Ferrington shouted and hurled the billycan across the stream in a rage.

When he was calmer, Jack suggested they go down. 'Nothing to eat here. You might be able to get a feed at a farmhouse.'

'How can we take the horses down these dangerous slopes in the dark? Have some bloody sense! And I'll have you know I don't beg for food.'

'Whatever you say.' Jack supposed the local blacks didn't either.

'We ought to go looking for those thieves,' the Major said, waving his revolver about as if a villain were still lurking.

'You can. What are you going to do – shoot someone for a loaf of bread?'

'I ought to. Give me that rifle. I'll stand guard.'

'Don't bother. I'll hear if there's anyone about.'

'You will? Good. Then I might as well get some sleep.'

In the morning they made their way down and and were riding back across the foothills when they came across five horsemen led by Rollo Kirk.

'What are you doing out here?' Kit asked him.

'Looking for an escapee. The rogue took off from a road gang yesterday. You seen any strangers about?'

'No,' Kit said excitedly, 'but I think your man's up in these hills. Someone stole all our food last night, left us not even enough for a cup of tea, and I'm damned starving, I can tell you that.'

'Only last night?' Rollo called to his men: 'We've got him, lads! Head uphill there, spread out. Good work, Kit! What are you doing up here anyway?'

'Just having a look around. You get a good view of the countryside from up there.'

'You would, of course.' Rollo feigned interest to please his friend, then jerked his head over his shoulder. 'Who's that bloke with you? He doesn't look much chop. Ugly bugger. I thought he was a nigger first up. What's wrong with his face?'

'Burns. He's just a labourer passing through. Listen.' Kit moved his horse further away from Drew, who was watching the riders hurling their mounts at the hills. 'He says his name's Jack Drew. Ring any bells with you?'

'No.'

'He's been at my place for some weeks now. You don't know of any absconders loose in that time? He says he's not a convict, but I thought you might know something about him.'

Rollo wheeled his horse about and confronted Drew.

'Where are you from, mister?'

'Who wants to know?'

'I'm the one asking the questions.'

'Good on you,' Drew said. He nudged his horse and rode on down the track.

'You come back here!' Rollo shouted, but Drew didn't look back.

'What are you doing with a hooligan like that?' Rollo asked Kit. 'A man has to wonder why he doesn't want to answer questions.'

'Could be your attitude,' Kit snapped, angry with both of them. Especially Rollo, who hadn't even offered him a biscuit.

'You did ask me!' Rollo said, offended. 'Would you like me to call in on my way back to town? We could discuss this character then. And I should very much like to see how your splendid house is progressing. I'd better catch up with those fools; they tried to tell me that the prisoner would attempt to cross the river, go south, but I knew he'd be up here somewhere. Thank you, Major, you've saved me a lot of useless travelling. See you later.'

He was gone, riding madly after his men before Kit could reply, and that depressed him. He depended on Rollo to keep him supplied with a good workforce, but if the truth be known, he'd found that caustic bird, Jack Drew, or whoever he was, better company.

Drew was waiting for him on the last rise, overlooking the flats. He pointed ahead of him. 'Look at that! I've never seen so many cattle.'

A half-dozen men, at least, were driving a huge herd of cattle along the road to Brisbane, so many that the herd stretched back out of sight.

'My word,' Kit said, 'that's something to see!' He gazed admiringly at the scene as the cattle lumbered on, raising clouds of dust, and the stockmen rode alongside, whips cracking, keeping the huge beasts moving steadily. 'There must be more than a thousand in that herd. I wonder who owns them?'

He didn't feel inclined to approach the hardworking stockmen with his curiosity, so he waited until the herd had bustled past, then, crossing over, headed towards the river.

'Where to now?' his companion asked.

'I want to get a look at a new place called Baker's Crossing. I think it's only a roadhouse, but I should be able to buy some food there.'

'I could catch a snake and cook it for you,' Drew offered, a smirk on his face.

'Don't bother, I'll never be that hungry.'

Kit was pleased to be back on the open road so that he could give the horse its head, and within an hour the river was once again in view. He followed worn tracks and was surprised to find not only a roadhouse, but a small hamlet almost hidden among the trees. It seemed such a quiet and peaceful setting that they were both surprised to hear shouts coming from the rear of the roadhouse.

They dismounted, hitched their horses to a rail by a wall that advertised

75

Baker's Store and Inn, Cooked Meal 1/-, and took their time walking down a track to see what all the excitement was about.

A man turned to shout at Kit even before he had asked what was up:

'Man in the river! Look! Man in the river out there!'

'Have you got a boat?' Kit asked. 'Something! To go out there and pick him up!'

'No. My boat sprung a leak. I've been meaning to fix it . . . Jesus, that current's strong. I don't reckon he's going to make it. Can't hurl a rope that far, poor bugger. But look out now . . . someone's going out for him.'

'Where?' Kit asked.

'Down there, ahead of the current as she rounds the bend. He must be trying to head him off, but it'll be tough going. With all the rain we've had, the river's fair ploughing along.'

He sprinted away, heading for higher banks to keep the drama in view, and Kit chased after him. Looking about for Jack Drew, because it suddenly occurred to him that the second man in the river, almost out of sight, might be him.

'They'll both be washed out to sea,' a woman screamed, and a man laughed: 'They'll be well drowned and got by crocs before then.'

'Who is he? The bloke in the river?' someone asked.

'I reckon it's that escaped prisoner the mailman was talking about. He bet he'd try to cross the river to get away from the posse.'

'Someone should have told that poor fool what's trying to rescue the bugger then. Let the rat drown . . .'

Stumbling through trees, trying to keep the river in view, Kit and several other men soon found themselves in a forest of mangroves that rose in twisted, slippery shapes from a sea of mud. Some men tried to push on, stepping carefully from branch to branch in an effort to stay clear of the mud, but Kit turned back . . .

Jack threw off his shirt as he ran down the slope and waded out into the river, keeping the struggling swimmer in view, then he began to swim too, cursing the wounded shoulder that ached and groaned at this sudden exertion, slowing him considerably, but he battled on and managed to grab the man as he was swept towards him.

The exhausted swimmer fell upon Jack, grabbing him so hard that he was dragging them both under.

'Let go!' Jack shouted. 'Let go. Lie back I'll get you in.' He was swallowing half the river, he thought, thrashing about like this, and was close to punching the man to save himself when the fool gave in and was quiet, allowing Jack to begin to pull him to shore.

He seemed to be going well, though slowly, when suddenly his companion came to life again and started fighting him.

Disbelieving, Jack was shouting again, but this time his quarry shouted back. 'Wrong side,' he spluttered. 'Get me . . . other side.'

'Bloody stupid!' Jack screamed, treading water furiously. 'No. This way. We'll drown out there!'

'Other side,' the man yelled through clenched teeth, and lurching against Jack managed to raise his arms a little, showing Jack that his wrists were bound.

'Oh Christ!' Jack spluttered, still hanging on. 'Bloody hell!' He had no knife, he couldn't undo those ropes here, so there was nothing for it but to push on. He guessed he had found their escaped convict. He pulled the man around angrily and grabbed the ropes – that made towing him easier, he had to admit, as he began the long, hard swim right across the wide Brisbane River.

They were swept a long way downriver but he finally managed to pull the bloke far enough in to grasp at mangrove trees standing waist-deep in the water, and from there to swim smoothly along in the shallows until they reached the end of the mud and were able to struggle on to a warm sandy shore.

'Thanks, mate,' the stranger said eventually. 'I'll do the same for you one day.'

'Heard that before,' Jack said. 'You nearly bloody drowned me.'

'For that I'm sorry, sir. But you see my circumstances.'

Jack did. His rough clothes might be soaked but the prison arrows hadn't washed off. He leaned over. 'Give me your hands.'

He soon tore off the ropes. 'Who are you?'

'The name's Harry Harvey, but you better forget me. Tell 'em I drowned . . .'

'I've already worked that out.'

'Then what are you? A beachcomber?'

'What's that?'

'That's a gent who lives by the sea and on its largesse. You've seen plenty of sun by the looks of you, that's why I thought . . .'

'You could be right. I wouldn't mind being a beachcomber.'

'What are you doing out this way?'

'My name's Jack Drew. I'm living downriver at a place called Emerald Downs. Now I've gotta get back. You all right from here?'

'As right as I can be. I'll take myself on to Ipswich somehow. I have good friends there.'

'I'll leave you then.'

'You sure you can swim back?'

Jack nodded. 'I'll get back. And you ought to change that name, since you died . . . drowned here.'

'True. Now I'd better be off myself. You're a good chap, Drew.'

Jack watched as Harvey climbed the high bank and shambled away, realising the man wasn't as fit as he should be at around twenty-eight years of age, the flesh hanging on his large bony frame. Starved, he was. Another reminder of the fate of gaolbirds. Jack shuddered, realising that

77

had they had the time he could have fed the poor fellow; plenty of *kudu*, choice fish, here.

He began the return swim, using the current to push him shorewards, even though it was taking him further downstream, knowing it would take longer to walk back to the crossing, but would give him an easier swim.

Once on the shore he climbed a tall tree to get his bearings, since the river had made a considerable bend here, meandering as it did across the valley. He noted that a smaller river ran into this one not far down, and saw he and Harvey had been forced to do battle with merging currents. As he turned back to make his way cross-country, he realised that the *murri* men bringing him in must have come that way, or they'd have sighted Baker's Crossing and probably left him there.

Kit was becoming impatient himself, but he wouldn't join the men who'd ridden down the road to see if they could sight the escaped prisoner or Jack Drew, the would-be rescuer.

'No point,' he'd said. 'You know that road leads away from the river, and that riverside scrub is impassable.'

'That's why they'd have to go for the road, if they survived,' one of the men said. 'And you're pretty cool about it, mister. Your mate could have drowned hisself, trying to save a useless felon.'

'He isn't my mate,' he retorted, sure that Drew wouldn't risk his life so easily. No, Kit thought cynically, Drew would make the swim and get back, turn up again like the proverbial bad penny.

He went back to the roadhouse, introduced himself to the proprietor, Ceb Baker, bought a pint of beer and a meal and sat at the counter listening to the locals. They were taking bets on who would survive the river, and Kit, not averse to a gamble, backed his own man for ten shillings.

He enquired about that big herd of cattle and was told they were from Montone Station.

'How can that be? Montone was attacked by blacks. It's closed down.'

'The cattle were still there. They went back for them.'

'They went back? Wouldn't that be dangerous?'

'My bloody word it would, I reckon, but they're a cheeky lot, those stockmen, they weren't gonna let go of their herds. And what's more . . .' Ceb winked at Kit, 'they brought down other cattle they found up there as well . . . said since the adjoining stations were also closed down, the extra cattle had been abandoned, and they could claim them.'

'Is that a fact?'

'Who knows? The boss of Montone says so. That Heselwood, he's a tough man. He called in here a few times, not one to cross.'

'He's a friend of mine,' Kit said, though his lordship was more of an acquaintance.

'You don't say? Is it true he's a real lord?'

'He is indeed.'

Eventually, there he was, Drew, standing in the doorway. No one had seen or heard him approach, but suddenly they were all upon him for the result.

'I couldn't get him,' he said sorrowfully. 'Tried to grab him but he was drowned; the body kept spinning away from me. Looked to me his hands were tied; he was floating funny, I couldn't make it out. I could be wrong on that, but I'm sorry, mates. His body'll likely end up down on your shores, Major.'

'The fool never had a chance,' Baker said. 'But you did well to try to save a man. Here's a beer for you. On the house.'

Money changed hands. Kit collected his winnings, ready to leave.

'What's that for?' Drew asked.

'He bet you'd make it back,' he was told.

'Is that right? Then you can shout me a feed.'

Kit had no choice. He had to wait about while Drew was fed, taking his time about it too, yarning to the locals as if he'd known them all his life. And when finally the fellow emerged, Kit warned him angrily: 'I hope you know that's not the end of it. The police will be looking for the body, and they'll be coming out to question you, so you'd better be telling the truth.'

'Was he an escaped prisoner?'

'They seem to think so.'

'What was he in for?'

'He was a robber. A scoundrel, they say. Held up coaches and travellers out on the lonely roads.'

'A real bad lad, eh?' Jack said.

They arrived back at the farm by about eight o'clock that night, and after checking that everything was in order, Kit sat down to a solitary meal with a map spread out in front of him.

'Do I feed himself out there?' Polly asked meanly.

'Who? Drew? Yes, give him something.' Kit was too excited to be worrying about any of them. He was determined to have a go at prospecting for gold, and now that he'd established that Drew had his bearings – that he could find his way out there in the back country, and return – it was only a matter of getting him to the same area where the blacks had given him the gold; or better still, where he had actually found it himself and wasn't letting on. He still hadn't worked out Drew's game, but surely the man wouldn't knock back the chance to go prospecting again? Not when he'd have company, horses, even a packhorse, as well as the best camping and prospecting equipment available.

The blacks seemed to be the main problem, but even so . . . He'd be armed. Safe.

Kit mulled over the fact that Drew had said he could probably move about there without being worried by the blacks. And why not? He looked like one, with his skin so dark. Kit wondered if he could darken his own skin too, dye it somehow, so that he looked more native. He'd heard some chaps did it in India to infiltrate tribes. But then they were able to wrap up their bodies and wear turbans, that sort of thing. Blacks here wore nothing much at all, dammit.

He found the Glasshouse Mountains on his map and marked them clearly. They would start from there. To hell with the range wars. Nothing to do with them! Maybe Drew wasn't worried about the wars at all. Maybe he just needed a rest before taking off again. In which case he'd jump at the chance to have all the proper equipment. Wouldn't he?

Kit decided to let him rest a few more days. Send him fishing tomorrow, that was always a saving on food expenses, then offer him a job here as an overseer. Give him Albert's job with better pay. Make him feel important.

'No thanks,' Jack said when the Major offered him the job. 'I don't know nothing about farms.'

'There's not a lot to know. Just make sure people keep working. I set the rules and routines.'

'And if they don't get them right, they get flogged! You must be mad if you think I'd take on a job where I could get flogged. Anyway, I wanted to talk to you about that.'

'About what?'

'This flogging. I've been thinking. I can't stay on here any longer. I appreciate you allowing me, but I can't stand by and let anyone get flogged. So unless I have your word it stops, I'll be on my way.'

The Major argued, blustered, shocked that this blow-in should dare to interfere with his business, until Jack offered a compromise.

'If you outlaw flogging on your property, I won't tell anyone. That way you still have your rules and the threat remains in place.'

'Certainly not. This is ridiculous. It's a juvenile proposition . . . I'd have to trust you not to tell them.'

'True. But then you wouldn't even be listening to me if you weren't trying to figure out how to get me to take you prospecting. And if I did that . . .' Jack said, watching him carefully, 'I would have to trust you. Say we did find gold? You might double-cross me and take the lot.'

The Major's eyes, caught unawares, faltered, and Jack sighed. Greed. It had some nasty playmates.

What am I doing here? he wondered.

It wasn't until the cattle drive could be heard rumbling down the road towards Emerald Downs that Kit recalled how he'd lost out on the cattle sales in Brisbane, and realised he'd been about to make another mistake. Who was to say this herd wouldn't be snapped up by agents and graziers too? Before they made it to the saleyards, like last time . . . Why couldn't he do the same thing? Purchase a herd from the drovers at his own price before they got anywhere near the yards. He was unsure of the protocol of these matters, being new to the field, but decided it would be worth a try.

He raced out to the stables, saddled a horse and took off down the track, waiting at the entrance to Emerald Downs, which, since there was no fencing, nor, of course, gates, was heralded by a timber structure of his own design, resembling a portal frame. The name was burned into a centrepiece that hung proudly by two chains for all to see, though the house itself remained hidden . . . private. Kit liked that.

But then the herd came rolling at him, moving much faster than he'd expected, the road more a measure of direction than a precise thoroughfare, and they might as well have been a herd of elephants as they surged and crashed ahead, mowing down bushes, smashing branches off trees, lowing and bellowing endlessly as if commiserating with each other at this long, forced march.

Kit had wheeled his horse away as soon as he saw them coming at him and rode round the flank of the herd until he found the chance to speak to one of the stockmen and ask if it were possible to buy some of these cattle.

'Ask the boss,' he was told.

'Which one is he?'

The stockman turned in his saddle and pointed to the rear. 'Back there. Red shirt. Grey horse.'

Kit had a busy time trying to get to the boss drover, dodging other horsemen racing after stray cattle, and excited dogs that streaked around, intent on keeping order, but he eventually managed to ride alongside the man in a dusty red shirt that had seen better days.

'Could I have a word with you?' he called, and the drover looked over at him to yell: 'What about?'

'Good God!' Kit shouted over the din. 'Lord Heselwood!'

'Yes. What do you want?'

He was the last person Kit had expected to find working on a cattle drive! Even if he did own the cattle. The Heselwood he'd met occasionally in Sydney was very much the gentleman, elegance personified, and yet here he was, unwashed, in muddied clothes, and managing the job at hand as easily as one of his employees! Kit had to urge his horse on to keep up with him.

'You may not remember me, sir. Ferrington. Major. I was—'

'Oh yes, I recall. You were an aide, were you not?'

'Yes, but I've bought this property here . . . Emerald Downs, I call it.'

'Good for you! Glad to hear it. Good to get out of the towns, better life in the country.'

His lordship looked tired, his face lined with dirt, but he was in excellent spirits, and that too was surprising. Heselwood was not known for his pleasant attitude; one could say he was generally found to be a haughty fellow with a mean and sharp tongue that he was never afraid to use, so most people, even Gipps, had treated him with caution. Kit quaked a little at his own temerity in approaching the great man like this, but Heselwood didn't seem to mind at all. He slowed his mount, looking about him.

'Good choice, Major. How many acres do you have?'

'Ten thousand, sir.' Kit wished he could get out of the habit of addressing men like Heselwood so formally, now that he was no longer an aide, and required to tug the forelock, especially since Heselwood was only about thirty. Though he looked fifty right now.

'This would make a handy agistment property,' he was telling Kit. 'Good spot to fatten up cattle being brought in from the west, where it can get as dry as a chip.'

'I'll keep it in mind. Last time I was in Brisbane I hoped to pay my respects to you and Lady Heselwood and extend my condolences for the loss of some of your people. It must have been a shocking ordeal, but I didn't like to intrude.'

'I appreciate that,' Heselwood said cheerfully. 'Not only were we in shock, and grateful to have made it back in one piece, we didn't have a stitch of clean clothes between us.' He laughed. 'These duds are hardly drawing room attire. Not that our Brisbane hotel is up to much either . . .'

Kit rushed in to offer aid. 'My home over the hills there is new and, I might boast, very comfortable, Lord Heselwood. If you and your good lady wish, I should be very happy to place it at your disposal . . .'

'No, no. Very kind of you, Major. We're settled in Brisbane for the time being, not getting in anyone's way, so to speak; things to sort out before we head back to Sydney and find a roof down there. Orphans we are, Major, the homestead taken away from us. Montone was blossoming into a very fine station . . .'

'Dreadful! I hope they catch those savages.'

'They will. I'll see to that.'

'This must have been a very long drive for you, bringing all these cattle so far. You must be exhausted. Can I offer you some hospitality now . . . refreshments, a meal . . . it wouldn't be any trouble.'

'Thank you, no, I have to keep going. Don't want the lads thinking the boss couldn't make it all the way. But I'm getting damned weary; those saleyards will be a welcome sight.'

'Yes.' Kit had almost forgotten the cattle. 'That was what I wanted to talk to you about. I was wondering if I could buy some of your cattle. Now.'

'Why not? How many do you want?' He grinned. 'You can have the lot if you like.'

'Bit much for my place, I think.'

'Yes, I imagine so.' Heselwood cast an experienced eye over Kit's land. 'How many cattle have you got now?'

'I'm still at the clearing stage. Only a few dairy cattle for domestic use.'

'These roughheads will do some clearing for you, the way they trample everything in sight. And you've got plenty of feed here. You could start with a couple of hundred. I'll have the lads cut out a herd and drive them on to your land. That herd will be happy to see your river; this mob's thirsty as hell but we can't slow up now.'

Before Kit could mention that perhaps a couple of hundred were quite a few more than he'd intended to buy, that figure being closer to fifty, Heselwood had whistled to a stockman and given him his instructions. Instantly the man rode away, whip cracking, to begin the process of separating two hundred cattle from the herd, and Heselwood bade Kit goodbye, urging his mount forward, obviously to oversee the operation.

'How much per head?' Kit called after him.

'They're good stock. The best!' Heselwood replied. 'You can have them for a pound a head. Give the lad an IOU on your bank.'

Kit was nervous about the number of cattle he'd bought, and the deal. His agent had said good cattle couldn't be bought for less than a pound, but this lot should have been cheaper without buyers around to push the price up. Two hundred pounds! he worried. His funds were running very low. Too low.

Old Bart knocked on his office door.

'What do you want?' Kit called, busy with his farm journals and ledgers.

'Them cattle out there, boss. They're getting to be a nuisance already, tramping into the maize fields and even around the vegetable gardens. You'll have them in the bloody house next.'

Kit pushed his chair back and came out. 'Yes, we'll have to build some more fences, two-rail, strong ones. Tell Albert to get some trees cut down and that sawpit dug out again; it has collapsed. Where is Drew?'

'He's fishin',' Bart sneered. 'Used to the easy life, he is.'

'He's helping to keep you fed! Tell him to get up here.'

That was true. Instead of idling the day away with a fishing line, Drew had built fish traps into the river's edge, with walls of sticks lashed together with twine. They covered an area about twenty yards long and four yards deep, for all the world like a miniature farm with small paddocks and gates, and Kit supposed that was what the traps amounted to. A fish farm. Anyway, Drew was trapping a good supply of fish every day, so in a mad way he was earning his keep.

'What's up?' Drew asked.

'I want you to give me a hand marking out some fences round the homestead and a couple of paddocks to keep those cattle out.'

'Righto. But what keeps them on your land, what with no fences out there?'

'That's another problem. They'll have to have my brand on them now.'

'Brand? With the hot irons? Those brutes are not going to like that.'

'I know, but they've got the Montone brand on them. That station was burned out by the blacks.'

He was beginning to feel the weight of being the boss now, only too

83

aware of his inexperience and the setbacks associated with his employment of cheap labour. He needed help, that was obvious. He had no idea how to handle all those cattle, though he'd tried to absorb the hasty advice offered him by the two stockmen who brought them in, while listening to their apologies that their charges had demolished his 'gate thing' down the track. That would have to be rebuilt too, or people would never be able to find the homestead. There were books one could buy on the maintaining of cattle herds, but he had no idea where one might be able to purchase them.

He worked with Jack Drew for several hours, marking out fence lines with string and stakes, and set him to digging post holes while he went back to his office and worried about finding an overseer, someone he could ill afford, who would require pay and keep.

If he could only find gold, how marvellous it would be! But it would be tricky getting his expedition underway, not to mention having to leave the farm for an indefinite time. How long did people plan for when they went prospecting? He couldn't stay away too long without an overseer, so he'd have to get on to that quickly. Go into town tomorrow and ask about. Maybe one of Heselwood's men. They'd be out of work now that Montone Station was closed and out of bounds.

But later that evening, as he sat on his veranda, enjoying a claret and his favourite part of the day, he did think of someone who could help him out. Adrian Pinnock! His future brother-in-law, who'd grown up in the bush and who would be an enormous help. He would invite him to visit, that was what he'd do, and encourage him to stay on for a while. That would be some saving. Adrian wouldn't expect to be paid.

And that brought him back to the wedding. To the inconvenience of having to take the time to go down to Sydney when he had so many other important matters on his mind. He hadn't heard from Jesse yet about his foolhardy suggestion that they get married next month. With luck she'd find the time too short to make proper formal arrangements, and ask for a postponement, which he'd gladly accept. The pursuit of that gold seemed to be taking over all his waking hours lately. He was sure the nightly bottle of claret was all that barred it from his dreams, allowing him a good night's sleep.

From the window of the Lands Office Hotel, Georgina Heselwood saw Jasin ride into the yard and she flew out to throw her arms around him in front of everyone, tears of joy and relief in her welcome.

'Careful,' he grinned. 'I'm absolutely filthy, it was a rough drive.'

'I'm so relieved you're back! You've been away for weeks. I was terrified something had happened to you. Are you sure you're all right? You look very tired.'

'Of course I am,' he said, dragging the saddlebags from his horse and lifting them on to his shoulder. A stablehand came for the horse and they went into the hotel through the back door, passing the proprietor, Mrs Pratt, who looked at them coldly and turned away.

'She wants her money,' Georgina whispered. 'I explained that we arrived here with nothing, naturally, and we're expecting funds from Sydney. But she has become impatient, and it's very embarrassing.'

'My dear, we have her money. In two or three days we'll be out of this miserable hotel and out of Brisbane.'

After he had paid the men, Jasin realised more than a thousand pounds from the sale of the cattle, ignoring the mutterings of graziers on the last day of the sale, and the hesitant enquiries of the district constable who had been sent to investigate the jumble of brands. The next day, having paid their debts, Lord and Lady Heselwood boarded a coastal steamer for Sydney.

But Georgina was confused. She had noticed that Jasin had been very happy on his return from Montone, from the ruins of their lovely homestead, spending money freely as if the cash he had raised on the cattle would last them for ever.

'You seem to have forgotten that the bank manager refused to extend the loan on Montone. I felt dreadful having to lie to Mrs Pratt.'

'I haven't forgotten. That fellow will pay for this. We could have been left destitute for all he cared. I'll see to it that he's out on his ear the first chance I get. I'll insist upon it.'

'Wouldn't it be better to take it quietly, Jasin? I mean, we're not out of the woods yet.'

'Ah, but we're well on our way. No need to be anxious. And we still own Carlton Park Station; that rent's very handy.'

Their cabin was small and musty. Jasin dropped the saddlebag that he'd insisted on carrying on to the bunk, and with it the new valise containing a few of the suitable clothes they'd managed to purchase in Brisbane.

He checked the door, but it had no lock. 'Stand here by the door, my dear. I have been bursting to tell you about this but I thought I'd wait until we were well on our way.'

He took a bulky canvas pouch from the saddlebag. 'I found some interesting stuff lying among the ashes of our poor old house. It didn't belong to us so it must have been dragged in by those savages. Probably collected it because it's shiny, the way some birds do . . .'

He emptied the contents on to the bunk, and the glittering ragged stones dropped so heavily, Georgina thought they were lumps of coloured lead.

'What's that?' she asked. 'What have you got there?'

He laughed. 'It's gold, pure gold!'

That night, Georgina couldn't sleep. She found herself reliving the nightmare of the attack by the blacks, unable to blot out the terror that now seemed embedded in her brain. Amid all the noise and confusion and the thunder of gunfire, she saw again the painted body of the blackfellow who had barged into the bedroom where she was hiding, and heard her own screams as he grabbed her. She'd thought he would kill her and she tried to fight him off, but he threw her on to the floor and pushed her under the bed! And then he was gone. Gone! Slamming the door behind him.

'It was as if he was hiding me from the other savages. Wanting them to bypass my room, Jasin,' she'd said.

'Nonsense! He probably took fright, heard someone coming and ran off. You imagined him pushing you under the bed. You wouldn't have gone peacefully, you must have fought him off and slid under the bed where he couldn't get at you. Or didn't have time to get at you . . .'

Jasin wouldn't have a bar of her story, said she'd become confused in all that chaos, imagining things. And she supposed he was right. It was such a terrifying experience, anyone would get mixed up. But there was something she'd been trying to remember, there was something, and it was close . . . She looked back into that room, their room, hers and Jasin's, with the mahogany four-poster bed she'd had made in Sydney and the chaise-longue sitting gracefully under the window, the lace curtains drifting softly above it, and then the wardrobe by the door. Jasin's sheepskin jacket was hanging on the hook behind that door; it hung there because it took up too much room in the wardrobe. And it was there that day, hanging on the door when that savage barged in. She remembered his eyes glaring at her, fierce green eyes . . . and suddenly it hit her! Green eyes? Since when did blackfellows have light eyes? Maybe he was a half-caste, that fellow. Unusual so far north. But that was it, that memory was true at least, if not the other part about the man trying to protect her. But it still seemed so real.

She sighed, preferring to forget it all if she could, and lay back listening to the chug of the engines as the little ship ploughed down the Brisbane River, making for the coast. Her husband, she knew, planned to return to Montone Station as soon as it was safe, and resurrect his cattle property. There was no stopping him, but she wouldn't return. Never. She couldn't ever sleep peacefully there again.

She thought of that voyage to Sydney on the *Emma Jane*, a difficult time, since the ship had carried more convicts than paying passengers. Jasin had complained bitterly but to no avail and, typically, he would not postpone their plans. They sailed from London as scheduled.

Georgina smiled. He was in a better mood this trip, thank God.

Chapter Six

Adrian was so anxious lately he could hardly sleep nights. Grandpa Marcus was still seriously ill, having suffered another stroke, the doctors said. As if that weren't bad enough, Mercia Flynn had come to town from Parramatta, to stay with the Pinnocks, and it hadn't taken her long to find out about Cissie Dignam.

'If you prefer Cissie to me, you should have said so,' she told him angrily. 'I wouldn't have accepted Jessie's invitation. It isn't my wish to embarrass you, Adrian. I shall remove myself in the morning.'

'Where will you go?' he asked, and that, apparently, was the wrong thing to say, since she rushed away in a storm of tears.

He hadn't meant to hurt her feelings. The real problem remained, though. He liked Mercia, more than Cissie really, but neither of the girls could hold a candle to dear, sweet Flo, whom he hoped to marry one day. First, though, he had to pluck up the courage to introduce her to his mother, a huge hurdle there. Blanche was the most awful snob, she wouldn't take to Flo, that was for certain. And yet dear Flo was so looking forward to meeting his family. He couldn't put it off too much longer; she was becoming impatient, even suggesting that he thought her not good enough for his people. And that was not true, he didn't think that at all, it was just Blanche . . .

'What did you say to Mercia to upset her?' Jessie demanded. 'She's packing. She says she's leaving in the morning.'

'I didn't say anything, she just took me up the wrong way, that's all. Anyway, you upset Mother bringing her here.'

'Rubbish. Mercia is always welcome in our house.'

'So she might be, but when she came bubbling in all excited about the wedding, that really set Mother off.'

'Set her off?' Jessie echoed. 'She's been sulking for a week.'

'Only because she didn't believe you'd go ahead with the marriage plans against her wishes, with Grandpa in hospital and all. I think when Mercia arrived she realised you were serious. Personally, I don't know what all the fuss is about. I mean, it's just a wedding and you've got weeks to get ready. If Grandpa is still sick, it won't affect him one way or the other.'

'Mother worries that he might die . . .'

'He won't die. The old coot's never going to let go, believe me. And if you need someone to give you away, I can do that.'

Jessie stared. 'Oh yes, of course! Oh, Adrian, thank you, I feel so much better. The way Mother's carrying on, she really depresses me.'

She threw her arms about him and Adrian hugged her with unusual warmth. That, surely, should put Jessie on his side, he hoped, for the up and coming family ructions. Which almost paled beside the impertinence of Alex Messenger at the Bank of New South Wales, who'd bawled him out about his spending, pointing out that he had no right to be selling bonds that his father had meant for the family.

Adrian had paid Messenger back by removing his accounts to the Bank of Australasia, away from prying eyes, and selling more bonds to boost the balance and impress the new bank manager, who was happy to have Mr Pinnock as a client.

He apologised to Mercia, persuaded her to stay on by insisting that Cissie was just a friend. 'We're all just friends, for heaven's sake,' he told Jessie, who looked concerned at that remark, but let it pass.

The following day he discovered just how much Jessie needed his support, and that cheered him. Weddings, he found, cost outrageous amounts of money.

On principle, Blanche flatly refused to have any part in the planning until Marcus was out of danger, leaving it to Adrian to discuss costings with Jessie. He proved a generous brother.

'You must have the best,' he told her. 'We Pinnocks don't need to scrimp. You go ahead, Jessie, and don't worry about the cost.'

With that he drove into town, still in a magnanimous mood, and bought a diamond brooch for Flo. It was shaped like a horseshoe and cost ten pounds, but he felt that since Jessie could spend up big, he could too. He hoped Flo would like it.

She did. She was thrilled. 'This is good luck for both of us, my love,' she said. 'I've never owned anything so precious before in all my life. Are you sure you can afford it?'

'Of course I can.' He swept her up in his arms and carried her through to the sunny bedroom overlooking the park.

Adrian loved this little house. It *was* little, the smallest house he'd ever visited, being only two rooms, but Flo had furnished it prettily and made it so comfortable that he loved coming here. He'd become so accustomed to their morning and very late-night trysts, to accommodate her stage hours, that it was a shock to hear that she would have to move.

'Why must you move?'

'Because the owner wants to sell and the person who is buying wants to live here.'

'I thought you owned it.'

Flo laughed. 'Don't be silly. I couldn't afford it. I only rent.'

Adrian wasn't to be deprived of their ideal love nest. Within days he had bought number 77 Garden Street in her name.

He placed her gently on the bed, his little doll, undressed her carefully, brushed her long hair until it shone, kissed her fingertips one by one, delighting in the sweet game they always played, and then, on her whispered instructions, removed his own clothing, all of it, until he was standing naked, amazed at his own temerity and good fortune to be her lover . . . until she beckoned him to her. And he made love to her, no longer the shy and bumbling lad.

'I love you, darling Flo,' he told her over and over, and Flo told him: 'I'll love you to the day I die, my Adrian, my sweetie. Always and for ever.'

Later he said, 'I think you should give up your job, Flo. It's too much for you, working nights and matinées and all that rehearsing, you know . . .'

'But I love rehearsing. Merlin is so clever, he's always thinking up the most amazing magics.'

'I didn't mean that. It's just that I don't like you having to go to work all the time. It would be different perhaps if it was some sort of hobby.'

'But it's not a hobby, love. It's my living.'

'It doesn't have to be your living. I'll take care of that.'

She hugged a pink satin robe to her and tied the belt. 'No, you're so generous, love, I couldn't ask that of you. Merlin pays me well. It was hard for him to find a girl tiny enough to slip in and out of those boxes, and someone who understood exactly when and where to do things, and a pretty one as well, he said. So he gives me fourteen shillings a week. That's kind of him, don't you think?'

Adrian finished dressing. She began to comb her hair into tight plaits, which had to be stuffed under a tiny red cap, covered in coloured sequins, once she reached backstage. He hated to see her lovely hair squashed down like that.

'He'll find someone else.'

'Not easily. It will be hard for him when I go.'

'Why don't you just go now? He'll have to find someone else sooner or later.'

She turned to face him. 'When sooner or later?'

'I don't know, Flo. It's just that I don't like my fiancée to be working. I mean, working on stage at that silly job.'

'But I'm not your fiancée, am I? Not to anyone but us. We don't live in the same place, but we live in my bed like married folk. I'm frightened I might have a baby before we're even engaged, and that would be awful. I'd lose my job, I wouldn't fit in the boxes, and then you probably wouldn't even want to make love to me any more.'

She began to weep, and Adrian kneeled to put an arm around her. 'Please don't cry, my darling. Everything will be all right. You'll see. Things are in turmoil at home right now, with my grandpa practically on his deathbed. Don't you understand how distracted we all are?'

'Of course I do,' she sniffed, 'and I'm so sorry. About the poor man I mean. But Adrian, much as I love you, I can't go on like this. It's too worrying, and that affects my work. I nearly got into the wrong box two nights ago, and that would have perfectly ruined Merlin's best magic. So I think it's better I don't sleep with you any more. Not till we're married.'

'Oh Flo, what difference would it make now?'

'That's not a very nice thing to say. It's very unkind. I don't think you care about me at all, Adrian Pinnock.'

'But I do, my darling, I do.'

'Then when are you going to announce our engagement?'

He felt little tingles of sweat on his face, and a positive rush of sweat in his armpits, at the thought of her common stagey friends who would have to be invited to their engagement party, and to his home, and along with Flo, socialise with Blanche Pinnock, who would be at her absolute worst. He'd get more grief than Jessie. At least Kit Ferrington, though a cold fish, was socially acceptable. But poor sweet Flo! Their mother probably wouldn't let her past the front doormat!

'Why don't we get married secretly?' he burst out. 'That way we won't upset anyone. You can give Merlin notice, so he will have time to employ someone else. It will work out perfectly. We'll elope . . . sort of.'

She looked at him, still on bended knee. 'Oh Adrian my darling, you are so romantic. Of course I'll marry you! When?'

When Adrian left, Flo turned to dress, and rush round to the theatre. It would be unthinkable to let Merlin down, even on this, the most exciting day of her life. She, Flo Fowler, was about to marry the love of her life, and she was still giddy with astonishment. She'd meant what she said to him. She'd fully intended to call off their love affair though it would have broken her heart, because already she'd seen too much misery from that sort of thing, too many girls left high and dry and too many old stagers telling them 'I told you so. You can't trust them stage-door Johnnies.'

Last night she'd sat by her window, looking out at the stars, and made the decision. Then she'd cried herself to sleep. Today was to have been the last of their loving. Adrian was a year older than her, she thought fondly, but much younger in his ways. Sheltered, you could say, even spoiled. So it had been necessary to speak her mind, let him be clear about their situation. Because she did love him and she would make him a good wife, but as she'd said, she couldn't allow things to drag on. Taking chances all the time of getting pregnant and losing him. They were both too young to be faced with a baby out of wedlock.

Anyway! It had happened. Surprise of all surprises! She couldn't believe he loved her so much he'd take fright at the thought of losing her. And they were to be wed!

How marvellous too that they could be married in secret. She was terrified of his family. She'd heard so much about them and all their high-society doings from Adrian, day in and day out, that far from finding all this stuff interesting, it had horrified her. He'd said that their main home was a sheep farm. Not the house in Rose Bay, with gardens bigger and prettier than that park out there. The greatest wonder of it all, though, was that Adrian, a real gentleman himself, had fallen in love with a nobody like her. For that he deserved her to be good and loyal and do everything in her power to see he lived happily ever after, with her.

'My dear Miss Pinnock,' the Bishop said, 'I am honoured that you should wish me to officiate at your wedding, but we must go about things correctly. There's protocol to be observed here. Now let me explain. First you must go to your own parish, to St John's in Parramatta . . .'

'But we live in Sydney.'

'Ah, but as I understand it from your mother, the Rose Bay house is a holiday home, and the family seat, so to speak, is in Parramatta. Now, you run along to St John's and speak to Reverend Nicholson about your plans.'

'We were hoping to marry in Sydney, sir. At St Andrew's.'

'Yes. One thing at a time. Reverend Nicholson in Parramatta will hear your request along those lines, with disappointment, I fear, and it will be up to him to refer you to St Andrew's parish in Sydney. When that is decided, one of those gentlemen will put your request to me. You see? And offer to assist me at the service. So you see, that's the general order of things. But I wouldn't worry, my dear. Leave this to your mother; the dear lady will have it sorted out in no time. And when is the great day?'

'I'm not sure. Major Ferrington asked me to set a date, which I have done, for next month, but there hasn't been time for him to reply as yet.'

Though privately Jessie thought there had been.

The Bishop laughed heartily. Patronising her, she thought. 'My goodness, you young ladies these days, you like to rush things. I can't see much point in visiting Reverend Nicholson until you have a definite date. You must wait on the Major's approval, don't you think? People have obligations, my dear. You'll understand that as you grow older.'

He ushered her to the door himself, telling her to 'run along now' as if she were a ten-year-old.

The expected telegram came from Kit, addressed to Adrian, but Jessie opened it anyway, since, she reasoned, the telegraphist and his colleagues would already know about her wedding from the previous telegram. She shivered with excitement as she took it from the telegram boy and stepped back inside in a most dignified manner, as if telegrams were to her commonplace, not a rarity, thinking that Kit must be observing some sort of protocol here, the word being in the air of late, addressing her brother instead of her. Maybe it was a formal approach to ask Adrian to be his best man, but that couldn't be, because she needed her brother to give her away.

Grandpa Marcus had pulled back from the edge, as Adrian had said he would, but his speech was badly affected and it would be a long time before he'd be able to walk again.

'Never mind,' she sighed, speaking to her faraway fiancé, 'you have a dozen good friends in Sydney who would be happy to stand with you.'

Which reminded her, she had forgotten to tell Kit that she had chosen three bridesmaids, who were as thrilled about the wedding as she was, so he would need a best man and two groomsmen.

The telegram was in her hand now, but it was all wrong:

COULD DO WITH YOUR HELP ON PROPERTY FOR A WHILE
STOP SAY YOU'LL COME UP STOP FERRINGTON

Not her! Adrian! No mention of the wedding. No special greeting for his fiancée. And worst of all, no reply to the April date she'd given him. What did he want Adrian up there for, anyway?

There had to be more to this telegram than was written on the page by the telegraphist, with his crystal-clear handwriting. That was it! There was a line missing, she was sure. Kit wouldn't ignore her like that. After all, he had asked *her* to set a date.

Jessie took her shawl from the hall stand, and as she threw it over her shoulders, her knees began to quake. Had Kit changed his mind? Was he calling Adrian up to his property so the two men could discuss the problem? The problem she didn't even dare approach for fear she would suffer her own heart attack. It was hard enough to breathe right now with her heart pounding in fright. Instead she forced herself to stand still and straight, by the open front door, dragged a deep breath into her lungs and released it slowly. Then again. And again, until she felt calmer, then she set off down the street, walking quickly, firmly, to complain about this telegram with half of the text missing.

The telegram was for him, but when he came home he found his mother and his sister in the sunroom, arguing about it. The yellow page set on the table between them like an unwanted child.

Jessie pushed it at her mother. 'What's been going on behind my back? What arrangements have you and Adrian been making to have Kit send this?'

'I told you. I know nothing about their arrangements. Nor yours, for that matter, except you went to see the Bishop, you silly girl.'

'I only went to seek his advice on some matters, since you won't help me.'

'Help you to do what? Have you both agreed on that rushed wedding date? Not as far as I know!'

'I've been waiting for Kit to confirm the date.'

'Then wait. And stop making such a fool of yourself. They don't make mistakes writing telegrams. And look at this! Is this your idea of a wedding invitation? This half-baked rubbish?'

'I was only practising . . .'

'I see. You are the daughter of . . . blah blah, but who are your fiancé's parents? Of where?'

'I don't know. I would have to ask him. But I want to know what Adrian has been up to.'

'Why?' Adrian had been standing by the door listening to this exchange.

'This telegram came for you,' Blanche said, passing it up to him.

'So I gather. Does anyone mind if I read it?'

He glanced at the short message and laughed. 'I knew he'd get himself in a tangle. But oh no. He knew what to do. Anyone can run farms. Any fool. Now he wants me to go up there and give him a hand. But you know that, you two, don't you?'

'Your sister seems to think the Major has a more sinister motive.'

'Like what?'

'Like we have all connived to put obstacles in the way of her wedding.'

'I didn't say that!' Jessie cried angrily. 'It just seems strange that I don't hear from Kit when I need to, and he suddenly wants Adrian up there. What could he do anyway?'

Adrian pulled up a chair and sat at the table, beside her. 'Is there any tea left in that pot, Mother?'

'No, I'll get some fresh . . .'

When Blanche had left, he turned to his sister. 'Now, what's up?'

She began to weep. 'I wrote to Kit agreeing that we could be wed next month, but I haven't heard a word since. Surely he knows he has to confirm it with me? And there are other things I need to know . . .' She lowered her voice. 'I don't know his parents' names or where they are, and that has to go on the invitations, it'll soon be too late to send them out. All sorts of things I need to know, and I'm running out of time.'

'Stop fussing,' he said. 'Kit probably hasn't received your letter yet. You should have sent a telegram.'

'I couldn't. There was too much to say. Adrian,' she clutched at him, 'do you think he wants you up there so that he can call off the wedding? To break the news to you first?'

'You've got some imagination, Jessie! It's clear he needs help, that's all. He has never lived in the country before. I think he has done well to last this long with all those convict blockheads working for him. I'll see when the next ship leaves for Brisbane and hop aboard.' He stood and threw his arms wide in a pose:

'Adrian to the rescue!'

'And where does that leave me? I still haven't a definite date.'

'Maybe he wants me to mind the property while he comes down here to be wed.'

'What?' Jessie wailed. 'You can't do that! Who's left to give me away?'

'Oh for God's sake!' Blanche snapped, as she brought back the tea tray with fresh tea and a plate of sponge fingers. 'He's to be your brother-in-law, Adrian; if he wishes you to assist him up there, then you should go. Wire acceptance right away. At the same time tell him that setting a wedding date seems now an impossibility with Marcus ill.'

'No!' Jessie cried.

'Did you mention that in your letter to him, Jessica?' she asked.

'I told him that in the letter that followed.'

'Letters he wouldn't even have received yet. Ships can't fly through the air like telegrams. We are not trying to upset your plans. I certainly have not been doing that. I simply knew from the beginning, with communication so difficult between you, that Kit was asking the impossible, even if Marcus were well. Wedding invitations have to be sent a month before, at the best of times; longer here with the distances so great . . .'

'Mother's right,' Adrian said finally, tired of the argument. 'You are cutting it too fine. I think the show would be far more pleasant if it isn't rushed and you don't forget things like wedding rings and top hats and cases of champagne. You know . . . the essentials,' he said, trying to make light of the situation.

In the end it was left to Adrian to sort things out, and he felt quite proud of his new standing. His telegram was sent, an expensive telegram because it contained advice that Adrian would board SS *Argyle* on Sunday, and a second message on Jessie's behalf that more time was needed to plan the wedding, due to Marcus Pinnock being seriously ill. No need for 'letter following'; he would deliver Jessie's next epistle himself, and upon arrival in Brisbane telegraph *her* that all was well. And with his hand at the helm of the Emerald Downs ship, restore order to their lives.

Telegram sent. Steamship ticket in his pocket, Adrian ran into Sam Dignam.

'Guess what?' he crowed. 'Old Ferrington's bitten off more than he can chew with that property up north. He wants me to come up and show him how it's done.'

'But he runs cattle. You're a sheep man. What do you know about cattle beyond they're bigger than sheep and don't need shearing?'

'I know enough. Anyway, I'm going up on the *Argyle* next Sunday.'

'You are? So am I. Got a job in Brisbane with a new paper called the *Courier*, so I expect you to give me all the latest. I'll see you Sunday, shipmate.'

The good thing about these sudden instructions, thought Adrian, was that he and Flo would have a little time to cool off. It wasn't that he didn't want to marry her; that was still on the cards, as he would tell her, but he had to go north on family business. He had no choice. He was the man of the family now and he had obligations, but he would be back as soon as he could.

* * *

94

She understood. She was very brave, no tears, only pride that her Adrian was taking responsibility in the family, with the grandfather so ill and his two ladies to think about. Obviously his mother and his sister relied on him. Flo was looking forward to meeting them one day. She giggled as she tripped happily down the hill to the Bijou Theatre; she'd be Mrs Pinnock herself then and, to be truthful, feel a lot more confident. His mother looked like ice to her even though Adrian said she was not, that she was actually a very sweet person. Flo had still only seen Mrs Pinnock from afar but her opinion hadn't changed. Not that she'd said so to Adrian; she hadn't wanted to hurt his feelings.

His sister, Jessica, was a different proposition. A real looker, she was. Vibrant, Flo thought, because of her colouring, that marvellous black hair, fair skin and bright blue eyes, a darker blue than the usual. Flo had seen her in the front row with Major Ferrington several times, and thought what a lovely couple they made, and now here she was preparing to become family with them. Adrian had said that his sister had a mind of her own, full of opinions, she was, and Flo couldn't see anything wrong with that. She had come to admire Jessica, whom they called Jessie. Though she couldn't quite work out what sort of opinions ladies had.

She'd thought Merlin would be pleased that there was no rush now to find a replacement, but he went on something awful, that he'd already offered the job to his niece, who lived in Bathurst, and sent her the money to come to Sydney, even arranged lodgings for her at the Onslow Boarding House behind the theatre. And paid the first week's rent.

'I warned you not to get yourself tangled up with that young buck. Told you you ought to stick to your own sort. But no, what do you do? Fall for his talk about getting wed. I suppose that got you into his bed faster than a leaping gazelle? Practising for the honeymoon?'

'It wasn't like that,' she said, her disclaimer sabotaged by a blush.

'So you say. Last week you were getting wed; this week the bridegroom has disappeared into the yonder. When will he be back? Of course you don't know. Well, you had your chance, Flo. My niece Patience is on her way, and when she gets here, I'll rehearse her for two days and then she goes on. I'd like you to help her with the little dance steps you execute as you walk in; it will be good for her to learn them.'

'All right,' Flo said meekly. It was her own fault this had happened, no use blaming anyone else, she should have kept quiet a bit longer, but it was her happiness that had spilled over, spoiling the cloth.

'I'll be back before you've had time to miss me,' Adrian said on the Saturday night before he sailed, as he kissed her goodbye, and Flo said she was missing him already. She hadn't told him that she'd lost her job as assistant to Merlin; she didn't want him to think she was less than a cheerful person, or even, God forbid, that she didn't trust him to come back soon so that their deliciously romantic wedding could take place.

Now she'd have time to make the wedding dress of her dreams, all white and frothy in tulle and lace with pink ribbons, instead of the nice floral dress she'd intended to wear at short notice.

'I won't come to the quay to see you off,' she said. 'Your family will want to be there and I wouldn't intrude.' Nor face up to the formidable Mrs Pinnock just yet.

'How I love you,' he cried. 'You're always so understanding, my darling Flo.'

They were at the quay, Blanche and Jessie, surprised to see that Sam Dignam was also sailing for Brisbane in SS *Argyle*.

'Where did Jessie get to?' Blanche asked Mrs Dignam, who was there to farewell her son.

'She went on board with Cissie to explore the boat. Sam has a job as a reporter in Brisbane, but why he'd want to leave the perfectly good *Sydney Morning Herald* to work in the back blocks, I'll never know. I mean, I consider it a backward step. Whoever heard of that other paper, whatever it is? But he says he's got a good story already lined up. Oh look, there's a platoon of soldiers boarding, I suppose they need them up there to protect folk from the savages.'

'Please don't say that! Jessie will be living there when she marries.'

The two women stayed talking as the crowds grew in number, and eventually the loudspeaker called for all ashore that's going ashore, and people hurried down the gangplank.

'Where's Jessie?' her mother asked.

'She's probably over there with Cissie, see. By the flagpole.'

Blanche didn't see, but she wasn't worried; the girls would be there somewhere. She pulled her cloak about her as a cool wind blustered in from the sea, wishing they'd get a move on taking the *Argyle* from the quay and out into the harbour, so that she could go home; it was tiring standing here all this time. She waved, though, stood and waved, her face turned into the wind that bore the chill of autumn already, until the ship pulled back from Circular Quay, ploughed about and headed busily down the harbour past the laconic grandeur of several tall ships that lay at anchor out there, and finally disappeared from view. Some people had run along the banks of the quay to be able to watch as *Argyle* passed the point, but Blanche had said her farewell. Adrian was safely on his way.

The crowd thinned out quickly, as if no incident of any sort had occurred here, and Blanche, among the first to leave, climbed into her carriage.

'Straight home, missus?' her driver asked.

'No. No . . . Jessie is still here. Somewhere.' She peered out of the open door. 'Where has she got to now?'

They waited, Blanche looking about her anxiously. 'Surely she hasn't forgotten the carriage is waiting? Joseph, would you walk over past those trees and see if she's there? She wouldn't have just wandered off.'

Joseph returned. 'Can't see her anywhere, missus. Do you reckon she got stuck on board? Missed the call?'

'I shouldn't think so. She's in such a state these days with one thing and another, she has probably wandered up to town, completely forgetting I'm here. I'll have a few words with her, I can tell you.' She sighed. 'Yes, we might as well go on home, thank you, Joseph.'

Blanche settled crankily into her seat, adjusting her bonnet from her reflection in the driver's window, thinking how much she hated wearing bonnets even though they did have their merits on breezy days like this. She sat very straight, looking neither left nor right as the carriage bowled up George Street. She was so cross, she determined not to see Jessie if she was walking up this way, the obvious path to the main shopping centre, but then she remembered it was Sunday. The shops were closed.

'Oh Lord,' she murmured. 'Maybe she went with those people who ran up to the point. But if she did, she'd have told me. How was I to know where she'd got to?' She considered turning back, and then shrugged. 'Jessie is quite capable of getting herself home.'

On board, Sam was pleased to discover that he was the only occupant of a two-berth cabin, and having settled in, he found Adrian's cabin.

When he knocked, Adrian slid out and tugged him away. 'Can you believe who I'm sharing with? Inspector Tomkins. Arnold Tomkins. A damned policeman!'

'Bad luck, old chap.' Sam laughed, but made a mental note to have a talk with Tomkins. No doubt he was to be part of the Commissioner's plans for the protection of farmers in the north, as were the soldiers who'd come aboard. His interview with the Commissioner hadn't revealed anything he didn't already know, except that urgent measures would be taken to remove the problem, meaning warlike blacks, Sam presumed. He had also asked if Major Ferrington was to be involved, but the Police Commissioner would make no comment on that subject. There was a good chance that Tomkins would, though.

'Who are you sharing with?' Adrian asked him.

'A very nice fellow. The luck of the draw, one could say. Come on up top so we can watch as we go through the Heads, always a spectacular sight.'

They moved aside to allow several other passengers to pass by them on the narrow companionway, went up a few steps, passed the entrance to the first-class salon as they headed for the outer door, and just as Sam pushed it open, Adrian stopped.

'I thought I saw someone back there. In the salon.'

'Who? Someone you know?'

'I think so . . . Wait a minute.' He went back, peered into the salon, saw a woman sitting quietly in a corner. And froze!

'What's she doing here?' he yelped.

'Who?' Sam came back to join him.

'Am I seeing things, or is that Jessie?'

Sam rushed on past him. 'Jessie! I didn't know you were travelling with us. How marvellous to see you! Why didn't you tell me, Adrian? He never said a word.'

'What are *you* doing here?' Adrian asked her through clenched teeth. 'Have you even got a ticket?'

'No, I'm a stowaway,' she said calmly. 'I didn't see why I should be left behind.'

Adrian looked about frantically. 'It's too late for you to get off! You could be arrested, you idiot. You must be mad. You can't just sit here in public view.'

'She can have my cabin,' Sam said gallantly. 'I'll find the purser and buy another ticket.'

'I see. And have my sister share with the other fellow in your cabin? What if there aren't any empty cabins? You're quite mad, Jessie, do you know that? We have to inform the purser you're on board, and you'll probably get shoved down to steerage and serve you right!'

Jessie laughed. 'Stop panicking, Adrian. I bought my ticket yesterday, bright and early. But thank you, Sam, nice to know someone cares what happens to me.'

'Mother didn't know, did she?'

'Of course not. I packed my suitcase and put it on board yesterday, and left a note for her this morning.'

'She'll be livid.'

'I daresay. But I'm out of reach now.'

Sam offered her his arm. 'We were just going up on deck to see the Heads as we sail out of the harbour. Would you like to join us, Jessie?'

'I'd love to.'

The voyage was more than Sam could have hoped for, the three friends together, as it should be. Except that Jessie was betrothed to a soldier who was too old for her. A father figure, he supposed, since she'd lost her own dear father. Nevertheless, Sam was determined to make the best of this chance, by being with her as much as he could without making too much of a fuss. On the second day, however, after a wonderful Sunday in their company, he planned to stay out of sight. A strategy, he decided, that might be helpful, have her miss him.

But that didn't work. It was Jessie who came looking for him. 'Wake up, sleepyhead,' she called. 'I've been up for hours. It's a beautiful morning and they're serving breakfast.'

'Where's Adrian?' he asked coolly, as if her brother should suffice for company for her.

'I didn't dare knock on his door and upset Mr Tomkins,' she replied from the other side of his door. Then she gave a gasp. 'Oh Lord! I'm sorry. Did I wake your other gentleman?'

Sam opened the door. 'There is no other gentleman. This is all mine. A porthole and all.'

'Oh, you rogue!' she laughed. 'Adrian will be furious. What's it worth not to tell him?'

'I'll think of something. We're going up to breakfast, are we?'

'Yes. Hurry up. The ship's heaving about a bit, I hope we're not in for bad weather.'

So did Sam. He'd envisaged lazy days on deck, with Jessie, and balmy nights under the stars, with Jessie. If he could shake off Adrian without giving the game away. But the weather was on his side. Not long after they took their places, Adrian came in to breakfast, but one look at greasy eggs and bacon on his plate, and he rushed for the door.

'Maybe I'd better go and see,' Sam offered, his voice vague, flat, devoid of enthusiasm.

'Would you?' she said, cornering him.

Adrian was hanging over the rail, having managed to make it across the deck without disgracing himself, but the sight of the churning waters and the perpetual rocking view of the sea and sky upset him even more, so he staggered away.

'I have to get down to my cabin,' he mumbled to Sam. 'Ate too much last night. That's what it is. I'll be better later.'

'Come on then.' Sam took the precaution of picking up a bucket from a nearby rack, and bringing it along as he assisted Adrian down the companion steps and along to his cabin, and that was just as well, since his friend's stomach rebelled again the minute he laid his head on the musty pillow.

Eventually he managed to settle down, promising to 'sleep it off', and Sam was glad to escape; the fetid air in that small cabin was beginning to affect him too. Certainly he had lost his appetite, so he waited on deck until Jessie came out to give her the news that her brother was tucked in his cot.

'He has always been inclined to seasickness,' she said. 'When we visited Hobart he hardly saw the light of day. Though that route is always very rough, they say.'

'Rough seas don't bother you?'

'No. I'm fortunate in that way.' She lurched against him. 'It's getting bumpier. I hope you can stay on your feet or I'll have no one to talk to.'

'Is that all I'm worth? A handy companion? Like the spinster aunt.'

'No, silly. You know what I mean.' She took his arm. 'Let's brave the winds and put in some promenading.'

Later Jessie thought it might have started then. He felt so comfortable, so just right, when they were walking together, close together, to stay on their feet as the deck shifted beneath them, and to shelter each other from the wind. Comfortable, like an old shoe, he would say in that self-deprecating way, and it *was* something like that. Sam had always been around. The Dignam property, Grosvenor Downs, was adjacent to the western boundary of the Pinnock head station, where their homestead was located. When she'd been very young, about eleven or twelve, she'd had a crush on him but it had faded, been forgotten somehow.

Sam had a meeting that morning with Inspector Tomkins, so she sat in the salon with other passengers, including a Mrs Kirk, who was travelling alone and therefore felt free to tack herself on to Jessie. Mrs Kirk was one of those ladies who affected gentility, aided by a repertoire of sniffs through a beaky nose ... sniffs, highly placed, that could register disdain, for instance. Another sniff, head tilted, could accompany approval, and the one where she sniffed chin lowered, listening, could only have been called crafty. In all, not the most pleasant of company, Jessie found, and a stickybeak to boot.

She informed Jessie within minutes that she was the wife of Mr Kirk, an important gentleman in the scheme of things in Brisbane, having been until recently commandant of the prison ... 'So I could not make my home in the town and of course not behind prison walls. It would not do at all, but he has been transferred to the police service, which should have happened years ago, since they all rely on Mr Kirk to keep the peace up there. He's the only one who knows what he's talking about. I could tell you a thing or two about what goes on up there, but it wouldn't be fit for young ears. Anyway, he is now the Inspector of Police . . .'

'Oh then he must know Inspector Tomkins, who is sharing a cabin with my brother. He's on his way to Brisbane also.'

'Tomkins? I do not know that name,' sniffed Mrs Kirk, leaning forward, her voluminous black dress smelling of mothballs. 'Why is he going to Brisbane?'

'I don't know.'

'What is taking you two young people up there?'

'My brother has business in Brisbane.'

'Would it be indiscreet to ask what business?'

Yes it would, Jessie thought. 'Goodness me, whatever business men have. Mainly I'd say we're just tourists.'

Sam was gone more than an hour, and by then Jessie had escaped to look in on her brother, but he was sleeping so she let him be and crept away, wondering where to go next. The lady she was sharing with had already announced that although she did not suffer from mal-de-mer, she intended to while away stormy weather in the cabin, with a collection of romance novels and a tin of toffees. To join her didn't seem much of a choice, so Jessie dashed in to collect her heavy cloak, the one with the hood.

'My dear!' her cabin companion exclaimed. 'You're not going out into the elements, surely?'

'Just for a little while,' Jessie conceded.

'Well, see you hang on. The way this tub is bobbing about, a person could get washed overboard and no one would ever know. Had one any sense, one should have waited for a berth on one of the big ocean-going ships, and enjoyed some comfort.'

Jessie nodded. 'I'll take care. By the way, Mrs Kirk was looking for you, Mrs Maykin.'

'Good God! That common woman, all manners and malice. Tell her I disembarked this morning.'

Jessie laughed. 'I wish I dared.'

'Have you met the husband, Rollo Kirk?'

'No.'

'A creature that one! Chief warden or whatever he calls himself of the prison.'

'Aha! Not any more. He's shifted over to the police force, she says.'

'He has? That's worse. To have the wretch let loose on *us* now. There has been a barrage of complaints about his shocking treatment of the prisoners; I shouldn't be surprised if the Governor hasn't quietly moved him sideways. I'd give that pair a wide berth if I were you, Jessica.'

'Yes. I'm off upstairs. Enjoy your books.'

The outer door was a challenge, with the wind barring her way. Determined, Jessie put her shoulder to it, muttering her irritation at what felt like solid brick wall, unable to move it an inch until suddenly it opened and she fell through to the deck. Sam had come from the other direction and wrenched it open.

Mortified, he grabbed at Jessie to help her up, but she pushed him away as she struggled with her long skirts to find a footing.

'Why aren't you more careful!' she snapped.

'I'm sorry. I didn't know you were there.'

'You didn't look. You could have seen me through the glass.'

He reached out and steadied her until she reached the railing. 'The glass in that door hasn't been cleaned in years. How can I be expected to see through it?

'Oh, never mind!' she said. 'Where are you going?'

'I thought I'd see what's happening in the salon.'

'Nothing. Too much seasickness. There are only a few people about, including that Mrs Kirk, who has claimed me, so I can't go in there. I'm going for a bracing walk instead. You'd better come with me, Mrs Maykin fears I'll fall overboard.'

'Righto. Come this side. I saw some dolphins a while ago.'

They made their way round the deck several times, not sighting any dolphins, then Jessie found a long box built into the bulkhead that offered shelter from the wind, and pushed over there to claim a seat with a shout of triumph.

'Look at this! Perfect. We have the sunshine and we've beaten the wind.'

Sam sat down beside her. 'It's a good spot. Would you like me to go down and get you a rug?'

'No.' She cuddled into him. 'This is fine. Tell me, who is Mrs Maykin? She seems to know my family, so I didn't like to ask about her, to her face I mean.'

'Graziers. Big estates on the Darling Downs. West of Brisbane.'

'Oh yes, I know. She's very nice. Funny. But how did your interview go with Inspector Tomkins?'

'Excellent. He's looking forward to his new post. But he didn't seem to know anything about the plans to chase the black fellows off station lands.'

'What plans are they?'

Sam had forgotten that her fiancé was in line to lead forays into areas reclaimed by the blacks, and thought it possible that those orders hadn't come through yet, so he shifted ground.

'I'm not sure. Just a rumour I heard. Obviously just that.'

'It's strange, though. Mrs Kirk says that her husband is now a police inspector. Is it usual to have two of them at the same office?'

'I don't know. Maybe it's a bigger town than we thought.'

They stayed there, huddled together, chatting over this and that, occasionally taking walks to watch seabirds scuttling after debris thrown from the galley, and to gaze at a majestic clipper ship sailing far out on the horizon, on its way south. The morning passed far too quickly for Sam. He was disappointed when they were interrupted by the clang of a bell.

'That's lunch,' she said. 'I'm starving.'

They played cards with another couple that afternoon, and read magazines until dinner, which was served at six, and then sat through a musical evening arranged by the Captain, who had a fine tenor voice, though the same could not be said for the songsters drawn from the company. But the evening was saved by a Russian gentleman who agreed to play his violin and stunned them all with his virtuoso performance.

He then handed out leaflets detailing his forthcoming performances at the Lands Office Hotel in Brisbane, and Jessie was delighted.

'We must go!' she said to Sam. 'He's wonderful.'

Sam grinned. 'By all means.' That was another thing he loved about Jessie, she was always so enthusiastic. And she gathered everyone else's enthusiasm to her, in bunches. Soon all the passengers were agreeing they should go in a party, give the gentleman with the unpronounceable name their full support.

He was confused, though, confused by this closeness with her and no mention of her intended. Not a word. But he wasn't complaining. He wished he had the courage to ask Jessie point blank if she could find it in her heart to care for him the way he wished . . . but he was afraid she'd laugh at him. Lines like that did sound soppy. Or she might even be offended. She with the blue sapphire on that all-important finger. Maybe it would be best, if he could find an opportunity, to take her in his arms and be done with it. She could only get cross with him, or call him a cad, or even slap him, but he and Jessie had had rows before. They were soon forgotten.

They called in on Adrian, before Mr Tomkins retired, but he was in a nasty mood, full of self-pity, complaining bitterly about the ship, the food that had made him ill, certain that he had been poisoned.

'You're just seasick,' Jessie told him. 'You're not the only one. Half the passengers are down with it. Is there anything I can get you? A cup of tea?'

'I have some there . . . I could hear singing. You lot must be enjoying yourselves.'

'Yes,' Sam said cheerfully. 'The Captain put on a concert for us, and tomorrow we're having a fishing competition from the stern, so you'll have to be up for that.'

Adrian groaned and turned away. But Inspector Tomkins was at his door and they moved out, once again lurching along the companionway in time with the huge swells that had developed over the last few hours.

'This is me,' Sam said at his door, and Jessie nodded. Then she reached up and kissed him. No goodnight kiss this; she kissed Sam full on the lips because she needed to, could not resist, and then came the thrill of relief that his arms went about her, and he responded, kissing her thoroughly, beautifully, she thought. It was as if they'd left reality behind, back there in Sydney, and out here on the ocean there was another life, sweet and uncomplicated.

'Perhaps you'd better go now,' Sam suggested without too much conviction.

'Do you want me to go?'

'Of course not, but it's late. Your cabin mate, Mrs Maykin, might not approve.'

She looked at him curiously. 'I thought you'd want to make love to me.'

'Don't be a tease, Jessie. It doesn't become you. Now goodnight.'

Jessie laughed and slipped away from him to let herself quietly into her own cabin.

She undressed swiftly, in the dark, and climbed nimbly into her bunk, hoping that she hadn't wakened Mrs Maykin, but a soft voice with a smile in it said:

'Nice night, dear?'

'Yes, thank you.'

'Nothing like a little shipboard romance,' the voice giggled.

Jessie was relieved that her companion wasn't upset. Mrs Maykin was old, close to forty she guessed, but so nice. She hoped they could be friends when she was settled in Brisbane. And that thought gave her a jolt of conscience which she brushed away in an instant. This lovely time she was having on board *Argyle* had nothing to do with Kit, she told herself, insisted. It just did not. She was just having fun.

She slept well. 'Beautifully,' she told Mrs Maykin in the morning, which turned out to be the start of a fine sunny day with a warm breeze and calm seas. Even Adrian had rallied, looking pale and peevish she thought, but on his feet.

Sam remembered to ask Tomkins about Inspector Kirk, since he too was curious that a police station in this remote community should sport two inspectors.

'Oh yes, him!' Tomkins said. 'He was a senior sergeant before taking on the post as chief warden up there. I haven't met the fellow but I believe he has been moved over to a position with a special operation that is in the planning stages. But nothing to do with me.'

'Would Kirk's new job have anything at all to do with the squad of troopers on board this ship?'

'He's civil. They're military. I don't see how.'

'But he has been promoted to inspector, and that leads me to think we're looking at a combined operation here. Civil and military.'

'That could be. I've been upcountry visiting my family, took leave as soon as I was given this appointment, so I don't know the latest.'

'Ah! I thought you might be holding out on me. Then I can tell you that the special operation is to send a squad back into the near north and chase away the hostile blacks who have been raiding properties and firing homesteads.'

'And you think this Kirk fellow will lead them? Highly unusual.'

'No. I'm guessing he knows the district and will add police powers to a volatile situation.'

'Then who will lead the troopers? I didn't see an officer with them.'

Sam shrugged. 'We'll have to wait and see.'

Chapter Seven

The Major came stamping up from his office to find Jack cleaning his fish on a bench outside the laundry.

'The police are here. I told you they'd want to question you, so don't go involving me in the drowning of that fellow. I want nothing to do with it. And the sooner they're out of here, the better.'

'Righto.' Jack followed him round the house to the barn, where a policeman was watering two horses.

'Where's your mate?' Ferrington said. 'My men saw two of you ride up.'

'That's right. The Inspector went over to the house. Said for me to wait here.'

'Is it about the fellow who drowned at Baker's Crossing?'

'Yes. We never found the body.'

Ferrington jerked his head at Jack. 'Come on then.'

They followed another path on to the back door of the house, where Polly was standing.

'I've been looking for you, sorr. There's a person at your front door.'

'Bloody cheek! Since when do these people use a front entrance? Got me coursing from door to door like a bloody greyhound!'

Jack padded after him as they followed the wide veranda round to the front door, where they found the visitor calmly seated in a cane chair. It was the same man they'd met with a posse in the search for Harry Harvey. He wasn't surprised, but Ferrington was.

'Kirk! You? What are you doing in police uniform?'

'I've returned to the force. Inspector Kirk it is now.'

'You've left the prison job?'

'Yes, and glad to be out of that place. No matter how hard a man works to keep order among those crims, you never get any thanks from the public. Just whines and complaints from namby-pambies who'd scream more if they got within a hundred yards of their houses, I tell you . . .'

'But who do I talk to about workers now?'

'Don't ask me. The new bloke, John Dempster, he'll probably fix you up if you cross his palm good enough. Likes a quid, he does.'

The Major scowled, making no effort to be sociable. 'So you're here on police business. What would that be?'

'I want to talk to your mate there.'

Now he was Ferrington's mate? Jack saw the Major's scowl deepen at that remark, but kept a straight face himself.

'Front!' Ferrington barked at him, so Jack ambled over with deliberate steps to counter the fact that he'd almost jumped to attention, a throwback to a convict career that he had to eliminate.

Kirk, still seated, took out a notebook while Ferrington moved away to stand, one foot on a bench, listening intently.

'Name?' the Inspector began.

'Jack Drew.'

'From?'

'London. Came in through Sydney. Been in the bush for years. Prospecting.'

'Found nothing,' Ferrington interrupted.

'What ship did you come in on?'

Look out, Jack breathed to himself. Ships' companies kept lists right down to the cook's cat, he'd been told. The *Emma Jane* would be no exception. 'Let me see now. 'Twas a Norwegian ship as I recall, a fine old lady too, two-master, the *Queen Sibil*, *Sabel*, something like that. Could never pronounce the name right.'

'What year did you come in?'

'Ah, no trouble remembering that. It was forty,' Jack lied. In truth he couldn't recall anyway.

'Any convictions?'

'Not me.'

'You got a trade?'

'Yes. I was a teacher.' He thought he heard Ferrington draw in his breath at that barefaced lie, but who could disclaim it? If a man could read and write, Jack figured in a flash of what he considered genius, he could teach. So old Clout's bashings to make him learn his sums and letters might have saved his skin here.

'Where did you teach?'

'St Paul's Mission School.'

'Where's that?'

Jack laughed. He was on solid ground here; this bloke wasn't English, he had a local voice. 'Next door to St Paul's. That's in London, you know.'

'You don't look like a teacher to me.'

'Yeah, well, that's what your sun does to a man.'

Kirk then went into detail about his attempt to save a felon called Harry Harvey, and Jack told that simply. He guessed he must have drowned. He couldn't catch the body. Saw it carried past in the current, tried to grab it – to save him. No luck.

'That's your opinion. There's no proof. As far as I'm concerned,' Kirk turned to Ferrington, 'Harvey's still at large. We'll get him sooner or later. But I wanted to have a private word with you, Major.'

'Very well. You can go,' Ferrington told Jack in a resigned voice. 'Tell

106

Polly to give the constable a meal. I presume you'll be staying for lunch, Rollo?'

'If you insist, Major.' He stood. 'How's the house going? Can I have a look around?'

The Major decided he might as well make the best of it if he had to share his lunch with Kirk, so he uncorked two bottles of white wine to keep himself in a civil mood, though in the end they did little to help.

When they were settled at table, Kirk presented a sealed letter to Kit.

'It's from the Governor General, Sir Charles FitzRoy himself,' he said. 'To be hand-delivered, so I took the honour upon myself.'

Intrigued, Kit took the letter and stepped down to the end of the room, to keep this important missive private. There he opened it, read it, read it again, and exploded.

'What the hell is this? What's this about troopers being sent bush to keep the peace?'

'I had an inkling you would be informed. I will be part of that cleaning-up operation myself.'

'Cleaning-up?'

'Yes. We've got to get out there and clean out the place, get rid of the savages that are terrorising people in the Wide Bay district. Wipe them out once and for all.'

'He isn't informing me! He's ordering me to lead a squad of troopers, who are being sent to Brisbane, in this action, at earliest.'

'You? Of course, Major! My word, we'll get the place cleaned out in no time. I will have a troop of my own. I'm to head a squad of Native Mounted Police.'

Jack didn't trust either of them. He delivered the message to Polly, who was in the herb garden, and went towards the back steps. Anyone watching might have thought he'd simply disappeared, because he didn't go up the steps, nor did he walk past. But in that second, Jack had slid under the steps and wriggled through slats to find himself under the house. He then crawled quickly in the direction of the dining room, where he could hear the men talking through the bare boards above him.

He'd been expecting to find out if Kirk had believed him or would be making further enquiries about him, but both men had forgotten him. The main topic of conversation chilled him to the bone. They were about to send a small army after Bussamarai and his warriors, who apparently now held a strong position on their home ground, north of the area they'd raided. North of Montone Station, where Jack had met the disaster of all disasters ... shot, burned and robbed of his gold. And who was to lead them? This pair of schemers! Although Ferrington didn't sound too enthusiastic. And well he might not! Here he was trying to persuade his 'mate', a stranger, to lead him to riches somewhere beyond the hills, and he gets caught up in government business.

'No use jawing about it,' Kirk was saying. 'You've got your orders. I consider it an honour to be chosen for such an important detail. All the folk with properties out there will be grateful for our presence. We can sweep through the countryside, wipe the blacks out of that district altogether. And come back heroes.'

'I'll ride back to town with you and talk to Lord Heselwood. He'll understand it's difficult for me right now, and ask Sir Charles to appoint someone else. He and Sir Charles are great friends.'

'Heselwood? He's gone. He and his wife left Brisbane a few days ago.'

'Blast!'

Jack heard the Major pacing about, the new flooring creaking under his weight.

It was dusty under the house and littered with offcuts of timber, empty paste tins and other debris that the builders had thrown down, out of sight of the master. It seemed to mar the spirit of the place, this mess, with the fine house above, as if ugliness lurked beneath the surface. He shuddered. Ugliness, and evil.

'Anyway,' Ferrington shouted abruptly, when his arguments were begininning to sag, 'I can't go! I'm getting married shortly.'

'Jesus! You keep your cards close to your chest! I didn't even know you had a lady in mind.'

'You can say that again,' Jack whispered, feeling a part of the conversation by this. 'Nary a word be spoke about the lad's private life, come to think of it.'

'Well I have, and I planned to go to Sydney shortly for my wedding.'

'When's shortly?'

'Any day. I have telegraphed an overseer to report to me as soon as possible, so that I can get away.'

Jack wondered whether Ferrington meant to get away to go gold-seeking, or to go a-marrying. He rather thought the former would be the winning bet, and the marrying bit only a tale. Anything to shake this job. And for that Jack wouldn't blame him. Bussamarai's men would have fled north until things cooled down, but the whole point of the raids was to establish his people's right to that land. Their tribal rights. They'd be back if need be, *because* they were undefeated. And they'd fight!

He wondered if either of them up there understood that. Certainly the Major seemed to have a healthy interest in dodging hostile blacks, but the other bloke, Kirk, he probably thought he could follow the old routine of ambushing blacks' camps and doing the big shoot-'em-up from cover. It might still work in lonely areas where peaceful families failed to recognise the danger from white men, but not this mob. Not Bussamarai's mob.

'You're a military man on the spot, Major,' Kirk was saying. 'There are a few others settled up here, but you outrank them. You must know it's not

108

done to question the Governor General's orders. You'd better tell your lady love to postpone the glorious day. If you have to. Though we'll only need two to three weeks, I'd say, to wipe out the blacks and their litters, once and for all.'

'What? What's this? Don't you get me mixed up in that sort of business. I'll have no part of it. And did you say your men are native police and not real police?'

'They're real police all right. They're trained.'

'Trained to kill! I don't want them. Won't have them. They're not in my orders.'

'No. I chose them. They're blacks themselves. We're just using fire to fight fire.'

'Bloody renegades, you mean. This is not on. Not on at all. I'll go into town and see about it myself. Who's in charge there?'

'Superintendent Jimmy Grimes. He's the boss. He won't take orders from you. Anyway, I thought you said you weren't going . . .'

Jack eased himself out of his listening post, dusted himself down and strode out to squat by the trees facing the house and think about all this. He ought to get out to the road, fast, he told himself, get ahead of that bastard Kirk and arrange an 'accident', put him out of action. A rock hurled from a tree would fix him, or a swipe with a heavy branch . . . dead easy to ambush him, smash him down from his high horse . . . but then Jack remembered the constable waiting over in the shed. He'd forgotten the Inspector had company. Protection, if only he knew it. Attending to Kirk would have to wait for another time.

He groaned. But what about the Native Police? Kirk was getting ready to sool them on to their own people again. Jack knew all about Native Police, the scourge of the back country. Not just renegades, he pondered angrily, that word was too kind for the likes of them; they were vicious killers, recruited by the military to locate and 'eliminate' pockets of blackfellers, including women and children, which they did with no compunction or pity. It was said in the black community that they revelled in the power bestowed on them by white officers, flattered beyond reason that they were given uniforms, horses, guns and tucker, and even pay. Jack recalled that the Major had objected to the use of those madmen, which was a consolation. At least some white folk were aware of their murderous reputation.

Not that Kirk cared; he was all for them, to get rid of the blacks in the area in no time. Didn't any of them understand why the blacks were putting up a fight? Even the Major had no objection to the chase; he was only concerned that these orders were interfering with his plans.

'Bloody hell,' he muttered, as he watched the two men emerge from the house and walk towards the shed. 'Someone has to warn Bussamarai. Tell him to pull his people way back for a while. Stay low.'

He knew they'd planned to withdraw, but since they'd won back their land, a source of great pride, they'd hardly leave it empty. Especially since it was good hunting ground. And how far would they have pulled back? This motley army the Major and Kirk were supposed to be leading wouldn't stop if they found the blacks had gone. Disappeared. That wasn't the nature of the beast. They'd hardly turn back and report to the powers-that-be that there weren't any blackfellers out there. Couldn't find any! They'd be a laughing stock! No, they'd have to push on until they engaged the enemy, even if it were only a family of blacks living by a waterhole, or on their pilgrimages to corroborees or sacred sites.

Someone had better tell Bussamarai to get his people the hell out of there! The chief wouldn't win a pitched battle against two squads of mounted troops. Nor could he handle a running fight with them, even if he recalled scores of warriors.

Someone. Yes. But who? Jack shuddered at the thought of heading back into that dangerous country, still carrying the painful reminders of his last encounter with local wars. He was not a soldier or a warrior. And right now he was engaged in working out how to make his way in the white world, in a strange country.

And not just make my way, he corrected himself, some of his old ambition returning. How to make a quid and live like this here Major. It can't be too hard, if I can just get myself started.

Come to think of it, he pondered ruefully, I guess me and the Major have got one thing in common. Neither of us wants to do our duty, because duty intrudes on our plans.

The realisation of his own duty had already come to him. He owed it to the blacks, his friends, to give them fair warning.

Ferrington made short work of farewelling his visitors, barely giving them time to mount up before turning away, and that surprised Jack, who had expected the boss to go into the town with them, to find out more about his Governor's orders, since they didn't sit well with him. Instead he tramped down towards the stables and Jack shot out to his fencing, fitting rough-hewn struts into the posts, a much trickier job than it had seemed at first glance. Especially when his workmates, two old lags known as Len and Laddie, took it into their heads to give him a bad time, gulping down all the drinking water, dropping logs on his bare feet, anything to annoy him without risking serious repercussions.

Today, though, he was in no mood for their games; he just needed to get this bloody job finished as ordered, so that he could take care of his own business.

Laddie, a bulky, balding Scot, who had once gained fame as a champion wrestler, Jack had learned, stuck a crowbar in the ground and leaned on it as Jack approached.

'Here comes the wee fancy man, Len. Do ye have a bench for him to sit on?'

110

'Shut your gob, Laddie,' Jack snapped, 'or I'll shut it for you.'

'Try, would ye, fancy boy? I dinna think so. Not without your boyfriend up there to mind you.'

'Get on with the work, you mongrel. I can't be bothered listening to your slime. Give me a hand here, Len, we could finish this job by tonight.'

Len scowled at him and squatted down on his haunches. 'We could if three kept working, not two. And you're not our boss, so don't go giving me orders.'

'Please yourself.' Jack knew the mini-strike wouldn't last long. He grabbed a strut from the pile left there by the woodsmen, jerked it free and swung about with it, inadvertently brushing against Laddie, the rough splintered edges catching in his worn shirt, tearing it. Jack could have sworn that Laddie had moved into his way deliberately, but no matter, the Scot now had an excuse to lunge at him with a yell of rage.

Even as the move began, Jack flinched instinctively, very much aware, and protective of his tender blistered skin, and that took him away from the huge hands grabbing for his throat. He spun about, tripped Laddie and poleaxed him from behind, disconcerted that his usual manner of attack had little effect on the tank-like trunk of his attacker, who had recovered his balance and was turning on him. Jack ducked back, rolled to the side and suddenly lashed out, kicking Laddie in the stomach with such force that it brought him to his knees, gasping for air.

'Sorry about that,' he said, helping Laddie up, 'but you should be careful who you call a fancy boy.'

'Look out,' Len called. 'The boss is coming.'

All three watched as the Major rode towards them. 'What's going on here?'

'I was showing them some wrestlings,' Jack said, searching for the correct words.

'I doubt that tactic would be approved,' Ferrington said, 'and you're not paid to amuse yourselves.'

Jack walked over to him. 'That's something else we have to discuss,' he said quietly. 'I'm not being paid to do anything.'

'We'll talk about that later. You! Laddie! What do you know about the fish farm? *His* fish farm.'

'What about it?' Laddie growled.

'Someone smashed it up last night, and I want to know who did it. Seems to me there's a lot of sabotage going on round the place lately, things broken, tools missing, gates left open, and when I get to the bottom of this I'll . . .' he looked at Jack, 'there'll be hell to pay, believe me.'

'We didn't do nothin',' Len whined. 'We never went down that way, boss.'

'I want it rebuilt, you hear me? You can get a team working there right away.'

'What about this fence?' Jack asked. 'I'll fix the fishponds.'

'I'll send some more men over here to get this finished. You come on now and have a look at the mess they've made of the fish farm.'

It seemed to Jack that the Major moved his workers about from job to job like blind bees, never getting anything properly finished. There wasn't much point in staring at smashed fish traps right now, but, he shrugged, if that was what the boss wanted, righto.

He whistled at the wanton destruction of his carefully constructed fish traps as the Major glared down the banks.

'See what I mean? I have to have discipline here or the brutes will wreck the place. Mindless vandalism this is; I'll put them on half-rations for a fortnight. No, for a month, if they deny themselves good food like this.'

Jack grinned, dropping down to the sand. He knew he was still out of favour with the workers, but this was a mad thing to do when it affected their rations more than his. Polly still fed him at the door to his room, as they would know, and better food than they were given, by a long shot. He stopped to look at clear footprints in the sand, and then froze.

'Jesus!' he shouted, and sprinted up the bank.

'Your men didn't do that,' he cried. 'They're not to blame this time. See those prints in the sand? They're paw prints.'

The Major dismounted and peered from the grassy edge. 'So what? Are you saying dingoes smashed up the ponds?'

'They could,' Jack said. 'They're capable of raiding them. But those prints are too big. That's a crocodile, and a bloody big—'

'What?!'

'A crocodile. Right beasts they are, kill a horse they could. Cripes, if I'd know they were in this river I wouldn't have gone in after the runaway, I'd have left him to drown on his own.'

Quick-witted, Jack remembered, in time, to keep Harvey secure in death, though he doubted Ferrington would have noticed; he was too intrigued by the prospect of a man-eating beast lurking at the bottom of his garden.

'Can you see him anywhere?' the Major asked hopefully, hanging on to a tree as he searched the river.

'No.'

'You stay and watch for him and I'll get my shotgun.'

'It'd be better to just tell your men to stay clear of the river for a while but keep an eye out, wait to see if the croc's a local or a lad looking for a mate. Could be a female with a nest around here.'

Ferrington hung about for ages, questioning Jack about these animals, in the hope the beast might reappear, but finally he gave up, vowing to arrange a crocodile hunt in the near future.

'You'd better be a good shot,' Jack warned. 'They're fast, them things, they come up the banks like lightning.'

As they walked back to the house, the Major, still fascinated, kept up his questioning. 'How do the blackfellows catch them? Did you say they eat

112

them? How big can they grow? Wouldn't it be something to get one of them! I've never been big game hunting, but I'd say this would count, wouldn't it?

'Not for me. I'd sooner look a lion in the face than one of them. That feller can have his river; you won't get me in there again.'

A few days later the mailman brought the responses that Kit had been waiting for, amid his other mail, which consisted mainly of country magazines and bills. He also bore news of a large crocodile sighted in the river, but Kit wasn't interested in being sociable on this occasion, so he cut the discussion short. He had a telegram from Adrian and a letter from Jessie, which could not have arrived in Brisbane on the same day, but that made no difference to this representative of the Royal Mail. He was very democratic about such matters, all missives being equal in his eyes; they were duly placed together in their slots, ready for his week-long country rounds, to be delivered when he and his horse were in good form, and when the various canvas bags had filled up every space in his cart.

Adrian was coming! He was on his way. 'Thank God,' Kit exclaimed. He needed him more than ever now, if he had to be caught up in the GG's bush fighting campaign. Adrian's telegram informed him that he would be on SS *Argyle* arriving Brisbane Thursday, and sadly that Jessica had had to postpone the wedding arrangements because of their grandfather's illness.

The latter confused him, since he hadn't yet received a response from Jessie regarding his suggestion that they marry next month, but then he turned to her letter, weeks out of date, to find the explanation. She had been amenable to the plan for an April wedding at the time, and was obviously very excited about it. Now, circumstances had changed for both of them, all of them, so they'd probably revert to the original arrangements.

His thoughts turned to the sudden illness of Marcus Pinnock. To be expected, of course. The old fellow couldn't go on for ever. And if he died, Adrian would be main heir to the Pinnock fortune.

And I'll bet he's well aware of it, Kit grinned, watching out of the window as Tom Lok hauled a chest of tea across the courtyard on a wheelbarrow.

He reread Jessie's letter fondly and sighed. He would respond this evening and post his reply in town. While he was there, he'd have a talk to Superintendent Grimes. He might know of an officer willing to lead the troops into battle for the Beyond. The land confrontations had nothing to do with him. If men like Heselwood had to have those huge estates out past the boundaries of civilisation, good luck to them, they could stake their claim on as much land as they wanted, but they shouldn't expect the government to protect them from irate black tribes. Everyone knew that the further back they were pushed, the more the blacks resisted. Kit remembered the Governor warning of the risks involved in taking up land in the back of beyond, of the very real dangers of attack by blacks, but he was ignored. Now they were coming crying for protection.

113

'I'll have something to say about this,' he muttered, but then remembered that his orders came from the Governor. Who had obviously capitulated under pressure from the rich squatters.

Anyway, he conceded, I'll go into town tomorrow. And I'll take Drew with me. Send him off to get the necessary implements for gold prospecting, because, dammit, I can't let him go. I'd lose the opportunity of a lifetime. I'll never find a partner with his qualifications again. He knows the blacks, he knows his way about out there, and from what I saw today, he's well taught in hand-to-hand fighting. Street fighter more like it, he mused, hardly good form, but effective.

And above all, the rascal knows there is gold out there. That much I believe. But as for him being a teacher in London before he came to New South Wales . . . Kit laughed. The bloody cheek of him! Teacher, my eye!

But he'd got Rollo's measure. Barely educated himself, Rollo could not make a judgement on that response, so Drew had won the round. He'd also made himself an enemy there, but that was his problem.

That night he invited Drew up to his veranda and offered him a whisky.

'I usually prefer beer on a hot night, but I've run out,' he said.

'Whisky will do. What's up?'

'There's no need to stand on ceremony. Take a seat there.'

He poured the drinks, neat whisky, double shots to put the man in a mellow mood, but Jack drank some and then reached for the water jug on the tray.

'I have to break it down. The taste's a bit strong for me yet, if you don't mind me saying, though it's surely a good drop. Never thought I'd see the day I'd be watering down good whisky, but that's abstinence for you. What's on your mind?'

'Tomorrow. I have to go to town tomorrow, thought you might like to accompany me. How long is it since you've seen a town?'

Drew flashed a grin, his even teeth looking whiter than white against his dark skin. 'I dunno. Years. Maybe I wouldn't know what to do no more.'

'Well for a start you'd need some cash. Here's two shillings.'

'What's that? Charity or pay? If it's charity, keep it. If it's pay, it's not enough.'

'How much is enough?'

'I want the same pay as your workers.'

That surprised and pleased Kit. He was almost at Drew's mercy on this subject. 'Good-oh. I'll give you two weeks' pay in the morning. But I have to make some plans now, I've got a lot on my plate.'

'Like what?'

'Private business. I have decided to try prospecting shortly. As soon as I'm free of certain obligations. And I would like you to join me on this expedition.'

'To partner you?'

'Partner? Yes, I suppose. But I need a definite answer from you. Are you game or not?'

Drew swallowed the whisky with a slight shudder and stared into the glass. 'I told you, I don't know where the gold is.'

'But you've had your hands on gold. I want the truth now.'

'That's the God's truth. I had a heap of it, sewn in a money belt. Weighed a ton it did, but there's your dead end. I don't know no more than you about where to find gold, and that's the truth too.'

'Prospecting, by the very word, as you are aware, means looking for gold. If folk knew where it was they'd go straight to it. I want to try to find gold, at least try, that's not asking much. You seem to have lost heart, but one more go . . . surely you owe yourself one more go, with the newest equipment.' He waited a few minutes and then added: 'Unless you have other plans.'

'No,' Drew said thoughtfully. 'No. Not exactly yet. When do you want to go? Right away?'

'Unfortunately, no. As I mentioned, I have some obligations to fulfil. I'll know more in a day or so. But can I count on you?'

Drew shrugged. 'I suppose I might as well.'

'Not too enthusiastic, are you?'

'Neither would you be if you knew what's out there.'

'Ah well, you can tell me all about it on the way into town tomorrow. And don't forget your boots.'

Brisbane! It wasn't like any town or village Jack had ever seen. Only a series of sheds and shops stuck between wooden houses with pointy roofs. Reminded him of a farm, more like it, with a wide dirt road running through it, and that big river circling about swollen with suspicion, as if eyeing the place off.

I would be suspicious too, Jack thought. All the peace and quiet trampled by these people with their animals and their stink. He looked to the river again, suddenly anxious about something, but unable to define it, then turned back to his new surrounds, as he rode beside the Major. His master, he grinned. Or partner . . . knowing Ferrington preferred the former. But there were ladies here, swishing about the streets in their pretty dresses, some even in shirts and men's pants!

'Hey, look at that!' he called to Ferrington as a pretty woman with a mop of red curls strode across the road in trousers, and swung on to a horse, but the Major had already seen her.

'Good morning, Roxy!' he beamed, his usually gruff voice dripping with honey, and Jack guessed this was the fiancée as he studied her firm tits and neat belted waist, deciding ladies in pants were a great innovation.

She turned to the Major, pouting. 'Kit! Where have you been? I haven't seen you in ages. Why didn't you let me know you were in town? I'm at the Lands Office Hotel, where I always stay. Where are you staying?'

115

Her question was almost a demand, and Jack was enjoying this. The fiancée was not one to trifle with.

'Whoa!' Ferrington cried. 'Hang on a bit, my dear. I'm just riding in, tired and thirsty, haven't yet made it to the Lands Office bar! And I didn't have time to write to you, business beckoned. But Roxy! You are looking as pretty as a picture. Did I ever tell you that before?'

She smiled, freckled face dimpling. 'You may have. You're not looking so bad yourself. How are you managing? Getting the hang of it?'

'More or less,' he said. The horses began to move restlessly at this delay, and Jack saw a horse trough ahead that was of more interest to the animals than this chatter.

'Miss Maykin!' A man came running out of a store, dashing across the road to her.

'The riding gloves you ordered. Here they are! They came in the last shipment. They're very nice, soft kid, the very best.'

'Serviceable, I hope,' she said, taking them and stuffing them under the handle of her saddle, which, Jack suddenly realised, was a man's saddle. He'd almost forgotten that ladies were supposed to ride side-saddle.

'Oh certainly, yes. Excellent wearing.'

'All right then. Put them on my account.'

She dismissed him and turned her attention back to the Major, so Jack let his horse trot on to the trough, where he waited, amusing himself by reading, and at times forcing himself to recall, the signs printed on the shop windows and walls.

'Gawd,' he murmured, 'I'd forgotten half these places existed. Drapers. Cafés. Tailors. Mercers . . . what's that? *Moreton Bay Courier*. A newspaper, for God's sake! What news could be worth writing about in this place?'

He saw a pie shop and thought he might buy himself a pie, but was suddenly uncomfortable at the idea of actually going in there. He felt shy of these town people now and realised it would take time to become accustomed to white folk and their ways again.

He climbed down from his horse, tethered it in the shade of a huge fig tree and stood staring at the pie shop, fingering coins in his pocket, a pocket in old trousers that back home he wouldn't have been seen in, even on the way to the scaffold.

'I've come down in the world all right,' he said to the horse. 'But I'm still a step ahead of the law.'

The Major joined him, having farewelled Miss Maykin, temporarily, Jack supposed, though he made no comment about her.

'We'll be here a few days, Drew. I'll be at the Lands Office Hotel. You find yourself some digs, then go to the store and find out about prospecting equipment. Make a list of what you need and the cost, and bring it to me.'

With that he rode away.

* * *

116

Kit stabled his horse and made straight for the bar, the source of all local information. He heard that *Argyle*, the coastal steamer from Sydney, was on schedule, but apparently a convict ship, *Randolph*, was headed upriver and causing all sorts of consternation.

'What's wrong with it?' he asked.

'What's wrong?' the barman boomed. 'It's a transport ship. Got a cargo of convicts on board and we don't want them here.'

'Why not? They're useful.' He saw Reece Maykin, Roxy's father, down at the end of the bar and pushed through to him.

'Good day to you, Reece. Why are they making such a to-do about this ship?'

'Because we don't want them. We don't want any more riff-raff from England's jails. Governor La Trobe wouldn't allow the captain to land them in Melbourne. He sent them on to Sydney, and FitzRoy wouldn't have them either. He ordered it on to here. But they needn't think we're going to let them be shoved on to us. We refuse to accept any more convicts here.'

'But they are a good source of labour, Reece.'

'They might be to you, sir, but not to us. We don't stoop to slave labour . . .'

'But surely working on the properties is better than prison?'

'Not when they're subjected to the sort of treatment meted out by the likes of you, Ferrington!'

Kit gasped, appalled at this rudeness, as Maykin turned away from him, and more upset to be facing hostile stares from other customers. He was inclined to demand an apology from Maykin, but had become aware that maybe he had placed himself in an unpopular situation. Few people called at Emerald Downs, certainly not the right people, like Maykin and his set, the bigwig squatters, but then they did live on distant stations, and after all, he himself was not ready to take on serious socialising until his house was completed. Or better still until after the wedding, when his bride could attend to the niceties. And bring her own family influence into the picture to even up their standing.

Kit left the bar and strode up George Street to call on the Superintendent of Police, Jimmy Grimes, the orders from Sir Charles FitzRoy firmly in his pocket.

The police station, lodged in a four-roomed house with a shingle roof overlooked the botanic gardens that had become the wonder of the town, so beautifully were they progressing, with native trees and fruits already growing in abundance. A rose among thorns, it was called by delighted locals, referring to the town's other claim to fame, or infamy, the Moreton Bay penal settlement.

Kit noticed a kiosk had blossomed near the gate and resolved to take Roxy there for a quiet talk away from the glare of her parent.

Obviously Grimes was expecting him. He was a hard, lean man with the

117

keen eyes of a bushman, a man who had served his time in the saddle, and was not about to brook any argument from a gentleman farmer. He stood.

'Mr Ferrington, is it?' he asked, his eyes cold.

'Major, sir.'

'Ah, but I hear you don't relish the role of an officer.'

'You could say that is very true, sir. I will do my duty, but I am burdened with responsibilities on my farm, and I have come to ask if you could recommend another officer to fill in for me. A name that I could present to Sir Charles for consideration.'

Grimes sank back in his chair, gesturing to Kit to be seated, and lit his pipe while his visitor waited, politely.

'The trouble is,' he said at length, 'we haven't got another starter. Captain Forrest would have helped. He's got a station up on the Downs, neighbour of the Maykins, but he broke his leg. Had a fall from his horse. Then we did have another major fellow, from the Guards they say, but I think he was a phoney. Took the widow Morpeth's savings and shot through. So there you have it.'

'I see.'

'And we've got troopers arriving tomorrow on the *Argyle*. They'll go straight to the military barracks to await your orders. We aren't well placed for troops here, only about a dozen resident now, under Lieutenant Clancy. A good bloke, Clancy, but he hasn't had much bush experience.'

'To be honest, I haven't either, Superintendent. And since I don't know the area, it will be very difficult.'

'Don't worry about that. That's why you'll have a squad of Native Mounted troopers with you.'

'And that's supposed to make me feel less concerned? I'm not such a new chum that I don't know about those scoundrels. I won't have anything to do with them, sir, and that's flat. If necessary I shall lodge my objection to Sir Charles immediately.'

Grimes sighed. 'Listen ... the blacks had a win out there, men and women were killed, homes burned. They have to be routed from that district to allow the graziers to get on with the job of opening up the country. That's a set fact. The government wants the problem fixed and so do the folk here, and that's that. As for those bloody native troops, I'd lock 'em up if I had my way; they're neither fish nor fowl, just plain bloody criminals, the only type that would join such a force. But we're stuck with them.'

'I'm not,' Kit said firmly. 'I refuse.'

Grimes shrugged. 'Well I have to say you're right on this, but Rollo Kirk reckons he can keep them in order.'

'The hell he will. Who's going to keep *him* in order? No. I still won't have a bar of them. I won't take on the responsibility of men who are widely known to assault and rape and worse, under the guise of orders.'

'What about your responsibility to your own men? Neither you nor

118

Clancy has bush experience. It's easy to get lost out there and you have to live off the land, you know. You've got a huge area to cover . . .'

'I know.' Kit climbed to his feet and looked at the maps on the wall. 'I will need the latest of these if I could have them.'

'By all means. So am I to report that you will take on the job without the Native troops?'

'Yes.'

'They will still be operating, separately then, as far up as Wide Bay, you understand?'

'Nothing to do with me. But I'm not taking my order lightly. I do know a bushman I can take with me, come to think of it. He knows the area well. Now, I will have to go home to make arrangements to depart, so I'll leave the new troops to Clancy for a few days.'

'Very well. I'm pleased to have met you, Major.' The Superintendent reached out to shake hands. 'Anything I can do, sing out. And good luck . . . By the way . . . keep your ears open talking to any of the station folk you come across; we're looking for the blackfeller chief. We haven't got a name yet, but they're so well organised of late we know there's a boss man out there giving the orders. If we can find him, we're halfway home.'

'Thank you, I'll certainly keep that in mind.'

The pies were still there. He wondered what was in them. Meat, he thought by the smell, but what? Pork, hopefully. But the two ladies were taking their time, deciding what they wanted to buy, pointing fingers, pursing lips, shaking heads, while Jack loitered outside, still unable to push past the door with the jingling bell that he'd listened to for the last half-hour. He was annoyed with himself for not going right in, pointing to a pie, handing over the coins that were hot in his hand and getting it over with, but he was off balance. Intimidated. Unable to make the move.

'Only because I don't know how much the bloody things cost,' he murmured to himself, excusing this weakness. 'I might not have enough, or he might gyp me.'

Jesus! There's a thought. Learning money all over again. I was always a good counter, but I have to know what I'm doing.

The ladies were digging in their purses at last. Buying buns. They looked good too, currant buns if he remembered rightly. Putting them in their baskets, talking, still talking to the pudgy-faced baker, and the pies remained in place, two pies, both as big as his hand. He would have to go in now; what if they were the last and someone else went in ahead of him?

The bell jingled and the ladies scrambled out, peering nosily at him, shying away as they passed, and Jack plunged for the door. The little bell announced his entry, but the baker lumbered round the counter and made for him, arms waving, shooing him!

Jack stopped in the doorway, confused. The baker was still coming at him. Pudgy hands shoved . . . pushed him back out the door.

'Get out of here! We don't serve niggers!'

'What?'

'You heard me. Get away from my shop or you'll get a kick in the arse!'

'Who are you calling a nigger?' Jack grabbed the baker's ear and twisted him back into the shop, the bell jangling now as if a yell for help, while the baker howled in pain.

'See those two pies?' Jack snarled as he threw his assailant across the counter, spilling the buns and sending a pile of loaves sliding to the floor.

'Yes,' the man whimpered.

'Now, when I let you go, mate, you're going to wrap up them bloody pies for me, or I'll crack your head open on your own counter.'

'Yes.'

Shaking, the baker moved swiftly round to the pies. 'I thought you was a nigger,' he whined, touching a hand to a reddening ear.

'You thought wrong. How much?'

'Naught. Just take them!'

'Now you're calling me a thief!'

'Oh no! No. Fourpence it is. Fourpence.'

The pies paid for, Jack turned on him before he left the shop. 'And remember this, next time I come into this shop you will call me sir. You got that?'

'Yes, sir,' the terrified baker quaked.

So, Jack mused with a grin, shopping ain't so hard after all. You just have to get the hang of it. Clutching his pies, he made for the shade of a big old tinai tree, called 'ironbark' by the men at Ferrington's farm, and was about to squat down when he saw a family of blacks coming towards him. They were skinny, pathetic, dressed in rags, two of the children covered in sores. And he felt ashamed of his objection to being called a nigger . . . a real bloody Judas, he thought.

He walked over to intercept them but they pulled away in fear.

'Just goin' down to da river, boss,' the leader, an old fellow called, but Jack shook his head and pushed the pies at him. He'd meant to only give them one, but there was only one bag. Anyway, they were both gone now.

'*Nerundama*,' he said, 'friendship', and they stared.

He fully expected that to be the wrong word, but the old man thrust the pies to the young woman walking beside him and threw questions at Jack in a familiar language.

'Who are thee? Where from do thee come? How do thee our words are knowing?'

The pies were already being shared and devoured and the woman handed pieces to the old man and to Jack, for which he was grateful. It was a pork pie, rich and fatty; he wondered if he could talk Polly into making them if she ever spoke to him again. But then, she was Irish, she probably didn't know how to make them proper.

All smiles, the group nodded appreciation and began to walk on, but the old man remained, waiting for the answer.

'Only a friend. My name is Jack. I knew some of your people.'

He was cautious. He couldn't afford to be recognised by blacks and linked to Bussamarai in this town, but the old man leaned over and stroked his dark skin.

'Long time you live in sun country.'

Jack nodded, and to retreat from this situation asked the old man's name.

'I am Berali of Turrubul people. This our river.'

'Thank you. I must go. But can thee meet me here by this tree after dark?'

As if he had already ascertained that it was necessary for them to talk more, Berali pointed to the base of the tree and walked away, leaning heavily on a stout stick. Jack hoped he was doing the right thing. This was an opportunity to send a message to Bussamarai. Maybe. But how could that be done without mentioning his name? So. A conversation wouldn't do any harm. He'd just test the air. But he didn't want white folk here seeing him consorting with blacks, if he had to play the spy for a while.

The pie shopping behind him, he decided then to go find a store that sold prospecting equipment, whatever that was, and then seek a bed somewhere.

Lieutenant Clancy was a forty-year-old Irishman, a stocky fellow with fair hair and a thick moustache and a perpetual toothy grin as if the world were as innocent as he appeared. On the surface, Kit discovered.

Clancy welcomed him warmly, showed him around the barracks. In normal times Kit would have ordered an immediate swab-down and scrub to remove the mould that powdered walls and sucked the air from the rooms, but he considered himself on loan, not responsible for the permanent billets.

'I have brought some maps I want you to study,' he told Clancy, who wasn't impressed.

'What's the use of maps when there aren't no roads, sir?'

'Terrain, Lieutenant. Rivers, hills are noted to the best ability of the map-makers. Including these mountains here. The Glasshouse Mountains. I've sighted them and they're a spectacular landmark, I can tell you.'

He was pleased he could at least spout that bit of knowledge. 'We could even use them as lookouts,' he said, a remark he was later to regret when he discovered it would take an experienced mountaineer to scale those perpendicular heights.

Clancy reckoned it would take only a couple of weeks to find good horses and have the dozen new troopers equipped and ready. 'Then Inspector Kirk will set our schedule to move out. His men are camped in our back paddock.'

121

'I give the orders here, not Inspector Kirk. This is a military patrol, not a police posse. Where they camp and what they do is not our business.'

'Yes, sir. Would you care for a cup of tea in the mess? Or a stronger drop? This being a tedious hot day.'

'No thank you, Lieutenant. I am extremely busy, having this duty put upon me at such short notice. But I shall be back tomorrow to inspect the new arrivals, their equipment and their mounts. You take charge when they disembark. I'll be there, though, just to look them over.'

'Yes, sir.'

When the Major left, Clancy made his way down to the mess for a little celebration. So! Ferrington wasn't Kirk's good mate after all. He was fed up with the interference of that greasy Inspector Kirk, lording it round the place as if he were leading an expedition into the Sahara.

What did they want police for anyway? Soldiers of the Queen didn't have to be backed up by civilians, just to chase off a few blackfellers with nary a firearm between them. What was the world coming to? No wonder the Major had scotched that idea. He seemed not a bad feller at all, this Major. Not bad at all.

The duty steward stuck his head in the door and Clancy called to him:

'Don't be rushing off now. I'll have me a whiskey. Irish whiskey, from that bottle there. Jump to it, lad!'

Roxy was in a flirty mood the next morning as they strolled through the gardens, not in the least interested in her father's bad manners as reported by Kit.

'Why are you fussing? He's rude to everyone. Why do you think my mother goes on so many trips to Melbourne and Sydney, and any other place she can think of?'

'But he accused me of being a slave trader.'

'Oh, darling. Don't be so melodramatic. Slave trader! What are you talking about?'

'Because I employ convicts, he claims they're slaves.'

'Oh yes, I've heard that before. People say that convict labourers are cheap labour, underfed and ill-treated. Is it true you actually flog them if they play up on you?'

'Certainly not,' he lied, sweating a little. Kirk had said it was legal and normal practice. He'd had no idea the locals were interested, let alone disapproving.

'There! I knew it was all an exaggeration. Oh dear, I'm quite puffed from the walk. Let's sit in here, quite a delicious spot really.'

She led him to a secluded park bench shaded by palms, and he sat with her, well aware that the short walk was nothing to a woman with her physical stamina. At the Christmas gymkhana she'd won the women's foot race and several riding trophies . . . but then she did have other physical attractions . . . He turned to kiss her mouth and explore those attractions.

Eventually they strolled down by the river and Roxy was pouting again. 'You haven't asked me about this evening.'

'You said you were dining with your family, and I have a guest arriving today on the *Argyle*.

'My mother is coming in too, hence the family dinner party, but afterwards,' she whispered. 'Are you in the same room as last time?'

'Yes.'

'Well then?'

Kit laughed, put his arm round her waist and swung her to him. She really was a delight, always so forthright and gay . . . and he needed cheering up these days.

'Wilt thou smile on me at the witching hour, my lady?' he asked with a bow.

'Verily, my sweet,' she giggled. 'In the meantime, come and have a look at the beautiful bay mare I'm thinking of buying.'

In his explorations of the town, Jack came upon a camp of blackfellers in unkempt, ill-fitting uniforms, and gathered these were the Native Mounted Police . . . Kirk's merry men. Except there was nothing merry about this mob. They reminded him of the vicious gangs that had roamed the dark streets of Soho in his early days. He'd been terrified of them until he grew bigger and stronger and learned never to traverse those streets after dark without weapons.

He stood watching them as they went about their chores, picking up some conversations he understood, mostly everyday stuff about women and booze. In all they seemed mightily pleased with themselves, swaggering about the place like little lords, but he saw in their eyes the flat coldness of killers. Killers specially chosen for this detail. Men with crocodile eyes. That was what the blacks called them; men with crocodile eyes! With good reason.

He wanted to go over and talk to them, ask them to think about what they were doing. Ask them to down tools and do a bunk. But no amount of preaching would work here. Someone like Ilkepala could probably scare them off, but where to find him?

That night he took some tobacco to Berali and sat down to have a yarn with him, saddened by the stories of the bad times that had come upon his people, upon whose lands they were now sitting. He talked a little of his wanderings, first from the lands west of Sydney and then on north with the families of the people, ending up here back with whitefellers on a farm.

Eventually he mentioned the name of Ilkepala, and Berali was startled.

'You don't go talking about that fella. Whitefella don't know him. He too good for whitefellas! Spit on them.'

He jumped to his feet, obviously afraid that this white man was trying to prise information from him, but Jack grabbed him, apologising, begging him to wait.

'I only mentioned his name because I wanted to get in touch with him and hoped you could help me.'

'No!'

'Listen to me. I wanted to warn him that the renegades, the crocodile men, are on the march again, and going out into his territory very soon.'

'You fool feller you! We got eyes. We see those bad men here.'

He shook himself free and drew himself up proudly. 'You think Ilkepala he no see these things?'

'Then you know more whitefeller troops are coming too? A journey of payback.'

The old man's eyes reflected pain at this news, but he was still suspicious. He turned and walked away without another word.

Jack was sorry that Berali wouldn't trust him, but at least he knew that the blacks were aware of the situation now, and that let him off the hook. He accepted too that he was a bit of a fool not to have guessed that the blacks hanging about this town would be passing on vital information like this to their friends inland. They had all sorts of communication systems, from signals left in the bush to the more urgent ones taken by runners who carried fire sticks to protect them through the night. He smiled . . . whatever was needed to keep them on the run.

He felt better now anyways.

That night, too intimidated once again to seek shelter at a rooming house, he slept soundly on a high bank overlooking the river, and in the warm early morning swam in a nearby creek. Later he joined a queue of stockmen waiting for a kerbside barber to get to work on their matted hair and heavy beards.

'Jesus! What happened to you, mate?' the barber said.

'Bush fire. Can you even my hair up? It's longer on one side.'

'You don't say! It's twice as long on this side. But them burns . . . there's some hair growing through. You'll have bald patches. Tell you what, I was a master hairdresser for ladies once, and I know all their tricks. I'll part your hair down the middle, take this longer hair down this side over the burn spots and pull it round the back, and put a band on it to keep it in place. Get me?'

Jack remembered that he'd worn his hair pulled back like that in his stylish days. 'Is it long enough?' he asked, surprising the barber.

'Almost, mate. Let it grow and come back to me next time you want it cut, and we'll have it right smart. Can't do anything about them scars on your face, though.'

One shilling and threepence that had cost, but he felt good when he bought some cooked fish and boiled potatoes at a stall and sat on a pier looking over that big river.

The storekeeper swore that no self-respecting prospector would ever head for the bush without this collection of spades and picks and crowbars, and

124

tin dishes of various sizes to 'wash' for the gold, as he put it, along riverbanks. Then there were axes and tomahawks, needed to cut saplings to build supports for tunnels when mines had to go deeper, following reefs.

'Reefs? What are they?' Jack asked.

'Long ledges of gold, mate. Once you find a reef you wouldn't want to stop, now would you?'

'No,' Jack breathed, astounded. Jesus! Was there a reef of gold where his friends had picked up the nuggets they'd brought to him? Bloody hell! He always thought gold lay around like dropped sovereigns. If he thought at all. So, with that he ordered every implement that was recommended, plus a few good strong knives and a camp oven that he'd found in a corner. Civilisation, he noted, was overtaking him at a fast rate now.

'Here's your list,' the shopkeeper said eventually. 'Tell your boss my prices are rock bottom. He'll never do better anywhere else.'

His boss didn't think that at all. He took one look at the total and yelled: 'What's all this? I can't afford all this stuff! This lot would fit out ten men. Why do we need ten axe handles?'

'They break. An axe head isn't much good on its own.'

'And what are sieves for?'

'To wash in rivers for alluvial gold.' Jack grinned, this being the answer he'd received to the same question. It didn't surprise him that the Major's lack of knowledge on this subject equalled his own, but he was interested to hear him claim he couldn't afford a few tools. He'd thought he was a rich man, with the farm and the fine house and all. But then a lot of rich men were said to be mean with their money.

'All right then,' Ferrington allowed. 'Tell him to pack it up and send it out to Emerald Downs.'

'Why don't we take it ourselves? If we go prospecting you won't be able to tell the bloke to send it on after us.'

'What do you mean, "if"? You agreed to accompany me.'

'Yeah, well, I'm not so sure now.' He was waiting for Ferrington to tell him about the other expedition – the military attack on the blacks – and wondering which one would be first. Some partner, this character, keeping shut on a show like that. Why all the secrecy?

'We'll talk about this later. I'm busy now. Get this stuff sent to the farm straight away and stop arguing about it. When we go we'll have packhorses. I mean, a packhorse. Now get on with it.'

Jack stared. He saw the eyes flicker. And heard the slip. Packhorses? What was the bugger up to?

'Bloody hell!' he murmured. 'That's what! He's going to combine the two. Fight his war and prospect at the same time! Probably getting paid for his efforts too.'

He can count me out, Jack decided, as he marched back to the store with his instructions. I've had enough of wars. Years of them.

'Where can a man get a good cheap feed?' he asked the proprietor.

'Carmody's pub, the Rose, down at King's Wharf. You on a ticket-of-leave?'

'What's that?'

'Convict. On parole.'

'No. Not me.'

'I didn't think so, mate. But why are you wearing them old clothes?'

'I dunno.' Jack said, perplexed.

'They put the mark on you, those clothes, mister. Now have a look here. I got good cheap shirts, this striped one would suit you, and some good-looking moleskins, they'd fit a big feller like you real well. You're working at Emerald Downs, are you?'

'No,' Jack said breezily. 'I'm the Major's partner.'

'Go on! Pleased to meet you, Mr . . . ?'

'Drew. How do we pay for that prospecting gear?'

'It goes on the Major's account.'

'Good. That's good. I'll take some of those clothes you got there. Put them on the account too.'

He finally left the store in a neat check shirt, a fine pair of breeches that showed a good leg, and a wide hat that went well in hiding the burns. He stopped to admire his get-up in a shop window.

'Nothing cheap about Jack Drew,' he laughed as he bent down to wipe a speck of dust from his new riding boots. 'Don't fool with me, Major. I might just hop on that horse and go.'

Right now, though, he wanted the good feed at Carmody's pub, but as he approached the wharf he saw crowds gathering and heard angry shouts from the pub balcony.

'What's going on?' he asked, and a man pointed to a ship lying at anchor downstream.

'That's the *Randolph*. She's carrying convicts, but we're not letting them land here.'

He rushed forward to listen to a gentleman address the crowd and Jack followed. That spruiker is money, he thought, a posh voice like the Major, greying hair and a trim beard, flash tweeds, all the makings. No gold watch, though; he supposed folk didn't wear them these days, not a one to be seen in the place.

'. . . We're not a dumping ground for their criminals,' the posh fellow was shouting. 'For all the riff-raff from their prisons! This has to stop, and we, ladies and gentlemen, will put a stop to it. Not one of those felons out there will set foot in Brisbane!'

He flung his arm wide to the river, and the crowd, now doubled, cheered.

'This is no longer the Moreton Bay prison settlement, it is a respectable town. I don't care what the Governor General says . . . that ship won't land here! Send it back to Melbourne, its original destination.'

'Send it back to England, Mr Maykin,' a voice yelled, and the speaker nodded. 'If need be, yes. They'll get the message then!'

'Good on you!' The voices shouted their approval, but then a policeman up on the pub's balcony had his say:

'In the name of the law, the captain and his crew will be setting their passengers ashore at this port, as instructed by Sir Charles FitzRoy, Governor General, and I'll brook no interference, so I recommend you all disperse quietly.'

Maykin was quick to respond. 'Sir Charles is making us the fools! He weakened when Melbourne and Sydney wouldn't take them, Mr Grimes; now he thinks we'll put up with it. Well, he's wrong. And how do you think you're going to brook no interference with only a couple of men to back you up?'

'I can arrest you for incitement to riot, sir.'

'I'm not inciting, I'm exercising my civil rights, as my friends here today will agree.'

There was a surge of approval, but an army officer pushed past Jack, smelling of whisky, Jack noted, though he didn't appear drunk.

'Have you no thought for those poor folk on that ship?' he called. 'Don't none of ye be pretending you don't know the foulness of the holds on transport ships, of the filth them prisoners have to suffer, and the horrible rations . . . You have to let them come ashore!'

'This is none of your business, Lieutenant.' Maykin sneered down at him. 'This is for the townspeople to decide.'

'Then let them ask how many prisoners have died on that ship, over months at sea! And let them speak up, or be shamed by forcing more suffering upon them . . . You're a miserable lot, you are!'

The Lieutenant, an Irishman, wasn't welcome at this gathering. The townspeople hissed; they emulated Maykin, sneering and snorting at him, and an apple flew past his ear.

In a second, Jack was up there beside him. 'Let them land! This bloke is right. You've got folk suffering out on that river, under your noses. By Jesus, you can smell that ship from here!' He could, but he doubted they had that capacity, though now noses were twitching, handkerchiefs were appearing, excitement turning to scowls.

'What's the matter with you?' Jack roared at them. 'You can't let them sail the seas for ever. And hands up who of you ain't got a convict in the family or been one your own selves. Let's see who's what here.'

'I certainly haven't,' Maykin called, and Jack turned on him.

'Of course not. I bet the rogues in your family are still safe in England.'

That drew a ripple of amusement from the audience, as hands were raised to declare familial purity.

'You put your hand down, Tilly Duckworth,' the Lieutenant snapped. 'You wore a number yourself, and your old man too. And the gall of you, Paterson, your daddy was one of the first inmates of Goulburn gaol as he was wont to boast. Now get along with you all before I call up the troops. And don't get smart with me, Maykin, my mate Grimes up there may not have too many troops, but I have, sir, and more comin' ashore this very morn.'

'Disperse!' Superintendent Grimes shouted from above, and reluctantly the townspeople turned away.

'What in the hell do you think you're doing?' Ferrington snarled at Jack, jerking him aside.

'Why? What's wrong?'

'What right have you got to be up there mixing in town business? You could have got yourself arrested! And . . . and . . .' He stopped, stunned. 'Where did you get those clothes?'

'At the Charlotte Street store. He let me have them cheap. What do you think of these breeches? They look a bit like yours, don't they?'

'No!' The Major stormed away to watch another ship plugging upriver.

'You want a job, mister?' The police boss was coming towards him.

'Doing what?'

'Helping us get those convicts off the ship. You did a good deed back there, backing up Lieutenant Clancy. I thought you might be inclined to help us. The poor buggers, men and women, will be proper legless by this, after being crammed in so long. There's a lot of them, nigh on two hundred . . .'

'No!' Jack said angrily. 'Get your blackfeller police to give you a hand.'

Grimes stood back to let the stranger pass, surprised by the angry reaction. But then he cheered up. Why not the Native Police? he asked himself. Let's see them do a bit of work for a change. Bloody good idea. They can clean the convict areas on the ship too. I'll work their arses off.

Jack strode away, but further on he stumbled, slipping along the bank of the river until he fell forward, vomiting, dry retching, grasping at a tree for support. He couldn't have agreed to assist those poor wretches because he couldn't bear to see them. It had taken too long for him to forget the misery of his own voyage, holding only to the good memories, like his confrontation with the captain of the *Emma Jane*, who couldn't intimidate him, and the few friends he'd made. Scarpy and the Irishmen.

'I must be getting soft in the head.' He groaned, straightening up. 'What do I care about them? They've got to take their chances like I did. Bugger them!'

A tall man watched him from a clump of mangroves at the water's edge, and he was amused.

'That Jack Drew, he hates to care. He likes being the hard man, gives no quarter. Life confuses him now.' He sighed. 'Me too sometimes.'

Ilkepala drifted back into the shadows and headed for the camp of the men with the crocodile eyes, their Dreaming lost.

Chapter Eight

First off *Argyle*, in his usual great rush, pushing aside Inspector Tomkins, who scowled at his rudeness, was Hector Wodrow.

Having failed to find his wealthy brother in Sydney, he had followed the advice of the lady who ran the boarding house he'd been staying in, and sought Jack further afield.

'Them as came here about the time you're speaking of, ten years ago or some, went north if they were smart . . .'

'Oh yes, he's a smart one all right, our Jack.'

'Then that's where he could be. They took up great sweeps of land up there because it was mostly all gone down this way; just walked in and claimed the land . . . Squatters, they called them, squatted, you see, Mr Wodrow. Cost them nothing for years, then they paid the govmint a pittance. Made their fortunes, they did. Would you like a cup of tea?'

'I wouldn't mind, Mrs Slade.'

'Right. Sit yourself by the door and I'll put the kettle on. I don't do this usual, you know. Tenants take a mile if you give them an inch, but you're a kind man, used to better than my poor establishment, I'm sure . . .'

'Where exactly is up north, Mrs Slade?'

'You could go to Brisbane by boat and search about from there. I know all this because me sister worked for a squatter family up there, the MacNamaras, before she married a shearer. In her day, though, they had to overland, took months to get to them great estates, but modern times we have now. People can travel there easy as pie. Here's your tea. You like it strong, don't you?'

'I do indeed. This Brisbane place. Do they speak English?'

'What else would they talk?'

'I heard the north is overrun with black tribes. Like Africa.'

'So it is. You wouldn't get me up there for smoke, but Brisbane's safe, they say. Civilised now.'

Stepping ashore from the *Argyle*, Hector breathed a sigh of relief. It wasn't until they'd rounded the last bend in the river that he'd made his decision to disembark. Prior to sighting the small township, he'd seen nothing along the banks of this wide river but thick green forest, where could be hidden thousands of savages, and he was preparing to about-face, return forthwith to Sydney. He wondered at the sheer boldness of men who would push into the wilderness, face savages and myriad obstacles, even death, to make their fortunes. But that would be Jack, if he set his mind to it. He was a bold one, that Jack! Hector had never lost his admiration for the young lad who'd run away and faced the cruel world on his own. Hector could never have done that. Never.

He picked up his bag and strode away from the wharf, puffing a little as he left behind the river breezes and encountered a hard sun blazing down on the few souls venturing out this midday. Hector hated hot weather.

Kit stood impatiently by the gangplank as the passengers streamed ashore, already beginning to doubt that Adrian was aboard. He saw two ladies coming down, one of them the lovely Madeline Maykin, mother of Roxy, and doffed his hat gallantly. There was a time when he'd caught Madeline's eye, and he would have taken up that delicious challenge had not Roxy intervened. But one never knew. There were always other days.

His smile was broad, mischievous as he welcomed her. 'A pleasure to see you back with us, Mrs Maykin. A great pleasure. I hope . . .' His voice trailed off as he noticed the young lady with her, and he had to take a second glance to convince himself he wasn't mistaken.

'Jessie,' he said weakly, so startled he was momentarily lost for words.

'Surprise!' she cried gaily. 'I don't think you recognised me, Kit!'

'But of course I did,' he spluttered, remembering to offer his arm as she stepped to solid ground. 'But what are you doing here? I mean, I wasn't expecting you . . .'

Madeline Maykin touched his arm. 'I must go. I see the boss is waiting. Very nice to see you again, Major.' She turned and embraced Jessie. 'Now don't forget, we must stay in touch, my dear. Do enjoy your visit, this is the very best time of the year, the climate's divine.'

She swept away. Jessie clutched his arm. 'You are pleased to see me, Kit? Aren't you?'

'My dear girl, I'm delighted. But I was expecting Adrian.'

'He's here. He's bringing my trunk. I knew you wouldn't mind my coming. Adrian thinks it's pushy of me, but we are engaged. Are you sure you don't mind?'

He supposed not. 'Of course I don't mind.' He remembered to kiss her on the cheek. 'Welcome to Brisbane, my love.'

Adrian finally came down behind two porters carting luggage ashore, and rushed to shake his hand. 'Great to see you, old chap. Sorry about the sister barging in on us. Not my idea, you know.'

'It's quite all right. I'm delighted to see her. Such a wonderful surprise.'

A few of the disembarking passengers joined them, including Sam Dignam, but Kit wasn't interested in standing about listening to their shipboard tales; he was too busy trying to figure out what to do with Jessie.

'We'll take the luggage over to my hotel,' he said to Adrian. 'I have a room booked for you. I think it would be proper to place Jessie at another. The Britannia is pleasant. Should you perhaps stay there as well?'

They finally sorted themselves out and Sam tacked himself on to the trio. He'd been heartened to see that Jessie's fiancé didn't appear to be overjoyed at her presence; the Major had only given her a perfunctory kiss on the cheek, whereas he would have thrown his arms about her for all to see, and kissed her madly.

But serve her right, he thought crossly. Only this morning she had insisted they'd simply been carried away by the fun of a shipboard romance, and he shouldn't make any more of it. They were very good friends, that was all.

'Sam, I'm engaged. You know that! Don't be tiresome. We had a lovely time and now you're spoiling it.'

'No I'm not. There appears to have been nothing to spoil! You used me, Jessie, kissing and canoodling to amuse yourself. I'm sorry it happened, and believe me, it won't happen again. I'm only hurt now to discover that you're a very shallow person.'

As they walked up the street, Jessie tried to concentrate on Kit's commentary about the town and the streets and general information, but she could still feel Sam's resentment. How could she have admitted to him that it was so nice to be kissed by a man she did care about, she really did. Because her fiancé hadn't yet learned to unbend with her. He was English-born, more formal than Sam, so his reticence was understandable. But it was mean of Sam to call her shallow, and claim she'd used him.

For heaven's sake! she brooded, as they made for the Britannia Hotel, a two-storey building on the next corner. Who is he to talk! It didn't bother him that I'm engaged and made no mention of becoming dis-engaged. What a hypocrite!

She was further annoyed when Sam took a room at the Britannia too. And he stood there watching, with a smirk, she was sure, when Kit instructed the porter to take her to her room.

'You have a rest, my dear. I would like to have a few words with Adrian. We'll have tea at four. Will that suit you?'

'I imagine so,' she shrugged, and dismissed, followed the porter up the stairs.

Mrs Rollo Kirk wasn't far behind. She was to meet her husband at the Britannia Hotel. She shoved up to the desk in time to hear a tall, good-looking Englishman introduce Jessica Pinnock to the proprietor as his fiancée.

'Well I never!' she frowned, turning to stare at Mr Dignam, whom everyone in first class had taken to be her fiancé. And why would they not, the way that pair behaved, goo-goo eyes all the time. And that one there,

131

the brother, taking not a whit of care what they did when backs were turned. She sniffed loudly at Miss Pinnock, and then at the brother, but they went their ways without even acknowledging her.

'Hussy!' she snapped and chose a comfortable chair facing the door to await Mr Kirk . . . Inspector Kirk.

'There's not much to see in this backwater,' Kit said, 'so I propose we leave first thing in the morning.'

'Marvellous!' Jessie said. 'I simply can't wait to see our future home.'

'No doubt,' he smiled, irritated that he would have to buy a horse for her. He'd already bought one, ready for Adrian, and managed a bargain, but cheap horses were few and far between. 'After tea you can inspect your mount, Adrian, and then we'll have to find one for Jessie.'

He came to regret that statement, since Jessie insisted on coming along to view the horses, and after wandering about the stables she sighted the bay mare that Roxy was considering buying.

'Oh Kit, I've found the most beautiful horse. I can't even look at any of the others. Come and see.'

As soon as she headed for the last stall, Kit knew she'd been looking at Roxy's horse.

'She's sold,' he said quickly, trying to turn Jessie away.

'No, not yet,' the stablehand said. 'Roxy was looking her over yesterday but she couldn't make up her mind.'

'Then she's too late,' Jessie crowed. 'I'll take her. She's just lovely. What's her name?'

'Honey Lou she's called, after her colour and Miss Lucy, the dam. Famous, Miss Lucy was, won the Darling Downs Cup twice. Good stock there, Major; fast, though. Is your little lady up to it? I mean, Roxy, she could ride a wild bull . . .'

'So could Jessie,' Adrian said proudly. 'Honey Lou will suit her just fine, Kit.'

'Don't worry, Kit,' Jessie said. 'I can handle this lady.' She dragged over a saddle. 'Here, Adrian, saddle her up for me.'

While Jessie rode the horse around the paddock, Kit strode angrily over to the Bank of New South Wales, where he had an uncomfortable conversation with the manager. He managed to extend his loan, though, and on his return forced himself to smile as he handed over eighty pounds. Twenty for Adrian's horse and sixty for the thoroughbred Jessie had claimed without the slightest enquiry as to the cost. Rich people! he sneered. They don't have to ask. But she'll learn to economise here.

Her arrival had so confused him he'd almost forgotten about the troops he was supposed to observe as they left the ship, until he saw the Lieutenant lining them up on the far end of the wharf, so in the afternoon he checked with Clancy, and finding everything in order, left him to it.

* * *

132

That night he failed to keep his assignation with Roxy. He could hardly knock on her door at that hour and offer apologies. He smiled to himself as he turned in.

'Brought to heel by the presence of my future wife!'

No doubt Roxy would be angry; she was fiery enough at the best of times, and the episode with the horse wouldn't help, but she'd get over it.

In the morning he was up at dawn, pleased to find Jack Drew sitting on the front steps of his hotel. Somehow, he thought fleetingly, he'd known the man would be there. Strange.

'We're leaving as soon as we can get away this morning, so wait here for me. My fiancée, Miss Pinnock, and her brother came in on the *Argyle* yesterday. They're coming out to Emerald Downs with us.

He hurried round to the Britannia Hotel, where breakfast was served from five a.m. to cater for long-distance travellers, and found Jessie and Adrian in the dining room.

They tucked into platters of steak and eggs, with tea and fried bread, all looking forward to the ride, because it was a perfect morning, skies blue, weather clear.

'You take Jessie to collect your horses, Adrian,' Kit said, 'and come on down to my hotel. I have a few things to settle up. My man will be there.'

'Who's your man?' Jessie asked.

'Just a bushman. Name of Jack Drew. I find him rather handy. He's riding with us. He lives at Emerald Downs.'

Jessie was so excited she could hardly contain herself. Kit had not been cross with her, as Adrian had predicted. In fact he was very nice, taking her presence for granted, as if acknowledging she had every right to be there. And he was looking just marvellous, very tanned and healthy; obviously the country air was good for him, after the office jobs he'd held in Sydney. He even had a sparkle in his eyes this morning. He was so happy and relaxed that she felt almost dizzy in his wonderful company, and so in love.

As they left the dining room she took his arm and he drew her close to kiss her quickly on the lips.

'I'm glad you're here, my dear!' he said, and Jessie's knees went weak.

They were saddling up the bay when a tall girl with unruly red hair came into the courtyard. She was dressed in an expensive black riding habit with a white silk blouse; showy stuff, Jessie thought, the sort of carefully tailored outfits that Blanche was always trying to make her wear. Jessie preferred her blouses and jumpers and favourite jodhpurs. Comfort before vanity, she told herself, a little supercilious, but she jumped when the girl shouted at the stablehand.

'What's that horse doing out? Who gave you the right to let anyone ride her, Leo?'

'This lady's got the right,' he said. 'She bought her, or at least her fiancé did.'

'You can't sell Honey Lou. I wanted her. I said I'd buy her.'

'You said you'd think about it.'

'I was only thinking about it because you were asking too much. You knew I would buy her, I just thought sixty was a bit over the top. Now you give this person her money back and we'll have no more of it. Honey Lou's mine, I've brought sixty pounds with me.'

'Can't do it, Roxy. First in first served. The bay's sold. She belongs to this lady.'

Roxy swung around to Jessie. 'Listen, there's been a misunderstanding. Here's the sixty. Take it. And another five if you like. And I'll have the horse.'

Jessie gulped. She disliked confrontations, but Kit had bought her the mare, she couldn't give her back; nor did she want to, she loved Honey Lou already.

'I'm really sorry,' she said, 'but I can't do that.'

'Why not? You can get another horse. Or did you pay more?' She rounded on Leo. 'That's it, isn't it? You got more out of them! What did she pay you? You little stinker!

'What did you pay?' she demanded of Jessie, who shook her head.

'I've no idea. She was a gift from my fiancé.'

Roxy wasn't one to give up. 'Who's he then? I'll give him ten more than he paid. Where can I find him?'

'I don't think he'll sell, miss,' Jessie said. 'I'm so sorry, but I'm fond of this horse myself and I really don't want to part with her.'

'We'll see about that. Who's your fiancé?'

'Major Ferrington,' Jessie said proudly.

'Who?' gasped Roxy. 'Kit Ferrington?'

Leo stepped into the argument. 'Let go, Roxy, for the love of God! I'll find you another horse. This lady got in first and that's all there is to it!'

'Kit Ferrington bought her the horse?'

'I told you. Yes!'

'We'll see about that. You wait here,' she yelled at Jessie. 'I'll get him.' With that she wheeled her horse about and raced furiously out the gate.

'I don't have to wait for her,' Jessie said angrily, but Leo was concerned.

'If you don't mind, miss, I'd rather the Major sort this out. Just hang on a little while.'

Roxy found him walking away from the hotel and jumped down from her horse to confront him.

'You bastard!' she shouted. 'First you stand me up, then I find you've got a fiancée right here in town.'

She went to slap him, but Kit grabbed her arm. 'Steady on! I'm sorry, Roxy, I didn't mean to upset you.'

'Upset me!' she shouted, pulling her arm away. 'Why should I be upset? I didn't even know you were engaged. You're a rat! An absolute rat! And then you go and buy my Honey Lou for your smirking brat of a fiancée.'

'I didn't mean that to happen. I'm sorry, Roxy, I really am.'

'If you're so damned sorry, then get down there and get Honey Lou back for me.'

'I can't do that. It's too late.'

'Is it really?' Roxy dug in her pocket and fished out the banknotes, shoving them at him. 'There's the cash. I've just bought her from you!'

He tried to push the money back to her but she turned on him in a fury. 'You'll take it, or I go back to your girlfriend and tell her you had an assignation with me last night.'

'But I didn't. I mean, I didn't keep it.'

'And she'll believe you when I tell her about the other times? And I won't be lying. You did arrange to come to my room. Take the money.'

'Roxy, my fiancée only arrived yesterday. I had no idea she was coming.'

'Obviously you didn't. Maybe she's not so dumb after all. Coming to check on you, was she? Well, I can give her . . .'

Kit tried to appeal to her better nature, but it was no use. People walking by turned to stare at them.

'I want that horse,' Roxy said. 'You get it for me or else.'

Jessie couldn't believe her ears. Here was Kit, her fiancé, handing the horse over to that hussy.

'The Maykins are powerful people in these parts,' Leo whispered to her, in an effort to explain, but it was all over in minutes. Roxy Maykin rode off on Honey Lou, leading her own mount, without even a backward glance.

'I hope she breaks her neck,' Jessie said to Adrian, and burst into tears when Kit came over to console her.

'She did choose the horse in the first place, Jessie. You don't want to start off with arguments and upsets, dear. I'll make it up to you. Leo is bringing up a another horse for you. Look, the chestnut, he's a beauty, isn't he?'

This was a fair to middling horse, not as refined as the bay, with a plain head, but Jessie saw Adrian glaring at her and realised she had better accept the gift with some grace or the ructions would continue.

'What's his name?' she asked in a small voice.

'This is Rufus,' Leo said eagerly, 'and a nicer feller you'll never meet.'

As Jessie went forward to make the acquaintance of the horse, Leo leaned back to Kit. 'And only half the price,' he added with a grin.

Kit introduced them to Jack Drew in a perfunctory sort of way, and soon they were riding through the town to emerge on to a bush road with the sun beating down on their backs.

Jessie was travelling comfortably, Kit thought, no problems with Rufus, but he was aware that she was still upset about losing the bay, so he went out of his way to cheer her up. He'd almost forgotten how gorgeous she was, with that striking colouring: black hair, creamy skin and those blue, blue eyes. She made the natural bush surrounds look drab.

He eased his horse over to ride beside her and held both mounts back a little to allow Adrian and Jack Drew to get well ahead of them on the narrow road.

'You're looking very beautiful today,' he said quietly. 'You seem to get more lovely every time I see you, Miss Pinnock. How do you do that?'

She blushed, suddenly shy, and he was surprised to feel a thrill of expectation as he reached out to touch her hand. This young beauty was to be his wife! He wished he could say what he really felt, that he wanted to take her in his arms and make love to her right now, over there under that tree . . .

'Thank you,' she was saying. 'That's so nice, Kit. So nice of you.'

'It's the truth. I'm so glad you're here, I really am, Jessie. And I do hope you like the farm.'

'I'm sure I will.'

'And do you still love me?' he whispered, looking down at the engagement ring he'd given her.

'Oh, of course I do,' she cried, turning to him anxiously as if she expected to see disappointment.

'And I love you,' he said, 'so all's well in our garden.'

Adrian would have to choose that moment to drop back to talk to Kit, so Jessie allowed her mount to follow them. She was thrilled that Kit was being so romantic, delighted now that she had made the effort to get here, but she could still feel an undercurrent of disquiet. Even fear. Fear of that woman Roxy. She was certain that there was something between her and Kit. She'd caught that look of Roxy's when she heard his name, and it was pure shock. Nothing to do with the horse.

She dug her heels into Rufus's flanks to keep up, as if letting herself know that that was what she intended to do, right from the start. Keep up. Keep ahead of Roxy Maykin, who hadn't been wearing a ring of any sort. Kit was so handsome, he'd obviously be a target for a single woman, and that had been worrying Jessie all along. Out of sight, out of mind, she'd heard said, and it was probably right.

'I'm very glad I came,' she told Rufus, patting his neck.

Adrian was full of praise for the lush subtropical countryside, with palms and umbrella trees splashed amid the grey gums as if none of them knew what sort of forest they were supposed to be presenting. Kit didn't bother to enlighten him as yet about the dry winters, the opposite to the climate Adrian was accustomed to. The main thing was to break the news that his future brother-in-law would be needed to manage the property in his absence.

136

'Where will you be?'

'Sir Charles has ordered me to resume my military status and take a squad of troops into the bush to re-establish law and order, since raids by blacks have gotten out of hand a hundred miles or so to the north.'

'Hold on! You're going on a campaign! How bloody exciting! I'll come with you!'

'Not possible. I need you to manage the farm, and anyway I can't take civilians, except Jack Drew. He's been written into my orders as a scout.'

'Surely you can get around them. Who's to know?'

'Adrian, your place is at Emerald Downs with Jessie. Try to keep that in mind.'

He settled them in, with Jessie's bedroom around the open veranda from his own and Adrian's further along, and on the first morning took them on a tour of his property, introducing Adrian to his workers as the manager.

Jessie loved it all, especially the homestead, with its view of the river down the grassy hill and across the flats. To her everything was just beautiful and an absolute credit to Kit, though Adrian took a more professional attitude, advising Kit later in the day that he seemed to be doing quite well, but was taking on too much at once.

'You have to give the place a chance. You're farming . . . trying to grow crops, agisting cattle, running dairy cattle, pigs and chooks, landscaping, nursing an orchard, a vegetable garden and an ornamental garden . . . What else, for God's sake?' he laughed. 'I can't see any sheep.'

'I had some but it was too wet underfoot. I had to let them go.'

'That's a relief. For now, I'd forget all the ornamental stuff, give the Chinaman the job of working the market garden, and only clear what land you need.'

'But the cattle need pasture.'

'Not those beef cattle. They're used to the scrub, they'll find feed unless there's a bad drought. And another thing, these blokes you've got working for you . . . I didn't see any of them straining themselves. The slowest bunch of slackers I've ever seen.'

That surprised Kit. He'd thought they were working as well as could be expected. But then Adrian was accustomed to employing men born and bred on these properties . . . and paying them accordingly.

'Then it's your job to whip them into shape, my friend. Get them working harder. That's probably the reason why everything round here is half finished . . . fencing, sheds, and pens and chicken runs, things like that. Half of them fall down before they are completed, because I had the only real tradesmen working on the house.'

Privately Adrian thought it was putting the cart before the horse to have built a splendid house before the farm started providing even enough food to support the occupants. The usual beginnings were log huts that expanded as more space was needed, until they grew into pleasant lined cabins and, over the years, more permanent houses. Even then it took a generation or so before a homestead like Kit's emerged. No wonder Jessie was so happy. She'd expected to be roughing it for a while, never dreaming that her first home would be as fine as this, and would feature a housekeeper-cum-cook as well.

When Kit took him down to the office and showed him the farm journals and ledgers, Adrian was shocked. His friend was already in debt and the future looked bleak. It would take years of perfect seasons for this place to become a paying proposition, even with the injection of funds that Jessie's dowry would bring in. Good money after bad, he thought dismally.

Nevertheless, it was a beautiful property and he told Kit that, pleasing him immensely.

'I hope you don't mind me saying you'll have to tighten your belt, though, Kit. Don't spend a farthing unless you have to. Push those workers of yours harder; the farm should be self-sufficient at least. Only buy what you can't grow.'

'Excellent advice,' Kit said. 'I'm greatly relived to be able to leave the place in your capable hands, Adrian, so believe me, I'm really grateful to you.'

That evening Adrian took his sister aside. 'Don't be buying anything you can't pay for with your own money, Jessie. Your fiancé has really gone overboard to make everything nice for you, at the expense of the business side of the farm.'

'What do you mean?'

'He's broke! He's built you this nice house, so now it's up to you to do your bit. Unless you want to break off the engagement and go home.'

'I will not,' she said angrily. 'How could you say such a thing! I'll work here with Kit, we'll make a go of it, just you wait and see.'

'We're going to be short of funds?' she said to Kit, more of a statement than a question.

'Not really, my dear,' he said, though he guessed she'd been briefed by Adrian. 'We'll pull through.'

'Of course we will,' she said, hugging him, and receiving a gentle kiss in return. 'I can economise. Let me think on it for a while. But do you really have to go away, Kit? I couldn't sleep last night after you told me. It's a very dangerous mission, stirring up the blacks . . .'

'They're already stirred up. All I have to do, with a squad of soldiers, is round them up and expel them from the settled areas. We don't have to get into any fights with them, just tell them to move on.'

'But what if they won't go?'

'Jessie, be serious. They won't have a choice against an armed force on horseback. I'll only be away a few weeks.'

'I think Sir Charles has got a damned cheek dragging you back into service because they're too mean to keep a permanent force of troops here, something they'll have to do eventually. There are more and more blacks further north; they won't just walk off their land as if they don't care. Actually, I feel sorry for them. I don't know why they can't stay on those big cattle stations. There's plenty of room.'

'Because they burn down the homesteads, Jessie.'

'Oh.'

'Have you seen Jack Drew?'

'Yes. He's round the back lining the storeroom to keep out ants.'

'Lining it with what?'

'Some sort of mud. He says it's foolproof when it sets.'

Sheer terror forced Polly to speak to Jack Drew as he worked. The tales about that great beast of a crocodile were frightening the daylights out of her, so when he came back from Brisbane with the boss and the Pinnocks, she chased after him in the yard.

'Would you tell me this then?' she said. 'Is there really a big crocodile in our river down there?'

'Yes. One at least, I saw the tracks.'

'And would there be more?'

'There could be a couple more. I wouldn't recommend swimming.'

'The men say they come up at night and prowl around looking to eat someone. That they're so big they could gobble a human person at a snap. Old Bart says he's seen footprints in the sand outside the men's kitchen. He says the smell of meat cooking brings them up.'

Jack laughed. 'They might lie about the banks, Polly, but they wouldn't stray too far from the river. You're safe as bricks up here.'

'Albert's been leaving hunks of meat up on the banks for it.'

'Poison?'

'Oh no, he wouldn't do that. He wants to see the beast, reckons he could make a pet of him. What's that if not encouraging the monster to be coming ashore, I ask you?'

Jack thought Albert would be better served preserving those hunks of meat for their own consumption, since from what he'd heard in the house, the new manager planned to economise in all directions, and he was certain to start with rations.

'Not a good idea, Polly. It still wouldn't bring a big old crocodile like him up here, but it's a dangerous game. I'll talk to Albert.'

'He don't like you any more, Jack Drew. He says you're a turncoat.'

'And didn't you think the same?'

'Might have. Did you see where he built me a room in the corner of the barn, with two wooden partitions? All private it is now.'

'No I didn't.' He'd never stopped to think where Polly slept, to be truthful. 'Comfortable, is it?'

139

'Enough. You can eat in the kitchen if you want, the boss said to tell you.'

Jack grinned. The Major had told her that weeks ago. Obviously his term of punishment was over.

He headed down to the river thinking that was just the sort of mad thing Albert would do. Pet, my arse! A croc would make short work of him, pull him into the river and roll with him till he drowned. Or maybe just take a leg off for starters. Jack had eaten crocodile, it tasted a bit like chook, but he had no idea how the blacks caught and killed the things.

That brought him back to the leaner rations and the Pinnocks. Buttering him up, the Major had invited him to join them on the veranda at dusk last night, his time spent mainly answering questions from Miss Pinnock, the fiancée. That was a surprise. Miss Maykin must have been just a flirtation.

Miss Pinnock was a pretty girl too, very sweet and obliging. Jack thought the Major had chosen to wed the better of the two. He wondered when the wedding was to take place. Her brother was not a likeable fellow, rather arrogant, overly full of himself, delighting in telling the Major where he was going wrong in this farming business, pointing out that the fine house was a mistake, an extravagance. Personally, Jack thought it was the best thing about the place. But where his sister, Jessie, was an open book, Adrian's eyes held a secret that he was keeping from them. And Jack wondered what this young whippersnapper could have been up to, that he needed to hide.

Up ahead on the river he saw two dingoes fighting over a lump of meat, and grinned. Your pet just missed out, Albert.

Jessie was absolutely fascinated when she heard that Jack was a bushman and had been living with the blacks for years and years, so there was no end to her questions about everyday things like food, clothing, shelter, language, attitudes, no end to them, but Jack didn't mind. It passed the time.

'You should write a book,' she said. 'People will want to hear all about this.'

'Yes, you should, Jack,' the Major teased. 'He was a teacher back in England, you know. Though you'd never think it now.'

'Good God! You can read and write?' Adrian was astonished.

'Of course he can,' Ferrington said, 'but he's not too good on reading maps.'

'Maps without towns or streets,' Jack growled.

'Ah. But look here, I have some new ones.' The Major unrolled the maps and spread one out on the long veranda table. 'Have a look at this one. There are few towns, but the sheep and cattle stations are clearly marked, even though the boundaries are vague as yet.'

Jack studied the map. Starting from Brisbane, which was quite a way inland from the coast, he followed the Major's pointer west to a town called Toowoomba, and listened to his explanation.

'This is the Darling Downs, excellent country, a plateau, and here are the outlying stations . . . not towns, big properties . . . McLean Creek, Wattle Creek, and so on. But looking north where I am going, we see Ballymalloy Station, Saturn Downs, Hanover, Juliana Plains, and up here, the furthest north. Grosvenor and Montone Stations.'

Jack stared. Montone? Where he had lost his gold? Maybe it was still there!

As they talked he looked at the rivers, working out finally how his rescuers would have brought him so far south. This stream ran into that fast-flowing river, the river that fair tore along in the wet season, and then they'd made their way on to this one, the Brisbane River. Looked easy now, but it would have taken skill to manoeuvre their frail canoes; they'd have to have been the best rowers . . .

A face came to mind. Moorabi . . . of course. He remembered now, heard him talking to him, soothing, realised it must have been him. But Moorabi was a very quiet man, known to be one of Ilkepala's offsiders; he wouldn't lift a finger without the magic man's say-so.

He shrugged. The connection was beyond him. The Major and his map suddenly a priority.

'. . . That's if he's joining us,' Ferrington was saying. 'He doesn't seem to be able to make up his mind. Have you decided yet?'

Jack grinned. 'Might as well.'

'Definite this time, is it?'

'Yes. When do we leave?'

'I'll give you a letter to take to town to Lieutenant Clancy in the morning. Tell him to get moving as soon as possible. We'll leave from here.'

'Oh, so soon?' Jessie was disappointed.

'The sooner I go, the sooner I'll be back, my dear. And then we should have a talk about the wedding. Would you give some thought to having it here? I really think it would be more practical.'

That night he managed to shake off Adrian, to find time alone with Jessie, and though it was late, he took her for a stroll across the hill to a glade of trees where she was at last in his arms. He kissed her passionately, surprised by her eager response, and she didn't object when his hands found her breasts and caressed them, so he brought her gently down to the grass with him and held her to him.

'I love you, Jessie,' he said over, and over, and she wept.

'If you knew how much I wanted you to say that to me, write that to me,' she said through tears of happiness, 'because I love you so much, Kit. I really do.'

He was kissing her, unbuttoning her blouse, to slip his hand into the warmth of her breasts, marvelling that she could only moan with pleasure, that she was not rebuffing him.

'You're so sweet, Jessie,' he murmured. 'I love you, and need you. My

141

wife.' He felt the thrill run through her at the sensation and at being referred to as his wife. She didn't pull away, but moaned again in sheer delight as he put his lips to her breasts, but suddenly, he stopped. Sitting up. Pulling her blouse back across her breasts. Standing, offering her his hand as she, confused and flustered, climbed to her feet.

He walked her back to the house without a word, and at her door he said, 'I'm sorry, darling, I shouldn't have . . .'

'No. No, Kit. Please.' Her hand was on his mouth. 'Please don't apologise, it was me. I've missed you so much. I wanted you.'

Kit knew he should have been firmer, but the temptation was too great. He took her in his arms again and said, 'Oh my darling girl, I think you do love me.' And went with her into her room, closing the door behind them.

There was a time, during the exciting and tumultuous night with this passionate girl that he hesitated, wanted to stop, thought they should, but his loving, and his sweet words about being wed soon anyway, and that this was his last chance to be with her before he had to leave had his lady hardly knowing what she wanted, except that she was desperate to please him. To be his wife. To prolong the joy of this rapturous first bedding.

But Jessie did know what she wanted, and it was him, Kit, her man. He was an experienced lover and she a virgin, but she felt she had to give him her all . . . all the loving she could, because that bold and brassy Roxy was still on her mind. She was afraid at first that he'd find her dull and disappointing . . . but soon all thoughts of anyone or anything else were swept away in the passion that erupted between them, and Jessie was overwhelmed with love for him.

He lay abed with her in the morning, and she whispered to him: 'Don't you think you ought to go back to your room? Someone might find out you're in here.'

'Let them,' he said drowsily. 'This is our home. We do as we please.'

'Our home!' Jessie echoed, needing the sound of those words to give her courage, for she really had been afraid that Adrian might find out. But then she thought, with a giggle, how bold Kit was not to care what anyone else thought. And why would he? Wasn't he right? This was their home, not home-to-be; it was already their home, so they could do as they pleased!

She slipped an arm around him, wildly aroused again, and kissed his back.

'We'll get married here, darling,' she whispered, starstruck. 'Why should we bother having to go all the way to Sydney and back?'

As it happened, Kit didn't leave for a few more days, but the bittersweet farewells only increased their ardour.

Jack carried three letters with him on his ride to Brisbane. The first, the most important, contained the Lieutenant's orders from the Major. Two others were to be posted. Adrian had slipped one to him on the quiet, with a wink. It was addressed to a Miss Flo Fowler in Sydney. The other was from both Adrian and Jessie, to their mother, also in Sydney.

Clancy was pleased to meet Jack officially. 'So you're the Major's scout then? I was looking about to be thanking you for standing up for them poor buggers on the *Randolph*. People have got short memories, I tell you. Would you care for a pint?'

'Don't mind if I do.'

'Have you known the Major long?' Clancy asked as they walked across to the pub, and Jack shook his head.

'Not long.' He wasn't in the mood for questions at this point, being not a little nervous at marching into a bar again after all this time, feeling as if he'd forgotten the protocol. He kept telling himself to just do what Clancy did, follow him, but the noisy crowd made him feel awkward and clumsy, so he hung back by the door.

To his dismay, Clancy noticed. 'Not used to towns yet, Jack?'

'I'm all right,' he replied, on the defensive.

'We get a lot of bushies up this way,' Clancy continued. 'They love the open spaces out yonder, fond of solitude they be. Never seem to take to towns again. Will you be stayin' or takin' yourself back out there when we've done our patrols?'

'Depends on which way the wind blows.'

Clancy was right about one thing. Towns had lost their appeal for Jack. He preferred to be out in the bush, in peaceful times.

The Lieutenant had explained that he'd set off with his troops at first light in the morning so the horses would be fresh, but Jack, having delivered his messages, decided to head home right away.

As he rode out of town, the *Moreton Bay Courier* was being distributed to eager local readers. On page six was the same small advertisement that Hector had placed in the *Sydney Morning Herald*, asking for the whereabouts of one Jack Wodrow of London; the same except that the address for reply was c/o the Post Office, Brisbane.

While Hector sweltered in a small hotel room, Inspector Tomkins was pleased with his new office at police headquarters, overlooking the Brisbane River. He opened the windows wide to catch the breeze, noticing the dark skies in the west.

Superintendent Grimes came in with an armful of files. 'Don't want to overload you too soon, but I thought you might look through these; we've always got a helluva lot of complaints about cattle rustlers and horse thieves. They seem to think there's easy pickings up here, and I suppose there is, we're so short-handed, but it's time we lowered the boom on them before someone gets shot. I think you'll find some of the files overlap, so it mightn't be such a big job.'

'Good. I'll sort them out.'

'Looks like a storm brewing,' Grimes remarked. 'Not surprised, it's still very hot, which means we're not over the rainy season yet.'

'Is that so? Only yesterday someone was telling me that the rainfall this year has been light, and I can look forward to cooler weather now.'

'In a couple of months,' Grimes laughed. 'I'll leave you to it. And you might check up on that story in the paper about the coach to Ipswich being held up. It doesn't tally with the facts we were given.'

The Inspector set the files aside and picked up the newspaper. His first priority on the new job was to acquaint himself with the local people and happenings. He noted the story about the hold-up by a lone bushranger, who had robbed the driver and five passengers of money, jewellery and, of all things, boots.

That's different, he grinned, harking back to his days as a London bobby, before he was recruited for the New South Wales police force. No self-respecting hold-up villains on the English roads would bother stealing boots. But then, he realised, distances were so great here, boots would wear out fast and be difficult to replace. As for the other discrepancies, the Inspector guessed how they might have arisen. Victims of these robberies would tell the truth to the police, but for publication they often boasted of losing much more money, and expensive watches . . . that sort of thing. Ego-tripping for the benefit of the readers.

Turning the pages, he glanced at the advertisements, all good insights into the town, and noted the usual list of missing persons that these papers always carried. Given the upheavals of convict transportation, and the defections from ships and the military, Arnold Tomkins was convinced that families would be searching Australian records for years to come.

He went to move on to other notices when a name caught his eye.

'What ho!' he laughed. 'What have we here? Jack Wodrow, I declare!'

Maybe the article about the hold-up on the Ipswich road had caused him to land on that name, he pondered. And so it should. Jack Wodrow! Highwayman of note. Wanted back in England for murder and robbery-under-arms. He wondered if it was the same fellow. If the rogue had ever been caught. What had become of him? And who was this asking after him? Hector Wodrow. A brother? A relation? Surely he wouldn't be dragging Jack's name into the limelight if he were the felon. Let sleeping dogs lie . . . Nevertheless . . .

The Inspector had left London six years ago, but he had a friend who had only recently arrived in the colony, former Police Sergeant Fred Watkins.

Fred had served in central London for most of his career and was a very knowledgeable man with a prodigious memory. On his retirement he'd emigrated to Sydney and set himself up, successfully, as a private detective.

Later that day, still curious about the fate of the infamous Jack Wodrow, Tomkins wrote to Fred asking what had become of the rogue, 'for reasons as herewith stated'.

He then requested a post office clerk to give him the tip when a man by the name of Hector Wodrow came to enquire about possible replies. And to hang on to any of those replies because the Inspector would like to see them before they were handed to Mr Wodrow.

The enthusiastic clerk not only remembered Mr Wodrow, he was able to tell the Inspector that the gentleman had said he was staying at the Post Office Hotel, just down the road.

At once, Arnold took himself down to that hotel and, recalling the description given to him by the clerk, soon sighted Mr Wodrow, finding the tall fellow with a sallow complexion and hawk-like nose very interesting. He'd never seen Wodrow himself, but this man, though rather stooped, came close to the description of the felon that he'd read often enough. He wasn't *the* Wodrow, of course, but Arnold smelled contact here somewhere.

He decided not to approach Hector until he heard back from Fred.

As he rode back to Emerald Downs, Jack found himself remembering a conversation with Miss Pinnock, who had been quizzing him about 'the outback'. Worrying about the Major. Wanting to know what sort of country he might encounter.

'Woods, woods and more woods,' he'd said, and she told him that 'woods' was an English term.

'We say forest, or just plain bush, Jack. But there must be more than trees. Is it just flat and ugly beyond the hills?'

He was surprised she would think that. 'No, it's good country, very beautiful.'

And it was too, he mused, but hard to describe in English words the beauty that the blacks had shown him: wondrous waterfalls, hidden springs, gorgeous flowers, deep, cool gorges, strange animals, and even stranger things like lights in the sky, and hills that you puffed to run down and sped up with ease. He couldn't in a lifetime recount all the marvels he'd seen and heard about, in that huge outback.

He stopped at a creek to water his horse and saw that horsemen had been here before him this morning, maybe a dozen or so, and as he sniffed about he realised he was following the Native Police. Few horsemen in this neck of the woods rode barefoot. It was them all right.

It took him about an hour to catch up with them, all looking official in their black shirts and white moleskins, to find out what they were up to, but their leader wasn't interested in his company.

'What are you doing here?' Inspector Kirk snapped.

'On my way home.'

'Then get going. And you can tell the Major that everyone knows he's dragging the chain, finding excuses not to do his duty. If he's too scared to take on a few unarmed blacks, why doesn't he say so and let Lieutenant Clancy get on with the job?'

'You can tell him yourself, you're going right past his place.'

'A lot you know. My men don't need to follow these roads. We'll be far inland before he even gets his boots on.'

'Bully for you.' Jack looked at the men riding with Kirk. 'Call these blockheads soldiers? The blacks out there will fix them.'

He turned to yell at them in Kamilaroi dialect: 'You won't get away with the killing this time, you devils. The big spirits know you're coming and they're waiting for you. They'll nail your ears to trees.'

They reeled back in shock at this whitefeller's threats, and pulled their horses away from him.

'What's he saying?' Kirk shouted, seeing the fear in their faces, and while some began to explain, others halted, not keen to go on, and arguments broke out between them in their own language.

Feeling he'd created enough trouble for one day, Jack rode away leaving Kirk to sort out the confusion. He stuck to the road because it was easier travelling, but over an hour later he began to get the feeling all was not well, an anxiety that was always a warning of trouble. Sure enough, a little while later, down came some of Kirk's men, riding hell for leather at him from a hilltop, shouting like banshees.

He put his horse to the gallop, but they were gaining on him, and it occurred to him to get off the horse and lose himself in the bush, but then he remembered these blokes were blackfellers, not ordinary soldiers, and would be able to track him. Instead he turned the horse uphill, pushing through the bush and turning again as he heard shots slamming into the trees.

'Jesus,' he spat, 'that'll teach me.' The Major was always on at him to carry a rifle but he could see no good reason. Until now.

He had no choice but to let the horse go, hoping it would draw them away for a few minutes at least, while he moved up into more difficult terrain where they too would have to dismount. The firing started again, wildly, he thought, bullets not landing anywhere near him. From his ground vision under a thick bush, he saw one of the troopers striding uphill take deliberate aim and shoot in another direction, well away from Jack's hollow, and he stared in amazement. Others followed, and he realised they were firing at someone else. But who?

He squirmed around on his back but couldn't make out their quarry. Nevertheless, they were pointing madly, sure they had an easy target, crouching, moving forward, right past Jack!

He still couldn't see who it was; the prey had lured them away from him, and suddenly he felt the hairs stiffen at the back of his neck as a quiet voice spoke: 'Go. This is not your business!'

For the life of him he could have sworn that he'd heard that voice before, but he could not see a soul.

But who's to argue? he asked himself as he dashed free of his shelter and raced downhill to where his attackers had tethered their horses.

He heard a scream from up the hill and looked back. A mistake. They'd left one trooper with the horses. Jack saw with surprise that the trooper still carried the native weapon, a waddy, as it bashed him across the skull, almost knocking him out.

Despite the dizzying pain, he had to rally and take on this bloke before he got to his gun. He fought him for the waddy, snatched it free, wielded the heavy club expertly so that the trooper stayed down, then smashed his rifle, grabbed a horse, shooed the others away and took off. Cross-country this time.

Eventually, as he neared the home stretch, he saw his own horse trotting sedately down the track and whistled him to wait. Not wanting to be accused of stealing a trooper's horse, he let it go and climbed wearily on to his mount, his head swimming.

The Major had been finding excuses all day to stay near the entrance to his property, to watch not for Clancy and the contingent of troops but for the delivery of his prospecting equipment. He didn't want Adrian to clap eyes on it and start asking questions. No one was immune to the lure of gold. If Adrian had any inkling of what he and, hopefully, Drew had in mind, he'd be pressing to join them right or wrong.

When he saw the horse wandering slowly up the drive with Jack Drew slumped over its neck, he was down there in seconds, shocked by the bloody wound on the side of Drew's head.

'What the hell happened to you?' he shouted.

'Got a whack over the head with a waddy. Help me down before I bloody fall off.'

Jessie was upset that Jack had been bushwhacked by those wretched so-called police troopers. She washed and bound the wound and brought him a whisky for the pain, but the Major wasn't so kind.

'What brought this on? Why would they suddenly attack you?'

'I met them on the road and had a few words with Kirk. Plus a few more to put the fear of the ancient spirits into his mob. Shook 'em up, I can tell you. I reckon Kirk sent them after me for payback.'

'You mean you asked for it?'

'No,' Jack said firmly. 'I wanted to see what sort of a command you've got with Kirk. And I found out, Major. He's madder than his troops. Maybe it would have been fair game to send them to give me a bit of a bashing for giving cheek, or stirring, but they were shooting at me. They would have killed me. And what for? Words? We only had words. You tell me what this little god is about. Who is he?'

'Former chief warden of the Moreton Bay prison settlement, a real martinet . . .'

'What's that? A tyrant?'

'Well, he wasn't popular, leave it at that. He helped me out when I was trying to get started. Forget about him, I don't encourage him to come here and I certainly don't approve of him having command of black troopers, but he wouldn't have sent men gunning for you.'

'The hell he wouldn't! Don't kid yourself. He's out for glory, that one. He's already boasting of his bravery and your cowardice.'

147

'My what?'

'Thought that would wake you up. He's competing with you.'

'Oh Christ, forget that fool. Go and have a rest. Clancy will be here tomorrow.'

Before Clancy could get there, though, Inspector Kirk and his men came galloping up the drive in a fury, coming to an abrupt halt in front of the house.

'Where's that bastard Drew?' Kirk shouted at the Major. 'Get him out here now.'

'I beg you pardon, Inspector,' Kit said, walking out to confront him. 'Kindly remember your place. I outrank you, sir, and I require proper respect. You do not charge on to my land like a pack of hyenas. Explain yourself.'

'I'll explain all right. I've come here to arrest that bastard Drew.'

'You have? That's rich, after your men shot at him and then bashed him. He is suffering a severe blow to the head.'

'He'll suffer a lot more when I get my hands on him.'

'We'll see about that. Ambushing and shooting at a person for no reason is a serious offence and I intend to report this matter to Superintendent Grimes, and note it also to the Governor General. Did those men of yours have your permission to make such an unprovoked attack, which could have resulted in the murder of Mr Drew, or were they acting of their own volition?'

'Never mind that,' Kirk raged. 'I've come here to arrest Jack Drew and you won't be stopping me when you hear what he's done. The man's a mongrel! I'll take him in and see him swing, the bastard!'

Kirk, still mounted on his horse, was in such a state, his plump face was bright red and perspiration dripped from under his cap, dribbling unchecked down his cheeks to the stubble of a beard. He was waving his arms about in a rage, causing his horse to prance forward, confused.

The Major jumped aside and thundered: 'Enough! Pull yourself together, man! Dismount.' He stepped forward then and shouted at the Native Police to dismount also.

'I am Major Ferrington,' he roared at them, since they seemed unsure of their orders. 'The Queen's man! Dismount and stand to attention!'

They did so, lining up awkwardly by their horses, doing the best they could, he supposed, but he had the impression they were scared.

'What's the matter with them?' he demanded of Kirk, who was opening his saddlebag.

'If you'd let me finish, you'll know,' Kirk said angrily. 'Do you know what he did? The bastard! He cut off Corporal Jojo's ears! That's what he did. That's the sort of criminal you're harbouring, Major . . .'

'Oh come on now! Where did you get that story from? Was that your excuse to have them fire on him?'

148

'Don't believe me, eh? You haven't got any use for me any more, of course. Fair-weather friend you are. Then see if this wakes you up to what you got in your house now!'

He threw down a bloodied cloth, and Kit drew back. 'What's that?'

Kirk opened it up with his boot. 'Get a good look at this!'

'At what? Oh my God! Oh Christ! Is that what . . . ?'

'Yes. Jojo's ears! Your mate Drew's handiwork. I had to send Corporal Jojo back to Brisbane for treatment, with an escort, so I'm already down two men. I might as well go back now and take that mongrel Drew with me.'

'The hell you will!' Jack was standing on the veranda with one of Kit's shotguns pointed at Kirk. 'I never cut off anyone's ears, Kirk, and you know it. They know it too.' He jerked his head at Kirk's men.

'Put the gun down,' Kit said, 'while I sort this out.'

'Sort it out now,' Jack countered. 'Ask those blokes if I did that to Jojo.'

Kit walked over to address the men, but Kirk remained standing where he was, too afraid of Drew to budge.

The Major talked to them for a while and established that they had been chasing Drew and yes, firing upon him.

'Why?'

'He bold to the boss, so boss said give him hurry-up.'

'You could have killed him.'

They looked to one another and shrugged.

'Did he attack Jojo?'

'No, he attack me,' one of the men said. 'He bash me, boss.'

'What's your name?'

'Trooper Wally, boss.'

'Did you bash him too?'

'Yeah. Got him good with the waddy.'

'Then who cut off Jojo's ears? Now I need to know, please. I am very sorry this happened to your mate. But who did it? One of you? Bit of bad blood going on amongst yourselves, eh? Some payback maybe?'

'No!' they all cried out, with certainty. 'No, boss, not us fellers.'

'Then who? Was someone else up there?'

They cringed back, eyes downcast. No one said a word. Nor would they talk any more.

'Put the gun down,' Kit shouted to Jack again. 'They're witness to the fact, you're in the clear. So who did it, Kirk?'

'Him!' Kirk insisted. 'That mate of yours. No one else could have done it.'

'Except you!' Jack yelled.

Kirk exploded in a rage and made for the front steps, despite the shotgun, but the Major grabbed him and held him back. With that Kirk's horse, spooked by all the commotion, bolted forward, scattering everyone.

* * *

149

Jack was stunned. He unloaded the shotgun and thrust it at Adrian, who had just come up with Jessie to see what all the fuss was about. He raced through the house and out past the dairy. Just running. He was moving so fast he hardly noticed that he was so far from the house until he came to the woods that hedged the farm. And then he leaned against a tree, afraid he was choking, unable to get his breath.

When the panic attack eased, he allowed himself to think of those bloody ears. What the hell had happened? Who had done that?

He had to force himself to recall that nonsense he'd thrown at the black troopers, that stuff about nailing their ears to trees. It had only been bluff, like threatening them with a bogeyman, sheer bluff.

So what had happened? One of the soldiers had had his ears cut off! Nailed to a tree? He wouldn't dare ask.

Who had done it? And who had sent him from his hiding place?

'Then who did it?' Kirk asked, swallowing the whisky Adrian handed him. 'It had to be Drew.'

'It wasn't,' the Major said. 'With your blokes chasing him and firing at him, he wouldn't have had the time to carry out such an act. In his place, a man would more likely just knife an attacker and be done with it. I think they must have run into some tribal blacks out there who simply took advantage of the chase, grabbed your man Jojo and gave him the works! Off with his ears.'

'How do you account for the fact that Drew threatened my men, prior to this, out on the road? They told me he said the wild blacks would cut off their ears and nail them to trees.'

'I don't know,' Kit said wearily. 'It must be a common threat, and common punishment among northern blacks. Jack would have known that.'

'He's more black than white, that mongrel,' Kirk said bitterly. 'I reckon he's gone over. He's on their side. You watch him.'

'As you did. I still want to know why you sent your men after him with guns.'

Kirk was sullen. 'I didn't. He threatened them and they don't like that. It's not my fault if a couple of them tried to run him down.'

'It's your responsibility, sir,' Adrian snapped. 'That's appalling. What sort of command have you got?'

Kit held his hand up to stop Adrian intervening further. 'At this point, all I'm prepared to say is that your bully boys got more than they bargained for. If you're returning to Brisbane, Kirk, then you'd best get going.'

'I've changed my mind. We'll stay on course, heading north. You needn't worry, Major, we'll make it safe for you by the time you venture out.'

Chapter Nine

The letter she received from Adrian and Jessie infuriated their mother beyond words. It was bad enough that Jessie should go chasing off to Brisbane. What was Adrian thinking of to allow his sister to carry on like this? He should have stayed with her at a respectable place in Brisbane, if there were any such thing, until the SS *Argyle*'s return voyage, and brought her home. Chaperoned her home, since she had proved how untrustworthy she was. Family was far more important than Kit Ferrington's problems.

But now . . . oh my God! . . . they were both staying out there in the wilds, both of them. In his house! Were they mad? Had Jessie lost her senses altogether? It was scandalous for her to be staying in the same house as her fiancé before the wedding.

The wedding! Another blow! Blanche rang for tea. 'Good strong tea, please,' she asked the maid, to help her cope with all this.

Jessie had informed her that the wedding would take place at that roué's house. Roué, that was what Ferrington was. What else would you call a man who entertained a single girl in his home with no other female to chaperone? Even if they were engaged.

'If I had my say,' Blanche stormed, 'there would be no engagement. It would be off, as of this very day. How dare they all flout the rules of decency like this!'

Ah, but the wedding she had planned for years wouldn't be taking place after all. Her only daughter. The beautiful wedding, in Sydney, with everything perfect, and hundreds of guests, and a lavish, romantic reception in the grounds of Government House, overlooking the harbour! She could almost weep, thinking about it. This was all too sad, too sad. That stupid girl! Nobody would go all that way for the wedding. And where would the guests stay? Had she thought of that? And who would cater? Jessie could cook everyday meals but she wasn't up to anything fancy.

Blanche looked at the note ending the hurried letter, asking her to have the dressmaker finish Jessie's dress and send it on as soon as possible, so that Jessie herself could make any alterations that were needed.

'I see,' Blanche said ominously. 'Send on the dress. And what else? I'll teach you to run off on me, my girl, leaving a note like some love-struck servant girl.'

151

She tore the letter into little pieces and dropped them in a dustbin. 'The mails are so bad these days, my darlings, one never knows where half the letters get to.'

That afternoon as she walked along Macquarie Street towards the hospital, a man wearing a long white dustcoat and a blue velvet cap glanced at her, and recognising Mrs Pinnock, followed her up the steps and along the main corridor.

When she made for the male ward, he stopped a nurse. 'Mrs Pinnock there, her son's sick, is he?'

'No, it's her father-in-law, Marcus Pinnock, a dear old man.'

'Ah yes. He is that, Marcus. Always the gentleman.'

'Did you want to see him?'

He stroked his grey-flecked beard. 'Not just now. I won't interrupt the dear lady. I'll come back.'

Merlin was a patient man, the wait didn't bother him, and it gave him time to think what might be made of this fortuitous incident. Flo Fowler was still at home mooning over young Pinnock. Only this morning she'd had a letter from him promising undying love.

'Easy said,' he'd told her. 'Men will write anything to keep you quiet. His promises are not worth a puff of smoke. You mark my words.'

'Don't say such things, Merlin. How can you be so unkind? What do you want anyway?'

'I'm short of the necessary. Temporarily, of course. I was wondering if you could lend me a pound.'

'A pound! Me? You've got a cheek. Why don't you ask your new assistant?'

'Because she won't have any money until I pay her, and I, as you see, am flat-strapped for the minute. And you're the only rich person I know.'

'Rich? Get out with you. I haven't a bean myself, Merlin, and you know that.'

'Ah, but what about the diamond brooch, that flashy jewel you've got tucked away. You could get a pretty penny for that at the pawnshop.'

'I wouldn't dream of selling it. I'd rather starve.'

'You probably will. If you don't want to stoop to being seen entering the pawnshop, I'll take it for you. I'll be back in no time. Give it to me, Flo, and we'll have a little celebration. You'll be rich; you won't have to worry about your daily bread. Your sweet Adrian can retrieve it for you when he gets back. And if he doesn't come back, you're sitting pretty.'

Flo held Adrian's letter to her bosom. It was horrible of Merlin to come here, spoiling the joy of this morning. Adrian had written as soon as he could, a beautiful, beautiful letter, telling her he was taking charge of his friend's farm, as the owner would be away for a week or so, and he'd write more, later on, to his darling Flo. The page ended in myriad kisses.

'If you don't mind, Merlin, I have to ask you to leave. I have work to do.'
'What work?'
'It's private. I'm sorry, but I can't give you any money, really I can't.'

But here now, in this hospital, was the prospective mother-in-law. Mrs Moneybags Pinnock, doyenne of the social set. There must be some way of prising a few pounds out of her.

Hours later, the woman emerged and he leapt up to assist her down the stone steps.

'Here now, let me help you, Mrs Pinnock. These steps are slippery after the rain.'

'Thank you,' she said, trying to unhand herself. 'It's kind of you, sir, but I am quite all right.'

'Walking, are you? I should escort you.'

'No! No thank you. I will be taking a horsecab.'

'Ah yes. Very sensible. I'm a friend of Adrian's, you know. Didn't want you to think you have some lecher after you.'

'Oh, I see.' She remained stiff as a ramrod, her son's name no help at all. 'Now excuse me, please, I must . . .'

Merlin was still smarting from Flo's rebuff, and now this hoity-toity one was at it too. He'd only wanted to make her acquaintance. After all, she was a widow and might have welcomed the company of a worldly gentleman like himself.

Now he jumped in. 'Just a minute, Mrs Pinnock,' he said silkily. 'I wouldn't dream of holding you up. I should introduce myself, though you probably recognise me . . .'

'No, sir, I do not. Now if you will let me pass . . .'

'Merlin's the name, Mrs Pinnock. Merlin, entertainer and magician extraordinaire.'

'Mr Merlin, I do not want to have to call for a policeman!'

'Dear lady, surely not. I wanted a word with you on an errand of mercy, that was all. To do with Adrian.'

'What about Adrian?' she asked him fiercely, her umbrella menacing.

'Well, of course, he's away, as we all know. But he has left his fiancée short of funds . . .'

'What fiancée?' she cried.

'Flo,' he continued capriciously, enjoying her shock. 'Adrian insisted she give up work, but he forgot to leave her provided for, you understand. Just an oversight, I'm sure, so if you could spare her a tenner, to tide her over, so to speak . . .'

She shook the umbrella under his nose, far too close for comfort. 'Get away from me, you nasty little man, or I'll have you horsewhipped!'

Merlin fell back a few steps as she whirled and retreated into the safety of the hospital. In case she returned with bouncers, he fled.

* * *

Blanche fled too, although to other people she appeared to be walking calmly, leisurely down the long corridor again. Far from it, though. Her heart was pounding, her whole body shaking. How dare that unsavoury person address her in such a manner! She was upset, furious, and not a little frightened by the encounter. Then, as she found an armchair outside one of the wards and settled herself, gathering the folds of her skirt in front of her as if to avoid further contamination, Blanche took stock of the situation.

The fellow was obviously a cad and a cadger all rolled into one, out to 'put the bite on her', as Marcus would say. Poor Marcus, he was only just hanging on . . . He had good days, when he was clear in the head and able to communicate, and bad days, like today, when he could barely stay awake, and the colour drained from his face and the doctor shook his head.

Why now? Blanche worried, suddenly feeling desperately lonely. Why do you have to be ill now, Marcus, when I need you? I don't have anyone else to talk to. You can't leave us now, you must not.

Ever since her husband died, Marcus had been there for her, the family rock, but now she felt her family was crumbling about her ears. And who was this Flo? What was this all about? For God's sake, Flo who? She probably didn't exist. It was all fiction to get a tenner out of her.

Fat chance, she thought angrily, using the anger to compose herself. I'll teach him to accost me. What was his name? Merlin! A stage name, of course. Outrageous! A liar and a cad!

'You're back, Mrs Pinnock?' Matron was standing by her. 'Are you all right?'

'Yes, thank you. I'm quite well. But it's rather hot out there. I wonder, could you send someone to find a cab for me?'

'Certainly. I've been meaning to say to you how sorry I am that Marcus is not improving. I know you hoped to take him home by this, but each time we get him up, just to sit in his chair, it tires him so awfully . . .'

'I know, Matron, I understand. It's just that it gets distressing.'

To her horror, Blanche burst into tears, and though she tried to insist that she really ought to go home, the kindly matron took her into her office and had afternoon tea brought in.

'We're doing our best for him,' she told Blanche, 'but this illness is so unpredictable. Be assured he is getting the best of treatment, round the clock.'

'I know that,' Blanche whispered unsteadily. 'I'm sorry to be teary, but I just had a rather unnerving experience and I really don't know what to do about it.'

When she heard what had happened, Matron was shocked. Especially shocked that such a thing could have happened right outside her hospital.

'Out there? At our very front door?'

Blanche nodded, feeling a fool, wishing she had shut up; it wasn't as if she'd been attacked, and after all, she'd gotten rid of the fellow herself.

154

But Matron was appalled. 'What a dreadful thing to happen! Trying to cadge money out of you, as if you haven't enough to upset you these days. One could understand if this sort of thing happened in The Rocks, but here in Macquarie Street, in the better part of town, with Government House only a few doors away! Shocking. We ought to report him to the police.'

'Oh no. I don't want to do that! Please, Matron. He said something about a person being my son's fiancée. I have no idea what that is all about. Adrian isn't engaged. But the last thing I want to do is bring the police into it. If you get me a cab, I'll go along home now. I feel so much better, it was so kind of you, really.'

'Mrs Pinnock. You can't leave a thing like that in mid-air. It will only make you worried that he'll accost you again. I know about these things; better to sort them out, but all right, no police. I know just the gentleman, he's very discreet.

'No, really . . .'

'Mrs Pinnock. I understand you're on your own at present, Marcus ill and the young ones away. Now I do recommend Mr Watkins, a private detective, London policeman, retired. Let him look into it.'

Blanche was about to refuse but changed her mind. Why not? If this Mr Watkins was respectable, it would seem to be an eminently sensible way of finding answers to her questions.

'If you think so,' she said meekly.

The following day at precisely two o'clock, as arranged, the maid admitted Mr Fred Watkins to her parlour.

From the name, and what little she knew of his occupation, Blanche had expected a rather seedy character, one that might be found loitering in dark alleys or on street corners, spying on people, but this man was tall and upstanding, well-built and neatly dressed, with a polite yet decisive air.

After the introductions, they were seated across from each other and he asked her to relate the incident to him.

This done, he made no attempts to sympathise, but noted Merlin's name and occupation. And the name of the woman he'd claimed was Adrian's fiancée. Flo, simply Flo.

'That's all I know about her, I'm sorry.'

She showed him a photograph of Adrian, and explained his absence from Sydney, and his business up north, saying as little as possible about Jessie, rather than admit she was living in her fiancé's house. Under his roof, indeed.

'And you don't believe your son is engaged to this person, Mrs Pinnock?'

'Certainly not. I know the girls he escorts to various functions, and I've never heard of anyone called Flo. I mean to say, this is a small town socially, one couldn't help but hear of anyone Adrian partners to any function. In fact, there is one girl, Mercia Flynn, of whom he was always quite fond. We hope something will come of that, Mercia is a lovely girl.'

'I'm sure.' Watkins closed his notebook and took a folded page from his waistcoat pocket. 'Here are my charges, madam. I will take the case if you wish me to. I should be able to get to the bottom of this within a day or so.'

'You wouldn't let that Merlin fellow know that I'm . . . enquiring, would you? He might take that badly.'

'Don't worry, Mrs Pinnock.' He gave her a quiet smile. 'He won't know you've given him another thought. Do you wish me to proceed?'

She glanced at his charges and nodded. 'Yes. Please. By all means.'

'Then with your permission I'll take my leave. Shall we say two o'clock on Thursday? I'll bring my report.'

'Thank you,' Blanche said, taken aback by this efficiency.

Back in his office, Fred set up a file for the widow, Mrs Blanche Pinnock, with the background given to him by Matron Carmichael, who greatly admired the lady and her father-in-law. He added the other family names – son, Adrian, daughter, Jessica – started a separate page for the villain of the piece, a stage character called Merlin. Then the name Flo, with a question mark.

That done, he checked his mail, frowning over a letter from his late wife's brother asking for a loan of twenty pounds, enough to cover his fare to Sydney, where, he had decided, he would very much like to live.

'Not on your life,' Fred said grimly. 'Your freeloading days with my family ended the day we buried Martha. I only put up with your sponging for the love of her, but no more. You stay in London, chum, find someone else to pay your bills.'

Come to think of it, he told himself, I really am free of the bugger at last; that's a cheery thought.

Next he read the letter from Inspector Tomkins and that brought a wide grin. 'By Gawd. Jack Wodrow, now there's a name from the past.'

Fred had met the rogue several times in his travels through the shady hangouts of the London underworld. Young Wodrow was typical of slum kids fending for themselves, up to any sort of mischief to earn a crust, except that he was a loner. He never ran with any of the vicious gangs that plagued the streets, and yet somehow managed to be regarded as a sort of boss. Never a ringleader, he nevertheless commanded respect, if that be the right word, Fred mused, for an apprentice robber.

By the time he had hit his teens, Wodrow was a fully fledged footpad, and from there graduated to highway robbery until he was a wanted man. Jack Wodrow, highwayman, was so adept at the job, so successful that he soon had a price on his head for robbery-under-arms, and eventually murder.

'And then what?' Fred quizzed the portrait of Queen Victoria on the wall. 'What became of Wodrow? He certainly wasn't caught, and that's a fact. Did he retire on his ill-gotten gains? Not impossible. But someone would have picked up on him. Unless he changed his name.'

With no response from Her Majesty, he reread Tomkins' letter.

No, he reasoned. He hasn't changed his name, if Arthur up there has stumbled on a brother or a relation, looking for him. Looking for Jack Wodrow.

On the other hand, it can't be our Jack Wodrow. They'd hardly advertise a search for a family miscreant; that sort of skeleton was usually kept in the closet.

'A mystery,' he wrote to Arthur. 'Our Jack just slipped away into oblivion. Forgotten until now. Maybe he died. I will check on that with London colleagues. Intriguing, though, that this man Hector Wodrow does resemble Jack. So we will see. All very interesting.'

Jack Wodrow, alias Drew, was at that moment riding west with a squad of soldiers, as their scout, and though he wasn't too excited about this escapade, he couldn't help seeing the funny side of it.

'And blow me,' he muttered to himself, 'if I can't see the funny side now of the robbery that was my undoing. Never did before!'

He had seen his career as a highwayman as strictly business, a stepping-stone to a better life. For years he had been cautious, trusting no one, and then misfortune had come upon him, tumbled on him like rocks from a cliff.

He had built a sizeable fortune in coin, almost enough to change his name and disappear up there to Liverpool, where, sailors said, folk didn't go in for asking questions. Maybe enough to buy a tavern and live grand. But while he was out one day, for less than an hour, a thief had broken into his rooms and stolen his carefully hidden savings. How he found the money, tucked deep under the floorboards, Jack would never know. But all of his savings were gone! Black Jack had been robbed! Bloody hell! A robber robbed.

As a result of that loss, Jack had redoubled his activities, and one night on the Birmingham road a merchant had lunged at him. Jack had only meant to shove him aside but his musket had gone off and he could still see the fellow sinking to the ground, astonished.

After that he'd gone hotfoot to London, sold his horse and remained lying low in his own district. Then the next bit of bad luck had descended.

He was walking home through the mists of a dark alleyway when he saw a dandy come stumbling, drunk, out of Minella's house. Easy pickings! In a flash Jack was upon him, and was rifling his pockets when the dandy's friends came out of the bordello, saw what was up, and fell upon Jack.

They delivered him to the parish watchman under the name he'd given them, Jack Drew, and the high, mincing voices, so self-assured, had saved his life. A parish watchman was unlikely to question information given him by gentry, and Jack entered the criminal lists as a thief, a footpad. Not as a highwayman wanted for murder.

Now he laughed outright, and Lieutenant Clancy turned to him.

'What's tickling you?'

'Nothing much. I've been robbed twice of my life savings. The first time was funny when I come to think of it, the second time not, by God.'

Ahead of them somewhere was Montone Station, and he'd been given an opportunity to search the place for his gold. It could still be there in the ruins of that homestead. If so, he decided, he'd resurrect his original plan. A moneyed person, he'd go to Sydney; he'd always wanted to see that town again. But not to stay. Jack now knew he wasn't suited to town life any more, but he'd discovered another option. This beachcombing business. He needed to find out more about that.

They passed the turnoff to Grosvenor, and with the Major in the lead, cantered steadily along the track that led directly into Bussamarai's territory.

Fred was at her door at the specified time, unperturbed that he had broken a promise to the lady. For her own good, he'd told himself. Checking on Merlin had been simple, everyone knew who he was. And several people had informed him that a girl called Flo Fowler used to work for him, as his stage assistant.

He found Flo in her cottage and had a little chat with her, ostensibly about Merlin.

'It seems Mr Merlin has debts, miss. I am trying to discover if he can pay and won't, or can't pay. You see?'

'Oh. Is that why you're asking about him? Well, I'm not one to talk but I could say that he can't pay because he's short of money.'

'How do you know this for sure?'

'He tried to borrow money from me, and I don't have any to give him. For heaven's sake, I haven't even got a job!'

'I hear you're engaged to Mr Adrian Pinnock.'

'I suppose Merlin told you that,' she fussed. 'Well, he shouldn't have. It's a secret. We're getting married soon, and it's our business to make the announcement when it suits us.'

'You must be very happy. I hear the gentleman is a nice fellow.'

'Oh he is, Mr Watkins, he's kindness itself. Would you like some lemonade? I make it myself using lemons from my tree out there.'

'I would love some lemonade, it's a thirsty day.'

'Well, you just sit there by the table and I won't be a tick.'

The girl was lonely, rather a sad little thing, happy to have someone to talk to. He stayed quite a while and even gave her some helpful hints with regard to her garden.

Merlin was next. He thought Fred was a policeman and Fred took it from there, interrogating him about accosting Mrs Pinnock . . . threatening to charge him with various offences arising out of that incident, warning him that he would be back after he and his colleagues had thoroughly investigated him, to see if other charges might be outstanding under his real name of Bill Jukes.

'These are serious charges,' he said as he was leaving. 'And I'm just the man to make them stick. I wouldn't be surprised if you're a candidate for Norfolk Island.'

'Oh Jesus, no! Listen, I didn't do nothing, true. I was just trying to get some money for poor Flo . . .'

'And look where it landed you.'

Fred went on his way, knowing that Merlin would be on his way too, hotfooting it out of Sydney like a shot. There was always another stage, another town willing to welcome a magician, fresh from the courts of Europe, as his posters read.

Blanche dined with Lady Georgina Heselwood, trying to concentrate on her friend's recent adventures.

'We'll be going back to Brisbane shortly,' Georgina said, startling Blanche.

'I thought you said you'd never go back there.'

'Oh no. I'll never go out into the wilds again. What a fool I was to think it was such an idyllic life, communing with nature, so far from the boundaries of civilisation. No, we'll be returning to Brisbane to farewell country friends, before we leave for England.'

'Even so, visiting country friends . . . would that be safe?'

'Oh yes. They have sheep stations on the Darling Downs, not to the north where Heselwood insisted on taking up our land. It is quite safe on the Downs now, well settled. But, this is what I wanted to tell you . . . we can look up Adrian for you. Where exactly is Major Ferrington's property?'

'I'm not sure. I'll have to find out.' Blanche paled at the thought of Lord and Lady Heselwood dropping in at Emerald Downs and finding Jessie living there with her fiancé. She felt quite dizzy, but managed to hang on until after dessert, before rushing away to an appointment 'at the hospital'.

She did go to the hospital, up the front steps and out of a side door, then to catch a cab and hurry home for her appointment with Mr Watkins, which had been bothering her for days. Merlin had receded into nothing more harmful than a tramp asking for a few pence, and his stories sheer poppycock. Blanche wondered why on earth she'd involved other people, especially a private detective. What on earth would Georgina say if she knew about that foolishness? Laugh, probably. Tease her like mad. Tell Jasin, who would want to know every detail, he was like that . . .

She made it to her front gate at the same time as Mr Watkins, who stood back and ushered her down her own path. He seemed unaware that she felt awkward, tottering along on her fancy high heels beside this bulky stranger, her long silk skirt with its overlay of fine georgette billowing in the wind as if to envelop him.

159

In her confusion, trying to think of a way to dismiss him before they reached her lobby, she rang her own doorbell, not noticing that only the wire door was closed, not the main . . .

'May I,' he asked, opening the outer door for her as the maid came tripping from below stairs.

'Oh! It's you, Mrs Pinnock.'

Fred didn't believe in frightening people with the ominous 'I'm afraid I have bad news' sort of stuff. He considered it better to relate his findings calmly and let matters take their course.

In this case he was able to say with a fair amount of certainty that she need not worry about Merlin bothering her again, '. . . since I hear he is leaving Sydney.'

'Good.'

'Now to Miss Fowler. Miss Flo Fowler.'

'I thought that she didn't exist?'

'Oh yes she does. I spoke with her. She seems a nice girl.'

'Who is she? I've never heard of her!'

'I don't suppose you have. Different circles. I can say on her behalf that she knew nothing of Merlin's attempt to cadge money from you, and it is my opinion that he intended to keep whatever money he could badger from you.'

'I wouldn't have given him a penny!'

'Miss Fowler is, however, engaged to your son.'

'She's what! I don't believe it!'

'I saw a brooch he gave her.'

'Some piece of glass she got from a fair, I suppose.'

'I checked with the jeweller, T.G. Poustie. Mr Adrian purchased the diamond brooch there and paid ten pounds for it.'

Mrs Pinnock was shocked. 'Ten pounds! That's a fortune! Are you sure of your facts here? Really, Mr Watkins, this is all a bit much!'

He continued: 'I had the impression that Miss Fowler was speaking of the cottage, in which she resides, as hers. Her own. Unusual for a single woman who relies on a wage. It turns out this is true. I checked the County Titles. The title deed is in her name. The former owner was not inclined to state the exact sale price, but he did say the cottage was paid for by Adrian Pinnock, even though it's not registered in his name.'

'That can't be. This is madness! Are you quite sure, Mr Watkins?'

'Yes. I have the written report here for you.'

'Oh God!' She cringed back from the folded pages he was handing her, as if they might burn her; then, resigned, she took them and placed them on a low table.

'Miss Fowler's address is there should you wish to call on her.'

'I wouldn't dream of it.'

'Yes. I think that's wise.'

160

'You do? It must be the first wise thing I've done of late when it comes to my son and daughter. I can't believe Adrian has a fiancée hidden away, that he's supporting and . . .'

Fred held up his hand. 'There might be a problem here yet. Adrian has been generous with gifts, but he's not supporting the young lady.'

'That's something, I suppose. Small mercy.'

'Is it? Miss Fowler is unemployed. She has no income at all. And little savings. She left her place of employment at the request of Adrian, who disapproved of her job.'

'Dear God! What was she?'

'Legitimate,' he smiled. 'She was a stage assistant to Merlin. I believe you saw her in his magical show. Miss Fowler was very proud that you came along and seemed to enjoy the performance.'

'Mr Watkins! Are you teasing me? I don't find this very amusing.'

'Of course not. But perhaps you can place her now.'

'I prefer not to.'

Fred climbed to his feet. 'Then we should leave it at that. If there is anything more I can do to help, just let me know, Mrs Pinnock.'

He handed her his business card.

She glanced at it and then looked up at him. 'Were you thinking I might hear from her if Adrian does not support her?'

'It's possible.'

'Oh Lord. This is more complicated than I thought it would be. I don't know whether to confront my son or not now. Oh dammit, Mr Watkins. Would you like a cup of tea? I need to think about this some more and I'll only get angry on my own.'

'I wouldn't want to intrude.'

'You're not intruding. I could do with your advice.'

Chapter Ten

They'd covered a lot of country – Jack had forgotten the power of horse travel – and not sighted a single blackfeller, which had them all in high spirits, joking abut this bush jaunt and the interesting equipment the Major had loaded on to the packhorse.

Listening to them, Jack shook his head, marvelling that white men would forge out into blackfeller territory without knowing a speck about the bush that had now enveloped them. They mightn't be able to see any of their so-called enemies, but once again they were here, not many, just enough for him to know they were being watched. He too began to leave signs, Kamilaroi signatures, hoping for peaceful progress, and now, reluctantly, he carried a rifle. There could come a time when he might have to defend himself, thanks to these fools, so the sooner they got to Montone cattle station, the better. That was to be his turnabout point; no matter what the Major said, he'd be heading back.

They followed stock routes that by the end of the day took them around a wide lake, home to a flock of pelicans.

'What do the blacks call them?' Ferrington called to Jack. Showing off, Jack thought, but he obliged:

'*Gulamboli.*'

'Go on!' Clancy was intrigued. 'What do they call pigeons then?'

'*Gulawalil.*'

'If you spot any, let me know,' Ferrington said. 'I'm partial to pigeon pie.'

They made camp at the edge of the lake, and while they sat around the campfire after a meal of boiled beef, Jack went exploring. He was not familiar with this area, but found it very beautiful, with its glades of tall, sweet-smelling trees and an abundance of native animals fortunate to inhabit such a land of plenty. Further out, he knew, the plains could dry out fast after the wet season and set the people on the move for sustenance.

The next morning they were on the track early, trotting along, all in good humour after a breakfast of eggs and bacon and black tea, so the Major decided to send patrols of three men fanning out into the bush, but keeping the main track within reach.

'I'll have you back at noon,' the Lieutenant cautioned. 'We don't want none of you getting lost on us.'

After a few hours, Jack pointed to tracks heading out into the bush.

'We've been following Kirk's men up till now,' he told the Major, 'but they've quit the track here. I'll take a look and catch up with you later.'

Though true, it was a good excuse to break up from the squad; he didn't feel comfortable riding with soldiers, thinking he might land a spear in his back. Ever since they'd left the Ferrington farm, he'd been careful to ride among them, rather than allow himself to be a target.

He followed the tracks of these horsemen easily, noticing that they would have been riding fast to create such a disturbance in the bush, and that worried him. They wouldn't have been hunting a kangaroo, not all of them, tearing at such a pace, tracks now spread out; they could easily have shot one by this. They too would have known they were being watched. Had they managed to turn the tables on a watcher? This thought made him very nervous.

The tracks had him so worried he kept after them and soon met up with three soldiers circling the area on patrol. 'Seen anything, Jack?'

'Only these tracks; Native Police have been hunting through here.'

'That's all right. They're on our side.'

'I can't see any tracks,' their corporal said, and Jack explained to them that the riders had spread out but were still searching in formation, showing them the crushed grasses, trampled bushes and twigs.

'A man would have to carry a magnifying glass to spot them things, Jack. How come you found them?'

'Because I know what I'm looking for. Not hard when you get used to it. I think we ought to tail them for a while.'

By this Jack could smell trouble, and he wanted to turn back, not know about this, but he pushed on, until the smell was in the air.

'Smell anything?' he asked his companions.

'Like what?'

He shrugged. 'We go this way,' taking them deeper into a gloomy forest, the canopy almost shutting out the light. Here the undergrowth was thick and the tracks through high grass simple to follow, so he reined in his horse and sent the soldiers on ahead until even they complained of the stink.

'Somethin's dead here,' the corporal said, walking his horse through the bush, and still Jack hung back, wanting them to find whatever was dead there, hoping against hope . . .

'Jesus! It's a dead blackfeller. Gawd!' The corporal stumbled away, retching, and the others, coverng their faces from the smell and the flies, peered up and followed his retreat.

'How do you know it was Kirk's men? It might simply have been the result of a fight among themselves.'

'Blacks don't hang people. Anyway, I'd say he was dead before they hung him up, he was so badly cut about. Looks as if they all had a go.'

'Could have been payback,' Clancy said. 'One of *their* blokes had his ears cut off.'

'Anyway,' the Major said eventually, 'you did bury him. That's all we can do. We have to push on.'

'I'd stick to the track as far as it goes,' Jack said. 'Forget the patrols.'

'Don't tell me what to do,' Ferrington snapped. 'We're not going to find blackfellows sitting on the track waiting for us. We have to find their camps and ask them to move on.'

'There won't be any camps once they find that grave. They'll know who did it, they'll be after Kirk's mob. You ought to keep riding, let them think you're just passing through.'

'But we're not,' Clancy said. 'We've got a job to do.'

'Whatever you say.' Jack shrugged. They'd be one short from now on. He'd keep an eye on them so they didn't get lost, but he wouldn't be riding with them. Whatever they thought they were about, he was just passing through.

Inspector Kirk was pleased with their operation so far. It had taken them days to catch up with one of the blackfellows his men had said were stalking them, and he got his deserts very smartly. Wally had sliced off his ears to take back to Jojo, and that was fair enough, and he'd ordered the body to be strung up to warn off any more blacks that came this way.

Now, according to his best tracker, they had a small group of tribal blacks on the run, and this would make for good sport.

He called to Wally: 'My boss told me that small mobs of blacks, families, had moved into the lake area.'

'Yeah. Plenty good tucker.'

'Then where are they?'

'They been here, camps empty now. Then all go five, six days back. Leave warriors to watch.'

'Why?'

Wally laughed proudly. 'They know we comen!'

'What! How did they know?'

'People see us uniforms in town. They bloody scared of us fellers, boss.'

Oh Christ! These idiots had known all along that there'd be no element of surprise, Kirk reflected angrily. He wondered how far the natives had gone. They'd be pretty cocky after all those raids on the cattle stations.

'You're not on a picnic,' he raged at his men that night. 'You be ready with the horses at dawn, we're going fast see. I want to know where all those blacks got to. Savvy? I want to find them.'

Kirk knew his job was to make sure there were no blackfellows about who would harass settlers; he also knew a lot of the black families were harmless, that in many areas of New South Wales they lived peacefully on sheep or cattle stations. However, he was of the opinion that it was an easier solution to simply wipe them out rather than try to tame them.

In the morning he had his troopers spread out, riding singly through the bush, looking for tracks, and soon they were on their way again, the men chortling and shouting to each other as they recognised signs and knew they were going in the right direction.

Their enthusiasm excited Kirk. He enjoyed hunting, mainly after wild boar, but this put any of those jaunts in the shade. He was glad now that he'd left the Major behind . . . that weakling who didn't deserve the rank he held.

'Bloody snob,' he muttered.

Bussamarai was granted an audience with Ilkepala under sufferance, because they had their differences these days. He had tramped with four of his men up to a cave near Beerwah, a day earlier than scheduled so that he would not appear tired after this climb, show that age was creeping up on him, and so, on this bright morning, he was feeling as fresh as spring water.

He looked out over the tips of the forest, enjoying the view, but reminding himself that as a young man he could climb these peaks with ease.

Never mind, he told himself. I still have a job to do and none of his spells will turn my face from my duty.

One of his men pointed to a faint curl of smoke, with a grin.

'Our pursuers,' he said.

'Yes. The crocodile eyes. Let them come. Where are the soldiers?'

'Far behind them. It not known what they do yet.'

Just then, Ilkepala appeared on the path above them, and that irritated Bussamarai for a start. 'He would!' he muttered; the magic man, of indeterminate age, was showing he was able to take on the heights.

The proprieties of conversation concerning families and law adherence were observed, and then they came to the business at hand.

'I know you believe it your duty to keep fighting but you must know this is a battle you can't win.'

'Which battle?'

Ilkepala sighed. 'The war. The war is over. I have discussed this with many wise men, and they give the same advice. Go north and this time stay there.'

'This is our land,' Bussamarai said sadly, waving his hand to cover all before him. 'Who are they to say it is no longer?'

'No one says that. Simply it is no longer safe for your people.'

'I will keep it safe.'

Ilkepala shook his head wearily. 'You watch the black soldiers?'

'Yes. They are doomed.'

'They have guns, fast horses. Cunning as rats.'

'So?'

'What about the white soldiers who follow?'

'Let them come. They'll get the same.'

'Did you know your war adviser is with them?'

Bussamarai stared. 'Who would that be? What adviser?'

'Jack Drew.'

'That can't be. He died in the fire.'

'No. He got back to white peoples and lives there now.'

'What's he doing riding with soldiers? The traitor! We'll have a special welcome for him.'

'I am not sure what he is thinking. But I can tell you he sent warnings to you of these invaders.'

'The warnings came from him?'

'Yes.'

'I always knew he was a warrior at heart.'

The magic man coughed, picked up a handful of nuts from the bowl Bussamarai offered him, and returned to his original argument. 'I see you must take this opportunity to wreak punishment on the crocodile eyes, they are the real traitors, but after that, don't attack the soldiers. This is too much to expect of your men.'

'I have my duty,' the chief insisted. 'This is our sacred land. I will not be the one to abandon it and it shocks me that you of all people should even consider running away. This is our spiritual home, where our spirits live too; they must be saddened to the very core of their hearts that you talk like this.'

Ilkepala was silent. Did not his old friend understand that his heart was breaking? That his advice was based on the necessity to save the Tingum people and the others who had joined them . . . to save them from certain death at the hands of the invaders, or the other cruel marauder, starvation, for their ability to find food was being seriously curtailed, and their land overrun by thousands of sheep and cattle.

Eventually he nodded. 'Do as your duty speaks.'

'But will you help me?' Bussamarai asked urgently.

'It may be possible, but know I will not desert you.'

'Where's Jack?' the Lieutenant asked as they made camp. 'I haven't seen him all day.'

'Don't worry about him. He wanted to prowl about on his own.'

'Do you think he's gone after them black troopers? He don't like them.'

'I hope he has. I didn't want to order him and get involved in their arguments, but it will suit me if he has decided to spy on them. This is a good spot here by the creek, don't you think?'

'Yes.' Clancy watched as Ferrington took the canvas cover off the packhorse and started lifting down some of the equipment, and began to understand why the Major had called a halt mid-afternoon. They could have covered another twenty miles or more by dusk.

'Give me a hand here,' Ferrington called to him. 'Help me get some of this stuff down to the water's edge; that pebbled section will do.'

'Are you up for a bit of prospecting then?' Clancy asked.

'A man ought to try, where possible. The government is offering huge rewards for anyone discovering goldfields.'

'Not to mention what the man himself might find,' Clancy laughed. 'And are you thinking this would be a good spot?'

'Could be. I've been reading up on it. Anyway, I'll give it a try, and the men are entitled to a break.'

Hooey! Clancy thought. A break for the men? Don't kid me, but if it's gold we're after this fine day, it's a walloping good idea. Then he said: 'You've got two of these sieves here, for sifting among the sand and pebbles. Do you mind if I have a go?'

'No. You might as well.'

It didn't take long for the men to see what the officers were up to, and they came down to watch and cheer them on, some begging to be allowed to have a go. It was the most exciting afternoon any of them had put in for as long as they could remember, even though in the end not a speck of gold was found, and the Major was deemed a good bloke. Clancy promised a half-pint of whisky to the first man to find gold, but drank it all himself in the final hours of light as he desperately washed the last scoop of alluvium.

Coming upon them on his return journey from the whitefellers' big town, Moorabi watched, fascinated. It had been Moorabi who had rescued Jack from the renegades, and cut off one man's ears, then he had seen them heading out into the bush, and later as he'd kept to his own track he'd observed Jack travelling with soldiers. A strange sight.

But here now could be their aim. They were all leaping and hooting around two men washing sand and he realised what they were up to. Ilkepala had told him that a growing number of white men were venturing into the bush to search creek and river beds for the yellow rocks that Jack Drew had always been talking about. The stuff he'd kept in his belt. They now knew it was called gold and was greatly prized for trade.

Moorabi shook his head at all those soldiers having such a good time, with no one on guard. He could have scattered their horses, burned their tents . . . but why bother? He had interesting news for Ilkepala now. Jack Drew and the soldiers were on a gold hunt.

Jack wouldn't have been surprised to know that the Major had already succumbed to prospecting, since he'd been studying a book on the subject every night since they left Emerald Downs.

'It's a great reader he is,' Clancy had observed to Jack. 'I'm never one for the books meself, but me brother James, he always had his nose in a book and that's what led him into trouble.'

'A book did?'

'Too much knowledge, me mum said. He read all about the Troubles in Ireland with the English, and damned if he didn't go back there to fight for them, ended up in jail, the fool.'

Jack was intrigued. 'I had some Irish friends transported to New South Wales; they were called politicals. Would that be for the same fight?'

'Indeed it would,' Clancy had said. 'I've been trying to get my brother transported here but they're stopping sending prisoners out now. Just his luck. The crowd we saw on the *Randolph*, I'd say they'd be among the last.'

Sometimes Jack thought he was fortunate to have been transported, despite the hideous transport ship and the violence of Mudie's prison farm, from where he'd finally escaped. Seven years in Newgate prison would have been just as bad. Worse. At least now he was fitter than he'd ever been in his life and had learned more than a bloke could hope to find in books.

He rode into a clearing and looked up to see the Beerwah peak, reassured that he was on home ground now; he knew every inch of this territory. Soon he was riding confidently through open scrub, on the trail of Kirk and his troopers, who seemed to have thrown caution to the winds, lighting large campfires and making no attempt to cover their tracks, even though they were riding deep into enemy territory.

But the bush was still the same, all a-tingle in the afternoon heat, cicadas buzzing, leaves glinting red on green, a little *dirijiri* fussing fitfully near its nest, and on further a python draped among the thick coils of a tree creeper, thinking he couldn't be seen.

He cut through a narrow pass at the base of the peak, causing a flock of cockatoos to shriek their irritation at this intrusion, but Jack was more interested in noting that no horses had been through here. That meant he'd gained a day on Kirk, who would have to travel around the high ground.

He smiled, pleased with his effort, and climbed above the height of the trees, some still in blossom, watching a great eagle soar above him and envying him his view; and then he thought of Ferrington and his soldiers and was angry. Why do people have to come in here and spoil everything? He knew that cattle and wild horses still trampled about the bush, under those treetops, and it would only be a matter of time before the cattle stations were all underway again.

Wearily, he walked the horse over stony terrain and headed down towards the place the blacks called 'water bubbling up' that he knew none of them bothered with during the wet season. It was a strange and lonely retreat with tropical palms and exotic flowering bushes crowding a small spring that ran down into a deep rock pool, and Jack loved the place. He hobbled his horse and let it graze nearby, swam in the pool, caught two fish in the creek lower down, had himself a fine meal and slept happily in the soft grass under the palms.

*   *   *

168

In the morning Kirk came upon Grosvenor cattle station, or rather an abandoned shepherd's hut with 'Grosvenor' burned into a wooden slat by the door. It was damp and musty inside where rain had seeped through the thatched roof on to a still waterlogged straw mattress, and the fireplace was a cosy home for an army of spiders.

'This bloke left in a hurry,' Kirk said. 'Didn't even wait to grab his boots.'

'I'll have them!' Wally said, but his leader made him put them back on the floor and ask permission. That done, the boots were taken, along with tins of weevily flour, tea and dried beef, all regarded as good loot by his troopers.

From there they fanned out again, looking for the main house, since the shepherds' huts were always a very long way from the homestead. In fact, Kirk mused as he mounted up again, being a shepherd in this country was a mug's game. Few were mad enough to take on such a lonely and dangerous job these days, sitting out there counting sheep or cattle, talking to yourself, waiting for a stockman to drop in your weekly rations or a blackfellow to come along and knock your brains out. If you had any.

They found it a good twenty-five miles away, a burned-out ruin with only the chimney left standing, but there they decided to camp as Bussamarai's men had guessed they would, with the hills at their back and the luxury of a well nearby.

As Kirk took his empty waterbag and walked over to fill it, one of his men warned him to be careful.

The Inspector spun about, reminded of prowling blackfellows, but Wally strode over to him.

'Look out for bad water there. Might be poison.'

Kirk pushed the wooden cover aside and sniffed the air. 'Smells all right. Obviously they haven't dropped a dead animal in there to pollute it.'

'Other ways,' Wally said. 'Better wait.'

They filled the bucket with water from the well and placed it by a tree, hoping some animals would volunteer to be tasters, but none appeared and they couldn't think of another way to test it.

'One of you taste the water. You should be able to tell if anything's wrong,' Kirk ordered, but they only growled resentfully and turned away.

'All right. We have to have water. You, Toby, you get all the waterbags, ride back to the river and fill them all while the other lads get our tucker.'

'Not much rations left, boss,' Wally said as he handed over his canvas waterbag. 'Only dry bacon now.'

'What? I didn't realise we were so low. You'll have to hunt then. Find us some food, plenty bush food, eh?'

Wally studied his bare feet. 'Better tucker than bush food here, boss.'

'Like what?'

He pointed to a lone cow grazing in a nearby paddock.

'I don't know about that. I don't think we're supposed to . . .'

169

Too late. Wally aimed his rifle and shot the cow. It looked up quickly, as if amazed, unsure of what was happening, lurched sideways and then slumped to the ground.

'Oh well,' Kirk said. 'I suppose it's better than kangaroo. You get down and butcher it.'

But there was no time. It was their good fortune that Toby had reacted quickly to the shot, turning his nimble stockhorse about in a second, and sighting the tribal warriors coming down the hill.

He screamed, pointing over their heads, then twisted his horse around again and made for the cover of the bush bordering the river. In a flash, the others were running for their horses, to gallop after him, while Bussamarai, from his lookout on top of the hill, raged.

'Who started that? Too soon, the fool! I told them to wait until the rats had settled. You run, get the men back. You . . . sound a call. Quick!'

He was running himself, running after his own men to prevent them doing, in their excitement, exactly what he'd warned them never to do. What Jack Drew had taught him. Don't run at guns.

Bussamarai was slow, but the warrior he'd sent was fast; he dumped his spear and hurtled down that hill, leaping over strewn rocks and tree stumps where the white men had cleared scrub, shouting over the war-cries of the attackers, and then he took a deep breath and let out a piercing whistle. They slowed down as he reached them, shouting at them to stop, turn back, take cover, but he couldn't reach the leader, the man whose determination to do battle had reached such a pitch that it had boiled over into action, too soon.

They all watched as the last fleeing horseman twisted about in the saddle and fired his gun, before urging his horse into the safety of the trees, and they saw the warrior stiffen, look about in surprise and, like that cow, lurch forward and slump to the ground, his spear sliding on ahead of him, its life wasted too.

All night they waited, but no attack came, even though the hostile blacks were still out there, blatantly advertising their presence by the campfires that studded the hillside. Tantalising them with the aroma of beef cooking . . . their dinner. Their cow.

'There must be more than a hundred of them,' Kirk whispered, petrified. 'Why didn't they attack again?'

'I tol' you,' Wally said confidently. 'Them blokes run scared of us fellers.'

'I see. Is that why they attacked in the first place? In broad daylight? Don't talk bloody hogwash.'

'Yeah, well I reckon 'tis so, boss. I reckon them fellows make a raid on us but their chief he says, "No, you don' do that! Not on blackfeller troopers," and he allasame maken sit down, see?'

'Have they got a chief out there?'

170

'Too right. You hear that whistling? Sure enough that a boss man give orders. Too right.'

'Who is the chief?'

'They say the Tingum chief, he strong fellow, got plenty warriors . . .'

'But what's his name?'

'Dunno. No one tell.'

Kirk wondered if he was up against that chief right now, not that it mattered what black bastard was out there waiting to attack again; they had to get out of here.

His troopers had resolutely refused to try and sneak away in the dark, claiming there'd be native warriors lying in wait in the bush for them to make exactly that move. They preferred to wait until light and try to swim the river with their horses.

'But they know we'll try to escape that way, surely?'

'We got guns but. We shootemup anyone come close here, and escape under cover. White officers teach us that. Bullets for cover, he say. Good joke that, eh?'

Kirk wasn't so sure. He trembled at the mournful notes of a rainbird drifting through the mist and jumped at every tiny movement. On this night, when he desperately needed to listen for natives infiltrating the surrounding bush, it was alive with the rustle and squeaks of nocturnal animals. For the third time in all those hours he fired point blank at what he thought was a blackfellow coming at him through the darkness, but it was only an owl, swooping low. That caused his troopers to open fire as well, the noise deafening, and when all the clatter died down and the echoes fled, their vigil seemed even more terrifying.

A hundred of them, he worried, and only twelve of us! Please God, let us get out of here before they attack again. And why would they wait anyway? He didn't for one minute believe Wally's boasts, knowing that those natives out there would be wary of guns, not men. And especially not renegade blacks, whose reputation for cowardice and cruelty would have preceded them. And that thought renewed his terror. What if the tribesmen out there wanted to take the troopers alive? And him too?

'Oh Jesus!' he muttered, pulling his coat about him and clutching his rifle.

Well before dawn, just as they were creeping over to their horses to take to the river, the Aborigines out there started shouting at them, beating sticks and stamping, yelling insults as if they knew what was taking place.

'See, they jus' want us to go away!' Wally said to him. 'So we gotta go quick before they change up minds.'

He leapt on to his horse and Kirk followed as fast as he could, his legs stiff from being stuck in that ditch all night.

The horse took his lead, moving quietly to the riverbank, and Kirk leaned forward to shove branches aside, at the same time ditching his pack and bedroll, lightening the load for the swim of his life. Of all crazy things to recall now, he remembered sneering at the Major for being a desk Johnny, a shiny-pants who'd never seen active service, when in fact Kirk himself hadn't either. He'd always managed to grab office jobs until he made it to the administrative areas, and certainly, never before had he forded a river on horseback, though he'd made it several times on big, sturdy wagons driven by someone else.

They had reached the sandy shore and were wading into the dusky waters when Kirk's horse began pulling back, spooked by the rush of the river, and while he wrestled with it, there was a gasp from his men.

On the other side of the river Kirk could only just make out the line of dark figures, tribesmen with long spears, waiting for them. Standing there silently, menacing. The awesome scene threw Kirk's men into confusion. Some started shooting, others, full of bravado, plunged their horses into the river, determined to get across further down, still others leapt from their horses to swim the river and get by on their own, unhampered by the horses. But by this Kirk had made his own decision. He realised they'd been manoeuvred into a position where guns were useless. He had turned his horse and ridden away hell-for-leather along the riverbank, heading back south, even before the roar came from the hillside and the tribesmen swept down to join the fray.

Some of the men who had chosen to swim had thrown down their guns, and Bussamarai ordered them to be collected, with the bands of ammunition, as he watched the river battle. Already four of the renegades had been speared halfway across the river and their bodies left to wash away. Another was fighting to maintain his seat on a frantic horse while two men, swimming beside him, were intent on dragging him off. Two of them had made it to the other side, to the waiting spears. Two were captured and a couple were still loose. That accounted for the crocodile eyes, but where was their white boss? He must be with the swimmers.

They were harder to locate in the half-light but they would have been carried downstream, so he ordered a careful search of both shores and waited until canoes brought the rest of the warriors back from the other side with the two prisoners.

'What about the horses?' someone asked him.

'Keep the saddles and mouth straps and let them go,' he said absently, gazing at the prisoners, two bedraggled black men.

'Why do you fight your own people?'

One of the men rattled off a reply in a language unknown to Bussamarai, and the other man hastened to explain. 'They make us, the white pigs,' he whined. 'They say they kill us if we don't fight.'

'And you are good fighters?'

'Yes . . . no. Not hurt blackfellers.'

Bussamarai ignored that, and turned to his men. 'We'll see how they can fight. Give them each a waddy. They can fight each other.'

Despite their protests, they were taken to a clearing and, as an audience of tribesmen gathered, ordered to fight.

'Loser goes back in the river,' Bussamarai said, and that set the pace. They fought viciously with the heavy waddies, until they were both so weak and bloodied they could no longer wield the weapons. In no time they were reduced to punching and biting as they wrestled on the ground.

'Fighters!' the Chief said, disgusted. 'They're no good at all. I thought we might see a good match.'

He kicked the nearest wrestler in the buttocks and ordered them to stop. 'Now what to do with them?'

There were plenty of suggestions as to how to deal with these traitors, most of the ideas put forward as brutal as the reputations of the black troopers, but eventually Bussamarai decided that since they carried guns, that should be the means of their own executions. To the great disappointment of his warriors, and even some resentment, Bussamarai sent for a gun and some bullets and gave one of his friends the order to kill them.

It was all over in a few minutes, the bodies dumped in the river, and the focus was once again on the search for the other survivors, especially the white boss.

Kirk threw off his police cap and uniform jacket with its silver buttons as his horse threaded through dense bush. If they caught him, those blood-thirsty heathens, he might get away with pretending to be just a stockman looking to collect roaming cattle or horses. He'd already seen a dozen or more huge bullocks grazing here and there among the trees, freed from the stockman's whip. One had frightened him, barring his way, the great horns lowered menacingly, but no bad-tempered beast was about to slow his race to safety. He jerked the horse's head aside, making it swerve, almost skidding on the damp undergrowth, detouring round the bullocks but barely slowing his pace.

Trouble was, though, this bush was now slowing him down. It was more like a jungle along these uneven banks, so he made the decision to quit following the river and make for more open country, where he could find a stock route and follow it back. After riding as fast as the terrain would allow for most of the morning, he was certain he'd out-distanced the blacks but was still too terrified to allow that he had escaped their clutches. The horse was tiring, but that couldn't be helped; he was feeling terrible himself, hungry, his stomach writhing for the want of nutriment, punishing him foully with stabbing pains and nausea.

The lush forests within reach of the river thinned out as he rode away, and he kept on and on, even when rain started to fall. He was in scrub country now, the tall trees well spaced, giving him room to urge more speed from the horse until suddenly lightning flashed and thunder cracked and his mount skidded to a halt, shivering in fright, almost unseating him.

Then the real rain came, a few dollops at first and then a deluge, a teeming, soaking deluge that almost shut out the light.

The Inspector grabbed the bridle to lead the horse as he tramped on, cursing the rain, the blackfellows who'd be out there searching for him, the stupidity of his so-called bush-savvy troopers, the idiots who had gotten him into this mess, cursing everyone and everything, plunging ahead, wishing he'd hung on to his jacket for some protection from the pelting rain and the tree branches that were now scratching and tearing at him as he lurched from one flimsy shelter to another.

By the time the rain stopped and the sun suddenly glared through the shimmering treetops, Rollo Kirk was exhausted; he could plod on no longer. He sank down beside a fallen log that was crumbling with decay, promising himself just a few minutes of rest, but his eyes were heavy as he leaned back, hands resting on his paunch, and the mouldy log became as comfortable as a soft feather pillow.

The horse waited, sniffing at the grass nearby, and as he moved quietly to explore a little further, the bridle slipped from the snoring man's hands. The animal wandered away, at times irritated by the trailing bridle, until eventually it stuck fast, caught in a sprawling tree root, and there he stood, not knowing what to do next. Until a pack of four dingoes came padding towards him, circling him, gradually becoming aware this animal was somehow in trouble. They began making runs at him, snapping, dodging the steel hooves that lashed at them, getting closer. Eventually the leader of the pack leapt up and bit that shivering rump, drawing blood, and that did it! The horse screamed, reared, snapped the bridle and galloped free, switching in and around trees with the ease of a dancer, leaving the disappointed dingoes – and his rider – far behind.

Rollo woke with a bump. He'd turned over and slid face-first into soggy grass, spluttering and spitting, reaching for the side of his four-poster bed, and then he remembered he didn't have that bed any more, it was back there in the rooms he'd occupied as chief warden. He was staying in a hotel now, he thought groggily, with his wife, but what the hell . . .! He staggered up, thoroughly disoriented, and stumbled forward, leaning against a tree for support as the shock of his situation began to filter into his brain.

'Oh Jesus,' he muttered. 'I've got to get out of here. Where's my bloody horse?'

Trooper Wally had sized up the situation and slid from his horse as soon as it entered the water. He dived straight out into deeper water and dived again, swimming underwater as far as his lungs would carry him, streaking along helped by the current, praying he wouldn't hit any snags as he duck-dived again and again. Then he was swimming. He could hear the screams from back there, and wondered fleetingly which of his comrades had been caught, but he had himself to look after; no one else mattered. He'd been in worse spots than this. Ripped away from his family, bashed and abused by missionaries, starved and flogged by a farmer and his wife who decided in the end that he wasn't worth feeding, so they got another black boy to work for them and strung him up on a tree. He still had the burn marks of the rope on his neck. And that bloody new boy, he just stood there watching. Didn't do nothing to try to help him. Just stood there. But a shearer, travelling through, came by in time, started yelling at them, cut him down. They were still arguing about it when he ran off.

A lot of times later he got jobs working in stables, ended up working in the police stables at Bathurst until they put him in the police force, got the surprise of his life at that idea. He didn't know they made blackfellers policemen. Or any bloody thing. But they did, and they gave him a uniform and all. Bloody good that. Bloody good. He could get his own back then.

He'd lost his gun now, though, bad luck, but he still had the knife strapped to his leg, another trick the officer had taught him, and it was a good strong knife too. Wally was confident as he waded ashore to start the trek back to Brisbane; no point in hanging about here any longer. It would be a long walk; he figured he had more than a hundred miles to go. Something like that. He wasn't too good at counting, but he remembered Kirk had been trying to count the miles all the time, and laughed. His boss never knew how long a mile was anyway.

'By Jeez,' he muttered, 'the warriors, they catch him, he get plenty hurry-up.'

As he set off, Wally amused himself by contemplating what the tribesmen might do to Inspector Kirk.

The next one they caught was Toby, who wasn't much of a swimmer, and finding that he spoke a Tingum dialect, the chief sent his man Nungulla to interrogate him. He wanted to know first-hand how many troopers were up this way and why white soldiers were following them.

'All going same way,' Toby said anxiously. 'All just for looking at the country.'

Nungulla belted him across the head. 'No lies.'

'All for getting your people out of here so they can bring back the cattle, start the farms again. Bring more whitefellers.'

'How will they be getting the people out?'

'Guns,' Toby shrugged. 'Why else would they go? And they look for your big boss too.'

'Who? Bussamarai?' Nungulla asked, surprised, then he began to fire more questions at this renegade, talking quickly, hoping he hadn't picked up on the slip he had made, mentioning that name. 'What big boss? No big boss, only elders, you mad pig! Even you know that! Our elders have big magic, turn you into a worm and feed you to the birds, they could. I only have to call them and they come down, put a spell on you so you waddle like a crocodile every day of your life. Me, I'm a big chief too and don't you forget it, see?'

Toby cringed on his haunches in front of this huge man, trying to think what he could offer for his life. 'Don't kill me,' he begged. 'I can help you. I see you have some of our guns. I can teach you how to use them.'

Nungulla spat at him. 'You think we are fools. We can use guns. White man teach us.'

'What white man?'

The punch was such a hefty blow, Toby was thrown backwards, his face numb, blood streaming from his nose.

'Do not presume to ask questions.'

'No. No,' he apologised. 'I did not mean to. Please don't kill me. I can help. Those guns, not many, not much ammunition either. Not for all your mob. I can get more for you.'

'Where from?'

'The soldiers coming. They have plenty guns and plenty ammunition. They fear you. Will not travel a step without plenty guns.'

'How will you get them?'

Toby threw his arms wide. 'They trust me. They will welcome me back to tell what happened to this mob of troopers.'

'So what about the guns? How will you get them?'

'Every night a man stands guard over the guns and ammunition in the camp,' he lied. 'So prized they are. In my turn to guard I could hand them all over to you if you are quiet enough.'

'How?'

Toby warmed to his tale. 'One by one. Box by box. Slide into the bush.'

'Sounds too easy.'

'Yes. Easy. Bye-'n-bye all gone while they sleep.'

Bussamarai agreed it did sound too easy. 'But we could let him try. We can pick the renegade off any time we like. Let him know that, and set him free. He can take a message to the soldiers that my warriors will wipe them out too, if they don't turn back.'

'I have to have a horse,' Toby insisted after he was given his instructions and the very real threats, which only made him even more determined to steer clear of the soldiers and Major Ferrington, and ride straight on to Brisbane. Bugger them all. He wondered if the Major knew that they were being watched all the way. Then he shuddered . . . watched by the very men who'd be waiting for him to hand over the guns. From a nonexistent stash.

That night they trussed him up like meat on a spit and tossed him near Nungulla's campfire, where he lay sweating with fear, listening to them talk. That one, Nungulla, he seemed to be pretty high up in importance. Several elders sat with him and his painted-up warrior mates, and they were all in good humour after this day's work. Toby heard them talking about him; some said they should throw him in the river just as he was, but Nungulla was hung up on the chance of getting more guns, and he kept arguing that the 'pig's' plan should be given a try.

176

'He could do it; those men have the run of the white men's camps.'

As the stars began to fade, Toby's hopes crept out of the fear, and he could see by the way Nungulla strode over to him that this was not his time to die.

Several of the warriors watched sourly as he was given a horse, and Nungulla lectured him on exactly what he had to do, warning him again that he would be killed if he attempted to disobey, and Toby nearly nodded his head off in his efforts to please.

'Yes,' he said over and over; he understood that the messages could get back to Nungulla very swiftly, and he knew they'd have scouts keeping an eye on him, and he would hand over the guns as soon as he was contacted by a man called Jungar, and they had no need to worry, this would all be done, until at long last he was sent on his way. So certain were they that they could keep him in their sights even as far away as Brisbane, they didn't even bother to keep him under guard on these travels. That would be something to tell the Major and his soldiers – that the big chief had so many warriors in this district that they knew their every move – if he met up with them, a meeting that was not included in Toby's plans. He had a horse and safe passage and he never intended to let himself get caught in their clutches ever again. The police could keep their uniforms. His was in tatters now, but he wouldn't need another.

Toby grinned slyly, and massaged his curly beard. He'd keep the horse and head for the hills down past Brisbane, live his own life.

There was no need to hurry. No one said nothing about hurrying, he told himself gleefully as he squatted on a sandy riverbank and cooked yabbies and mud crabs for his breakfast the next morning. The meat from the shellfish was so sweet, he ate the first catch hungrily and went off to find more, but storm clouds were brewing, another downpour like yesterday, he guessed, so he took the horse and searched about for some shelter.

He'd only just found a cave hidden behind a crush of bushes when the rain thundered down and he hurried in gratefully, pulling the unwilling horse behind him before replacing the disarranged foliage. The walls carried paintings, Dreaming stuff, Toby realised, and he was studying the characters when a voice from within the cave called out in amazement.

'Toby! By Gawd! Hey, is that you?'

It was Wally. Trooper Wally! The two friends fell upon each other in relief, hardly able to believe that both had survived the ambush.

'What about Kirk?' Wally asked. 'He get away too?'

'I dunno. Never seen him. Don't think so.'

'He ain't no loss,' Wally shrugged. 'You see any of the other blokes?'

'I think they all drowned or got killed by them wild blackfellers.'

'But you got away with a horse! How did you do that? Pretty bloody smart I'll say, mate.'

When Toby explained his mission, his mate roared laughing. 'They think you gonna give them guns? Who gonna give you the guns?'

'Not the Major,' Toby grinned. 'And wouldn't he like to know his squad is being tailed all the way?'

'He sure would. Give you nice bloody present for the information.'

'That's nothing,' Toby boasted. 'He'd give a double extra present for what else I know.'

'Like what?'

'Well, you know how they keep trying to find out who the big boss of the wild blacks is, the one making all the war rules, and no one knows and not even the town blacks will let on? Well, I know, mate. I got his name allasame!'

'Go on! What's his name then?'

'Bussamarai, that's it.'

'Jesus. I heard talk of him years gone. Thought he'd be long dead. He was a big war chief even then. By golly, the Major like as not give you a good present this time.'

The thunder rolled, the rain teemed down, but they were snug in their cave, talking about their lucky escapes and the fate of the others, and all the while Wally was looking at the horse. He was on the run, not Toby. If the wild blacks caught him they'd kill him in a flash, but they wouldn't kill Toby. Not even if he lost the horse. They'd soon round him up another one; there were plenty of brumbies – wild horses – roaming loose in the bush these days. Toby ought to give him the horse. It was going to be hard enough to get back through this dangerous country without having to hoof it. Wally worried the matter of the horse all the time they talked, and he listened angrily as Toby told him of the best feed he'd just had of crab and yabbies, knowing he didn't have the luxury of exposing himself like that, of being able to sit calmly by a campfire cracking crab shells and stuffing himself with the meat. Wally was starving.

Suddenly he lunged forward and shoved his knife into Toby's stomach, then pulled it out and lunged again, the knife sinking into his chest.

'It's the horse,' he said as Toby's body rolled down the dusty floor of the cave. 'I have to have the horse. I knew you wouldn't give it to me.'

Moorabi loved horses. They were the most magnificent animals he'd ever come across, so powerful and yet so gentle, strength and beauty combined with such intelligence that he was sure they were true gods from another world. There were so many running wild now that they had come together in small mobs, family mobs, the strongest male in the lead, as it should be. Many a time he'd proposed that his own people should adopt the *yarraman*, explaining how much easier their lives would be if they allowed *yarraman* to help them as did the white men . . . and ladies, but they'd laughed at him. Hadn't they lived content for mountains of years without those prancing beasts? Why would they want to use them now?

The more serious thinkers pointed out that though they'd examined every avenue of information available, they could not find a *yarraman* totem, nor could any of the elders and magic men find a place for them in the Dreaming, therefore they had to be otherworld beings. And another 'therefore' – they did not belong. Could even be taboo.

Moorabi disagreed with their arguments. He said it was only superstition that *yarraman* were not welcome in the tribes like dogs were, and that harked back to the old days when blackfellers first saw men on horseback and fled from them, believing they were seeing men with four legs.

'That was ignorance,' he said. 'We know better now. If we befriend the *yarraman*, they will make us as strong as white men.'

All the talking in the world made no difference to their attitudes. Even Ilkepala, the wisest of all, saw no use for them. 'They run off. They're not as patient and loyal as dogs, for all their cleverness.'

Even Moorabi had no answer to that, nor did he dare mention that fences could be built to keep them surrounded, because fences were much hated. Nevertheless, despite their attitudes, Moorabi never missed a chance to ride, instead of trekking long distances like everyone else.

'You'll see,' he'd say quietly. 'One day all of our people will be riding the horses. It makes for sense.'

He had become adept at catching horses. He taught himself to rope them in like the whitefellers did, at first surprised that some fought him, not wanting to be ridden, but gradually, with plenty of sweet talk and sweet fruit, they didn't mind. Moorabi was never one to boast, to tell anyone that he had lots of horses, eventually, and he never built a fence. His operation was simple. He would go about his business, mostly long treks on behalf of Ilkepala, always carrying a rawhide rope, and always on the lookout for stray horses. He preferred the animals that had recently strayed from their owners, rather than having to cut one from a mob with a big man-horse watching angrily. They were so pathetic when they'd strayed and were lost, these *yarraman*; the big eyes would look so sad and confused, and they'd come to him for comfort.

Moorabi always rode bareback, using his rope as a halter, and when he no longer needed the horse he would simply let it go, and pick up another one next time if he could find one. Otherwise walk, as the spirits intended. Often, though, he would come across a friend, a horse that remembered him, and that was always a joyful encounter.

On this day, still travelling north, he was hoping to sight a horse, since he'd recently endured trudging on through heavy rain, and could do with a ride, but it seemed they'd all gone to ground somewhere, until he saw this one threading through the scrub, still fully rigged!

Well, this was luxury, a saddle and bridle provided for him! He whistled to the horse, but it only lifted its head to gaze at him for a few minutes, and went back to grazing.

Moorabi circled around it, looking for the rider, obviously a white man, so he dared not raise his head and maybe meet a bullet.

He waited a long time, but no one came for the horse, so he crept towards it, grabbed the broken bridle and leapt into the saddle, urging it to move away quietly, without any fuss. Once away from there, he found a bush track and sat back, pleased with himself as the horse broke into a canter, unconcerned that its new rider was a naked blackfellow with a grizzled face, barely discernible behind a full beard and steely black hair.

As the days passed, Nungulla was informed that his pig trooper was riding down the valley as instructed. So far so good.

Jack had been trying to catch up with Kirk's men, but the heavy rain had wiped out their tracks and he wasn't clever enough at the game to fall back on the myriad other signs that would have shown their route. It was at times like this, when he was unsure which direction to take, that the sheer size of this land threatened to overwhelm him. Years back, when he'd first joined a mob of blacks and gone on the trail with them, he'd actually had a fit of the horrors . . . a bloody nasty experience, he recalled . . . unable to grasp the dimensions of the huge plain they were crossing. He could see the horizon in all directions, trees he could see, and a massive flawless blue sky, but nothing else, not a house, a post, not a stick upon a stick . . . nothing out there, nothing at all.

He'd sat down heavily, feeling a bloody fool, unable to get up, so bad was his anxiety. The black women, bewildered, had fussed over him, brought him water, felt his forehead for fever, but could find no cause for what ailed him, and Jack was ever unable to explain the fit that had caused his legs to turn to jelly.

They couldn't leave him behind in that state, so the women called on one of the young bucks to carry him, and there he was, being piggy-backed for miles, until the fit wore off. To this day it seemed stupid that a grown man should have to be piggy-backed for no obvious reason, but every so often, after that, when they'd move out into new big country, he'd had whimpers of the same thing, though never that bad again.

Right now, he was in two minds: he knew he should go back and see how the Major and his party were getting along, but having come this far, it would be more interesting to see what new trouble Kirk's bad lads had managed to find.

He came upon a derelict shepherds' hut and stayed clear of it; the stink of those filthy old huts had always bothered him, and he would have passed on by, but suddenly he thought he saw a flicker of movement behind the broken glass of the single window, maybe only the shadow of restless leaves from the wattle tree drooping by the water tank. Whatever it was, Jack did not react. He'd long learned that danger lurked in every corner in these volatile times.

He rode on by, keeping his distance, doubled back to observe the rear of the hut, and dismounted to approach the dilapidated door on foot.

A voice shouted at him: 'Get back! I've got a gun!'

Jack stood still and sighed. 'So have I, you clown. What are you doing in there, Kirk? And where's your horse?'

'Oh Lord, it's you, Jack!' The Inspector wept as he staggered out of the hut. 'Thank God you found me. They're all dead, my men. Those savages killed them all. I thought you were one of them, with your dark skin and all.'

He clutched at Jack. 'We have to get out of here, there are thousands of them. You got any food? I'm starving, I'm dying of thirst and I'm sick too, Jack. See how sick I am, I'm burning up . . .'

'Yes, you're sunburned,' Jack said, pushing him away. 'Settle down and I'll get you some water.'

'No, don't leave me!'

'I'm only going to the horse. Now squat down there.'

'We better get inside. They might see us and kill us.'

'Stay here. I'm not going into that fleabag of a place.'

He fed Kirk some berries and nuts he was carrying with him and listened to the story of the ambush, all very familiar to him. No point now in asking why Kirk didn't have men on guard.

'You rode clear. Where's your horse?' He looked about, thinking it was probably wandering around here somewhere.

'I was exhausted. I fell asleep, that was yesterday, and it got away on me. I've been walking ever since. You have to get me out of here. Where is the Major, are his troops nearby?'

His horse got away? Jack shook his head, disgusted. Ferrington wasn't nearby, and he was not about to share a horse with this rat, who might turn on him first chance.

'You'll have to stay here,' he said, ignoring Kirk's angry protests. 'Keep down, keep out of sight. I spotted you at the window. The blacks won't come in here, they know the place is full of fleas.'

'So do I. It's frightful. You can't force me to stay in here.'

'No, I can't. You can start walking again if you like, and it'll be a hundred to one you'd be lucky enough to have Ferrington find you. There ain't no highways out here.'

'How long will you be?'

Jack didn't know; it depended on how fast the Major and his soldiers had been travelling. 'Not long,' he said.

'Can't you leave me some food?'

'I haven't got any, but you got enough fat on you to survive a while.'

Kirk was livid. If he'd really had a gun, Jack was sure he'd be grabbing for it now instead of rushing at the horse in a vain attempt to jump aboard and ride away.

Jack hauled him back and shoved him at the hut. 'Now get in there and shut up. You got yourself into this mess, not me.'

'And you're not going to ride away and leave me to the savages,' Kirk screamed. 'You're a savage yourself! I know you're not coming back, you filthy black! You're one of them, think I don't know it, you scum, fit only for the knacker's . . .'

Jack shook his head again as he rode away. Keep that up, mate, and the lads with the spears will turn up on your doorstep.

So now to find Ferrington. This was causing a delay in his own plans. According to the Major's map, Grosvenor cattle station was next door to Montone, next door meaning something around fifty miles from homestead to homestead in bush talk. In other words, he thought angrily, he was only about fifty miles from his gold . . . if it was still there. Jesus! Wouldn't that be something! To just pick it up and walk away, back to that town, exchange it for cash, and a man was free to go and do what he liked. Cripes! To be rich and free! Was it possible for Jack Wodrow to get that lucky?

He blinked, surprised that his real name had entered his thoughts, but pushed that aside for more serious considerations. Ferrington was heading this way, a leader who seemed to Jack to be only slightly better at the job than Kirk, with less experienced men than Kirk had, and all that didn't add up too good at all, especially if Bussamarai had only half the men Kirk claimed he had. Though it wouldn't take too many men to pull off an ambush like that . . . Suddenly he worried that he was going in the wrong direction. Should he go north instead? See Bussamarai, prevail on him to allow the soldiers to come through in peace. Maybe even send a delegation to sit down for peace talks. Why not? This war couldn't go on for ever. It was sad to say, but with that town growing down there at the port, white folk would come pouring through here soon like an army of ants.

Would Bussamarai listen, though? Jack wasn't sure at all. He could likely get a spear in his chest for talking such treason. Henry the Eighth, whose deeds had fascinated young Jack, had nothing on Bussamarai, he mused, when it came to his commands and his rule. You didn't need to be standing close if you even thought of disagreeing.

But Kirk was muddying the waters. He was in danger there, and had to be brought out as soon as possible, so the only choice was to find Ferrington and take him to Inspector Kirk, then try to get about his own business.

Business, he thought, that's a funny word. Biznez. That's London, busy streets, crowds pushing, women hissing and skipping to keep their skirts off street dung, merchants haggling, noise, yells, shouts, trundle of wagons, all that and more, that's where business is carried on, not here, not at the end of the world. One day he'd ask the Major if he could see a world map, for he knew only the map of England, could draw it for Mrs Clout to show off to the do-gooders. But this land he didn't know. Didn't know where it was placed on the map, only that it was a long way away, because it took three months of floating hell to get here. And sometimes he wondered about how to get back, if he chose to do that, like.

These ramblings eventually told him that the day was passing beneath his feet. He had no hint of the whereabouts of the grand Major and his mob, and he should have picked up some sign of them by this.

None the wiser at dusk, he rested the horse awhile and set off again in the direction of Beerwah, seeking hills that would give him a chance to spot campfires.

They were there all right, studded on the slopes of the dark hills to the north, blackfellers' camps, plenty of them, but down this way, no sign of Ferrington. He hitched the horse to a tree branch and climbed further up and around the hill, but all he could see at this stage was the silver ribbon of a big river winding through the blackness that was forest.

He was sitting, irritated, perched on a slab of rock, stroking the stubble on his chin, wondering what to do next, when he saw a faint curl of smoke over to the west, and automatically looked back to Beerwah. That was camp smoke! That couldn't be the soldiers, he reasoned, they were too far off. But if it was them, they were headed west, where they'd only run into the big hills, the mountains that the blacks said were the spine of this side of the country. After that, he'd been told, there were great plains and then red desert, but he had never accepted offers to show him those lands. Too bloody far for these feet.

And where the hell were the soldiers?

They had veered off course, but the Major hadn't noticed because they'd been combing the area for several days and were relieved when they came upon the river again. Except it wasn't their river; it was a tributary, smaller, less aggressive. That wasn't questioned, and even had it been, he and Clancy would have agreed that it was to be expected of the upper reaches of any river, before it got into its stride and jollied along full flow.

Another thing kept them close to the river; once again, never listed for discussion, it just came about almost as routine, that as the men were setting up camp, out would come the sieves for panning, and the great race would begin again, better than any card game or horseplay they'd previously engaged in around campfires. This was the ultimate game. Some had become so immersed in the concept, in the simplicity of such an awesome project, that there were whispers of desertion, only whispers though, among the poorly paid regular soldiers.

Then the Lieutenant had gone down with the fever, which Kit blamed on a chill from the drenching rain, though some of the men declared sullenly that Clancy was only suffering from lack of booze, his last bottle tossed to the wind a couple of days ago.

The sick man had clung on with a soldier riding by him to offer support, but that left Kit as sole navigator, taking the lead, and that responsibility made him nervous. At least, though, he reassured himself, he could still see the strange cork-like peak of one of the Glasshouse Mountains, with its two companions. It didn't occur to him that they could have been moving in an arc, with Beerwah keeping to his left, so he didn't bother to consult his compass.

One of the soldiers was heard to remark that no matter how far they travelled they never seemed to shake off that ruddy peak.

'I seen a picture like that once,' his mate said. 'In my auntie's house. No matter where you walked in that room, the eyes followed you. Rum it was. Real rum.'

'We ought to climb up there and paint eyes on the peak,' another suggested, and then he shouted: 'Look out! Clancy's over!'

The Lieutenant crashed to the ground, so Kit had to call a stop and set up tent for the patient, who was seriously ill, even delirious at times. Frantically he ordered that Clancy be swabbed continuously to cool him down, and he himself added antiseptic to the water, to kill the germs. He put four men on patrol, instructing them to keep a wide circle around the camp, and placed two on guard, exploding when they dared to suggest guards weren't needed in daytime.

'That's an order!' he yelled at them. 'Get on with it. The rest of you look to your equipment, your horses. Sharpen up, make use of this time!'

But while he sat with Clancy, fanning him, wiping the sweat from his face and chest, one by one the men without specific duties sneaked from the camp and ran the half-mile through thick scrub to the sandy riverbank.

Fortunately Jack spotted their early-morning campfire, and rode quickly in that direction, hoping it was them, otherwise he would have wasted almost two days, at the same time angry with them if he were right.

He came upon them on the second day of Clancy's illness, relieved to meet mounted guards first, but further annoyed to find a practically empty camp in a state of disarray, possessions lying about like litter.

'What the hell are you doing?' he shouted at Ferrington.

'Clancy's very sick!'

'I know that. Your guards told me. But what are you doing stuck right over here? You said you'd be heading for Montone Station; you're heading away from it.'

'We are not. I know exactly where we are, and where have you been? You should have reported to me four days ago.'

Jack took him aside and gave him the bad news of the attack on Kirk's party.

'You'll have to make a quick decision now,' he said. 'And in the meantime I need your packhorse, to bring Kirk in.'

'I can't spare the packhorse! We can't move on without our supplies!'

'You can share out the supplies and dump all the rest, including this stuff...' He kicked at the prospecting equipment, and the officers' folding table and chairs. 'You don't need any of this.'

184

Ferrington was about to argue with him but changed his mind. Instead he worried about Clancy. 'All I can do for the Lieutenant now is to leave a man with him, and hope he can throw off the fever. I thought you might know of some bush cure.'

'No,' Jack said flatly. 'I'm sorry to hear he's crook, and I'm trying to be sorry about all those Native Police getting killed, but you better get the message. There's a big war party on the loose, so you're headed for a fight. Montone Station is about sixty miles from here.' He pointed. 'In that direction, by the way. But you please yourself where you go. Personally, I'd turn about and go home if I were you. In the meantime, remember that ambush. I wouldn't camp with my back to the river like this. Look for safer ground. I'll grab some grub and get going.'

Kit was glad to see the back of Jack Drew and his nagging criticisms. He went back into the tent to sit by Clancy, praying he'd come round and help him with the decisions he had to make, but the Lieutenant was still very ill, cold now, in need of more blankets.

Kit called to the next in rank, Sergeant Rapper, a man he couldn't take to. He was a burly fellow with sandy hair and a complexion to match, and though he'd had years of service, Rapper never seemed to have adjusted to taking orders. He could hand them out with ease and determination, but his attitude was one of resentment when it came to his betters. Kit had discussed the fellow with Clancy, who'd laughed.

'Don't worry about him, Major. He's just ag'in the world. Got a chip on his shoulder the size of Gibraltar. You'd get more out of him if you asked him to do things rather than tell him.'

Bloody rot, Kit thought now, recalling that conversation. I don't have time for prima donnas.

He threw open the tent flap and shouted to Rapper: 'Get some blankets for the Lieutenant, he's shivering now. And get this camp cleaned up. We're leaving immediately.'

'What about Clancy?'

Kit flinched at the lack of respect, but carried on: 'Choose a man to stay with him. Someone who will look after him.'

'Then what?'

'Get the blankets, Sergeant!'

He hadn't told Drew that they were short of rations, out of sugar and with only a bag of flour left, and some tea, and salt. They'd been living on scrub turkeys and whatever wild meat the men could shoot, mainly wallabies, but the packhorse had carried spare ammunition as well as the camp equipment, so that had to be shared out. Kit himself took spare waterbags to hang by his sword, but he could hardly be expected to carry other equipment.

By noon, he had his troops stand to attention to pay their respects to the

Lieutenant they would have to abandon, with his guard, then they mounted up.

Kit rode over to Rapper. 'We are making straight for our destination today, Montone Station. It's about sixty miles in that direction.'

The sergeant nodded, with a faint sneer. 'I been saying that for days, but no one listens to me.'

'I do not have to explain my orders, Sergeant. But now I want you to alert the men that there could be trouble ahead.'

'Looks to us that the niggers have all done a bunk, sir. They're gone from this area now. I reckon we're safe.'

'Then you're wrong.' Kit had been trying to decide when, or if, to tell them about the fate of Kirk's men. Soon enough they'd hear it all from Kirk, if Drew got him out safely, but . . . He sighed. He might as well get it over with.

He turned his horse about to address the men. 'I have some bad news,' he said. 'The Native Police were attacked by a war party and wiped out. As far as we know, only Inspector Kirk has survived. Mr Drew has gone to rescue him . . .'

His announcement had the expected reaction of shock, fear and then anger, and he allowed them a few minutes to digest the situation. 'I hope your weapons are in good order, that you stay keen and alert. It is our duty to make this area safe for settlers, and we can only do that by running off these savages.'

'How many in the war party, sir?' a trooper asked.

'At this point I could not say. Kirk will provide us with that information.'

'Didn't Mr Drew know, sir?'

'He wasn't sure. Now carry on, and God save the Queen.'

They talked again, Bussamarai and Ilkepala, and celebrated the destruction of the savage troopers.

'The soldiers are next,' the war chief crowed, and Ilkepala groaned.

'It is my opinion the renegades will not be much mourned by the whites, but killing soldiers will only bring more. And you said yourself you were trying to avoid going up against guns.'

'True.'

'Then why not make peace with them?'

'You think they want peace? They do not. They want to turn our bones to ash.'

Nevertheless, Bussamarai was worried about the guns and was trying to think of another way to overcome the soldiers without losing any of his men. Nungulla was still boasting he could steal their guns with the help of that renegade pig, and Bussamarai was prepared to allow him to try, but he thought it was a ridiculous notion, bound to fail.

'You should make them turn back,' Ilkepala was saying. 'Make them go away and avoid a battle altogether.'

'Good. I'll just stroll down and tell them go away.'

They argued this and other matters, and Bussamarai remembered Jack Drew. 'Is he still with the soldiers?'

'No. They say he is roaming about on his own.'

'Why?'

'Maybe seeking his own Dreaming. He took time to visit the place of the bubbling waters, where he always liked to sit and contemplate.'

'He has no Dreaming out here, but still now . . . he's not with the soldiers?'

'Not this day, it is said.'

'Then we strike now!'

'What! You can't. There are eighteen soldiers all with guns and you have only a few men down here with you.'

'Sixteen. Didn't I hear that one of the headmen in a red coat is sick, left behind with a guard?'

'Only yesterday they left him, but that is still too many. You must not attack them.'

Bussamarai's broad grin brimmed with confidence. 'I did not say attack, I said strike. They have two headmen, both with the swords, one badly sick. What would the rest of the soldiers do if they had no leader?'

'I am not sure.'

'Then we'll find out. I'll send a man to kill the other leader. The one who rides before them.'

Chapter Eleven

On his way to the office of the Stock and Station Agent, who was now selling town blocks at a fast rate, Sam came upon a fellow he'd met in the corridor outside his Sydney office, unmistakable in that long coat and cloth cap.

He bade him good morning and asked how he was getting along, at the same time remembering that the gentleman had wanted to place an advertisement in the *Sydney Herald*.

'Not too well at all,' came the response. 'I haven't had a response to my enquiries either here or in Sydney.'

'What were you enquiring about?'

'My brother. Mr Jack Wodrow. He migrated to this country ten years ago and apparently he's done very well, but I'm unable to locate him.'

'Maybe I can help. Perhaps an article in the paper might serve you better.'

'What do you mean, an article? What would that cost?'

'Not a farthing. I'm a reporter, I'd be glad to write an article about your search.'

'Would you? I'd appreciate it. This is most fortunate. It would be sad to have to return without being able to at least acquaint him with family affairs.'

'Well then, what about coming over to my office and we'll have a talk?'

Hector Wodrow was afizz with excitement, though he wouldn't show it. He was to be famous! This man, Sam, wanted to know all about him, and his brother, so that he could compose a little story about them, and put it in the paper. He wondered if it would be on the front page, though that seemed to be given over to advertisements and notices. He took off his cap and began to relate their background to the reporter.

Their father, Mervin Wodrow, was a fine man, a missionary, as was their mother, Clara. A saint she was. The parents were generous to a fault, always giving to the poor of their money, their kindness and their prayers, though they did keep some aside for the upkeep of the family home, and for the servants who ran the household while they were out . . . day and night, they were . . . rescuing the poor and destitute from the streets and from their sordid lives.

'Jack and I attended St Thomas' Academy in Edgware Road, and I went on to follow in Father's footsteps, though I was more suited to parish work. Jack, though, he preferred farming, not given to church, even pastoral work, at all, which really saddened the parents. They were upset that he wouldn't at least carry on with the mission, and I feel the family disagreement on this matter was too much for Jack. He simply left.

'It was only recently, upon the death of our dear father, that I learned Jack was in this land. A sheep farmer, it seemed, something along those lines . . . Is this enough for your article?

'Yes. It will only be a paragraph or two.'

'I can give you more. On board ship I won the quoits contest and was appointed Honorary Recreation Officer. Quite an honour, don't you think?'

'Indeed, Mr Wodrow. But I think what we have will do fine.'

Before he left the building, Hector cancelled his 'whereabouts' notice, since the article would be sufficient, and retrieved his shilling.

The next day Inspector Tomkins read the piece, with great interest.

'Mervin Wodrow! I remember him. A creepy little parasite. He ran a seaman's mission, with about as much human kindness as an alley cat. So Hector and Jack are his sons! Still doesn't tell me much, except that Hector's painting a pretty picture for publication. And wait on . . . how old is he? In his late thirties, I'd say. He couldn't have gone to St Thomas' Academy, it was only opened about twelve years ago, if my memory serves me true.'

He laughed. 'Unless you were a particularly slow scholar, Hector, still there in your twenties! Bunch of lies, this stuff, enough to make a man give it more thought. I'll send it down to Fred Watkins.'

Unfortunately, the two paragraphs in the *Courier* about his long-lost brother did not attract any response, so Hector decided to return to Sydney on the next sailing, but he left his Sydney address with Sam Dignam, who had pointed out to him that outback stations only received newspapers once a month, if that. This meant that Jack or any of his colleagues could still see the story . . . Hector had surreptitiously bought five copies by dint of several visits to the shops that offered the *Courier*.

He planned to stay on in Sydney because he found the climate pleasant, much less humid than this Brisbane backwater. He might even take a wife, if one were available with sufficient funds, and retire.

A week later he boarded the steamer *Arabella*, bound for Sydney, by no means disappointed in his quest. These things take time, he told himself, I have yet to study ships' passenger lists of a decade ago, and I'll see exactly where he disembarked. That could be a pointer to the chosen district.

On the Sunday morning, the huge bell on the wharf clanged fiercely, and people came running, bursting with curiosity, only to fall back in shock as two fishermen shouted the news that the *Arabella* had been wrecked in Rous Channel, between Moreton and Stradbroke Islands, and so far no survivors had been found.

Sam Dignam wrote the sad story for the *Courier*. The doomed ship had sailed down the Brisbane River, crossed Moreton Bay in a severe storm, run into even more dangerous waters in that channel and never even made it to the open ocean. It went down with the loss of forty-four lives. No survivors.

Hector Wodrow made front-page news that day.

Inspector Tomkins read his name on the list of those lost at sea, but he had known several of the other passengers much better, including Miss Grimes, the Super's aunt, so Hector was swept to the background in the wave of grief that overcame the town.

In Ipswich, formerly known as Limestone, there was a day of mourning for the loss of their police chief, Inspector Crotty, who had also gone down on *Arabella*, but Harry Harvey and his mates, holed up in the high country between Ipswich and the Darling Downs, were celebrating. Crotty had been getting too close for comfort of late, employing men to guard the road across the plains, and the difficult climb up the range, from attacks by bushrangers. Several of Harry's plans had gone awry thanks to these guards, but the townspeople weren't impressed. They disapproved of council funds being spent on civilian guards, and with Crotty gone, Harry thought there was every chance they'd be given their marching orders.

'Sent back to the coalmines,' Scarpy laughed as he reached for the tattered copy of the newspaper. 'I reckon they'd be better off joining you than working down those bloody mines. I wouldn't go down there for quids.'

Scarpy wasn't an active member of Harry's gang, which was composed of three men who lived in the camp and another who lived and worked in the town, to keep them informed of local comings and goings. Scarpy – no one knew him by any other name – owned a heavily wooded property out on the plains where he had a cottage, a few horses, an orchard and nothing much else it seemed, bar a few chooks, but he'd turned out to be a man who could keep his mouth shut. Even hide a bloke or two in a cellar when the coppers were out on the hunt.

He wasn't one to socialise in the town; he preferred the company of bushmen, even though most of his acquaintances out here were hardly law-abiding, something that didn't bother Scarpy one bit. They'd generally gained the impression that he'd been a convict in his day, being closer to fifty than not, with a voice that still rang of the Bow bells, and made his own way after that. His own way, they guessed, could easily have been bushranging, because of his habit of homing in with glee at their misdeeds. He loved to hear what they were up to, but could be relied upon never to open his trap to a copper. He had no time for the law, no fear, not Scarpy.

So there he was on a visit, sitting at a makeshift table, poring over the newspaper and the story of the wreck, snorting a bit at Crotty's demise – Crotty, who had given him a prod of suspicion every so often – and peering at the other names.

'By God, there's a great name here. Wodrow! Any of you blokes know Jack Wodrow? No, you wouldn't. He was famous back in the old country. A highwayman. Before your time. Smart man, he was. I knew him, though. Changed his name . . .' He hesitated, and Harry looked up, interested. 'Went bush. Took up with the blacks, he did. Last time I saw him, years ago, me and a mate were rounding up brumbies, an Irish mate, O'Meara, and Gawd he was a one, look out if you crossed him, and coppers, he hated them too. Agin the government, that's what he was, every bleedin' time.'

'What about Wodrow then?' Harry asked.

'I was coming to that. Me and O'Meara, we had these cattle penned in . . .'

'Thought you said horses,' Harry laughed. 'Doing a bit of rustling, were you, Scarpy?'

'We never did!' he said defensively. 'Anyway, you could have knocked me down with a feather. There comes Jack, out of the bush, as dark as spades, wearin' only a rag over the goods, so to speak. Frightened the life out of me. I thought he was a blackfeller . . . He went over, you see. Went native.'

'What happened to him after that?'

'I dunno. Never saw him again.'

Harry gave this some thought. He recalled the fellow who'd pulled him out of the river, skin blackened from years in the sun, and turned quickly to Scarpy:

'But he goes by the name of Jack Drew now?'

'Yes,' Scarpy said, and then retracted. 'No! I didn't say that. I said his name was Wodrow, not Drew! You're getting me all mixed up.'

'That's too bad, because I was just about to inform you that I met your Wodrow. Or, as he said, Jack Drew.'

'Go on! You never!'

'Have it your way. But I say he's the gentleman who helped me swim across the river. Got me away from my pursuers. Doesn't that sound more like the deed of a man who has reason not to be fond of the law?'

'Might.' Scarpy pushed the paper aside and climbed to his feet. 'I gotta go. There's more flaming rain on the way. Fancy that Crotty getting drownded, eh?'

'And fancy your highwayman popping up in these parts.'

'You got it all wrong, Harry. I never heard of a Jack Drew.'

'What did Wodrow change his name to?'

Scarpy trudged over to his horse, knowing he'd said too much already. 'Don't suppose it matters now,' he said to Harry. 'The poor bugger's probably dead by this. He looked as skinny as you when I saw him in the bush. Yeah, he called himself Brosnan in those days, linked up with the Micks.'

As he walked his horse down the steep incline, Scarpy was tickled pink to have heard of Jack again, but sorry he'd made such a mess of things. Harry was sharp, but he might have swallowed the cover tale. Poor Brosnan. His name had sprung 'fast to the tongue', as he himself would have said. He got shot in the breakout from Mudie's farm. O'Meara never forgave them. He went back years later and gunned down the man who'd killed his friend.

But whoa, he thought, none of that is any business of Harry's. Nothing to do with him. And if Jack did him a good turn, wasn't no reason to be prying. A man doesn't ask questions in this end of the world, Harry oughta know that.

He hoped Jack was all right. Would be good to have a yarn with him, Scarpy, thought. Tell him I did all right after all. And I've still got a good stash of cash put away in case I have to do a bolt again. If I ever get caught, it can rot, buried out there under the outhouse. He wondered why Jack was still using his convict name of Drew. Maybe he thought they'd forgotten him. Could be.

Scarpy had never told anyone his own name, but it was still on the prison records, he supposed. Clarence Covington. What a handle. 'Best forgot', as the Micks would say.

Harry watched him as he trundled down the hill. He didn't care if the fellow called himself Diddlydoo. The man he'd met in the river had done him a great service, whoever he was . . . No need for old Scarpy to be so prickly.

Adrian read the account of the tragedy and shuddered. He'd had no idea that the strait between those two large islands was dangerous. Certainly no one aboard *Argyle* had been concerned. The passengers had found it rather exciting to be swishing through the gap from ocean to bay, with views of sandy beaches and green forests on either side.

His sister came down to the office. 'Who was your letter from?'

'What letter?'

'The one addressed to you, Adrian,' she said. 'I think it is a lady's handwriting.'

'Then you could be right. They could have a lady clerk at Jameson's Drapery. I told them to send me up the work shirts I like, but they're out of stock. Did you read about the wreck?'

'What wreck?'

'Here in the paper.' He handed it to her. 'A coastal steamer was wrecked leaving the bay. Every single soul on board was drowned.'

'Oh dear Lord! Anyone we know?'

'I don't think so. Take the paper with you up to the house. I'll have time to read it all later.'

'But I wanted to talk to you about managing the finances. I have some rather good ideas.'

'All right. But can't we talk about it later? I have to sort out these bills, see what can be paid and what can wait . . .'

By this time Jessie had found the story of the shipwreck and was completely immersed in it, wondering if Sam had written this piece, since the author was not identified.

When she left, Adrian turned back to the mail and to that letter. It was not from Jameson's but from Flo, and he opened it gently, as if her fragrance might flow from the pages and be lost to him if he didn't take care.

It was, as usual, the sweetest letter, with some news of the town, mainly that Merlin had left, which was a relief to Adrian, removing as it did any temptation Flo might have had to return to work for him. She wrote that she wouldn't be surprised if Merlin had joined one of the gold rushes because people were going mad for gold all over the place, and really finding lots.

'That's what Kit needs here,' he murmured. 'He's still losing money and seems to think the bank will wait indefinitely.'

Adrian was doing his best. The convict labourers were entitled to a small wage of a few shillings a week, compared to more than a pound a week paid to free men, but they were hardly worth their keep. Clearing was patchy, deep roots still littering land that was supposed to be totally cleared; ploughing was rough and haphazard; the horses were poorly shod, buildings leaked, everywhere he turned there was something wrong.

To try to smarten up the work, he had ordered that tobacco rations were no longer to be handed out as a right, not until the work improved. The workers complained, but Adrian stood firm. He stopped work on the continuation of the veranda on the western side of the house and sent the two carpenters to work in the fields. But these items, he knew, were trivial. They wouldn't hold back the floods.

Returning to Flo's letter, the sweet and loving letter, he took a page of Kit's stationery to respond:

'Dearest of my dear . . .' It was such a joy to write to her and forget the problems of this place.

Since this was to be Jessie's home, Adrian believed she had a serious responsibility to assist, beginning with the dowry, and brought that subject up when they sat in the dining room to compare notes.

'The dowry has been decided upon, that's no problem, but Mother won't allow it to be paid until the wedding, so you'd better get that over with.'

'You make it sound so unromantic,' Jessie said crossly. 'A wedding here, on this veranda, with that lovely view, will be absolutely beautiful.'

'Don't be silly, Jessie. You know Mother won't approve of that. She'll insist you marry in a church, and that little church we saw in Brisbane, in

Charlotte Street, will do very well. And I think the hotel where Kit was staying could handle the reception.'

'I told her we could have the wedding and the reception here. It will save money.'

'What the hell for? Mother's money doesn't need saving! Kit's does. She'll be paying for everything. And you can't have people here, visiting the shell of a house. You don't have curtains and you have a bare linen press, precious little cutlery and dining room accessories! What were you thinking of? You told me none of those extras were necessary just yet, and at the same time you're talking about having the reception here!'

'I know,' she said miserably. 'I got carried away. I thought if Mother could send us the dowry first, I could buy all the manchester I need.'

'Let's get something straight. The dowry is the property of the husband, to do with as he wishes. He won't spend it on household linens and whatnots, that's your department. And Mother's. I'm surprised there was no letter from her in this delivery, she's had time to answer. And I wrote again explaining that since Kit wasn't in a position to be paying fares to Sydney and back, as well as expending for the entertaining he'd have to do while in Sydney, and a honeymoon on top of that, it would be more sensible to have the wedding up here. I didn't mean in this house. You'd better write to her again and I'll ride in to the post office store and mail it.'

As well as my letter to Flo, he added to himself.

His mother *had* received that advice from Adrian. She was appalled that the pair of fools she had bred should be taking all this so lightly.

Major Ferrington, broke? Should she be surprised? she asked herself. She never had trusted him.

'Yes, I should!' she exclaimed angrily. He had given the impression that he was well off and very much able to sustain her daughter in the manner accustomed. He'd spoken of his property, of the lovely homestead he was building, and indeed, had even said at one stage that Jessie would want for nothing.

That in itself wasn't so bad. It wouldn't kill Jessie to learn the value of money the same as any young bride, even though, Blanche admitted, she herself had not had the experience, having come from a wealthy family to marry into an even wealthier fold of sheep farmers. But that was beside the point. Ferrington had deceived her and Marcus. Her son was deceiving them too, and Jessie had chosen to go chasing off to visit her fiancé without a thought for the proprieties. And now . . . the visit had turned into permanence!

'Well not in my book, miss! You get yourself home or there'll be no wedding, not if I have any say in it.'

She worried about Jessie staying there with the two men, and prayed again that Adrian was chaperoning his sister.

'Oh God,' she moaned. 'Pray Jessie has the sense to resist any untoward approaches that fiancé of hers might make.' And she worried again that if she were having such thoughts about them, what would other people have to say? The worst of course. The very worst.

What should she do? She wished she could talk to Marcus about this, but now he was recovering she dared not upset him. Then she remembered that Adrian, in his last letter, had not even enquired about his grandfather. That was about the last straw!

She was walking down from Macquarie Street when she met Mr Watkins, who was extremely pleased to see her, complimenting her on a most beautiful chapeau.

'Thank you,' she said, appreciating his kindness, because she needed a little cheer on this miserable damned day. First the worries about Adrian and Jessie, and then to the hospital, where Marcus, obviously improving, was in a cranky mood, demanding that he be taken home, out of 'this mortuary'.

'How is your father-in-law these days?' Watkins asked, guessing where she'd come from.

'Improving,' she said grimly. 'Turning from a teddy bear into a grizzly.'

Amused, he said: 'Men aren't the best patients, Matron tells me.'

'If Marcus is any example, she's right.'

'Are you walking to the shops, Mrs Pinnock?'

'Well, no, I was only going to the cab station. I'm on my way home.'

'My conveyance is over there in front of my office. Don't bother with those cab drivers. Allow me to take you home.'

Blanche made small noises about putting him to the trouble, but didn't really protest, because she was glad he'd offered. She was feeling poorly. Truly poorly. And friendless. Forsaken by her family, by the very people who should be caring for her.

'Do you have any family, Mr Watkins?' she asked, sitting beside him in the black-upholstered gig.

'Two sons,' he said. 'My wife, bless her soul, passed away.'

'Then I hope your sons are better behaved than mine is,' she said peevishly. 'I'm fed up with Adrian. Absolutely fed up.'

He sighed. 'My Andrew was apprenticed to a solicitor, a friend of mine, who took the lad on as a favour, but he now finds he doesn't like the work, and my elder son, Bede, who is twenty-two, married and in the police force, has run off to the goldfields in Victoria. With his wife!'

'With his wife?' she said. 'I suppose that's some consolation. Most of them leave the wife and children behind, to fend for themselves.'

'I hardly feel it's consolation for me. I've had her mother on my doorstep, berating me for allowing this to happen to her daughter, and demanding I get her back. I agree it's no place for young ladies, but what can I do?'

'Oh dear. Young people these days, they seem to be losing their sense of order, of propriety. But it's not just the young ones. This gold talk is everywhere; now that there are diggings in New South Wales as well as Victoria, people don't seem to talk about anything else. Responsibilities are going out the window and people are leaving their jobs at an alarming rate.'

'I know! It's incredible! They don't seem to realise the dangers of disease as well as violence on the diggings.'

Blanche nodded. 'And I fear this is only the beginning.'

He slowed the gig. 'There's a very nice teashop on the other side of this park. Would you care for afternoon tea?'

'I couldn't think of anything nicer,' she said firmly. 'I often have tea there, being rather partial to cream puffs.'

Mr Watkins was pleased to know that she hadn't heard from Merlin, or Miss Fowler, and they settled to a pleasant tea under potted palms, as if they were old friends. Then Blanche brought him up to date with her troubles, appalled with herself for spilling the part about Jessie staying in *his* house, spluttering that she was sure everything would be above board.

'Of course it would be,' he said kindly. 'Despite your disagreements, your daughter sounds like a very nice young lady. And didn't you say she was a very resolute sort of lass, rather strong-minded?'

'You can say that again.'

'Well then, I shouldn't worry. She'll be fine.'

'That's as may be, but I'm so angry with them all that I refuse to write to them. I simply will not answer their letters.'

'Mrs Pinnock,' he said quietly, 'if you don't mind my saying, you really ought to write. Keep in touch with them. Let them know that you are not pleased. No letters at all will have them thinking you're busy, or the mail's lost . . .'

'Or that I'm cross with them?'

'No, provide excuses to sidestep your obvious disapproval. I would write.'

'I'll think about it.'

'And perhaps you'd consider having tea with me again next Wednesday afternoon, so that we can discuss our wayward offspring.'

Blanche smiled. 'Very well.'

She did write. To Jessie. Irritated that she could barely put her instructions in a telegram:

YOUR BEHAVIOUR IS DISGRACEFUL. YOU CAN REDEEM YOURSELF BY RETURNING HOME IMMEDIATELY, SO THAT THE ARRANGEMENTS FOR YOUR WEDDING MAY BE FINALISED. MOTHER.

They did not spend the following Wednesday afternoon at the tearooms. Blanche had to call in at Watkins' office to request a postponement, because that was the day the doctor decided to release her father-in-law from the hospital.

Mr Watkins was very understanding. 'It's quite all right. I don't mind at all, but do you need help with Mr Pinnock? Is he able to get about under his own steam?'

'Not really,' she said. 'He's unable to walk more than a few feet as yet. I will have to buy a wheelchair, though goodness knows how I'll get him, and a wheelchair, home.'

'It's very simple. Buy the wheelchair. Have it delivered to your home. I'll come with you to collect Mr Pinnock and between us we'll take him safely home. If you want me to, that is. If you have other plans . . .'

'No. Hospital staff would help me get him into a vehicle, but I was wondering how to get him inside the house. We only have female staff. I think Marcus would like your help.'

He did. Not being a man who could tolerate fuss, he appreciated the firm hand of the former police officer, and his matter-of-fact approach to the old man's difficulties.

'Where did you spring from?' he asked as Watkins lifted him down to the wheelchair that was waiting at the side entrance to their house.

'Friend of the family,' he said. 'Glad to help.'

'I won't need this bloody wheelchair for long, you know.'

'Shouldn't think you would. Get a bit of meat on you and you'll be up and around in no time.'

'Did you hear that, Blanche?' Marcus called. 'I'll be up and around in no time. And I don't want you women treating me like a baby. No more of that hospital muck. I want decent food. Starting with a big steak and plenty of pudding.'

'Yes. You can have anything you want. Cook is delighted you're home. Would you like to lie down before dinner?'

'There you go already! No I wouldn't. I want to sit on the back veranda and look at the bay, and have a nice cold glass of ale. Want to join me, Mr Watkins?'

'Wouldn't knock back a cold ale on a hot day, sir.'

'Call me Marcus.'

They sat out there enjoying their ales and talking amiably until sunset, when Mr Watkins took his leave.

'Do you play crib?' Marcus asked.

'Yes.'

'Then come and have a game with me, Fred. Looks as if I'll be stuck here for a while. Come any time.'

Over dinner, though, Marcus had his questions. 'Nice fellow, Fred. Good solid chap. Retired police. Did you know he's a detective?'

'Yes, he did say.'

'So how did you come across him? What have you been up to? Planning to rob a bank or something?'

'Yes, of course,' she laughed, but Marcus wouldn't be put off.

'Something fishy's going on. What the hell is Adrian doing swanning around Kit's farm? And what's Jessie doing up there? When's the wedding anyway? I figure you've been keeping me in the dark, Blanche, and I think Fred's been called in to do a bit of checking for you.'

'What did he say?'

'Nothing that gave me any hint of how he met you, or how you became friends. You do seem to be friends. I have no objection to him, believe me, but it's curious all the same.'

'We'll talk about it in the morning, Marcus, so don't be worrying. A lady referred me to him, I just wanted him to do some snooping, that's all.' She patted his hand. 'Nothing to get excited about.'

'So you say,' he growled. 'I don't like to be left out of family matters, Blanche. Keep that in mind.'

As promised, and only because she couldn't get out of it, Blanche began to tell him about her problems with 'the children'.

She made light of Adrian having a 'girlfriend' she hadn't met. And admitted that she hadn't known or approved of Jessie's going to Brisbane with Adrian. And told him that Adrian had discovered that Kit was in serious financial trouble.

'He can't afford to come to Sydney for the wedding, so—'

'Can't afford what?' Marcus exploded. 'What's this?'

'Now I told you I didn't want you getting upset, and already you're getting all het up.'

He sat back in the easy chair, all too aware of his condition, and took a deep breath. 'Right. I'm a reformed character as of now. Peaceful as a dove. But let's take things one at a time. Which one of them caused you to call in Fred Watkins?'

'Oh. Dear oh dear, what with one thing and another, I forgot that incident. A fellow accosted me in the street, demanding money. He said he was a friend of Adrian's girlfriend, something like that. This was outside the hospital.'

Marcus drew himself up with a snort of rage.

'But don't get upset, it was over in a minute or so,' she smiled, adding, 'I threatened him with my umbrella.'

'Good on you! What's the world coming to?'

'Anyway, I told Matron, who was very cross about it, and she called Mr Watkins, just in case the fellow decided to accost me again.'

'And Fred got it sorted, eh?'

'Yes. He had a word with the fellow, who has left Sydney now anyway, so that's all.'

'Except for Adrian's girlfriend. What part did she play in this?'

'As it turned out, nothing.'

Marcus had nothing but time on his hands. He mulled over Blanche's story. I think I only heard half the tale, he mused. Someone putting the bite on her, on behalf of the girlfriend? Where does she fit into this? I daresay Fred knows more than he's letting on, but he wouldn't be in a position to speak. I'll have to dig about myself.

He wrote, in his none-too-steady hand, to Alex Messenger at his bank, asking him to call, and Messenger was on the doorstep the next day, fortunately while Blanche was out shopping.

He was surprised and relieved that Marcus took the information he could offer very calmly.

'Adrian gets a sizeable allowance for doing nothing much at all,' Marcus told the bank manager. 'But he was overdrawn, you say? And digging into a family nest-egg?'

'Exactly. He also sold the last of the shares Barney left to him.'

'What about the rest of the family share certificates?'

'They're still intact, in the safety deposit box. In Blanche's name.'

Marcus sat back. 'Good. Now here's what to do. Get me a pen and paper from that drawer behind you and make out a letter to the Parramatta branch of the bank, where my accounts are kept, as you know, cancelling Adrian's allowance. It was supposed to be a wage, Alex, but he's getting too high-handed for farm work.'

He watched as Messenger wrote the short note.

'Do you know where he is now? Managing a mate's farm. The blind leading the blind, I say. You'd think with me being crook, he'd have gone out to my place and given a hand, right? You finished there?'

He read the note written in the bank manager's clean, sloping hand-writing. 'Let's see. Yes. To whom it may concern. Goodoh, that will do fine. Give me a pen and I'll sign it.'

He leaned forward and laboriously signed the note and handed back the pen.

'This'll give him a shake-up. He's not getting another penny out of me until he starts earning his keep at our Parramatta properties.'

After Messenger had left, Marcus sat waiting for Blanche to come home. No need to tell her about this move, she'd hear soon enough, he decided. He wanted to hear about the mysterious girlfriend, and the wedding, wondering if Kit was relying on the dowry for financial rescue.

'Nothing wrong with that,' he murmured. 'A business arrangement after all.'

'When's the wedding?' he asked his daughter-in-law cheerfully, when she came in. He was quite pleased with his morning's work.

'You're looking so well,' she said. 'A quiet morning in the sunshine has done you good. As for the wedding, I've no idea when it will be.'

'You'd think he'd want to get on with it, if he is short of spondulicks.'

'Yes, you would. I'm just waiting for Jessie to come home to finalise the arrangements.'

He nodded, satisfied with that answer. 'Reece Maykin's got a fine sheep station up there. On the Darling Downs, magnificent sheep country, they say. Has Jessie met him yet? He was a great mate of Barney's, you know. Tell her to look him up. Nice family. You know Madeline Maykin, don't you?'

'No, I've never met her. They've been up north quite a while, haven't they?'

'Yes. And by the way, who's Adrian's latest girlfriend?'

'I've no idea.'

Flo sat by the window, admiring her diamond horseshoe brooch, set in gold. It really was beautiful, she'd starve before she'd sell it, but she had now received another letter from Adrian and still no mention of money.

She could quite understand it, because rich people didn't think about money, it was just there for dipping into whenever they pleased, like dipping into a well. But it was different for poor people. She'd been walking the streets, day in and day out, trying to find a job, any job, doing anything people wanted, but couldn't find anything. Now she was walking further out, into the posh parts of town, knocking on doors, asking if anyone wanted a servant, or a laundress or something, but mostly the back doors were opened by maids who shooed her off fast, closed the door in her face. Still, she wasn't going to ask Adrian for money, she wouldn't do that. She just wouldn't.

But she only had a few pence left.

She'd come from Tasmania in the first place, running from a brutal stepfather, and joined the Summerville Show Troupe as a seamstress and general help, when it sailed for Melbourne. Totally stage-struck by then, she yearned for a chance to tread the boards, and although she had to admit she couldn't sing a note, and dancing was beyond her, the owners kept her on because she was an obliging girl, and could handle the ticket office without getting tangled up.

After the show moved to Sydney, she got her big chance with Merlin, and was happy as his assistant . . . in the limelight at last.

She'd ever be grateful for that job, because that was how she'd met dear Adrian. He'd come to the stage door, just like it said in the penny love stories, just like that.

Only yesterday she'd gone back to the theatre to see if she could have her old job back, and they were pleased to see her, to have her back, because they were going south again, to Melbourne and then on to the booming gold towns . . .

She couldn't leave Sydney, leave Adrian. She wouldn't dream of it. She'd go down and see them off at Circular Quay, all of her friends, her only friends in the town, apart from Adrian, but it couldn't be helped.

She looked at her shoes, worn out now, lined with newspaper, and wondered where she could get enough money to buy another pair. She had some sideshow dolls; perhaps she could sell them, and maybe some of her furniture, by putting a sign outside.

200

Walking past one day, Fred Watkins saw the sign: SOFA. FOOTREST. TABLE. TWO CHAIRS. FRAMED PITURE. FOR SALE, printed on the side of a packing case.

He shook his head sadly and knocked on her door.

'What's this?' he asked as she peered out of the window over the tiny porch, his voice as jovial as he could produce. 'Having a cleanout, are we?'

'Yes, Mr Watkins,' she said in a small voice. 'Yes, a cleanout.'

'Anything I might like to buy?'

'I don't think so. I should take the sign down. I've sold out really. Would you pass it to me, please?'

He obliged, collecting the packing case and bringing it to her door.

'Can I carry it inside for you?'

'No thank you, it's all right there, just turn it about so the sign doesn't show.'

'Did all right with your clearout, eh?'

'Yes, good.'

'And how are you this fine day?'

'Good, thank you.'

'Ah. Well, I'll bid you good day, miss.'

'Yes, thank you,' she said and disappeared from view, but anticipating her withdrawal he had time for a quick glance into the sitting room, empty except for two chairs, looking lost and lonely on the bare boards. He wanted to try again to speak to her, but realised she was clinging to her dignity and could resent his intrusion, so he walked away. Best to leave her be, he thought, for the time being.

Flo was right. It didn't occur to Adrian to send her money. Even if he hadn't been busy trying to organise these fractious convicts, threatening them with a flogging if he had any more slacking off. As a matter of fact, he would have ordered floggings by this, especially for that ugly carrot-head Albert, the ringleader in outright insolence, except he didn't know the protocol. He'd never had anything to do with floggings, though like everyone else, he was aware that they were an integral part of the lower echelons of colonial life. He had forgotten to ask Kit who actually carried out the sentences. Did he wield the whip himself, or appoint someone as flogger? In which case, who?

And another thing. He had seen Albert's bare back with the signs of what had to be a recent flogging, and didn't imagine a man could order the fellow to be whipped again. Not on top of those scabs and sores.

So what to do with him? He was bringing the work almost to a standstill, the men moving about like zombies, sneering at Adrian when he passed by. Farm implements were left lying in the fields, the vegetable gardens trampled; a tin of paint had been splashed on the veranda, right by the front door. Things were getting worse. He considered locking the men in at night, but that would mean barring the windows of their quarters, and the building itself, only wattle and daub with a thatched roof, wasn't even secure.

Finally he sat down to discuss the problems with Jessie.

'No wonder Kit couldn't make a go of this place,' he said. 'The workers are useless! Uncontrollable.'

'Kit could control them. He never had this trouble.'

'No, because he flogged them.'

'He did not! How can you say such a thing?'

'Ah, leave it. I'm not here to argue with you. I've come to a decision, though. I'm going to sack a fellow called Albert. He's an overseer of sorts, so Kit says, but he's more like a ringleader, he's at the back of all the trouble I'm having. If I get rid of him, and maybe one of the others as well, the rest of them might sharpen up. And that's a saving, little though it be, of two wages. Kit can do without them, and at this stage every penny counts.'

Jessie agreed enthusiastically. 'Grandpa always says pennies make the pounds, and he's right. I was thinking along the same lines. We'll have the wedding in Brisbane as you suggest, and that means we won't be doing any formal entertaining here for a while, so ... I'm not going to waste money on curtains and linens, and things we don't need. I'll tell Kit that every penny I have has to go towards the upkeep of the farm. Until we get on our feet, house expenses will have to be kept to a minimum.'

Adrian nodded his approval. 'I'm glad you're seeing sense. The man is doing his best, you mustn't lumber him with non-essentials.'

'I know,' she said, 'and what's more, I intend to make myself useful, and not sit about like the lady of the house, in daffy poses. That's not me at all. I can do the cooking and the housework. There are only the three of us, and just Kit and me after the wedding. I don't need a cook, and with a brand-new house, there's hardly any housework to do. I'll put Polly off.'

'Good idea,' Adrian said. 'Now we're getting somewhere.'

'Yes. I'll tell her tonight,' Jessie said thoughtfully. 'But I was just remembering ... She's still a convict, isn't she?'

'They all are. If they're fired from here, they have to go back to prison.'

'I don't care about those men, but it's a shame for Polly. I'll write her an absolutely glowing reference that she can take back with her, so she won't have any trouble getting another job. That will do, won't it?'

'More than fair, I think.'

'Good.' Jessie jumped to her feet. 'I might as well get this over with. I'll explain to her that we can't afford her, she'll understand that. And I'll tell her about the reference ...'

When Miss Pinnock had finished her short speech, she said:

'You do understand, don't you, Polly?

And Polly stood, stayed on her feet, clutching the kitchen table to stop herself from swaying with the dizziness that had suddenly swum in on her . . . stood steadfast, for she wouldn't let this stupid, stupid female see her plight.

'I do,' she said through clenched teeth. 'That I do.' And as the stupid, stupid, smug apology for a woman marched out of her kitchen, Polly let go and crumpled into a chair.

Oh God, let this be a bad dream, let me be wakin' to a normal evening and puttin' the beef in the salt barrel, like I was about to do before she came in, but she did come in and she stood there by the breadbin and it's never a dream at all. Oh God, she'd never do that to me, would she? And why would she not? The hussy. What am I to her, with my worn hands and crone face? Just another thing! A thing. To be thrown out when it's not for use no more. Thrown back on the heap of trash in that prison, and why? Because she's sitting up in the Major's house, eating like a duchess and crying poormouth, that's why. But it won't wash with me. Poormouth be damned! Lying bitch. Soon as she gets rid of me she'll probably bring her own flash maid from Sydney, one of them pitcher-book colleens, poncing round in their black and white, like sniggering magpies. But . . .

'Oh God, no!' Polly cupped her hands to her face as the tears began to fall, and her voice came out a croak. 'No. I can't go back to that prison. I can't. I thought I could stay here for ever. I don't want to go no other place, even if the bitch's reference can wheedle me out of the prison gates. And what if it can't? I heard say folk aren't taking government people no more.'

She hauled herself up, picked up the carving knife, and sliced the round of beef in half, placing the pieces on a large platter, then she took them out to the pantry and put them carefully into brine, with a sigh, a long, aching sigh, for hadn't this been the best job she'd ever had? And wasn't this the prettiest place she'd ever seen, with its rolling green hills and the grand old gum trees all around, as untidy as all getout, them straggly trees, but they never give a damn, them being kings of the forest here, and no getting away from that.

She stepped outside into misty rain and looked about her, uncertain where to turn, wondering if she should go down and tell old Bart what was happening to her. No use trying to talk to Albert, he was almost off his head over that flogging, as if no one else ever got tied to a triangle and whipped till the skin and blood dripped. There was a time, Polly recalled, when she nearly got flogged herself, when a judge had sentenced her to a flogging for her crimes. Atrocious, he'd said they were.

'A matter of bloody opinion,' Polly muttered, setting off for the barn. 'I was new to that house, a raw colleen come to learn servanting in the manner of things, but I wasn't raw in the ways of rutting men and I knew what the master, old Moffat, was after when he pinned eyes on me, rattlin' his privates at me from the shadows when no one was looking.'

She walked along the side of the barn, thinking of Belfast, where you ran from the cold of the rain, not wandered about in it, and she kicked at an empty box left lying in her way.

He got me, though, she reflected, like he got all the maids anywhere under forty, when it suited him. 'Twas my turn at the back of the stables, held down for his pleasure by two of his lackeys, and no amount of kicking and biting could put a stop to it.

She brushed wet hair from her face and walked into the paddock to look out over the river, but there wasn't much to see on this dark night, and that depressed her even more.

I should keep on going, I should, while the courage is in me, throw myself in the river and be done with it. I had courage once, by God I did. The time old Moffat wanted his feet rubbed and the butler gave me the hot oil to run on up with while it was still hot, and put a little on a sponge to warm his feet and then give them a good rubbing.

'Why can't you do it?' I asked him, and he pushed the sponge and the pot of oil at me, and told me to get a move on.

So I gets on to his room and he's sittin' there in his chair with his putty feet on a towel ready for me to get down and do the rubbing, but no sooner do I put the pot down and look up to start, wondering if that flamin' butler hadn't made the oil too hot to get me in trouble, than the master flicks off the linen over his lap and there he is bare, all spread for me . . .

'I don't have that sort of courage any more,' she sighed aloud. 'I got it beat out of me! I'm done now. Though I did lie, said it was an accident . . .' Polly took time out to laugh.

''Twas an accident, milords, just an accident, I pray thee, have mercy.' Then she chortled. 'Sure it was an accident that I tipped the copper pot with its hot oil on his crotch, and the screams could be heard a score of miles away.'

Atrocious. She nodded. But somehow they'd forgotten the flogging and sent her away on a prison ship.

She was slipping on the wet grass, moving slowly down to the river, with the vague plan in her head of jumping in, getting this misery over and done with.

'I'm never going back to prison,' she warned herself. 'And that's a true fact. I'd be better off dead. The river will finish me quick, just take me under its warm waters and carry me off . . .'

She could hear her own voice now, younger, stronger, braver, asking why she had put up with the depravity of that prison ship and the hideous prisons all that time. Why hadn't she put an end to it sooner?

'But didn't I have meself a nice job here in the end, here at Emerald Downs, and isn't that a love of a name?'

You had. Haven't any more. And you're too old now. They'll never give you an outside job, you'll have to finish your time locked in.

It was true. And when she'd done her time, and maybe more for being sacked, what then? The streets?

204

Determined now, she began walking to the river, when all of a sudden she stopped with a screech.

'Jesus, Mary and Joseph! The monster! The crocodile!'

The return journey was harder, clambering back up the hill, the rain pelting down now, not at all kind and refreshing, but beating, punishing her, and she wept for all the anguish of her miserable life, for the waste of it and what might have been, had she come across some good fortune somewhere.

She staggered into the barn, sobbing, heartbroken. 'I nearly made it,' she managed to say, 'right here.' And her hard-hearted youthful voice found pity for her. But you didn't, you poor love. That's over. And you've no one to care a whit for you in the whole world. They saw to that when they sent you off, and no one in your family gave a damn about you. They were too ashamed.

'I had a letter written telling them where I was,' she offered sadly.

And who wrote back? No one. Not even the mater. Give over, Polly, you said it yourself. You're done for.

'Yes.'

She lit a candle by her bunk and carried it out into the barn proper, placing it on a ledge so she could see to search for a rope. That done, she climbed up on to a bench and flung the rope over a rafter, mildly pleased that she'd got it right first go . . .

Chapter Twelve

The hut looked innocent enough, but Jack skirted it with the spare horse to be sure, and finding no hint of trouble, rode up to the door and called softly to Kirk, who came dashing out.

'About bloody time! A man could have been murdered by this, and saved you the trouble. Did you bring me some food? And water? I haven't got any water left.'

'Get on the horse. There's a waterbag hanging by the saddle. And here's some food.' He handed over the small parcel. 'Now shut your trap and get going.'

'Where?'

'To meet up with the Major. He's still coming north.'

'I'm not. I don't care where he's headed. I've just survived a battle.'

'Where no one fired a shot.'

'Where my men were massacred! I'm returning to Brisbane. I can't be expected to suffer any more.'

To his surprise, Jack agreed. 'Clancy is sick with the fever. You can help escort him back after I check in with the Major.'

They rode for hours with little to say except for Kirk's complaints that they were going in the wrong direction.

'You think I don't know east from west with this bloody sun beating down on me? We're going too far west, we should be travelling due south now, you're avoiding Ferrington. What the hell are you up to?'

'Ask the Major. He veered west, he should be heading back this way now, so with luck we'll find him.'

Kirk bucked up, pleased. 'He got lost? The Major and the Lieutenant got lost? Led their troops in the wrong direction! Wait till they hear about this back home. He's not so bloody smart after all! If he and his men have strayed off course, how the hell are you going to find him now?'

'I found him before . . .'

'Bloody fluke that must have been,' Kirk growled. 'I demand that we forget him and press on. You said Clancy needs help; then that's where I'm going. You take me to where I can pick up the stock route again. I'm ordering you!'

Jack ignored him; he was watching a horseman riding slowly along the crest of a hill far ahead of them, and wondering who it could be.

Eventually, as they came closer, the rider brought his horse to a halt and sat, observing them.

'Who the hell's that?' Kirk asked, and began shouting: 'Hey! Over here! Who are you?' He was about to ride on to meet the mysterious horseman when Jack grabbed the reins of his animal and jerked it back.

'Stay here! That's not a white man.'

'Are you sure? Then it must be one of my men; someone must have got away from the savages.'

'It's not one of your men, unless he's taken to wearing a bone through his nose.'

'Then if it's a savage, shoot him. Get him, quick! You never thought to bring me a rifle, did you? I'd pick him off bloody quick smart.'

'Shut your trap and stay here. Don't move. I'll see what's going on.'

He advanced quietly towards the rider, and then nodded his head in recognition.

'I should have known,' he smiled. 'Who else rides *yarraman*? Greetings to thee, Moorabi. What brings you here?'

'The soldiers are coming. The people would like them to turn back.'

Jack shrugged. 'Can't be done. They have to go north as far as the place of the fire . . .' He touched his face gingerly. 'Then they will return. They want to be able to tell the white people that they can return to their houses and farms in safety.' He looked squarely at Moorabi. 'Can they?'

'Not wise to do so. Yet.'

'Why not yet?'

'The magic man seeks peace. Bussamarai wants war.'

'Surely the man Ilkepala can cast great spells and spirit songs to force peace.'

'He is much powerful, but Bussamarai has the warriors and a burden of grief that he cannot put down.'

Jack understood the reference to mourning and the protocol involved, knowing that it would take powerful magic to interfere in tribal matters of such importance, but he was interested to know that not all the people wanted war. That was a good start.

'The man leading the soldiers,' he said, 'the man in the red coat who carries a sword, he does not want war either. He wishes for the white people to live here in peace and the black people to be able to walk safe too.

'It would be thus good if the two chiefs could talk,' he added. 'Two warriors, say. Might you take that message? And while I'm here, where are they? The soldiers.'

Moorabi turned and pointed. 'Come on through bunya-bunya lands.'

'Ah yes, I know.' He remembered that the bunya pine trees had edible seeds that were very popular, and families would travel to the area to harvest them.

'Better you help the other chief who has the heat sickness.' Moorabi handed Jack a small bag of white powder. 'Give him this medicine quick or he die.'

'What is it?'

'Same stuff Ilkepala gave you when you sick from the gun and the fire.'

Jack was amazed. 'Ilkepala did that? He helped me? Why would he do that?'

'Maybe he sees you useful still.' The black man shrugged. 'Maybe he practised medicine on you.' Jack didn't know if that was meant to be a joke or not. But Ilkepala's messenger added: 'He says thumb scoop of the powder in water, dawn and dusk.'

'Is he still at the camp where we left him?'

'Yes. Do you know the Kianga high country?'

Jack nodded, pointing west. 'Why would I go through there?'

'Because down the other side are plains, easy for the horse to run fast.'

'But that way I'll miss the soldiers. I have to meet them.'

Moorabi gazed about him, losing interest in the conversation. 'Who is the man down there?'

'Just another scout,' Jack said casually, suddenly remembering Kirk's mission. 'Thank you for the medicine and for bringing me downriver when I was sick. But there's a crocodile in that river. I could have been grabbed and eaten where you left me!'

Moorabi patted his horse's neck as if to placate it at the mention of the great enemy crocodile. 'No. That feller, he is new there, he come out of another river looking about for a mate.'

Kirk was spluttering with rage. 'My horse! Didn't you see? That painted savage was riding my horse! Why didn't you shoot him? Are you that stupid you didn't notice my saddle? It's the best tooled leather I could find!'

'Come on, we have to hurry.' Jack urged his horse into a gallop. Of course he'd noticed the saddle and bridle, and he'd guessed it might have been Kirk's, but who cared? He hadn't been inclined to pick a fight with Moorabi over it. Fair go. Kirk had let it wander off, so it was just his bad luck.

And now what to do? Head down to meet up with the Major or scale that hill and get to Clancy as soon as possible? No choice really. Clancy was the priority; this powder stuff might work.

The Inspector caught up with him as they began to climb the hill. 'Who was that blackfellow anyway? And what did he have to say?'

'He's a tribal bloke I know. And don't carry on about the horse. You lost it, he found it.'

'I never heard of blackfellows riding horses. Is he a chief or something?'

'Yes,' Jack lied, enjoying himself. 'A big chief, that one. He's a top-notcher. He let me have some medicine that could cure Clancy's fever.'

'Did he tell you where his war parties are?'

'No, but he said we could have safe passage over here.'

'So that means there are war parties round here still.'

'I don't know,' Jack said wearily.

'How long before we catch up with Ferrington? I don't feel safe just the two of us out here, no matter what the savage told you. We're probably riding straight into another ambush.'

To get away from Kirk and his questions, Jack took a side route to the craggy hilltop, and soon found himself looking down on another river valley, with, sure enough, a long flat stretch this side of the river that would take them to Clancy's camp by nightfall.

Moorabi nodded complacently as he watched them gallop away. Jack Drew was going exactly where Ilkepala wanted him to go, well away from the danger that was stalking the soldiers. It was only a small war party; Bussamarai liked to keep the main body of his warriors near him for a quick strike, like that success by the river.

'Will this powder cure the white man?' he'd asked Ilkepala, thinking it might only be a ruse to lure Jack Drew to safety, and the magic man was offended.

'Of course, unless the sick man is too far into his other life. I would not have Jack Drew think me a trickster. He is our best bridge over the gulf between white and black tribes; some day he might be useful.'

Had they known the large seeds littering the ground under these trees were the remnants of a good crop, Ferrington's men could have had a feast of the prized bunya nuts, but they rode on by, anxious to be through the gloomy pine forest and back to open country.

Kit was peering at an odd plant as he rode at the head of his troop . . . it was half tree, half fern, very odd . . . when he felt the jolt. Not pain, at first, just a heavy jolt that lifted him right out of the saddle before it dropped him across his horse's neck, and he was falling to the ground, clutching the reins, trying to hold the horse that, taking fright, plunged forward, dragging him with it.

The Sergeant saw the long spear lunge into the Major's back and wheeled his horse so fast that the thrower, dodging away, was taken by surprise as the animal bore down on him. A boot clipped him in the head and he reeled into a tree, but as he tried to stagger away, wiping blood from his eyes, he saw the horse coming back at him. He saw only that great horse, not the gun that was trained on him by the rider, who shot him and flew on past shouting: 'Dismount! Load up! Take cover. Tight here! Stay tight. Stick together.'

While he was shouting orders, the Sergeant kept his horse moving about in case there were more enemy spears in the wind, and he cantered up to hurry the two men who'd gone after the Major, now lying groaning, the spear embedded in his back.

'Get it out!' he yelled. 'Pull the bloody thing out, don't let it wave in the wind, making the wound worse.'

A soldier looked up at him, stricken. 'He's bleeding, Sarge. I don't want to hurt him no more.'

'Jesus!' Rapper urged the horse closer, leaned over, yanked the spear out and hurled it away. 'Now carry him back fast. Get him to cover.'

He collected their horses and brought them back to be hitched to trees with the others, roared at his waiting men to 'Look lively! Make a circle! Keep cover, keep close! There'll be more, so keep your eyes peeled.'

Sergeant Rapper was in his element. He was in command in a real battle situation, and they wouldn't find him wanting. No, sir. Not Tom Rapper. Let the bloody blackfellers come now and they'll get what-for! Regretfully, he climbed down from his horse – it felt good being up there, in charge – and strode over to the Major.

Already the two men had placed him down on a blanket readied by one of the others, and the Sergeant dropped down beside him.

'You'll be all right,' he said as Ferrington tried to speak. 'Just hang on. You got hit by a spear. I have to cut your jacket to have a look at it. And your shirt. You're bleeding a fair bit . . .'

He saw the Major nod, whether approval or simply understanding, he didn't know. He took his bayonet and sliced the clothes from the bloody mess, hissing at the men nearby to get swabs and bandages from the medicine box, and snarling at the others to 'Look out! Not in!'

'Keep watch, you bastards!' he muttered at them as he worked, relieved that the Major had gritted his teeth stoically, barely allowing himself more than a groan, though the jagged wound in his back was deep. All the time, though, the Sergeant was trying to work out what to do with him, finally coming to the conclusion that like it or not, Ferrington would have to ride. They couldn't take the chance of the attacker being a loner, nor could they sit in the forest waiting for a full-scale raid that could easily happen now.

But which way to go? Keep on or turn back? The Major didn't turn back when Clancy went down; he said they had a job to do.

He leaned down to Ferrington. 'We can't stay here. I can give you some rest for a while, but you're gonna have to ride, Major. Do you think you can do it?'

Ferrington sighed, his face twisted in pain, then he took a deep breath. 'Yes.'

'Orders were to go on. Right?'

Again: 'Yes.'

'Then we'll get out of this forest, out into the open, and I'll find a safe place for you.' He sat back on his haunches. 'Well, we found what we were looking for, didn't we? And I got the blackie who speared you.'

Ferrington nodded. 'Good. Water . . . could I have some water?'

The blackfellers were out there; because the horses were so spooked, they were dragging at their straps and milling about nervously. Watching them, Rapper knew they had to vacate this spot before dark, when the blacks would be able to creep up on them, which was why they probably hadn't attacked already.

So we have to go on the attack, he told himself. We're here to get rid of the buggers after all. If I'm wrong, and we're all alone here, no harm done; if I'm right, we have to give 'em a fight first up.

Quietly he addressed his men, feeling good, feeling like Wellington, he was that proud, and put them at the ready until he had carried out the hard business: getting the Major, who was a big bloke, on to his horse with as little hurt as they could manage, and setting him there with one of the men detailed to mount up and stick by him.

The order Rapper gave was not to sneak away but to charge, to hurl their horses out of this place, firing their guns into the bush around them. So, quietly, they slid on to their horses, and at the Sergeant's shout they were off. Startled tribesmen who, they discovered, had them surrounded, obviously waiting for nightfall as Rapper had guessed, sprang up from their cover when bullets slammed about them, screaming as random shots found marks and twenty horsemen thundered over those who couldn't get out of their way in time, trampling them unmercifully.

They were cleared of the threat of attack now, but Rapper wasn't finished. He shouted, 'Turn!' and his troops knew what to do. Two men rode on with the Major, the others wheeled about and charged again, this time at the blackfellers who'd chased after them, and who were dropping back to yell their frustration, but without cover now, taking the full force of disciplined troops armed with shot and steel.

Some managed to escape, but after the attack Rapper's men counted fifteen dead tribesmen, while their own tally was a leg wound from a spear that had lost its momentum too soon. They rode away from the scene of the fight and caught up with the Major just as he and his two aides had reached the outskirts of the forest and were entering open country.

Rapper borrowed the Major's compass and set a course due north, eventually sheltering, before dusk, in a cluster of huge boulders that gave them cover and a good view of the surrounding plain. This, Sergeant Rapper decided, after he found a spring running from a nearby rocky outcrop, would be his headquarters. But first things first.

As soon as the men had Ferrington bedded down in his tent, Rapper took him a mug of hot tea, and squatted beside him.

'It's bad luck having to lie on that side all the time,' he said. 'Can I get you something to prop you up a bit? A blanket, eh?'

'I would appreciate that,' the Major groaned. 'My back feels damp. Is it still bleeding?'

'Could be, after bumping about on the horse, but I don't want to lift the dressing yet. I put antiseptic on the wound so it should be all right, but I think leave well alone, what do you reckon?'

'The pain subsides a little if I lie still. I'd rather not disturb it.'

'Good. We're camping here tonight, it's safe, so you get a good sleep.

Pity Clancy finished off his grog before he got sick, you could have used a shot or two now.'

He left the tent and strode round the camp checking everything from the horses and their hobbles to equipment and weapons, before he would allow meals to be prepared.

'This is the procedure every night from now on,' he told the men, 'and no one gets a feed until everything is in tip-top shape. This will be our base until I say different. And see here, a lot of you blokes are farm boys. I want you to keep an eye out for plant food . . .'

'Like what?' someone asked, and Rapper roared at him:

'Like I don't bloody know, but you find some. The blackfellers live here, none of those bodies I saw looked starved. We can get meat easy enough, kangaroos, bush turkeys, plenty of game, but there has to be stuff growing.'

'I grabbed some of those berries lying about this morning,' a soldier called. 'I ate them, they're pretty good.'

'You could have poisoned yourself,' someone said, but he laughed.

'I don't think the good Lord would make poison taste that good.'

'And you didn't think to get more for your mates?' Rapper bellowed. 'Now listen to me, anyone who brings back growing stuff that we can eat will be in line for promotion. Now build up that fire and get the grub going. I'm starving.'

They made loaves of damper using the last of the flour mixed with water and a handful of currants, and Rapper flapped the empty flour bag at them to make his point about the necessity to gather edible vegetation.

'Don't be thinking we're turning back just because the rations are almost done,' he said, and was tempted to add "thanks to Lieutenant Clancy's miscalculations". 'Because we're not. Every man is expected to forage the same as any army does on the march. There's grub here; find it or starve.'

The Major was in agony, his side on fire. He called for help and a young soldier came.

'Who are you?' he asked weakly.

'Billy Freeman, sir. The Sergeant said I'm to be your sentry.'

'Tell the Sergeant I want to see him.'

'Can't do that, he's gone out on patrol. There's only me here.'

Kit lay still for a while, preferring help from the rough sergeant than that of this sprat, but in the end he had to ask.

'Would you help me up? I have to go outside to relieve myself.'

'To what?'

'Help me up!' Kit snapped, and bit his tongue as the move to climb up from his ground bedding sent more pain shooting through his body. He couldn't recall when he had ever before experienced such agony, and prayed that it would stop, begged God in silent, teeth-clenched prayers, to put a stop to it, but He had no pity, and when he stumbled back with the lad, he asked to be laid down on his stomach.

'What about some tea? We kept some damper for you. You should have that first while you're up.'

Kit was too dizzy with the pain to care any more, so he handed himself over to his aide and passed out.

They were riding in formation, four abreast, uniforms buttoned, caps on straight, bandoliers slung across shoulders, gleaming with cartridges, and rifles in the light holsters by their knees. Even their boots were polished. They looked dangerous, Rapper thought, and he liked that. He urged his horse into a canter and began a methodical search for campfires. Black-fellers' campfires. He didn't know where they were, but at least he could see where they'd been and work from there.

Bussamarai heard about the loss of so many good men in the bunya-bunya forest and mourned. Now doubt plagued him. He had said they could carry out raids against the white men without having to go up against guns, but this time it hadn't worked. Though surrounded and outnumbered, the soldiers had gone on the attack so unexpectedly that the guns were able to do their vicious work.

Some of his men were beginning to lose heart in this fight anyway. Pleased with their win against the crocodile eyes, and with the sweet taste of revenge, quite a few had retreated to their new camps further north, where they could resume normal lives. They argued that the whites would be back and would settle in eventually, so why not give way now and be done with it?

'That's not the point,' Bussamarai had said, over and over again. 'We own this land. If the whites want it they must fight for it. Have you no self-respect? Would you just walk away and say take it, take our food, our sacred places, just take, please yourselves. No! No! Don't be fooled into thinking they won't chase you off your new lands, because they will. It's only a matter of time . . .'

Sadly, they knew that too. They understood what was happening but they wanted to enjoy life while they could, live with their wives and children and explore the new lands with the permission of the tribes that had taken them in.

An elder explained harshly: 'They do not seek death.'

Enraged, Bussamarai ordered him from the camps. Expelled him from Tingum country, risking severe retribution, but the ancient one merely looked at him sorrowfully and tramped away.

This brought Ilkepala to his *gunyah* a few days later, trailed by several women.

'What are they doing here?' the war chief demanded.

'They are travelling through to be with their menfolk.'

Bussamarai turned on the woman leading the group. 'Go back. You are not wanted here.'

213

'Our sons and our husbands need us,' she said sternly. 'I want to see that my sons are properly fed, and you can't stop me.' With that she marched away, and the other women padded nervously after her, but the chief let them go.

'They're not the only ones,' Ilkepala told him. 'There are women in a lot of the camps here now, just to forage for the men while they await your orders. Will there be a corroboree for the people to sing their grief over the dead warriors?'

'No.'

Bussamarai would give no explanation for that unusual decision. It was an order, that was all. His reasons, though, were plain to Ilkepala, who thought it best, given the chief's present ill temper, not to voice them. The magic man knew a meeting of all the warriors would present an opportunity for this disquiet to spread, infecting the many who were still eager to fight.

'What do you plan now?' he asked.

'That is for me to know,' Bussamarai said angrily, because in fact he did not yet know. The soldiers were still moving north at a snail's pace, so he had time to plan a raid that would eliminate them and yet not cost him any more casualties. He hadn't told Ilkepala that for every one of the fifteen men killed, two or three were leaving, and that was very worrying.

'What about the guns?' Bussamarai turned to his friend Nungulla. 'It is urgent now that your spy returns our generosity in freeing him.'

Nungulla shivered. 'The spy was seen riding south but he seemed not to know where the soldiers were, which is understandable; they were in different war parties.'

'Then he should be given guidance.'

'This was agreed upon, but then he could not be found.'

'What do you mean?'

'He disappeared.'

Nungulla suffered the humiliation of the abuse that his leader heaped on him, before members of their inner circle, with his head down, for he dared not look up in case that magic man could read the rest of the news from his face.

There were only a few of his men left in that southern area. Most of them had become bored, lost interest in a job that was a waste of time, watching bush tracks empty of travellers, and so they'd quit. Nungulla deemed it safer to say the spy had disappeared than admit his own men had let him escape. As for the others, trailing the soldiers, they had reported that these troops were a gentle lot, just riding their horses along at an easy pace, stopping for games at the riverbanks. They weren't like the crocodile eyes who had killed and hanged one of the scouts, and who rode hard searching for prey. Everyone was mightily relieved when Bussamarai wiped them out. But . . . the scouts trailing the soldiers had joined up with the small war party for some excitement. And – Nungulla dreaded having to repeat the latest bit of information that had come to him – they had told the leader of the war party that the soldiers were easy prey. Not like warriors at all.

They'd found out, too late, that it wasn't true. The soldiers had fought like sharks, turning on them, teeth bared!

They'd collected their dead and brought them back, so right now there was no information from that area. The soldiers hadn't been seen since then, and he hoped Bussamarai wouldn't ask exactly where they were. Nungulla had no idea. As a matter of fact, he was thinking seriously of defecting, of going back to his young sons, who had a great need of their father to protect them and teach them the ways of the new clans they had encountered.

Sergeant Rapper and his men had wasted no time searching the bush to their north and had already come upon two recent campfires. He insisted that his 'farm boys' examine the immediate areas to work out what the blacks had been eating. They found charred animal bones that were of no interest to Rapper, but then they came across leftover berries, shells from nuts, and pieces of a tuberous plant akin to sweet potato.

'There you are!' he crowed. 'You live and learn. Now we know how to raid the blackies' pantry, and I'll bet there's a lot more besides. But down to business. We're going after this little party, so mount up. We've got work to do.'

Stragglers from the decimated war party were still nursing their grief when they came upon the shepherd's hut, that symbol of the white man's temerity in building houses on Tingum land without permission, even a small structure like this. Soon the hut was ablaze, and for good measure a wild pig was slaughtered and thrown on to the fire. It sizzled and spluttered and the delicious aroma of fat crackling skin drifted into the air with the smoke and wafted through the crisp scrub. Dingoes sniffed the air and set off at a trot for the source. To small animals like wallabies and bandicoots and wombats, smoke was danger, and they scurried away. A hawk, its wings rust-red against the blue sky, hovered inquisitively, while bold currawongs flew down to observe proceedings and, hopefully, steal a morsel or two.

Others saw the smoke. Tingum men in the hills knew the smell of old timber and laughed. It was about time somebody burned down that eyesore.

An eagle-eyed soldier saw the smoke, called to the Sergeant and pointed. Rapper nodded, and he too pointed, leading his mounted troops in that direction, waving them forward with a twirl of his arm and a large flat hand indicating quiet.

By the time they were spotted in the bush, the naked blackfellows were hanging over that campfire, poking at the half-cooked pig, eagerly awaiting a meal, and Rapper couldn't blame them; he too was salivating at the smell of roasting pork so close to them.

But he couldn't afford to waste any time. The blackies might hear them any minute, so it was cut and dash. Now! Straight at them, guns firing, surrounding them, lashing out, a fight of shots and grunts and yells and horses neighing in consternation at the suddenness of it all, then silence and heat. It was hot in that little clearing, from the spitting fire, from the sun, from the sweat of men and horses. Dingoes dived through the thud of hooves to try to grab some of the bounty, but were driven back by the heat. One body lay in the fire and a young soldier, sickened, dismounted and pulled it out, dragging it over to lie beside two of its comrades. Then, recovering, he looked about with an embarrassed grin.

'Another win, eh, Sarge?'

Rapper dismounted, walked around the still smouldering ruin, pushed at the chimney with his boot, took a discarded spear and jabbed at the roasting pig.

'Who'd want to live in an isolated place like this?' he muttered. 'It'd be bloody asking for trouble.'

There had only been six men at this feast, and they'd got them all. A good day's work, he concluded, and ordered his men to carry the bodies far into the bush and dump them.

'We can't have them stinking up the place while we take our share of the spoils of war,' he grinned. 'Roast pig for lunch. But leave some for the Major and the lad back at the post.'

Nevertheless, he rostered the diners carefully. Eight men on guard at all times while the others ate. Rapper wasn't about to make the same mistake as his victims.

For two days Jack nursed Clancy, administering the white powder as directed, happy to see the fever subside and the Lieutenant, though weak, able to take a little food, and all the time Kirk complained bitterly.

'I demand to be escorted back to Brisbane. You can spare that soldier. Give us some rations and we'll leave.'

'Trooper Sutcliffe is under orders from Ferrington to stay here with the Lieutenant. I don't have any say-so about it and neither do you. If you want to go home, no one's stopping you.'

'You deliberately steered me away from the Major and his party so that I can't get back and report the massacre of my men. A massacre that I think you set up!'

'I did what? You were happy to come straight here.'

'You gave me no choice. Too busy helping the blacks.'

Jack bent down, grabbed a snake from the undergrowth and hurled it at him, laughing as Kirk ran screaming into the bush, trying to untangle himself from the reptile. Then, when he returned still shouting abuse at him, Jack produced another snake.

'Do you want this one too?' he called, holding the squirming reptile up by its tail.

Kirk jumped back in fright, and Jack stormed over to him.

'If you open your trap at me again you'll get one of these snakes. Now go away and shut up.'

Another day went past, and Clancy was stronger.

'I'm indebted to you, Jack, and your blackfellow mate. I won't forget your kindness, but I think me and Sutcliffe out there have to get going.'

'Back to Brisbane?'

'No fear. I'm well enough to stay on a horse. I must report to the Major. You wouldn't be inclined to be our guide, would you? I could never find the squad on my own.'

For that matter, Jack hadn't reached his goal either. He had no intention of returning, having come this far, without searching the ruins of Montone Station for his gold, so he agreed to lead them north the following morning.

But when Inspector Kirk heard of their plans, he berated the Lieutenant mercilessly, demanding that he be escorted back to civilisation. He argued that Clancy wasn't well enough to carry on, he claimed Jack Drew would get them all murdered, he insisted that Ferrington wouldn't be expecting them, so to follow was pointless, but all to no avail. Clancy was adamant. He had his orders.

'What about me?' Kirk wailed. 'You can't expect me to go on!'

'I'm sorry, Inspector. You'll have to ride with us.'

'I will not!'

'Then go!' Jack said. 'Get on to stock routes and follow them back.'

'They'll be wiped out by the rain.'

'No they won't. Just keep your eyes open for a change.'

Kirk hung about the camp all afternoon, trying to decide what to do, but in the end, heading for Brisbane, even alone, still seemed the safer alternative.

'You'll hear more of this,' he warned Jack in the morning. 'I'll get back and report you as a spy. You're not a white man, you're a half-caste bastard. I saw you talking to the enemy; don't forget that, because I won't. You could have taken my horse back but you let that savage have it . . . I'm laying charges against you as soon as I get back. I'll have you locked up the minute you show your nose . . .'

Jack had had enough of his ranting. He picked up the slush bucket that the trooper had been using to wash the cooking utensils, hurled the greasy contents at the Inspector, and snapped at him:

'I should have left you in that hut, you mongrel.'

They had expected on their return to the headquarters late in the afternoon that the Major would be feeling a little better, but he was not, and Rapper guessed the wound was infected.

He made a great to-do about this misfortune, dressing the wound himself, and going to great lengths to make his patient as comfortable as possible, but in fact he was delighted. He could hardly keep his joy from

217

showing, because he was still the boss, the leader, the commander of the troops. And hadn't he done well? Better than the two officers put together. He'd engaged the enemy twice and won. He couldn't wait to write up his report in Ferrington's journal. He thought it might be a bit of a cheek, but so what? Ferrington wasn't capable, someone had to keep a record of their progress. He would also report that he'd done his best to give aid to the Major by trying to keep the wound clean, but it needed stitching, he was sure, and what to do about that? Rapper was truly concerned; he discussed the problem with his men and could only come up with a remedy of tight bandaging, which was of little use around the Major's broad back. In the mean time he forbade the men to touch the blue bottle that contained the precious antiseptic, no matter what minor cuts and abrasions they had suffered. It had to be kept for the Major, and him alone.

The next morning he led his troops out into the field again. He had advised the Major that he could be away overnight this time, depending on circumstances, because according to his calculations, they were within striking distance of the Montone boundaries. The maps showed the terrain there was good open country with undulating hills, excellent grazing land of course, and the river they would encounter was the Mary River. Since no land had, so far, been taken past this point, as long as the blacks had been chased out of this area, the troops could turn back.

Privately, Rapper thought the expedition a bit of a swindle on behalf of the powers-that-be, to shut the settlers up and send them back to the farms, because what if they did kill blackfellers and chase the rest out of the way? What was to stop them coming back as soon as the soldiers left? Nothing. Nothing except the settlers themselves. He reckoned they'd be fighting it out for years. Not that anyone listened to him . . . But he had a job to do, like the Major said. And soldiering was a good job. Down here in the Antipodes you weren't up against guns and cannon like they were in Europe. Rapper had already planned to quit the military when his regiment was ordered home to England, and was thinking about what he might do then. This gold prospecting didn't sound too bad at all. Even the Major was more interested in that field than fighting.

Once again he had his squad riding in formation whenever possible. The loss of Inspector Kirk's Native Police was a good lesson, and Rapper was mindful of the dangers ahead, but he wanted the blackies to know the soldiers were serious now, and to take the hint: get the hell out and save everyone a lot of trouble!

They passed the burned-out hut and rode on to the ruins of the Grosvenor Station, knowing this was where the Native Police had got themselves cornered, so they didn't dally. Instead they raced further north, until Rapper ordered a halt beside a small creek, and immediately had the men dig in. Within an hour their perimeter was well protected by short trenches and once again his men were rostered for guard duty.

It was Bussamarai's move. He was still wary of the guns, delaying a decision, but his men were complaining that they should either fight or leave.

'They're saying we've been waiting for the soldiers,' Nungulla told him. 'And now they're here, so why don't we attack? We still have twice as many men as they have.'

'Is that all?' Bussamarai was shocked. 'We should have more than that. Many more! Where are they?'

'Gone home for a little while,' Nungulla said edgily.

'Gone home? Call themselves warriors? I should have brought their women instead,' he shouted angrily. 'And you say nothing to the belly-achers! I do not answer to them and I do not explain to them. If any man has a complaint, let him come to me himself.'

His inability to think of a plan was infuriating him, so he called to his favourites to join him in the river to cool off, and afterwards had them dress his thick hair into a topknot with wet clay and paint his face and body with white daubs, denoting his rank. He then added his prized possessions – two massive teeth that had belonged to giant animals of the Dreamtime, far too large to have belonged to any living today, setting them in his hair to resemble horns.

Stuck in the clay between the two horns, to draw more attention to them, was the gleaming yellow stone that he'd found at the same time, way up in the Gimpi Gimpi hills. Ilkepala had said the stone was gold, the stuff Jack Drew was always going on about, and they'd had a good laugh about that.

'Maybe he'll want to fight me for it?' Bussamarai chortled.

So. That filled in time. He decided to meditate on the problem and let the spirits have a chance to bring a solution, as had happened so many times before.

The news was bad. Six more men killed by the soldiers. Shot! Those guns again.

'I told you so,' he shouted at Nungulla. 'How many times do I have to tell them to keep away from the white men's guns?'

Nungulla shrugged. 'The soldiers have passed by the place they called Montone.'

'Where are they headed?'

'I don't know.'

'Well find out!' their chief shouted.

A few hours later, Nungulla returned to report that they were making camp by Warrul Creek, and Bussamarai sprang to his feet.

'Come,' he shouted. 'Let us go now and view the white warriors.'

By the time they arrived, observing from a distant hill, he was told that the intruders had dug holes outside their campfire, cooked meat that smelled like birds and were just talking.

'Why the holes?' Bussamarai asked suspiciously.

'I will discover,' a volunteer said, and raced away, but the chief hardly noticed. He was depressed, knowing the soldiers had chosen the camp site wisely. Then he said: 'Where did that man go? Tell him to come back. It is obvious. The holes in the ground are for shooting places.' The concept was new to him, since a man would have to stand back to throw a spear or a boomerang, but a gun needed no force, so he guessed he was right.

Then a shot rang out, clipping the air so suddenly that they jerked back as if they themselves were the targets.

Instead, a man crawling forward through the undergrowth to get a better view of the enemy camp was shot in the head by the sentry dug in on the western side.

All six of his sentries began firing then, and Rapper shouted abuse at them, demanding they save ammunition.

'There's no ammo store out here! Just lie low now and see what happens next.'

'I said to call that man back,' Bussamarai said sadly.

'We did,' someone answered. 'That wasn't him, it was somebody else.'

'That means we can't go at them in the daylight,' Nungulla sighed.

'Night is a risk too! Don't you understand? I don't want anyone to be killed.'

'Then you've lost your heart for war,' Nungulla said angrily, 'because that *is* war.'

Bussamarai stood defiantly, scanning the area, his face grim, but inside, deep inside, he was trembling.

Was this right? Surely not? Surely not! He was just trying to be wise, to be cunning, to win this battle his way.

In the end, against his better judgement, he had to give the order to attack that night, with the moon flitting from cloud to cloud, casting light on the assault as if to get a better view of Bussamarai racing ahead of his men.

Spears flew, stones thudded, guns cracked, men leapt at the soldiers who were kneeling to fire, and were caught by shots from the trench snipers. Many a heavy spear found its mark, lobbing among the defenders, but the soldiers stood their ground and the attackers fell back into the darkness. A sullen quiet settled over the night, broken eventually by the shuffles and whispers of the men whose duty it was to retrieve bodies, aid the wounded and take score.

Rapper had two dead and four men wounded, and he was furious, his pride severely dented. He'd begun to believe that this squad, under his command, was invincible.

Bussamarai suffered the loss of eight men, and some slightly grazed by bullets, which told him the soldiers were well trained in the use of their guns. Most of his warriors had never even seen a soldier before. They understood they were white warriors but had not grasped their accuracy with guns, especially in darkness. Bussamarai looked at his men, grouped miserably around their campfires, too shaken to sleep, and he scowled. Now they knew!

'I suppose you'll want to attack again as soon as the sun comes up?' he roared. 'Anyone stupid enough to want to do that can go now. The rest of you will have to put aside the mourning. Nungulla needs a lot of men to keep the soldiers in; men who will stay alert this time. So you mob there, get down to him now. The rest of you, I want that hard string they call wire, that makes fences. There is plenty still in the fences close to the burned house. Get it all and bring it to me!'

'Why is this?' a man asked.

'So their horses can't get out. They make fences to keep them in. With their wire we can do that too. Fix it from tree to tree, thus we have them surrounded. Go there now and be quick! That soldier boss will want to get his men out as soon as he can, like last time.'

They had water, some food, and there would be more to be found in that creek, Rapper was sure. He had bought mussels and other shellfish from blackfellers in Brisbane after seeing them fossick in Breakfast Creek. A basketful for a penny was good buying, and you got the woven basket thrown in. He always ate his fill and sold the rest, including the basket, for which he charged a halfpenny. Rapper picked up a waterbag and took a long drink, noticing a beehive in a tree overhead. Fortunately the native bees didn't sting, but this was no time to be bothering about honey. He examined the wounded men, now lying in a hollow by the creek bank, and ordered two of them on their feet.

'They're only flesh wounds, you'll live. But stay here and look after your mates. Bertie here's badly injured, he got speared in the chest, and Pratt, he's broken his leg. I've set it as best I could . . .'

One of the men interrupted him: 'My arm's still bleeding, them spearheads is bloody sharp!'

'Keep it bound,' the Sergeant snapped, but the other man, who had a shoulder wound, was more concerned about Bertie and Pratt.

'What will happen to them? They can't ride. How will they get out of here?'

'If the Major can ride, they can. Now get them water and try to keep them cool.'

He left abruptly rather than have to discuss this subject. They could get Pratt on to a horse, but Bertie? Rapper shook his head, worried.

Later in the morning a sentry whistled to him. 'Look there, Sarge, is that a rope between those two trees?'

'Looks like it. Or twine, something like that.' But it was strung very tightly, so it couldn't have been there last night. He turned away and, keeping low, called to the next sentry. 'Do you see any ropes strung between trees?'

'Ropes! What ropes?'

'Look again.'

The sentry was quiet, and then he called: 'By cripes. Yeah. Wire! There's wire strung all over the bloody place. What the hell is that about?'

'Work it out,' Rapper snarled, and went back to the creek.

That exit was closed also. He could see the makeshift fence on the far side of the creek, while on the other side of them, saplings dumped in the creek itself made a barrier that was too difficult for the horses to jump.

So, he worried, unless we can get out there and cut the wires, the horses are boxed in! Rapper wasn't one to panic, but his heart was thumping as he went among his men, ordering them to keep down. Cutting the wires wouldn't be easy, they'd be sitting shots. But it would have to be done, sooner or later. He'd have to ask for volunteers.

In the meantime, he could do with this delay to make a decision about Bertie. He shuddered, unwilling to face that prospect.

He wondered, idly, where the scout, Jack Drew, had got to, and if he'd found Inspector Kirk. And that reminded him of the Major. When he didn't return on schedule, the Major, in normal circumstances, would raise the alarm. But here in the back of beyond, there was no one to turn to. No bloody troops anywhere.

'Where's Sergeant Rapper?' the Major asked when his sentry peered in.

'He's out on patrol, sir.'

'Already? It's only just dawn!' He jerked back in pain. 'Oh God! This bloody wound, it's giving me hell.'

'I'm sorry, sir. What can I do? About the wound?'

'Nothing. I just have to put up with it.'

'They didn't come back last night, sir. The Sergeant said they might be a day or so and we're to stay here and wait for him.'

'A day or so? When did they go?'

'Two days ago, sir. They'll probably be back today. They were only going to the line marked on the map and back, so we should have them here soon.'

Kit lay on his side, trying to piece things together. He remembered the Sergeant coming in crowing about a successful raid on a mob of blacks, and that was good news, though he had noticed a bit of extra bragging aimed at his own failure to engage the enemy. Not that Kit cared. The way he felt right now, Rapper could wipe out a whole Aborigine tribe if he wished. He still couldn't believe he'd actually been speared! Nor how much his bloody wound hurt. He cursed himself for allowing Sir Charles to push him into this in the first place, and determined that as soon as he got back he'd resign the military once and for all, even if it meant losing his pension. Nothing was worth all this.

'Would you like some tea, sir?'

'Yes, please. What's your name?'

'Freeman, sir. You're looking much better this morning.'

'Feeling better too. Though I think I lost a couple of days.'

'Don't think you'll miss them, sir.'

'Who else is here?'

'Just us, sir,' Freeman said as he dipped under the tent flap and went about his business.

'Good God!' Kit exclaimed. He had never felt so vulnerable in his life. Just the two of them? Him and that young fellow with fluff on his chin. He struggled up, puffing at the exertion, needing to dress, knowing he'd feel a lot safer if he had his breeches and a shirt on, and his revolver close to hand.

'Freeman,' he called. 'Give me a hand here! And tell me, where is Jack Drew?'

Jack Drew and Lieutenant Clancy were riding north, searching for the Major and his squad. Jack decided to camp on high ground, at one of his favourite lookouts, where he hoped to catch sight of them, and Clancy was impressed with the view.

'Look at that now! All them trees like a deep carpet and that sky so pink and lovely. It's such a peaceful spot, it is.'

'Give it a half-hour and look again. It might not look so peaceful.'

'Why is that?'

The half-hour to darkness revealed the lights of campfires on the far hill.

'There they are. Your blackfellers, Clancy. Somewhere around Montone Station. If we can catch up with Ferrington, you should tell him you've come far enough. Once he gets that message, I reckon he'll agree. No point in looking for trouble.'

Clancy stared at the pinpoints of light. 'How many tribesmen would there be?'

'Plenty. And they're not sitting there for fun. They're waiting for you.'

'But we have to chase them off these properties, Jack. If we don't, what will happen to the settlers?'

'Stay home if they have any sense,' Jack said sourly.

'We'd have to tell them the blacks are still here if we turn back, and admit we failed in our mission.'

'Then they will stay home.'

'You don't understand, we have our duty . . .'

'So have they. Their chief can't back off, he'd lose face too.'

'Who is this chief? Do you know him?'

'Light a fire, Clancy. I'll find some grub.'

'Is it safe to light a fire?'

'Might as well. Keep an eye out for the Major's camp somewhere out there.'

Chapter Thirteen

There was talk of gold in the back blocks that were much more accessible since the establishment of the port of Brisbane. The pastoralists were anxious to return to their huge estates west of the port, for fear other squatters like themselves would claim their land. Until such time as the government surveyors were able to keep pace with the rush of settlers, it was a case of first come, first served; take up or squat on as much land as you wished and legalise the boundaries at a later date.

'All very well,' the pastoralists were now complaining, 'but we're not only having to deal with Aborigines, we now have to contend with settlers coveting our properties.'

The argument held little sway with the government. Down there in Sydney, more than five hundred miles from the disputed lands, Sir Charles FitzRoy felt he had done his best by sending troops to assist. He passed the complaints on to Parliament, where they triggered a move to limit the size of graziers' runs, the accepted name for pasturelands.

This sudden turn of events sent shock waves through the wealthy Pastoralist Association, and members were advised, in the absence of fencing, impossible on such huge properties, to mark their boundaries clearly via blazed trees and well-positioned signs.

All of these matters had the residents of Brisbane in a restless state, needing to know how much longer people would have to wait for the authorities to issue the all-clear.

Superintendent Jimmy Grimes could only advise patience until the police and military squads returned. Only then could he give the word that the countryside was safe. As it was, he could not do anything to stop people travelling. 'No law against going out there and getting plugged by a spear,' he shrugged. 'But they won't want to come crying to me.'

In the meantime, small farmers had begun to trickle out with their families into the lush surrounds of the town, and settlements, later to become suburbs, were springing up in all directions.

Baker's Crossing was prospering. The store now boasted a post office, as well as a stock and station agency, which served as a bank depot every third Monday. It all seemed to have happened overnight, as Ceb Baker himself was proud to say.

'One minute we're here at the end of the line, if you don't count them big cattlemen, next minute there's farms further on for miles and miles. Folk just leapfrogging on from one holding to the next. We had to smarten up, start getting more goods in, I can tell you. And that meant most of the folk living here already don't have to go right into town any more. Baker's Crossing will never look back, I tell you. We're doing all right, we are . . .'

It was one of those settlers, a poor farmer working hard with his wife and daughter, clearing their block so they could get a crop in as soon as possible, who saw the bedraggled fellow, coming down the track on a lame horse, and ran to help him.

It was the same settler who brought Inspector Kirk in to Baker's Crossing on his wagon, anxious to be first with the awful news that savages had massacred the whole squad of Native Mounted Police.

Kirk was exhausted, surprised that he had managed to find his way back to civilisation somehow. For days he gratefully accepted the hospitality of Ceb Baker, and the awe of people anxious to hear, first hand, the terrifying account, a tale that they would be able to tell their children and grand-children in the years to come. Of how they, as pioneer farmers, had to live among savages in the hard fight to put bread on their tables. They could tell, too, of the bravery of Inspector Rollo Kirk, whom they actually met, and whose hand they shook, a man who single-handedly fought two savages to get his horse, when his men had panicked and run down to the river, there to meet their deaths. Once on the horse, he'd escaped . . . ridden through the enemy lines, using a discarded spear like a lance to ward of a huge fellow who tried to drag him down. He'd ridden hard for a while, turned about to search for survivors, finding none, had made his desperate way back to civilisation, a difficult task as he often found himself riding in circles.

The poor man was starved. They fed him the very best fare and saw him well rested before Ceb Baker himself took him to town in his dray, the lame horse loping along behind.

Wally came home by a different route. He made for the coast and kept it in view, knowing he couldn't help but tumble upon the big town sooner or later. He came through the original settlement of Redcliffe that had been abandoned for the better site of Brisbane Town, on through Petrie, where some looked askance at a blackfeller on a horse, but thought him to be a stockman perhaps. He stopped at Breakfast Creek to have a yarn with blackfellers, who kindly gave him a good feed, not realising he was one of the dreaded Native Mounted Police, since he'd long discarded the uniform jacket. Wally thought that was pretty funny.

A determined man, though, he rode right into Brisbane, right to police headquarters before he spoke to any whities, for fear they'd belt him and take his horse.

The constable on duty stared as the blackfellow marched in the door. He was bare-chested, barefoot, with dark trousers hanging on skinny hips. The heavily whiskered face was as dark and leathery as a mask.

'Get out of here!' he shouted, diving around the desk to add push to his words. 'Get the hell out!'

But the blackfellow resisted. 'Doan you touch me, mister. I want the boss.'

'Well the boss don't want you. Now about turn and shove off.'

The arm he grabbed was like steel, and the skinny black body might have been cemented to the floor for all the good his shoving did, and he stumbled angrily, calling for help to remove or, by this time, jail the intruder.

'What's going on?' Inspector Tomkins was about to wind up his day's work and head for the National Hotel's saloon bar for a drink with Sam Dignam.

'Mounted Police, sir,' the blackfellow yelled. 'Inspector Kirk and them blokes allasame dead.'

'What?' the constable and Tomkins responded as one.

Tomkins, an obliging man, acted as secretary, taking down Trooper Wally Faith's report as told to Superintendent Grimes. He made notes as they went over the story again, question and answer, but it appeared that the whole of the squad was lost in the ambush. Wally had managed to swim downriver and find a horse for the ride of his life before the tribesmen could catch him, but he hadn't seen any of his comrades again.

'Did you search for them? To see if there was anyone you could help?' Grimes asked, and Wally was taken aback.

'Me? No fear. They all bloody dead.'

'What about Major Ferrington and his men? Where were they?'

'They follow. Supposed to follow, but me I never seen them.'

'You didn't find them on your return journey?'

'No. I get out of that district bloody fast. Cross over to the sea side and come down that track. Safer over this here side.'

'So they wouldn't be warned of what happened to your comrades.'

Wally shrugged. The questions went on and on, annoying him. And it mightn't be a good time to tell them that the Major was being tailed all the way by the tribesmen. As it was, he'd chosen a safe track home rather than warn the Major, knowing he'd miss out on a reward for the information. But there was, he decided, a better chance of a reward here, before he went bush once and for all.

'This all good information, eh?'

'Yes,' Grimes said. 'Very sad, very sad.'

'Then I get a present for bringing the information eh?'

'A present? What sort of present?'

226

'Shillings. We get good shillings for information.'

'Yes, I suppose so,' Grimes agreed. 'You've had a dreadful experience. The constable will take you back to your barracks and get you fitted out with a new uniform.'

'Better shillings and a feed first.'

'All right,' Grimes said, digging out two shillings. 'You can find something to eat at the barracks.'

'Do you believe him?' Grimes asked Tomkins.

'We have to. For the time being. There'll be hell to pay over this disaster! He doesn't seem too concerned about the fate of his comrades, or Inspector Kirk, does he?'

Grimes nodded. 'Given their own reputation for murder and mayhem, I'm not surprised that a little thing like having their mates killed doesn't bother those blokes. I thought Kirk was mad to take on the job in the first place, but he was all gung-ho about the show, poor fellow.'

Sam Dignam stuck his head round the door. 'What's this I hear about a raid? Word has it in the pub that one of the Native Police is back in town under arrest. I saw him walking past the pub with Constable Brown. What's going on?'

The Superintendent asked him to come in and shut the door. 'We have extremely bad news but we can't release it until we have a word with Mrs Kirk.'

'Rollo Kirk's wife? Why? Has he been hurt?'

'Worse than that, I'm afraid. They were ambushed by blacks. The fellow you saw with Brown isn't under arrest, he's the only survivor.'

'Holy hell! They were all killed?'

'As far as we know. We only have that trooper's word, Sam, so I'd go easy on this . . .'

'But I could write "feared lost", couldn't I? And the paper won't be out until the morning, so you've got plenty of time to speak with Mrs Kirk.' He tipped his hat to Tomkins: 'Forgive me, Inspector, I'll have to skip that drink. I want to talk to that Native Trooper, and take the cameraman with me. That's all right, isn't it, Jimmy?'

The Superintendent couldn't see any reason to hold back on the news, so Sam disappeared and the other two men remained, discussing the report and worrying about the Major and his men.

'They should have been on hand to back up Kirk's men,' Grimes said. 'I don't know what to make of this. But we'd better get over and prepare Mrs Kirk before she gets wind of it herself.'

Rollo Kirk's return was not what he had expected. He saw himself the centre of attention, just as he had been at Baker's Crossing, the bearer of awesome news, the sole survivor struggling back to civilisation.

People stared as he came into town on Ceb's dray, and squinted at him.

He did look a bit different, he had to admit, from the clean-shaven, spick and span inspector who had ridden proudly with his troops, now dressed in a borrowed check shirt and moleskins, and featuring a rough sandy beard. This he'd retained for effect, not even allowing the folks at Baker's Crossing to give it a trim; it lent a true picture of how he'd had to survive out in the bush. And as well, he'd lost weight, the fat had fair fallen off him with all the riding and starvation rations, a shock to a man used to four good meals a day.

He waved, sadly, and pointed ahead to his destination, the police station, while they nudged each other, confused.

Someone shouted, 'Good on yer, Rollo,' and he acknowledged it grandly, but then they were laughing, smiling, cheering him, and it was all wrong, there was nothing amusing in the tale he had to tell, a tale that would wipe the smiles off their faces.

A man ran alongside, shook his hand. 'We'll have to call you Lazarus, mate,' and others took up the call.

'Lazarus!' they shouted at him, happy to see him, and Rollo was affronted.

Jimmy Grimes came out to greet him. 'For God's sake, Kirk! We thought you were a goner. Any more of your men with you?'

'None of my men are with me,' he said angrily. 'I thought that would be obvious. We were ambushed by the savages and—'

'I know,' Jimmy said gently. 'You've had a real bad time of it. Come on in. You too, Ceb. We'll get a cuppa tea and then you can give us your account . . .'

Rollo thought someone else from Baker's Crossing had come to town before him and stolen his thunder. He said: 'You've heard? I would have come in sooner but my horse is lame. I was lucky to get as far as Baker's Crossing in one piece.'

'Yes. Trooper Wally Faith got back. He thought everyone was killed. He didn't think anyone else had escaped. Is that true?'

'It certainly is. We must be the only survivors. It was shocking, screaming savages waving tomahawks, terrible . . .'

Grimes interrupted him. 'Good Lord! We'd better send you home first, Rollo. Your wife thinks you're missing believed dead. I'm so sorry to have upset her for no reason.'

Instead of being able to astound everyone with his news of the massacre, he was bundled off home, where his wife fell about weeping for joy, showing him the newspaper with Wally's black face on the front page under the heading MORE GRIM NEWS FOR BRISBANE.

The article went on to tell of another catastrophe so soon after the loss of the *Arabella* with all souls, explaining that a squad of Native Mounted Police, led by Inspector Rollo Kirk, had been ambushed by blacks and, it was feared, all killed, except for Trooper Wally Faith (picture) who had managed to escape and bring the frightful news back to Brisbane.

That was the only time he rated a mention in the paper. The only time, and Rollo was furious. Instead of returning to the police station, where Grimes was waiting for his report, he went to the office of the *Courier*, where Sam Dignam was only too pleased to hear his story from go to whoa.

'It'll be interesting to get another angle,' he said, but was corrected by the Inspector:

'The official angle!'

Rollo talked and talked, and Sam filled page after page about the ambush and the fate of Kirk's men, before beginning his questions regarding the Major's part in making the area safe from attack.

'Ferrington? That's a laugh. He's hopeless. He couldn't protect a cat from a mouse, so what hope did I have with him as backup?'

Sam found this interesting but was determined to be fair when it came to Jessie's fiancé. Very fair.

'When I got back to the camp, where he'd left Clancy, after I escaped from the savages,' Kirk was saying, 'I found they'd veered off in the wrong direction. He didn't have the sense to know he was travelling nor-west, instead of following us . . . so you see, I didn't have a chance. Nor did the poor men in my squad who lost their lives because of him.'

'What's this?' Superintendent Grimes was in the doorway. 'Inspector Kirk, we have been waiting for you, sir! I would have thought an official report back at the station would be more pressing than this!'

Sam looked at him curiously. 'The Inspector was just saying that Major Ferrington let him down.'

'Exactly!' Kirk said. 'That's exactly what I was trying to say. He failed us. He let my men ride to their deaths thinking we had a platoon of experienced soldiers bringing up the rear. Had they been there, to counterattack, between us we could have mown the lot down. And what's more . . .'

'Back at the station, Inspector, if you please!' Grimes ended the interview abruptly, and Sam wasn't surprised. But he was interested. He'd catch up with Kirk again before this day was out.

Once again Grimes and Tomkins listened to a report on the ambush, which differed very little from Trooper Faith's version, except for their methods of escape. The trooper swam to safety, then found a horse, and the Inspector rode free. Having told his story, Wally, a blackfellow himself, was only interested in earning some extra shillings, but Kirk had plenty more to say and the two men comprising his audience were extremely concerned, and questioned him closely.

'You say the Major made no attempt to keep on the established route?'

'I told you. He veered off. I think he was lost. But he could have been doing some prospecting again.'

'What do you mean, prospecting?'

'The soldier guarding Lieutenant Clancy told me the Major had them all panning along riverbanks for gold at every opportunity. They said they were having a great time, because Ferrington was in no hurry.'

'Gold?' Tomkins said. 'Are you sure?' He was confused at this, and worried the subject until Grimes decided they'd look into it further at a later date.

'You said Lieutenant Clancy was ill?'

'Yes. The fever. Ferrington left him behind. With a guard.'

'Couldn't do much else, I suppose,' Grimes said, rubbing his chin.

'You said that Ferrington had veered off course. So how did you find him when you survived the ambush?'

'Ha! That's another matter we'll have to look into. I was riding south and I took refuge in a shepherd's hut. While I was checking to see if it was safe, my horse got away and I was stranded. Next thing, along comes that traitor Jack Drew, riding through dangerous territory as calmly as if he was out there in Queen Street.'

'Why wasn't he with Ferrington?'

'Good question. Because he's a spy. He was in contact with the savages all along. I saw him with the chief!'

Grimes shook his head. 'Don't get carried away, Rollo. He's Ferrington's friend, I doubt he'd do the dirty on him.'

'He's no friend of mine. He left me in that hut for another twenty-four hours. Wouldn't take me back with him.'

'How did you get out then?'

'Drew reported to Ferrington, who sent him back to get me, with a spare horse.'

Tomkins leaned forward. 'It seems Ferrington did have your welfare at heart.'

'Rather late, don't you think?' Rollo said angrily. 'Drew would have told him my men had all been killed. But that's not the half of it. Listen to this. On our way back south, just Drew and me, we spotted a blackfellow watching us. A big fellow, covered in war paint. Who was . . . get this . . . riding my horse. The one stolen from the hut.

'Well! Drew says for me to stay there and he goes over and has a chat with the blackfellow. I got a good look at him and I swear he was the big chief, the one who led the raid on us. But was Drew worried? Not a bit of it. He pulls his horse up and the two have a pow-wow. Probably comparing notes on how many of my men that war chief killed.'

'Leave probability,' Grimes snapped. 'What happened then?'

'I was waiting for Drew to shoot him. He had his rifle and ammo, and the blackfellow, on my horse . . . didn't even have a spear. But no. Drew turns his horse about and rides back to me and says something like: "We gotta get going." '

Tomkins stared. 'You're saying the scout, Jack Drew, had a friendly conversation with the chief of those blackfellows, right in front of you!'

230

'That he did. And he warned me to keep my mouth shut or else.'

'Or else what?'

'He threatened me with live snakes. Threw them at me. Later on, at Clancy's camp, he flatly refused to guide me out of the area, just left me to my own devices and, fortunately, my own good sense of direction.

'But I want to put it on record that Ferrington was derelict of his duty, and Jack Drew was keeping the blacks informed every step of the way. They are responsible for the deaths of eleven of our men, and probably more.'

'More?' Grimes echoed.

'Ferrington's such a blunderer; he has probably been caught pottering about riverbeds with his men, or walked straight into an ambush like I did. Drew said he'd take poor Clancy and his man to catch up with Ferrington, but I wouldn't trust him. I told Clancy to come back with me but he would not.'

When they finally allowed Kirk to depart, Grimes slumped wearily in his chair. 'I could do with a drink. This is a bloody awful mess.'

'I hate to say this, but it sounds factual.'

'Close enough, I'd say at a guess. He's crook on Ferrington but with good reason, and he's got it in for Jack Drew as well, though it sounded to me as if Drew, who doesn't fear the blacks, got him out of a tight spot, by bringing him the horse.'

'He's an unpleasant fellow, though,' Tomkins said. 'He will cause a heap of trouble before he's finished. There could be a court-martial.'

'Yes, but my concern now is for Ferrington and his men. I can hardly send a posse of volunteers out there to aid military men.'

'Hardly,' Tomkins said bleakly.

The bar was filled with angry drinkers and would-be heroes calling for posses to get out there and do the job properly, string up every last one of the savages, and Rollo was enjoying what he regarded as his proper place in the scheme of things.

'My brave men, game enough to take on their own kin, would be alive today if it wasn't for the cowardice of Ferrington,' he railed, thumping the bar.

'That'd be right,' someone allowed. 'Rollo here says Ferrington and his tin soldiers were too busy prospecting . . .'

'What?' Sam Dignam had just come upon them. 'Come off it, Rollo, that's a bit much. He wouldn't do that.'

But the word itself set up its own clamour.

'Prospecting for what?' people began shouting.

'Gold, of course,' Rollo yelled. 'What else would they be prospecting for? Women? Out there?'

He was laughing until he realised he was being shoved aside, by the fever the very mention of the word 'gold' could cause. Everyone was talking at once. Experts came forward insisting they'd known all along about gold being out there in the back country. Others were keen to form parties, not posses, and get going. A storekeeper tapped Sam on the shoulder.

'I wouldn't go criticising poor Rollo there, mate. I sold Ferrington the equipment he needed to prospect for gold. Did you hear that, Sam? Gold! So don't tell me he had his mind on the job. I say he ought to be lynched.'

'He must have had the tip from someone in the gov'mint,' a stockman standing nearby put in. 'I reckon the gov'mint knows gold's out there and sent soldiers to search for it. You know what they're like, they don't want us to get to it first.'

'Jesus, mate, you could be right,' another stockman said. 'I wondered why they sent two different squads out there! Police *and* military. The police were there to chase the blacks out of the way so the soldier boys could fossick about in safety.' He turned to the storekeeper. 'I'll buy you a drink if you open your shop. I want some of the prospecting jiggers.'

'Make it a whisky and the doors are open,' the storekeeper replied smartly.

He already knew, with others listening to the conversation, that he'd be sold out within the hour, not only of prospecting equipment, but also of all requirements for outback treks. A gold rush could make his fortune.

Sam Dignam listened to all this in astonishment. He watched as the bar emptied out, men muttering plans and promises as they left. He glared at Rollo Kirk, leaning drunkenly over the bar.

'You're mad, Rollo,' he said. 'You're bloody mad.'

The morning had its own madness, streets bristling with activity, shop-keepers beaming and cursing as the buying spree continued and their employees downed tools and quit. Wagons were lining up, packhorses were in demand, and men with swags on their backs were already trudging down the road as the exodus began.

Jimmy Grimes was an early riser, but the noise of excited dogs barking and children screeching had him dragging on his pants to see what the hell was going on. He was nearly skittled by a gig as it flashed past him, and a neighbour staggered over the road, bent double with a bag of potatoes on his back.

'You shouldn't be carrying that, Corky,' he said, taking the load himself, 'not with your crook back. What are you doing?'

'The missus and me, we're off to the goldfields. She's over there packing up the dray.'

Jimmy strode over and dumped the potatoes on the dray. 'What goldfields? What are you talking about?'

'The goldfields. Out there.' Corky waved his hand vaguely. 'There's a rush on and I'm not going to miss out this time. You oughta come along, Jimmy. Come with us, it's better to go with a mob.'

232

'I didn't hear anything about a gold strike.'

Corky walked around the dray. 'Word travels fast in these parts. The news came in only last night, there's a strike all right. A big one. Sing out if you want to come with us, but we'll be gone within the hour.'

Everywhere he went, the Superintendent heard the same story, but he couldn't track down the source; he couldn't find the man with the gold.

'I think this is false, it's just a rumour,' he said, relieved to find that a few people agreed. But that didn't stop the rush.

'They're bloody sheep,' he said angrily, after trying to convince a party of twenty, including women and children, to wait for confirmation of the news. 'All follow-my-leader. They're determined to go.'

He walked over to his office, took a loudspeaker and walked along Queen Street calling on people to remain in town, at least to wait for confirmation.

Constable Brown came by. 'Why don't you just let them go?'

'Because it's bloody dangerous out there! Have you forgotten what happened to the black troopers? I want you to get on your horse and ride after those people. Read them the riot act. Warn them they could get killed. Tell them we have no information whatsoever about a gold strike.'

'I told some blokes and they didn't believe me. They said the government is keeping it secret so ordinary folk can't get a look-in.'

Irritated, Grimes turned on him. 'Go! Get going!'

There was no stopping them. The road out to Baker's Crossing was soon a quagmire as the last of the summer rains set in with a vengeance, and thunder rolled over the determined travellers. After the crossing there was no road as such, just tracks born of the stock routes, and they had spread out like channels in a delta, more so now, since they were awash with mud. Not that the rain and the mud and the bogs had any effect on the would-be prospectors. Buoyed by gold jubilation, they surged on, their eyes set on the future more than a definite destination. They disappeared into the distance, into the endless forests, losing touch with each other, pressing on, and rushing headlong into the perils and pitfalls of a seemingly lush and benign land.

In the morning Tom Lok dashed out into the teeming rain and ran up the track to Polly's kitchen. He was out of currants and needed some for his pudding. As he slid along the back veranda, he heard Miss Jessie and her brother in the kitchen and, from habit, stood back to listen to them. He liked Miss Jessie, she was a kind young lady, always interested in tasting what he cooked, and congratulating him on being able to cook for so many, so very well. She even wrote down his recipe for hash beef made with stale beer, which she said was very tasty.

'Polly must have slept in,' Miss Jessie was telling her brother. 'She'll

233

probably be up soon. I don't suppose she'll be very happy at being put off, but it can't be helped.'

'Yes, it's a pity for her, but I've no sympathy for the other two, Albert and his mate. I've written the letter to the authorities to come and collect the three of them. It's not our place to take them back. And I'll get Tom Lok to ride over and post it. Get it out of the way. What a day it is! When it rains up here it really rains.'

'Light the stove, will you, Adrian? At least I can have it going by the time Polly gets up here.'

Tom Lok moved into the open doorway. 'Dry wood for the fire out here, missy. In this box.'

She looked back, surprised. 'Thank you, Tom.'

He had given the impression that he'd just filled the wood box, rather than ask for the currants in front of her brother, who might not like the borrowing, him being tight-fisted with supplies, and was just turning to leave when the missy called to him:

'Tom, run down to the barn and tell Polly to hurry up, Mr Pinnock is ready for his breakfast. And ask her to bring some eggs up with her. The basket is empty.'

'Yes, missy.' This was a nuisance. He had to get back to his cookhouse; the men had finished their breakfast of mutton stew but they wouldn't have gone out into the fields in this rain. Left hanging about, some of them would steal anything edible from his kitchen if he didn't keep watch.

He dodged from tree to tree, for shelter, as he made for the barn, noticing that Albert and some of his mates were squatting under the awning at the far end, having a smoke. They were well out of sight of the main house and the office, so Mr Pinnock would have to find them to get them to work. He giggled. The Major would have them all on the job by this and blow the rain. He never took the nonsenses from them. He was a good tough boss, the Major.

Around the corner he sped, in his gumboots, and bowled into the barn, hissing at Polly to wake up, since there was no movement in the huge dim shed.

'You wakey, Polly! Them up there, look see their brekkie. Missy get the stove going . . .'

He stopped, knowing something was awry here, peered into her makeshift room, nodded approval that she was up and had made her bed, guessed she must have gone the other way, around the far end of the barn, but he still felt tense. A tingling he felt, on his neck, at the back of his neck, and he drew his lips tight across his teeth, the way he did when people made him nervous, and headed for the feathery light from the open door, but before he reached it, he saw the overturned bench and her! He saw her hanging there, all lopsided, her dress hitched, looking shocking, shocking! And then he realised Polly was dead and he ran screeching to the men taking a smoko behind the shed, and one of them threw a clod at

234

him to make him shut up before they listened to him proper and heard: 'Polly, she hang, dead. In the barn.'

They were on their feet, past him, running past him on into the barn, where Albert yelled at her for doing this as they cut her down, and he was weeping and crying and asking why the hell would she do this, and trying to wake her, insisting she wake up, until his mates pulled him away and they covered her poor body with a blanket, and he was still asking why.

Tom Lok knew. He told them he knew why. And they all turned to him. Civil. Speaking proper to him now. No more rude lingo.

'Why, Tom?' Albert asked. 'Why would she do this?'

'Because they sack her. No need for house cook no more.'

Albert stared. 'They what?'

'Put Polly off. I hear them say. True. They put her off. She goin' back to plison . . .'

Albert let out a roar that seemed to shake the rafters. 'They'd do that? They'd sack her! All she ever wanted was to stay here. Jesus, she'd have worked for nothing . . .'

They stood around, muttering, threatening. 'They shouldn't be allowed to get away with this,' Old Bart said.

'No bloody fear they won't,' Albert said, through his tears. 'By cripes they won't.'

'We'd better be careful, though,' one of the men warned. 'They could send us back too if we don't watch out.'

Tom Lok spoke. 'I hear more.'

'More what?' Bart said absently as he took Albert's arm to lead him away.

'Albert, he being put off too, and someone else. Back to plison.'

They stood very still at that information and Tom Lok quaked, but he needn't have feared for himself.

'Ring the bell!' Albert said, sniffing heavily to finish off the tears. 'Ring the bloody bell, Tom, as loud and long as you can. Send them all up here.'

The bell clanged and clanged, and Jessie ran to the back door to see what was happening and Adrian came after her.

'What's going on?'

'I don't know,' she said.

'I'll get my jacket,' he said. 'You stay here.'

The rain was easing to a soft mist as he ran down to the men's quarters in time to see them tramping through the paddock to the barn. He shouted after them but no one even looked back, so he dashed into the cookhouse, only to find it deserted.

He went after them, of course, angry and confused, wondering what had brought on a sort of walkout. Maybe it was just the rain, and they were staging a sit-down. Whatever it was, he'd take it calmly, no point in getting too fussed over a wet day; he'd even let them have their own way, since he'd soon be rid of Albert, who was the ringleader.

Sure enough, there was Albert standing outside the barn, facing the men, laying down the law by the looks of things, judging by the mutterings his words engendered.

They were silent, though, when Adrian approached, and they stepped back to allow him to pass. Politely, he thought, mollified.

'What's going on here?' he demanded.

'Show him,' Albert ordered, and old Bart took him inside the barn.

He was shocked when he saw the body, and fell back with a cry of horror. She looked hideous, her face . . . Adrian turned away:

'What happened to her?' he cried, moving back to the door.

'You killed her,' Albert cried. 'You killed her!'

Menace was all about him. 'Me? I did not!' he retorted. 'How did she die? The poor woman!'

'She hanged herself,' old Bart called out. 'She hanged herself because you was getting rid of her.'

'What?'

'You heard,' Albert said. 'Let's hear you deny it. Were you getting rid of her? Putting her off? Sending her back to that prison?'

'Yes, but . . .'

'So you killed her.'

'No!' Adrian was shouting. 'No. Listen! We were only putting Polly off because we couldn't afford to pay a cook. My sister told her she'd get the best reference, she'd get a good job . . .'

'She liked it here,' Albert said, looming over Adrian and grabbing him by the collar of his jacket. 'She liked it here, didn't she, mates?'

Adrian broke away from him, demanding he be heard, trying to explain, but they picked up wet clods of dirt and threw them at him, until it became too much and he was forced to retreat, run, back to the house, shouting at Jessie to lock up, hurling himself up the front steps and staggering in the door dripping mud and slush.

'What on earth are you doing?' she cried. 'You're leaving mud everywhere. You should have come in the back way! Just look at the mess!'

But Adrian slammed the door. 'Lock up, I told you. They're after me!'

Jessie peered out the window. 'Why? Who is after you?'

'They are. The workers. All of them!'

'No they're not. There's no one out there, Adrian. What has got into you? You look terrible. Take off your boots and go through to the laundry and clean up.'

He left his boots on and stormed past her. 'I said lock up. Now do it! This is all your fault!'

'What is?' She followed him into the dining room, where he slammed the French doors and, looking down, kicked angrily at them.

'There are no locks or bolts on these doors!'

236

'I know that. We don't need them. What's got you in such a state?'

Adrian ignored her, hurrying through the house to close all the outer doors, including the door that shut them off from the separate section of the house containing the kitchen and laundry and the tiny bedroom that had been occupied by Jack Drew. It was connected to the dining room by a short covered pathway, from veranda to veranda.

'Polly's dead,' he told his sister. 'She hanged herself and they're blaming us.'

Equally shocked, Jessie burst into tears. 'No! That can't be right! Surely not! Adrian, that's terrible! She hanged herself? I can't believe it! Why only last night . . .' Jessie sobbed, 'only last night she was all right.'

'You sacked her,' he said numbly.

'Yes, but I told her about the reference, she didn't seem upset . . .'

'She was. She hanged herself, and that mob of felons out there is blaming us.'

'I'll go out and talk to them.'

'No you won't. We'll just have to wait until they settle down and send Tom Lok to bring over the pastor from that little church near the store.'

'He's Lutheran. I think she was a Roman.'

'We'll just get him here anyway, so we can formally report the death and the circumstances, and let him decide the burial service.'

Jessie sat at the end of the table, too stunned and upset to speak, appalled that she was being blamed for the tragedy, and beginning to accept that it was true. Had she caused the poor woman's death? Could she ever forgive herself?

Stricken with remorse, she ran through to her bedroom and flung herself on to her bed, weeping bitterly.

They retreated to the cookhouse, where Tom Lok made fresh tea in the big enamel teapot, and handed out biscuits to each man as he filed by with his mug. He'd never seen them so distressed, or heard such laments.

'She was a good woman, poor old Polly.'

'Had a hard life.'

No one seemed to know what else to say.

'The Major always said she was a good cook . . .'

'She was, by God. That she was. What's he gonna say when he gets home and finds out she's dead?'

'Why would he care?' Albert thundered. 'He'll have the fiancée to cook for him now, and keep his bed warm as well. He left the Pinnocks here to do his dirty work while he went off playing soldiers. Wouldn't know one end of a gun from the other, the bastard.'

As Tom Lok listened, the voices grew angrier and more belligerent. The sun came out but still no one mentioned work.

'I reckon we should have a wake for her,' Albert said. 'A good old Irish wake.'

'Be a bit careful,' old Bart said. 'Pinnock up there'll report us if we muck up any more.'

'I don't have to be careful. I'm being put off too. You ask Tom Lok up there. That's right, isn't it, Tom?'

Tom nodded so enthusiastically his precious embroidered cap fell off, but no one laughed this time. They didn't even attempt to grab it and throw it away.

'We'll give Polly a good send-off,' Albert promised. 'There's liquor in her pantry. I say we go and get it.'

'What about Mr Pinnock?'

'He hasn't got a say in this as long as we stick together. I'm betting that with Polly hanging herself, we'll all be shoved back to jail, and the way things are going, I'll be on a boat to Norfolk Island, so I might as well make hay while I can, mates.'

Albert marched outside and picked up a hammer, which he pounded on the windowsill like a magistrate's gavel. 'I hereby order all hands to attend Polly's wake or suffer a punishment of fifty lashes!'

He had such a wild look about him that none of them knew whether or not he was joking, but the challenge was there and the liquor too much of a temptation.

They marched up to the kitchen, pressing near the door as Albert walked straight in and disappeared into the pantry. Minutes later he appeared with a box of the Major's claret.

'There's more,' he cried in triumph, passing the claret to willing hands. 'There's whisky too, and another box of wine bottles.'

He hurried back inside but the door that faced the house opened, and Miss Pinnock stood there.

'What do you think you're doing, Albert?'

'We're having a wake for Polly,' he said belligerently. 'And you're not invited.'

'You're stealing from that pantry,' she pointed out, and he laughed.

'Well, now ain't that a shame?'

'I want you to put that liquor back, please. It belongs to the Major.'

'It belongs to the Major,' he simpered, copying her. 'Well, not any more. You killed Polly as sure as you stabbed her, you and your brother.'

'We didn't,' she said quietly. 'But I'm terribly sorry . . .'

Albert's patience gave out. 'Sorry don't help. Now you get back out that door where you came from or I'll give you a hiding.'

She was about to continue the confrontation when one of the men who were witnessing the scene called out to her: 'You heard him! Go back, miss, if you know what's good for you!'

There were roars of laughter as she retreated and the ransacking of the pantry went on without further disturbance, to the increasing joy of the revellers, then it was back to the cookhouse to let the wake begin. The bottles were broken out, uncorked, and set upon the table, to be passed

238

round for a swig, starting with the claret, then the white wine, then on to the hard stuff, and a shout went up for Polly.

'That was a stupid thing to do! Damn stupid,' Adrian said. He had come back from trying to barricade the front of the house to find she had actually gone out there when she heard them in the kitchen. 'Anything could have happened to you. Don't ever do that again.'

'I was only trying to keep them away from the liquor. It'll be horrible if they get drunk.'

'Nothing we can do about it. Let them drink themselves stupid and pass out. I'll get everything back to normal tomorrow.'

'Will you?' she asked nervously. 'We have to get through tonight yet. I don't like the idea of them being drunk, God knows what they'll get up to.'

'Don't worry, Sis; I'll look after you. Fortunately Kit keeps his spare guns in his room. A couple of shots will keep them in order, believe me.'

Some of them, unused to liquor after years of incarceration, soon fell by the wayside; others sang songs, bawdy and sentimental, woven together like a sour blanket, while Albert rambled on about Polly, about her death, her murder, and the injustice and the cruelty. He harked back to the transport ships, the filth and degradation, until his utterances struck chords among them and they grunted their agreement. Several whiskies later, he was prowling about the cookhouse, cursing the high-and-mighty lords and masters who treated fine Englishmen like oxen, beasts of burden.

'That's all we are to them,' he ranted, 'beasts of burden, to be sent to the knacker's when we're too old to work for them any more. The knackery! That's where we'll end up, alongside that old horse out there; he's nearly done too, but would they put him out to pasture? No, they keep him working, dragging logs . . .'

'They wouldna send us to the knacker's, Albert, they couldn't do that,' a voice slurred from the back table, but he was in no mood to brook disagreements.

'How do you know? You know nothing! You wouldn't even have yer bloody head on straight if it wasn't for that cracked mirror over there. So you shut yer gob.'

He rounded on the others. 'There's poor Polly up there dead, and what do we do about it? Nothing. Supposed to be her mates. Well I reckon we ought to do something!' He picked up a tin plate and banged it on the table. 'Give her a cheer, mates. Make it loud so she can hear!'

So began the banging and crashing of everything from plates to buckets to washbasins and boards as they marched out of the cookhouse, delighting in the racket, tramping round the cobbled courtyard, thumping away as if they were proud bandsmen in smart uniforms and tall hats, and the marching led them past the Major's office, around the corner and up the hill towards the homestead.

They were getting ahead of him, and he couldn't have that! Albert had to run to take his rightful place as leader, pushing aside old Bart, who was having the time of his life, singing his favourite sea-shanty and beating a saucepan with a ladle.

The singing turned to jeers when young Pinnock appeared on the side veranda and ordered them back to their own quarters, and then the jeers turned to abuse, sending him back inside very swiftly. Some threw a few stones, for something to do, since the life was ebbing out of the party, and a few more were thrown and then it was a hail, noisemakers tossed aside as the Emerald Downs workers ran at the house again and again, caught up in a new sport, in the cheers and the clapping when another window went. Until there were no windows, not even any fancy fanlights left intact.

It was then that Albert came into his own. It was then that he took his revenge for that flogging, for the years he'd spent in prison and for the worse years ahead of him. He came roaring past the front line carrying a fiery torch of rags and kerosene and hurled it into the house, the hated house that had cost so much but couldn't afford to feed Polly.

He ran back for another and was joined by drunken comrades calling for a bonfire!

They heard the gunshots from the house but took no notice; the shots were not real, they were fireworks, to be expected on a gala occasion like this, with freedom afoot and defiance in the air.

'A bonfire!' was the shout now, and the torches glowed like shooting stars as they soared towards the house, and the sky itself was soon aglow.

Adrian couldn't bring himself to shoot at them. He'd thought the gunshots would frighten them off, and was amazed when they kept coming, ignoring him! He grabbed Jessie and rushed out to the kitchen, where he ran into Tom Lok.

'You take missy 'way from here!' Tom cried. 'I got horses saddled, you come quick!'

They followed him across the dark paddock, past the dairy to a clump of trees where he had the horses waiting.

'Go quick!' he ordered.

'What about you, Tom? You come with us.'

'No. I be all ri' here. Fix up mess in the morning.'

'Get on the horse,' Adrian hissed to Jessie, and turned back to the Chinese cook. 'Thank you, Tom. I won't forget this.'

They galloped away from the house, and then, out of range of the rioters, reined in the horses and looked back at the shocking spectacle of Kit's lovely homestead wreathed in flames.

'Will he ever forgive me?' Adrian wept, and Jessie turned sharply to look at him, hardly believing her eyes. Her brother was always so adamant about being right, knowing what to do at all times. He was the last person she'd have expected to break down, even in these extreme circumstances. The Adrian she knew would have been full of excuses and blame by this. There were plenty of people to blame still running amok up there. But he was genuinely distraught and obviously prepared to recognise his responsibility as manager.

'Forgive *us*,' she said, correcting him, unable to contain her own tears. She doubted she could ever forgive herself for causing Polly to commit suicide, and, too, for triggering a disaster that had now wrecked Kit's home and his dreams.

'I can't see how he could,' she added hopelessly. 'I don't think he'll ever forgive either of us.'

The flames had died and the house was smouldering. The men, so hell-bent on rampaging only a little while ago, were quiet now, nowhere to be seen.

'Where are we going?' she asked him.

'To town. The horses are fresh. Think you can make it in one ride?'

'Yes.'

'Good. I don't feel like explaining to anyone out this way, there's nothing they can do. I want to go straight to the police and report the riot and Polly's death, then we can deal with all the rest.'

Jessie was relieved. She was so shockingly depressed, she didn't want to talk about this to anyone either. Or face anyone for that matter. Her shoulders shook with another bout of tears as the horses gathered speed, heading for the road, and the long ride to Brisbane.

Chapter Fourteen

Needing some extra warmth to bolster his frail state, the Major climbed out of his tent and creaked over to the huge old log that lay beside the ashes of the morning campfire.

He clasped his side as he lowered himself into a sitting position and breathed a sigh as the sun filtered through the trees. He had figured out that he had three broken ribs behind the wound, to add to his troubles, but they would have to mend themselves, nothing he could do about them except try and keep straight and nurse them along. The wound caused by that damned spear was still oozing, and Freeman was struggling to provide dressings for him, coping only by washing the bandages and drying them in the sun at every change. They were stained and ugly by this, but they had to do.

He was anxious about the men, but Freeman had said that there was no need to worry, Rapper would bring them back soon, then they could all head back to Brisbane. It sounded feasible, but Kit was anxious, very anxious . . . anything could go wrong. They could have been ambushed and suffered the same fate as the Native Police. He hoped Rapper had the sense to simply ride into that area to show the flag, and above all, keep moving. It was one thing to take on small groups of blacks, quite another to hang about in a district where they now knew a large body of tribesmen were located, according to Kirk, and he had no reason to doubt him.

The nagging worries persisted, so he turned his attention to Jessie. These last few days, thoughts of Jessie had kept his mind off the pain, and the mosquitoes, and the vulnerability of this isolated little camp. He had forgotten how lovely and how sweet she was, while he was working to get his farm and house organised, and when she arrived in Brisbane, it was almost as if a strange girl had suddenly attached herself to him and, he admitted, he'd handled it very badly. He should never have let Roxy have that horse. A damned disloyal thing to do. Disloyal to Jessie. Then when she was in his home, she had lit up his life, cheerful, loving and, he'd been astonished to find, she adored him.

He smiled, picked up a twig, and crumbled it in his fingers. Not for one minute did he regret making love to her, as he probably should, because she had been eager and anyway, the first night with her had really sealed his love for her. Their love. He'd been totally taken aback by the accord, by the completeness of their lovemaking, as if it were meant to be, and when he'd held her in his arms the next morning, he'd known they had a rare and wonderful union. Kit raised his face to the warmth of the sun, feeling a little more cheerful, yearning for Jessie, thinking of the good years ahead of them.

'When I get out of this mess,' he muttered.

Freeman had taken the horses through the scrub to the waterhole below the spring, but he seemed to be taking his time about it and Kit's anxieties were set in motion again. He'd found that when he kept very still, the pain of the broken ribs could subside, as it had now, so he was loath to move about, but decided he'd better check. One of the horses might be giving Freeman trouble, or he may even have fallen asleep in that pleasant grove, a dangerous thing to do. They had to stay alert.

He dragged himself up and limped through the waist-high grass, noticing how green the bush was after all that rain, which also meant there would be plenty of pasture for his cattle back home. And that reminded him; he hoped Adrian was keeping an eye on them. It was still strange to him how those beasts were allowed to wander about the countryside, and he was determined to invest in more fencing when he could afford it.

A shout shattered the quiet of the bush and Kit plunged forward only to stumble on to a fight! Freeman was desperately trying to fight off two blackfellows armed with waddies, all three grappling about on the slippery rocks! He cursed himself for not having a weapon with him and hurled into the fray, grabbing one man by his long hair and yanking him away, dragging the waddy from him and swinging it wildly, whacking and whacking at the attackers in a fury. Every move caused him such pain that he fought harder, retaliating, as if these men had caused his injuries, until they ran off, disappearing into the bush.

Freeman leant against a boulder. 'Thank you, sir. They just sprang at me from nowhere. But are you all right?'

'More or less,' Kit said, taking Freeman's arm to steady himself, already dreading the walk back to the camp. 'But from now on, neither of us moves without a weapon. Do you hear me? We're both on report! Come on, Jenkins, help me get back.'

That night neither of them slept. They packed up the tent and stayed by the campfire, taking it in turns to stand guard.

'We can't stay here,' Kit said eventually. 'We will have to leave in the morning.'

'Which way will we go?'

'Home. We'll leave a message here for Sergeant Rapper. It's the only way. We'll never find the squad on our own.'

'Sorry to wake you,' Jack said to Clancy and Trooper Sutcliffe. 'But we have to go. I've spotted a campfire over to the east. It could be Ferrington and company. At least I hope it is!'

He left them to get themselves organised while he made his way up to a higher spot to try and make out other landmarks that would help him find his way as they crossed country at ground level, but it was still dark and the moon wasn't high enough to be of much help.

As he turned about, a voice called to him:

'I have some information for you.'

Jack squinted into the shadows. 'Is that you, Moorabi?'

'It is. I wished to show you the camp over there.'

'I've already seen it. Who is it?'

'Your officer. The other one.'

'Good. I was getting worried about finding them.'

'There are only two in that camp. The others are all in Bussamarai's country, caught in a trap.'

'What do you mean?'

Moorabi went on to explain that there had been fighting, and the soldiers were presently surrounded and in danger, and Ilkepala was most worried.

Jack gave an involuntary jump at the mention of the magic man, who obviously could still rattle him. 'Why would he care?'

'He does not like the fighting. He wants peace.'

'Hard to come by,' Jack shrugged.

'Something else. Bussamarai is angry that he did not catch the leader, the other officer with them. Ilkepala thinks he might talk to the boss officer if you bring him.'

'Where to?'

'Back to where you were nearly slain. If you will go there.'

'I'll do that.'

'Save time then, I show you through to boss officer and his soldier.' He looked at Jack with a grin. 'We can't have him killed before he plays his part.'

Jack thought about that as he went to inform the others that they had a guide, and he wondered if he had free passage through their land only because he had a part to play. And if he would still be safe when the part was played out. He shuddered. He had never kidded himself that he was one of them; he was only tolerated and, at times, useful, but he had no totem, as they would say, no Dreaming, no clan obligations or accountabilities.

The Lieutenant, riding beside him, was full of questions about Moorabi, fascinated that Jack could speak his language, and thoroughly confused about the placement of the troops and how they came to be separated from Major Ferrington, but Jack was deep in his own thoughts. He was reminded that he had no white clan connections either; he was just as alone in his own world, tolerated, used, not a person anyone would miss if he fell off a cliff.

By the time they came upon Ferrington's camp, he and his companion had left, so they had to rely on Moorabi to track them down.

'Why would the Major be leaving if his men are up north?' Clancy asked Jack. 'This isn't right. Are you sure this feller isn't up to some trickery?'

'No,' Jack said despondently. He was tired of them all.

They soon found Ferrington, who had been travelling rather slowly, and learned the reason. He was struggling with a spear wound and broken ribs.

'They're both out of action,' Jack said. 'Both officers. That one still weak from the sickness and the other with a spear wound. They'll have to keep going back to the town.'

But Moorabi wouldn't agree. 'No. The boss officer must come with us. Ilkepala say!'

It took a while for Jack to get through to the Major that all of his men, including the Sergeant, were under siege, and when he understood the situation he was distressed. 'Of course I'll go back.'

'A long ride in your condition won't be too good,' Jack warned, 'and I can't say it will help. They might kill you too.' He was thoroughly depressed about the whole show by this. He'd thought it would be a comfortable ride to Montone and back, over in a few days, with the blacks smart enough to keep out of sight and Ferrington smart enough not to look for a fight. Now the whole thing was out of hand.

'Why did you let Rapper go off on his own?' he asked angrily.

'Because he was doing so well on patrols,' Ferrington said. 'He turned back and got the mob that attacked us in the first place, when I was speared, and killed fifteen of them. The next day he ran down another group of fellows in their camp and got them too. He was doing well.'

Jack glanced nervously at Moorabi, who snapped: 'We know about that!'

'But he says your people attacked first,' Jack told him.

Moorabi shrugged. 'We must go. Bring him. Send the others on.'

In the end, because they were out of rations, Ferrington ordered the troopers to escort the Lieutenant back to Brisbane.

'I'll go, under orders,' Clancy said, 'but it's a mad thing you're doing, Kit. They probably want your scalp as a trophy. You can't help your men by waltzing into the enemy camp. Besides, you've got that wound . . .'

But the Major would not be deterred: 'I'll need your jacket, Lieutenant. Mine was cut off me. I have to look the part. On your way back, call into my farm and give my love to Miss Pinnock, my fiancée. I'd appreciate it if you could do that for me.'

Bussamarai was pleased with himself. He sat back, listening to the men, who had procured and made a fence with the wire, a word Jack Drew had taught him. Where was Jack Drew anyway? Now that he had won this battle, against real soldiers, he wanted to let him know that his friend was still the boss out here. He'd destroyed a whole mob of crocodile eyes, and he'd taken all of the real soldiers prisoner. He had them fenced in with their horses. Was this not a day of triumph? His men were celebrating with a feast of bullock, one of many strays left behind by the settlers he'd chased out. Useful animals, he had to admit, their meat excellent, their skins good for all sorts of purposes, from ropes and bags to piccaninny slings.

Ilkepala came to join his mob seated by the river, and congratulate them on overcoming the enemy.

'We can finish them off in our own time,' Nungulla said. 'They can't get out.'

'Then there is no need to finish them off,' Ilkepala said silkily. 'They are beaten. We should send them back now, without their weapons, to show we are merciful.'

Nungulla was tired of this old man's interference. He had often said if his magic was so good then why didn't he use it to keep the whites out for ever?

'Why do you use "we" when you didn't even lift a hand to help? Who are you to say what we will do? This is for us to decide,' he snarled.

'Us?' Ilkepala's leathery face creased into a thin smile, but his eyes were flint. 'Us?' he asked again.

'Yes. We've wasted too much time on them as it is. They've killed many of our warriors, children have lost their fathers, wives their husbands, so they have to die. It is only the way they die that we have to decide. And . . .' he looked about at his friends, 'we believe the relatives of the dead men should have the honour . . .' He stopped speaking, aware that something was wrong.

'Since when do the men in this tribe speak for their chief?' Bussamarai demanded, bristling with rage, and Nungulla knew that the old man had deliberately drawn him into this confrontation.

'We only say what we know you will do,' he stammered.

'Then you know nothing, for I have not decided. Leave us! You do not have enough respect to sit in this council.'

Bussamarai was still smarting from Nungulla's charge that he had no heart for war, and was pleased for an excuse to be rid of him before he caused any more irritations.

'The officer bosses are not with their soldiers,' he said, changing the subject. 'I find that a great disappointment.'

'One was killed with a spear,' a warrior said, but Ilkepala shook his head.

'No, he was only wounded. The other man was ill with the fever and has gone back to his own people. The wounded officer is called Major, and I am informed that he wishes to come forward and meet your great war chief.'

Ilkepala was unconcerned that this was not strictly correct, and that the officer might not agree to accept the invitation, issued by Moorabi, to meet with the war chief. But it was the best he could do for now. He knew that if all of those captive soldiers were slaughtered, the white powers would descend again with the force of thunder and lightning and no one within reach would survive. That would include other tribes living in neighbouring districts who had no part in this particular battleground. The spirits had given him the warning, he'd seen it in the clouds, but it was not an argument that sat well with Bussamarai, who was more concerned with his duty. Recently, though, his duty to fight off the whites was being eroded by his understanding, at last, of the unfairness of battles against guns. Jack Drew had taught him not to openly go at guns, but those weapons existed, and it was up to the chief to outsmart them. Or lose warriors, as he had done already. He was almost ready to come round to Ilkepala's way of thinking, but not quite, which left a dangerous canyon there. Any minute he could stand up and issue orders that would mean the end of the soldiers. Even burn them out.

Burn? It might be difficult, though. The bush was green, still damp. It would probably only smoke, smoulder and die out.

Bussamarai interrupted Ilkepala's thoughts. 'The boss officer wishes to meet me?'

'Yes. He will speak to you on behalf of his soldiers.'

'When will this be?'

'Within two days. He is on his way.'

Bussamarai grunted. 'The soldiers could be dead by then.'

The magic man hid a flinch. There was the canyon.

'In which case there would be no meeting.'

'He need not know. If I captured him, that would be a great prize. What would they give me for him, I am wondering.'

'Not as much as they would give you for all of those soldiers!'

The chief thumped his fist on the ground. 'True! That is something! What would they give?'

One of his elders leaned forward. 'But you have to ask yourself what it is they *can* give you. They have nothing you want except the right to live on your land, and they'd kill you first before agreeing to that.'

Ilkepala fumed and the elder was suddenly struck with a ferocious toothache, causing him to fall moaning to the dirt.

The chief shrugged and turned to Ilkepala. 'My men fought well and took risks to tie those wires, keeping the soldiers in. They deserve some recognition.'

'You mean payback?'

'A small attack, perhaps? I will think about it.'

So did Ilkepala. He sat away from them, meditating, but keeping an eye on them. He did have an arsenal of his own, but he would have to be prepared mentally, and it was difficult to attend to these two things at once.

The thinking didn't last too long; they soon had a plan, which Ilkepala was told would allow warriors to attack unseen.

'What magic is this?' he asked, and Bussamarai, coming along behind him, laughed.

'Not magic! Smoke! We will make clouds of smoke to hide the throwers of the short spears . . . you'll see.'

Yes, Ilkepala thought. I will see.

He watched as they tested the wind and began gathering damp leaves beside three tall trees, excitement in the air again, and looked down towards the soldiers' camp, where all was quiet, a breathless, expectant quiet that told him death walked among them, waiting.

Bertie was dying. They kept asking how he was and Rapper kept saying, 'He's coming along, he's a fighter, Bertie.'

'But when will he be well enough to ride, Sarge? We have to get out of here.'

Pratt called to him: 'You wouldn't leave me here, would you?'

'No. We'll shove you and that bloody leg on to that nag of yours. You'll be right.'

'But we're fenced in.'

'Don't worry. We'll cut through them.'

'You're waiting for Bertie to die, aren't you?'

'I wouldn't say that.'

'I would. He's a goner and you know it. He's suffering terrible bad, why don't you shoot the poor bugger?'

'You shut up! I don't want any of that talk! I'm running this show and you be bloody thankful.'

He could smell smoke and hear panicky whispering among his men.

'They're gonna burn us out! Jesus, we'll fry! Get the Sarge!'

This was the time to go, Rapper knew. Right now. Cut the wires, get the horses and bolt before the fire took hold. But there was Bertie. He crept back to Pratt to tell him to drag himself over to the horses. At least he should be ready . . . but there wasn't much flame, just thicker clouds of smoke.

Of course. The woods were spongy, wet after the rain. The savages would know that. So what were they up to now?

Smoke!

'Keep down,' he hissed. 'Keep your rifles loaded. Pass that on. I think they're coming at us again, through the smoke.'

'We shoulda gone!' a man complained. 'We should go now, mates! Through the bloody smoke while we can.'

'Too late now. Look at that,' his friend yelled. 'Here's your bloody fire!'

Rapper stared. 'No!' he shouted. How could he have been so wrong?

Flames leaped out of the smoke and roared up into a huge tree! Beside it, another tree went up in flames, and then a third, sending out a ferocious

248

heat that caused everyone on both sides to retreat very quickly. The massive trees burned like huge torches, lighting the land all about them, a spectacular sight that had the onlookers gazing up in wonder . . . wonder that soon turned to gaping amazement as the trees kept burning. There were no sparks, not a branch fell; the sturdy trunks, more than four feet in diameter, neither bent nor swayed nor crumbled. The trees were burning but not burning; they remained upright, three incredible torches that could be seen for miles around.

'What the hell?' Rapper cried. 'Are those trees on fire or not?'

'They're burning all right,' the soldier next to him said. 'But they ain't, if you get me.'

They all stood, mystified. No ash blew down and still the branches reached out strongly, silhouetted against the flames. And still the three flaming trees burned.

'I'd never have believed it if I hadn't seen it with my own eyes,' the Sergeant said. 'I don't know what to make of it.'

Pratt called for help and Rapper hurried over to him. 'What's up?'

'What's bloody up? It's them trees. The devil's work, that's what it is. We're among a pack of devils.' He began to cry. 'God save us from evil, we'll never escape from them naked devil-worshippers!'

Rapper shoved him aside. He looked at the horses, surprised that they were so calm. A phenomenon like trees burning above them should have them spooked out of their brains, but it didn't seem to bother them at all.

Rapper pushed his cap back and scratched his head. The men were spooked, not their horses. Weird that was. Were the trees really burning, or were they seeing things? The horses . . . they weren't seeing any fiery trees. They were too calm.

As the men drew back, they were still watching the trees, petrified of them, because the flames were dying down and yet the trees appeared to be unscathed. Rapper, too, was unnerved, though he couldn't admit it.

'Strange things happen in these strange countries,' he told them. 'Probably an everyday event to the blackies. We just take no notice.'

'Bertie's dead,' someone called. 'He's gone.'

'See, I told you,' Pratt snivelled. 'Them devils got him when we weren't looking.'

'And they'll get you too if you don't shut up,' Rapper snarled. He was sad about Bertie, and apprehensive. What now? Try to break out or hang on? For what? He wondered if the blackies knew about white surrender flags.

Ilkepala returned to his own campfire to thank the spirits who had aided him in that difficult spell and turned back the raid which would certainly have reawakened Bussamarai's waning popularity. When they came to him, though, the chief and members of his council, they were humbled, asking him to speak to the spirits on their behalf and discover the meaning of the trees of fire.

'That will require patience,' he told them, 'but sit down with me while I ask.'

They waited for hours, until a great loud voice was heard proclaiming the three trees a barrier between two worlds . . . to step past would be to step into the white man's world for ever. Never to return.

The listeners cried out in fear and turned to gaze at the trees as if they might burst into flames again to emphasise the new law, and when they turned back, the magic man, powerful friend of their powerful chief, had disappeared.

Rapper heard the voice booming through the bush and turned to the men nearest him. 'Now what? What do you reckon he's saying?'

'Who?' they asked.

'The blackie with the big voice shouting orders at them.'

'I never heard anyone shouting orders.'

'I never either.'

'You must have,' he said angrily. 'It nearly deafened me.'

'No, Sarge. I reckon the devil trees must have you hearing things.'

He was embarrassed. He slunk back to Bertie's grave and stood there, trembling. 'I bet you heard it, Bertie. 'Twas enough to wake the dead!'

It occurred to Rapper then that those trees could be a demarcation line – the area a no-man's-land – and that the voice might have been telling him to stay on his own side, the speaker thinking he understood the blackie lingo.

I dunno, he said to himself. But with patience and a good hard think, I might be able to figure a way out of this mess. Maybe they want something. It's more than twenty-four hours since they attacked. What are they waiting for?

In the morning, Tom Lok cooked the stew and plonked it on the table as if nothing had happened, and some of the men staggering into the light of day took the ladle and served themselves while others hung about outside.

'What's to happen?' they were asking themselves.

'We have to bury Polly,' old Bart said.

'There isn't time,' men argued. 'All the farmers in the district will be down on us. Where's Albert?'

'He's gone. Run off. Who would blame him? He burned the house down.'

'We can say that. We can say it was just Albert.'

'They won't believe us. They'll say we should have stopped him. I'm bolting too. And so should you lot if you've got any brains. Get running now, I reckon. Make for the hills. Or it's Norfolk Island for the stayers!'

Old Bart looked wildly about him. His head was splitting from that liquor. They were right. Someone else would have to bury Polly. He went back to their quarters and rolled up a couple of thin blankets for a swag, marched into the kitchen, ignoring the Chinaman, grabbed a saucepan and a knife, some bread rolls and a lump of cheese. Tom Lok handed him a canvas water bottle and, accepting it, he nodded. Then he went down to the empty stables, too late to claim a horse, and looked for more handy items, especially a strap to parcel up his possessions in the swag. None of them would ever be free men now, he knew, but for a while this would be the next best thing. Maybe he could hook up with the blackfellers like Jack Drew did.

He was the last to leave.

Tom Lok watched him tramp across the fields into the bush, heading inland, and set about cleaning up as he always did when they left for work.

Lieutenant Clancy didn't forget his promise to the Major. They had some difficulty identifying the property as, according to his recollections, there should have been a house, a fine house on the second hill overlooking the river, but there wasn't one to be seen. Eventually they found the long drive that led in from the road, which confused them again, as it seemed to lead nowhere, but they kept on and were confronted with burned-out ruins.

'Jesus, Mary and Joseph! Are we in the right place or going mad here?'

'This is it all right,' Sutcliffe said. 'I remember we came here before we left, and that barn was over there to the left. And downhill the men's quarters.'

They rode on down and were met by a Chinaman, who told them about the breakout.

'Miss Pinnock?' Clancy cried. 'Where is she? Is she all right? God Almighty, they didn't hurt her surely?'

'No. She go away with Mr Pinnock. Get away quick in the dark.'

'And what are you doing?'

'I not good at digging. You help me, eh? Got to bury Polly.'

'Someone's dead?'

'Polly. She got herself hung.'

Clancy was shocked. 'We'd better wait for the police on this.'

Tom Lok agreed. 'Yes. I wait for the policeman coming soon I think.'

Clancy rode around the ruins. 'Poor Kit. This will break his heart, he was so proud of his house. What a homecoming he'll get.'

Adrian took Jessie to the Lands Office Hotel, saw her settled in a large cool room, and went to the police station, where Inspector Kirk took a long and detailed statement with unashamed enthusiasm. Adrian didn't like Kirk and knew he'd blundered by involving this fellow, but he'd been so tired when they rode in, he wasn't thinking straight. To retrieve the situation, he asked for Inspector Tomkins, whom he'd met on the ship, but Kirk would not let go.

'Tomkins is down at the docks. I can handle this. I always knew Ferrington wouldn't be able to deal with those felons,' he said. 'So spare

251

me your excuses. It was only a matter of time before they turned on him. Burned his house down, eh?'

'You have that on record, sir,' Adrian said stiffly. 'And I want those men charged.'

'They'll be charged all right. Where are they now? Sitting on the stoop waiting to be arrested, I don't think. But I've got all their names. They won't get far. Tell me again, the cook hanged herself, you say?'

'Yes, sir.'

'Why?'

'I don't know. Why do people do such things?'

'She didn't leave a note?'

'I don't think so. There was such confusion when we were informed of her death that I didn't think to look for one.'

Kirk sat back in his chair. 'You're trying to tell me that Ferrington's cook, who has been working for him for quite a while without any disagreements, suddenly killed herself? To my personal knowledge, having been a guest in that house, he was pleased with her services, wouldn't you say?'

'I would indeed. I would go so far as to say the Major appreciated her. She was a good cook, the poor woman.'

The Inspector slapped a ruler on his desk. 'Then what went wrong? You say the Major appreciated her services. In what manner? As a cook and a bedmate?'

'Certainly not! How dare you make such an assumption!'

'I'm asking, Mr Pinnock. Your sister is the Major's fiancée. That, I can tell you, is news to his friends. It was only just before Miss Pinnock arrived that he even mentioned he was considering marriage. Not a word about it. Let us establish, then, that Mrs Pohlman, the cook, would not have known either. In truth, Mr Pinnock, was Mrs Pohlman surprised when your sister arrived?'

'Yes, she was. But as housekeeper she could have expected notice that a lady visitor was arriving. Unfortunately the Major was unable to do that because he did not know that my sister was accompanying me.'

'But she was surprised?'

'Yes, but not disconcerted.'

'As far as you know. It seems to me that Mrs Pohlman saw herself displaced as the lady of the house. Your sister wasn't an ordinary visitor, but a fiancée!'

Adrian bristled. 'I don't like what you're implying!'

'What am I implying? That Mrs Pohlman's life fell apart when her lover suddenly produced a fiancée? Yes. It's the only explanation for a contented woman to go off and do away with herself.'

'It's not an explanation! It's preposterous!'

Kirk ignored him. 'And you say her death triggered the riot?'

'Yes. But I will not have any talk of intimacy between the Major and

Polly. I mean, the woman was so much older than he, and by no means fetching in appearance.'

As he said that, Adrian wished he could retract it, since Kirk's sallow features were far from fetching, and his wife, the dreaded Mrs Kirk from the ship, was downright ugly. It crossed his mind that even Polly would have won over her.

'It's amazing how you young people seem to think that beauty is your own exclusive right,' Kirk snapped. 'Well let me tell you, Mr Pinnock, I'm betting in your case it doesn't equal brains! Mrs Pohlman, a woman scorned, hangs herself and the workers riot in sympathy. And what were you doing all this time?'

'What do you mean?'

'There were guns in that house. I've seen them. Did any of the rioters get hold of them?'

'No.'

'So there you are. Armed. Unable to defend yourself.'

'I did try. I fired over their heads.'

'Not at them?' Kirk's disbelief was evident. 'Don't you know what guns are for?'

'Of course. But I didn't think they'd go that far. They were all drunk.'

'On liquor you allowed them to steal from Ferrington's store!'

'That they stole before I could stop them . . .'

'You expected drunken rioters, known felons, to stumble away and sleep it off! Is that what you do on drunken nights out, Mr Pinnock? Down there in your safe Sydney mansions. Well let me tell you, up here it's frontier country, you shoot first. I myself have just had a most harrowing experience, my Native Police were murdered by blacks . . .'

Adrian was shocked! 'The squad that came through Emerald Downs? All of them killed?'

'All but one. I only managed to escape by the skin of my teeth. No thanks to the cowardly Ferrington, who stayed well away from danger.'

'Where is Major Ferrington now?'

'Who knows? Still swanning about the safe districts, I expect. But he'll have an interesting homecoming. First a ruined farm and homestead, then a court-martial. I suggest your sister looks elsewhere for a more eligible beau.'

'What my sister does is none of your business,' Adrian said angrily. 'I'm sorry to hear about your men, truly sorry, but I find your attitude offensive. I shall put it down to agitation as a result of your recent dreadful encounters with the blacks, and hope you see matters more reasonably in due time.'

He picked up his hat to leave, but Kirk remained seated. 'My job is to enquire speedily into this matter and find a posse to search for the dangerous felons that you have let loose on the countryside. I doubt your neighbours will be feeling reasonable, Mr Pinnock. Good day to you.'

'Why on earth did you talk to Kirk?' Jessie exclaimed. 'You know he hates Kit. You know he's an awful fellow.'

'I had to. Tomkins and the Superintendent weren't at the station. But never mind. He was all business. He took down the particulars and is preparing to organise a posse to round up the escapees.' Adrian felt his version of the unpleasant interview was more appropriate at this point, because Jessie was so tired and distraught. She seemed to have aged overnight.

'I think you should see a doctor,' he said. 'He'll give you something to put you to sleep for a while.'

'No doctor! For heaven's sake, Adrian, we have to do something. We can't just sit here . . .'

'Do what?' he asked, slumping into a chair. 'I've told the police everything. I don't know what else I can do.' He groaned. 'Jessie, for the life of me I don't know what to do now. I wish I did. I'd give anything to be able to do something, to try to make amends . . .'

She was weeping again so he stayed until, exhausted, she fell asleep. Even then he cringed at the thought of having to leave this room and make for his own, further along the passage. He dreaded meeting anyone, even a housemaid, for fear of questions or commiserations, and he knew worse was to come. When the town heard about the tragedies at Major Ferrington's farm they would be overwhelmed by public curiosity, and maybe criticism.

Inspector Kirk's hostility had undermined what little self-confidence remained to him, so he kept watch on the door in a state of trepidation, nerves jumping as footsteps approached, and settling gratefully when they passed on by.

Sam Dignam was their first visitor. He'd heard about the fire at the Major's farm when he returned to the office after attending a meeting of the Pastoralist Association. The meeting had turned into a celebration since news had been received from Sydney that surveyors were already at work defining boundaries that would eventually be the borders of a new colony north of New South Wales. Most of the pastoralists present were from the Darling Downs, and their chairman, Reece Maykin, was delighted to advise that their district would be part of the new colony, with the capital here in Brisbane. That pleased Sam too . . . A new colony, a new governor and parliament! Now they were talking! With all that interesting stuff swirling around, the *Courier* could become a daily instead of just a twice-weekly publication.

By the time he reached his office, the publicity-seeking Inspector Kirk had been and gone, leaving a lurid tale with the editor, who called to Sam, excitement jigging.

'Come and hear this! It's the best story . . . I tell you, Brisbane is kind to us. One tragedy after another. But this is good. How about this headline? DEATH, DISASTER AND SEX!'

'Clumsy. What's it about?

'Sit here and have a look. Sex and suicide. Arson. Cripes, this is a good story, Sam. I want you to follow it up.'

Sam began reading the notes. Then he jerked the pages up as if his eyesight was failing him. 'What? What's this? Ferrington's farm burned down? The convict cook hangs herself. Jesus! This can't be right. My friends are managing his property while he's away.'

'They're not doing much of a job of it. Remind me not to hire them.'

'Where are they now, Adrian Pinnock and his sister Jessica?'

'In town. They're safe. I think Inspector Kirk said they're at the Lands Office Hotel.'

Sam was up and running, tearing down the street and dashing into the hotel to demand Miss Pinnock's room number. He was told that she was in Room Four, on the front of the hotel, with a balcony, and he tore up the stairs and rushed to knock on the door.

At first there was no answer, until after a delay it opened cautiously. It was Adrian. On the far side of the room Sam could see a four-poster bed swathed in mosquito netting and barely made out Jessie lying there.

'May I come in?' he asked softly, and Adrian shrugged, stepping aside.

'I heard you had terrible trouble out there. Is that true?'

'Yes,' Adrian said numbly. 'I suppose . . . yes.'

'Are you all right? And Jessie?'

'I don't know. Jessie finally fell asleep. She's practically hysterical . . .'

'Should you call a doctor for her?'

'No. She won't hear of it.'

Sam closed the door and led Adrian out on to the balcony. 'You look done in, mate. But do you mind if we have a talk? We have a story about happenings at Ferrington's place but it's very important that I get it straight. I don't consider Kirk's version reliable.'

Adrian shuddered. 'Oh God help us! If you're taking his word you'll get the worst of it. Sam, it was bloody awful. Things went wrong and they steamrollered from there.'

'Someone died. The cook. She hanged herself. Is that right?'

'Yes. That was the start of it. Kirk says she was Ferrington's lover, but she wasn't. That's garbage!'

'Why did she suicide?'

'How do I know? She was the cook and housekeeper. She just did her work. She didn't confide in us.'

'Who found her hanged?'

'I don't know. Ah yes, I do. The Chinese cook.'

'He cooks for the workers?'

'Yes.'

'What happened after that?'

255

Sam listened carefully as Adrian described the events of the night, realising it must have been a terrifying time for them, but he still couldn't fathom what had triggered the riot. Would men like that be so fond of the Irish cook that they'd go berserk because she'd quietly hanged herself without a word to any of them? He felt there was a stone missing in this path, one that wouldn't be identified until they located some of the rioters. There had to be an explanation . . .

'Who's there?' Jessie called from the bedroom, her voice sounding high-pitched and querulous.

'It's me,' Sam called, jumping up to greet her as she pushed the lace curtains aside and stepped out through the open French doors.

He was shocked by her appearance. Her hair was awry, understandable since she'd just awakened, but her face was grey and her eyes were red and puffed from weeping. She seemed unsteady so he put an arm around her, but she jerked away from him. 'Don't,' she said. 'Please don't!'

'I'm sorry,' he said, as she moved away to stand behind Adrian's chair. 'I just came to see how you are.'

Jessie made no attempt to push the hair from her face or straighten her blouse and skirt, leaving them twisted at her waist. 'We're all right, thank you.'

He turned to Adrian. 'Is there anything I can do?'

But Jessie answered. 'No, Sam. There's nothing anyone can do,' she said, and went back into the room.

'She's very tired,' Adrian said. We rode all night. Didn't get in until early this morning.'

'That's all right. I understand.'

They walked along the balcony to the outer staircase, where Adrian clutched Sam's arm. 'I'm in a terrible mess, Sam. I don't know what to do. What should I be doing now? Can you imagine what it will be like having to face Kit? I never dreamed I'd make such a mess of things. I've thoroughly let him down, haven't I?'

'Come on downstairs and I'll buy you a beer. I think you need a drink more than anything. You can't be blaming yourself for everything that happened. You should be counting your lucky stars those felons didn't attack you.'

'They were too drunk. I thought gunshots would scare them off. I swear, Sam, I had no idea they'd burn down the homestead. Kit was so proud of it. He'll never be able to afford another one. He's ruined.'

Sam was surprised to find himself feeling sorry for Ferrington. 'Well, we'll just have to see what we can do to help out,' he said. He didn't add that if anyone needed friends now, it was Jessie's fiancé. He'd be coming home to a heap of trouble, and a nasty enemy in the form of the law as spake by Inspector Kirk.

* * *

The days were milder now, sunnier, released from humidity as the rainy season drained away, but for Adrian they were grim and grey. He had to face days of intense questioning by Police Superintendent Grimes and the warden of the jail, as well as by various people who were either enquiring after unpaid bills or merely curious. To make matters worse, the local paper had given the impression that Kit's farm was a den of iniquity, though Sam had tried to temper his editor's enthusiasm for what Adrian regarded as downright vulgarity.

When he had the chance, Adrian talked to a master carpenter about clearing the ruins of Kit's house and rebuilding, relieved to know that this was the very man who had provided most of the construction materials for that house, as well as several tradesmen.

'A terrible shame,' he said, 'to have a fine house like that destroyed. And so soon. Three of my tradesmen worked with his blokes out there to show them the ropes and keep them on track. When I went out to inspect, I thought they'd done a damn good job, considering. Then they go and burn it down. Mad! That's what I say about them transported convicts, they're not right in the head by the time they get 'em here.'

'Then will you start rebuilding as soon as possible?'

'Can't do that. Not until the first bills are cleared. The Major owes me more than sixty-three pounds, Mr Pinnock. When that's paid I'll order the timber he'll need. Might take time, though. The Major, he wanted the best cedar, so do a lot of folks. There's a shortage.'

'Order it anyway. I'll pay whatever's owing. I'll arrange it right away.'

'Good on you. You bring me the cash and I'll dig up the specifications.'

Adrian found the Bank of Australasia in Albert Street and persuaded the manager to arrange to draw funds from his Sydney account, after he'd managed to establish his identity by calling in Sam Dignam.

'I should have done this when I first arrived,' he told Sam, 'but I forgot. Anyway, this fellow will telegraph Sydney and he says I can draw cash in a few days.'

'What about now? Do you need any money?'

'I could do with a few guineas. We left in a rush.'

'You should have said so before this! You have Jessie to look after as well. Will ten guineas be enough?'

'Plenty. Why don't you come with me and see if you can cheer Jessie up? She's very low. Not coping at all.'

Jessie hated this room. She hated having to listen to all the cheerful voices coming from the street below, and she hated the view of the rooftops framed in the hard blue of the sky, so she wrapped herself in a blanket and sat in the armchair, her back to the closed French doors. And there she sat, determined to remain there until Adrian came back.

* * *

'I didn't mention to anyone that we had told Polly her services were no longer required,' Adrian warned her. 'It won't help, really it won't.'

'That *I* told Polly she had to go, you mean?' Jessie wailed.

'I haven't mentioned any of that. It isn't necessary. She suicided and the crazy lot of men who worked there used that as an excuse to get drunk and go berserk, so you stop this overblown dramatic act you're putting on and shut up about it. We've got enough problems without you trying to play the martyr. Now pull yourself together.'

'Don't you speak to me like that! You're trying to make me lie about what happened. I won't do it.'

'You will do it. And you'll be nicer to Sam Dignam, if you please. I know you were flirting with him on the boat. Did you think I was blind? You had a last little fling with him, and that's all right, but don't go taking our problems out on him now. He's our only friend in this damned town until Kit gets back.'

He slammed the guineas on her dressing table. 'Tomorrow you get out and buy yourself some decent clothes, or by God I'll move out of this hotel and leave you here. Already people are beginning to wonder who the hell that woman is, holed up in her room like some loony.'

Jessie stared at the coins. 'Did Sam give you that?'

'Yes.'

She sank back in her chair. 'Oh God! I wish we'd never left Sydney.'

Which reminded Adrian that he intended to send her back to Sydney as soon as possible.

Inspector Kirk was addressing a crowd outside the police station, calling for volunteers to round up the escapees from Emerald Downs, and Adrian had walked into the group before he realised what was going on. By that time it was too late.

'What about you, Mr Pinnock?' Kirk shouted. 'I expect you'll be anxious to join us. You know them all by sight. That's Mr Pinnock, gentlemen! He was managing the property for Major Ferrington when the workers decided to take a holiday.' Then he grinned, adding: 'After they'd had a party at Ferrington's expense.'

A man in the crowd objected. 'This is no laughing matter, Kirk. As a farmer myself I take no pleasure in another man's misfortune. It's hard enough to get started as it is. How many men do you need?'

Superintendent Grimes strode forward then, and asked for twenty men.

'We need to search the area around Baker's Crossing, but they'd know they're running into blackfellow country if they go too far, so I'm guessing the smart ones will be heading south. Inspector Tomkins will take ten men towards the crossing, and Inspector Kirk, you and your men head out on the Ipswich road.' He turned and called to Adrian.

'A word with you.'

'Yes?'

'I'd prefer you stay in town, Adrian. You can't be in two places at once. I'll need you here when they bring these characters in, to make certain we've got the right blokes. It wouldn't be the first time posses have scooped up law-abiding citizens and caused no end of trouble.'

'Thank you,' Adrian said. 'My sister is still very upset. I wouldn't want to leave her just now.'

'No, of course not. It must have been a terrible ordeal for a young lady. If there is anything I can do to help, let me know.'

Adrian breathed a sigh of relief at having escaped riding with a posse, and headed for the bank to see if there had been a response from Sydney.

'Yes,' the manager said, 'your man down there did reply, but he says there are no funds in your account, in fact you are overdrawn.'

'I can't be! I have an allowance paid in there every month. Are you sure you got my name right?'

'I'm afraid so. It sounds as if it is just a mix-up. They'll probably pay double next month.'

'But I can't wait for next month. If I were in Sydney I would have this sorted out in a second! Could you advance me fifty pounds?'

'Goodness me, no. Not without collateral and a formal application, which would have to be approved in Sydney anyway . . .'

No amount of arguing about the status of his bank balance made any difference, and Adrian strode out into the street furious. He decided to write another letter to his mother straight away and ask her to send them some money, irritated that he would now have to explain everything to her, since they had moved into town and were staying at a hotel.

'God, what a mess,' he muttered, as he walked into the hotel lobby. 'She'll be wondering what's happening about the wedding!'

A clerk called to him: 'Mr Pinnock. The mailman was looking for you. He has a letter for Miss Pinnock. Says he's been carting it about the countryside for days, and then when he finally got to Emerald Downs and saw the house was gone, he thought he'd better bring it back . . .'

'Good. Where is it?'

'Here. Thin it is. Someone didn't have much news, eh?'

Adrian took it up to Jessie. 'You've got a letter from Mother.'

'Oh. What does she say?'

'I don't know. It's your letter.'

Jessie opened it. 'Well! I'm ordered home or there won't be a wedding. That's exciting, isn't it?'

He picked up the page she'd tossed aside, read the terse lines, and nodded. 'Not in the best of moods, I see. But going home right now would be the answer, Jessie. I'm sure Kit will understand.'

'Are you? Did you know all about this?' She held up a newspaper. 'It's days old. There's been fighting and killing in the back country. Kit is out there in the thick of it. I would go home because he certainly won't want to see me, but I have to make sure he's all right. I just have to make sure he gets back safely.'

'He'll be all right,' Adrian said lamely. 'Sam says Kit and his men should be back any day.' He'd seen the papers but couldn't bring himself to talk about the news with Jessie. Sam had filled him in on some of the details, saying that Superintendent Grimes wasn't inclined to trust Kirk's version of events entirely, so all they could do now was wait for news.

'I'll go and write to Mother then,' he added. 'And try to explain what has happened.'

As he walked down the hall, he looked forward to writing to Flo after he'd finished the chore of explaining matters to Blanche. And he wondered how Marcus was, feeling guilty now that he'd almost forgotten his grandfather's illness. I'll write to him as well, he decided.

Then it occurred to him that happenings in this distant county might be reported in the Sydney newspapers.

I must ask Sam, he said to himself.

Chapter Fifteen

The *Sydney Herald* was now a daily publication, with room to expand on the new skirmishes with the blacks in what they referred to as 'our near north', accepting that the very northern tip of the colony was a good thousand miles on from Brisbane and known as 'the far north'. The confrontations had been expected, following the raids on cattle stations such as Grosvenor and Montone, and the resultant demands that the Governor send troops to defend settlers, but suddenly came the news that fourteen, or even as many as twenty, Native Mounted Police had been massacred in their sleep by black savages.

Inspector Kirk was remarked upon as the hero of the day, having fought off the raiders and ridden hard for four days to bring home the shocking news of the fate of his men.

Marcus was reading this with great interest, remembering the days when outback New South Wales was dangerous territory too, when he noticed that a detachment of troops was also in the area, this force led by Major Kit Ferrington, former aide to Governor Gipps.

'Blanche!' he called. 'Have a look at this! Your future son-in-law is back in military service! He's chasing wild blacks!'

She hurried out to the sunroom. 'What do you mean, he's chasing blacks? It must be someone else. He has the farm . . .' She stopped. 'Good Lord! That must have been why he wanted Adrian up there. To manage his farm while he was away on duty. Then why didn't he say so? Heavens, Marcus, why didn't Adrian mention it?'

'Probably didn't want to worry you.'

'Couldn't be bothered, more like it,' she snapped.

'Don't fuss, they probably only expected him to be away for a few days, show the flag, frighten off the blacks with their guns, that sort of thing. But it looks a lot more serious than that now.'

Blanche plucked dead flowers from a large bowl of pink and red azaleas. 'You don't think they'll be in danger at Emerald Downs?'

'No. Too close to town. Heselwood was telling me the troublemakers are much further out . . . His station is about a hundred miles further out, if I recall.'

'I can't believe he and Georgina actually lived out there, beyond the recognised boundaries . . .'

'He got good land, though. I forget how many square miles. The blacks will give over eventually.' He peered at the paper, as if trying to look into the future. 'I wonder how our Major is coping with blackfellow tactics?'

'I don't know. It's all very worrying. I've told Jessie she must come home. When I'm out this morning I'll call at the shipping office and see when the next ship from Brisbane is due.'

'Where are you off to today?'

'We're taking the paddle-steamer ferry to Manly. It's such a nice day, it should be lovely on the harbour.'

She gathered up the dead leaves and flowers, swept them into a small bin and was making for the door when he called to her: 'Who's we?'

'Mr Watkins and I,' she called from the passageway.

'I thought so,' he mused. 'Fred might win fair lady yet.'

Flo wandered aimlessly along Circular Quay, just looking at the boats and the ferries and peering down at little fish darting about while a larger silvery-pink fish swam lazily among them, hardly deigning to notice them.

People were boarding the Manly ferry, and Flo stopped to watch, recalling the picnic day the theatre company had enjoyed on that very same ferry, when they'd first come to Sydney. Beautiful it had been. Beautiful.

She saw a grand lady in a heavenly pink organza dress, with a lovely cashmere shawl draped about her shoulders, walking down the pier towards the ferry, escorted by a familiar gentleman . . . and suddenly she realised it was Mr Watkins. And. Oh Lord! He was with Mrs Pinnock! She was sure of it! She darted into the crowd to get a better look, and nodded to herself. It was her all right. Mrs Pinnock. Adrian's mother. She wondered how Mr Watkins knew her, but supposed rich people knew everyone in their class. And Mr Watkins was so nice, he'd be gentry too, no doubting that.

He was very attentive to the lady, taking her arm to go up the ramp, and they looked real nice together, she being a good-looking lady, tall and stately, and he a big protective type of fellow. And of course, she remembered, Mrs Pinnock was a widow. Well there you are!

Flo wished she'd seen them earlier so that she could go over and speak to Mr Watkins, who would then introduce her to his lady, Mrs Pinnock. And she'd be able to say to Mrs Pinnock that she knew her son, in fact she and Adrian were dear friends, and Mrs Pinnock would say something like, 'Oh,' and she could say, tell her, that actually they were engaged and they'd been meaning to tell her, but Adrian had had to go away, and so on . . . But they'd boarded the ferry now and Flo couldn't afford a ticket, so she couldn't just happen to be on board and come upon them by chance.

The men pulled up the short gangplank and the paddlewheels ploughed the boat away from the pier, leaving Flo feeling bereft, as if they should have asked her to join them and have an enjoyable day together, and she could have got to know Mrs Pinnock.

She wandered away then, following the shoreline and on down worn steps to the grim shops and shanties of the Rocks district, home of the seamy elements of the Sydney community. It was a filthy, depressing slum, but always full of life, though most of the residents were at odds with the law. Because it was so busy, so overcrowded, Flo had chosen The Rocks for her enterprise. She dodged down Maple Lane and took up her position on a corner outside a sly grog shop, hoping for a few pennies from the boozers who stumbled in and out of the place.

Flo didn't feel so bad begging here, because the police never cared what went on in The Rocks, and the inhabitants took begging for granted. There were beggars everywhere, from ragged children to old crones and cripples. She'd been on this corner often lately, and rarely failed to earn less than threepence, so she was managing quite well . . . except for the men who thought she was a whore, and abused her. But Meg Flite, who *was* a whore, agreed to stand with her and take the men off her hands.

This morning, though, the woman who owned the sly grog shop called her in, and Flo was nervous, afraid that the woman, Bonnie Hunter, a bossy, tough type, would tell her to move on. Which Flo didn't want to do. She felt safe there with Meg and Bonnie to protect her from ruffians.

'Listen here,' Bonnie said, leaning across one of the big casks that formed a counter in the dingy shop. 'Meg says you're engaged.'

'Yes.'

'Well it seemed to me a saucy-looking little bint like you was wasting your time begging, when you could rake it in on your back. But she says you don't want no part of the game. So I been doing a bit of fishing round. Is it true you're engaged to a Mr Adrian Pinnock?'

'Yes,' Flo gushed. 'That's right. Do you know him?'

'Not exactly. But now, you tell me . . . have you met Major Ferrington?'

'No, but I know who he is. Adrian told me he's his sister's fiancé.'

Bonnie stood back, hands on hips. 'Well bugger me breeches! You tell me the truth now, girl, or I'll kick your arse all the way back to George Street. Are you engaged to Pinnock?'

'I told you, yes.'

'I don't see no ring.'

'He gave me a house, and . . . other things. He's away, he's up there staying with Major Ferrington . . .'

Bonnie started to cough. 'Get me the mug on the shelf over there,' she wheezed, 'and put some whisky in it . . . not that bottle, the one behind you. Now give it me!'

She drank the whisky, coughed and wheezed for several minutes and then poured herself another, downing it in a gulp.

'Are you all right?' Flo asked.

'No, I'm not all right,' the woman barked at her. 'I've got a throat full of razors. But leave that be. I can't make you out. Why in the blazes are you begging, with Pinnock's money in your purse?'

'Oh, that's the trouble. I haven't got a job now, and with Adrian away I haven't got any money and I can't get a job. It's terrible not having any money. I don't like to write to ask Adrian for some; he's been so good to me.'

'For the love of Luke, give over! Write to the bastard. Go round and see his mum. I never heard of such a piffling lot of carry-on as you're feeding me.'

'I wouldn't do that,' Flo said stiffly. 'I'd rather beg.'

'Where do you live?'

'In Prince's Lane.'

'Gawd! This I have to see. I'll walk you home tonight, and don't you bloody go without me.'

'This is your house?' Bonnie was astonished.

'Yes. I'm sorry, but I haven't got any furniture.'

'So I see. You've got a little garden, though. It's real pretty.'

Bonnie swished quickly about the two rooms, her black and orange taffeta dress seeming to dominate Flo's house, so much so that Flo had to ask:

'Excuse me, Bonnie, but why are you here?'

'I'll tell you why I'm here, girl. Its because I'm crook. I'm sick. And a doctor friend of mine tells me I'm gonna get a lot sicker, with this throat, see. And I was looking for someone to sort of look after me.'

'Oh dear. I'm so sorry, Bonnie, sit down.'

'Thank you.' She sank on to the hard chair with a puff of taffeta. 'But I don't want you feeling sorry for me. I'm no charity case. I can pay my way.'

'I'm sure,' Flo said politely.

'I didn't want to die in that filthy hole behind the shop. I was saving to do better in life, see, but it's beat me to the post.' She looked about her. 'Jesus! A person can be bloody unlucky. But listen to me now. You want to sell this house?'

'No.'

'Well you can't keep begging. What say I pay you to look after me?'

'Like a nurse?'

Bonnie nodded. 'I suppose that's what, yes. Like a nurse. If you won't sell me this house, I'll find one nearby. What do you say to that?'

'All right.' Flo supposed it was all right. She didn't know what to think.

'Good. And later we can have a talk about our gentleman friends.'

Bonnie Hunter seemed to have friends everywhere. She bought a house three doors down from Flo's place, a house that the owner refused to sell at first, because he and his wife had only been there a couple of months, but somehow she persuaded him, and soon a lorry arrived with her goods. Then a gentleman brought furniture for Flo's house, everything

264

brand new, and a grocer arrived with boxes of provisions for her kitchen.

'Who will run your grog shop?' she asked Bonnie.

'No one. I sold it. Might as well have a bit of peace and quiet now, eh?'

'Yes,' Flo said shyly. 'What exactly do you want me to do, Bonnie?'

'Come along here every morning, get me meals, clean up, all that stuff, and I'll pay you ten bob a week.'

A few days later, Flo went with Bonnie to see her doctor in Macquarie Street, and the genial old gent was delighted that his patient was so organised.

'Now, dearie,' he said to Flo. 'You know where I am. I live upstairs, so if the clinic is closed, ring my night bell. If Bonnie needs me at any time, you run over here and get me.'

Flo was impressed. 'What a kind man,' she said, and Bonnie laughed.

'So he ought to be. He went up on a charge of sodomy, but I gave evidence he was in my place the night it happened.'

'How awful for the poor man! Just as well you could prove he was telling the truth.'

Bonnie seemed to almost choke on her cough as they crossed the street. 'Where did you say you came from?' she asked.

When Blanche arrived home that evening, Lady Georgina Heselwood was in the sitting room with Marcus.

'Why, Georgina!' she cried. 'What a pleasant surprise! Had I known you'd be calling on me I'd have hurried home. I hope you haven't been waiting long.'

'No, dear, don't fuss. I've been royally entertained here by Marcus, who is looking better than ever, might I say.'

'It's the company,' he beamed. 'Beautiful ladies have always been good for my constitution. Blanche – listen here. Georgina has news of our northern contingent.'

'About Jessie and Adrian?'

Georgina nodded. 'Yes. Heselwood heard it from the Governor. But don't worry, they're all right.'

'What then?'

'Give her a go, Blanche. All in good time.'

Blanche glared at her father-in-law, but sat quietly on a nearby sofa, her hands clutched together on her knees.

'Well, you know the Native Police suffered severe losses when they were attacked by blacks?' Georgina began. 'Apparently Major Ferrington and his men headed into the same area but they had serious setbacks. First, his second-in-command, Lieutenant Clancy, went down with the tropical fever, then in a skirmish, Major Ferrington received a severe spear wound.'

'How do they know all this?' Blanche asked urgently.

'Because Clancy, still weak from the fever, was withdrawn to Brisbane.'

'What about Kit?'

'He's still out on patrol.'

'With a spear wound? Are they mad?'

'The Lieutenant said it was the Major's decision. So he can't be too bad.'

Blanche sighed. 'That's a relief, but still . . . infections, you know. He should have turned back.'

'I agree, but Jessie and Adrian have had their problems too. You know they were staying at the Major's property, Emerald Downs . . .'

'Adrian was there to manage the property,' Blanche said, feeling heat in her cheeks and hoping it wasn't showing. 'Jessie went up to view it. Emerald Downs is to be her future home, you know.'

'Don't be too sure of that,' Marcus muttered, and Blanche looked to him.

'Why? What's wrong?'

'The poor things,' Georgina said. 'They're so young. They probably didn't realise what management of that particular property meant. The staff were all convicts . . .'

'I'm aware of that,' Blanche said.

'They rioted,' Marcus said bluntly. 'Got into the booze store. Burned the house down!'

'Good God!' Blanche screamed. 'Where was Adrian? And Jessie?'

'I understand they had no choice but to leave, for their own safety. They're in Brisbane.'

'Oh heavens, how terrible! How awful! Anything could have happened to them with a pack of felons running wild. It's terrifying to think about it. Ferrington should never have left them there! Especially Jessie. What are those men thinking of?'

They discussed the shocking news over sherries, to calm Blanche's nerves, and Georgina informed them that she'd be going to Brisbane shortly.

'I thought you said you'd never go back,' Blanche said.

'To Montone. I don't mind accompanying my husband to Brisbane, but I won't go out to Montone again. Heselwood is busting to return to Brisbane, so that he is closer to what's going on out there. It seems the Major is on his way to Montone land at present, and may even be there by this.'

'But wild blacks are still there! They killed the native policemen.'

Marcus intervened. 'Those blokes weren't trained soldiers. The blacks won't get it so easy if they challenge a military squad.'

'You say if?' Georgina asked. 'Do you think there's a chance they'll retreat now?'

'Might be. They have their myths and legends of the Dreaming, but I don't recall them throwing up martyrs.'

'I hope the situation out there can be resolved. We had blacks living and wandering about Montone until hotheads came along stirring up trouble.

266

But Blanche, I wanted to ask you if there's anything I can do to help Adrian and Jessie while I'm up there.'

'Yes,' she said firmly. 'Yes you can. Send them home. And . . . oh my Lord! If that house was burned down, what about their clothes?'

Georgina was pale. 'I went through that. After our house was burned down, we rode into Brisbane with only the clothes we stood up in, and no money. It's the most horrible, embarrassing feeling. Perhaps you could telegraph them that Heselwood and I are on our way, and we'll look after them.'

'Telegraph them where?'

'The post office will do. It's only a small place. They'll be found.'

'I should come with you,' Blanche said, but Marcus disagreed.

'They're not babies. You'll only get in the way. It's not as if you have a house to go to. Leave it to Georgina.'

They were on Montone land. Disputed land. Property of the Tingum clans, claimed by Lord Jasin Heselwood as his cattle station, and Jack remembered it well. He could have found the site of the homestead blindfold, since he'd spent so much time reconnoitring the area before the raid. There were the blue hills overlooking the station, and among the heavily wooded areas over there was a small creek, Wurrul the blacks called it, for the bees who lived there. It ran down into a deep gully that carved its way over to the big river on the other side of the valley. Jack had seen it in flood and that was a scene to behold. Water for miles across. He was reminded of the Brisbane River then. When he was in that town, something about the river had bothered him, and of course, he mused . . . that was it! All those buildings clustered along the banks of that river! They'd better watch out. There was another mighty river that could rise up to great heights like this one, and storm across the land. For the first time he realised that the cattle station hadn't been there long enough to see a good flood in action. Then he grinned.

'What's so amusing?' the Major asked, riding alongside him.

'I was just thinking that even if a fire hadn't got that house, a flood would have sooner or later.'

'But you said the homestead used to be on that rise over there.'

'Might be, but still not high enough. Not in this country. Big rains up north send mountains of water down these rivers.'

Worried, the Major wanted to know about Emerald Downs. 'Would the Brisbane River flood like that?'

'I reckon it would. In the town anyway, with the river winding around it like a noose.'

'What about out my way?'

'Yes, probably. You don't get all that green for nothing.'

'But my house would be safe, wouldn't it?'

'I think so. Hard to tell.'

He asked Moorabi, who gave the matter some thought and then answered in his own language.

'He says your house is high enough, but not what he calls the other houses. The men's quarters, stables, all that stuff.'

'Oh Christ!' the Major groaned, and Jack took his horse closer to him. 'How are you feeling? Do you want some more of Moorabi's pain-stopping potion?'

'I could do with it, please.'

'Righto. Hang on.'

All three dismounted in the shade of tall pines, and while Jack was mixing the white powder with water in his tin mug, Moorabi glanced over to the nearby foothills.

'Bussamarai waiting there.'

The Major turned painfully. 'Is he the chief?'

'The big boss,' Jack said. 'Be careful of him.'

'What do you think he wants of me?'

'I don't know. A bit of glory. We'll walk up there. Give us time to look about.'

'Where are my men?'

Jack put the question to Moorabi, who replied, pointing.

'They're camped in that scrub over there beside a creek. It's dense bush there, hard to see anyone, but Moorabi says they're in there. And the warriors have them surrounded.'

'Fence,' Moorabi said proudly, and Jack nodded.

'Yes, I suppose like a fence,' he smiled. 'Come on then, Major. Let's go and see the boss.'

But Kit stood firm. 'No. Help me mount up. I will not see him until I've spoken to my men. Not on any account.'

Both Jack and Moorabi were dismayed. 'Not a good idea,' Jack warned. 'We don't want him taking offence.'

'I want to see my men first. I need to know their exact circumstances. It shouldn't be difficult for mounted troops to break out of there. I will see them, then meet with your fellow.'

'You'd have to ride through the blacks surrounding them.'

'I know that. Tell Moorabi I want safe passage. Tell him to ride ahead of me.'

'Why should he? He could get shot! Oh, all right, I'll go with him. You're making it bloody hard on us.'

He discussed the situation with Moorabi, who insisted on going over to the blacks' camp first, for instructions on the change of plan.

'By all means,' the Major said, riding out into the open where he knew he could be clearly seen by the Aborigine watchers and, Jack guessed, by the men under his command.

Eventually Moorabi returned, walking across the open country, indicating they should follow him.

'I think he means us to walk too,' Jack said.

'Yes. You can walk. But my regiment is cavalry. We ride.'

Caught in the middle, Jack decided to ride too, thinking it might be safer if hostilities broke out. He looked back to the overgrown orchard beside the burned-out ruins of the Montone homestead, wishing he could leave this lot to their own arguments, because he was impatient to search for his gold. It was all he could do to keep riding in the opposite direction. It seemed he was the only one with any interest in the actual station right now; the rest of them were all too busy figuring out how they could kill each other.

As they entered the scrub, they saw Bussamarai's men moving carefully aside. Suddenly a great cheer was heard as the soldiers recognised Major Ferrington, and then Moorabi stopped, holding up his hand.

'What now?' Jack asked, and then he saw the rough wire fence. 'Bloody hell, Major. Look at this.'

'I can see it,' Ferrington said angrily. 'Sergeant Rapper!' he shouted. 'Report, please. What conditions do you have there?'

'Three dead, sir. One injured. All others able. Not much protection, though.'

'Then mount up.'

'Yes, sir!'

'Good man, that,' Ferrington said to Jack. 'Doesn't ask questions.'

'What are you doing? What's the point of them mounting up stuck in there?'

'Just to be on the safe side,' he said, turning his horse about. Then he called to Rapper: 'Smartly, at the whistle, single file!'

Jack stared. 'What? Do you want them to do exercises in the bush?'

'No. I want to even up this meeting. No better time than now, with their keepers distracted.' He gave a piercing whistle and sent his horse galloping through the scrub, back to open country, and with that Rapper's riders came streaming out, single file as ordered, through a narrow opening between two trees, and Jack guessed that Rapper had taken the hint and cut one wire. Just enough. The horsemen thundered past him, struck out across the grassy plain and fell into line behind Ferrington, dropping back to a trot.

Moorabi was aghast and Jack felt sick. 'Now we're for it,' he said. 'The bloody fool's mucked everything up.'

He heard Ferrington shout, and Sergeant Rapper repeat the order, and prayed they weren't about to attack, but that didn't happen. As Aborigines emerged from their vantage points, weapons poised, the horsemen began to drill. First two lines only, trotting forward, falling back into various formations, riding into neat figure-eight circles, criss-crossing each other, dropping into pairs and peeling off as they neared the Major, who kept shouting instructions and beating time in the air as if conducting a brass band.

269

Jack watched in astonishment, and then realised he was enjoying the show. They were good, those soldiers, bloody good, he thought . . . they probably didn't have much else to do but drill, he supposed, sitting in their Sydney barracks.

He looked about him to see that the blacks, who loved nothing better than a good corroboree, were thoroughly enjoying the show too. He began walking around the outskirts of the makeshift parade ground with Moorabi, until suddenly, there was Bussamarai. Not the expected angry chief, but one of the audience, spellbound as the horses went through their paces, a wide grin on his face.

Hardly turning aside, so as not to miss anything, he clapped Jack on the back, indicating he watch. Then, when the long drill finally ended, Bussamarai was wary again, and hundreds of spears rattled around them, but the Major had brought his men to a halt. They were lined up in two rows, with Rapper in front of them and their commander ahead of him. Their rifles were still in holsters, Jack noticed, thankfully, as Ferrington dismounted stiffly, took his sword and placed it on the ground.

Then Rapper called for a cheer, 'Hip hip!' and Jack realised what was happening.

'They are honouring you,' Jack said urgently to Bussamarai. 'They put on the horse dance in your honour and now they make three cheers in your honour. That is their gift to you.'

As the last cheer rang out, Bussamarai nodded, pleased. He strode up and down, still not making any effort to go any closer to the soldiers but peering at them curiously. He clapped his hands and turned to Jack.

'Bring up the officer boss.'

And that was when Jack's attention was taken, not by the cone-shaped headdress that the chief always wore, or by the two huge teeth stuck in clay on either side of his forehead, but by the glittering gem sitting squarely between them. He jerked back in shock; he pointed at it, stuttering, and then Bussamarai noticed him, knew he'd recognised the yellow stone as the precious gold he'd always been seeking, and roared with laughter. He doubled up laughing.

'You want one, eh, Jack? I got the best one, eh? Bussamarai he can even beat you at the yellow gold hunt!'

'Have you got any more?'

'No.' The chief began to walk away, shouting to Moorabi to bring up the officer boss.

'What about the soldiers?' Moorabi asked, but the chief had lost interest in them for the time being. He brushed the question aside with his hand, but then changed his mind.

'You tell them we have more horse dances later. Good corroboree.'

'Where did you get the gold?' Jack asked, chasing after him, but the set of the broad black shoulders charging on ahead of him told him this was not the time to irritate his old friend.

The Major staggered forward, leaning on a stout stick that Jack had found for him, but Bussamarai gave no hint that he had noticed the man was injured. At the same time Jack was disappointed that the chief had washed out the clay headdress, and now the thick, wiry hair was held back by a band of plaited twine. There was no sign of the gold nugget.

'I think it is a custom for him not to admit that you have been wounded, something to do with sit-down talks,' Jack said, and Ferrington nodded.

'I see. Protocol. Very well. What is my role?'

'Try to hold on. He's testing you. Moorabi is bringing you a drink. Get it down quickly, you'll feel better.'

'He can't be allowed to have the upper hand, though. I have protocols of my own.'

'Forget them. You got away with double-crossing him once already. Don't try it again.'

I'll make sure of that, Jack told himself as he helped Ferrington to sit on the first tier of a small natural amphitheatre where corroborees were often held. I'll be translating.

Already the Aborigine dancers were busy painting themselves for the various stories they would tell. Food was being prepared and handed around by the women, many of whom remembered Jack and brought him tasty morsels which he shared with an unwilling Major Ferrington, telling him it was bad manners to refuse to eat snake or grubs, which was not true. None of the blacks ever took offence when he had refused strange food, as he had often done until he became accustomed to their diet.

Behind them, though, Rapper and his men ate everything they were offered, sitting quietly, waiting for what Jack heard them referring to as a 'concert'.

At dusk, more Aborigines appeared, taking their places on the other side of the fires, and noting that they were well outnumbered now, Jack leaned over to the Major.

'You better get your protocol right, mate.'

The music was supplied by a single didgeridoo, beating sticks and voices, and the dances lasted for hours, with the audience on both sides giving them noisy ovations. Suddenly the corroboree was over, the fires died down and the darkness became ominous.

'What now?' Rapper was heard to whisper, but no one answered.

Then Jack saw Bussamarai stand and beckon him. He pointed to Ferrington, a question, and the chief nodded, indicating that they should both join him in his *gunyah*, a large half-hut sheltered by sheets of bark. Jack was relieved that no one else was invited. Until now he'd expected that they would have to meet with Bussamarai and his council of elders, which would have complicated matters, because there were always too many opinions being pushed forward at a meeting like that.

They were finally seated on the grass, across from Bussamarai, who immediately began laying down the law about white men trespassing on his land, and there was no way that Jack could cover up his angry accusations, but Ferrington took them calmly, without interruption.

'Tell him that everything he says is true. And I apologise.'

Expecting an argument, Bussamarai was surprised. He leaned forward, his heavily creased faced glowering suspiciously.

'Then go away. Get out!' he shouted.

'With your permission, sir, we shall do so,' Ferrington said quietly, and Jack raised his eyebrows at this bit of flattery, by no means displeased to pass it on.

Bussamarai was well aware that, though outnumbered, the officer had the guns, so he allowed himself to accept the compliment.

'Why then do we sit here?' he cried.

'Because I do not wish war and neither do you. But after me will come settlers, whether we like it or not. As inevitable as rain.'

Jack translated and Bussamarai sat very still, his dark face set like a bronze, then he began listing all the clans who lived or had lived in his homeland, and the tribes that made up the great nation. He stood and pointed to the landmarks that emanated from the Dreaming, telling the stories of how they came to be, from back in ancient times when the giant animals and birds roamed this land, lizards as tall as trees and birds so big the emus were tiny in comparison. Jack had heard most of this before, so he translated with ease, and the Major was fascinated.

'The most marvellous stories,' he told Jack. 'You must write them down when we get home. Even more important, I'm sure people who study prehistoric birds and animals would give anything to learn more here.'

'The officer thinks your stories are the best he ever heard,' Jack said, and Bussamarai nodded gravely.

Once again he began to debate the problems, going over the same ground until Ferrington repeated a previous answer.

'The settlers will come. It is sad for your people. But they will come, as inevitable as rain.'

Bussamarai jumped to his feet and strode away, then turned, beckoning Jack to join him.

'Tell me, Jack Drew, will all those white people come whether we fight or not? Is what he says the last truth?'

Jack gave him a dismal nod, and Bussamarai took his arm. 'Some of me wished the officer would lie, tell a story of hope, but I see he cannot.'

'Then let him tell you a story of change. Talk to him of peace arrangements.'

And so the meeting resumed, but the Major was weakening. 'Ask his permission for me to retire, Jack. I think we have established enough goodwill to end hostilities for the time being. That's all I can do. It's up to men on both sides to hold the peace.'

Permission given, Ferrington announced he would be taking his troops and departing in the morning, and Bussamarai nodded his approval.

Dawn found Jack riding swiftly towards the ruins of Montone Station. He leapt down from his horse, rushed through the overgrown orchard and stood back, taking in the outline of the large homestead, recalling how he'd dashed in the back door.

The chicken run was still standing, and he shuddered. The wide yard between there and the house had been a battleground during the raid. He'd raced across that perilous open stretch, close to screaming in fear as people in the house opened fire. It had seemed a mile wide, and though he had tried to erase the scene, looking around now he could still see bodies strewn about, cut down by gunfire, and a woman, her head bashed in, lying sprawled beside the body of the blackfeller holding a bloodied waddy. Victim and attacker dying together, side by side.

He pulled his hat down over his forehead as if to shut out the horrific scene and tramped into the ruins, stepping over blackened timbers to walk through the dusty ashes and concentrate on this section, which would have been a passageway.

He found a stick and poked about, past what would have been doorways at the front of the house where he'd actually opened a door and seen that white woman! He couldn't have saved the woman in the yard, but he'd tried to help this one . . . pushed her out of sight, shut the door behind him to urge the blackfellers on down the passage . . . and then nothing. Nothing.

Here. It must have been here somewhere. He searched carefully, first in a small area where he must have fallen, then wider, on and on; then, covered by ash now, he realised he could have lost his money belt when they carried him out of the burning house. But which way? Would it still be in the house, or maybe it had fallen off outside. The blacks wouldn't care about his belt.

In the end he knew it was no use. He had searched for hours. There was no belt, probably burned to ash in that great fire, and no gold. Not a skerrick. It was gone.

You knew it wouldn't still be here, he told himself angrily. Those stockmen came back for their cattle; they'd have scratched about to see what could be recovered from the ruins. Someone would have found those nuggets lying about; the fire wasn't even fierce enough to burn all these timbers, so my gold wouldn't have rated a singe.

He marched around to the front of the house, where he saw roses struggling to survive, but their plight failed to touch him. He strode into the open and shouted at the house, at the Montone Station homestead:

'Who took my bloody gold?'

Only an echo responded.

He thought enviously of the nugget Bussamarai had, a much bigger specimen than any in his former collection, and wondered how he could

273

go about acquiring it. Ask for it? Definitely not; no one would dare such disrespect. Bartering? For what? Could he ask to be shown where it came from? No. Not now, not in this delicate stage of truce. He could always come back another time and have a serious talk about it. Let Bussamarai have his fun.

When he arrived back at the camp, he found the Major preparing to leave.

'Your friend Moorabi gave me a honey-like potion to smear on the wound. I think to guard against infection,' he said, and Jack grinned.

'I thought you smelled familiar.'

'Thank you. It's frightful, but soothing. And Sergeant Rapper has me strapped up like a mummy. We did a morning drill for the chief, who was pleased as Punch, so now we're off.'

Jack watched them leave and rode up the hill to say his own farewells to Bussamarai. The chief was not wearing his ceremonial headdress, and there was no sign of the gold. Jack sighed, and clasped hands with his friend.

'Time for me to go.'

'Yes. Time for us to part again.' Bussamarai wished Jack a long life and many children.

'Got to find a wife first,' Jack laughed. 'Can't say I've got much to offer a woman.'

Bussamarai was surprised. 'Our girls never complained,' he grinned.

Ilkepala saw them standing together, laughing, two good men, and was pleased he'd had the foresight to rescue Jack Drew from the fire. He had thought Bussamarai might part with his gold, make a present of it to Jack Drew, but that hadn't happened and so be it. They were parting friends, that was the main thing, some solace for a man who, the magic man knew, was heading for stormy times. He wished he could warn him; maybe the spirits could help. A way of thanking the white man. Doubtful.

Chapter Sixteen

This was more to Rollo Kirk's liking . . . a posse of local men, his own sort, who enjoyed a hunt. They'd be searching through settled districts, with civilised folk to help out and offer shelter this time. The convicts who'd worked for Ferrington were old hands. Only the dopes would head inland towards Baker's Crossing; the rest would know their only real chance was to go south.

'We'll get the bulk of them, lads,' he told his men grandly. 'We'll ride the road to Ipswich, scour the town, and if we haven't got them all by then, we'll chase them down on the flats. Mount up, and remember they're desperate characters, felons all of them, so don't take any chances.'

He saw the excitement in their eyes, mostly young blokes, out for adventure, saw them pat their rifles into place and set their hats at a jaunty angle as they turned on to the open road.

'Keep your eyes peeled!' he shouted. 'We'll bail up every soul we see, be they on the road, in the fields or in houses. Search everyone and everything!'

They caught two of the absconders plodding across a ploughed paddock, within the first hour, and the farmer didn't take kindly to horsemen trampling his crop, but when told that the two strangers were dangerous escapees, he was pleased to assist. The prisoners were chained to a tree and left for the posse to collect on their return journey.

Though they trawled the farms and lanes, they didn't have any more success, except for information on which people in the town were the lawless type and likely to harbour criminals, so Rollo and his men swept into Ipswich, making straight for a large house at the end of a secluded street.

Dogs barked and women screamed as they surrounded the house, firing shots into the air when Rollo demanded, in the name of the law, that all inside step out on to the front veranda, forthwith!

They did, they rushed out, women and children and servants, behind a very large irate gentleman who announced he was the Mayor of Ipswich and would have the law on the lot of them for trespassing.

Inspector Kirk's apologies notwithstanding, the Mayor called upon his own police to search the town for these absconders and insisted that Kirk take his men beyond the town and cease creating a nuisance. More subdued, they made for the coalfields, where they caught another man, but only because he ran when he saw Kirk's black police uniform.

He turned out to be a common thief who'd been pilfering around the pitheads and offices for weeks, and the miners were grimly pleased to see him in custody. They sent him in to the local lockup, and as several were just coming off their shift, everyone soon adjourned to the nearest pub, where Kirk and his troops were treated to a round of beer.

After that, Kirk had difficulty assembling his riders, since they were enjoying the company of the miners, but eventually he prevailed upon most of them to return to duty, leaving two men behind. The stayers waved cheekily from the bar, promising to catch up later, but the Inspector was glad to be rid of them, since they didn't take the search seriously, once the liquor took hold.

They were out on an open road when they spotted a man dodging among the huge prickly pear trees that plagued the area, but they couldn't ride after him because the trees were a scourge on horses, so they dismounted and continued the hunt on foot.

Kirk ran towards the fellow, shouting at him to halt, and saw him look back before he dodged away.

'That's Minchin!' he shouted. 'Albert Minchin. He's one of them!' He was so excited his voice was almost a shriek, with the result that their quarry ran faster than ever.

'Spread out!' he yelled. 'Get around him! Catch the bastard. He's the ringleader.'

He dragged up his rifle and fired, and then there was a volley of shots as others in the hunt followed the Inspector's lead.

'Head him off!' someone shouted. 'He's getting into that thick bush!'

The hunters were taking more care to avoid the savage thorns of the prickly pear than Minchin, who was obviously too desperate to care about the scratches and so made it to the cover of the bush. Undeterred, a man leading the pack plunged in after him.

Albert was waiting for him. He felled him with a heavy stick, grabbed his rifle and dropped into the high grass beside the unconscious man, checking that the gun was loaded. Then he shot the next man dashing towards him. Shot him dead! He sighed with pleasure. That felt good. He fired again, ran forward and grabbed the gun from beside the dead man, took another shot at one of his pursuers, who was skidding to cover, got him, heard him yell! Heard him yell he'd been shot in the leg.

'That's not half of what you pigs will get!' he screamed. 'Come anywhere near me and you're dead.'

The unconscious man stirred, so Albert shot him.

'Dead like him!' he shouted, leaning down to grab more ammunition.

Gossip among the tradesmen who'd called at Emerald Downs had always held that the bush at the base of the plateau leading up to Toowoomba was a hangout for outlaws, and when the mailman had told them about the absconder who'd drowned in the river, Albert had always had his doubts. He figured that the escaped prisoner, Harvey by name, had made it across the river with help from Jack Drew. And why? Because he could make for Ipswich and then head on to outlaw country.

And Albert was nearly there! If it wasn't for this mob on his trail, he'd have made it. Still could. One thing was for certain; they'd never take him in. Never. He wasn't going back to any jail, let alone that death pit, Norfolk.

He chuckled as he sat down to examine the guns. One was a beauty, the first one, very modern; the other too old. He smashed it and then pushed the body over to grab its jacket, brown tweed it was, like the one young Pinnock used to wear, lording it round the farm. Lucky he was, not to have had his head bashed in, mused Albert. He'd thought about it several times but never got round to it.

So. Now. He peered through the dappled light of the bush. It smelled good, fresh. Couldn't see any of the hunters. They were calling to their mates, asking if they were all right. Let them come in now if they dared.

He pulled on the jacket, smoothing the fine cloth. 'Real nice,' he said. 'Real nice.' Then he backed away, watching furtively, retreating further into the bush, knowing that each step would take him closer to outlaw country. He'd heard you couldn't miss the cliffs; 'twas said they reared straight up from the plains, and he'd seen them for himself now. There they were in the distance.

Voices were hollering, worrying, outside there, calling to their mates, so he sent off another shot to keep them occupied, because he'd had a good idea.

Albert crept away, but instead of heading for the high country as he'd planned, he ran swiftly in a half-circle, keeping well away from the voices until he found their horses, all hitched, waiting, unguarded.

He leapt on to the first one and scattered the rest, then he was galloping along that road, straight at the plateau.

Inspector Kirk was furious that his posse had let Minchin get away, and steal a horse as well, and they all went half-silly with shock that two men had been killed. That, he supposed, was understandable, but it was bloody stupid of Mick Devine to go bowling into the bush in the first place. Did he think he was chasing 'roos or something?

Anyway, they had to take the bodies into Ipswich and deliver the other bloke to the doctor to get his leg seen to, and now they were on the job again, this time for real, as he'd told them.

'Did you think you were on some sort of picnic?' he asked them angrily. 'Well you're not. You've lost mates! We're hunting a felon, a killer. Get that straight. There's a track ahead that goes up through Cunningham's

Gap, and the police say if he makes it to the top their own men will nab him, but they think he'll hide out in the foothills. So that's where we search. Every blasted inch of the foothills if we have to stay here for a week.'

They growled agreement. No more cheers. Instead a determination to get Minchin, dead or alive. It was now recalled that Minchin was a lifer, sentenced for murdering his own brother in a fit of rage.

One thing the Native Police had taught Kirk was to watch for campfires. They'd been searching this rugged country all afternoon without success, but Kirk had been waiting for darkness, and there they were. Two small fires. Not that he expected Minchin to light one, him being alone and without any equipment or food, but others could help him on his way, or recruit him.

This time they made their way through the scrub carefully and quietly, heading for the nearest campfire, bursting in to train their guns on three men who were sitting about, unconcerned by this intrusion.

'Stand, in the name of the law!' Kirk shouted at them, although they were already climbing to their feet to see who these visitors might be.

'What can we do for you gentlemen?' a lanky character asked them.

'Stand aside while we search your camp.'

'Nothing much to see, matey. Some bunks there in the hollow under the cliff edge, our pantry's there too, and the cave next door belongs to a million bats.'

'We're looking for an escapee by the name of Albert Minchin. He's a dangerous man, a murderer. Have you seen him?'

'Never heard of him,' the lanky man said, lighting his pipe. 'Who did he murder?'

'Some of our men,' Kirk snarled, 'so don't try to be smart. He's around here someplace. Anyone who harbours that felon will be charged with him, so here's your chance. I ask you again. Have you seen him or any stranger today?'

'No we haven't. We like to keep to ourselves. We don't like strangers.'

Kirk knew it would be a waste of time asking for their names, so he stayed with them while his men searched the surrounds.

They didn't find anyone else around the camp, so the Inspector called to them to hurry back to the horses so they could investigate the other camp. They were well up the track when one of his men, a young stockman called Mitch, tugged at his arm.

'Don't look back yet, boss, but they've got our man there.'

'How do you know. Did you see him?'

'Saw fingers. He's standing on a ledge just past that makeshift bunkhouse.'

'Why didn't you grab him?'

'Couldn't. He was down below ground level. I thought of pointing the gun at him and ordering him up, but I reckon he wouldn't have been there if those other blokes hadn't shown him the quick way out.'

Kirk spluttered his rage. 'Why didn't you just shoot him? Kill him! Jesus, he shot your friends without thinking twice.'

'Because I reckon if we go back quietly we'll catch him,' Mitch said. 'I want to take the bastard back and see him swing.'

Two of the men made a noisy exit scrambling towards the horses, calling to each other to hurry up with the lanterns, while Kirk and the other three waited in the shadows until they heard laughter, and a new voice.

'That's him,' Kirk whispered urgently. 'That's him. I know the voice.'

They charged in, shoved the others aside and lunged for the latest member of the outlaw camp. Mitch grabbed him, punched him to the ground and ran a rope round his neck while their guns were trained on his mates.

'I ought to take you three in too,' Kirk said, although he had no such intention; he didn't feel up to handling four prisoners with only five men, 'but I'll let you go this time. And don't think I won't report you to the Ipswich police.'

He walked over and pulled Minchin around to face him, but stopped.

'This isn't Minchin,' he yelled. 'This is . . . For cryin' out loud, mates, this is the late Harry Harvey! Drowned in the river at Baker's Crossing, he did. What's the matter, Harry, cat got your tongue?'

He was jubilant, Minchin forgotten. This was a prize catch! Kirk knew he'd been right all along.

'I never thought you'd drowned, Harry, not for one bloody minute. And I never believed that Jack Drew. What is he? A mate of yours? Birds of a feather, eh? I'll have him too when I get back.'

They trussed Harry and pulled him up the trail. 'It's Norfolk Island for you, Harry,' chortled Kirk. 'I might even come and visit you. See how you're getting on.'

The outlaw had nothing to say. He spoke only when spoken to, and then he was polite. He heard Kirk's men complain when he decided to call off the search and head back to Ipswich. He listened carefully to everything that was said, because this was his way. Harry was a practised escapee. He never missed a chance, and he couldn't afford to this time. His constitution wasn't up to the rigours of that island; he'd have to watch and wait for an opportunity.

His friend Scarpy heard about it two days later from one of the men who'd witnessed the arrest.

'Terrible bad luck it was. Harry slid over the edge of the cliff on to that ledge where only eagles could spot him, but this time they came back. Looking for another bloke who shot up the posse, a real bad'un. The police in town are hopping about like jumping jacks because the bloke's still in the district. They found his horse; he never made it to the top and the whole mountain's on the search for him.'

'Why?'

'The reward. There's a reward for him already. A hundred pounds!'

'How come Harry got arrested? What did they charge him with?'

'Being dead! The boss copper recognised him. And wasn't he pleased with himself. Said he knew he hadn't drowned, that a mate of his had helped him get across the river.'

'Did Harry mention his name. The mate?'

'No fear. The copper did. Jack someone, he said, and he told Harry he'd get his mate too.'

'Is that so?' Scarpy said thoughtfully.

They found Albert Minchin's horse, as he'd known they would, since he'd sent it trotting down the steep track to lead the posse away from him. Then he looked up to the heights and took a deep breath. The single track, barely a wagon-width, was a trap in itself. He couldn't afford to go near it, so his only alternative was to scale the cliffs. Albert knew it would be a tough climb, hampered by heavy undergrowth and hidden gullies, maybe even gorges. He'd already come face to face with a dead end, and had to try another route, but he'd get there. He was determined to reach the top of the plateau.

After that it would be easy going. He was armed, that was a good start. For many long years Albert had pondered various aspects of an escape, if an escape became necessary, and now as he struggled through a clump of coarse brambles he reached for the best plan.

Once he made the top, he'd skirt the town, steal a horse and get going. As far south as possible first up. Then down to business. The gun would get him food, money and more guns. Sometimes he'd give money to the poor farmers so they would look out for him. Pay them to be on his side.

Albert's ambition now was to be a bushranger, a real outlaw. No one would want to argue with him or give him orders ever again. Prison lore had been rife with stories of these bushrangers, who were hard to catch because they'd rob stores or banks sometimes a hundred miles apart, and disappear into their lairs in the hills, where they were safe.

Two days later he scrambled on to flat land with his clothes in tatters, but the gun carefully tended, and hid in the scrub until nightfall. He was starving, but refused to deviate from his plan. First a horse.

Inspector Kirk was back in Brisbane with four absconders and Harry Harvey. Several of the others had been captured on farms out past Baker's Crossing, and the one known as Old Bart had been found on a roadside, dead from a heart attack.

The remainder, it was decided had hidden themselves among the folk caught up in the so-called gold rush, heading into the wilderness.

'They won't last long out there,' it was said, and no one bothered much about them for the time being. The jail was already full of prisoners awaiting the magistrate's pleasure.

Kirk wasted no time in taking the story of his recapture of Harry Harvey to the *Courier*, boasting that he'd promised to bring him in, though no one actually remembered him saying that. It was a good story, though – the criminal, presumed dead, who comes to life – and it tied in with Kirk's other claim that Jack Drew should be investigated.

'Jack Drew is no good,' he told the editor. 'How many times do I have to say this? On top of everything else, we now know he deliberately helped Harvey escape, and that's a crime in itself.'

Harry Harvey, one of the few prisoners who could read, studied the newspaper, pleased to find himself famous again, boasting that his name had been mentioned right here in print four times. Four times! His fellow prisoners were impressed.

He also pondered the inclusion of Jack Drew in this story, remembering Scarpy's story of the famous highwayman Jack Wodrow, who may or may not be the same bloke.

'I think Kirk's got it in for Drew,' he murmured. 'And where is this gentleman? Why haven't they arrested him? Makes you wonder, all this.'

Never one to procrastinate, Harry asked to see Inspector Kirk, who swaggered to the barred window eating a sausage.

The sight of the fellow with grease on his piggy face almost made Harry change his mind, but Norfolk with its torture chambers loomed, and he thought better of it.

'What do you want?' Kirk grunted. 'You in a hurry to get to the island?'

'No, sir. I was reading about you in the paper. I hear your exploits feature quite regularly.'

'You could say that,' Kirk allowed, finishing the sausage.

'It's a wonder you don't have them placed in a book that you could sell, and become even more famous.'

Kirk's eyes flicked at him, interest raised.

'Yeah, I've thought about that,' he lied. 'What did you want anyway?'

'Me? I didn't know you had a book in mind already. I wanted to say to you that's what you ought to do, sir, after I read here of your exploits. And I could help you with that enterprise.'

'Why would you help me?'

Harry laughed. 'To make sure you didn't forget to mention me. Make me famous too.'

'Ah, get out with you.' Kirk started to walk away, but Harry called to him:

'I was just thinking, Inspector. If you caught a really big fish from the criminal class, you'd sell more books and probably get a promotion to boot.'

Kirk nodded, suspicious now but listening. 'What big fish, Harvey? Not you, I can tell you that.'

'Have you ever heard the name Wodrow?'

'No.'

'He's famous back in the auld country.'

'What for? Spit it out, Harvey. What do you want?'

'It's what I don't want. You keep me off Norfolk and I'll give you a big fish.'

'Who? This unknown Wodrow? Forget it.' He turned to walk away again but Harry called after him:

'He's famous, I tell you. A highwayman. One of the glory boys. And you can be the one to nab him. If the other police up there heard this, they'd be down here in a flash.'

'Good. Try your tales on them,' Kirk said, and strode away.

But the question lingered. What if Harvey did know something? He asked Grimes if he knew the name Wodrow, and surprisingly, he did.

'Yes. Hector Wodrow. He was here recently. Went down on the *Arabella*, poor chap.'

'Ah, that's the end of it then. I'd heard he was famous back in the old country. A highwayman.'

Grimes shook his head. 'I don't think so. I caught a glimpse of him one day, can't see him a highwayman.' He called to Tomkins: 'Rollo here seems to think that Wodrow chap was a highwayman. Looked more like a preacher to me.'

Kirk saw Tomkins' sudden interest and warning bells rang.

'No, he wasn't the type,' Tomkins said. 'He was here searching for his brother, who he said was a wealthy grazier, something like that, but he never found him. I thought the brother could have been Jack Wodrow. There's still a warrant out for his arrest, according to my mate Fred Watkins. It was a murder charge as well, so it would still be on the books. Why? Do you know where the brother is, Rollo?'

'No. Someone must have seen his name on the *Arabella*'s list and it rang a bell.'

'Who would that be?'

'I forget now. Someone in a bar. Didn't mean a thing to me.' He dived out of the station and across the road to the pub . . .

'Didn't mean a thing to him,' Grimes commented acidly, 'but he remembers the name and asks about it.'

So. Wodrow exists, the Inspector mused as he tossed down a cheap whisky. And where is he? Tomkins would like to know. He'd be interested in what Harvey had to say. So am I now. But how to get the rest out of that tricky character?

He went back to the jail and had Harvey brought out to a single cell near the main entrance.

'It appears there could be a bloke called Wodrow who fits your picture,' he said. 'Only could be. Where's your man?'

Harvey sat back. 'Where's the proof I'm not going to Norfolk?'

'Give me a go, I need a bit more than this. Where's Wodrow now?'

'I told you. No result for me, no result for you.'

'Hang on. I mean, is he in this country? No good to me if he isn't.'

'Yes. He's in this country.'

'And still wanted by the law?'

'You know he is or you wouldn't be back here. That was a quick turnabout, Inspector. What did you find out so fast?'

'Never mind. I'll speak to the magistrate if you give me Wodrow's whereabouts.'

'Can't do that. Sorry.'

'I'm not making any deals until I find out if this is the same fellow. Was he transported?'

'Might have been. Talk to the magistrate.'

Much as he hated having to confide in Tomkins and maybe lose half the kudos, Rollo had to know more.

'I chased up the bloke I met in the bar, since you were interested in this Wodrow character, but he couldn't tell me much more, so let me ask you this: was your highwayman transported out here?'

'Not according to the records. If he's in this country, as I think you are saying, then he must have gotten himself here under his own steam. That would tie in with Hector Wodrow's search. We think he might have retired out here with his ill-gotten gains.'

'He's a rich man?'

'Hard to say. One thing wrong with that argument, Kirk. Hector advertised for Jack Wodrow by name. He actually put the name in the paper. Not the sort of thing family members would do to a known felon. We could be barking up the wrong tree.'

'When did they last hear from him in England?'

'Ten years ago.'

That took the wind out of Rollo. 'Ten years? Hell, who'd care after ten years?'

'The law would.'

'Don't know if I could be bothered,' he mumbled. But later that day he rewrote his report on Harvey, claiming that he had 'come quietly' when arrested, and was co-operating with the police in the apprehension of several other known felons. Recommending leniency and the necessity to keep him incarcerated in the Brisbane gaol so that he could be on hand for further interrogation. He took it straight over to the Clerk of the Court, and retrieved his original report, which thankfully had not yet been viewed.

Who cared what gaol Harvey ended up in? His mind raced on then to that thrilling suggestion about a book. Wouldn't that be something! He'd discuss it with Mrs Kirk. She was an educated woman. She'd know how to go about something like this. He practically skipped down the steps of the new courthouse, making for the gaol again.

The magistrate's court was stifling, and the man himself was not in the best of moods.

'They told me the rains would be over by this,' he complained to his clerk, 'and the place is like a bathhouse.'

'Yes, the showers are hanging on, sir,' his clerk apologised.

'You said that last week.' He turned to the papers and files on the desk before him, then looked out over the audience, grumbling to himself about the damp smells arising from their presence.

Called before him one after another and dealt with swiftly were twelve convicts, all formerly employed at Emerald Downs by Major Kit Ferrington. They were accused of arson and absconding from lawful custody.

'What do you plead?' he asked each one, barely waiting for the 'not guilty' response before banging his gavel and sentencing every wretch to Norfolk Island for the term of his natural life.

'You can't do that!' a thug called Lennie Hobbs shouted at him. 'Me and Laddie had nothing to do with it. Albert torched the place, not us.'

He was dragged away, still shouting. Lucky, the magistrate thought, that he didn't cop a flogging as well, for that outburst, but he wanted to get out of this stinking sweaty room as soon as possible.

'What do you plead?' he asked the next one.

'Not guilty, Your Honour.'

Down went the gavel, and the sentence was almost pronounced when the prisoner began bellowing and the clerk jumped up to explain.

'He's not one of them, sir. This is Harold Harvey. You might note . . .' the clerk's voice dropped to a whisper, 'that he wasn't connected with Emerald Downs. He is an absconder but is remorseful and now co-operating with the police in the matter of apprehending several known felons.'

The magistrate peered at the fellow, whose bellowing had subsided. 'I ought to charge you with contempt of court, Harvey. You shut your trap while I look at this.'

He glanced at pages, turned them over as if the backs might contain vital information, breathed in a wave of foul air and made his decision.

'Adding six months to your sentence,' he announced, 'to be served in Her Majesty's Brisbane prison. Next?'

All eyes swivelled to the accused who was the cause of the sudden upsurge of interest in court proceedings, Olivia Fernwood. She was a young woman with a mass of dark curls framing a pretty face, accused of drowning her employer, Jancy Cribb, by pushing him into the river.

The magistrate smiled as her blue eyes looked up at him imploringly.

* * *

284

'Where is he?' Kirk said, grabbing the prisoner as he was being taken out the back door in chains, and Harry laughed.

'Talk about a sleuth! You'd better sharpen up, Kirk. You had him.'

'Who?'

'Wodrow. You had him right under your nose. Name of Jack Drew!'

'How do you know?' Rollo could hardly believe his luck.

'One of his old mates told me.'

'I thought as much,' Kirk muttered, walking away. Neither man offered thanks for the favours. The deal was done, no more to be said. And Harry already had enough information about a crooked warder in Brisbane gaol to ease himself out of there in due time.

After only a day's ride, which was already taking its toll on an exhausted Ferrington, the troops were astonished to see a wagon trundling towards them.

The old couple on board greeted Sergeant Rapper warmly, and asked the way to the goldfields.

'What goldfields?'

'They're out there somewhere, everyone knows that.'

Rapper grinned. 'Believe me, mister, if I knew where there were any goldfields, I'd lead you there.'

The other soldiers gathered around, endeavouring to convince them to turn back, but it was Rapper who solved the impasse.

'I'm commandeering your wagon anyway,' he told them. 'Our officer was wounded in a skirmish with the blacks and he needs transport. And one of my men is struggling to hang on with a broken leg. You've come by just in time. You can take both men on board.'

'I don't see any officer,' the old man argued. 'And I'm not turning back for anyone.'

'He'll be along shortly. It's hard going for him to have to ride . . .'

'You can tell your officer we'll take him back, and your soldier,' the woman called. 'I'm not going any further, Corky. Didn't you hear what the Sergeant said? That the officer was wounded by blacks! You turn this wagon around right now, do you hear me? Do you want to get us killed?'

The Sergeant didn't enlighten them that the area was probably peaceful now, and when the Major and Jack Drew finally caught up with them, he was relieved to be able to hand over Ferrington, who was pale and weak, and had blood seeping through his shirt. Rapper doubted that the sick man could have stayed on his horse much longer.

The woman, Mrs Corkland, upset that he should have been riding with such injuries, soon had him comfortable in her wagon.

'He must be in terrible pain!' she told Rapper, who agreed. He'd seen the agony on Ferrington's face while they carried out those parade-ground manoeuvres for the entertainment of the blacks, and known what an effort he was making, not only to stay on the horse but to lend style to the performance as well.

When she'd finished attending to the Major, Rapper leaned into the wagon. 'How are you feeling, sir?'

'A bit woozy, Sergeant, but help me up, there's a good chap. I want a word with the men.'

'You mustn't!' Mrs Corkland cried. 'You'll only start it bleeding again. I absolutely forbid you to move from that bed!'

'The lady's right,' Rapper said. 'Now that you can, you have to give it a chance to heal.'

'I will. But I need to at least sit up for a few minutes.'

Grumbling, the woman propped him against folds of canvas, so that he was able to thank Sergeant Rapper, in front of his men, for a job well done.

'After the first attack, when unfortunately a spear got me,' he continued, 'Sergeant Rapper followed through, letting the hostile blacks know that you were a force to be dealt with.'

'Until they turned the tables!' a soldier shouted.

'Let's say both sides discovered the cost of confrontation. I know that their chief did; he was ready for peace, especially after the raids carried out under the command of Sergeant Rapper. Persuasion, one could say.

'Also, I was most impressed by your discipline in trying circumstances,' he said to the men, 'and your self-control in keeping the peace with the blacks, the last few days we were there. If both the blacks and the settlers follow your example, we should expect peaceful times in this area. Thanks be to God.'

Hearing this, Corky began to complain that he'd been tricked, that there was no risk of attacks by the blacks, but his wife wasn't taking any chances.

'You heard the man say "if". If folk behave! I don't recollect seeing too much of that nowadays. We're going home and taking the Major and Trooper Pratt with us.'

Having promised to go straight to Emerald Downs to let Jessie and Adrian know the Major was on his way, Jack set off with Sergeant Rapper and his men.

'I had the idea you and the Major were more interested in gold,' Rapper said to him.

'Just interested, Sergeant. But the trouble was, like old Corky back there, we didn't know where to look. I've been poking about for years and I never actually found any.'

'You going back to try again?'

'No.'

'What about the Major?'

'I don't know what he wants to do. Why?'

'Because if he does decide to go prospecting, you might put in a good word for me. I'd like to go along. I reckon we'd make a good team.'

Jack almost choked on that. Ferrington a team man? Bloody hell! Tell his workers that when he handed out fifty lashes. But then he looked at the other side of the man, from Rapper's point of view. Rapper was a tough man. The Major had won his respect, not an easy thing for a desk soldier to do.

'Wonders will never cease,' he muttered.

He had already decided to move on when the Major got back from the farm. He'd have a horse and a few pounds, more money than he needed to take him down to Sydney. It would be a long journey, but he was in no hurry, and he was looking forward to exploring the coastal route. He felt that if he could see that harbour again he could start his life once more, get it right this time. He was no longer interested in chasing elusive fortunes, thinking he might seek to live in a quiet village somewhere, close enough to the bush he'd come to love, where he could settle down and live a normal village life.

The troops were keen to get back to town now and Rapper set a cracking pace, leading them in a race across open country as if tossing aside all their cares, and Jack kept up with them, enjoying their company.

That night, though, they came across a large camp of travellers, all en route to the non-existent goldfields. Rapper managed to convince some of them to turn back, but most insisted they had the right to go wherever they wished, and he couldn't stop them.

In the morning, though, several men claimed that they were entitled to the protection of these troops, from blacks and bushrangers, annoying Rapper, who shouted that his men were not police, and if they needed protection they should turn back. After that, he refused to stop for any of the travellers, taking his troops past them without even an acknowledgment, which pleased Jack, who was impatient to keep moving now.

Eventually they reached Baker's Crossing, where Rapper decided he'd earned a drink of beer after weeks of drought, but Jack was anxious to press on, so he left them at the turnoff to the river and kept riding, heading for Emerald Downs.

He didn't have the same trouble recognising the terrain as Lieutenant Clancy had; he rode straight through the bush to avoid the twists and turns of the road, and came upon the scene with a gasp of horror.

'What the hell's happened here?'

Shocked, he rode around the deserted property, came back and stared at the ruins of Ferrington's house. Then he rode about again and found the Chinaman in the barn.

Tom Lok showed him Polly's grave, and he was immensely saddened at such a waste of a life.

'Tell me what happened,' he said gravely to the Chinaman. 'Tell me from the start.'

Only a few hours later he was joined by his companions of the previous days. Rapper had heard the news at Baker's Crossing and called in on their way past to see if they could offer any assistance.

'Kind of you,' Jack said wearily. 'But not much anyone can do until the boss gets back. Not much at all.'

Sergeant Rapper strode about, picking up the remains of a dining chair. 'What a bloody shame,' he said. 'What a bloody shame. You coming into town with us then, Jack?

'No. I'll wait for him.'

'Yeah,' Rapper said, understanding.

The squad mounted up and rode slowly, silently, down the track to the road, and Jack watched them until they were out of sight, unwilling to have to turn back to this misery.

Late in the afternoon he watched a huge flock of budgerigars performing their nightly fly-round before settling down. The ritual, carried out by various birds, even crows, always intrigued him. They circled way out beyond the hills then came back to float lazily over the other side of the river and back again, their flashing colours even more brilliant bathed in the bright orange of the setting sun. It always seemed to him that it was a family outing, a get-together, one and all, playing in the thermals, sweeping across the skies like a wash on a giant canvas, maybe even encouraging young ones to stretch their wings. But whatever it was, this time they depressed him. A sort of envy, he supposed, that he was so earthbound and so very alone, waiting to deliver sad news, while up there, joy and harmony wheeled above him.

Superintendent Grimes was an easy-going man, a country man, appointed to this post because he understood that a certain amount of disorder would be inevitable in the growth of a port, especially this port, named after Sir Thomas Makdougall Brisbane, which had begun life as a convict settlement. He found he could cope when he came to accept that everything in the north seemed larger than life . . . The Aborigines were more belligerent than their southern brothers, the graziers more ambitious, the townspeople in more of a hurry to get things done, and the working man more knowledgeable as to his rights. He learned that patience and prayer solved a lot of problems; patience in being able to explain to people the reasons for the many difficulties and delays they had to overcome in frontier situations, and prayer that his advice was close to correct. Even so, his patience with Inspector Kirk was running out and his prayers were far from kindly.

Sergeant Rapper and his troops had ridden back into town, quietly and without fanfare, because they'd lost three men, and their commanding officer had been wounded. The Sergeant presented his report to Lieutenant Clancy, who invited Jimmy Grimes to attend, since he was responsible for the law in the district, and they were delighted to hear, at the end, that a peace of sorts had been established. That, in fact, both the soldiers and the

288

blacks had been able to sit down together for a corroboree. An unexpected and gratifying result.

Rapper was able to inform his interrogators of the cause and extent of injuries sustained by Trooper Pratt and Major Ferrington, and the discussion naturally led to the misfortunes at Emerald Downs.

'We saw the place on the way in,' he said. 'Jack Drew stayed there to wait for the Major and, I suppose, try to soften the blow. A terrible shame it is to think Major Ferrington is coming home to that disaster, when he should be riding in with flags flying.'

Clancy looked to Grimes as if pushing the next chore over to him, but the police superintendent leaned back in his chair.

'The Lieutenant has a problem he needs to discuss with you, Sergeant. He has invited me to remain in the room as a witness.'

'Why? What have I done?' Rapper demanded.

'Nothing,' Clancy said. 'Nothin' at all, Sergeant. Let me explain. Our friend Inspector Kirk has lodged a complaint with your colonel in Sydney, concerning the leadership of Major Ferrington.'

'What complaint?' Rapper bristled angrily.

'Hold your fire, man. In his turn, the Colonel has required that Major Ferrington answer the charges in writing, which I have to tell you, Sergeant, is only a flea's breath away from an official enquiry. The charges are thus: that Major Ferrington did take his men prospecting, in defiance of his military orders; that Major Ferrington did deliberately take a western course away from the agreed-on route, thereby distancing himself from the Native Mounted Police, and placing that squad in danger.'

Rapper's swarthy face was almost purple with anger. 'A load of tripe, sir.'

'Maybe. But we did do some prospecting . . . ' Clancy said.

'Only at campsites.'

'We did veer away from the stock route.'

'By mistake,' Rapper said stoutly.

'And we were not there to go to the aid of the Native Mounted Police when they were attacked.'

'Because they hurtled north at a much faster pace. We were patrolling as wide an area as we could as we moved north. We didn't know they'd been attacked. That Kirk is a miserable little . . . Excuse me, Mr Grimes. But I reckon he's just whingeing for the sake of. Easy seen he doesn't like the Major.'

'Which doesn't alter the fact that Major Ferrington will have to answer these charges as soon as possible. With your permission, Lieutenant Clancy will submit both of your statements to the Colonel at the same time, to support Major Ferrington.'

'Good,' Rapper said sharply.

Dismissed from that depressing scene, the Sergeant gave a concerned whistle. He didn't like the sound of those charges, by God. He didn't like the sound of them at all. They could be made to stick. He hoped the Colonel and Major Ferrington were mates, as officers often were, or this gentleman, wound and all, could be in a heap of bother.

He went searching for Inspector Kirk, but was waylaid by Sam Dignam from the *Courier*, who'd got wind of their exploits and wanted the full story.

'I'll buy you a drink or two, Sergeant,' he said, 'on the strength of your story. I believe Major Ferrington was wounded?'

'That's correct.'

'I met a couple of your men who say he's a hero.'

'That is also correct. Lead on, Mr Dignam.'

When the Sergeant had left, the two men discussed their other problem.

'It won't take long for Kirk to find out that Jack Drew is at Emerald Downs,' Clancy said. 'The man was invaluable to us. Can't you re-call that bastard Kirk? You don't need two inspectors. His job is done. Couldn't you have him sent to Norfolk as a warder?

'I can't stop the momentum now. As his superior I have to follow up the information he has unearthed. Not only is Jack Drew an escaped convict – one of the Major's workers said he'd been at Major Mudie's prison farm years back, so Kirk followed that up swiftly – but Drew is an alias. His real name is Wodrow . . .'

'So Tomkins said. He had no idea Drew was Wodrow; he likes the man, and is desperately sorry he let the cat out of the bag to Kirk, of all people.'

'Yes,' Grimes said. 'He seems a nice fellow. I'd have let his history slip into a bin, given the chance. We've got enough villains to chase without going after reformed characters like Drew.'

'What can we do then?' Clancy was worried. 'Recommend him for valour?'

'Wouldn't do any good.'

'What would?'

'Damned if I know. I'll think about it.'

Sergeant Rapper made it his business to find the Pinnocks, and Miss Pinnock received him in a quiet corner of the hotel garden.

'The Major asked me to pass on his best regards,' he said, tactfully avoiding mention of Emerald Downs.

'Thank you, Sergeant.'

He thought she looked drawn and thin, not the clear-eyed beauty he'd seen before they set out on the expedition.

'Lieutenant Clancy said he'd been speared,' she continued. 'That was such a shock. Has he recovered?'

She spoke dully, as if he were tiring her.

'Can't say that he has, miss. He's still rather sore and sorry, but he'll be home in a few days.'

290

'Oh? He's not with you?'

Sergeant Rapper was finding this conversation very odd. If the Major had arrived back in Brisbane with his men, surely he would not have sent a stand-in to speak to his fiancée. He would have been here himself.

'No, miss. Some wagoners are bringing him in to save him having to ride.'

'Oh. Yes. I see.'

There was something else he wanted to discuss with the Pinnocks, but now that he'd seen the nervous state she was in, he decided he'd have to speak to the brother.

'And how is your brother, Mr Pinnock?' he asked.

'Quite well, thank you.' She fingered a handkerchief in her lap.

'I thought I might pay my respects to him also.'

'Yes. He would most likely want to hear from you. I presume all went well. Apart from the Major's injury. Thank you for coming to see me, Sergeant. I am most appreciative.'

'My pleasure, miss.' He rose quickly, tipping his cap. 'Where would I find Mr Pinnock then?'

'I really don't know,' she said, peering about her as if he were loitering behind the hydrangeas. 'Somewhere, I suppose.'

'Thank you, miss.'

Rapper wondered if there might be more to the story of the riot at Emerald Downs. She was definitely not the same person. She and the brother had escaped, but what had happened beforehand? Maybe she'd been attacked by those felons? Frightened out of her wits?

'That's what it seems like to me anyway,' he murmured. 'Damn shame, a nice girl like that.'

He found Adrian Pinnock in the bar but did not accept his invitation to join him in a drink, believing that it would not be correct to be pushing himself into an officer's family circle.

He explained that the Major was being brought in by the Corklands, in their wagon, and would be back in a few days.

'But I just wanted a quiet word with you, sir, that's all. I wanted to warn you that the Major might be facing an enquiry into the conduct of our mission . . .'

'Ah yes. Lieutenant Clancy did say something about that, but he said it was all a lot of tomfoolery. Nothing to worry about. But thank you for bringing this to my attention.'

'If you'll forgive me, sir, I think due attention should be paid to this matter, and I ask you to warn the Major, as soon as he comes in.'

'Poor Ferrington. I rather think he'll have more urgent matters to see to when he gets back than Kirk's miserable complaints. We're all sick with worry. Sure you wouldn't like a drink?'

'No thank you, sir.'

'Bloody fool,' Rapper growled as he marched out of the bar. 'I wouldn't have left that whippersnapper in charge of a chook pen. A couple of years in the army would straighten him up. That's what he needs.'

When the wagon rolled into Baker's Crossing, the Major was recognised by the locals, who rushed to tell him the news, such news! That his workers had burned down his fine new house and absconded, some even running this way only to be rounded up by posses, and the manager of Emerald Downs and his sister . . . they'd hightailed it for town.

'Leave the poor fellow alone!' Mrs Corkland snapped at them. 'You've given him a God-awful shock, you men, with your big mouths. Here, Major, you'd better take a drop of the doings.'

She handed him a shot of whisky, but swallowing it, he muttered: 'They must have the wrong place. It couldn't be mine.'

'Sounds like it,' Pratt said. 'Cripes, having your place wiped out by a bush fire, that's bad enough, but to get it burned down on you, that's terrible. I'd get after them blokes, sir, I'd strangle them with my bare hands.'

Kit had come to hate the soldier with the broken leg and the whining voice, who had shared the back of the wagon with him for long days, but now he'd had enough.

'When I want your opinion, I'll ask for it,' he snarled. 'Get my horse saddled up.'

'My leg, sir. I can hardly move.'

'I reckoned you'd want to get going,' said Corky. 'I've watered your horse and he's already saddled. I hope they're wrong, Major, by God I do.'

Kit thanked Corky and his wife, and managed to ride away in a dignified manner until he was out of sight of the curious folk at the crossing, and then, seized by panic, he urged the horse on. The animal, having spent days trailing along behind the wagon, leapt forward easily and sped down the road, hooves flying.

Jack had no words for him, no words to console, nothing that he could think of to say that might alleviate this man's pain, so he sat by the woodpile and smoked a cheroot Tom Lok had given him. He tried not to feel sorry for Ferrington, despising sorriness, wondering if there was such a word, maybe not, rethinking it as pity, knowing that was the last thing the Major needed.

He wanted to say, about the house, that it was only a thing, it could be put back together again, and the land was as green and fertile as ever, but this wasn't the time. He watched as Ferrington questioned Tom Lok for a third time, and as if a wind of change had blown up from the river he saw the man storm from despair into towering rage! He strode over to the barn, shouting revenge on the men who had done this, cursing them to the depths, flinging aside farm implements that Tom Lok had collected and placed neatly along the side of the barn.

'Why don't I burn this down too?' he shouted at Jack. 'Burn the lot down! What bloody use is it to me now?'

Jack shrugged. 'If it makes you feel better, burn it.'

'Of course, that's exactly what you would say, wouldn't you? A man who has nothing, who is content to sponge on others! Who doesn't even own a bloody chair! What do you care if I burn the rest of the farm to the ground? It doesn't mean a bloody thing to you . . .'

He stormed away, still ranting, shouting, threatening, and Jack thought how complex people were. Here was a man willing to make peace with blacks who had almost killed him with that spear, who had almost taken his life, but the men who had burned his house down . . . no mercy for them. Ferrington was in a murderous mood; had any of them been about, the floggings would have been on again in real earnest. Maybe that soldiering business had him so well trained he'd just gone by the book, while out here he had to write his own book, day by day.

Come to think of it, so do I, thought Jack. I've had the blacks making all my decisions for me for years . . . what we do, where we go, who we visit, where we hunt or harvest . . . His meditations were interrupted by Tom Lok, who came up with a message:

'The boss says you can go. Me too. I can't go, Mister Jack. They put me back in plison.'

'Are you a convict too?' Jack was surprised.

'Yes. My daddy velly good cook in Sydney Town. White man bash him, take his money. Same man come back, bash him again, take the money, this time my daddy he die. So I wait for that same white man near that same alley and I cut his throat.' He laughed. 'That fixed him, eh?'

'You better hang around here then. He might change his mind.'

'He might beat me.'

'You can run faster than him.'

Tom Lok nodded. 'That is true.'

Ferrington slept in his office. Jack bedded down on a bunk in the men's quarters. Tom Lok slept in his kitchen. He cooked steak and eggs and mashed potatoes for breakfast, serving the Major in his office and Jack in the cookhouse.

'Boss going to town, see his lady,' Tom said, as they observed him heading for the stables. 'You tell him he better shave first, Jack. Clean up nice for missy.'

'Not me, Tom.' He was surprised, though. Ferrington rarely looked as unkempt as that, even in the bush.

'You didn't tell him about Miss Pinnock sacking Polly, did you?'

'No, no say. You tell me no say.'

'Good. We can't have him cross with her.'

293

'No,' Tom said seriously. 'This morning he bloody cross with Mister Pinnock. Wring his neck, he said.'

'Gawd!' Jack sighed. 'Oh well. Now . . . thank you for that breakfast, it's the best feed I've had in a long time. But we've got work to do. We'll hitch the horse to the dray and start cleaning up the mess, we'll cart the ash and debris away and dump it in that hollow over the back of the house.'

Tom bridled. 'Me, I cook. Not coolie.'

'Get some shovels!'

Someone had to start somewhere, Jack decided, and he'd got nothing else to do. Then he realised that thought had a familiar ring. Strangely, when he'd been living with the blacks, having nothing to do wasn't a concept, it wasn't thought about as such.

'Oh well, one thing at a time,' he said as he remembered his idea of an excursion to Sydney, that leisurely five-hundred-mile ride. 'It can wait.'

The old horse pulled the dray up to the front of the house, and Jack picked up a shovel. 'What a waste,' he said, as he dug deep into floury ash.

Chapter Seventeen

Whenever ships came into port, whether from over the great oceans or from the coastal cities, people turned out to greet the passengers, ask for news, or see who came ashore . . . sometimes even for the excitement of seeing a ship coming up the river.

On this day there was whispering and pointing as Lord and Lady Heselwood stepped ashore, the aristocrats who'd been evicted from their land by a horde of savages. They were met by Reece Maykin, who produced an umbrella for Lady Heselwood, despite the fact that it was a glorious April day.

She was wearing an elegant blue gown with a crinoline skirt, and a perky hat that some of the ladies thought foolish for this clime, but they all agreed the Heselwoods were a handsome couple.

'Him especially,' one woman giggled, making syrupy noises with her lips. 'I'd have him any time. And who's the natty one?'

They stared suspiciously as a neatly turned-out officer in a red military jacket with an abundance of gold braid joined the Heselwoods on the wharf and was introduced to Maykin. Uniforms made the freewheelers in this frontier town uneasy, they brought to mind vague misgivings about rules and restrictions, so the crowd of onlookers by the Custom House shuffled back a little.

Colonel Gresham, a tall, spare man with white hair and a thick waxed moustache, didn't even notice them. He was delighted to have made the acquaintance of the Heselwoods on board ship, and had no intention of relinquishing their esteemed company so soon. He was sorry now that he hadn't allowed his wife to accompany him on this short voyage, so that she too could have met this couple, and gained an opportunity to foster a friendship. The Colonel was always careful to mix socially with the right people, and to be able to claim this pair, the darlings of Sydney society, as personal friends would be quite a coup.

He heard Mr Maykin say that he had booked them into the Lands Office Hotel, and was about to inform them that he would be staying there too when Lady Heselwood flatly refused that accommodation.

'Definitely not,' she said. 'That woman treated us like poachers when we were last here. We shall stay at the Britannia.'

'By all means, my dear,' Maykin said.

The Colonel beamed. 'That hotel has been recommended to me. I'll be at the Britannia also. Could you direct me to it, Mr Maykin?'

'Better still, I'll take you, sir! My carriage is across the road, there's plenty of room.'

Anxious to please, Maykin didn't notice Heselwood's grimace, and Lady Heselwood's mischievous smile.

'My dear, you've made a new friend,' she said to her husband when they retired to their room.

'A bloody bore,' he retorted. 'What's his name again? Colonel who?'

'Jasin, I keep telling you . . . Gresham. But he says call him Charles.'

'I'll call him nothing. Do not make arrangements with him, Georgina. I'm not here to socialise at all, let alone put up with that dullard. I thought I'd cast the fellow overboard if I had to listen to any more about India.'

'Actually, at lunch you were quite rude to him about that.'

'Lunch? Who invited him to lunch? No one, he just tacked himself on to us. Anyway, I wasn't rude, I simply said that if I wished to know about India I should go there.'

'I think he was offended.'

'Nonsense. You can't offend people like that. And did you notice he kept looking in the mirror and stiffening that moustache?'

'He is quite handsome.'

'Spare me! Is there fresh water in that jug?'

Kit wasn't interested in the goings and comings at the port; he rode straight to the barracks, where Clancy was delighted to see him.

'You're looking a darn sight better, Major,' he said. 'Those ribs still giving you trouble?'

'Not too much. I've come to fill out the forms and get the report out of the way.'

'Right you are! Come on through to the office. I was terrible sorry about the trouble at Emerald Downs, sir, terrible sorry.'

'Did they catch any of them?'

'Some. They're headed for Norfolk prison. One fellow they called Bart died on the road. Another, Albert Minchin, he's trouble. They say he was the ringleader.'

'Where is he now?'

'Disappeared. They had him to ground out Ipswich way but he got his hands on a gun, shot and killed two men, wounded another and took to the scrub. They're still searching for him. People warned to shoot him on sight. No quarter.'

'Good. This will do, I'll sit here. I'll need several pages . . .'

He picked up a pen and examined the nib as Clancy gave him the necessary stationery, and opened a window to air the office.

The Lieutenant was concerned for Ferrington, surprised to see him looking so wretched, unshaven and untidy, wearing only his uniform trousers and shirt and a bush hat.

'Is there anything I can do for you, Major?' he asked. 'Sergeant Rapper says you did a mighty job.'

'A stiff drink would help.'

'Aha! That I can do. I happen to have a drop of the best Irish.'

He dashed away and returned with the whiskey. 'A double here to get started,' he grinned, but Ferrington had no smiles left in him, Clancy feared, for he only nodded and downed the drink in a gulp.

Clancy decided it would be best to let the Major get on with his report before he mentioned Kirk's charges, since it was obvious Ferrington hadn't heard about them.

'Did you come straight from Emerald Downs?' he asked.

'Yes.' The voice carried an edge of irritation, so the Lieutenant retreated, his guess confirmed. Anyway, he thought, it would be easier to finish the report without the distraction of Kirk's lies. He was still fuming that, as well as the other muckraking, Kirk had referred to him as an alcoholic, which Clancy emphatically denied. He liked a drink, that was true, he argued, but he was no drunkard.

'Just because I have a drop in my saddlebag,' he told the Sergeant, 'doesn't make me a tosspot.'

Sergeant Rapper wasn't interested in defending Clancy, whom he considered to have been a dead loss for the whole operation.

'Weak as piss,' he'd said to his mates, 'and his drinking does no good mentioned in the same breath as the tripe Kirk's puttin' about. He's no help to the Major, never was.'

Rapper had come to the conclusion that the combination of field soldier – himself – and office soldier – Ferrington – would work, given tricky situations like the ones they'd encountered, and was pleased to sing Ferrington's praises at the barracks, backed up by his men, but that didn't alter the scurrilous stories doing the rounds of the town, and he was at a loss to know how to combat them.

'Short of catching up with Kirk on a dark night,' he'd muttered.

The Sergeant, always correct, sprang to attention and showed not an inkling of the surprise he experienced when Colonel Gresham walked in the gate.

'Afternoon, sir!' he shouted, saluting.

The Colonel acknowledged the salute but didn't bother to stop. He knew these barracks, he'd designed them himself, and he was pleased that the lawns and gardens either side of the path from the gate to the administration centre were well kept, flourishing in fact. No doubt the rainfall and good soil played a part, he supposed, barracks being notorious for neglected gardens. He nodded his approval as he passed, noting the trees were flourishing too, good English oaks that he had recommended. In all, his design had worked admirably, something that he must point out to Lady Heselwood, who had mentioned that she'd called in a landscaper to prepare the grounds of their new house in Point Piper.

He opened the fly-wire door and strode inside, to a small unmanned reception area, then through an open doorway, where he found Lieutenant Clancy at his desk, a bottle of whiskey on the sideboard behind him, and on from there, someone out of uniform lounging at a desk.

Clancy leapt up. 'Colonel Gresham, sir!' he said in a voice loud enough to alert the fellow at the other desk, who simply turned about, recognised him and nodded.

'Gresham.'

'I beg your pardon, Major!' Gresham said, ignoring Clancy, who was hastily buttoning his jacket.

Ferrington turned to him, his face cold. 'How are you, Gresham?'

'You are out of uniform, sir!'

'Ah, yes. My uniform got cut up to make way for a spear. Sorry, Clancy, I just remembered your jacket. I'm afraid it got ruined too. What are you doing in this neck of the woods, Gresham?'

The Colonel was stunned. 'Major Ferrington. I expect the courtesy of my rank, sir!'

'Very well, you have it. Sorry about that, but I'm busy writing my report, having just got back to town, and then I have a lot to do.'

'Excuse me, sir,' Clancy interrupted. 'Major Ferrington hasn't been well. He's not himself.'

Gresham stared at them. 'What's wrong with him?'

'Tropical fever, sir.'

'Yes, that'll do,' Ferrington said, and went back to his work.

But Gresham wasn't about to allow that. 'In which case you are relieved of duty for this day, Major. You may repair to the infirmary.'

The Major turned and glared at him. 'For Christ's sake, I'm here for a reason, I have a job to do. Will you let me do it?'

'So do I, Major. I have a job to do also. To enquire into the charges against you of dereliction of duty causing the deaths of men under your command.'

'What men? What are you talking about?'

'He doesn't know about the charges yet,' Clancy cried anxiously. 'He has just come in from the wilds and found his house—'

'Shut up!' the Major snapped at him. 'What charges?'

'Yes. We're paying attention now, aren't we? Suddenly no tropical fever evident.'

Gresham walked over to the desk. 'I see you are lodging your report. Very well, complete it and then you will have plenty to do. I can promise you that.'

The Colonel was served tea in the shade of the eastern veranda and Clancy took the opportunity to present himself again, correctly dressed this time, and beg permission to speak on behalf of Major Ferrington.'

'I believe the man is capable of speaking for himself, thank you.'

'And there you'd be wrong, sir,' Clancy said boldly. 'For he has his wounds . . .'

'I know about that. I have read your version of matters up until the time you returned to Brisbane, which was after the Native Police engaged the enemy, and before our troops took action, under the command of Sergeant Rapper.'

'Ah no, sir.' 'Twasn't that at all I wished to mention. It's that the Major has suffered personal loss. He would have only just discovered that in his absence his workers rioted, burned down his home and skedaddled.'

The Colonel turned a mean eye on Clancy. 'What the hell are you talking about?'

'It's the shock, sir. Can you imagine your shock when you come home from duty to find your house burned to the ground?'

'And this happened to Ferrington?'

'Yes, sir. While he was away.'

'I see, but what has this to do with my business here?'

'Well now, the man's upset and there's your reason. But might I say, about that other business, which I'm thinking you're here to investigate . . .'

The Colonel sipped his tea. 'No you may not, Lieutenant. I shall hear your statement when I'm ready. I've read the others held by Superintendent Grimes. When Ferrington's version is complete, bring it to me, and tell him to present himself here in correct dress tomorrow at ten a.m. No earlier. No later.'

'I don't think he has another uniform, sir.'

'Then tell him to buy one.'

'We have none in the stores and the shops here don't run to uniforms.'

Colonel Gresham gritted his teeth. 'Get out of my sight, Lieutenant!'

Kit had meant to find Jessie and Adrian as soon as he had rid himself of his last military obligation, but after listening to Clancy and Sergeant Rapper, he headed for the police station in search of Kirk.

Inspector Tomkins greeted him sincerely and sorrowfully. 'We owe you a debt, Major Ferrington, for your forbearance with the blacks, despite a severe wound. Your men speak highly of you.'

'But not Rollo Kirk, I understand. Where is he?'

'He's not here at present, Major. You look all in. Would you care to join me in a nice hot cup of tea?'

Kit glanced at the clock. Nearly five now. He wondered where Kirk was. Just the same, a cup of tea wouldn't go amiss right now, and Tomkins was a pleasant man. Sane, he thought. Sane, by way of a change.

The tea was strong and sweet and served with butternut biscuits. His host was quiet, apologetic. He explained that he was pleased to have this chance to apologise to the Major . . .

'We'd hoped this would have all blown over before you came home. And we certainly didn't count on Colonel Gresham arriving so quickly. That had to do with availability of shipping, unfortunately. Apparently *Argyle* was due to sail when he decided to investigate matters, and he hopped aboard.'

'Could I see Kirk's statement?'

'We gave it to the Colonel.'

'But you would have made a copy.'

'It just so happens . . .' Tomkins opened a drawer and took out a folder. 'Here you are.'

As he opened it, Kit asked: 'What about Grimes? Where does he stand?'

'Very much opposed to Kirk bypassing his authority. Opposed to Kirk at any time, I suppose you could say. But it's out of his hands now. It's a military matter.'

Tomkins disappeared to replenish his teapot and Kit read Rollo's version of their operation. About the hero Kirk and the villain Ferrington. He tossed it back on the desk in disgust, and sat back angrily until the Inspector returned.

'I want you to know,' Tomkins said, 'that we are all happy to give you whatever support we can, including personal references. There'll be no shortages in that field, let me tell you.'

'Thank you, but I won't be needing them.'

'Please, Major. Take care here. These enquiries can be difficult. References can be crucial.'

'No. This is a military matter, and I'm finished with the military. If they hadn't forced me to leave my property and take on a mission that any officer with an ounce of sense could have handled . . .'

Tomkins shook his head. 'Don't underestimate yourself, Major. You were able to make peace with that chief, a marvellous achievement, considering his reputation.'

'No it wasn't. The fellow wanted peace. He sent for me. The real peacemaker was my scout, Jack Drew. Anyway, I will not defend myself against this twisted statement. I refuse. Under no circumstances,' he said hotly, 'will I allow the likes of Rollo Kirk to question my conduct.'

'I can't see that you have a choice,' Tomkins said kindly, but Kit shrugged as he drank the fresh cup of tea.

'Thank you. I appreciate your time. I must be off now. Could you tell me where Mr and Miss Pinnock are staying?'

'Yes, of course. They're staying at the Lands Office Hotel. I presume you know that Adrian made his full report on the riot at Emerald Downs as soon as he and Miss Pinnock got into town. It's all here if you want to read it. A most regrettable business, Major. Young Pinnock was distraught.'

Kit declined. 'I've had enough of reports for one day. I'd rather see Adrian and my fiancée now, and come back tomorrow if I may.'

'By all means.' Tomkins walked him out to the street. 'Don't forget, if there's anything we can do . . .'

'There is,' Kit said coldly. 'Tell me where I can get my hands on Kirk.'

'You've had a long day,' the Inspector said wearily. 'Take a rest, Major. We'll have another talk tomorrow.'

The noise in the bar at the Lands Office Hotel dwindled to a hush, the last loud voice left hanging, agape, as Major Ferrington was recognised at the door . . . a tall dark figure against the glare outside, but him all right.

Then there was a curiosity, a general glancing around the room, to find who would respond, for what was he after? They knew by the cut of his shoulders that he wasn't here for a quiet drink, a thirst-slaker. Few knew him personally; he'd always been aloof, a presence you could say, a man who minded his own business, but now his business had become town property and so the silence in the bar began to crumble. Shoulders turned slowly, seeking out, with asides and wry comments, a possible connection, finding it in a young bloke drinking with his mates by the open window.

'Who?' they asked, as the name sped about and heads jerked in that direction.

'Pinnock,' came the mutterings. 'You know . . . the young bloke who managed Emerald Downs.'

'Jesus! Some sort of manager!'

As Pinnock walked over to the door, with the smile of a man extending a hand to a gallows attendant, the hard humour of the back-country men bit into the dusty air.

'Oh well. As they say,' a joker remarked, 'if it isn't one thing it's another. Isn't that right, Major?'

'Where's Jessica?' he asked, moving back to rest against a low stone wall.

'She's upstairs.' Adrian rushed forward. 'Are you all right?'

'Yes.' Kit stifled a groan; the ribs were giving him hell and the wound was itching as if attacked by ants. He told himself that was supposed to be a sign of healing, that itchiness, and hoped it was true.

'I'd rather have a word with you first,' Adrian said. 'I'm so awfully sorry about what happened, Kit. I really am, and I take full responsibility . . .'

'Full responsibility?' Kit thundered. 'Like how? Bring Polly back to life? Rope in the absconders, who, I believe, have already murdered two of the men who were out trying to recapture them? Doing your job!'

'If you'd let me explain . . .'

'It's a bit late for explanations. You lost control of the bastards and let them wreck my farm. But what caused Polly to hang herself? What was that about?'

'We'll never know, Kit. She didn't leave a note. It just happened.'

'And now your solution to your responsibilities is to hang about in a bar.'

'I've been trying to raise money to help you . . .'

301

'Oh for Christ's sake!' Disgusted, Kit pushed himself up and walked away, resisting a need to nurse his injured ribs with his arm, but Adrian followed him.

'Couldn't we have a talk? Before you go up and see Jessie, I mean. She's not well, you know . . .'

'Not well?' Kit turned abruptly. 'What's wrong?'

'She got a bad fright, remember? The riot terrified her.'

'Of course it would . . .' He resumed the walk along the hotel corridor. 'She's been resting here, I hope?'

'Yes, but I'd better let her know you're here.'

Kit felt that his life was almost too chaotic to contemplate with any measure of accord, and he'd been trying to contain his anger, but suddenly Adrian was in front of him, barring his way, just when he was reaching out to Jessie, the only person he really wanted to see.

'You look exhausted,' Adrian was saying. 'Come up to my room, you can share my room. I'll pour you a drink, then I'll get Jessie.'

'You'll get out of my way!' Kit said, shoving him aside. 'I'll see Jessie, then I shall take a room of my own.'

'What with? You're broke!'

Kit didn't miss a step at that unwelcome reminder; he kept on to the lobby, enquired at the desk and hurried upstairs.

She took a while to answer his knock, with a thin 'Who is it?' and there was silence again when he responded, forcing him to repeat: 'It's me, Jessie! Kit.'

Finally she opened the door, and as he took her in his arms in a rush of emotion at being reunited with her at last, he did notice that she looked untidy, her long dark hair needing a comb, her clothes crushed, so unlike her, and he blamed himself for intruding without warning, without giving the poor girl time to attend to her dressing.

He kicked the door shut and was kissing her passionately, telling her how much he had missed her, when he realised she was turning her face away, gently trying to extricate herself.

'I'm sorry, my darling,' he said. 'I shouldn't have rushed at you like that, but I have missed you so much. I wanted to tell you that right away, because I've been thinking about you so much . . .'

'But you were hurt,' she said. 'I was frightened when people said you'd been struck by a spear . . .'

'You knew I'd be all right, though, didn't you?' He grinned, seating himself on the bed and taking her hands, looking up at her. 'But think what a fright I got when I first heard those lunatics had rioted at the farm! I should never have left you there.'

'I was all right,' she said sadly, moving away from him to sit primly in the armchair by the window as if they were expecting afternoon tea, but Kit didn't complain; he was happy to see her there, safe and well. She did look rather pale, but against the tangled curls her face seemed lovelier than ever,

302

ethereal, he thought, different from her usual bright and bouncy self.

'We rode away,' she said. 'There didn't seem to be anything else we could do.'

'Of course not. You should have left, gone to the Crossing at the first sign of trouble.'

'Too late, I think. It all happened so fast. Odd, isn't it?' she said. 'That you should be attacked by black savages and we get attacked by white savages. Really odd.'

He glanced anxiously at her, thinking that was a peculiar thing to say, and deemed it wiser to steer away from the subject of the farm.

'I'm glad you had the sense to come here, Jessie. Are you finding the room comfortable?'

'I suppose. It doesn't matter. Did they bury Polly?'

'Yes. I'll put a nice headstone there for her. Why don't you come and sit over here with me?' He patted the bed. 'Come and let me give you a cuddle.'

'No,' she said firmly. 'We have to talk. About the farm.'

'Don't worry about the farm, Jessie, not now. You're safe, that's all that matters.'

'Adrian's upset.'

He nodded, but made no comment. He didn't want to criticise her fool of a brother in her company.

'Obviously you are too, my dear, but don't be. We'll sort it out.'

'But it wasn't Adrian's fault.'

The hell it wasn't, he thought; riots don't just happen, they build, and they're triggered by events. Adrian should have seen trouble was brewing and done something about it . . . settle the staff down or call for backup from neighbours or police.

'Don't worry about that now,' he sighed.

'But I must. Did they tell you why Polly hanged herself?'

'We don't know, Jessie, we simply don't know. It's very sad when someone dies like that, very sad, but what's done is done. No use dwelling on it.'

'But we do know. We know very well why she went down to the barn and did what she did. And we should be dwelling on it. Or I should, anyway.'

'Now, now, Jessie, don't—'

'Please, Kit, let me finish. Polly was perfectly all right. She cooked us a nice dinner, and afterwards I told her . . . You see, I was trying to help. I can cook a bit, simple dishes, things like that, but I would have bought a cooking book or borrowed one of my mother's. Anyway, I'd have learned. See what I mean? And as for the housework, it's not all that hard . . .'

As she was waffling on about housework and laundering, he felt a prickle of anxiety at the nape of his neck, and found himself praying he was not anticipating the outcome of this tale, praying that he was wrong, because anger was building. Surely she, they, couldn't have been that stupid . . .

'. . . and I wanted to help you, by economising, see what I mean? It would save money, I didn't want to be useless, I wanted to show you I could be just as useful as her. You were always saying what a good cook she was, I know that, but you really couldn't afford her, so I did what . . .'

'You did what?' he asked, leaning forward ominously. 'What did you do?'

'. . . what I had to do. To save money. I put her off.' Jessie breathed a sigh of relief, as if she'd finally been able to jettison this burden. 'Kit, I'm so sorry. I think that's why she was upset, why she . . .' Her voice trailed into tears.

He was stunned. He stared at her, digesting the effect that being sacked would have had on Polly. Though she had been under punishment at the time, living in a sectioned-off corner of the barn, behind temporary walls that they thought he hadn't noticed, she had no reason to think her job was in jeopardy.

'I said I'd give her an excellent reference,' Jessie added plaintively.

Kit scowled. 'You sacked her for the few shillings that she earned per year, less than what you'd pay for two handkerchiefs! Less than what you people put in the plate at church on Sundays!'

He shook his head as if to rattle out the truth. 'And you left her facing prison again? Didn't you know that if they're sent back to prison, for whatever reason, they face severe punishments? Polly! She was a harmless woman. What had she ever done to you?'

Jessie began to weep. 'Please don't raise your voice, Kit. I'm so sorry, you have no idea how terrible this has been for me. Your farm! I will never forgive myself . . .'

'Bugger the farm,' he stormed. 'The woman's dead. You intended to give her a reference? God Almighty! This isn't Sydney society, you stupid girl. A reference for Polly would have been nothing more than a cruel joke. And now you sit here crying. For whom? Are you sorry for Polly or sorry for yourself? More the latter by the look of you!'

He stood up and made for the door. Then his world seemed to come crashing down on him as he turned the brass knob. He turned to look at her bitterly, about to say: 'All that misery over a few shillings!' but couldn't bring himself to spit the words at her. It was bad enough knowing.

When she was eventually able to control her sobs, Jessie washed her face and dressed her hair with the cheap brush and comb that Adrian had bought for her, winding it into a single loose plait. It hadn't occurred to her that Kit would react so angrily. She'd gone over the scene so many times in her mind that she'd convinced herself of the ending . . . a bittersweet reunion, after she'd insisted on telling him the truth, begging his forgiveness for causing so much trouble, and receiving that forgiveness from her loving fiancé. But instead he'd shouted at her, as if she weren't upset enough. Now she was totally devastated! There would be no forgiveness.

No wedding. How could she possibly have got it so wrong? Hadn't she herself said that she doubted he would forgive them . . . but he had, before she'd told him about Polly. Adrian had warned her not to mention that, but she'd had to.

Jessie sighed. She was a truthful person. Tried to be. She knew the guilt would have weighed on her until she confessed, so it had to be done.

She remained in the chair by the window until Adrian came knocking at her door, ever so quietly.

'Where is Kit?' he asked anxiously.

'I've no idea. He was angry with me, really angry . . .'

'Oh no! You told him about sacking Polly?'

'He said I was stupid,' she said dully.

'And so you are! For crying out loud, Jessie! Don't you see that will make him even angrier with me? Where did he go?'

'I've no idea.'

'What will you do now? I mean, about the two of you.'

'Nothing. I don't think he's speaking to me.'

'He'll come around. It's just a lovers' spat. And he has a lot of problems at present.'

'I don't think he will.'

'In that case you're on the next ship back to Sydney.'

Jessie flinched. 'I am not. I will not go back and have Mother gloat over me, and be made a laughing stock after rushing up here to see a fiancé who has now dumped me.'

'Don't be so dramatic. He hasn't dumped you. But he hasn't any place for you to live, so you'll have to go home.'

'Never!'

Barging down Queen Street, Kit had gone several blocks before he realised he had no money and nowhere to stay in this town. He supposed he would have to figure a way out of this mess, but why bother? Every time he thought of Emerald Downs, he felt bruised. He didn't have the heart to start again, so why not muster the cattle, sell them, and let the place rot? As for Jessie and her brother, he hoped they would stay clear of him. In his present state of mind he could easily do Adrian a damage, and Jessie! Words failed him!

He shook his head once again, as he thought of her and her part in the farce of managing the farm. How dared she interfere like that? And why on earth had Adrian allowed it? He had carefully quizzed Tom Lok about the mood of the workers prior to Polly's suicide, and heard they had been sulky, as Tom put it. 'Cross and sulky, boss. They no like Mister Pinnock.'

'So what? They didn't have to like him. Just get on with their work. They didn't like me either, so what's the difference?'

'Ah, but you the boss. He only all talk.'

Kit knew what he meant. He wished Jack Drew had heard that, with his holier-than-thou disapproval of flogging the bastards. He remembered that

305

Adrian had fired the gun, over their heads, and the rioters had ignored him. If he'd shot a couple of them, two local men who'd volunteered for the posse would still be alive. That would have ended the riot quick smart.

Would you have shot at them? he asked himself.

Under those circumstances, bloody oath I would have.

But then, had he been there, Polly wouldn't have been sacked. That was another thing Jessie hadn't considered. Her fiancé appreciated good food. Jessie again. Did he really love her, or had he been won over by her surprise appearance in Brisbane and, never forget, her unrestrained pleasure in sex? The girl had practically lusted after him, wildly enjoying every minute of their lovemaking. He'd loved that. What man wouldn't? Rare in a gentlewoman, and even more exciting than practised sex with someone like Bonnie. He hadn't thought about Bonnie in a long time, and wondered mildly how she was, until more pressing matters took over.

The barracks! Of course! He could take refuge there for a while. He walked on to Fortitude Valley and once again presented himself at the barracks, where he showered and shaved and was soon confronted by Lieutenant Clancy, who was relieved to see him.

'For your interview with the Colonel tomorrow, you can wear my uniform. I'll have the brass sewn on for you, Major. They can pick it off later . . . unless I get to like wearing it.'

'Don't bother. I won't be needing it. But could you see the paymaster and draw my pay for that command?'

'Sure I'll do that, you'll be wanting every penny now I don't doubt, to be replacing your lovely house.'

Kit nodded, covering his bitterness with another request. 'Where's the telegraph office?'

Shown the way, he sent two telegrams, at regimental expense. One went to the Governor General announcing the success of his mission and his immediate resignation. A second, almost identical, went to the Minister for Home Affairs in the Parliament of New South Wales, whose portfolio included the military and a paper navy.

Like it or lump it, he thought, I'm out. Where that leaves Colonel Gresham I'm damned if I know, nor do I care.

Having done that, it was hardly correct to dine in the barracks and stay overnight, but Kit figured he'd earned a little extra. He met Sergeant Rapper at the gate early the next morning, and Rapper, who, as usual, knew everything that was going on, did not salute. Instead he grinned as Kit rode out.

'What shall I tell the Colonel, sir?' he called.

'Tell him I said to stick it!'

Rapper's laugh rumbled after him.

The rain started again that morning and Scarpy cursed as he dragged his horse down the muddy slope to the ferry. At the best of times the animal hated the ferry, and now the slippery approach had him really spooked. He reared and jerked about, agitating two other horses and causing so much commotion that a ferryman lost patience and ordered the horse to be taken back up the bank.

'No bloody fear,' Scarpy said. 'It's the bloody storm's upsetting him, that's all.'

'What storm? Bit of rain don't hurt no one.'

'There's a storm coming all right, you mark my words. This here horse knows better'n us.'

'Ah, get out with you. That nag just got no balance in the mud. Get him out of the way.'

'No, he's settling down now. See, he's coming aboard like a lamb. Maybe he got it wrong this time.'

'You can say that again,' the ferryman laughed. 'I wouldn't place no bets on his forecasts if he can't tell a summer shower from a storm.'

He hauled in the heavy ropes and whistled to the men to pull up the gangplanks as the ferry moved out into the Brisbane River. Most of the passengers huddled under the canvas awning, but Scarpy stayed with his horse. He unrolled an oilcloth cloak and buttoned it over his shoulders, took off his knitted cap and replaced it with a rawhide hat, looked down at his boots, almost new they were, and decided to preserve them too. He whisked them off and tied them to his saddle.

When he saw that the ferryman was watching him, Scarpy shrugged, as if to say: best be on the safe side, and the ferryman glanced at the sky, shaking his head.

The ferry travelled down the wide, meandering river before rounding yet another bend and heading for the wharf at Cafferty's Creek, but no sooner had it begun slewing to a halt than a massive clap of thunder shook the vessel to its boards. Scarpy made a point of tapping the ferryman on the shoulder when it was time to lead his quiet horse to shore, in the midst of a crackling storm, with the rain now a torrent.

His triumph was little compensation, though, as he had to weather the storm along the river road into town. He didn't like this place; it still smelled to him of the prison settlement, which had been his home for five hard years before he got his ticket-of-leave and married Nelly, the barber's daughter. She was a nice girl, but delicate. He'd promised Ted, the barber, he'd look after her. That was the time when Scarpy finally realised that outlawing was just as unrewarding as plain thieving and decided to give it away in favour of a straight life. He was telling Ted the barber this just before he was due to be released, and Ted, a widower, pricked up his ears.

'You go straight, Scarpy, and take on my daughter and I'll give you a dowry.'

'Dowry?' he laughed. 'What's a bloody dowry?'

'Just goes to show you're ignorant! A dowry's ten pounds, and her linen box, what go with a lady when she marries.'

'Ten pounds? You'd give me ten pounds to marry Nelly?'

'If you look after her; she's sickly.'

So he did, Scarpy reminisced, and it wasn't a bad arrangement. They both did their best, bought the little farm, raised chooks and geese, sat under the big fig tree of a night for a bit of a singsong while she played her guitar, and counted stars. She hung on as long as she could but the consumption got her in the end. It wasn't until her auntie turned up for the funeral in Ipswich that Scarpy discovered that Ted's wife had been a black gin. Nelly was therefore a half-caste. Not that it mattered.

After that he'd seen her family about from time to time, just enough to say good day or give them a feed if they came by, which wasn't often. But he'd turned to her auntie recently, needing some information, and she'd told him exactly who to talk to in Brisbane, so that was his destination now. To find a blackfeller called Moorabi, who, he'd been assured, knew everything about everything.

This was a cloudburst and a half, he told himself as he took shelter from the teeming rain in stables that, fortunately, had a spare box for his horse.

'I don't like to leave him out in the weather,' he said, 'so don't go moving him, mate, or I won't take it kindly.'

The stablehand looked at this stocky little man with a voice like a rasp and a face to match, and decided the horse could stay there, but wished he'd charged more in the first place. That box was usually reserved for classy horses, not stockhorses like this bloke's grey.

'Orright,' he shrugged, and watched the stranger tramp out into a street already beset with flash flooding.

He found some of Nelly's people sheltering in their humpies at Breakfast Creek and enquired after Moorabi, but was told he had gone up into the hot country, by which they meant north.

They broke into a chorus of laughter when he put his question to them.

'I'm looking for a whitefeller who looks like a blackfeller.'

But an elderly woman knew. 'He bin here, talk to people allasame some time. He name Jack, eh?'

'Yes! That'd be him. Jack Drew. Do you know where he is now?'

They shook their heads.

'He be a mate of Moorabi,' the woman said, and Scarpy nodded wryly.

'Just my luck. When will Moorabi be back?'

'Maybe tomorrow. Maybe Sunday,' she told him, being as helpful as she could, but Scarpy knew their concept of the days was, at best, unreliable.

'Kind of you, missus,' he said. 'I'll come back again. And you tell people I'm looking for him, eh?'

From there he trudged through the rain to a sleazy tavern near the wharves, bought himself a whisky and started yarning to the landlord, who was always a good source of information.

He heard about the posses which were still rounding up the absconders from a prison farm, and feigned interest until he could get the subject round to Harry Harvey and his sentence, hearing that Harry, being another absconder from custody, had got off light. The others were sentenced to the dreaded Norfolk Island, but Harry was set to do his time here in Brisbane.

'I reckon some coin changed hands there,' the landlord said with a wink.

'Who would have his hand out to Harry?'

'Word has it he's sweet with a copper called Kirk. Nasty piece of work he is.'

Scarpy bought another whisky and sat morosely in a corner, even more anxious now. He knew Harry Harvey was broke; he wouldn't have had enough to bribe his way out of a sugarbag, so he could have traded information. Scarpy hoped he was over-reacting to a guilty conscience for telling Harvey about his old mate, but what if Harry had seen value in that information? He could have. Only a chance, but he owed it to Jack to warn him. If he could find him. With any luck he'd gone off into the bush again by this, so this worrying might be all for nothing. Just the same, he had to be sure.

The storm had turned into relentless heavy rain, and though the streets were awash, Scarpy spent the next few days searching the gloomy town in the hopes of spotting Jack, checking at the blacks' camp and returning to his headquarters at the tavern. He thought of visiting Harry in the gaol but doubted that would achieve anything, so he set his sights on this fellow Kirk, only to find that he too was out of town.

But Scarpy was a patient man; he stayed on, hoping his farm was getting a share of this rain.

Colonel Gresham was appalled that his enquiry was being ignored. Not only by Ferrington, but also by the local police, who insisted that it had nothing to do with them, so he had to wait, with growing anger, for the return of Inspector Kirk.

In the meantime, though, through a stroke of luck, he'd been passing the post office when a clerk called to him.

'Colonel. We have a telegram here for Major Ferrington. It's very important. Will you be seeing him or should we send it out to his place?'

'I'll take it for him.'

He did indeed take it, and placed it on record with the rest of the papers he was preparing for his enquiry.

The telegram was from the Minister for Home Affairs, and it read:

REQUEST FOR RESIGNATION DENIED UNTIL OUTCOME OF ENQUIRY STOP

It made the Colonel very happy. So happy he couldn't help crowing about it to Lord and Lady Heselwood.

'This fellow Ferrington seems to think he can dodge the enquiry by resigning from the military. I mean to say, he seems to have no idea of procedure at all.'

'One would imagine that Major Ferrington would have an excellent grasp of procedure and protocol, given his stints with the Governor,' Heselwood said tartly. 'Perhaps he simply can't be bothered with your enquiry.'

'That's preposterous!'

'From what I hear, those charges against Ferrington are preposterous.'

'They are not, sir, they are not! And I am here to do my duty, while he dodges about, behaving, I might note, more like a thoroughly guilty man than a person willing to face his accusers.'

Heselwood frowned. 'I fail to see why you are bothering with an enquiry, Colonel, since you seem to have already made up your mind.'

His wife, a sweet woman, intervened before he had to put up with any more of Heselwood's impertinence. 'I believe it's the weather, Colonel,' she said. 'I've never seen such persistent rain. They say the roads are blocked and the river is rising. People are being held up everywhere.'

That was hardly an excuse for the fellow to try to resign, the Colonel thought, but he let the matter drop. 'I'm sure you're right,' he said, 'and what a shame that you have to suffer such inclement weather while you are here.'

'Where is Ferrington anyway?' Jasin Heselwood asked her as he paced moodily on the wide veranda closed in by a curtain of rain. 'I wanted to have a talk with him. If he really has arranged a truce with the blacks, it would be a good idea for him to take me to meet that chief. Then I could be sure of resurrecting Montone Station without any more trouble.'

'I don't know. He called in to see Adrian and Jessie a few days ago and then he disappeared. It's all very odd. Jessie is still quite shocked from the effect of that riot out there, not coping well at all, which surprises me. She seemed like a girl who could take something like that in her stride.'

'Not like *my* girl,' he said with a grin, 'enduring a vicious raid on her home by blacks, and having to ride for her life. You took that in *your* stride, my love. You must be made of sterner stuff!'

'I don't think so. I was a nervous wreck by the time I got back here. I'm going to see Jessie this afternoon. She won't go back to Sydney, though her brother thinks she ought to, but don't you think she should discuss it with the Major first? I mean, she is his fiancée.'

'Let her go. The fellow has more important matters on his mind.'

'More important than his fiancée?'

He shrugged. 'Find out where Ferrington is. The sooner I get to talk to him, the better.'

* * *

310

Georgina was more concerned about Jessie than she let on to her husband, but there was little she could do.

'Perhaps you'd like to move to our hotel, Jessie. It's up on the terrace and not as stifling as this place.'

'No thank you. I'm all right here.'

'Oh yes,' Georgina sighed. 'But it's a shame we're all boxed in by the rain. I was looking forward to a picnic lunch in the botanic gardens, but that has had to be postponed. It's so humid. Can I get you a cold drink, some lemonade perhaps?'

'No, nothing, thank you.'

'You can't sit in here all the time, Jessie. Let's go down to the lounge.'

'I'd rather not, Georgina. I think I'll lie down for a while.'

Lady Heselwood had seen enough. Her friend had asked her to look after her daughter but the girl seemed hell-bent on sitting around feeling sorry for herself.

'I think it's time you pulled yourself together, my dear. What happened happened. It's over. Do you intend to sit in that chair for ever?'

'No,' Jessie said meekly.

'Then what *do* you intend to do? You can't stay in a hotel room indefinitely.'

'I've nowhere else to go.'

'Yes you have. I think the Major will agree that you should go home until he sorts everything out.'

'The Major doesn't care what I do.'

Georgina sighed. 'I'm sure he does. Has he gone out to the farm?'

'I suppose so.'

'When do you expect to see him again?'

'I don't. The engagement is off. I posted his ring back to him.'

'Why?'

'Just because. I don't want to talk about it.'

Exasperated, Georgina stood at the foot of the bed, trying to get some sense out of the girl, without success, so she went in search of Adrian, and found him emerging from the hotel office, looking every bit as woebegone as his sister.

'What is happening with you two? And what's this about Jessie's engagement being off?'

'They had a fight. He went off not speaking to her. And I'm even less popular with him. I'm going to see if I can get us on the next ship out of here.'

'Shouldn't you wait and at least talk to the Major about Jessie? She doesn't want to go home, so I think she's hoping to make up with him.'

'No she's not,' he retorted. 'Look, Lady Heselwood, I'm sorry, I don't want to offend you because I know you're trying to help, but I'm making the decisions now. I have no choice. We have to leave the hotel as soon as possible whether she likes it or not. We haven't any money; as it is, we're living on borrowed funds.'

'Good heavens. We'll cover your bills here, Adrian. There's no need to rush off on that account.'

He shook his head. 'There's no point in staying on here. We must go home.'

When he returned, he informed Jessie that he had booked them on a ship leaving port the following afternoon, and he had telegraphed their mother to meet them.

'I'm not going!' she said.

'Then stay here and get tipped out into the street. I have paid the hotel bill up until tomorrow, and that's it. You haven't got a penny. For once in your life you'll do as you're told! You never should have come up here in the first place, before the Major was ready to receive you! You've brought all this down on your own head. No wonder he's fed up with you.'

Sensing trouble, Georgina called on Jessie the next morning. She had bought a long summer coat and some light clothes, including a pair of canvas shoes, for her to wear on the ship. Tucked in the pocket of the coat was a beaded purse containing twenty pounds.

Jessie, however, was refusing to accept them.

'Yes you will,' Georgina insisted. 'I remember what it was like landing in town with only what I had on when we had to flee Montone, so just take these pieces gracefully, and stop making such a fuss.'

'But I'm not going home, Georgina.'

'Then where are you going? There's no accommodation for you at Emerald Downs.'

'I thought perhaps I could go round to your hotel. You did ask me.'

'And you refused. That was before Adrian made the decision for you both to return to Sydney. I know your mother will be delighted that you are coming home, she was extremely worried about you, especially after all that trouble at the farm. It's for the best, believe me, and by the look of you, a sea voyage will do you the world of good.'

Jessie shrugged and perched on the edge of the unmade bed. 'What a fool I've made of myself! What will I say when people ask about the wedding?'

'My dear! Under the present circumstances your wedding would have to be postponed anyway. The poor man had a lovely home for you to go to, I believe, and now that has been destroyed. He will have to start all over. The thing for you to do is write him a nice letter and make up for the little tiff you had . . .'

She held up her hand to silence Jessie's attempt to protest. 'I know, one doesn't like to back down, but at times it's necessary. Now you write that letter, and don't mention the ring. You can tell him you're leaving for a while so he doesn't have to be worrying about you. It's your role to support him when things are not going well, and be as helpful as possible.'

'Helpful?' Jessie said angrily. 'I have already learned that one must never attempt to help Major Ferrington. I will not back down, as you call it. He was rude to me. He will have to apologise or he can rot for all I care.'

Lady Heselwood raised her eyebrows. 'Well! I see you are feeling better. I do believe a little anger is far more attractive than the vapours you've been nursing. Now let us pack you up, and I shall take you to lunch before you leave.'

She looked around the room. 'Oh dear. How silly of me. You haven't a valise! I should have known that, shouldn't I? Come on, we'll see if we can buy one. You can hardly travel with your clothes in a saddlebag.'

When Major Ferrington didn't appear for the interview as instructed, the Colonel had issued an arrest order, and Lieutenant Clancy was dispatched to bring him in.

A party of four soldiers, led by Clancy, immediately set out for Emerald Downs, only to be told by Jack Drew that the Major was not at home, such as it was.

'Forgive me, Jack,' the Lieutenant said. 'Me heart's not in this, but I have me orders. I have to bring in the Major.'

'What do you mean? Bring him in? What sort of an order is that?'

'He has to answer the charges laid against him.'

'What bloody charges?'

'Military stuff. Didn't he tell you?' Clancy climbed down from his horse, ordered his men to dismount and explained the situation to Jack, all the while keeping his eyes peeled for the owner of the farm.

'He can't be held responsible for the deaths of the Native Police!' Jack said angrily. 'He had nothing to do with them. He said that all along. He wanted no part of the bastards. And he told Kirk that right from the start.'

'I know, but his orders said different, if you get what I mean. He was to liaise with them, work with them, so to speak.'

'They ploughed on ahead, too cocky to need backup, that's what happened. Those buggers attack defenceless blacks wherever they come across them; they never expected to run into the real war parties that you find up here. Kirk was the same; to him the tribes were just dumb niggers that he could attack in safety, surrounded by armed men. Well he was bloody wrong, wasn't he?'

'He says he relied on backup.'

'Ah, I get it. Kirk has to put up a front like this to cover his own mistakes. He walked straight into disaster like a right idiot. He under-estimated the blacks.'

'Well, you could say . . .' Clancy admitted. 'But he's police and so were his men, and they were under military orders, meaning the Major, you see.'

'Bloody hell!' Jack shouted. 'Whose side are you on?'

'Just doin' my job. Now I'd understand if you was hiding the Major here, true I would, Jack, he being a mate of yours, but it'll do no good.

313

We'd just have to keep on after him. Now you're sure he's not hanging back in the bush there, waitin' for us to depart?'

'I'm bloody sure! Major Ferrington has no need to hide from a weasel like you. Or from Kirk's bleatings. You said there was an enquiry, do I get a say?'

'Only if Ferrington calls on you, but if I was you, Jack,' Clancy added stiffly, 'I wouldn't be throwing me weight around. There's talk in the town that you're on a wanted list. They be sayin' you're a mite dodgy yourself. I wouldn't be gettin' too smart.'

Clancy was disappointed Jack had taken that attitude. He was only carrying out orders, and besides, the powers-that-be had woken up that Brisbane needed more troops, because it was well-known that there were hundreds of belligerent black tribes on past the areas now declared safe. It would be a mighty job, never-ending, to keep some sort of control in the north . . . and, as Gresham had told him, it was ridiculous that they'd had to call Ferrington in the first place. They needed more ranking officers, and because of his recent experience, he, Clancy, was in line for promotion to captain, recommended by Gresham, who wasn't a bad sort of bloke after all.

But where was Ferrington, if not at his farm?

When Kit left the hotel, still angry with Jessie and Adrian, he was determined to find Inspector Kirk and soon discovered that he'd gone out to Redland Bay, on a tip-off, to arrest Albert Minchin.

Kit wouldn't have minded a few words with Minchin either, so he too headed in the direction of Redland Bay, calling in at lonely homesteads, finding himself always a day behind Kirk and his men, but somehow less stressed than he'd been for a very long time. The solitude was a relief, the quiet ride, bayside, sheer pleasure. He camped on the shores, watching Aborigines leisurely fishing the shallow waters, marvelling at the birds that nested around him and the animals quietly grazing in the shady bush. He knew that nature was just as bountiful on his land, by his river, but he'd never taken the time to sit, to simply gaze about him, to enjoy what he already had, a wonderful stretch of country, all ten thousand acres of it. More than he'd ever dreamed he could own.

'More than I deserve,' he told himself sadly. For what had he done but gone at it like a steam train? Running mad over it, instead of taking the time to look at the land as a whole. Working out which sections should be utilised and which areas of forest should be left in a natural state. He wasn't sure how one could go about this, with minimal knowledge of the bush, but it was possible Jack Drew could help him. While Jack didn't know farming, he did understand the wildlife in the area.

Finally, though, it was the rain that put an end to his communing with nature, and his search for Rollo Kirk, and he turned back to Brisbane.

When he led his horse off the ferry, there was Lieutenant Clancy, waiting for him. Waiting to arrest him.

Chapter Eighteen

The rain had stopped at last but the humidity was intense, as the sun bore down on the cloud cover that remained, turning Brisbane into a sweatbox, but Georgina Heselwood kept her promise. She accompanied Jessie and Adrian to the *Argyle* and saw them safely on board, hoping the Major would suddenly materialise, but there was no sign of him.

At the last minute, Sam Dignam came racing across the wharf and up the gangway, thrusting a tin of sweets at Jessie and shaking hands with Adrian.

'I hope you've brought your sea-legs this time,' he said to him before turning back to Jessie.

'Now you have a good rest, Jess.'

With that he gave her a hug, and Georgina noticed that Jessie was weeping quietly as she bade him farewell. She wondered who she was weeping for. Herself, her fiancé or this handsome young reporter? Oh well, she sighed. Time would tell. And if truth be told right now, she was greatly relieved to have Jessie off her hands. She was a stubborn girl, and posting her engagement ring off to Ferrington at the farm was a silly, reckless thing to do, especially when Adrian insisted they'd only had a foolish quarrel. That it wasn't serious. He seemed to think the Major would be shocked when it was delivered to him.

Sam assisted her down to the wharf and stayed with her until the ship pulled away.

'May I escort you back to your hotel, Lady Heselwood?' he asked.

'Thank you, Sam, but there's no need. I might have a look about the shops now that the rain has stopped.

He raised his hat and departed, and Georgina walked over to a jeweller's shop, peering at the motley display, wondering, also, about Sam Dignam. He seemed very keen on Jessie. Had she changed her mind about Ferrington? Was she using a lover's tiff to withdraw from the engagement and turn to Sam? It occurred to her that Ferrington was far from well placed at present as regarded marriage. She'd heard he was in financial trouble even before the disaster at Emerald Downs. Surely that wasn't the reason Jessie was backing off? Turning to the wealthy Sam Dignam as a more appealing choice, now that Ferrington was down on his luck.

No, she said to herself. I wouldn't accuse Jessie of that. She's a naughty girl, jumping on that ship without a word to her mother, but I don't believe she's that calculating. Rather the opposite. Jump first, think later is more her style.

She saw some horsemen ride past, reining in their horses and dismounting at a hitching rail across the road from the police station. The leader, she realised, was the police inspector Kirk, the darling of the local newspapers, it seemed, though she and Jasin were far from impressed by the wild accusations he was making about Major Ferrington. And it further irritated Jasin that Colonel Gresham seemed to set great store by Kirk's statements.

Georgina smiled, a little sadly. Her husband was well known to be a very self-centred man. Apart from baiting Gresham, he would not involve himself in the Major's problems, even though she had reminded him that this was Jessie's fiancé.

'It's all a lot of rot,' he said. 'All these civil servants trying to outdo each other. Let them sort it out and then I'll have a serious talk with Ferrington about the truce. I want to meet the chief.'

The newspaper photographs were kind to Kirk, she thought, frowning at the Inspector as he removed his hat and wiped his swarthy face with a dirty cloth. He turned to say a few words to the other three men, before taking his rifle from its saddle holster and setting off across the wide street.

Georgina, too, was set to go about her own business when she heard someone shout to Kirk, and looked back to see a dark-skinned man storming down the street.

'Kirk!' he shouted again. 'Get back here, you lying bastard. I'll have a word with you . . .'

The Inspector glanced back, and recognising the man, seemed to panic. Georgina gasped as she saw him frantically trying to load his rifle from a bandolier slung across his uniform jacket, but he was too late. The stranger caught up with him, grabbed the rifle and flung it away, and with a crack that could be heard all over the town on that quiet sultry afternoon, he slammed his fist into Kirk's face.

Georgina gave a small scream. The few people standing about, including the men who'd just parted from Kirk, all seemed rooted to the spot as the dark fellow pounded him again, pounded him to the ground and kicked him hard in the buttocks.

As he turned away, leaving Kirk sprawled on his face in the dirt, the stranger caught her eye and hesitated, looked at her again, and then strode on past.

She watched as he disappeared round a corner, knowing she'd seen him before somewhere, believing that she knew him. But she didn't know any black men! Wait, though, she thought, he wasn't a blackfellow. The voice was English, home English even, not a local accent.

Georgina began to walk away, turning up the steep hill towards the terrace, her long sleeves and rustling skirts a hindrance in this heat. Puffing, she took refuge on a low stone fence in the shade of a clump of bamboos, and went over the violent scene again. And it was then that she placed him.

It's him, she said to herself. It's the man who grabbed me and pushed me under the bed at Montone the day we were attacked by those savages.

But how could it be? How could it be?

'But it was him,' she said firmly. 'I swear to God it was.'

She'd seen him. He *was* one of the raiders, the savages, who'd attacked the station that day . . . but he wasn't a blackfellow at all, and that accounted for the light eyes in the dark face that she'd never forget. But what had he been doing fighting with the blacks? Because he certainly hadn't been on the other side.

Georgina shuddered, remembering the terror, and jumped up to hurry towards her hotel as if to leave those dreadful memories behind, but already the tears were welling. Tears for poor Mrs Gwyder, their cook, who been bludgeoned to death in the yard, and for the stockmen who'd been killed, good people who'd died simply because they were there, going about their daily chores.

By the time she reached the hotel, she was so angry she felt like turning about and going straight to the police station to identify that man as a member of the raiding party that had attacked Montone Station. She could tell them that he had entered her bedroom during the fighting, and he was as close as any white man could get to looking like a blackfellow then, his body black and dusty, almost naked. It was the first time she'd ever seen him, but under the circumstances, she could hardly forget him.

She began climbing the stairs. A maid stood aside for her at the landing. She reached out to her.

'Are you all right, madam? You're looking ever so pale.'

Georgina lurched away from her and almost fell, so the girl took her arm to assist her up the next flight and Georgina found herself transfixed with fear, as if that man had hold of her again.

'Here's your room, madam. Do you want me to come in and—'

'Thank you, no . . . no!' Georgina stumbled inside and sat heavily on the bed as the wind caught the door and slammed it shut. As he had done! He had come in, stared at her, as if shocked to see her there, then he'd run at her, giving her the fright of her life, but he'd grabbed her and pushed her under the bed and then she'd heard the door slam and she was in there alone, with howling savages invading her house and guns firing like cannons over the mayhem.

Heselwood had come for her, pulled her out through the French doors to make a run for the horses . . . and they had ridden for their lives, looking back to see their lovely homestead going up in flames.

She'd told Heselwood about the man several times, but he'd never believed her. He might now if she could point him out. But would she? The fellow had tried to protect her, by pushing her out of sight and closing the door so that, obviously, the storm of murderous blacks would pass on by! She sighed, confused, and reached for the water jug, pouring herself a long glass of the tepid water to calm herself down. But what was the wretch doing there in the first place? She should report him to the authorities. He must be a madman. Look at his behaviour today, attacking the police inspector.

When her husband returned, she was about to tell him what she'd discovered, but hesitated, realising that if he did believe her this time, there'd be hell to pay. He'd have been out the door with a shotgun to find the fellow himself.

I'll just wait until I can positively identify him, she decided. It won't be hard to find out who he is now. That incident, the fight in the street, won't go unnoticed by the local newspaper.

Scarpy loved newspapers, though he never bought any. Wherever he found them, he read every line, right down to the page number, and on this afternoon, seated in the cool of the tavern with its stone walls and flagstone flooring, he saw the boss dump a pile of papers by the back door.

'What're you doing with them?' he wanted to know.

'Giving 'em to the butcher for wrapping meat for his customers.'

Scarpy slid out of his seat and grabbed a few copies, returning to begin scouring them for all the worldly happenings.

Hours later, he was still happily working through them when he came across an advertisement.

'God help us!' he spluttered. 'Here's someone advertising for Jack Wodrow.'

'What's that?' The innkeeper peered down the counter at him.

'Nothin',' Scarpy muttered, reading it carefully again. Then he changed his mind.

'There's a fellow here, name of Hector Wodrow, got his name in the paper ... like ...' Scarpy was choosing his words carefully. 'Hector Wodrow,' he emphasised. 'I used to know him.'

'Hector Wodrow?'

'That's what I said.'

'Then you might have used to know him, Scarpy, but you ain't gonna get to know him any more. He drowned. Went down in the *Arabella*. If that day's paper is still there, you'll find the list of them as drowned, poor souls.'

'Well whaddaya know?' Scarpy buried himself in his reading for quite a while after that, all the time wondering who the hell this Hector was, to be blaring Jack's name out like that. Scarpy himself mentioning it to Harry Harvey was bad enough, but this fool coming right out and putting it in the papers left his effort in the shade. It was a wonder he didn't add Jack's alias.

'Bloody fool!' he muttered, wondering if Jack had seen this.

Surreptitiously he tore the page out, folded it carefully and stuffed it in his pocket.

Men ran out to aid Rollo Kirk, among them Constable 2nd Class Griffen, a newcomer to the Brisbane Police Corps, who had heard the ruckus out there but missed the attack.

He could hardly believe his eyes that a police officer should be bashed in the main street, and right in front of the police station! His father had warned him that this was a rough town, and as he bent over the semi-conscious officer, who was bleeding from a cut over his eye and another by his mouth, he made a mental note to tell Father he'd been right. Inspector Kirk was a real mess.

Superintendent Grimes came down and took over.

'Who did this?' he shouted, but no one seemed to know. A stranger.

'Drew!' Kirk managed to say, blurting blood on to his jacket, and a couple of teeth as well, the constable noticed.

'Jack Drew?' Grimes asked, and Kirk nodded, grimacing in pain as he tried to get up.

'He went that way!' An onlooker pointed, and Grimes called to Griffen: 'Get after him! Now! Go! We'd better get Rollo over to the hospital.'

Griffen raced in search of the attacker, asking people if they'd seen him, dodging in and out of lanes and ending up at the waterfront, where he poked his head into a tavern.

'I'm looking for Jack Drew,' he shouted.

'What's he done?' Boris, the innkeeper, growled from behind his counter.

'Bashed a police officer.'

'Good on him! When did this happen?'

'Only a little while ago.'

'Which one? Who did he bash?'

'Inspector Kirk.'

That brought a hearty cheer and Scarpy stepped forward. 'I'm Jack Drew.'

Boris twisted round in surprise, but he caught Scarpy's half-closed eye and signalled to acquaintances of the volunteer not to comment, as Constable Griffen dashed forward.

'I'm arresting you, Jack Drew, in the name of the law for assault and battery, and you'd better come quietly.'

Scarpy nodded morosely. He was thrilled to know Jack was in town, and best of all that he could take the coppers off his tail for a while. He allowed this one to clap shiny new handcuffs on him and went quietly, as instructed, knowing that the minute they left there'd be hilarity in their wake.

They plodded up a long street, with people staring at them, and took a short cut through a lane that led up to the rear of the station, where he was shoved inside to share a small cell with a couple of stockmen who weren't averse to some rounds of dice.

Before long, another policeman came down to see Jack Drew. An officer, a fair-haired fellow with a sandy beard.

He opened the cell and looked in. 'Where's Jack Drew?' he asked, confused.

'Must be in the other bin,' one of the stockmen said.

'No. There's no one in there.' He peered at Scarpy. 'Who are you?'

'Mr Covington.'

'What are you in for?'

'I got picked up for bashing a copper, but it weren't me, Officer. I was just sitting . . .'

The door slammed shut.

'Who did you bash?' the stockman asked cheerfully.

Inspector Tomkins found the constable laboriously writing up the arrest in the daybook.

'Who's that you've got in the lockup?'

'Jack Drew, sir.'

'That's not Jack Drew. Throw him out.'

'But he said . . .'

'It's not him, Griffen.'

'It's not?'

'No.'

'Why would he say he was?'

Tomkins nodded. 'Why? A joke I suppose. Or there could be more to it. He could be a mate of Drew's, drawing your fire, so to speak.'

'I'll charge him with obsteructionaling justice!' Griffen said indignantly.

'Forget it. Just release him.'

Griffen headed for the back door and Tomkins retreated to his office. He wished Drew had thought twice about assaulting Kirk, though God knows Kirk's wild claims about Ferrington's leadership and Drew's association with the blacks were reason enough to confront him. Sending him to hospital, though, would only aggravate the situation.

Having been unceremoniously tossed out of gaol, Scarpy decided he might as well call in at the blacks' camps again, to see if there was any word of this fellow Moorabi. He still had to find Jack, who'd probably done a vanish after bashing the copper. He wondered why he'd done that. A man would have to be bloody angry to pull a stunt like that in broad daylight. But that was Jack. Still the boss. Never did take no pushing about from no one.

He ambled along the riverbanks on the outskirts of the town but was unable to locate any of the blacks in their usual haunts, so he sat down under a tree to wait a while, in case any of them showed up. Then he must have dozed, because he awakened, startled, to see a strange blackfellow standing nearby.

He was handsome fellow, with high cheekbones, a straight flat nose, his mouth smooth and curved like a woman's over even white teeth. His thick hair, standing out from a centre parting, was cut evenly at the jawline to meet a curling beard. It was against the law for blacks, men and women, to be in town areas, even out here, unless they were dressed in some manner, so this bloke wore a sleeveless shirt and moleskins which did nothing to hide his muscular frame.

'Why did you want Moorabi?' he asked quietly.

'To ask about a friend,' Scarpy said.

'Who is this friend?'

'Name of Jack Drew.'

'You a fren' to Jack Drew?'

'Old friend.' Scarpy hoped he had chosen the right side. 'He's in a bit of trouble. I have to warn him. I thought Moorabi could tell me where to find him.'

'I am Moorabi,' the blackfeller announced. 'Do you know the place on the river?'

'No.'

Moorabi scratched his head and frowned, obviously trying to work out how to give directions, and then he had an idea. He beckoned Scarpy to follow him and went over to the sandy riverbank, where he drew a map of the river with a stick.

Scarpy was fascinated. He had no idea that this river had so many twists and turns. Then he watched as his guide drew the road that left town, following the river for a start and breaking away into the valley until abruptly he plunged the stick into the sand.

'There?' Scarpy asked, and Moorabi nodded.

'What kind of place is it?' he asked, trying to align the spot with the bends of the river, but when he looked up, the blackfeller was walking away.

'He was only walking along the riverbank,' Scarpy told Boris, 'no shelter of any sort in sight, and suddenly he's gone, quicker than I could blink. He disappeared right then. Gone!'

'Getting arrested was too much for you, I'm thinking,' Boris said.

It was too late then to do any travelling, so Scarpy stayed for a few serves of the tasty stew Boris cooked up every night, then took to his cot in the Seamen's Mission round the corner.

The next morning he collected his horse as the sun was rising to deliver a clear day, and set out along the river road. Soon he lost sight of the river, as he'd expected, and rode on, not knowing whether he was looking for a village or a farm or what, but he could ask about. Since Jack was, so far, a free man, able to walk the streets, and thump a copper for good measure, and be fingered for it right off, then he must be fairly well known about the traps, Scarpy mused. It wasn't as if he was talking out of school.

I'm off the hook altogether now, he thought, what with Hector Wodrow sticking his bib in and saving my bacon. I've no need to mention Harry Harvey, and what I might have said to him.

He whistled cheerily as he rode away from Brisbane, admiring this countryside, a lot more interesting than the flats out his way, and by midday found himself at a place called Baker's Crossing.

'You've come too far,' he was told. 'Jack Drew lives at Emerald Downs, about ten miles back. River side.'

This time he had a more detailed description of his route and a rundown on the adversities that had beset the farm and its residents; they were a talkative, pokey lot, he thought, asking a man more questions than a hive had bees. None of his answers were truthful. On principle.

Moorabi knew he would shortly be going in the same direction as the whitefeller friend of Jack Drew, but he had a few more people to see yet.

He had been sent to warn people still living by this river that most of the near-inland clans, of which a lot of them were members, were preparing to move north, for good, and this would be their last chance to join the exodus. The Tingum tribal elders had decided that they would not just be moving north of the white settlers; they were going far, far north into the rainforests, into the great mountains, where they would be welcomed by distant tribes who had been informed of their predicament. And where their children would be safe.

Several of the local black people had already left, but quite a lot chose to stay, refusing to leave their own familiar lands, claiming that it would be too dangerous to travel through strange country where many tribes were known to be even more savage than the whitefellers. Moorabi couldn't deny that, nor would he try to persuade people. His duty, as outlined by Ilkepala, was simply to inform. Not to take responsibility for decisions.

As he picked his way through mangrove swamps right down at the bend of the river, he found himself thinking of Ilkepala more and more, for the magic man had begun to teach him important old ways and wisdoms, things only the chosen ones were permitted to know. And he had explained that if Moorabi lived a good life, it would be permissible for him to aspire to know more. Moorabi understood that it would take many years, and many more initiations, before he would be ready for spiritual instruction in the great meanings of life, and beyond that . . . he dared not even contemplate. Many elders reached that point, but few were considered worthy enough to know more, to become magic men like Ilkepala, men who were blessed with awesome powers.

Not that Moorabi, a humble man, ever expected to reach that level of spiritual awareness, but he found it exciting to contemplate and he was mightily surprised that Ilkepala should begin to show him the paths, when he was only thirty years of age. These honours were usually reserved for older men.

The noise of the cicadas was deafening, and it seemed to be getting worse, so he clapped his hands to his ears and ran down to wade into the river, trying to escape it. The shrill sound reached screaming pitch before it suddenly ceased, and Moorabi found himself standing waist-deep in the water, in total silence. He couldn't hear a sound. Not the rush of the river, or the cicadas, or the birds, or those high tree branches swishing in the wind. The silence seemed to leave his mind blank, so he just stood, unable to move.

Then he heard a great wailing. A terrible wailing. And women's high-pitched crying. And it was so sad he wept, until it finally ceased and he could hear the wind again, and the hiss of the leaves, but the cicadas were silent.

Unable to interpret the dream he'd experienced, he went about his business, staying a few more days for personal farewells, which were sadness themselves, maybe part of his dream, for his aunties wept to see him go.

No horse this time, he smiled to himself as he set out on his trek, choosing not to travel with the others because he'd already learned from Ilkepala that solitary travel was the second perfect time for meditation. Stillness and solitude being the first.

'I never thought I'd see the day,' Scarpy laughed, when he rode up to the burned-out site to find Jack and a Chinaman working hard, pilling ash and debris into a dray.

'Who are you?' the familiar voice challenged.

'What sort of welcome is that for an old mate?'

'Cripes!' Jack stared at him. 'It's you, Scarpy! Well I'll be blowed. What are you doing here?'

Mild-mannered Tomkins could have asked the same question of Lord Heselwood the next morning, if he'd dared, for the gentleman was at the front desk trying to lodge a missing persons report, insisting that Major Ferrington was nowhere to be found.

'I am reliably informed by reporters of your *Brisbane Courier* news-paper that Major Ferrington is not at his farm. Nor is he in the town. He has not left by ship . . . I checked the passenger list. So,' his lordship leaned forward to quiz the duty constable at the counter, 'where is he?'

Unfazed, the constable picked up a pen. 'What name was it again?'

'The name of the missing person is . . .'

'Excuse me,' Tomkins said to the constable. 'I'll handle this.' He turned to the enquirer: 'Inspector Tomkins, sir. Am I addressing Lord Heselwood?'

'You are indeed, Inspector.'

'Good.' He beckoned Heselwood aside and lowered his voice. 'We have unofficial information that the Major is under military arrest at the barracks.'

'What?'

'It's not generally known. They're keeping it quiet.'

'You mean that fool of a Gresham is keeping it quiet! Why would he do that?'

'Something to do with his enquiry, I suppose. We're not even supposed to know; we just got the tip from an NCO at the barracks.'

Heselwood brushed his fair hair from his face. 'This is a damned nuisance. I want to talk to the man. In the barracks, eh?'

'Yes, sir.'

'Thank you, Inspector. I shall pay him a visit.'

'I gather he's not permitted visitors.'

'We'll see about that.'

Colonel Gresham was fed up with this town . . . with the weather, the humidity and, worst of all, the attitude of the people. They had no respect for his rank, no idea of hospitality . . . not one person had even invited him to tea . . . and at the hotel he had been given a side table on his own. When he protested that the usual seating had him with the Heselwoods, the woman in charge told him baldly that Lord Heselwood preferred to dine alone with his wife. Gresham was concerned that it could have been a snub, but then couples often preferred their own company. Anyway, all round, he was having a perfectly miserable time, so all he wanted to do was get this enquiry over and done with. He'd already been held up for days thanks to the absence of the chief witness, Inspector Kirk, who seemed to think the enquiry could await his pleasure.

But finally Kirk was back, calling in casually as he rode back into town with his posse, having achieved nothing at all on their manhunt, to inform the Colonel – 'inform him' was the instruction left with the sentries in the gatehouse – that he would be available at nine in the morning.

The arrogance of the man was insufferable, and the Colonel only permitted the enquiry to proceed now, at nine a.m., to get it over and done with.

He sat at the desk he had allotted himself, placed papers in order on the desk, took a glass of water, looked at his watch and called to Lieutenant Clancy:

'Tell your clerk to come in and be seated at the end of this desk. You will take the seat here on my left. The three junior officers waiting outside will sit over there facing the court.'

Clancy didn't think it was actually a court, this enquiry, but shrugged off Gresham's pomposity as yet another cross he had to bear.

'Tell Sergeant Rapper to bring in the prisoner. He's entitled to hear my interrogation of his accuser . . .' He stopped, seeing Rapper at the door.

'What is it?'

'Inspector Kirk, he's in hospital, sir.'

'He can't be. I'm expecting him here this morning.'

'He's there all right.' Rapper's face creased into a mean grin. 'He got thrashed yesterday. By Jack Drew. He's in no state to turn up here. Sir.'

'Get out!' Gresham shouted at him. 'Get out, all of you!'

Not long after that, Sergeant Rapper, still pleased with the morning's news, was called to the gate, where a civilian was demanding to see Major Ferrington.

Rapper restrained himself from whistling with surprise when he recognised the visitor as a real nob, a lord no less, big enough in the pecking order to make mincemeat of Gresham. He considered his day was going extremely well.

'Can't let you visit the prisoner, sir,' he said, straight-faced. 'But Colonel Gresham might see you.'

That put a spur in the lordly tail, he crowed to himself, as the aristocrat reacted well:

'Might! You take me to Gresham immediately, Sergeant.'

'Yes, sir!'

He wasn't able to hear exactly what went on in the Colonel's office, but the voices got louder and angrier until Lieutenant Clancy rushed out and yelled at him to bring up Ferrington.

'Has that clown started his enquiry?' Kit asked Rapper.

'Not as you'd notice. He can't seem to get it off the ground. Kirk was supposed to come along this morning but he can't get here.'

'Why not?' Kit asked sourly.

'Because he's in hospital,' Rapper laughed.

'Cholera, I hope.'

'No. Better than that. Jack Drew gave him a hiding. Blacked his eye, took out a few teeth, and put the boot in his rear end so he won't be happy sitting for a while.'

Kit shook his head. 'I don't think that's going to help.'

'But you've got a visitor. He's been giving the Colonel the rounds of the kitchen.'

'What?' Kit was astonished. 'Who?'

'His lordship. Lord Heselwood.'

'What the hell is he doing here?'

As Kit walked up the steps, he was nervous. Heselwood's name was enough to intimidate him. He wondered for a second if he'd paid for those cattle, remembering with relief that he had, but hardly reassured; this was obviously something else that had gone wrong.

He straightened his shirt and wished he hadn't refused to shave for his appearance before Gresham, squared his shoulders and strode into the room where the Colonel and Lord Heselwood were waiting.

'I wish to state that I have resigned my commission,' he began without waiting for the formalities.

'Oh no you haven't,' Gresham barked, pulling out a telegram and slamming it on the desk.

Kit glanced at it, and then snatched it. 'This is addressed to me!' he shouted. 'Why wasn't it delivered to me?'

'You're seeing it now,' Gresham said, 'so don't try to shelve your responsibilities, Major, any more than you already have.'

'If you gentlemen don't mind, I'd like a word,' Heselwood said. 'It seems your enquiry isn't happening today, Colonel, so we'll just have a quiet chat.'

'There is nothing to chat about, Lord Heselwood,' Kit said angrily. 'I refuse to acknowledge an enquiry that would give any sort of credence to trumped-up charges brought by a person of low—'

Heselwood interrupted him with a raised hand. 'I was just about to suggest we take a short cut, so to speak. You told me you have Inspector Kirk's written report, Colonel. And you have Major Ferrington's written report. And you have to hand the statements of an officer and soldiers who were under the Major's command. So well done. All in order.'

'I will not have any part in this,' Kit said, but once again, Heselwood stopped him.

'Do be patient, Major. It seems to me that you have all the relevant information here, Colonel, so I'm wondering if either Kirk or the Major will be changing their stories when you question them in your search for the truth.'

'Not me,' Kit said.

'And Inspector Kirk?' he asked the Colonel.

'How would I know? And this is none of your business, sir.'

'That is correct to a certain extent. But I have a vested interest, one might say. I need the assistance of Major Ferrington, and I bloody well can't get his assistance while you keep him locked up! You have all you need to know about your bloody enquiry at your fingertips, so get on with it, man!'

'When the witnesses are available,' Gresham said firmly.

'One witness. It appalls me that, as the Major says, you give credence to that fellow over the word of a gentleman. And I might warn you that you are on shaky ground. Despite the appearance you are trying to convey of fairness, with these reports, as I told you before, I had the distinct impression, from your own words, that you had already made up your mind. My wife was also a witness to that conversation. A matter that I shall take up, personally, with the Governor General.'

Amazed, Kit watched as Gresham, looking even more uncomfortable, spluttered: 'Are you trying to sway my judgement, sir?'

'No, no, no,' Heselwood said airily. 'Dear me no. I am merely pointing out that you have made up your mind, so why waste more of the military's time and fees by prolonging the matter. We have to get on with our lives, Colonel. Now when can we have the result of your enquiries?'

'My report will go to the Minister for Defence.'

'Excellent. But I meant when will it be completed?'

'This evening. But it's confidential.'

'Very good. Is there anything more you wish to ask the Major?'

'No.'

'Then I presume he's free to go? After all, you only make recommendations here, don't you? It's not a court-martial.'

The Colonel looked as limp as a wet rag as he shuffled papers about, peering over his spectacles at certain pages, marking them with a pencil, scratching his neck, glowering at his prisoner, stretching time like a rubber band in the hope that somehow Heselwood might disappear, but the band bounced back into normalcy and Heselwood, friend of the GG, was still there. His lordship sat back in his chair, totally at ease, took a monogrammed handkerchief from the pocket of his tailored tweed jacket and mopped his brow, though Kit hadn't seen a drop of sweat on the fine forehead.

As they waited, he turned to Kit: 'Dreadful, that assault on Inspector Kirk. One just never knows these days. You wonder who's next.'

Kit could have sworn that was a threat directed at Gresham, though his lordship seemed to be cheerfully patient now, awaiting the Colonel's pleasure.

Suddenly Gresham looked up, and glared at Kit. 'You may go, Major. I shall apprise you of my recommendations in the fullness of time.'

Heselwood smiled. 'For the earth is the Lord's and the fullness thereof, as the good book says.'

He stood and held out an elegant hand. 'Thank you, Colonel Gresham. These little conflicts must be the very devil for you. Come along, Major, we have work to do.'

Sergeant Rapper brought up Kit's horse. 'What happened?'

'Damned if I know,' Kit said. 'No doubt I'll hear eventually.'

As he rode away with Heselwood, he tried to thank him, but milord wouldn't hear of it. 'No trouble. I need your help. I want you to take me to meet the tribal chief, the fellow who runs the show round my property at Montone.'

'I don't know about that, Lord Heselwood. I wouldn't know where to find him. You'd have to talk to Jack Drew.'

'Oh yes, we'll do that. I'll be very interested to meet that fellow. We need him on our side. But the soldiers have been singing your exploits in town. They said the chief was impressed with your status, you know, uniform, sword and all. Though you don't look too impressive today.'

'I haven't got a uniform now. Only a ceremonial.'

'Better still!' Heselwood laughed. 'I ought to get one too.'

'Come to think of it,' Kit shrugged, 'I haven't even got that.' But Heselwood appeared not to notice.

Bewildered by Heselwood's effrontery, Kit was still trying to digest the man's nerve at interfering in a strictly military affair. Had he been Gresham, he'd have sent him packing, title or no title. Which reminded him of Gresham's report.

'I'd like to know what that bugger intends to recommend,' he said, and Heselwood glanced at him with a shrug.

'Don't worry about it. It's my bet he'll recommend a dishonourable discharge and that will be the end of it.'

'What!' Kit almost turned back, but they were passing the Lands Office Hotel and he automatically looked towards it.

'She's gone,' Heselwood said. 'Miss Pinnock and her brother sailed for Sydney yesterday. I must say, there was some curiosity observed that you were not there to wave farewell.'

Kit wouldn't comment. He was not surprised that they'd gone home, both of them, but he was so numb from multiple shocks that he couldn't bring himself to think about them, not even about Jessie. He seemed to have nothing left inside, and having shed the ignominy of confinement in a military prison, he felt like a stunned mullet washed up on a muddy shore, lacking the motivation to struggle.

Further down the street, Heselwood pointed out a barber. 'That fellow's quite good. You have a shave and a tidy-up and come up to the Britannia Hotel. We'll have morning tea with my lady wife before we leave.'

'Leave for where?'

'Emerald Downs for a start,' he called, reining the horse aside to allow a long bullock train to pass. 'We have to enlist your friend Jack Drew.'

Mrs Kirk bailed up the matron at the bush hospital, demanding that her husband be released, insisting that he would be much better off at home with proper care and decent food.

'I quite agree, Mrs Kirk. I told your husband he could go home yesterday but he seems to think his injuries are much worse than they are, and hung on to his bed. It would suit me if he left, I have serious cases to attend to.'

'My husband is a police inspector, very highly thought of in this town I'll have you know, Matron. It's obvious to me that you can't tell a serious case when you see one. Which is exactly why I'm taking the Inspector home from this dump. It's no better than a collection of bush huts.'

'If you want better, get on to the gov'mint,' the Matron barked, and strode away.

Mrs Kirk rallied some gentlemen visiting the hospital to assist her poor battered husband out to their gig, and took the reins herself.

'Drive me to the barracks,' he said. 'I have to see the Colonel so he can get on with his enquiry.'

'No you don't. He called in at the house yesterday afternoon. I told him you were still in the hospital, so he left a message to say that his enquiry was completed.'

'It can't be. I didn't get to speak. I was to be the chief witness.'

'Well, that was what he said.'

Rollo moved uncomfortably on the hard seat. 'How do I look?'

She glanced at him. 'The swelling's gone down on your face, but there's still black around your right eye and bruising on your chin. My word, that Drew fellow has something to answer for! I never heard of a police officer being attacked in a main street before. And no one coming to your aid. It is disgraceful. We ought to leave this place, Rollo.'

'Have they locked up Jack Drew?'

'No they have not, and I told Grimes off about that, but he said no charges have been laid. And I said I'd lay the charges, but he said it would be better for you to do that yourself.'

'I'll lay them all right,' he mumbled. 'The bastards. They should have grabbed him there and then, but no, Grimes and his mates, got it in for me they have, because I'm the one gets results.'

'Of course you do, Rollo. They're just jealous. But listen, I heard them talking about a spot for an assistant chief warden on Norfolk Island. They say it's the most beautiful island, with a wonderful climate, not like this stewpot of a place. And they say the married quarters are simply divine. Prison officers live like kings, with lovely houses, and gardens overlooking the ocean, plenty of servants, and what's more, a proper regiment of soldiers based there permanently. Now I want you to apply right away.'

'I will when I finish with Drew and Ferrington,' he said, mushing his words thanks to missing teeth and a swollen tongue. 'Did you ask the dentist about my teeth?'

'He said with front teeth missing it would be better to take the lot out, then you can have false teeth and it's goodbye toothache for ever. You might as well, Rollo, you know how bad your toothaches get.'

He nodded. 'Yes, all right. After I see Drew put away. Did you ask Gresham about his enquiry, like what happened?'

'Yes. But he'd only say he would release his findings at a later date.'

Rollo groaned. Today he would take it easy. Tomorrow he'd arrest Drew himself. Now that he had something concrete to go on.

When the Major rode in with Lord Heselwood, he was surprised to see the house site completely empty of debris, and though he didn't care whether the wreck was cleared away or not, he made an effort to thank Jack and Tom Lok and the fellow named Scarpy who was helping them.

'Some of the men from Baker's Crossing came to lend a hand too,' Jack told him. 'They finished the fencing and did all sorts of odd jobs round the place.'

'I'll have to thank them,' he said dully, introducing Lord Heselwood to the three men. Heselwood's title didn't mean a thing to Tom Lok, but Jack and Scarpy drew back like startled deer, and regarded the lord with suspicion. Typically, Heselwood didn't seem to notice.

'Lovely spot,' he said, dismounting. 'Mind showing me about?'

'Not at all,' Kit said. He turned to Jack. 'Lord Heselwood owns Montone Station. He was there with his wife when the blacks attacked. Barely escaped with their lives.'

'You don't say?' Scarpy said, unimpressed, but Jack mumbled that he had things to do and strode down towards the river.

So there it was at last, he mused, staring down at the rushing, rain-swollen waters. He hadn't known what had become of the woman in that house, in the bedroom, during the raid, and he hadn't wanted to know. Too fearful too ask anyone, not the Major, not Bussamarai, and not even Moorabi. He'd seen the dead white woman in the yard, that was enough; he didn't want to be told about the other one, the woman with the lovely face and the soft brown hair . . .

But she'd escaped. And she had a name. Mrs Heselwood.

He wanted to sigh with relief, but it wouldn't come. The burden he'd carried since he'd regained consciousness in the barn was still a lump in his chest, undigested. Montone had been the climax of the war in that area, he mused, and they'd both won. Bussamarai had pushed out the white folk and their cattle, and burned down the house and outbuildings, and here was Heselwood on his way back. They both must have known it would only be a matter of time before the rebuilding began, hence Bussamarai's lack of enthusiasm for the recent confrontations with white folk. It occurred to Jack then that the savagery of the assault against Kirk's troops was in marked contrast to Bussamarai's failure to act against Rapper and his men. So that must have been personal. Straight-out revenge against savage blackfellows who had been given weapons by white men to murder their own people.

Heselwood. He didn't remember him at all from the attack on the farm. Several white men had been there, firing at them. One of them had shot him.

What would Bussamarai say about this chance meeting? Jack wondered. He'd probably be amused.

He noticed then that the water level of the river was a lot higher than before, and he jumped to his feet, remembering the crocodile, and trudged back up the hill.

The next day, as Tom Lok served their meal, four men, the most unlikely of company, sat glumly at the long table in the cookhouse, eating their lunch from tin plates.

Heselwood did most of the talking. Scarpy said nothing at all. He'd said his piece, told Jack about this fellow Hector, wishing he'd been a little more respectful in the telling, when it turned out to be Jack's kid brother.

'He didn't know I was a robber by trade,' Jack said, overcome by melancholy. 'The poor bugger, came all this way trying to find me and

330

then got himself drowned. He must have found out I was here, God knows how, never thinking I might have changed my name. Why would he, Scarpy? Him thinking I never had the need.'

Jack managed a wan smile. 'It's a peculiar thing, what with Hector being my brother and all, but I can't get as downright miserable about him as I did about Brosnan.'

'Ah well, Brosnan was a lovely feller. We never thought he'd get shot, he wanted no part of breakouts from Mudie's.'

Jack sighed. 'Yes, he left a sort of gap, Brosnan did. The blacks call it a space, something like that, left where he should be standing. But they never mention a dead man's name.'

'Don't want to be upset, reminded of the dead one?'

'You'd think so, but I found it had the opposite effect. You'd go to say the name and have to stop and think about it, and that's when you notice the space.'

'Sounds rum to me.'

'Yeah, but what about the other business? The tip you had they're looking for Jack Wodrow?'

'I reckon Hector set the ball rolling.'

'Not on purpose, though.'

'True. But your mate Inspector Kirk is on to it.'

'So that's what Clancy was talking about.'

'Who's he?'

'No one that matters.'

'Then I say we'd better get the hell out of here, Jack. You can come to my place and figure out your next move from there. Stay as long as you like . . .'

'I might. There's no rush. That rat Kirk won't get me.'

Scarpy finished his meal in double-quick time and turned his attention to the others at the table. Heselwood was still nagging them to go with him up to his cattle station, to make sure he didn't get done by the blacks again, and putting up all sorts of reasons why they had to go. By this he was offering to pay them, and Scarpy thought Jack should grab at the opportunity to dodge the law and make a few quid. But he kept out of it.

As usual, Jack couldn't make up his mind. He'd always thought that when he returned to civilisation he'd be a rich man, able to do as he pleased. Well, he *could* do as he pleased, as long as he kept a jump ahead of the law, an aspect that hadn't featured in his plans, but it was still hard to make a decision and he didn't know why. He felt like a deer blinded by light, unable to make that escape until the last second, when choice fled first. Like going in and giving Kirk a hiding. That didn't require a decision. It just had to be done.

He looked over at Heselwood, who was offering to loan the Major some of his stockmen, to get him started here again. They'd also mind the place while Ferrington was away, and Jack thought that offer was hardly tactful under the circumstances. Ferrington didn't miss the irony.

'Yes,' he exploded, 'why don't I do that? It's a good idea to have men mind the place; none of these buildings have been burned down yet.'

'Take it easy, old chap. Why don't we go over to my digs and have a port?'

Jack nodded, wishing they *would* go. Heselwood's 'digs' were in the Major's office, while the rest of them slept in the men's quarters. Yesterday, when he discovered they were short of rations, Heselwood solved that problem by taking Tom Lok to Baker's Crossing to buy supplies, and some liquor, while Jack and the Major tidied up around Polly's grave and built a small timber fence to keep it safe from dingoes.

'I think I'll have another cup of tea first,' the Major said, and Tom Lok rushed to oblige.

Kit had been trying to convince himself that he didn't have to go with Heselwood, but he was so depressed he didn't care much what he did. He'd been shocked earlier, when the mailman brought a small parcel for him . . . and he'd been foolish enough to open it in front of the others, curiosity-induced folly. When Jack saw the ring he was troubled, a mite embarrassed, not knowing what to say, but Heselwood laughed.

'Looks like you'll have to woo the lady all over again.'

'Which I can't do if I'm trekking inland again,' Kit snapped, but milord had an answer for everything.

'On the contrary, absence makes the heart grow fonder!'

Whose heart? Kit wondered. He was still profoundly annoyed with Jessie, it wasn't a matter that could simply be turned over and forgotten, but he had been very rude to her, and that worried him. He didn't think Jessie would be warming to him after that episode.

Maybe, he sighed, this was for the best. She'd called off the engagement, there was nothing more to say. After all, what had he to offer now but sheds for a homestead and a pile of debts? And, he groaned, the possibility of dishonourable discharge. The Governor General hadn't responded to his resignation, and rightly so. It was absolutely not done to try to involve His Excellency in the matter. Kit couldn't imagine what had got into him to have committed such a breach.

Blanche Pinnock waited anxiously as the coastal steamer docked at Circular Quay in Sydney. She'd been a bundle of nerves from the minute she'd received the telegram from Adrian, advising that he and Jessie were coming home. She still hadn't overcome her shock at the loss of the *Arabella*, the other coastal steamer that plied the Brisbane–Sydney route, and for the last few days her heart had travelled with them every inch of the way. She'd felt some relief when Marcus let her know the day the ship would have cleared the danger zone and be sailing safely out into the open ocean, but she was still so concerned, she studied the map of the coast carefully, working out where the ship might be, until she heard it had been sighted coming through the heads into Sydney Harbour.

People were streaming ashore, and at last there was Adrian, looking surprisingly healthy after their ordeal. He was very suntanned and had lost weight, which he'd needed to do, she thought, since he was inclined to overeat, and make too much of a good thing of luncheons and dinner parties. But then she saw he was helping Jessie to clamber along the gangway, and she looked dreadful!

Blanche rushed forward and flung her arms around them. 'My dears! I'm so happy to have you home. I've missed you both so much. Now you get the luggage, Adrian, and Jessie and I will wait in the carriage . . .'

'Mother,' he said tersely, holding up a valise, 'this is all the luggage we have. We got burned out, remember? But we have to get Jessie home as soon as possible. She's not well, she's been seasick the whole time.'

'Oh, you poor girl,' she said, taking Jessie's arm. 'But don't worry, now that you're on solid ground you'll be fine. Mal-de-mer doesn't last, you'll see. Now I want to hear all about the dramas, you must have had the most terrible time. And to think Kit was wounded in action against those blackfellows . . .'

'Mother, please . . .' Jessie stumbled and almost fell to the ground, but they managed, between them, to help her to their carriage, the driver jumping down to lend a helping hand.

'I'm taking Jessie straight home,' Blanche said. 'You run and get the doctor. This isn't just seasickness, she's very ill.'

With the help of the maids, Blanche only had time to put Jessie to bed in her own room before the doctor came. He went straight up to the room to see the patient, in his usual jovial mood, but soon came out and beckoned Blanche into the upstairs sitting room for a private discussion.

'What's wrong with her?' Blanche asked breathlessly. 'I hope she hasn't caught one of those dreadful tropical sicknesses, she's so pale and weak.'

'No, it's not that,' he said.

'Oh, thank God. But I had to call you, she's usually such a good sea traveller.'

He drew her into the room and closed the door. 'It's not seasickness either, Blanche. Your daughter is having a miscarriage.'

'What?' Blanche almost screamed. 'That's not possible!'

'I'm afraid it is, my dear, and we have to help her right away.'

'You're wrong!' she cried, rushing for the door. 'I won't have this. I'll talk to her myself.'

'Blanche,' he said firmly. 'You can do that later, but unless you want this to be public knowledge, you'd better listen to me.'

The seriousness of his tone stopped her before she opened the door. 'What do you mean?'

'She should be in hospital, but it will cause less talk if we look after her here. Get towels and old sheets, quickly, and I'll want hot water and an oilcloth if you have one . . .'

'How is she?' Adrian had been hovering outside.

'She's all right. Go down quickly and tell your grandfather there's no need to worry. Just too much seasickness. She's dehydrated.'

When the maids offered to help, Blanche managed to smile at them. 'Thank you, no,' she said. 'I haven't seen Jessie for a while. I want to do for her myself.'

As she climbed the stairs with jugs of hot water, the smile disappeared and she gritted her teeth in rage. She helped the doctor, throwing a pile of towels and stained linen into a corner to be burned, for they certainly wouldn't be seen by anyone else in this house, and smiled again, obeying his instructions.

Her voice was soft as she tried to comfort her daughter, who didn't seem to be able to control her weeping, but a voice inside her was railing against Ferrington, that seducer of innocent young girls, that hound! 'I'll have his hide,' she said under her breath, when it was over and she was washing Jessie down and putting her into a fresh nightdress. 'I'll kill him.'

They tucked her into bed, and the doctor was very matter-of-fact about the whole business, which Blanche found even more humiliating than if he had frowned and lectured the girl.

He took Jessie's hand, patted her forehead and beamed at her. 'There you are now, my dear,' he said. 'You're a good strong girl. You'll be quite all right now. Nothing to worry about. She can have a light tea, Blanche, and get up for a while tomorrow.'

Blanche saw him to the door and looked at the time. The maids would have gone off for the afternoon. She called in on Marcus, who was settling down for his afternoon nap.

'The doctor took his time,' he said.

'Oh yes, he likes a chat. Where's Adrian?'

'He's gone out.'

Wearily Blanche climbed back up the stairs, furious that Adrian had let her down yet again. She needed him to dispose of the soiled linen she'd stuffed into a large suitcase and hidden in her room. The doctor had been under the impression that she'd taken it down to the laundry – after all, Blanche's linen was of the best quality – but she wanted it out of her house and dumped on the rubbish tip as soon as possible. In the morning she'd buy replacements.

But of course, Adrian would have to go missing now! Typical!

Blanche sat on the edge of her bed and wept bitter tears.

*　*　*

Relieved to be able to hand over responsibility for his sister, Adrian took out his much-loved brougham and before long was driving swiftly into town to confront his bank manager.

I'll give him a piece of my mind, he vowed as he strode into the lofty portals.

But the manager wasn't perturbed by his belligerence. 'I can quite understand your annoyance, Mr Pinnock, believe me. You were placed in an awkward situation, but the fault lies not with us. No, not at all. It seems your allowance was not paid in as you expected, so when I heard from you, I made enquiries on your behalf, and discovered that it has been cancelled, or so I was told. A mistake I feel sure, but I was unable to proceed, you understand . . .'

'Who cancelled it?'

The bank manager fiddled with a pen on his neat desk, impatiently tapping a time's-up signal. 'Mr Marcus Pinnock.'

'That can't be right,' Adrian cried. 'He wouldn't do that!' He then found himself moving with the manager, who had risen from his chair, walked round the desk to open the door, and hold it open.

Once back in Castlereagh Street, with only a few pence left of the money Sam had given them, Adrian postponed questioning his grandfather; that hitch could be sorted out any old time. He climbed back into his brougham, slapped the reins on to the horse's rump and went dashing away to see his beloved Flo.

From her open front door she could see the flash vehicle prancing down the narrow street, but she didn't realise it was Adrian until he jumped down. Then of course she ran, Flo ran, and threw herself into his arms, and he picked her up and carried her inside, slamming the door behind him. By this, with Bonnie's help, she'd managed to refurnish her little house, but Adrian didn't notice anything different. He carried her straight through to the bedroom and began undressing her so frantically, Flo was overjoyed. This was the homecoming she'd dreamed about. Her darling Adrian made love to her as if he'd been away for ten years instead of a few months, his love so passionate Flo wept tears of happiness.

At dusk she lit the candles and opened a bottle of claret, which they shared, sitting up in bed, while he told her about the disastrous and dangerous times he'd had on the northern farm, and how his friend, Major Ferrington, had been speared by savages, but was all right now, thank God.

'How terrifying,' she cried, aghast, 'to have them set fire to the house while you were inside. What sort of people worked there?'

'Felons,' he said. 'But we got away. I was really sorry about the house, though. It was a nice house.'

Adrian drank the last of the claret and pulled her over to him, running his hands over her body. 'You're so beautiful,' he said, kissing her neck.

'You're so soft and white and luscious, I missed you so much. I can't believe I'm back at last.'

He stayed late, making love to her and dozing, and woke up suddenly, starving, so Flo gave him a meal of giblet soup and cold baked ham with pickled onions and pease pudding.

The glow was still with her the next morning when she ran down to tell Bonnie her darling was back.

Bonnie was confined to bed now, and having trouble breathing, but she still liked to know everything that was happening around her. The old doctor from Macquarie Street called every day, giving her medicines and lotions, and her other friend Dr Bamberry, an apothecary (they laughed that Flo could never pronounce that word), brought her opium to ease the pain. On the quiet, they told Flo that Bonnie didn't have long to go, and she hated to hear that; it was heartbreaking to have to watch a friend die.

Nevertheless, Bonnie guessed as soon as she saw Flo that morning, and demanded to know everything. Everything meaning every intimate detail, and Flo blushed at the telling, but it made Bonnie happy.

'Did he give you any money?' she rasped.

'Oh no. We were too much in love to talk about money.'

'Well don't let him get away again. Tell me once more about Major Ferrington. Are you sure he's all right?'

'Yes, Adrian says he's well now. He's a hero, that friend of yours, isn't he?'

'Always was to me, luv.'

In the morning, Blanche began by treating Jessica tenderly, but she couldn't maintain the role, and within the hour she was snapping at her to stop feeling sorry for herself.

'You brought this on yourself, my girl, so don't try my patience with your crocodile tears. You sit up and pull yourself together. I have never been so humiliated in my whole life, to have the doctor tell me that you were pregnant!'

She stormed out of the room and into Adrian's bedroom, yanking him awake.

'Get up! It's past seven o'clock! What time did you get in last night? Out there carousing again. Don't think I don't know what you get up to, you wretch! You get dressed immediately. I've got a job for you.'

'What sort of a job?' he mumbled, sitting up.

'I've got some garbage to be disposed of.'

'I'll do it later.' Adrian was tired; he slumped back on to the pillows.

'You'll do it now! Do you know what state your sister was in when you brought her home yesterday? Do you have any idea? You damned fool! She was pregnant!'

'Hell's bells!' he exclaimed. 'Who to? I mean, who's the father?'

'Her precious fiancé, of course. Who else would it be?'

336

He shrugged. 'What did she say?'

'She didn't say anything, not a word. She had a miscarriage! I had to help the doctor! Myself! I couldn't allow anyone else to find out. What a scandal! In my own home! Now you get dressed this minute, and I'll tell you what you have to do . . .'

To get rid of her and her ranting, Adrian climbed out of bed and began to remove his nightshirt. That made her run for the door like a startled rabbit.

Jessie pregnant! The little villain! No wonder she was off-colour and teary. Well, she was in for it now. Blanche would never let her live this down. And as for Kit! God help him!

When he walked out to the passageway, Blanche was waiting, and picked up where she'd left off. 'You come with me! And let me tell you, I will never allow that rogue Ferrington in this house ever again! He's banned from our circle! He can stay away. There'll be no wedding. How dare they put me through such a hideous day! I ought to have the law on him . . .'

'Don't worry about the wedding. It's off. They had a row and Jessie called the engagement off. She sent the ring back.'

Blanche staggered and reached to the wall for support. 'She what? She was pregnant and she called off the engagement? What was she thinking of? She couldn't do that!'

Adrian shrugged. 'Thank God for the miscarriage then.'

'That's a dreadful thing to say! Oh my God! Was she wearing that ring or not?'

'No. I told you, she returned it.'

Blanche almost fainted. 'And there I was telling the doctor she was engaged, trying to make the whole miserable business seem not so bad, and she wasn't wearing her engagement ring! Is there no end to this humiliation?'

Adrian had made up his mind to tell her about Flo today, but decided it wasn't a good time. Anyway, there was his allowance; he had to talk to Marcus this morning.

'Does Grandfather know?'

'He does not, and he mustn't know.'

'Won't he wonder why you're banning Kit from the house?'

'Don't bother me! Just come with me and do as you're told.'

Marcus was waiting for him in the study, peering over the roll-top desk like a white-capped eagle, ready to attack.

'Morning, Grandfather,' he said, and dropped into the easy chair beside the desk.

'Are you finished gallivanting? You sure you have time for a few words?'

'As long as they're pleasant words on a fine morning like this. I wanted to ask you—'

'You'll ask me nothing until I'm ready. I want to know exactly what happened on that farm that the workers mutinied while you were in charge. Is it a prison farm or not? The papers don't seem to be clear on that.'

Adrian relaxed; he had plenty of time. 'Not exactly,' he said. 'Kit employed convicts who were finishing their sentences. They weren't locked up at night as they would be on an actual prison farm, and they weren't supervised by guards.'

'In other words they could bolt when they felt like it?'

'Yes, but the consequences were harsh. Norfolk Island when they were captured.'

'*If* they were captured. I read that the ringleader, a murderer, is still on the loose.'

Adrian went on to explain the course of events, from the time they realised Kit was in financial difficulties, avoiding mention of Polly's sacking, and the old man shook his head as the sorry tale unfolded.

'A risk taking them on in the first place, without guards. Foolhardy.'

'They were cheap labour. If Kit had employed guards it would have cost a lot more.'

'So he was pennywise. What will he do now?'

'I've no idea.'

'He is your sister's fiancé! It was your responsibility . . .'

'No it isn't. The engagement's off.'

'What? Why?'

'I don't know for sure. You'll have to ask Jessie.'

Marcus reached for his pipe, and packed it with tobacco. 'Pass me the matches from the mantelpiece.'

Adrian obliged, and the old man cupped his hand and lit the pipe, one eyebrow raised to begin his questions again, but Adrian cut in.

'About my allowance, sir. Did you stop it?'

'I did.'

'Would you mind telling me why?'

'Because you're a rogue and a spendthrift and you don't get another bean out of me, or your mother, until you get back to work!' He puffed a cloud of smoke at Adrian, who shook his head miserably.

'Look . . . I'm sorry, Grandfather. I realise I was a bit slack, but I am entitled to an allowance. When you stopped it, you left Jessie and me stranded in Brisbane without any money to pay our hotel bill.'

'You seem to have managed. Now . . . your allowance will resume when you get back to work at the Parramatta properties. It will be paid weekly, instead of monthly, into your hand. Which means you have to be there, get it?'

Adrian didn't comment.

'You will report to Joe Somers, who is now manager of the head station, and we'll have no more to say on the subject. Is that clear?'

'Yes. But I can't go out to Parramatta just yet.'

'Why not?' Marcus demanded angrily.

'Because I'm getting married.'

'To whom, may I ask? The floozy from the concert hall? Grow up!'

Adrian was surprised that he knew about Flo, but he wasn't about to stay and argue. He simply said, 'Her name is Miss Fowler, sir, and she will require your respect.'

With that he picked up his hat and left.

'Why didn't you tell me you were pregnant?' Adrian asked Jessie.

'I didn't know, honestly, I was feeling so awful . . .'

'Did Kit know?'

'Of course not, you idiot. If I didn't know, he didn't know, and don't you tell him. Are you really going to marry that girl? Mother's livid!'

'Yes I am,' he said, but now that he'd made the announcement and was faced with having to bring Flo home to meet the family, he wasn't so sure. In fact he was petrified. Though he loved her and adored making love to her, he'd seen her through different eyes on his return from Brisbane. She did seem a little cheap. And it wasn't just the family – he and Flo could suffer them – but his friends. How would she fit in with the Parramatta squattocracy?

'Oh God,' he groaned. 'Poor Flo.' He wished he was back at Emerald Downs.

Blanche couldn't believe her ears when Marcus told her that her son was to be wed.

'Please, Marcus, don't joke about something like that. I've enough on my mind with Jessie and her failed engagement. We'll have to return those engagement presents, too, it's just dreadful.'

'I tell you, it's true. I told him no work, no money, so he'd better get back to Parramatta quick smart. Because there are no handouts here. Then he says he can't go to Parramatta because he's getting married. Do you suppose he's got the girl in the family way?'

Blanche jumped nervously. 'You've pushed him into this, Marcus. He had a bad time up north, you should have given him a chance to settle down first. He probably just said that to give himself some breathing space.'

'Breathing space be damned! There's plenty of breathing space out west, acres of it. You're too soft on him, that's the trouble. He can't marry without any money; you tell him to get out there and earn his keep before he volunteers to support someone else.'

Adrian didn't wish to discuss the matter. 'Not in the mood you're in,' he told his mother. 'Jessie's got you all upset, so don't you go taking it out on me!'

339

'But is it true? Give me a straight yes or no. That's all I ask. I have a right to know what's happening.'

'All right. Yes!'

'What?' she screamed. 'What? If your father were alive he'd knock you down! How dare you carry on with this person behind my back! I presume you keep her hidden away because she's not up to our social standing. Otherwise why the secrecy? Well you listen to me, what you're doing is an insult to her, an insult. If she had any sense she'd tell you to go to hell.'

'I don't have to listen to this,' he snapped and marched away, leaving her to fume until the doorbell rang. Driven to the limit of her endurance that morning, she fell into the arms of Mr Watkins, who listened to her woes, all except the one about the nature of Jessie's illness, and dried her tears.

'You're such a comfort,' she sobbed. 'I don't know what I'd do without you, Frederick.'

'It's the other way around,' he smiled. 'You're the light of my life, Blanche, and I wanted to talk to you about that. I would like to make it official, our walking out together. Would that be all right with you, my dear?'

'Oh yes, I'd be very happy about that, but I think we won't mention it round here just yet.'

Laughing, he gave her a peck on the cheek. 'Now, Blanche, what did you say to Adrian? That you resent all this secrecy. You mustn't do the same thing. We could start by telling Marcus, and then perhaps you'd like to go to the band recital in the botanical gardens.'

'I'd love to, but I'm upset with Jessie and Adrian . . .'

'Then it's time you let them work out their own problems. Give yourself time off, I always say, when botherations mount up.'

Chapter Nineteen

Inspector Kirk was so angry, livid, with Jack Drew when he walked out the door the next morning, his uniform spick and span again, dust and blood removed, the tear at the elbow neatly sewn by his wife, that he was almost blinded by his rage.

He banged into the gatepost, lurched aside and stormed down to the stables, where he was subjected to snide remarks about his black eye and other bruises as the grooms saddled his horse for him. Even making jokes as he lowered his bruised rear end to the saddle.

It occurred to him then that he would get a worse chiacking at the police station, and thought better of reporting in.

Why should I? he pondered moodily. Why should I have to put up with that? I'm my own man. An inspector. I can do my job without having to front up there. Especially since Jack Drew's at the top of my arrest list today. If they won't arrest the bastard, I will.

It did cross his mind that maybe he ought to take a constable with him, but his rage rejected that suggestion out of hand. He had no need of assistance to arrest a felon like Drew, and he certainly would not share the glory with another lawman. This was his own arrest, and it would blossom into a good newspaper story when he announced that Drew was an alias to cover the famed Wodrow name. It was exciting when put like that. Kirk licked his bruised lips and spurred his horse into action. He'd go out to Emerald Downs, find Drew and arrest him at gunpoint. There was nothing Ferrington or anyone else could do about that. And if he tried to escape, preferably in front of witnesses, he could shoot him. Easy as that.

The ride turned out to be more harrowing than he'd expected. His rear end, his bum, hurt like hell, bouncing on the saddle. That kick Drew gave him had found its way right through to the bone, and the longer he stayed on the horse, the more agonising his injuries. Time and again he cursed Drew and everyone associated with him, vowing revenge on the lot of them.

Another man was heading in that direction, walking cross-country, though, and only using the winding road when it became part of the straight line in which he walked. To Moorabi, roads were for vehicles, winding to avoid massive trees or the steep hills and gullies that patterned this land. He was

341

padding along at a good pace now, rid of the irritating shirt and trousers, and wearing only a fur string belt with a boomerang stuck in it, and when he came to a fast-flowing creek he waded across, pleased with this season's good rains that brought bounty to the valley.

He couldn't resist checking the creek banks, and sure enough he came across *nulaga*, the feller Jack called 'crab'. He was big and fat, too tempting for a man to ignore.

Soon he had lit a small fire and cooked the crab, breaking the hot shells and sucking out the delicious meat piece by piece. Pleasantly satisfied by the light meal, he climbed up the rise and stood there for a while surveying the countryside, which was still green and healthy. It wouldn't be long, he knew, before the tall trees would have to brace themselves against the long dry season.

As he set off again, he noticed a rider coming along the road but took no notice. He had just realised that he would be crossing the road near to the entrance to the farm where Jack Drew lived, and thought it might be all right for him to go in and have a sit-down with Jack for a while. See if his friend had found him.

Kirk saw the blackfellow stamping out a campfire off to the right of the road, and resented this intrusion. 'The bloody blacks,' he growled to himself, 'they think they can squat anywhere they like. They don't care who owns the land. I'll give that bastard a piece of my mind.'

As he rode closer he was further offended, realising the man was almost naked, and that he could arrest him. This wasn't exactly within town boundaries, but plenty of white people used this road and they didn't want to be faced with this obscenity. Imagine ladies seeing this bloke now, his black bum naked; you couldn't call that string clothing, by any stretch of the imagination! And when he turned round, they'd probably faint right away! Blackfellows enjoyed exposing themselves to white women, Rollo thought, he bet they got a real kick out of it.

'Hey, you!' he called, and when the blackfellow turned, Kirk yelped at him: 'You!'

He grabbed for his rifle. 'Don't you bloody move, you horse thief! You took my horse! You're the one. You'll hang for this. You're under arrest!'

But the horse thief wasn't waiting to be arrested. He took to his heels and raced away as Kirk loaded his gun, spurring his horse into action.

The blackfellow dodged across open country, making for the safety of the bush, but Kirk soon caught up with him. He even had time to halt his horse to get a better shot while the horse thief was racing for that thick tea tree.

When he fired, he saw the fellow fling up his arms, but he still kept running, and Kirk grinned at the spectacle, comparing him to a headless chook, until the black man began to stumble, and fell, within a hand's reach of the bush.

The Inspector dismounted and looked down at the body. 'You should have run faster,' he said, irritated that he'd have to move it; he couldn't leave it in the open. He considered covering it with tea tree branches, but changed his mind and dragged it into the bush, pushing it further in with his boot.

He wiped his hands on his trousers and walked back to his horse. That episode over, it was now Jack Drew's turn to face the music.

'Someone's coming!' Tom Lok called.

Kit made for the door of the cookhouse. 'Who is it?'

'The policeman, Mr Kirk, he riding on down now.'

In seconds Kit was out the door and charging up the hill. 'Get off my property!' he shouted. 'Get off or I'll take to you with the horsewhip, you lying bastard!'

Kirk ignored the outburst. 'I am here on police business, you can't order me off.'

'I can throw you off! Get out of here.'

Kirk dismounted. 'Where's Jack Drew?'

'He's not here.'

'Yes I am.' Jack came out of the cookhouse, followed by his friend Scarpy. 'What do you want, Kirk?'

'I'm arresting you for assault and battery, and for suspicion of highway robbery.'

'You and what army?' Scarpy growled.

'You keep out of this, mister,' Kirk said, 'or I'll have you up on charges too.'

'What charges?' Kit demanded.

'Obstruction of justice. And that applies to you too if you make any attempt to aid and abet that felon. It would suit me fine to lay civil charges against you, Ferrington.'

Kit lunged at him but Jack held him back. 'Come over here.'

He took Kit aside. 'I've been expecting this. The bruises look good on him. I won't run from Kirk. You tell him you'll bring me in yourself.'

'I will not.'

'Listen to me. I can't let him take me in, he's got the gun, I could have an "accident". But I will front up on the charge. It's not a serious one. I knew what I was doing and I'd do it again.'

They argued until Kirk shouted at Jack to step forward, undoing the rope hooked on his saddle peg.

'Are you gonna hang me?' Jack asked him.

'Don't get smart. You're under arrest, Jack Drew.'

'You're talking funny, Kirk, is there something wrong with your mouth?'

'There'll be something wrong with your mouth in a minute.'

'Wait!' Kit called. 'I heard you threaten Mr Drew, so you listen to me, Kirk. He's willing to let you arrest him for bashing you . . .'

The Inspector looked at him suspiciously. 'He's what?'

'You heard him,' Jack said. 'So I'm under arrest! That surprised you, didn't it?'

He turned back to Kit. 'He's trying to make a big fellow of himself again. Thinks he can't lose. If I disappear, he can call up a posse again and hunt me down. If you cause trouble, the great Inspector can bring the law down on you too. So I give up, Kirk. I'll come quietly.'

'But not with you,' Kit said. 'I'll bring him in.'

'You expect me to believe that?'

'All right. You take him in, but I'm coming with you.'

'Me too,' Scarpy said. 'We'll all come with you, make sure he don't escape, eh?'

'Thanks, Scarpy,' Jack said with a grin. 'Will you get the horses?'

'Sure I will. Come on, Tom, give me a hand.'

'Just a minute!' Heselwood was at the door. 'What's going on here?'

Ferrington jerked his head at the Inspector. 'This bastard is arresting Jack for assault and battery on his person, as you see.'

'*You* did it, Jack?'

'On my honour, sir.' Jack bowed to the company.

'Cut that out!' The Inspector frowned, not quite catching what was said but taken aback by Heselwood's appearance. 'I'm surprised to see you in the company of this lot, sir.'

'Don't be. Like you, I have business here. But surely you're not taking him in today. That's a long ride, Inspector.'

'I have my duty . . .'

'And rightly so.' Heselwood turned to Kit. 'Despite your differences, Major, one would have thought common courtesy would have you offer the gentleman some refreshments. I'm sure Tom Lok could scratch him up a meal.'

As he spoke, there was an expression of benign innocence in his clear blue eyes. 'Am I being too forward in making this request?'

'No, of course not,' Kit stammered, realising Heselwood was up to something again, but what, was beyond him.

'Why don't you step over to the office with me, Inspector, and have a glass while we wait?'

Kirk, too, was confused, but the offer was too tempting to refuse. 'I surely would appreciate that, Lord Heselwood. Kind of you. But what about him?' he asked, pointing to Jack. 'I'd better bring him along. I don't want him bolting on me.'

'I said I'd go with you,' Jack growled.

'Good,' Heselwood said quickly. 'That's settled. Jack will wait. Come along now, Inspector, I'd like to hear first-hand about that shooting outside Ipswich where two men were gunned down. How on earth did that happen? The escapee wasn't armed, was he?'

'Stupidity,' Kirk said pompously. 'Plain stupidity. You don't mind if I bring my rifle, do you, milord?'

Heselwood blinked. 'Your rifle? No, I suppose not. No. Quite all right.'

The Inspector tried not to show it, but he was beside himself with delight at being invited into the company of this important man, who made no effort to have even Ferrington join them. He could see the irritation on the Major's face at this snub, and too bad!

'You'll have to forgive my digs,' Heselwood said, taking him into the familiar office. 'No homestead, so I sleep in here on a bunk in the corner. Have a seat, that chair's quite comfortable, I'll squeeze here at the desk. Now, I've got rather a fair whisky, best Baker's Crossing could offer, but not too bad.'

He poured two whiskies and handed one to Kirk. 'Your good health, sir!'

'Pip pip,' Kirk responded, thinking it sounded fitting, and launched into the story of the hunt for Albert Minchin, an absconder from this very farm, and his own daring dash into the woods, under fire, to bring out the wounded. He had only just reached the part where he was congratulated on his bravery by the Mayor of Ipswich when he saw a big red kangaroo in the yard.

'Look at that!' Heselwood said, interrupting. 'My word, he's a big fellow. I wonder what he's up to?'

They watched the animal thump over to the men's sleeping quarters, peer in and casually bound away.

'As I was saying,' Kirk continued, 'the Mayor said the people of Ipswich were grateful for my—'

'The wildlife on Montone Station was marvellous,' Heselwood observed. 'We had mobs of kangaroos and wallabies, and there were always emus skidding about. My wife loved it. And the birds! She'd never seen birds by the thousands before. Of course there was that other wildlife, the blacks. They made short work of our dream. You've been up there yourself, I believe?'

'Yes, once again I was lucky to escape with my life. Those murdering savages killed my troops. A massacre it was. They didn't stand a chance against those vicious hordes.'

'Incredible!' Heselwood murmured, refilling the glasses. 'The trouble is, though, I want to go back. You've experience of the area; would you say it is safe yet?'

'No fear. I wouldn't trust blackfellows. The sooner they're wiped off the map, the better. Then you'll be safe.'

'But Major Ferrington says it is safe, that he made peace with the chief.'

'I wouldn't trust Ferrington either.'

Heselwood sighed. 'I have to trust someone. I decided to have them take me up to meet the blackfellow chief. A sort of warlord, I understand. The Major as the negotiator, and Jack Drew as translator. That way I could find out for myself.'

'And you could get yourself killed.'

'I'm not so sure. I think a truce could work if I, as a settler and a neighbour, could get to know the fellow. I am given to understand the blackfellow chief knows he can't win against white folk, and that makes sense to me. But as usual, something always goes wrong.'

'Like what?'

'Like you're taking the Major and Jack Drew back to Brisbane just when I have persuaded them to escort me inland.'

Rollo gulped down the whisky. 'I'm sorry, Lord Heselwood, but I have my duty to perform. That Jack Drew is an all-round bad egg, believe me. I am almost certain he is an escaped prisoner himself. Ferrington doesn't have to come to Brisbane, but Drew is headed for jail.'

'How damned unfortunate,' Heselwood said, rising from his chair to walk to the door and stare out. The others had disappeared and the former centre of the farm's activities now looked desolate.

He turned back suddenly. 'Am I right in saying that it was you who charged Ferrington with neglect of his military duties?'

'Yes,' Rollo said angrily. 'And I won't go back on it, if that's what you're asking.'

'My dear fellow. I wouldn't dream of it. But cast your mind back. You claimed that Ferrington spent precious time prospecting for gold. Was that true?'

'Yes. I had that from his own men. It's true all right.'

'But did they find any?'

'No.'

'Good. Excellent.' Heselwood pulled the chair back and sat facing Rollo. Then he changed his mind and refilled the glasses, taking a gulp as if to fortify himself. 'I have something to tell you in the strictest confidence, and I'm sure, you being a senior police officer, I can rely on your integrity not to discuss this with anyone else. Most of all, the people here.'

Rollo was intrigued. He'd taken it for granted that Lord Heselwood was a friend of the Major's, but maybe not.

'You can surely rely on me, sir, my word you can, yes,' he said to encourage his confidence. 'If I can help you in any way . . .'

'Thank you, Inspector. Now first of all, let me tell you that the reopening of Montone is not necessarily a priority with me. As you are no doubt aware, I own Carlton Park, a substantial cattle station down south that keeps me busy. But I do want to go back to that property urgently and make peace with the chief, and the only way I can achieve that is by being introduced to him by Major Ferrington and Jack Drew.'

'If it's not urgent to reopen Montone, why the urgency to meet the chief?'

'This.'

Lord Heselwood dipped into his waistcoat pocket and withdrew a small suede bag. He opened the flap and drew out something wrapped in white silk. Undoing that, he placed a gleaming gold nugget, about half-thumb-size, on the desk, sitting back to allow Rollo to view it unhindered.

'Gold!' Rollo breathed. 'It's gold.'

'Yes. An excellent sample.'

'Where did it come from?'

'Montone.'

'What?'

Heselwood reached over and closed the shutters. 'Montone. I found it on my station.'

'Is there any more?'

'There were a couple more, I sold them. But I was about to begin to search the surrounds when the blacks chased us off.'

'Oh Jesus! Where did you actually find the gold?'

'In the wall of a cave,' he lied, 'where I took shelter from the rain one day. I dug them out myself with my knife. It was a huge thrill, I can tell you.'

'I can believe that!' Rollo's heart was beating like a drum. Absent-mindedly he poured himself another whisky, drank it down, and stared at the gold nugget. 'Can I pick it up?'

'Of course. It won't break.'

It was heavy, and it was worth a lot of money. Rollo loved the feel of it in his hand. Raw gold! Picked out of the dirt just like that. Picking up money. Men were already finding heaps of gold down south, making fortunes . . . everyone said there was gold up here too. There had to be. Rumour had it that Jack Drew was behind Ferrington's dabble in panning for gold, but that was a waste of time. This was the real thing.

'I kept that one for a souvenir,' Heselwood told him, taking back the nugget and turning it over in his fingers.

Rollo sweated, his mind in a turmoil. He was still overwhelmed at the attention shown to him by this illustrious man, and his brain was bounding away ahead of him on the trail of gold, willing to agree to whatever milord wanted. But he was trying to hold back, to comprehend what was going on here. Anxiety strained his voice when he tried to discover where he might fit into this . . . this field of good fortune.

'What . . . what . . . will you do about the rest?' he stammered. 'The rest of the gold. I mean, you'd be foolish to leave it there, Lord Heselwood; someone else might find it, and it being on your land doesn't make it yours.'

Heselwood sighed. 'I am aware of that and I'm quite frantic about it. That's why I need Drew and Ferrington to take me to Montone and introduce me to that chief.' His smile was cheerless. 'After all, I don't want to end up a rich corpse.'

'Do they know about the gold?'

'Good heavens, no.'

'Anyone else?'

347

'Not a soul.'

'I could take you. I know the area.'

'With all due respect, you don't know the chief and you can't speak the language. And anyway, if you came with me, what about the arrest of Jack Drew?'

'That can wait,' Rollo said eagerly. Measured against a reef of gold, Jack Drew was not worth a minute of his time.

'Splendid! I knew you'd see it my way,' Heselwood said. 'So here's what we do. We postpone arresting the fellow. They take me up and introduce me to bosso without any further delay. Then, if I'm sure it's safe to reopen Montone, I'll do just that. I won't need Ferrington or Drew any more. As soon as he gets back, you can arrest him.'

Rollo waved that suggestion aside. 'What about me?'

Heselwood looked pained. 'I thought you would be interested in gold mining with me! I will need a partner, and one can hardly invite stockmen into such an endeavour. If any of them knew there was gold in the area, how much work would get done?'

'Your partner,' Rollo breathed.

'Fair enough. It's the least I can do. One hand washes the other, Inspector. You help me and I'll help you.'

Jasin Heselwood ushered the fool out of the Major's office, and raised his silky eyebrows to the heavens. I'd rather partner a hyena, he said to himself.

To the west, the skies were darkening, a strange green tone spreading over the gathering clouds, and a sudden gust of wind scattered dry leaves as Heselwood escorted Kirk over to the cookhouse.

'Is the meal ready, Tom? The Inspector's hungry.'

'Boss say no meal,' Tom sulked.

'You get him a meal immediately,' Heselwood ordered. 'I'll speak to the boss.'

'About what?' Kit asked, coming in to join them.

'About common courtesy, sir. And I might tell you, the Inspector has decided not to arrest Mr Drew after all.'

'What? Why not?'

'I'm entitled to change my mind,' Kirk said with a shrug, and sat himself down at the table.

'Oh well, good. All right. I'll tell him.'

'If he's still here,' the Inspector smirked. 'Given that start, he's probably bolted.'

Kit glared at him. 'He's still here.'

'Excellent,' Heselwood said. 'I want a word with both of you.'

He put it to them bluntly: 'I've got the Inspector to drop the charges on condition you finish the job, Major, and take me to meet that chief. Then we'll all know, once and for all, if the truce exists. That means bringing

Jack along as an interpreter. It is only a few days' ride for the three of us, there and back, not an onerous exercise. I'm quite looking forward to it.'

In the end they agreed to go, on their terms. Jack to be paid. The Major to be loaned one of Heselwood's experienced stockmen for a year to help him run his cattle property efficiently.

With that, calm was restored. Heselwood went off to take a nap and the other three men walked down to check on the river.

'Do you think it will flood?' Kit asked nervously.

'No,' Jack said. 'The level's a lot higher than usual, but it's just flexing its muscles. You watch out when Meewah does flood, though; he can come down like an avalanche.'

'I thought this was the Brisbane River,' Scarpy said.

'New name,' Jack said. 'Who's Brisbane anyway?'

'He was a governor,' the Major said. 'That storm's going to hit soon. More rain!'

Jack sniffed the air. 'There's no rain in those clouds.'

'Well it's damned dark, it looks like it to me. We might as well go up, nothing we can do in this light.'

The wind increased, howling down the valley, and Jack shuddered. Over all the years he'd spent in this country, he'd never heard a howling like that. It sounded like a thousand dingo voices, mourning, crying. It terrified him and he began to hurry as if needing to find safe shelter.

And then he heard Tom Lok screaming. Screaming and screaming!

They ran, stumbling and shouting. The screaming stopped abruptly. Dust-filled wind howled around them and they could hardly breathe as they fought their way uphill. Horses in the stables whinnied pitifully and pounded on the walls as they ran by. The big red kangaroo that had been wandering about before, shot across their path, almost flying as it sped for the bush.

Heselwood came up fast from his nap at the first blood-curdling scream, and wrenched open the door of Ferrington's office.

At first he couldn't make out what was happening through the dust and the gloom, but the screams drew him to the Chinaman, who was pointing at something before he suddenly fainted, falling to the ground in a heap. Heselwood peered about him and eventually focused on a huge man, a fierce-looking blackfellow, who must have been seven foot tall if he was an inch. His face and body wore white ceremonial stripes and his eyes were ringed by yellow ochre.

Jasin staggered back. 'God Almighty,' he shouted. 'Who the hell are you?'

As he spoke, the man seemed to disappear into the gloom and then reappear, but this time he was carrying someone.

'Who is that? What is this?' Jasin demanded, only to fall back in horror. The giant was carrying a dead body, holding it in front of him, the body of another blackfellow, and he just stood there, making no attempt to speak

349

or move any further. He just stood there, holding out the body, grief personified.

The spirits had led him swiftly to Moorabi's side as he lay in the sweet-smelling tea tree, his life ebbing away.

'I had a dream,' Moorabi whispered. 'Was it of this I dreamed?'

'No, it was the death of your father. The great man's heart stopped beating when he was bathing in the river, and they laid him on the soft sand to recover, but he chose not to stay with us.'

'Who will lead the people now?'

'We will see. You can go now, your loving father is waiting for you.'

He closed Moorabi's eyes and wept over him as he set up a howling for the good and brave man who, he'd hoped, would take his place one day. The howling alerted hill people, who came down to take Moorabi and bury him in the proper manner, and begin the crying for him.

Then he stood and hurled a rock into the sky, watching it travel up and up. Lightning flashed, illuminating his face as it changed from grief to grievance, from the gentleness of a man who has laid a dear friend to rest to an avenger, to the man called Ilkepala who had seen the bullet wound in Moorabi's back. He walked to a stream and bathed before addressing the spirits about this terrible crime, then he applied the appropriate daubs of white paint, not of mourning – that would come later – but of retribution. Moorabi was a chosen one. A terrible loss.

The dust storm swirled and howled about him as Ilkepala went forth.

Tom Lok came to his senses and crawled away. Rollo Kirk heard the screaming, looked out, thought he saw some sort of monster and hid in a corner of the cookhouse. Heselwood remained, shocked by this apparition but needing an explanation.

Jack motioned to the Major and Scarpy to stay back. He went quietly up to Heselwood and asked him to walk away.

'Why. What the hell is going on?'

'I think I know who it is,' he said. 'You need to keep clear. This may not be real. You don't need to get mixed up in it.'

He waited for a few minutes and then spoke to the tall figure in his language. 'You know me. Is it permissible for me to know who that is in your arms? I am beset with a terrible sadness.'

Suddenly he felt a shocking pain thud into his back, as if he'd been shot, and he fell down, but when he climbed to his feet he was looking into Moorabi's dead face.

'Oh no!' he cried out. 'Oh no! What happened to him?'

It came into his mind then that Moorabi had been shot in the back, and the earth shook beneath his feet as he looked up at the giant whom he knew as Ilkepala, the magic man, who it was said could transform himself into any shape. Though Jack thought these magics were probably some

350

sort of trickery, he was not immune to fear as the huge blazing eyes glared down at him and Moorabi's image faded.

He felt his legs buckling but managed to speak. 'I am so sorry a friend has been lost to us. It will take a long time to put down this crying. I am sad for you too and for all the people.'

The giant, the impossibly tall painted blackfellow, seemed to fade just as Moorabi had done, and the howling stopped, and the wind dropped, dust falling gently around them, but somehow the eyes remained. Yellow eyes.

'Who did this terrible thing?' Jack asked. 'Who shot him?'

From over near the office that he called his digs, Heselwood gave a shout, pointing at the cookhouse, which was suddenly on fire, timbers ablaze.

Kit began to run towards it, but Jack ordered him back. 'Keep away. This is not your business. Remember Rapper's story of the trees. This may not be real.'

'You can't let it burn down,' Kit shouted, running towards the water tank and nearby buckets, but Scarpy grabbed him and held him back.

'Looks as if it's burning down to me, mate, but I wouldn't interfere in this blackfeller stuff for quids. That bloke was carrying a dead man; there's evil afoot somewhere.'

They'd forgotten about Kirk, who was forced to run from the building. He looked towards the blackfellow, screamed, and tried to run away, but found he was unable to move.

'Help me,' he shouted to Heselwood.

'Oh bloody hell!' Jack exclaimed. 'It was you! You shot him! Oh Jesus! Why did you do that?'

'I never did,' Kirk blubbered. 'I didn't. Someone else shot him. An accident. It was an accident.'

He began to scream, tearing at his hair.

'What's happening?' Heselwood called.

'I don't know,' Jack said.

'My hair, it's on fire!' Kirk screamed, running down to the tank. 'Help me, I'm on fire.'

'No you're not,' Jack said urgently, grabbing him. 'You're imagining it.'

But then his hands seemed to be on fire, so he let go with a yelp of pain, staring at the very real burns on his palms. Then he knew nothing could be done for Kirk. No one would be allowed to interfere. He watched the Inspector reel drunkenly about, screaming in pain, screaming for them to help him. Heselwood wanted to run to his aid, but Jack restrained him.

'Keep away. It's dangerous to touch him.'

'What's wrong with him?'

'He's telling you. He's burning up.'

But the Major could stand it no longer. He ran over to take hold of Kirk and try to convince him he wasn't burning, but a bolt of fire shot up his arm and he was thrown to the ground.

351

All was still now. Jack could feel the presence of Ilkepala but he could not be seen. Kirk kept on staggering about, trying to make for the river to quell the flames, and he was only a few feet away from the water's edge when he fell, within a hand's reach of the river.

Scarpy was first to reach him. 'He's dead, I reckon. Someone make sure.'

Gingerly, the Major bent down, fingers outstretched to touch, but Jack saw those yellow eyes again. They seemed to be reflected in the river and were moving closer.

'Look out!' he screamed. 'Look out!' He leapt back, dragging Ferrington with him as the massive crocodile tore out of the water, grabbed the body, rolled with it in his huge teeth and disappeared in a flash, the waters rushing on, recklessly.

'God Almighty!' Heselwood shouted. 'I think I'm going to be sick.'

Shocked and bewildered, they stood well back, staring at the river, petrified. Then they looked to each other, too dazed to speak. Because nothing could be done.

Though no one was hungry, Scarpy cooked breakfast the next morning, since Tom Lok had packed his few belongings and fled.

'He got such a fright, he probably prefers prison to any more of our ghosts,' Kit said, 'but I won't turn him in.'

'I don't blame him, I'm not hanging round here either,' Scarpy said. 'But tell me this, Mr Heselwood. How did you persuade Kirk to change his mind and decide not to arrest Jack?'

Heselwood yawned. 'Immaterial now. But if you must know, it was just talk. I told him what he wanted to hear.'

'Which was?'

'Ah now, every man has his price.'

'I'm not so sure. Depends on the man.'

The four of them talked over the events of the previous day, going over and over the phenomenon, amazed that the building they were sitting in showed no sign that it had been touched by fire, and yet Jack's hand and the Major's arm were now blistered.

'But why would Kirk want to kill that blackfellow?' Scarpy asked, and Jack said sadly: 'He'd met him before.'

He'd had enough of the talk; it was futile trying to work out exactly what had happened and how it had happened, and he couldn't bring himself to talk about Moorabi, so he left them to it and went for a long walk through the bush.

Eventually he came to the mangrove swamps, formerly a weird forest in a sea of mud, but now waist-deep in water, and he felt a little better. All the swamp creatures would be enjoying this renewal . . . another inevitable cycle. Life went on, he sighed, relentlessly.

Bloody relentlessly.

As he turned back, a black man fell into step beside him as if this walk were prearranged. He was a man of normal height with wiry white hair and a leathery face, and he carried a boomerang in a belt of possum fur. Nothing extraordinary about him at all, nothing to set him apart from any other men of his tribe, but Jack knew it was Ilkepala.

There seemed to be nothing to say, so they kept on through the bush as birds darted about and the noses of small animals twitched from their hollows. A curlew's mournful cry could be heard and Jack wondered why they always sounded so far away. Ilkepala would know, he thought, but he couldn't bring himself to break the tranquillity of the lovely surrounds.

When they came to the cleared fields, Ilkepala stopped and held out his hand.

'The great chief, our friend, is with the spirits now.'

Bussamarai dead? Jack was shocked. 'He is gone too? What was wrong? He looked well when I last saw him.'

'I am thinking the heart broke. He wanted you to have this.' Ilkepala held out the large gold nugget that had been part of the chief's headdress, and Jack accepted it politely.

'He knows I would rather see him here than his gift. But I thank him for his great kindness.' He put out his hand to Ilkepala. 'I thank you too, for your wisdom, and ask you to honour me by shaking my hand.'

The elderly man's grip was hard. Then he patted Jack's face, on the side where the scars were becoming fainter, and nodded approval before turning to walk back into the bush, gradually disappearing into the dewy night.

When he returned, Heselwood called to him: 'Where have you been? Now that Kirk's out of the way there's nothing stopping you coming with us.'

'Yes there is. There's no point in either of us going with you any more. Bussamarai, the big chief, is dead.'

'How do you know?'

'I was told. Believe me, he's dead, and I've no idea who will take the lead now. The truce will probably last, though, because Bussamarai was greatly respected. No one will dare challenge his rulings, not for a long while, and by then, with luck, they'll be used to having white settlers in the district. Thanks to the Major, you can take your men and open up the station again.'

Kit had overheard the conversation. 'I'm really sorry about the chief, and I suppose there's no point in asking who told you?'

'No. Just accept it.'

The next few days brought strange happenings. Superintendent Grimes, accompanied by Inspector Tomkins, came out to investigate the death of Inspector Rollo Kirk, having been advised of the tragedy by Lord Heselwood.

353

'His lordship did his best to explain these extraordinary events, Major, and you should thank your lucky stars he was a witness,' Grimes said, 'otherwise the whole thing looks a bit suspicious.'

Kit reacted angrily. 'Do you take the word of a man just because he's titled over everyday honest men?'

'We take the word of one we consider a bystander, sir, over those of men who have had recent serious conflicts with the deceased.'

'Did he tell you that your precious inspector murdered an Aborigine called Moorabi?'

'We have no evidence of that and no body has been found. Lord Heselwood did insist that it went on record, though.'

The two police officers walked about the property and, with great care, along the section of riverbank from where the body had been taken, but could find no evidence of a crocodile in residence.

'No body either,' Grimes said dismally. 'Lord Heselwood suggested we tell Mrs Kirk that her husband drowned, that it was accidental drowning, and we did that, rather than try to explain the rest of it. But she wanted to know what he was doing in the river.'

'He fell in,' Jack growled.

'No. We had to tell her the truth, that a crocodile got him, and she appeared to prefer that end, said she intended to write a book about his life. And she couldn't hide her excitement that he was on the front page of the paper again, victim of a crocodile attack. The woman is positively basking in the limelight of Rollo's spectacular death.'

Before they left, Tomkins had a word with Jack about the late Inspector Kirk and his suspicions.

'He seemed to think that you were someone called Wodrow, but that fellow has long gone. Then there's the matter of Mudie's prison farm, which I found in his notes. Do you know anything about that?'

'No. Never heard of it.'

'I didn't think so. Kirk could be very vindictive, not caring whose reputation he tarnished. We thought it best to destroy those notes, since you have been of service to the community, Jack. But one more thing . . . now that the slate's clean, see that you keep it that way.'

Heselwood was back in town, full of news about the bizarre happenings at Emerald Downs, and Georgina could hardly get a word in.

'Incredible it was, the whole affair, from beginning to end; did I tell you that the Major and another fellow there actually did sustain burns when they tried to assist Kirk?'

'Yes,' she said.

'Damnedest thing I ever saw, I'll dine out on it for years, but the end result was all my way. The countryside up there round Montone is cleared now as safe. I can reopen the station. And all thanks to Jack Drew.'

'Who?' The name leapt at her, the name she'd found in the newspaper.

'Drew. A most interesting fellow, a bushman. He was the one who secured the peace. The papers have it all muddled up thanks to the Kirks and that bloody old Colonel's interference. Drew took Ferrington right into the enemy camp, where they negotiated the release of his soldiers . . .'

'Why would he do that?' she asked. After all, as she recalled, this Jack Drew was on the side of the blacks.

'For peace, of course. That's what I've been trying to tell you. He knew the boss man, the chief. People in high places, as it were, even that witch doctor who loomed up at Emerald Downs. Bloody shook me up, I can tell you. I mean to say, a man wouldn't want to cross a bushman like Drew, not with the sort of friends he can muster. I wanted him to come with me to Montone, but he said he'd had enough of the bush.'

'I should think so,' Georgina said. 'It sounds to me as if he was altogether too friendly with the blacks.'

'Oh no! Never say that. He told us that the chief had died very recently, and don't ask me how he knew that, but his legacy of wanting peace would remain. For a while, anyway, as long as both sides behave. Drew is the man we've needed all along, someone who stayed with the blacks long enough to get to know them. Now he's a mediator. I'll tell you this right now, my love: if we get any more trouble on Montone, I'll come looking for Jack Drew to sort it out.'

Georgina sat back in the comfortable armchair and listened to him rattling on while he dressed for dinner, feeling better than she had for days. She had considered it her duty to report Jack Drew for his part in that raid, but the fact that he'd tried to protect her had held her back. Rather selfishly, she thought.

But now, by all accounts, the bushman had redeemed himself, and she could allow herself to be grateful to him for the gesture. She had no wish to meet the man, to face her flawed hero; it was enough that at last the mystery was solved. She hadn't imagined him after all. And it would be nice to acknowledge his rough chivalry . . . somehow.

When the mailman came, his dray packed with bulging mailbags and a collection of parcels and supplies piled up on the tray, Jack guessed he'd come in this direction first, to view the scene of the horrors that had taken place at Emerald Downs, and maybe pick up a little extra information about the strange events.

'Is there a cuppa going?' the mailman asked Kit, who nodded towards the cookhouse and told him to help himself, because the telegram he'd received had him thoroughly confused. It was from Adrian.

ARE YOU COMING TO SYDNEY STOP I AM TO BE WED SHORTLY STOP BONNIE HUNTER DYING STOP ASKING FOR YOU STOP

Bonnie Hunter? How did Adrian know Bonnie? And what was this about Adrian getting married?

He didn't think to ask Jack what was in the neat parcel he'd received, and since he didn't ask, Jack had no need to try for an explanation. He'd been sent a beautiful lace handkerchief with a G embroidered in one corner, and guessed it was from Lady Heselwood. She'd seen him in the street that day, and, he was sure, remembered him from Montone. He'd been so relieved to hear she'd survived the attack, it had taken a little while for him to realise that she was the one person who could get him hanged, if she ever spoke up. But it seemed that his secret was safe with her. He gazed at the handkerchief . . . he would treasure it. There was no note, though, and Jack guessed the gift had fulfilled an obligation to thank him, and at the same time allow forgiveness, but did not extend to friendship.

'Fair enough,' he said with a grin.

Kit thrust the telegram at him. 'Can you beat that? He's getting married. He never said anything to me about having a girlfriend, let alone a fiancée. I wonder who the lucky lady is?'

'Could be a Miss Fowler. He wrote to her a couple of times.'

'Never heard of her.'

'Who's Bonnie Hunter?'

'An old friend of mine. I had no idea Adrian knew her.'

'If she's asking for you, you'll be able to see the poor woman while you're in Sydney.'

'Who said I'm going to Sydney?'

'You are, aren't you? You can't just leave Miss Jessie there.'

The Major frowned. 'Things aren't too good in that department. Anyway, I haven't much money, I'd have to travel second class.'

'If you want to go, I'll hang on here for a while. But if you think your ladies aren't worth the ticket . . .'

Chapter Twenty

The streets of Sydney were crisp and cool after the dragged-out northern summer that rode roughshod over any portent of autumn, and Kit strode through a busy arcade, encouraged to feel a mite cheerful after a long absence from that emotion. It seemed disloyal to be glad to be away from Emerald Downs, but for the present, he'd had enough of the place.

When he emerged from the arcade and turned left, heading for the post office, he was across the road from the Officers' Club, but he had no wish to pay a visit, and that surprised him. It had been his club and all his cronies that he'd missed most of all when he first landed on his newly acquired Downs. Kit admitted to himself that being broke might have some bearing on his restraint, but it didn't bother him to pass on by.

As soon as he arrived, he had sent a message to Adrian asking him to meet him outside the post office, since he preferred not to call at the Pinnock house, not yet anyway, and there he was, looking very much the dandy again in a stylish suit and straw boater.

He greeted Kit effusively, as if there'd not been any friction between them. 'So glad to see you again, Kit. You're looking really well. A bit thin on it, but you'll build up again. Everything all right back home?'

'More or less. What's this about a wedding? You never mentioned getting married before. Why all of a sudden? Have you got someone in the family way?'

'Not me. At least I don't think so. Let's walk up to the gardens. I can't afford to buy you lunch, they've cut off my allowance.'

'Why?'

'A few things, not the least the marriage.'

'Who are you marrying?'

'Flo Fowler. You never met her. She was one of the theatre girls, the magician's assistant. A really lovely girl, Kit. You'll like her. I have to go back to work on the family properties, to get my allowance restored . . .'

'That's fair enough.'

'Oh yes, but Mother is being very difficult. About the wedding, you see. I want Flo to come with me to the house, but she's too shy.'

Kit was impressed that Adrian was standing by his girlfriend, despite his mother's attitude, and wondered what Jessie thought of it, but he had his own worries.

'How is Bonnie?'

'Oh yes. Sorry, old chap, she died, passed away two days ago. My Flo was working for her. She nursed her through all the sickness that took her off.'

'Oh God. She was a good old girl.'

'What's your connection with her? Flo won't hear a word against her, but I understand she was nothing but a whore.'

'I'd prefer you didn't speak ill of the dead,' Kit said stiffly. 'Bonnie was no fool. She made the most of the hand she was dealt. She loaned me money to help me get Emerald Downs going. I would have repaid her eventually, she knew that.'

'Cripes! You've probably got bailiffs after you now to pay the money to her estate. I'm sorry, have I caused you even more bother?'

'No,' Kit said dismally. 'I shouldn't think so. But how did my name come up?'

'Easily. When Flo said she was engaged to me, Bonnie told her she knew of the Pinnock family, and that my sister was engaged to a friend of hers. And then as soon as Flo mentioned I was up at your farm, Bonnie brightened up, wanting to hear all about you. She said she wanted to see you, that it was important. Still sounds to me like she was after her money.'

'No. Bonnie and I always got along well.' He found it hard to accept that such a strong, confident woman was no more. Did not exist.

'I hope you're right. I've got a note from her lawyer; he wants you to call on him. Settlement of her estate. You must go, because I think she's left her house to Flo. There's no one else. He's down in Pitt Street; why don't you go there right away? I'll wait outside. Then we'll go out to Flo's place. She'll give us lunch.'

Though it was irritating to have Adrian organising him, Kit agreed.

'Mother nearly had a fit when your message came,' Adrian said. 'She expressly forbade me to meet you. She gets almost apoplectic when people ask when the wedding is. You're definitely *de trop* in our household after what happened to Jessie.'

'It was Jessie who called off the engagement, not me.'

'No, I didn't mean that. She had a miscarriage, you pair of rascals. Right under Blanche's nose!'

'She what? Is she all right?'

'Of course she is. Good stock and all that, you know. She's fine.'

'Oh my God!' Kit blundered on in a daze, too upset about Jessie to think straight. Too late for Bonnie. Too late to help Jessie.

'When's Bonnie's funeral?' he asked Adrian, hoping to make restitution somewhere along the line.

'The funeral? Oh yes. It was this morning. Flo went along. Sorry old chap.'

The lawyer was a genial fellow, with a bald pate and puffy hair like cotton wool billowing over his ears.

'Ah yes, Major Ferrington. I was about to write to you but they told me you were coming to Sydney.'

Kit sat back on a firm leather chair, trying to appear at ease, but he had already decided to sell Emerald Downs to meet the debt owed to Bonnie. You might as well, he told himself. Jessie will never forgive you for forsaking her at the worst possible time. Her family wouldn't have a bar on you after that. Emerald Downs has been nothing but disaster.

The lawyer opened a file. 'Ah yes, here it is. Let me see: Last will and testament of Bonita Hunter, et cetera, et cetera.'

He looked up and smiled indulgently, peering over his glasses. 'The wording is a little unusual, Major, but we're all friends here. You're the only beneficiary. It reads: "To my friend and lover Major Kit Ferrington, all my worldly goods. I sold the grog shop, did well out of it, so forget your debt. I didn't make the real money until it was too bloody late so you might as well have it. I heard your paradise is hell. This might make it paradise again. Kisses. Bonnie."

'So there you have it. Short and sweet. I'm pleased for you. Bonnie had many lovers but you were her favourite. As you would know, she was a very sensible woman; when she knew she was going, she settled her affairs and listed her assets. Let me read this to you.

' "A house and contents in the suburb of Miller's Point . . ." ' The lawyer smiled sadly. 'That was her home, where she died. Then there's an account at the Bank of New South Wales to the amount of five hundred pounds and three shillings. And lastly, this is interesting: "A half-share in Pomfrey's Department Store in Elizabeth Street." Old Charlie Pomfrey died a year ago and left his shares to his pal Bonnie, much to his family's chagrin. Only recently they agreed to buy her out at a nominal price of three thousand pounds, but the sale hasn't been finalised. She drove a hard bargain, did our Bonnie. It will be up to you now to make the decision to sell or retain the shares.'

'I'd sell,' Kit said, as if the question were hypothetical. None of this seemed real. 'Would you mind reading all that to me again, sir? I can't quite . . .'

'Certainly, Major. Now let me see . . .'

'What did he say?' Adrian asked anxiously.

'Nothing much. She forgave me the debt . . .'

'She turned out all right after all, eh?'

'You could say that. And she left me a few pounds in her bank.'

'Good on her. How many pounds?'

'Enough.' Kit resisted the urge to shout with glee. Five hundred pounds was a fortune . . . and there was more to come. He steered Adrian across two streets so that he could pass by Pomfrey's Department Store.

359

'Who gets the house?' Adrian asked.

'No one. It's to be sold and the money goes into the estate, such as it is. Legals and what have you will probably fritter it away.'

'Damn! I was sure Flo would get it.'

Flo gave them lunch in her tiny house . . . fricasseed chicken with sippets and pickled mushrooms; oddly, a meal that Polly had often prepared for him, Kit mused. She used to sprinkle the fricassee with nutmeg, he recalled.

'Bonnie lived just up the street,' Flo told him. 'A much bigger house than this, of course. I liked her, she was very kind, and she paid me well.'

'But you took very good care of her,' Adrian said.

'Well, she was real sick, and she got worse and worse. It was sad it was, and me tryin' to help.'

'So she should have left you the house.'

'Why do we want another house? Besides, after we're married we'll be going out to Parramatta, won't we?'

Adrian frowned. 'You wouldn't like it out there, Flo. The people out that way are all so . . . stuffy.'

'Are you sure that's all it is?'

'Of course.'

She turned to Kit. 'I think I don't match up to his family and friends, and that has been worrying me.'

Kit saw a glint of steel in the wide blue eyes, and had the feeling the girl was in the process of gaining the upper hand in the relationship. He passed the buck quickly, gazing at Adrian.

'Is that the trouble?'

'There isn't any trouble,' he snapped.

'I haven't even met his family, right here in Sydney.'

'Then you *can* meet them!' Adrian said. 'I'll take you there whenever you like.'

'I don't want to now,' she pouted.

'Then don't. What *do* you want?'

Their argument continued in a series of twists and turns, irritating Kit, but he couldn't escape because Flo was taking her time in serving the dessert, more interested in staying at the table with them so as not to miss a point. They were like a couple of children, he thought, logic as wobbly as jelly. He was convinced they deserved one another, when they did manage to come to an arrangement. Of sorts. They would marry, the question of Flo meeting the family left unresolved. Adrian would go to work in Parramatta and his wife would remain here in the cottage.

'Flo, you could have a nice house at Parramatta,' Kit said, trying to help. 'His family would see to that, believe me.'

'I don't want to go there. You heard Adrian say they're stuffy, by which he meant they'll look down their noses at me. Bonnie told me to look out for that. She said you never were like that, Major.'

360

No, he thought, because she was a rollicking joy in bed. He wondered what else Bonnie might have taught her.

'If Flo wants to stay here in this house . . . she loves it here . . . then she can,' Adrian told Kit. 'Parramatta isn't so far away. I can come home any time. And she can catch the ferry to visit me too.'

Flo jumped up from the table and kissed Adrian. 'Oh, lovely, it's all fixed.'

Kit smiled. 'I think it's time I withdrew.'

'No.' Flo bounced back and ran into the kitchen. 'You must have dessert, I've got dumplings and golden syrup.'

They both walked as far as Argyle Street with him after lunch and Flo pointed out St Anne's Church.

'Isn't that so sweet, with its little garden and roses by the door? That's where we should be married.'

'And we shall,' Adrian said, mellowed by the expectation of an afternoon's pleasure with his love.

'You are so sweet, my darling. He's always so sweet to me, I just adore him. We ought to have the wedding before the Major goes home. When do you think, sweetheart?'

'Whenever you say, sweetness.'

'Next Saturday then. We'll have a quiet wedding, we don't need a lot of people . . .'

Kit practically staggered away from all the cloying endearments, walked to the nearest pub and downed a hearty rum.

'Well,' he said, 'that was quite a day.'

A whore approached him. 'Buy me a drink, mister?'

'It would be my pleasure,' he said, placing a shilling on the bar as he left.

He called at Flo's place the next day. 'Would you ask Adrian to give this letter to Jessie, please, Flo? I don't think it would get past her mother if I posted it.'

'That's a shame. People are so unkind. I'll see Adrian takes it to her. The wedding is at ten on Saturday. You will come, won't you?'

'Short notice, isn't it? For you, I mean?'

'Oh no. I made my own wedding dress from materials Bonnie gave me. I've had it ready for weeks now and it is so pretty, I can't wait to wear it.'

When he left there, he walked up to Bonnie's house and peered through the windows, but had no wish to investigate any further. He had business matters to attend to now, instead of skulking about, a pauper, so his first effort was to remove himself from his cheap lodgings and take a room at the gracious Grand Hotel in Castlereagh Street. Then he went out and, gratefully, with a whispered prayer of thanks to Bonnie, bought himself some decent clothes to replace the complete wardrobe destroyed in the fire.

More confident now, he returned to the lawyer's office and signed the necessary papers to obtain title of Bonnie's house and issue instructions to sell. He repeated the exercise when it came to the shares in the department store, transferring them into his name and agreeing to sell at the price stipulated by Bonnie.

'You had no trouble at the bank?' the lawyer asked.

'Not at all, sir. I was surprised that the funds were made available to me so soon.'

'My clerk arranged that. He's a very efficient fellow. The other matters will necessarily take a little longer.'

'Yes, of course.'

Still a little dizzy at the pace of the change to his life, Kit went out to Cemetery Hill to visit Bonnie's grave, where he paid a stonemason to replace the small wooden cross with a more substantial headstone, feeling that it was the least he could do. But as he walked back, his mind was on Jessie. It was disappointing now to find that though he had much to celebrate thanks to Bonnie's legacy, his heart wasn't in it. He missed Jessie too much. In his letter he had apologised for his rudeness, begged her forgiveness for pushing the burden of Polly's death on to her young shoulders and declared his abiding love for her; finally asking her to, at least, meet him somewhere, so that they could talk.

He took a cab to Flo's house, seeking a response from Jessie.

'She got your letter all right,' Flo said. 'Adrian saw to that, but she said she didn't want to see you. I'm terrible sorry, Major, knowing you were soon to be married and all, but I wouldn't give up. I'd go out there. Don't let old Mrs Pinnock tell you what to do.

'Adrian didn't,' she added proudly. 'He stood up to her.'

All very well, Kit thought, but he's her son. And there was the terrible calamity to be overcome. A miscarriage! Poor Jessie. And having to suffer Blanche and her recriminations on top of it! He wasn't surprised that she didn't want to see him.

So what was to be done? He couldn't just do nothing. Go home and forget Jessie? The more he thought about it, the more he was inclined to believe that Flo was right. He would go to the Pinnock house. Demand to see her! Ill-mannered though such an intrusion might be, he had no other course.

'Rose Bay,' he called to the driver of his cab, and sat back on the worn leather, a mass of trepidation, listening to the even pounding of the horse's hooves on the sandy road.

'Miss Pinnock is not at home, sir,' the maid said.

'Are you sure?' he asked, trying to peer round her.

'Of course, sir.'

'Where did she go?'

'I don't know,' she said, a little bewildered by the question.

'Then would you kindly bring me pencil and paper? I wish to leave a message.'

He could have told her that the necessary stationery was kept in the hall stand drawer, for such occasions, but left her to it, and soon she returned, waited until he wrote his message, and accepted it.

This girl didn't know him, fortunately, so he slipped a shilling into her hand. 'Could you see that she gets it and no one else?' he asked, with a wink, and a broad smile lit the girl's face.

'Oh, sir, surely, and thank you.' His note was tucked safely into the hidden reaches of her long skirt, behind the flimsy apron.

Kit felt he'd made some progress as he climbed back into the cab. At least Jessie now knew where he was staying and that he was desperate to see her.

Yes, he mused, that's what I wrote, desperate. And I meant it.

The maid took Jessie aside and, giggling, slipped her the note. 'He was so handsome, miss, a shame you weren't home.'

'Thank you,' Jessie said stiffly, knowing already who it was from.

He was staying at the Grand Hotel, and desperate to see her. She hadn't answered his letter. She couldn't, she was so embarrassed and humiliated, especially when Adrian admitted he'd told Kit about the miscarriage. She never wanted to see Kit again. Never. It was all too awful. Her mother, still angry with her, had called her selfish and bold, with no regard for other people's feelings, and looking back, Jessie supposed she was right. But she hadn't meant to be like that. How could she have got everything so wrong? she wondered bleakly.

She was so glad she and her mother were out when he called; that would have been dreadful! Adrian said he had warned Kit not to come here; Blanche hated him, he was the enemy now. Jessie was certain he'd have met a flood of abuse at her door, which would have been even more embarrassing.

'Oh God,' she sighed, 'could things get any worse?' She supposed not. But he'd said he was desperate to see her. What was that about? Was there something else happening?

She placed the note in her satin handkerchief sachet with the letter he'd written her. It was a beautiful letter, full of love, the sort of letter she'd always wanted to receive before all this happened. Before she'd rushed off to see him, uninvited, and messed everything up from that minute on. Even flirting with Sam. Another escapade she'd prefer not to recall. She hadn't heard from him since she came home, which was a relief.

It occurred to her then that if Kit wasn't welcome in this house, maybe she could call on him at the hotel. Just to listen to what he had to say; what he was so desperate about. Maybe something else was wrong. But how could she face him? If he brought up that miscarriage, she'd die.

* * *

363

Despite all this, Kit had not forgotten Colonel Gresham's enquiry, so he took the cab on to the Victoria Barracks and found a friend of his, Captain Jim Bignall, on duty.

'Delighted to see you,' Jim said, rushing out to welcome him. 'I hear you're the great hero, soothing the savage breasts and all that.'

'Not from where I stand,' Kit said, with a grimace. 'All I'm trying to do is get on with being a farmer, and I keep getting sidetracked. I've had Gresham on my back like a bloody leech, and I'd like to find out what he ended up pinning on me.'

'Yes, I heard something about that. Leave it with me, Kit, I'll snoop about and see what's going on. Where are you staying?'

'At the Grand.'

'Ah, very swish. Farming must be kind to you. I'll see what our Colonel has been up to, and get back to you as soon as I can. By the way, is it true you got speared?'

Jim's question necessitated a much longer visit to the barracks than he'd counted on, since one thing led to another and Kit could hardly dash away after asking a favour, so it was almost five o'clock by the time he reached the hotel desk to ask anxiously if anyone had been looking for him.

'No, sir,' the desk clerk said.

'Any messages?'

'No, sir.'

'Saturday!' Blanche almost shrieked the word at him. 'You're getting married on Saturday!'

'That's what I said,' Adrian told her calmly.

'It's impossible! How do you expect people to know? I mean, the invitations. And good heavens, is it still that showgirl? Jessie! You talk to him, he's not making any sense. Doesn't he understand . . .'

'I have to get back to work because I haven't any money,' he said. 'That was your doing and I don't have any quarrel with it. You are right, I am needed at Parramatta and I have to get on with it, so the wedding will take place on Saturday. We'll have a short honeymoon and I'll report forthwith.'

'Mother, you know Adrian is marrying Miss Fowler,' his sister said, 'so stop pretending you don't and I suggest you stop referring to her as "that showgirl".'

Adrian nodded. 'Thank you, Jess. Now, as I was saying. Miss Fowler and I will be wed at St Anne's Church in Argyle Street . . .'

'Where? Oh my God! That's down by The Rocks. What are you thinking of?' Blanche strode over to the door. 'I don't want to hear any more of this. You do what you like. We will not be attending. You two seem utterly determined to bring shame on this family at every turn.'

As the door slammed behind her, Adrian shrugged. 'I really can't be worried, Jessie. Weddings always seem to me to be more about the pomp and people than the two who count most. Which reminds me, did you answer Kit's letter?'

'No. I really don't feel like talking to him. But he came here today when Mother and I were out.'

'Just as well,' Adrian laughed. 'She might have biffed him.'

'He left me a message, though; said he was desperate to see me.'

'So he would be. I think you're being too hard on the poor fellow.'

'Is that all? I thought it might be something else. That he could have more problems.'

'Don't you think getting wounded, losing his house and his belongings and his fiancée are enough? You're some support, Jessie! Flo would never let me down like that. And yes, there was something else. I heard round town that he's about to be drummed out of the army.'

'What do you mean? How could that happen?'

'It's a bloody shame really. All to do with Kirk's lies. I'm glad a crocodile got him. It was probably bilious for days. They call it a dishonourable discharge.'

'I know what it's called. Couldn't you do anything to help?'

'What could I do? I wasn't there. But I'm still his friend, not like some people I know.'

He walked towards the kitchen and she heard him calling to the cook that he wouldn't be home for dinner. Jessie fought off the tears that always seemed to be hovering close to the surface lately. Did Kit really need her support? She supposed it must be an awful thing to be given a dishonourable discharge, and looked down upon by all his friends. She really ought to go to see him, but it would be so hard, so humiliating, after all that had happened. And she was so nervy lately, she didn't know if she had the strength to face him.

Major Ferrington sat in the foyer of the hotel that evening, reading newspapers and country journals, keeping in view of the reception desk in case a message came for him, or a letter, or, he dared hope, Jessie herself.

He had her ring in his waistcoat pocket, ready for that eventuality, and in the other pocket a gold locket in the shape of a heart, with a ruby set in the centre.

As he turned the pages of the *Sydney Morning Herald*, he came across an article noting that skirmishes between Aborigines and white folk in the back country west of Brisbane were at an end, 'thanks to the heroic efforts of the late Police Inspector Kirk, who sadly, was only recently the victim of a vicious crocodile attack. His body was never recovered. His shocked widow is presently writing a book about Rollo Kirk's many exploits and adventures, and this paper will be bringing the book to our readers in serial form. We are eagerly looking forward to the first instalment.'

The desk clerk was startled to see Major Ferrington tear a page from a newspaper and hurl it into a nearby bin, and people in the busy foyer turned to stare. Among them an old friend who came dashing over and threw her arms about him.

'Darling! How are you!' Roxy cried. 'How marvellous to see you again, you rascal. I was so sorry to hear about your lovely house, darling, really I was. Everyone said it was a homestead anyone could be proud of. But what are you doing sitting here on your own? I'm staying in the hotel. Are you too?'

He nodded, nervously, eyeing the entrance as she prepared to seat herself on the plush settee beside him.

'Then we simply must have a glass of champagne. You're looking so lost and lonely . . .'

'I'm waiting for someone, Roxy.'

'That's all right, I'll wait with you. We'll have champagne. I insist. I want to hear all the news. You call a waiter.'

He knew that if he told Roxy who he was waiting for she'd either set out to annoy him, or tease him unmercifully, but she certainly would not leave, so he managed to send her into the front lounge while he organised the champagne, and gave strict instructions, and five shillings, to the desk clerk to send for him immediately if there were any callers or messages for him.

She had found a table near the window and looked up, smiling radiantly, as he approached. She certainly looked very much at home in these surrounds, Kit noted, with her red hair now coiffed into long curls under a fetching little hat of beaded satin.

'You're looking very smart,' he told her, to keep the peace, and she preened.

'Thank you. You're looking pretty good yourself. You've got a gaunt, interesting look about you. I must say you've been busy, though, darling, one drama after another. And we were all very upset about your troubles at Emerald Downs, even Father! My God, what a time you had!'

'It's all over now, Roxy. Don't worry about it.'

'But I do. Jasin Heselwood told me that old Colonel Gresham had really harassed you, so I gave him a piece of my mind the other day. Met him down the street from here and told him if I were a man I'd knock him down.'

Kit groaned. 'Thanks a lot. I'm waiting on his report.'

'Who cares about his silly report? Why don't you have dinner with us?'

The waiter brought the champagne, giving Kit a chance to change the subject.

'Are you down here for the Royal Show?'

'Yes. I'm riding in two more events. I've already won a blue ribbon with Stargazer.'

'I thought he'd be getting a bit old for show work.'

'Not him. No fear. I say, this is very decent champagne. Thank you for that. I'd heard you were a bit strapped. Now, why don't you come out to the show tomorrow . . .'

Jessie had managed to persuade herself that she should go into town, and possibly see Kit, find out if he needed her help, or even advice. You never know what exactly troubles people, she thought. Maybe he simply wanted to make an end to the engagement, officially. Another thought crossed her mind that gave her a start. What if he'd found someone else and was desperate to clear the decks, so to speak? No, surely not. It was too soon.

The shops were well lit now that dusk was settling, and everything looked so attractive, even the people bustling in and out.

She caught her reflection in a shop mirror and noted that the Italian straw hat, which her mother had chosen, looked quite good after all. Trimmed with flowers, gauze ribbon and blond lace, it really was very pretty, and set off her smart town dress very nicely. Since she'd returned with hardly a stitch to her name, Blanche had carted her to all the best salons in Sydney to replenish her wardrobe with the most attractive and fashionable outfits available. Even though most of the gowns were so tightwaisted, like this one, that she practically lived in corsets these days, Jessie hadn't complained. She knew how much her mother enjoyed shopping and let her enjoy herself for a change; what with all the happenings, Blanche was rather miserable lately.

Jessie had to admit, though, that the new clothes did give her badly-needed confidence, and Blanche was delighted when heads turned to gaze at her beautiful daughter.

'See,' she would whisper. 'You look quite splendid. I told you the right outfits would make such a difference.'

Just then, it occurred to Jessie that her mother was probably glad that her own choices had gone up in smoke. One way of getting rid of frumpy clothes. She wondered if Kit would notice that she had turned into quite a fashion plate.

The Grand Hotel was just up the street and she was beginning to dawdle, taking longer to look in windows, nervous, trying to ward off excuses not to go in, and she found herself looking into the brilliantly-lit front lounge of the hotel, where café society people liked to gather.

She peered at the superb chandeliers and the gold-trimmed walls, then, at the next window, took in the fashionable folk all enjoying themselves immensely by the look of things. Now she was worried that Kit might not be in, and that she'd look foolish asking for someone and having to slink away like a mouse. And she was looking at a woman sitting there on the other side of the glass, drinking champagne, who was wearing a beaded satin hat the same as one that Blanche wore. And it was Roxy! Roxy Maykin. Down here for the show, she supposed. Drinking champagne with . . .

It was like a physical blow. As if someone had punched her in the stomach. Jessie was gasping for breath as she turned away to retrace her steps along the footpath, away from the hotel, when she ran straight into a woman coming the other way.

'Oh, I'm so sorry,' she muttered, head down.

'Why, it's Jessie!' the woman said. 'How nice to see you again. I haven't seen you since our voyage on the *Argyle*. How have you been keeping?'

'Very well, thank you,' Jessie said, recognising Mrs Maykin. Roxy's mother!

'We must have a chat. I'm so glad you're well. We were all so upset to hear about Emerald Downs; it must have been dreadful for you.'

'Would you excuse me, Mrs Maykin, I have to go.'

Madeline Maykin was surprised that the girl should rush off like that, and wondered what on earth was wrong, but as she went on her way she saw Roxy sitting at a table by the window with Major Ferrington, Jessie's fiancé – or ex-fiancé, if the gossip were correct.

'Well we can't have that!' she said, and ran back down the street after Jessie, ignoring the astonished stares of passers-by.

She caught up with Jessie at the next corner. 'Where are you off to, miss?'

'Home, Mrs Maykin,' Jessie said angrily. 'I was just about to call a cab.'

'But you mustn't, darling. Do come back, you can't run and hide.'

'I beg your pardon, Mrs Maykin!'

'Oh come on, you saw Roxy back there with Ferrington, and obviously it upset you. In which case it is silly to rush away, especially when you look so gorgeous. Now come on, tell me what this is all about.'

'It's about nothing,' Jessie said defensively, drawing back into the doorway of a darkened shop as if still afraid to be seen. 'Kit left a message for me to call on him at the hotel, but obviously this is a bad time.'

'I won't ask why you have to call on the gentleman and not the other way round,' Madeline laughed, 'but did he specify a time?'

'No.'

'Well then, you're within your rights. Come on now, straighten up. The gentleman is expecting you.'

'I can't. You don't understand.'

'She got your horse. Are you going to let her get your man? No, of course you're not.'

With that, Madeline took Jessie's arm and walked her back to the hotel, encouraging her all the way. Together they crossed the carpeted lobby, and Madeline almost pushed the girl towards the lounge.

'In you go now,' she said. 'He's expecting you, don't forget.'

'Will you come in with me, Mrs Maykin? Please?'

'No. You have to stand on your own feet. You're a big girl, it shouldn't be hard.'

But it was hard, because there was a lot of noise and the room seemed hazy. She couldn't focus, and she had to get past people who insisted on moving about, and negotiate her way around armchairs and sofas, and legs stuck out there to trip her, and dodge waiters with flimsy trays of glittering glasses, and answer someone who called hello to her, but keep going because he was over there and he was getting to his feet, pushing back the chair, his face beaming, incredulous, joyful . . . 'Jessie!'

His arms flung out to welcome her, nearly knocking over a potted palm, but he caught it in time, and took her to him in a bear hug of a welcome that had people smiling, sharing their happiness, and then he looked at the table, crestfallen. It was only a table for two and Roxy hadn't moved. She simply looked up in that patronising way of hers.

'Kit was just saying how crowded it was in here,' she said, intimating that Jessie was intruding, despite Kit's warm welcome, and Jessie blinked, the haze clearing. She was unused to such calculated rudeness in company, but she couldn't allow Roxy to get the better of her again.

'That's because there are so many country bumpkins in town,' she said. 'Will you be long, Kit?'

'Afraid so,' Roxy said. 'He's dining with us this evening. The engagement's off, isn't it, Kit?'

Jessie imagined she heard a threat in that question, but dismissed the idea when he spoke.

'Good Lord, no!' He glanced at Jessie's left hand, and she was glad she still had her gloves on, since the fourth finger was bare. 'You'll have to forgive us, Roxy, but we do have plans for this evening.'

Once again Jessie found herself being ushered along at quite a pace, this time across the foyer and out the front door.

And over by the grand staircase, Madeline Maykin nodded as she waited for her daughter to emerge from the lounge. She and her friend Lucy Dignam had plans for their children, for Roxy and Sam, and they were proceeding very nicely. She had no intention of allowing Major Ferrington to rock the boat. Sam Dignam, a wealthy bachelor, was a much more suitable prospect, especially since he'd gotten over his crush on Jessie and was now mad about Roxy. So it was Roxy who had to be kept in line, and Madeline would see to that.

'How dare you invite me over and entertain her at the same time?' Jessie exploded, but he hurried her down the street.

'Where are we going?' she cried.

'I've no idea. And I didn't invite Roxy, she parked herself on me while I was waiting for you. If you'd come earlier it wouldn't have happened.'

'I don't like you associating with her. I'm not blind, you know.'

'I'm sure you're not.'

'Well, where are we going?'

'Let me see. The hotel is out, and your place is out; wiser people are deserting the streets . . . what do you suggest?'

'You could take me home in a cab . . .'

369

'Or we could ride around in a cab for a while. Then I'll take you home.'

'So we're re-engaged, are we? Or did you lie to her?'

Kit laughed. 'I sweated on that with the ring in my pocket and not where it should be.'

'Really? You've got it with you?'

'Yes, I was hoping you'd take it back.

'Mother will be furious.'

'Oh well, one wedding at a time. Here's a cab.'

The next morning, Kit rose early and walked for miles around the foggy waterfront. He was overjoyed that all was well with Jessie again, but they still had a lot to talk about, especially from his side. Explain, he thought, would be a better word. Explain where his sudden wealth had come from. No use dodging that. Explain that there was every possibility that he would be disgraced . . . dishonourably discharged from his regiment. And tell her that he'd only built a cottage to replace the house, and that would be the residence. He couldn't make the same mistake twice. The farm was his financial priority now, and after that, to make sure this never happened to him again, he intended to buy more land as an investment, as well as a buffer against the bad seasons that farmers always complained about. Commercial land, he mused, as he watched the fog lift over the harbour and heard the ferry bell clanging.

They were expecting Mr Watkins to join them for lunch, since he'd just arrived back from escorting Marcus out to his Parramatta home, so Jessie waited until they were settled at table, with the guest for protection, to break the news to her mother that she and Kit had renewed their engagement.

'See,' she said, holding out her hand with not a little bravado. 'See! The ring! Kit insisted I take it back.'

'What?' Blanche almost bounced out of her chair. 'What? When did this happen?'

'Yesterday. I saw him yesterday evening. When you were at the church charity meeting.'

'Did he come here? That fellow? To my home?' She was livid.

'Yes and no. Look, it doesn't matter, Mother . . .'

'It doesn't matter that you're sneaking around behind my back again? I won't listen to you.' She clapped her hands over her ears. 'I won't! I forbid you to see that scoundrel ever again!'

'Then don't listen!' Jessie threw her napkin down and jumped up. 'What do I care? We are engaged and I will marry him. I intend to tell him that we ought to marry while he is in Sydney so that I can return with him, with my husband. Now if you didn't hear that, too bad!'

She flounced out of the room.

Blanche burst into tears. 'Do you see what I have to put up with?' she said to Watkins, but Jessie stuck her head back round the door. 'And don't forget that Adrian's wedding is tomorrow at ten!'

'I couldn't care less,' Blanche snapped back at her. 'I won't be there.'

'Please yourself!'

This time the door slammed.

Blanche sniffled into her handkerchief: 'Oh, let them do what they like! You were right, Fred. I shouldn't take on so. Letting them upset me all the time. What say we take the ferry to Manly tomorrow, and have a picnic right up on the Heads. I hear it's a fine view of the entrance to the harbour. We may even see some big ships come by.'

'That's a splendid idea,' he said quietly.

'Excellent. I'll have Cook do a hamper with all our favourite foods, and a little wine perhaps?'

'Yes, but I think Sunday would be more convenient.'

'Oh. Do you think so?'

He nodded. 'We ought to have a talk about Saturday, Blanche. I've always believed family to be very important. And now that I've met them, I've grown rather fond of Adrian and Jessie. We'd better think what can be done about all this.'

The little church of St Anne was decorated with a sprinkling of gumtips and frangipani, and an organist played softly as Adrian sidled nervously from the vestry to take his place at the altar, attended by a young gentlemen friend whom Kit hadn't met before.

'Went to school with him,' Jessie whispered.

The priest walked across the altar to engage the young men in earnest conversation, and peer at the pews as two elderly ladies came in to take their places.

In a loud whisper, one of them told the other that her husband would be giving Flo away.

'We're Flo's neighbours, we are. Lovely girl. And look, that's her hubby-to-be, up there on the left with the fair hair. Handsome lad he is too.'

When the organist changed to a stirring march, Kit turned to look for the bride, but was astonished to see Blanche and a very large gentleman sitting a few pews back.

Equally surprised, Jessie was nudging him. 'I can't believe what I'm seeing. Look at Adrian, he's positively gaping!'

'Who's that with your mother?'

'The gentleman I've been telling you about. Her friend Mr Watkins.' She giggled. 'He's a really nice man. I think he's her "hubby-to-be".'

But then Flo came into view on the arm of her neighbour, her short stature almost overwhelmed by a white silk crinoline hung with myriad ribbons and bows and lacy frills. Kit thought it overdone, a little like a lampshade, but conceded she'd got the bodice right. It was cut so low, and so loosely, the décolletage was, to his eyes, splendid, showing her full creamy breasts to great advantage. And Flo herself shone! Her fair hair, circled with a confection of small flowers, set off her doll-like prettiness, and she was blushing a little, which seemed to emphasise the flawless skin and big blue eyes.

He was pleased that Jessie stepped out into the aisle to welcome the bride, and Flo, meeting Adrian's sister for the first time, was clearly thrilled by this surprise. When she moved on down the aisle towards Adrian, her face was a picture of bliss.

Proudly, Adrian stepped forward to take her hand.

'Isn't it romantic?' Jessie whispered, and Kit glanced back at Blanche, who obviously did not hold to that sentiment.

Later she took Jessie to task, insisting she sit down at the dining room table with her and make notes.

'I am not going through that humiliation again. I could have screamed seeing Claude Finley standing up there with Adrian. What on earth will he tell his family? Not a soul at the wedding!'

'There were a couple of people . . .'

Blanche ignored her. 'If you insist on marrying Ferrington before he returns to that place, you set a date right away and get his family details. I will make the arrangements and have the invitations hand-delivered. Now, make a list: church, reception, wedding party . . . who will be your bridesmaids?'

'Mother, I don't—'

'I asked you who will be the bridesmaids. If you won't choose them, I will. And you can tell Ferrington you will be married in the cathedral, I'll allow nothing less.'

At about the same time, Kit found Captain Bignall waiting for him in the hotel foyer.

'You're looking very spruce,' Bignall said, walking over to meet him.

'I've been to a wedding. Good to see you. Have you been waiting long?'

'Not long at all. I have some news for you. Could we step outside for a minute?'

'Of course,' Kit said nervously. He'd kept telling himself that he didn't care what conclusions Gresham had drawn, he had his own life outside the military, but he knew that was only bravado.

'Well now,' Bignall said as they stepped out into the warm sunshine, 'it seems Gresham took a very hard line with you. He recommended a dishonourable discharge, Kit.'

Though it was not unexpected, it was a jolt, and Kit felt himself sag. 'He did, eh? Bloody hell!'

'Yes. We were all very sorry to hear about that, so a group of your friends from the Officers' Club, yours truly included, lodged a protest on your behalf, claiming that Kirk's statement was not only uncorroborated, but had been challenged by Sergeant Rapper and several troopers. Those first-hand statements were in the file but Gresham had ignored them.'

He stopped, flicked some dust from his uniform jacket, and frowned. 'I couldn't tell you about that before, because we were waiting on the outcome. But I've just come from Government House . . . I'm taking up your old job as the GG's aide . . . and I can tell you safely now that Sir Charles upheld it.'

Kit was stunned. 'He did? He upheld the protest?'

'He did indeed. He said the northern graziers were in your debt, and the outcome of your expedition was exactly as he himself had predicted when he appointed you to command. As a matter of fact, Sir Charles was rather cranky with Gresham for interfering. Wasting his time, as he put it. He said you had resigned your commission anyway. He just hadn't had time to attend to the details. I believe there's quite a backlog of work in that office.'

'Good God. I hadn't heard from him and thought I must have offended him.'

'Certainly not, you're the white-haired boy.'

Kit was mortified that he'd been so wrapped up in his own affairs on this visit to Sydney that he'd ignored his old friends at the club. At a time when they were, generously, going out of their way to help him.

'How good of you fellows,' he said to Captain Bignall. 'How very kind of you. I don't know how to thank you.'

'You can come over to the club and shout us a drink. And didn't I hear you were to be married shortly? I hope we're invited.'

'I was thinking you might do me the honour of being my best man . . .'

Coda

The first thing Jack wanted to do, with the newly-weds settled in their cottage, and the Major busy reorganising his farm with the help of experienced stockmen, was to see the place where his brother had drowned. It still pained him that he'd missed young Hector. That his brother had come all this way to see him, searched for him so diligently, and lost his life in the attempt. It didn't seem fair, but then not much was fair in the scramble of living, he mused.

He put his hand in his trouser pocket, checking that Bussamarai's gold nugget was still there, and headed for a jeweller's shop to get this over with.

'I might be a bushie,' he said to the first man behind the counter, 'but I'm no idiot. Ten bob be buggered! Get your boss.'

To prevent a gold rush into Aborigine territory, he told the jeweller that he'd brought this nugget from the southern goldfields, and settled down to haggle over the price, emerging with a hundred and four pounds in his pocket, including the money that the Major had paid him.

A princely sum, he told himself cheerily. But this time hang on to it.

Having lost his first fortune to thieves, and the gold in his money belt to the fire and some stranger, this, Jack decided, was his last chance. He had to get it right! He proceeded uneasily into a bank and handed over most of his money, instructing the teller to keep an eye on it.

A clerk in the Land Office showed him on a map where the *Arabella* had gone down in the straits between Moreton and Stradbroke Islands as it made for the open ocean.

'How do I get to this Stradbroke Island?' he asked the teller.

'Go on down to New Farm; a fisherman might take you across for a shilling, but there's nothing much over there, only blackfellows and a little settlement called Dunwich.'

Jack tramped through the town to Fortitude Valley and followed the tracks down to the New Farm area, which was under cultivation by market gardeners. From there he went on to the river and eventually came across some fishing boats tied up at the wharves.

After asking about, he was referred to a lugger called *Ladybird*. The skipper was a swarthy Greek known as Stamos.

'You want to go to Dunwich? Cost you two bob. Climb aboard, you're just in time.'

As the lugger, a two-master, set sail, Jack stayed on deck to make the most of this voyage. He was interested in everything about him, especially the chance to follow the river out to sea, but he gasped when the boat eventually headed into the great expanse of Moreton Bay, not certain that crossing these heaving waters was such a good idea after all.

Stamos called him into the wheelhouse and pointed out various islands that they passed, amazed to learn that Jack had never travelled these waters before.

'How did you get to Brisbane then?' he asked.

'Overlanded. I overlanded from Sydney.'

'Jeez! That's some hell of a ride, mister.'

'I suppose so. I walked.'

'Go on!'

Stamos was impressed. He invited Jack to have a meal with him and they talked – of course – fishing. Their mutual love, as it turned out. Stamos explained that the lugger was rigged for seine fishing, and that it stayed in the bay for two or three days at a time, depending on the catch; and that fascinated Jack, who had never seen net fishing on such a scale before.

'Are you in a hurry?' Stamos asked Jack. 'If you like, you can come fishing with us. I can always do with an extra hand, and I'll drop you off at Dunwich in a couple of days, instead of going straight there.'

'I reckon I'd like that,' Jack said, 'and would it be out of order to throw a line over the back of the boat while we're going along?'

'The back of the boat!' Stamos chuckled, shaking his head. 'You mind a big-feller fish doesn't yank you into the sea, mate.'

When he came to think of it, later, Jack counted those couple of days on board *Ladybird* as the most enjoyable he'd had in years. Like a holiday, that being something else he'd never experienced before. He had a great time fishing, and sorting the fish in the nets, and thoroughly enjoyed the company of the skipper and the crew.

They pulled in at the Dunwich jetty, where they dropped Jack off and delivered supplies to the villagers before setting sail again.

'Pick you up at the end of the week,' Stamos called to Jack. He hadn't asked Jack's business on the island and Jack hadn't volunteered the information. He liked that. He liked Stamos, he decided, as he trudged away from the village, a good bloke, and what he didn't know about fishing, and the fish in these waters, wasn't worth knowing.

He deliberately avoided the village for a start, preferring to keep his intentions to himself, as he trudged along the edge of the island thinking of the *Arabella*, which had come ploughing over this way from the mouth of the Brisbane River on its last voyage.

Even before he reached the northern point of the island, Jack was finding flotsam and jetsam high up at the tide line on the otherwise pristine beach.

He turned over smashed timbers, ragged pieces of canvas, bottles, a mattress, a woman's shoe, all sorts of stark reminders of the terror that had ridden the storm out there in the channel, between these two large islands.

He climbed up on to a sand dune and stared at the sea that had claimed the *Arabella*, that had dragged his only brother to its depths.

'What did you do with him then?' he shouted. 'Feed him to the sharks? Cast him on another lonely shore?'

They'd said there were no survivors; not one soul had made it to this shore, or the shores over there. It didn't seem so far for someone to strike out for a beach. Hard, he supposed, with a storm smashing about you.

Poor Hector. What had those last minutes been like? Had he been thrown into the cauldron to drown? Or gone down with the ship among all the other panicking, despairing souls?

Jack stood on the dune in the breeze and called to his brother: 'I'm bloody sorry, Hector. I wish I'd known you were here. I'd have been damn glad to see you and that's the truth, you were always a good lad. But it wasn't meant to be. I suppose the parents are gone now; if not, they'll hear in good time what happened to you. Authorities will chase it up. They're like that.'

He went to walk away, but his conscience turned him back to finish his eulogy.

'Go with God,' he called, a little self-consciously, and bowed his head.

That night he camped on the beach, thinking he might build a memorial to Hector with the timbers the sea had washed up, but he decided not to overdo his brotherly duties, Wodrow was a name best forgot.

In the morning, thousands of seabirds woke him, so he pulled back into the bush, and finding it no different from the mainland, went in search of food.

For days he explored the island, meeting several friendly Aborigines, and spent some time with them, exchanging stories. They told him that the correct name for the Dunwich area was Goompie.

The scenery on the oceanfront was spectacular, and having run along that beach for miles, just for the hell of it, he marched across to the more sheltered bay side and pottered about on the muddy shores before walking back to Dunwich.

The people there, mostly fishing families, were pleased to meet the visitor and invited him to stay. He learned that the settlement and the jetty-ramp had been built by convicts, but the place wasn't suitable for prisoners, so the authorities abandoned the idea. After them came missionaries from Europe, earnestly resolved to convert the Aborigines to Christian godliness, but only one of them spoke English, and not one understood the Bundjalung language, so they were sent elsewhere, the mission abandoned.

On the return journey, Jack worked his passage, since Stamos wouldn't accept payment, and as they sailed back up the Brisbane River, the skipper surprised him by offering him a job.

'I wouldn't mind,' Jack said. 'I like this boat. And I'm taken by that island back there. I'd like to live there.'

'Forget it,' Stamos said. 'They're turning it into a quarantine station for the typhoid cases that come off the ships. Where do you live now?'

'No place in particular.'

'Then you could do worse than New Farm. I've got a house there overlooking the river.'

Jack thought about that, but as the lugger drew close to the wharves, he studied the banks carefully, and when they'd docked he walked over to Stamos.

'What is over there on top of those high cliffs, on the other side of the river?'

'That's called Kangaroo Point. Just houses, that's all.'

'Then take a tip from me. Move up there where it'll be safe from big floods.'

'How do you know?'

'Blackfeller savvy. I've got a few things to do. When do you sail next?'

'Next Thursday. Can you sign on then?'

'I'll be here.'

As he walked off to find himself some lodgings, Jack had a real spring in his step. He cut across a field of turnips, hurdled a fence and spoke to a wallaby that was grazing nearby.

'I'm going fishing, *burrai*! And I'm getting paid for it. What do you think of that?'

The animal glanced up, considered him for a few moments, and it seemed to Jack that it gave him the nod before returning to the tasty lettuce.

One year later, when the river rose up and high floods inundated Brisbane, the lugger *Ladybird* was moored safely near Stradbroke Island, and there the new owner/skipper, Jack Drew, and his Aborigine crew stayed until the muddy waters spewing into the bay finally washed away. His friend Stamos, who'd retired because of a back injury, looked down on the dismal sight from his house up there on the Kangaroo Point cliffs and thanked his stars that he'd taken Jack's advice.

The flood waters, hurtling down after rain-filled cyclonic storms had lashed the surrounding hills, caught Emerald Downs by surprise, and though the farm buildings were above flood level, the Major lost thirty head of cattle and four of Jessie's goats. And low-level crops of barley and maize were washed away.

Taking the lead from his wife, who was no stranger to floods, he was sorry about the animals but philosophical about the financial losses, realising it was all part of the highs and lows of farming.

More than three weeks passed before they learned it was safe to enter Brisbane again. Townspeople and assigned convicts were still busy cleaning up the mud, but the cholera outbreak caused by polluted water had been checked. In all, nine people had drowned and seven died of cholera, five of the latter being children, so local folk were in mourning. There was a severe shortage of supplies, as Kit had guessed there would be, so they had brought along farm produce to donate to the hospital, and having done that they made their way to the post office.

'You ordered some books, Mrs Ferrington?' the postmaster asked, and Jessie rushed over to him. 'Yes. Are they here?'

'Sure are,' he said, 'out there with the rest of the mess. They got ruined, I'm afraid. You'll have to try again.'

'That's bad luck,' Kit said to her, 'but come along, we'll put in the order for supplies, even if we have to wait a while longer. And did you remember to list tea, that Indian tea? We're nearly out.'

'Yes, dear,' she smiled. 'The Indian tea, the Irish whiskey, the English dining setting and so forth, but where can I get some more goats for my little herd?'

'We'll ask around. But we can't waste time, we don't want to be here overnight and we have to see Jack.'

He was on his boat, moored again at New Farm, when they came aboard to surprise him with a letter.'

'A letter for me?' Jack was mystified. 'No one writes to me.'

'Well someone has,' Kit said. 'It came to me first, before the flood, with instructions to hand-deliver it to you as soon as possible.'

Jack took a knife and slit the red seal, peering at large lettering on costly parchment, then at the signature.

'Who's this Charles someone?'

'The Governor General,' Jessie said excitedly.

'Why's he writing to me? Does he want to borrow a quid?'

'It's a pardon,' the Major grinned. 'I never did believe that teacher story. And I had heard a whisper, at home, about Mudie's prison farm, so I checked. Then I worried that you were a sitting duck if another character like Kirk came along, so I set about fixing things.'

'How?'

'I wrote to a mate who is the Governor General's aide.'

'His what?'

'His offsider. I told him that you negotiated the peace with the blacks, which is still holding, and that you are now an upstanding citizen of Brisbane, and—'

'You want him to return the favour?'

'Something like that. Anyway, Sir Charles went along with it, put his name to a pardon for Jack Drew, and so there you are.'

'Well I'll be damned! This is the pardon?'

'Yes. You're a citizen of New South Wales now. A free man.'

After they left, Jack took the letter and locked it in his sea chest. Funny, he thought, Jack Drew's for real now, and that's all right, but in my head I've always been a free man.